Hard as Stone

Trilogy Omnibus

Beatrice B. Morgan

AUTHORS 4 AUTHORS PUBLISHING

Marysville, WA, USA

Published by Authors 4 Authors Publishing
1214 6th St
Marysville, WA 98270
www.authors4authorspublishing.com

Library of Congress Control Number: 2022948040

E-book ISBN: 978-1-64477-164-8
Hardcover ISBN: 978-1-64477-168-6
Paperback ISBN: 978-1-64477-165-5
Audiobook ISBN: 978-1-64477-166-2

Edited by Rebecca Mikkelson
Copyedited by Brandi Spencer

Cover design ©2022 Practically Perfect Covers. All rights reserved.
Interior design by Brandi Spencer

Authors 4 Authors branding is set in Bavire. Headings and story signage are set in IM FELL English Pro. All other text is set in Garamond.

Beatrice B. Morgan

Hard

as

Stone

Trilogy Omnibus

Authors 4 Authors Content Rating

This title has been rated 14+, appropriate for teens, and contains:

- strong language
- graphic violence
- brief sex
- moderate fantasy drug use
- negative mild illicit drug use
- moderate alcohol use

Please, keep the following in mind when using our rating system:

1. A content rating is not a measure of quality.

Great stories can be found for every audience. One book with many content warnings and another with none at all may be of equal depth and sophistication. Our ratings can work both ways: to avoid content or to find it.

2. Ratings are merely a tool.

For our young adult (YA) and children's titles, age ratings are generalized suggestions. For parents, our descriptive ratings can help you make informed decisions, but at the end of the day, only you know what kinds of content are appropriate for your individual child. This is why we provide details in addition to the general age rating.

For more information on our rating system, please, visit our Content Guide at: www.authors4authorspublishing.com/books/ratings

Dedication

To the girl team I didn't know I needed,
Jackie, Kaylyn, and Cathy.

And everybody upstairs too.

Moorin

Gracita

Kusmerk

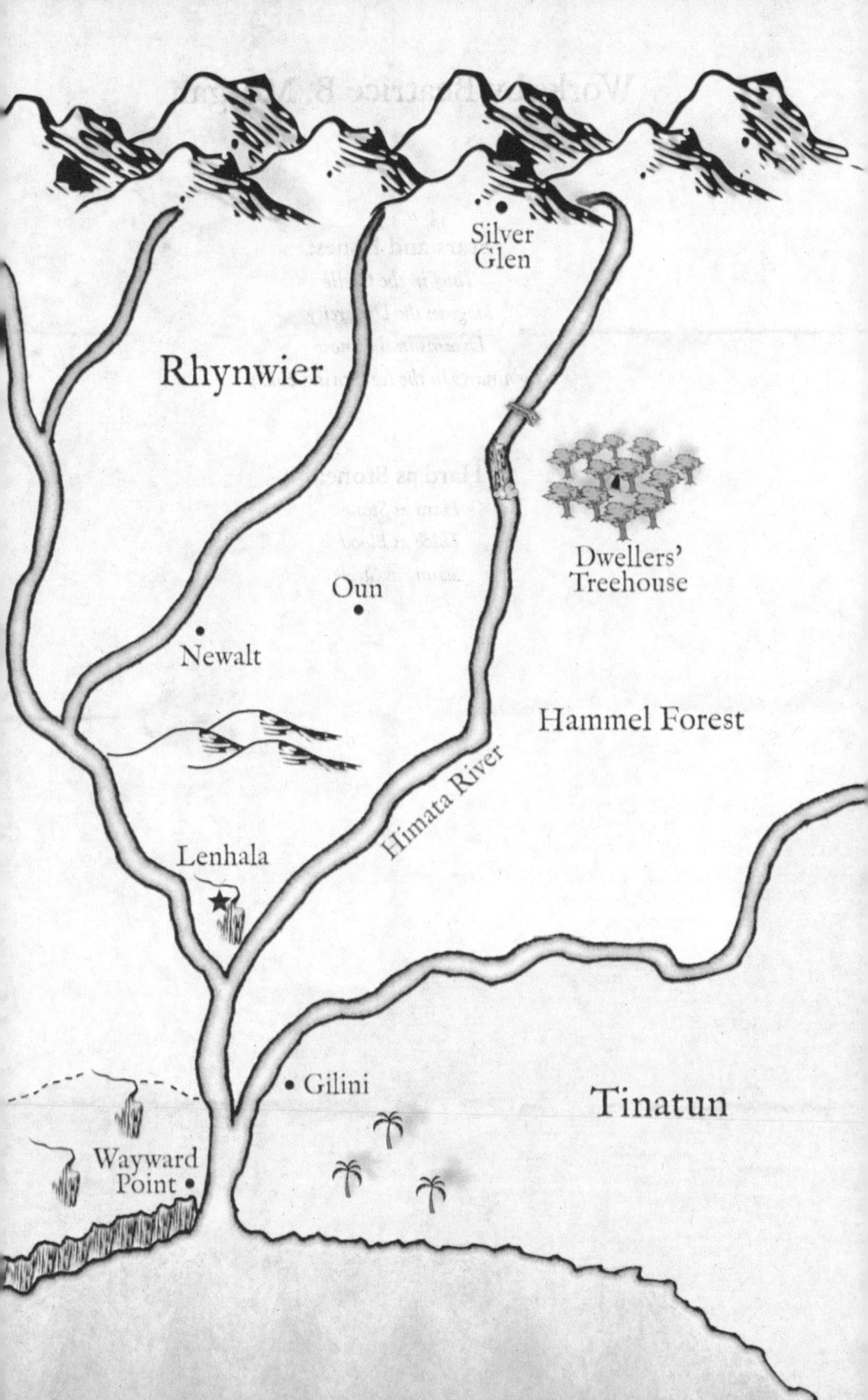

Silver
Glen

Rhynwier

Oun

Newalt

Dwellers'
Treehouse

Hammel Forest

Himata River

Lenhala

Gilini

Tinatun

Wayward
Point

Works by Beatrice B. Morgan

Stars and Bones:
Thief in the Castle
Mage in the Undercity
Dreams in the Snow
Nightmares in the Ice (Spring 2023)

Hard as Stone:
Hard as Stone
Thick as Blood
Strong as Steel

Table of Contents

Table of Contents

Hard

as

Stone

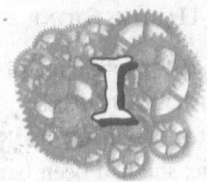

R aven Thane spotted a glint of metal among the shifting greens of Hammel Forest, and her entire body stilled in reflex. Her heart stilled and then skipped a beat. On the other side of the oaks, the sunlight glinted off metal.

Metal. An automaton.

Raven flattened herself against the trunk of an oak. Had it seen her?

The dappling sunlight shifted as the wind rustled the leaves; the metal itself did not move. After her heartbeat returned to normal and her nerves had hardened, she stepped away from the tree. She picked up the few blackberries that had fallen out of her basket in her rush to hide and set the basket on the ground.

She knew she should turn around and head back home, but her curiosity won out. She dusted off her skirt and slowly made her way through the summer's thick foliage toward the glint. She squeezed between two ageless oaks and into a clearing.

A soft gasp escaped her lips at the sight; within the clearing, tree roots, saplings, and weeds had ruptured what had once been a white stone structure. The walls and ceilings had long since fallen, leaving sun-bleached chunks of stone tangled and half-swallowed in the weeds. The glint of metal came from the far side of the ruin, amid a pile of crumbled white stone.

Raven shuddered, despite the warm air—she had stumbled upon a forgotten temple of Wilyn, Goddess of the Forest and Keeper of the Stars. Wilyn's temples had been made of white stone, Raven recalled. Marble.

A prickle started at the base of Raven's neck and worked its way down her spine. She had never seen one of Wilyn's temples; she had only heard about them, and she had the strangest feeling that she had invaded something private.

A hundred years ago, Wilyn's temples and shrines had dotted the northern forests of the kingdom of Rhynwier, just as her sisters' temples had: Minerva, Goddess of the Sea and Wind, prevailed in the south and along the coasts; Solen, Goddess of Stone and Steel, prevailed to the west and the mountains. According to folklore, the Sisters had gifted magic to the ancient people of Rhynwier, who worshipped them. The Sisters did not show such favor to the ancient people of their neighboring kingdom of Gracita, where they favored machinery over magic.

The followers of the Sisters had been the first slaughtered when Gracita invaded and the war began. For one hundred years, Gracita's automatons and war machines fought against Rhynwier's magic, leaving villages and towns devastated along the border. Entire cities had been reduced to rubble and ash. Legends told of a river turned black with the ashes of a port city.

Then, fifteen years ago, Gracita ended the war with the assassination of Rhynwier's king and queen. The Gray Elite—Gracita's military—took control. Their automatons scoured the countryside for remnants of the magic they fought to stomp out; magic became illegal and punishable by death.

After three years of Gray Elite rule, magic had vanished.

Raven didn't remember magic; she had been barely two years old when the war ended. What she knew of her kingdom's history came from word of mouth, passed down stories, and books bought from the rare trader.

Even those were becoming fewer.

Raven took a steadying breath and tiptoed to the edge of the crumbling foundation. Would Wilyn be angry that Raven disturbed her temple?

She scoffed silently at herself for such a thought. Of course not. Wilyn didn't exist, or she would have saved her people from their slaughter.

She climbed onto a wide piece of marble. She kept her eyes open for movement in the surrounding forest and her ears alert for any sound that shouldn't be there—be it man, beast, or automaton.

She ran a finger along the ebony hilt of her favorite dagger, tucked safely into the buckles of her leather boot. Just in case.

As she listened to the sounds of the forest, the sounds that she knew by heart, one became apparent. No birds chirped from within the clearing. No birds perched in the young trees. Her feeling of invasion became something sickeningly like sacrilege.

No threat from the forest made itself known. She straightened, tore her eyes off the empty trees, and carefully made her way across the uneven foundation. Tree roots and vines threatened to trip her, and the sun's reflection off the stone threatened to blind her. She kept her eyes pinned on the glint of metal.

The glint came from what had once been the sanctum, where offerings and prayers were sent to Wilyn. Now, it was a ruin. As Raven approached the sanctum, the glint became weathered brass.

Not an automaton—a piece of one. An arm.

The body of the automaton had been crushed by the fallen sanctum, and the left arm had been bent at the shoulder, jutting upward in a grasp of survival. The brass panels and steel plates had rusted and dulled, and the smallest finger on the four-pronged hand had rusted entirely off, leaving a skeletal three-bolt mechanical bone behind.

Raven listened harder to the forest for the crunch of gears or the hiss of steam, but it never came. She had never been this close to an automaton, dead as it was, and her heart rattled with every tiny step closer she took. She had read that automatons had the strength of one hundred men, could withstand magic and bullets, and understood only logic; they were incapable of compassion or emotion. The Gray Elite had programmed them with their laws, and automatons understood those laws and only those laws.

She imagined the automaton bursting from the rubble, its red-gleam eyes focusing on her, its gears churning, its engine whirring, steam hissing from the joints.

A bird darted overhead at such speed that Raven ducked; the bird vanished in the trees. She scanned the sky but saw nothing. Her stepmother often said that birds carried the first warnings of disaster, but Raven had stopped believing those silly stories years ago.

Raven closed her hands around the automaton's wrist and gave it a hard yank. Metal creaked and whined, and with a few more strong tugs, rusted bolts gave, connecting wires snapped, and the arm came free of the crushed shoulder. A few pieces of scrap metal fell out of the arm's shoulder joint, and Raven scooped them into her pocket.

With no small amount of triumph, Raven started home with the automaton arm slung over her shoulders and her basket of blackberries hanging from her elbow. She stayed within the thick shade and kept alert for any stray automaton that happened to have wandered this far north. Rare but not impossible.

Maybe it would come looking for revenge for its fallen comrade, if automatons could understand such a thing as revenge.

She jumped over a fallen tree, jostling the arm and the berries. What a find! She couldn't wait to see the look on Brent's face. All she had to do was get the arm past her father first.

Raven had lived her entire life in Silver Glen, a small village nestled into the shadow of the mountains. A century ago, it had been a booming mining village, but with the war, the silver depleted. Most of the village had fallen into ruin. What remained of Silver Glen consisted of a few lopsided houses, a trading post, an inn that rarely got used, a few farms, livestock, a tannery, the mill—the things simple people needed to survive. The woods reclaimed everything else—old homes and buildings. Tree roots grew through stone foundations and timber walls, slowly returning the minerals to the earth.

On the surface, Silver Glen looked small and rundown, sparsely populated. The majority of the village couldn't be seen from above ground; it had been built into the mine.

Raven walked through the old streets—now grassy paths—and down the alley between the trading post and the inn. The narrow path led underneath a thick canopy of oak and pine and led into the mine's main entrance. An old wooden sign leaned against the pale gray stone of the mountainside and warned of dangerous caves, loose rock, and instability. Another warned of a cave-in. Raven walked past the signs and straight into the mine. The sunlight illuminated the entrance enough to see by, though it diminished with each step. Rather than go straight, to where a cave-in had blocked the main shaft, she turned right, into an old room.

"It's me," Raven announced to the dark room. Her voice echoed. "Open up!"

"I'm going to need your password," came a female voice from the speaking tube hidden in the shadowed corner.

"Oh, come on, Sweets! It's me, Raven."

"Password," repeated Sweets.

"Sweets!" Raven pleaded.

"For all I know, you could be the Revenant," said Sweets. "I've heard he can steal voices."

Raven scoffed; the Revenant was a ghost story they told to small children to scare them into good behavior. It was a ghost of a monster that swooped from the darkness to snatch its victims without witness, without prejudice.

"Password," Sweets chimed.

Raven groaned and began to tap her foot. Sweets had told her the password just that morning. Sisters, why couldn't she think of it? "'Gooseberries,'" she guessed.

"That's the old password, Rae."

"I know it is!" She huffed. The arm over her shoulder rattled. "Just let me in. You know it's me."

Sweets sighed. "Fine. I'll let you in this time. By the way, your password was 'jackrabbit.'"

Raven cursed under her breath. She remembered it now. "Thanks, Sweets."

A thunk resounded from within the stone wall. Locks released, and with a powerful hiss of steam, gears began to revolve—the stone wall opened to reveal a spiraling metal staircase. Bioluminescent fungi grew along the ceiling, lighting the space in a pale yellow-green glow. Raven started down the stairs, and the door closed behind her with the same thunks and clanks.

Down, down, down into the mines of Silver Glen she went. At the bottom of the stairs, she came to an iron door. She kicked it twice.

"Open up; my arms are full," she said.

The door opened with a vicious creak. Sweets stood in the doorway so that Raven could not pass. She wore her dark blonde hair in a bun on the top of her head; a crossbow hung across her shoulders, and a pistol hung at her side in an old leather holster.

"Not the Revenant," Raven motioned to herself. She tried to step past Sweets, but the other girl stepped in the way. Her eyes fell on the automaton arm, and her straight-line mouth fell into a frown.

"What is *that*?" Sweets asked.

"I thought Brent would enjoy it," Raven said with a smile.

Sweets knew better than to argue. Rolling her eyes, she stepped aside. "Password."

"'Gooseberries,' right?"

"Raven," Sweets sighed and put a hand to her temple.

"Right, right, it's 'jackrabbit.'" Raven skirted through the doorway. "Thanks again, Sweets!"

Raven quickly left the entry hall and whatever lecture Sweets had been preparing. Despite being only a few years older than Raven, Sweets often acted more like a mother than a friend.

Raven made her way through the old mine's tunnels, which had been reinforced with steel and wood to accommodate its inhabitants. The bioluminescent fungi grew along the ceiling in every hall and most of the rooms, lending its sickly light. Raven made her way to the cannery and stepped through the door basket-first. No one paid her mind. The girls were working furiously, washing, mashing, spooning, and canning berries into preserves for winter. Steam from the canners vanished into vents, pulled upward by humming fans. Raven set the basket on the front counter and cleared her throat.

"I've brought you blackberries," she said.

Raven took a step backward toward the door when her half-sister, Lena, appeared from the kitchens. Both girls shared their father's brown-blonde hair, but Lena had her mother's vibrant green eyes, whereas Raven had her mother's brown eyes. Or so her father said. Raven had never met her mother. She had died when Raven was small.

Lena's green eyes fell onto the basket of blackberries, and she smiled. She had a beautiful smile, one that spread like a plague. Raven found herself smiling back. Even at fifteen years old, Lena would become a beautiful woman, and everyone knew it. She would grow into a beauty, while Raven would remain plain.

But that was how their lives had been: Lena excelled; Raven sufficed. Despite that, Raven loved Lena. Her insides were as beautiful as her outside.

Lena picked one of the berries and rolled it between her fingers. "Nice and ripe. Great for canning or eating." She popped the berry into her mouth and hummed her delight.

Raven took another step backward, toward the door. "Well, if that's all you need..."

Lena frowned. "Oh, come on, stay a while. You need to learn how to can."

Raven jostled the arm. "I'll think about it. I've got to drop this treasure off with Brent first."

Lena's eyes wandered the length of the arm, and her frown deepened. In that moment, she looked so much like her mother.

Raven left the cannery before her sister could start lecturing her about the importance of food preservation and roles within society or whatever else she thought Raven needed to hear. She'd heard it all before, and she doubted it would stick any better this time.

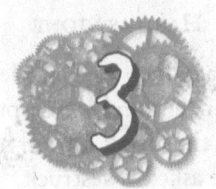

R aven made her way to the other side of the mine, to the workshops and smiths.
She kept her eyes open for any sign of her father—she didn't feel like a lecture
from him either. Luckily, she didn't see him, and she made to the Corridor of
Smiths—as she had always called it. They had built the tinker shops and metalsmiths
on the far edge of the mine for safety, as they were prone to mess and destruction,
and for the noise. The banging of hammers and saws against metal and wood
clattered from the dozen workshops. The Corridor of Smiths had a strong stench of
molten iron and grease.

Brent's tinker shop was on the far end. Unlike some of the others, his iron
door was propped open. Mechanical innards and scrap metal cluttered the narrow
entrance to his shop and formed a single-file path to the workshop itself. Brent had
stationed Alarms—tiny metal birds that tweeted at detected movement—about the
clutter.

Only Raven knew the secret to the Alarms. If one moved slow enough, they
would not tweet. Feeling up to a challenge, Raven crept into the room one tiny step
at a time. She held the arm and herself still as possible. The birds did not sing. After
what felt like ages, she made it to the other side. Once through, she relaxed, glanced
over her shoulder at the silent Alarms, and walked straight into something large and
metal.

She stumbled backward with a yelp—she'd walked into the Scrapper, a machine
that Brent had built from salvaged parts to grind other salvaged parts—those he
couldn't use—into easy-to-smelt pieces. Glad no one had seen her stumble, she
pushed herself back to her feet, rubbing the bruise forming on her backside.

Brent stood hunched over at his worktable. The thick leather strap of his
goggles stretched across the back of his head, further messing up his brown hair.
Like the entrance, the workroom was cluttered and piled with salvaged machine
parts, steel, brass, copper, and metals she didn't recognize. Though the
bioluminescent fungi grew along the ceiling, a lantern on the worktable lit the
workspace in bright yellows and whites.

"Hello, Brent," Raven announced.

"Hello," he said absently in the same calm, distant tone he used when he
worked. "I've told you about sneaking past my birds. You're giving the children bad
ideas."

"I'm helping you improve them." She navigated through the scrap metal maze
to the middle of the room, where Brent kept the space around his worktable clear.
"I've brought you a present." She jostled the automaton arm. It clicked and rattled.

Brent straightened; his magnified eyes settled on the arm and widened. Dropping his tools with a clatter, he fumbled to pull his goggles off his eyes. He blinked at the arm a dozen times, then took it from her.

"Where did you get this?" he asked, awestruck.

"I stumbled across it while picking blackberries," she said innocently.

He slowly moved his gaze from the arm to her. His stare became suspicious. "Picking blackberries? This arm is old. It wouldn't have been by the bushes. Unless you went farther than the bushes." When she didn't deny it, he sighed. "Raven, we've talked about this. Scavenging is dangerous beyond the borders. What if an automaton had caught you? Samuel would be furious if he knew where you'd gone."

Raven heaved a sigh and tried to look as though Brent's mild threat of her father's reprimand didn't frighten her. If her father had his way, she'd be off scavenging duty and canning fruit and making soap with her sister.

"But..." Brent started, gazing longingly at the arm. His fingers twitched with excitement. "The parts this arm contains may well have been worth the trip. But, please, promise me you won't go looking for treasure beyond the safety of the borders."

She didn't answer. Instead, she pretended to find his cabinet of bolts, nuts, and screws fascinating. He knew as well as she did that there wasn't any treasure left within the borders.

"Raven," Brent warned.

"I'm not a child anymore," she said, setting her hands on her hips. "I'm nearly eighteen. Practically an adult. I can hold my own."

"Against one of these?" He held up the arm. "And this is an old model too. The automatons now are twice the size. If you met one of these out in the woods, there'd be no helping you. You'd either be killed on the spot or hauled to the capital."

She rolled her eyes. She knew the risks.

"And you're not 'nearly eighteen.' You just turned seventeen." Brent heaved a sigh and brought the arm to one of the few clean spots on his worktable. He grabbed for tools without looking and began to uncover the insides of the arm. "These parts are old but look to be in decent shape. Oh, there are some miniature parts in here, too small to make with the tools I've got. Oooh...this looks like silver."

Her pride swelled. She knew Brent wouldn't tattle on her to her father. Since he had been taken off scavenging duty to work in the tinker's shop, he had less and less scrap metal brought to him. It didn't seem that long ago that Brent, Sweets, and Raven were scouring the forests around Silver Glen for pieces of the old world. Both of her friends worked in the mines now. Her father had given them grown-up jobs, as he said, because scavenging and berry picking was something to keep the older children entertained and busy.

Raven couldn't fathom not being able to go outside, to be stuck underground, under the sickly, glowing light.

She found a place on the other side of the worktable and leaned forward to watch Brent work. He had the arm apart in no time. It would have gone faster had he not stopped to admire each part. He sorted the pieces into buckets: gears, wires, valves, nuts, and things she didn't recognize. She found it hard to believe that all those parts fit into the space of the arm, and she found it harder to imagine how they would all work together.

What had the completed creature looked like? She tried to picture it—the monstrous human-shaped metal contraption, limbs plated with steel, brass, and copper, bolted together and steaming at the shoulders and hips.

"The old automatons were clunky," Brent said. "They were built for durability, not maneuverability. The newer ones have been streamlined, but the old ones like this arm were full of little parts and things." He pulled out a tiny gear that looked like two gears smashed together. "Oh, I already know what I'm going to use this for."

A memory came back to her, of a trader who had told them a haunting story about an automaton so finely built that he appeared human, but the eyes had given him away. They had been empty, wholly dark. Soulless.

"There was a whole automaton," she said casually, "but it was crushed by one of Wilyn's sanctums."

Brent gasped and dropped the scrap metal he'd been holding. It clattered into the bin. He blinked at her, his eyes wide. His lips formed the word "sanctum," and then he slowly pushed his goggles to the top of his head. His voice came out grave. "Raven, that's far beyond the border."

She cursed herself for the slip.

According to the Gray Elite's border laws, wandering automatons could not cross the border of an established town, but anyone caught outside those borders without the proper authorization was considered a refugee. The bigger the town, the higher the risk—as her father always said. Which was why the people of Silver Glen had taken to living in the mine, underneath the Gray Elite's border laws.

Raven crumpled under Brent's disappointed gaze. Sighing, she said, "I'm careful. It's not like I've got magic in my blood, or they would have caught me years ago, right?"

His frown deepened, and she cursed herself again. She had admitted to having gone beyond the borders more than a few times. She had, many times. Enough to know her chances of running into an automaton were slim.

Brent released an exasperated sigh. He knew there would be no talking her out of going back. "Just be careful. And don't try to bring back too much."

Brent fell into silence as he made his way deeper into the arm. The buckets slowly filled. Raven didn't move until an Alarm sang out a sweet tune, mimicking real birdsong. Booted footsteps made their way toward the back room.

A tall, lean bronze-skinned boy appeared in the doorway. He wore the top half of his dark brown hair long and tied back; the bottom half, he kept shaved. At the sight of Raven, a smirk stretched across his shapely jaw, and his sapphire eyes glittered. He wore scuffed leather boots, a dagger tucked in the buckles of each, and patched trousers. Another set of daggers were on his suspenders, half hidden by his unbuttoned vest. He'd rolled the sleeves of his white shirt to his elbows and tucked his hands into his pockets.

"Zander," Brent said with exasperation, "please explain the dangers of the woods to Raven."

Raven groaned. She didn't need Zander in the debate too.

Zander puffed his chest with importance. "Brent's right, Rae. Those iron beasts are more vicious than a hungry bear. Some have spears for arms that tear through a man's chest like a knife through a tomato." He withdrew a pistol from the leather holster slung low on his hip. "Next time you're itching to break the house rules, take me with you. I can keep you safe." He winked.

"Or I could run face-first into an iron maul," she deadpanned. "What do you want?"

Zander laughed. "This isn't your house, Raven. I can be in here if I want. I didn't come to see you. I have business with Brent."

She motioned at Brent, still meticulously picking apart the arm.

Zander frowned. "Just Brent, not you. Get out."

"This isn't your house," she chimed back at him. "I can be here if I want."

Zander chuckled, a retort on his tongue, but Brent spoke first. "I've finished the adjustments you asked for."

Brent set down his tools and reached underneath the worktable. He straightened, holding a cloth-covered something. He turned to Zander and pulled back the cloth to reveal a polished pistol.

"Here she is," said Brent.

Zander let out a sigh of longing and turned the pistol over in his hands. It was an old gun, hundreds of years old, but Zander and Brent kept it in good shape. The barrel was medium length and dark steel. The grip was dark red leather. Zander referred to his gun as *her* and had named her Birdie.

"There's my girl," he said lovingly to Birdie.

Birdie never missed her target, Zander would proudly tell anyone who would listen, no matter how many times he'd already told them or how often they had seen him shoot.

"Go test the new calibration," Brent advised, eyes fondling the gun. He knew Birdie as well as Zander did by now.

Zander didn't need more of a suggestion. His eyes roamed over Raven, and he said lazily, "Want to come see Birdie in action?"

She shrugged; she didn't have much more to do, unless she counted her chores, and if she had the choice between trying to infuriate Zander and making soap, she'd choose the first.

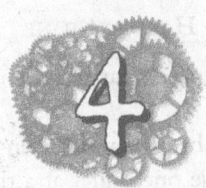

Zander, Brent, and Raven went to the shooting range, a shaded clearing up on the mountain, accessible by a mine shaft. The trees leaned toward the range, and their collective canopy shaded much of it from the sky. At the far end, hay bales, logs, and dirt-filled bags had been painted white, gray, and yellow. The colors of the Gray Elite. Most of the painted faces had comical grimaces, ogre teeth, large noses, and pointed ears.

Raven took up a spot near the front; Zander took a position a toe away from the ditch—the line separating him from the range—and Brent pulled open a fake tree trunk to reveal the control panel of the Cycle. With the pull of a lever, gears in the hidden track began to crank; steam hissed through the vents. The Gray Elite targets jittered to life and started to move along the tracks.

Zander pulled Birdie from her leather holster. He held her in one hand, his unnamed pistol in the other, and took a shooting stance—boots apart, knees slightly bent, body turned so Birdie aimed first. He let out a slow breath, blue eyes focusing with a predatory intensity that gave Raven a shiver. He looked ready to kill.

"Give me the count." Zander's voice mirrored his eyes: husky, deep, and focused.

Raven cleared her throat and raised her hand into the air. She held up three fingers and put each down as she called, "Three, two," and paused for dramatics with her index finger pointed to the sky. "One!" A fist in the air.

Bang! Bang! Bang! Birdie's blasts shook birds from the trees, scattering them in all directions. The Gray Elite targets absorbed the impacts, sending splinters and splatters of dirt into the air. Bullet after bullet, enemy after enemy, until Zander emptied both guns.

Not a single bullet missed.

Zander tossed a haphazard smirk over his shoulder at Raven. "One more for good luck?" He loaded a single bullet into Birdie without looking; he kept his stare on Raven. Her cheeks heated like they did sometimes when he looked at her, and with the blushing came a terrible embarrassment. Zander's smirk widened. Her blush and embarrassment intensified. Had he done that on purpose?

He snapped the cylinder back into place with a flick of his wrist and pulled his gaze off Raven to aim. As he pulled the trigger, Raven pulled the level on the machine. The belts pulling the targets jerked—

Bang!

The bullet missed.

"Oh?" Raven said haughtily. "Never misses?"

"You cheated," Zander spat. "You did that on purpose."

11

"What if I did? You can't expect your real enemies to parade in a conveniently predictable line."

Zander grumbled under his breath, and Raven pretended not to hear the name he'd called her. He reloaded Birdie one bullet at a time and slid her into the leather holster. He started to reload his second gun.

"Let's do a second round, Brent," Zander said, snapping the second gun's cylinder into place. He sneered at Raven. "Without cheating."

Raven opened her mouth to argue, but the trap door to the mine shaft opened with a creak. Sweets stuck her head out and squinted at the daylight. Her pale skin looked nearly white.

"There you are," Sweets said to Raven. "Your father is looking for you."

Raven's heart fell into her stomach, but she stood straight and set her hands on her hips. "What did I do this time?"

Sweets bit her lip. "Well, someone, not me, might have seen you walking through the mines with an arm over your shoulder. And, well, you know, word gets around."

"Someone's in for it," Zander taunted.

Raven groaned.

"Best not keep him waiting," Sweets said, her voice small. She shrank, letting the trapdoor creak toward the ground until only her eyes were visible. "He's in a bad mood today."

"Of course not." Raven kicked at the ground and started toward the trapdoor. She couldn't get out of this one. "When has he ever *not* been in a bad mood?"

"When were you born?" Zander asked.

She stuck her tongue out at him.

"And Zander," Sweets added. "Watch the bullets you use. The foundry's been slow this month."

He harrumphed his acknowledgment.

Raven followed Sweets back down into the mines. It took several steps for her eyes to adjust back to the dreary light of the fungi. They reached the main level of the mines, and Sweets vanished down a passage saying, "He's in his office."

Raven huffed. She could only imagine what he had to say this time. She made her way to his office in the middle of the mines, between the workshops and the living quarters. The door was shut. Raven straightened her shoulders and lifted her chin. Another lecture. She'd handled plenty of lectures. She could handle this one.

She knocked.

"Come in," came her father's reply.

Raven stepped into the office. Her father stood on the other side of his desk, an old wooden desk that had belonged to the mines, with his thick arms crossed and his trimmed beard barely hiding his scowl. Her stepmother, an older version of Lena in both looks and temperament, stood beside the desk.

"Ah, I must be going." Her stepmother kissed her father's cheek and then kissed Raven's temple. She lingered and whispered to Raven, "He means well, darling." Her stepmother left.

"Sweets said you wanted to see me?" Raven asked innocently.

"Close the door."

Oh... She knew that tone. Not good.

He wasn't just angry. He was *furious*. Raven gently pushed the iron door back into the frame. The latch clicked; the finality of it pulled her heart further into her stomach.

"Sit down," he said.

Raven sat in one of two chairs in front of his desk, both originally made of wood, both patched with metal. She started to slump forward but thought better of it. She held her shoulders square and crossed her ankles like her stepmother had taught her, and she folded her hands in her lap. She schooled her face into calmness and met her father's glare.

Her father was the overseer of the mines, of Silver Glen; he kept it running, and he kept the people safe and cared for. Sitting before him, Raven had no doubt how he had become overseer. He stood tall and broad and had an imposing presence. He radiated authority. As a child, Raven had wished that she would inherit that authority, that people would look to her as they looked to her father.

She didn't. They didn't.

Finally, he said, "You brought back an automaton's arm?" Though his brown-black eyes glared, his words were calm.

She nodded. "Brent said it was a good find. I watched him take it apart. There were loads of pieces inside of it."

"Where did you find it?"

She swallowed. "It was by luck. A bird tweeted, and I happened to spot it near to where I was."

"Which was where?"

Her fingers twitched. He knew exactly where the old temple was. He would know exactly how far outside the borders she had gone.

When she didn't answer, he growled, "Raven."

"By an old Wilyn temple," she said quietly.

He slammed his fist onto his desk, rattling the brass cup of quills and an ink bottle and knocking off a small tinker cat whose tail ticked with the time. It clattered on the stone floor of the office and rolled to a stop. Still, it clicked.

"You know where the boundaries are." His tone was venomous. "The automatons will not attack you within our borders, but outside them, they will cut you down on sight. That's their merciful punishment. Do you know what happens to the people they take back to the capital?" His eyes burned.

She twisted her hands in her lap. "You've told me."

"Then please, elaborate on what happens, what could happen to you. And then please, explain your reasons for disregarding those warnings."

She swallowed. Eyes on her fingers, she said, "When the automatons take a person to Lenhala, one is thrown in jail, killed, or sold as a slave."

"You know what fate would befall you? A seventeen-year-old girl?"

She didn't answer.

"If you were lucky, you'd be warming the bed of some military general."

He didn't say what befell the unlucky girls. He never did.

"I'm sorry, I—"

He slammed his fist down again. "You're sorry? Raven, the border laws might not exist underground, but they exist above ground, and you are not an exception to them. Going outside the borders is putting yourself in direct danger and not only defying the Gray Elite laws, but the laws of Silver Glen." He balled his fists. "What is wrong with you? Why must you continually do this to me? Your sister doesn't give me a fraction of the trouble you do."

Raven held her lip between her teeth to keep it from quivering. "You could stand to be more like your sister," her father had once told her after she had abandoned her chores to play in the summer rain.

She waited for him to admit it, that he preferred Lena over her, that she had been a mistake. She knew it; the whole mine knew it. Who could possibly prefer plain Raven, who did everything wrong, to lovely, perfect Lena, who did everything right?

Raven felt the tears welling behind her eyes, but she held them in.

"You've deliberately disobeyed me for the last time," he said darkly. "I've had it with you pushing aside the rules. Starting tomorrow, you're in the kitchen with your sister."

Raven snapped her gaze up at him. "What? No!" She jumped to her feet. "I won't do it again, I promise."

He shook his head. "I won't hear it. You've strayed too far." She tried to argue, but he held his hand up. "No. Tomorrow morning. The kitchen. Lena already knows, and your stepmother is going to be there to make sure you don't shirk your duties. It's high time you grew out of this wild streak, Raven. You're soon to be a grown woman. You're not a child."

With that, he turned his back. The discussion was over.

Raven stood on legs that didn't feel like her own. She set her hand on the door handle; then her father added, "Don't forget, you are on watch tonight."

Don't screw it up.

She let herself out of the office. She heard footsteps in the hall, but she didn't look up to see who. She didn't want to face them, in case they'd heard everything, and she didn't want anyone to see her cry. She started toward the living quarters, then turned down an empty hall. The tears pushed harder, wetting her eyelashes.

She headed for the quickest way out of the mines. When the ladder came into view, she bolted. She climbed as fast as she could and pushed through the trapdoor.

The calming breeze rushed through her hair and kissed her cheeks. She set the trapdoor back in place. Moss and stone had been affixed to the iron lid to hide it, but she knew how to get back in again. She started down the mountain to her favorite place in Silver Glen, where no one would tell her what to do.

15

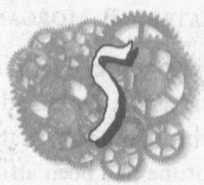

Raven knew the way to her tree. She could run it blindfolded. She weaved through the forest, her skirts rustling, her boots pounding on the dirt and grass. All around, the birds chirped, flaunting their freedom. They could fly about all day, wherever they pleased, while Raven couldn't even leave the boundaries of the mine.

Her tree—she had carved her initials into its thick trunk—stood a short distance outside the boundary. She came to the wooden fence that encircled their small corner of the kingdom and jumped over it in a single leap. Her boots hit the ground on the other side, and she ran all the way to her tree. It stood taller than the others, and its branches had grown in such an array that they begged to be climbed.

Raven climbed up and up and up until her head and shoulders burst through the topmost branches. Only then did she paused to catch her breath. Before her, the Hammel Forest sprawled to the horizon on rolling hills of blue-green. Above her, puffy white clouds lingered in the endless blue sky. The world went on forever.

Somewhere up there in the endless blue, sky cities roamed freely, going wherever they wished, whenever they wished. What would it be like to look down on the world from the deck of an airship? To live in one of the sky cities? The passengers were not confined to a life of hiding underground or in the cover of trees.

Raven knew there had to be more to the world than picking berries and surviving the winter. She knew there was more—Zander had proved it. Six months ago, he had escaped from Lenhala, the royal city of Rhynwier. He had shown up, ragged and dirty, in the middle of the night. But he never wanted to talk about it. Whenever someone mentioned Lenhala, he got a distant look in his eyes.

Somewhere to the south, Lenhala stood proud. A city of metal and stone stretching toward the sky. One day, Raven would like to see it. If only just once. Just to see what it was like, what the world could be like outside of the musty, dingy mines.

Raven inhaled the sweet scent of the outdoors, then slowly released it. The odds of her leaving Silver Glen were next to none, and her father would never permit her to leave. She would live here for the rest of her life, preserving food, tending to the children, and cleaning.

She climbed down to the fork in the tree and sat on the wooden plank she'd stolen from the workshop. She rested against the right fork and draped her legs off the plank, either side of the left fork.

She did not want to spend the rest of her life daydreaming about the rest of the world, but what choice did she have?

Raven sat, listening to the birds, the bugs, and the whispers of the forest, watching the sun make its steady path across the sky, until her hunger demanded she

16

return for whatever grub the kitchens had made. She started down to the earth without enthusiasm. Her foot slipped on the hem of her skirt, and rather than grasp to hold on, she jumped the rest of the way down. Her feet slammed into the ground; the impact traveled up her legs and into her shoulders. Shaking it off, she started home.

Hands grabbed her shoulders and slammed her into the tree trunk, hard enough to knock the breath from her throat. She started to scream—a hand covered her mouth.

"You'll get their attention faster that way," growled a male voice.

She blinked—Zander had grabbed her. Her panic subsided and turned to anger. She tried to pry his hand off her mouth, but he didn't budge. His eyes flickered about the forest to her right, intent and focused. She mumbled for him to let go, and he shushed her.

She glared at him, and then she heard it.

A buzzing, not like bees or wasps, but a mechanical buzzing. Miniature gears clicking so fast, they hummed. An automaton.

The buzzing came closer. Her blood ran cold. Zander moved his free hand to his unnamed gun—he'd covered her mouth with the hand that would have grabbed Birdie. He slowly lifted the gun at firing lever and cocked it.

Her heart pounded. Her hands clutched Zander's. He wasn't shaking. He stood steady and sure. He wore his predator's face, a wolf ready to seize his prey, waiting, listening, and then—

The automaton came through the trees. Gears turned, thunking and clicking; steam hissed and gurgled. It looked like a birdcage with wings. The wings moved like a hummingbird's, so quickly, they blurred into a sheen of brass and steel. Steam issued from the bulbous head of the automaton, white-glass eyes turning in every direction, clicking as it searched. The body was a brass cage large enough for a grown man to sit in.

The automaton came closer, and Zander aimed.

Bang! The bullet smashed into the head, right through the left eye. It exploded into a spray of scrap metal. The wings sputtered. The cage crashed to the forest floor and stilled.

He didn't return the gun to his holster. For a moment, the forest quieted, and all she heard was the creaking and groaning of the dying automaton. Zander's hand slipped from her mouth, but she hadn't the words.

"Zander," Raven whispered, but he shook his head.

"Cage Birds travel in threes," he said. "We need to move. Now."

She nodded. Zander took point, and she followed a step behind. He walked with his unnamed gun at the ready, predatory eyes on the lookout. Raven scanned the forest as they walked, ears alert for the humming of mechanical wings.

The boundary fence came within sight, and for the first time in her life, her heart leaped at the sight of it.

And then she heard it—the hum of wings.

"Careful," Zander whispered. He adjusted his fingers on the gun and slowed.

How could she be careful when the boundary was right there? The automaton couldn't follow them over it.

They crept closer to the boundary, but Zander halted them. The second Cage Bird appeared in front of them, between them and the boundary—patrolling it, Raven realized. A rock fell into her gut. It hadn't been there when she had left. She would have seen it, heard it. Her chest tightened as she thought—it might have been there, and she had been too distraught to see it.

Another set of humming wings came from behind them. Neither Cage Bird had yet to spot them, but if they moved—

Zander aimed faster than Raven could blink. *Bang.*

She jumped; the Cage Bird's head exploded into scrap metal, and the body crashed to the ground. Zander spun to shoot the last Cage Bird behind them. He aimed over Raven's shoulder, and in the heartbeat that followed, his eyes widened.

The humming changed pitch.

"Raven!"

Cold metal hands fastened around her upper arms and yanked her backward. She yelped, but the sound evaporated as her back slammed into the bars of the cage, and the jaws of the Cage Bird snapped shut, shutting her inside.

Zander stood on the other side of the bars, Birdie in his other hand, both guns aimed at the Cage Bird, looking more like a predator than she had ever seen, teeth clenched, eyes wide and fierce. Angry.

But he didn't take the shot.

The Cage Bird started into the forest, away from the boundary fence. She shouted his name, but the Cage Bird moved too fast.

Raven's heart hammered. She kicked the doors, pushed them, beat them with her fists, but nothing worked. The cage wouldn't budge. Above her, the engine of the Cage Bird rumbled and clicked and crunched. The wings beat furiously, faster than before. Below her, the forest floor rushed past.

"No!" Raven slammed her hands against the cage doors one last time. The tears she had denied pushed against her eyes.

You've always wanted to fly, a dark voice in her mind said.

She sank to the bottom of the cage and brought her knees to her chest. Wouldn't her father be in a rage when he heard. A small amount of spiteful joy rose, knowing that Zander would be the one to tell him. Her father might even hit him. Too bad she wouldn't get to see it.

The Cage Bird lurched to the side, throwing her into the bars. It crashed into a tree with a sickening crunch of metal. It tumbled to the forest floor and rolled to a stop. The wings to her left had been crushed; the gears tried and failed to move.

For a moment, nothing happened. Her heart pounded, the sun glittered through the canopy, and the Cage Bird *clunked, clunked, hissed*.

Through the bars, Zander appeared. She'd never been as happy to see him. He knocked the butt of his unnamed gun into the jaws of the cage, and the lock sprang open. Raven crawled out from the cage, relishing the feeling of grass beneath her fingers. She stood on shaky legs, and when she stood clear, Zander shot the Cage Bird in the head, putting an end to the sputtering buzz of the remaining wing.

And then the forest was silent again.

Raven leaned against a tree trunk, hand over her racing heart. She could still hear the clanking of the Cage Bird's insides, the humming of the wings on either side of her, trapping her. Zander glared down at the Cage Bird with cold hatred, Birdie and his unnamed gun still in his hands.

With every heartbeat, her panic eased. Automatons, in Silver Glen.

If Zander hadn't been there... Then, another thought formed. Zander had been there, at her tree. "What were you doing?" Raven snapped at him.

"I could be asking you the same thing." Zander holstered his unnamed gun. A smirk replaced his grimace. "And after your father scolded you for wandering beyond the borders."

Her face reddened. It had been Zander in the hall.

"You should have shot it back there," she spat, turning toward the boundary. "You almost let it take me."

He holstered Birdie. His smirk lessened into something serious. "I didn't want to risk shooting you."

She laughed bitterly. "I thought you never miss."

19

"You'd rather I tempt fate? There was also the chance of the shrapnel taking out an eye or giving you a nice laceration." He ran his finger across his left eye.

She huffed, and they started back toward the boundary fence. They walked a while in silence, and then she said, "Thank you."

He made a small sound, and she knew he wore that arrogant smirk of his. "Good thing I followed you, or else you'd be on your way to Lenhala." A note of fear eased into his voice. "Raven, seriously though, Cage Birds have never come this far north. Don't leave the boundary without protection."

"You're saying I can borrow Birdie? I'd feel safer with her."

"No, you're not allowed to touch her," he said quickly. "But, if you are planning on leaving the boundary again, say something. I'll go with you."

She blushed at those words and turned her head so he wouldn't see. "My father would be angry that you'd suggest such a thing."

Zander chuckled. "He'd be angrier if he knew I let you wander into the forest alone."

She held her tongue. That way, Zander got to be the hero. She tried not to let it bother her. He *had* saved her from the Cage Bird.

The boundary came into sight, and she felt a relief and a burden. She also felt bruises forming along her shoulders and knees where the Cage Bird had crashed.

"No doubt, you heard my father take me off scavenging duty," she said.

Zander didn't respond.

She sighed. "I guess this means I'll be making soap and working with Lena in the kitchens."

Zander still didn't respond. He wasn't even looking at her. His intense stare looked through the forest, his hand resting on Birdie.

She yanked her attention away from him. She could ignore him too. She took a step toward the boundary when she felt it: a taut rope against the top of her foot. She glanced down. Thick wire stretched between two trees, into which she had walked.

A click—a *thwomp*—Zander grabbed her arm and yanked her back. She felt air move against her neck, and then a bolt embedded itself into the tree. Raven stumbled backward and lost her balance—a bolt had nearly gone through her throat! She fell, and Zander fell with her. Her back slammed into the ground, and Zander landed on top of her, his fist slamming into the ground beside her head.

She took a gasping breath—Zander's lips hovered a hair's breadth above her own. She couldn't move. Not because his weight pinned her, but because her limbs had turned to lead. She blinked, he blinked, and for a terrifying, exhilarating moment, she thought he might kiss her. For that same moment, she wanted him to. That terrified her more.

Zander blinked, then scrambled to his feet. She pushed herself up, face burning like fire.

She remembered—the bolt.

"What happened?" Raven asked.

"Someone set a trap." Zander touched the shaft of the bolt and followed the line it had traveled. He uncovered a narrow box attached to the opposite tree. The wire had been the trigger, releasing the bolt at her.

She took in the plain wooden bolt, and her face paled. "That's not one of ours."

Zander shook his head. "No. And, this bolt would have gone through your throat. The only animals in this area this could possibly be for are deer. Tell me, what else would a hunter use a bolt for?"

She swallowed. Understanding washed over her. "People."

He nodded grimly. "I was going to say, we should forget this happened and not tell your father, but this changes things. Come on."

Automatons and people hunters? Had they been in the forest that morning too? Raven followed a step behind Zander, glad to have him with her. She didn't want to tell her father about anything that had happened, but Zander was right. He needed to know.

Zander led the way to one of the trapdoors into the mine and waited for her at the bottom. In the dimmed light of the fungi, his dark brown hair appeared black, but his sapphire eyes stood out.

"Rae," he said, his voice soft. "Go on ahead. I'll talk to your father alone."

She hadn't expected that. Zander had never thrown aside a chance to get her in trouble. "Are you sure?" she asked.

"He's already yelled at you once today. I haven't gotten a good yelling for a few days. I don't want him to forget me."

She frowned. "Why? You used to thrive on my being in trouble."

He mirrored her frown. "Well, if you're so adamant, you can go with me. I'll let you explain why you were out there by yourself and how I saved your ass. Twice." He held up two fingers.

Her face reddened. Her stomach threatened to growl. "Fine, but don't make me look worse. I don't need him angrier."

He shrugged, and before he could change his mind, Raven headed toward the kitchens for something to eat.

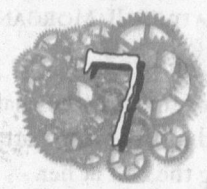

Raven headed through the cannery, not through the kitchen; she didn't want to meet anyone. No doubt, word of her insubordination and subsequent reassignment had spread. If she walked into the cafeteria, she would be greeted with pitied looks or about time stares from the older women. She still felt the puffiness of her eyes too, and she didn't want anyone to think she had been crying over it.

The cannery had quieted down since morning. The girls were gone, the blackberries had been processed, and the basket had returned to the stack in the corner. The smell of preserved berries floated through the air, tart and sweet, and it made her mouth water.

Raven slipped into the store for something quick.

"Back so soon?" asked Lena. Raven jumped; her half-sister stood on the other side of the storeroom, stacking jars of blue and red berry preserves. She gave Raven a knowing smile. "You missed lunch earlier." If Lena noticed Raven's puffy eyes, she didn't mention it.

"I did," Raven said.

Lena stood, waiting for an explanation. Raven bit her lip. She didn't want to tell her anything more than she had to, but she hadn't prepared an excuse for why she'd been gone. No doubt, Lena knew.

"I know this isn't the kind of job you want," Lena said softly. "But it's not so bad. At least we'll get to spend more time together. And you'll get to know everyone, and—I don't know—maybe you'll find a boy you like."

And settle down, she could hear her stepmother saying.

Raven shifted on her feet. She didn't want to have that conversation with Lena, with anyone. She placed a hand over her stomach. "Can you spare anything to eat? I'm famished. I'm on watch tonight, and I can't pass out from hunger, can I?"

Lena retrieved a few strips of dried venison, a stale slice of bread, and a bit of last year's preserves. Raven sat at the counter in the back while her sister worked, cleaning the dishes they'd used that day and giving Raven a quick rundown of all the chores in the kitchen. She included notes on how each worker had an important role, as to not make anyone feel less needed than another.

At Lena's behest, Raven washed her own plate and put it away. With a quick goodbye and a promise that the kitchen wasn't so horrible, Raven sulked back to her bedroom. Most of the people who called the mine home were still in the cafeteria, drinking and laughing after a day's work. Raven had no will to join them.

Raven shut the wooden door to her bedroom and let out a heavy sigh.

Her small room had only enough space for a narrow bed, a clothing trunk, and a bookshelf where she kept interesting stones, a few tinker toys, and what books she had managed to collect from traders. Raven collapsed onto her bed.

One thing she liked about her room was the ceiling. She had carved airships and stars into the stone and coaxed the fungi to grow in the lines so that the stars and airships glowed.

Kitchen duty. She'd much rather scavenge. There was so much more to see in the world than the ruins of Silver Glen, and she couldn't see any of it while stuck underground.

After the foot traffic of people returning from dinner quieted, Raven got up. She could put off her watch duty no longer. She grabbed her cloak, tucked one of her favorite books under her arm, and headed across the mines to the lookout tower.

The lookout tower jutted up from the highest point in the mines. On the outside, it looked like a thick tree. Its iron body had been covered with vining flowers, climbing ivy, and tree bark. From its top, the entire forest could be seen. Its purpose was to sound the alarm for danger, and someone stood on watch in the lookout tower night and day, every day of the year. It was a duty that they shared among the capable.

Raven's boots clicked on the iron steps, and the sound echoed up the tower's dark interior. On the last flight of steps, the last gleams of twilight gilded the lookout tower's landing in golds and blues, deep and mournful.

Carl was sitting at the desk, looking deathly bored. At the sight of Raven, he sat bolt straight and jumped to his feet.

Raven straightened her shoulders and put her hands on her hips. "I'm here to relieve you."

"Thank the Sisters," Carl breathed. He let out a wide yawn. He pointed to a basket. "My wife made biscuits. There's a few left. Help yourself."

"Thanks," she said.

With that, Carl made his way down the stairs. Halfway down, he started to whistle.

Raven sulked to the edge of the tower. She could see for miles, all the forest twilit and gleaming in dark golds. The pitiful town of Silver Glen sat nestled in the forest, vaulted wooden roofs dull, even in the twilight. The sun edged underneath the low-hanging clouds, turning them all purple and orange and pink. The summer haze glowed. A glorious sight. It made it look as though the very air glowed.

The colors dimmed, stars appeared one by one, and the night took control of the world. Millions of stars glittered from horizon to horizon. What would it be like to sail through them? To have the stars within reach? To fly between the stars and the clouds?

She let out a sigh and plopped down into the singular chair. A crossbow leaned against the wall, and a dozen bolts lay in a tall basket underneath the table. A chain hung from the warning bell, which, when pulled, would echo down the tower and into the mines. One ring for traders or visitors, two rings for everything else.

Raven had never rung the bell. She slumped onto the table and scanned for any sign of anything. She could still hear the buzzing of the Cage Birds, feel the metal hands close around her arms. She looked harder, but she saw no glint of metal in the night.

They couldn't cross the border anyway. The border laws didn't allow it.

But why had they been there? Had they wandered beyond their usual path? How had Zander known about them? Either he had followed her and spotted them, or he had spotted them and then gone after her. Either way left her stomach in knots.

But why?

The only thing Silver Glen had lay at its deepest point, far under the mountain. It was an ancient temple of the Three Sisters, one of the few remaining untouched by the war. Raven had never prayed or given an offering; few people still did, except for her stepmother. The ninny. The old temple was mainly used as a meeting for the council. Raven had always found its dark walls and dim light eerie.

Still, the attack that day had left her shaken. She watched, waited, and watched, but she saw nothing. As the night went on, time seemed to slow. Even the stars paused.

Raven felt the tug of sleep. To keep herself awake, she reached for her book. She propped her boots up on the counter and started to read. She'd read the book countless times; it was an adventure of a young boy named Leon Stark, who stowed away on a ship, thinking he would escape his life as a slave. However, the ship he boarded was a pirate ship, and through his adventure and bravery, he became captain.

Even though she knew the twists and turns of love and betrayal, she lost herself in the story. She stood with the boy on the pirate ship's deck as it shot out of the waters and into the sky, taking flight. She felt his awe as he saw the flying ship for the first time, when he felt the blast of the cannons, when he touched a cloud.

A bird cawed from the tower's roof, pulling her out of her fantasy. She blinked; the wind rustled the leaves. The moon had gone behind a cloud. She heard the flap of a heavy wing, then nothing.

She heaved a sigh. Tomorrow, the kitchens. She wouldn't step outside the mines again for a long while, not if her father had anything to say about it, and she would never see an airship—let alone ride in one. She would live and die in Silver Glen.

With that thought, she buried herself in the story once more. Her only escape.

R aven read until her relief came to take over the watch. She thanked him vigorously and then jogged down the stairs, yawning. She walked to her room in a sleepy daze, with sky cities and airships and pirate captains flying through her thoughts amid a flurry of adventure and romance. She tiptoed through the living quarters, which were humming with the soft breaths of sleep, and shut herself in her room.

She undressed and set her dress and her corset inside her clothing trunk. She slid her dagger from her boot and set it beside her bed. She always kept it and her boots within easy reach at night. It made her feel more prepared should something happen—not that anything ever happened.

She undid the clasp on her locket—the only thing she had of her mother's. It was a simple golden locket with a delicate floral pattern etched onto its front. She tried to open it, but like always, it remained shut. She'd never been able to open it.

She set her locket by her dagger. In just her chemise, she curled underneath the thin blankets.

In her mind, she could picture it: her own airship, a sky city unlike any other, of bright colors and with a full library. Flying through the stars. Flying alongside the clouds. Where magic existed, free as the wind, bright as a sunrise. High above the world, away from the Gray Elite, from their automatons, from their sprawling empire, from the shadow of the war.

She fell asleep to her fanciful thoughts, and too soon, a hand was shaking her awake.

"Jusaminmore," Raven mumbled, but the hand persisted.

"Now, child," came the deep, soft voice of the elder, Mel.

Raven snapped awake.

The older woman stood at the bedside, her silver hair braided over her shoulder, her dress the color of the darkness around her. Her piercing eyes reflected the yellow of the fungi.

"Mel?" Raven muttered, sitting up.

"Up, now," Mel urged. "There isn't time to chat."

Mel glided into the hallway with the grace of a ghost, and Raven scrambled to her feet. Had she overslept? Enough that Mel had come to fetch her personally? Guilt and shame coursed through her limbs like a dull ache, and she felt separate from herself as she hurriedly dressed. Raven rushed into the hall after Mel.

Raven yawned. She could have used a few more hours of sleep. She felt like she had barely gotten any at all.

All the other doors in the living quarters were closed. With every step, Raven's thoughts cleared of sleep. Mel did not lead her into the kitchens. She led her down, deeper into the mine, deeper and deeper. Raven's stomach flipped and flopped in rhythm with her hurried steps. What was wrong?

They walked deeper still. With no small amount of nervousness, Raven realized that Mel was leading her to the Temple of the Three Sisters. Her heart sank. Did this have something to do with the arm she had found? The arm she took from the ruined temple?

They descended a wide staircase carved from the dark gray stone. The stairs and the temple they led to were ancient, older than the mine, far older. The smooth steps and walls had no markings of carving tools, and Raven's stepmother often said the ancients had used magic to shape the temple. As she descended deeper, Raven felt a prick of fear that her stepmother might have been telling the truth. The stale air of the mine mingled with something else, something metallic and floral; the deeper they walked, the stronger the scent.

A chill sent gooseflesh over Raven's arms and legs. She hated going to the temple.

They finally reached the bottom of the stairs, and Mel led her through a set of iron doors. Each had been carved with a thousand interlocking whorls and starbursts. The main chamber of the temple held the statues of the Sisters, each carved from their respective stone: marble for Wilyn, sandstone for Minerva, and granite for Solen. The fungi grew along the walls and ceiling, shadowing the Sisters' stone faces.

Mel led Raven into a small side room without fungi. A single candle burned on a wooden podium. Raven didn't like how small the room felt and how full of shadows it was.

"The door," said Mel.

Raven quietly shut the door; her hands shook on the handle. To be called upon by the elder in the middle of the night...it couldn't be good. Raven turned, going through all of the possible things she might have done wrong, trying her best to hide her trembling nerves, when movement in the shadows caught her eye. A third person stood in the room.

Zander leaned against the wall, half hidden in shadow, with one foot propped against the wall and his arms crossed. His eyes met hers. The candlelight flickered shadows across his face, and his eyes appeared black. He wore a dire seriousness that turned Raven's blood cold.

She balled her fists in her skirt. Had Zander told Mel what had happened? Had he told her father? Her heart skipped a beat, then sped up like the beating wings of the Cage Bird. She wanted to shout her accusations at him, but not in front of Mel.

"Raven." Mel folded her boney hands in front of her. Her calm voice soothed a minuscule amount of Raven's anger toward Zander. "The time has come for you to prove yourself. The time of change is fast approaching; the winds have told me as much. From here, your decisions will shape your future, and ours."

Raven bristled. She doubted her decisions in the kitchens would shape anything, unless her food poisoned everyone in the mine. She glanced again at Zander. Why did he have to be here for this? He seemed to hear her thoughts; a smirk broke his serious mask, and he winked. She bit back the urge to stick out her tongue at him.

"Something was stolen from us this night, something of great value," said Mel. "It must be recovered at all costs."

Raven blinked at Mel; her surprise stole whatever thought she had had. "I'm sorry, what?" she whispered.

"We have been robbed," Mel said plainly. "I am charging you with finding the thief."

Raven gawked; surely, she still slept. Sleepwalking. That had to be it. She shook her head and rubbed her temples, trying to wake herself up. She glanced back at Mel, who hadn't removed her stare. Zander leaned against the wall, his eyes focused on Birdie.

Raven's stomach turned over, and panic set in. Had she missed something? "I'm sorry. I-I don't understand. What thief? What's been stolen? When?"

"When you were on watch," Zander said dryly. His sapphire eyes flashed from Birdie to her. He wore no emotion she could easily read. "A thief snuck into the mine, stole from us, all the while the person who should have sounded the alarm didn't."

Her heart skipped a beat. She had been reading. Under Mel's knowing glare, Raven's entire face flushed. Even Zander looked angry.

"I-I'm sorry... I didn't..." Raven glanced between Mel and Zander, shame weighing her shoulders down. She started to shrink but realized what Mel had said—that she would be the one to retrieve the stolen something. Raven jerked her chin up and straightened her shoulders. "I'll get it back. I'll have the thief by sundown. Just tell me what was stolen and from where."

Mel didn't look convinced. "The thief stole a relic from the temple, something as ancient as the stone and as valuable as the stars," she said darkly. She lifted her chin and looked down at Raven, making her feel even smaller. "The thief has already fled into the night."

Into the night... Raven gasped. "Outside?" The mere word sent a jolt down her spine and into her toes.

Mel was sending her *outside*?

Mel nodded. "Yes. Outside. You are familiar with the terrain. And since it was your negligence that allowed the thief access to the mines..." Mel hesitated to let those words seep in. "I am charging you with the relic's recovery."

The thrill of chasing down a thief rose and then subsided. "But my father's orders—"

Mel held up a hand to silence her.

"He does not yet know of this," Mel said.

Raven blinked several times. Surely, she had misheard. Mel would defy her father's orders?

Her confusion must have shown, for Mel said, "This is a matter of the utmost importance. I will speak to him come dawn and explain why I have sent you."

After she had gone—which wouldn't give him a chance to scold Raven for messing up her patrol or refuse to let her leave.

Mel was helping her.

Then, why did it feel like punishment?

Raven held her shoulders straight. "Yes, of course, I'll go. I might not have the thief by sundown, though. Is there anything to go on? A direction? A face to go with this thief?"

Mel's stern stare faltered a fraction, and something like exasperation slipped through. "I am not sending you alone."

Raven's hope withered, and realization settled in. She cast a glance toward Zander. He gave her a crooked smile and slid Birdie back into her holster.

"That's why I'm here," Zander said. "We're going together."

Something caught in Raven's throat, then she blurted, "Why must it be Zander?"

"Because I know the terrain better than you." Zander patted Birdie. "And as you know, you wouldn't survive out there without me."

She balled her fists in her skirts. "I could arm myself."

"It would take too long to teach you how to shoot," Zander said, stepping off the wall. "And our thief is likely heading to Lenhala. If we get stopped by Gray Elite, you're going to need me."

Raven fumed. "I will not."

"He is right, Raven," said Mel. "Should you encounter the Gracitan forces, they will require identification."

"Yes, but why does it have to be Zander?" Of all the people in the mine!

"Because," Zander said, his words grim, "I'm from the capital. I have papers. My name has meaning. It'd be easy to explain that I met a girl and ran away with her, and that's why I've been gone so long. It wouldn't draw suspicion. Otherwise, the automatons might think us refugees."

His words sank in. *I met a girl.* Raven paled, and the heat of embarrassment made her legs feel like sand. "You're saying we would be undercover as..."

"Lovers," said Zander, the word a purr on his tongue.

The sand in her legs liquified, and she feared she might melt into a puddle. She might have, had Zander not shot his arrogant, knowing smirk at her. Her embarrassment became anger. She couldn't believe this! Finally, her chance to see the world beyond this forsaken village, and she had to go with pigheaded, show-off Zander.

"Absolutely not!" Raven stomped her foot.

"Stomping isn't very ladylike," Zander murmured.

"Shut up," Raven spat.

He rolled his eyes.

"I am not going to play that game with this..." She couldn't think of a proper insult for Zander, at least not one she could use in front of Mel.

He raised his brow at her, waiting for it.

She growled and continued, "Why can't you send someone else?"

Mel sighed. She started to speak, but Zander spoke for her. "Because I know my way around." His sneer vanished and became a serious demeanor that Raven hadn't seen on him before; she didn't know if she liked it or not. "Because I'm *from the capital*. I lived in Lenhala." He hesitated, and a darkness came over his face. Then, he whispered, "I'm Gray Elite."

A heartbeat passed. Then two. Three.

"You..." Raven started, then paused.

She had to be sleepwalking.

Zander, a Gray Elite? Part of the military who had scattered deadly machines throughout the kingdom to hunt people like mice, who had destroyed magic and those who wielded it, who had forced the people of Silver Glen to live underground out of fear. Raven stepped back; her back hit the wooden door. She bent over, eyes on Zander's scuffed leather boots, the well-made leather boots that he had always worn.

She thought back to that day six months ago when she had first seen Zander. He was sitting in the trading post on the surface, a tankard of ale in his hands, talking to her father. His trousers had been torn and dirty. His shirt had slept-in wrinkles. His hair had been filthy. His sapphire eyes had met hers—full of defeat, ceaseless worry, and desperation. He had been withdrawn for the first few weeks, barely talking to anyone, and then he and Brent restored Birdie. Zander taught a few of the other boys how to shoot, and her father put him on scavenging duty.

He had started to talk more, and to make him feel welcome, Raven talked to him. She had sought him out a few times; she had asked him about the world outside the mine, but the details he gave were short. Eventually, she stopped asking. They talked more and more. She started to consider him a friend. He lost his shyness and wariness and relaxed into his cocky self, and while those eyes of his had been intriguing at first, every time he opened his mouth, she wanted to smack that smirk off his face.

All that time, Zander had been a Gray Elite? An enemy?

Zander wasn't smiling now.

Her voice came out small. "I thought you were an escaped refugee."

Zander's eyes lingered on her; then he shrugged. "It sounded better that way. If people knew I was a deserter, they would either turn me in for the money or kill me on sight."

Raven took a deep, steadying breath. None of this made sense. It all felt silly, strange, and she expected herself to be jolted awake at any moment by her sister, urging her to walk with her to the kitchens.

Zander's lips twitched upward.

Suddenly, she burned with embarrassment. "This is a joke, isn't it?" she asked, her voice wobbly. "You're pulling another joke on me."

Raven tightened her hands in her skirt, turning her knuckles white. Zander knew how badly she wanted to see Lenhala, to see the world outside this bloody village!

Zander frowned. "Rae, I'm not. Listen—"

She turned to leave, but Zander jumped between her and the door. He threw his arms out to block her path.

"Move!" Raven demanded.

Zander stood firm.

Mel's calm, quiet voice came from the other side of the room, "This would be a good time to explain yourself to her, Zander."

Raven looked over her shoulder at the elder. She stood half in shadow, the candle's light reflecting in her dark eyes. She was looking at Zander, not Raven, and the piercing look gave Raven a chill.

Zander huffed. "Fine."

Raven looked between Zander and Mel; something had passed silently between them. Another secret.

Zander took a deep breath, lowered his arms, and set his sapphire stare on Raven. Calmly, he said, "I was born in Lenhala. While my father served in the Gray Elite forces, he and my mother believed in the resistance against Regent Dunel's reign."

She blinked. "Resistance?"

"There are those who strive to rid Rhynwier of Gracita's rule and restore the kingdom to its former glory," he said. "They do so by freeing slaves, scrapping automatons, stopping the Gray Elite from expanding any more than they already have, and striking at the Gray Elite from the shadows. My father was a general to King Reginald, and my mother was a lady in waiting to Queen Katerina. Though they swore their allegiance to Regent Dunel, they remained loyal to their kingdom."

Raven hugged her arms around her chest. She'd never seen Zander so serious and so nervous at the same time. She didn't like it. It reminded her of that first meeting.

Zander looked down at his scuffed leather boots. "My father gave me something to hide as far away from Lenhala as I could," he said, his voice near a whisper. "Somewhere the Gray Elite wouldn't come looking for it."

"And you came here and hid it among the relics of the Sisters," Raven finished for him.

Zander nodded.

Her stepmother would be sick with shame at such an act. Raven shrugged and added, "Well, what is it?"

What could be so important that his parents would send him, an eighteen-year-old boy, to the edge of the world?

"I can't tell you," said Zander.

"Oh? Keeping more secrets?"

He frowned. "I don't know what it is. Only that it is very valuable and rare. My father sealed it in an iron box. I've never looked inside."

A part of her didn't believe him. She huffed. "Why me? Why not pick someone else to go with you?"

He gave her a lopsided grin. "Well, considering it *was* your fault for not paying attention on watch..." She swatted at him, but he jumped out of her reach. "And you are good at navigating the terrain. You're skilled at not being detected, at least, when you're trying. With a few lessons, you could pass for aristocracy."

31

"Why would I need to pass as aristocracy?" The word tumbled ungracefully from her lips.

His grin faltered. "Because that's the part of Lenhala I'm from." He took a step toward her. "This is serious, Raven. My parents put their trust in me to keep that box safe. I will get it back."

"But..." She gaped between Mel and Zander.

"We leave now," Zander said. "We need to be as far from here as possible when everyone wakes."

"Why?"

"Because I do not want your father sending a team after us," Zander said.

She wanted to ask if her father knew about this iron box, but Mel spoke first, "I agree. Now is best. Things have been packed. If you leave now, you will have several hours between you and here by dawn."

Raven sighed. Though the thought of such a journey thrummed through her veins, the idea of walking until dawn—several hours—exhausted her. Zander appeared beside her with a pack over his shoulders and another for her in his hand. She took it, glad she had dressed earlier, and slung the pack over her shoulders.

"Let's get on with it, then," she groaned. "You better have packed breakfast."

The walk through the mine didn't feel real. Zander led the way to the trapdoor farthest from the main entrance. Outside, the stars blinked, cool air blew down from the mountains, and the animals of the dark scurried, chittered, and hooted.

She could almost hear her stepmother croon, *Wilyn is watching. The stars are her eyes.*

"Where are we going?" Raven asked as she followed Zander down the hillside. She felt glad to have Zander leading the way, but she would never tell him so.

Zander looked up at the stars. "We need to head south for a day; then we'll head southwest along the river."

"I thought we were catching a thief?"

"We are. That's the best way to get to the old kings' highway, which is where our thief has most likely gone. We'll be able to catch up to him this way."

He started down the slope, and she started after him. Questions of his plan popped up, one after another. "But how do you expect us to find this thief?" she asked. "What does he look like? What if he didn't head south? What if this thing of yours was taken by one of the kids or moved so someone could clean underneath it and put somewhere else?"

Zander huffed. "Because it wasn't in a place anyone else but Mel went. *Hidden.* It's something the Gray Elite would pay dearly for. We won't be dealing with a common street thief, Rae. For someone to have snuck into the mine unnoticed and poked around enough to find the thing, we're dealing with an expert thief."

Raven wanted to ask about the contents of the box, but Zander's dark tone made her tongue curl against her teeth. He glanced back at her, predatory gaze piercing through her.

"Forgive me for having questions," she muttered.

He shook his head. They didn't speak again until they had reached the boundary fence. Raven quickly glanced around for any more Cage Birds. She saw nothing, nor did she hear anything strange underneath the scurrying and chittering.

"And," Zander continued, "we're going the same way our thief would have gone."

"And if he went east? Or west?"

Zander shot an annoyed glare at her as he lifted his boot over the fence. "Then, we'll take a nice trip together." He brought his other foot to stand with the other so that the fence stood between them. "From this point on, things will be dangerous. This is your last chance to turn around and beg Mel to put you back on kitchen duty."

Raven straightened her shoulders and held her chin under his disbelieving glare. "Isn't this why you asked me to come along? Because I refused to balk at danger?"

Zander's glare didn't relent. "There are worse things out there than Cage Birds," he said grimly. "Much worse. Bigger. Meaner. Ruthless. Trust me, I've seen the monster machines the Gray Elite have made."

She huffed. "You expect me to go running back to the mines with my tail between my legs?"

He shrugged, his serious mask shifting. "It's a fair warning. And"—he stepped aside to let her climb over—"it is your fault it got stolen."

She rolled her eyes and climbed over the fence. He held his hand out to her, but she ignored it and jumped to the ground instead.

They had walked a short distance when Zander said, "That trap you triggered earlier also suggested the thief would take this route."

"How so?"

"Because it had been set along this path, see?" He pointed to where the trap lingered against the tree. "It had been set so that if someone caught him and came running after him, the trap would distract or kill his pursuers."

She blinked at the trap. "Oh." She cleared her throat. She hadn't thought of that at all. "Well, then, I feel more confident about our direction."

Zander chuckled and shot her a smirk. She groaned and started to walk a little faster. He matched her pace, and they headed steadily south.

10

The sun slowly rose, and the inky shadows of the forest lightened from gray to misty blue to sun-warmed yellow. Raven had never been above ground during the sunrise, and she hesitated to blink lest she miss one of the colors of the forest. Beside her, Zander didn't seem at all fascinated with the waking world as the birds started to chirp, as the night bugs grew quiet, as the sun warmed the leaves and bushes and ever-shifting foliage. Fog rose in low places, small dips in the forest floor, and hovered above ponds and lakes. As the sun's rays tumbled over the treetops, the fog and mist burned with the sun's light until nothing remained.

It was beautiful, more so than she had ever imagined.

The sunlight made Zander's bronze skin glow golden, while it made her look ghostly white.

She had never been more than a few hours' walk from the border of Silver Glen, but the trees didn't look that different, nor did the bushes, berries, or rocks. She knew the landmarks around Silver Glen, and when she spotted new rock formations or trees she didn't recognize, a tingle of excitement worked its way up her spine. She spotted sparkling lakes and ponds through the trees, reflecting the rising sun's light.

Zander spoke little, mostly to point out possible traps or snares within the natural world and what plants to avoid at all costs. The farther they walked, the greater her exhaustion became. It weighed on her limbs, her mind, until she felt as though she moved through mud. She followed Zander's back between the sun-parched trees, alongside whispering creeks, and along ancient stones that might have been the remains of homes, waystations, or roads.

Finally, when she didn't think she could go on, they came upon a waystation. Its walls were rough-cut logs, its roof unevenly vaulted. Horses were tied in a small stable beside it, and a hammered metal sign advertised ale, wine, trading, and beds. A dirt path stomped into submission by generations of horses wound east and west; it vanished out of sight through the trees.

"We rest here," said Zander, and Raven hadn't the thought to argue.

They walked through the door of the inn. One side was devoted to a small tavern; the other side, a trading post. It smelled like stale ale and sweat. The trading post was a counter—a metal sheet held between two barrels. A woman stood behind the counter, sorting buttons by shape and size.

"Morning, ma'am." Zander put on a weary smile. "Is there a room available for travelers?"

Her crisp eyes flickered between Zander and Raven. "There's room."

"I have money," Zander added meekly, and he withdrew a silver coin from his pocket. "Is this enough?"

34

The innkeeper eyed the coin, then eyed them again.

Raven glanced at the coin—a silver coin with a hard-nosed face stamped onto either side. A Gracitan token. Raven held in her surprise as best she could. Zander had Gracitan money? Of course, he did. He was a Gray Elite, she reminded herself.

"I-I have trading also," said Zander, a strain in his voice she'd never heard before, a desperation.

His pleading voice worked on the woman; her brow curved in pity.

"The token is acceptable." The woman took the token and deposited it underneath the counter. She placed a heavy iron key on the counter. "Down the hall, second room on your right. Number two. Key works the water heater too."

"Thank you, ma'am," Zander said with a bow of his head.

The woman's eyes ran up and down Zander, then shifted to Raven. She took in her home-sewn dress, her leather corset, her dusty boots. "You both look a little worse for wear," said the woman.

Before Raven could reply, Zander spoke quietly, "We've been traveling most of the night." He glanced around the mostly empty tavern. A few men who looked like travelers were sitting at the far table by the open window. A group of older women, all knitting, sat on the other side of the room. None were looking in their direction.

The woman made a small hum.

"We were..." Zander paused, glancing at Raven. He wore fear in his eyes, and her heart thudded against her rib cage. He lowered his voice. "We were attacked last night, and I couldn't bring myself to make camp in the woods."

The woman's eyes grew softer. "There's been more trouble to the north recently. Bandits or worse?"

"Cage Birds," he whispered.

The woman pulled her bottom lip into her mouth. She gave a subtle shake of her head.

Zander swallowed and glanced his sorrowful eyes at Raven. "One nearly took Rae." He reached out and took hold of Raven's hand, giving it a gentle squeeze. She nearly ripped it away from him but then remembered their roles. Lovers. She let him hold her hand and tried to look at him with what she hoped was kindness, while pretending her heart didn't flutter at the touch.

"It could have been worse," the woman whispered. "I've had travelers tell me they've seen Goliaths in the woods."

Zander made a small sound of shock. He shook his head in disbelief. "No," he whispered. "Sisters, there's getting to be fewer safe places in this kingdom. Soon, Gracita will have us all enslaved."

The woman nodded. "You'll want a warm meal later, I suppose. We don't have much, but my girl and I can cook up a fine stew from the ingredients the wood offers. Wilyn hasn't abandoned us entirely."

"Thank you," Zander said.

"Take care," said the woman. "I'll send word when the meal is ready if I don't see you."

Zander thanked the woman again, and then he led Raven down the hall. An iron number two had been nailed onto the lopsided door. He unlocked the door with a heavy clunk and pushed it open. It was a small room, but a room. Raven walked past him and dropped her pack onto the floor before collapsing onto the metal frame bed that took the majority of the space.

"I'm exhausted," she grumbled.

He dropped his pack on the floor and threw his jacket over it. "Don't hog the bed; scoot over," he grumbled.

She blinked and pushed herself onto her elbows. Indeed, their room had only a single bed. Two pillows. One blanket.

Her face burned. "There's only one bed?"

He put his fingers to his lips and hissed, "Because we've lovers, remember? *My love?*"

She swallowed and glanced down to the bare wood floors. "Maybe you should sleep on the floor."

He half laughed. "Why should I sleep on the floor?"

"Because you're the gentleman," she said flatly.

He lifted a brow at her and laughed—his low laugh sent a shiver down her spine. "I'm a gentleman, she says," he said, a smirk on his lips. He unfastened his holsters and hung them on one of the brass coat hooks nailed unevenly on the wall. He sat down on the other side of the bed and started to unbuckle his boots. "I'm sleeping right here. You are free to sleep wherever you see fit."

Zander reclined back on the second pillow and let out a sigh of relaxation.

Raven glanced at the floor; it looked horribly uncomfortable. Beside her, Zander's face had already relaxed, his chin dipped to the side—asleep. Or pretending, like he had done for the past six months, like he had done with the innkeeper.

Raven sat up, untied her corset, unbuckled her boots, and set them on the floor. She unclasped her locket and slid it inside one of her boots so she wouldn't lose it. Gritting her teeth, she climbed underneath the blanket beside Zander. The space between them felt too small, and she could feel the heat coming off his body. She could feel him there, breathing, his heat pressing against her back.

Despite the oddity of his proximity, she tried to find comfort. She needed sleep; she was exhausted. Sunlight seeped through the wooden shutters on the narrow window, making the room much brighter than her bedroom back at Silver Glen. She had never before tried to sleep in the sunlight. When she closed her eyes, the shadows were tinged with orange and gold.

"The Gray Elite will pay for the capture of anyone with magic," Zander whispered. "There are some who would eagerly turn in strangers for a chance of a few tokens."

"Is that why the innkeeper was hesitant?"

"Yeah. But when I told her about the automaton almost taking you, she got that sympathetic look in her eye. She's not one of those." Zander shifted, and the whole bed shifted with him. The metal frame creaked. When he spoke, he sounded closer. "People are wary of strangers. People are quick to point out magicians. The Gray Elite have turned the people against them. People are terrified of magic now."

"Why is that?"

"Anyone caught harboring a magician will also be put to death," Zander said grimly. "Even if they knew nothing about it."

Her heart skipped a beat. "That's awful."

"I didn't say it wasn't. Gracita is serious about stomping out magic."

"Why, though? It never made sense to me."

"To prove their machines superior," he said bitterly. "And, Gracitans, by nature, can't use magic. My father used to say they feared it, so they strove to make themselves stronger, and when they could, they invaded Rhynwier. They are always striving to make sure magic doesn't come back."

"Come back?" Raven rolled onto her back. Zander had rolled onto his side, facing her. His exhausted sapphire eyes met hers.

He half laughed. "Magic isn't something you can stomp out, though the Gray Elite try. They see magic as a disease and think killing all those with it will make it go away. But that's now how magic works."

"How does it work?"

He didn't answer immediately. His gaze turned curious and searched hers. Those eyes fell to her lips, and her heart stopped. "They don't know," he whispered, and his gaze returned to her eyes. "No one does. And the Gray Elite want to keep it that way."

They stared at one another for a long moment; then Raven turned her gaze to the ceiling. She didn't ask any more questions; Zander didn't offer up any more history. Soon, gentle snores came and went with the rising and falling of his chest. Soon, exhaustion pulled her far into sleep.

Raven woke feeling better rested than she had in a long while. Her body had never felt more relaxed. She didn't want to move. She inhaled, and the scent of dirt and sweat filled her nose. Sunlight gleamed on the other side of her eyelids, warm and welcoming. Birds flitted about, tweeting and chirping to one another. Voices drifted from somewhere. Outside, maybe.

Then the night before came back to her.

The inn, she realized. She blinked her eyes open. Judging by the golden sunlight streaming in through the gaps in the shutters, it was afternoon. She'd slept most of the morning. She inhaled, filling her drowsy chest with the stale air of the inn, and rolled onto her back.

Her arm grazed something warm. She turned her head; Zander slept beside her. Right beside her. Her arm grazed his. It took a heartbeat and a half for her to feel the heat from him pressing into her, and another heartbeat for that heat to flush her face bright pink. She moved her arm away quickly.

Zander shifted but continued to sleep. Gentle snores escaped his parted lips.

Trying her best to ignore the rapid thumping of her heart, Raven carefully scooted off the bed and tiptoed into the small adjoining bathroom. Shutting herself inside, she heaved a breath.

Copper pipes of varying sizes ran along the back wall, connecting the water basin, the toilet, and the showerhead tucked into the tiled corner of the room. Underneath the main water tank, the heater looked like something Brent would salvage together from scrap metal.

She unbuttoned her dress and hung it over a wooden chair. She laid her underdress on top of it, followed by her socks and underthings. She stood on her tiptoes to turn on the water heater, but it had no knob or level. Only a keyhole.

Of course, the key. It started the heater.

Raven reached for her clothes but stopped. It would be a burden to redress only to undress a few seconds later. And Zander was likely still sleeping. She glanced around and found Zander's overshirt hanging off a hook—he must have gotten up sometime in the night and left it here.

Slipping Zander's shirt over her naked body, Raven tiptoed back into the bedroom. She spotted the heavy key at once, sitting on the small table at the foot of the bed. She closed her hand around it, and then someone cleared their throat.

She whipped around, holding the key out like a dagger. Zander stood by the open window, canteen tilted toward his lips. Water dribbled down his chin, and his eyes had gone wide.

A fire burned through her cheeks. She wore nothing but his shirt.

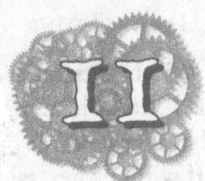

Zander gaped at her, unblinking, while the water dribbled from the canteen and onto his undershirt. Raven yanked the hem of the shirt as far down as it would go, but her knuckles still only grazed the tops of her thighs. It covered the necessities but left her legs bare. Zander's wide eyes wandered up and down her exposed legs, and her skin prickled under his gaze. She had never seen that look on his face—hunger.

She flushed from head to toe. "Stop looking!" she hissed.

He blinked several times. His parted lips curved into a mischievous grin, and he said, "If you didn't want me to look, you shouldn't have come out half naked."

Her skin felt like fire. She stormed back into the bathroom and shut the door. She thrust the heavy key into the water heater. With a hard turn, the heater started. Steam hissed through the pipes, heating the water in the tank.

How dare he! Her skin burned, and one look in the broken mirror told her she'd gone entirely red. She yanked off his shirt and left it on the floor.

She didn't wait for the water to heat all the way. She pulled the chain to release the water into the shower's pipes; it streamed out of the head. She welcomed the cooler water against her burning skin. After that episode, she needed a cold shower.

When Raven reentered the bedroom wearing her dress, Zander was gone. She combed her light brown hair and braided it back. She tied up her corset and slipped on her boots, taking care to make sure her dagger was secure. She was slipping her locket underneath the collar of her dress when the door opened, and Zander sauntered through.

His eyes ran along her body before he met her gaze; her cheeks burned. He cocked a grin, and if she had been holding something, she would have thrown it at him.

"Dinner's nearly ready." Zander shut himself in the bathroom.

She sighed through her nose and opened the shutters. She could see people coming and going from the tavern and trading post. There weren't that many more people than in Silver Glen, and they all looked ragged and weary. The few houses and buildings she could see looked to have been there a long time, the wooden logs weathered to gray, nails rusty and orange, shutters lopsided, and fences patched in several different shades of newness.

It looked like the ramshackle surface town of Silver Glen, a ghost of its former self. Another town the one-hundred-year war had torn through. Another town the Gray Elite had left to rot.

At the thought of her home, her chest tightened. Her father would know she'd left by now. Zander too. What had Mel told him? Had he sent a search party to retrieve them? Had Mel convinced him otherwise?

The mines would be better off without her, said a mean little voice in her head. She didn't hold an important job. Maybe that was why Zander had chosen to take her along—the mines wouldn't miss her.

Zander stepped out of the bathroom. His hair was wet, and his shirt clung to the water between his shoulder blades. He sat on the bed beside her, and she feared he'd bring up that he'd seen her nearly naked.

"Here's the plan," he whispered, and her chest loosened. "During dinner, I'll keep everyone in the tavern distracted. You sneak into the other rooms and see if our thief is staying here."

"And if he is?"

"Then, you steal back the box."

She huffed. "What kind of plan is that?" He frowned, and she added, "What kind of thief would leave his goods lying about? How am I supposed to know which room to search? How am I supposed to steal it back?"

"Then, I guess you'll have to go through their things," he said. "We don't have much choice. We need that box. I don't know how else to search without holding them all at gunpoint and demanding they empty their pockets. That won't go over well."

She nodded. As much as it pained her to admit, he was right. "You expect me to knock? The doors will undoubtedly be locked."

Zander threw her a smirk. "I know how good you are at picking locks."

At that, she didn't balk. Brent hadn't invented a lock that she couldn't get through. At his smirk, her cheeks burned, and her pride swelled.

They went to dinner together. More people lingered in the inn than before, everyone in the little town it seemed. The innkeeper, the woman who'd given them the key, and her husband and daughter ran the place. Her husband looked like a much more agreeable person, laughing and talking to anyone within range of his booming voice, which was most people. He clapped Zander on the shoulder like an old friend and gave him a wide, friendly smile that Zander returned.

Zander and Raven accepted steaming bowls of wild stew and joined a local couple at a table. It was a logging town, they quickly discovered. It had the best supply of white oak and red pine, but the Gray Elite had stifled business when their machines took over. They preferred metal to wood, and the logging industry had declined.

The view of the Gray Elite was poor here, just as it had been in Silver Glen. As the loggers and farmers began to drink and talk, Raven understood why Zander had been nervous about spending Gracitan tokens; no one liked the Gray Elite, and several promised horrible deaths to any unsuspecting Gray Elite foolish enough to be caught alone.

Raven didn't contribute to the talk. She kept her eyes on her stew, looking carefully at the chopped meat and roots. Rabbit, maybe?

One hundred years of war had taken its toll on Rhynwier, and the past fifteen years had only been worse. The Regent, Marco Dunel, had brought poverty to the countryside while building up life for the rich and powerful in Lenhala and making Gracita's people richer.

Rhynwier suffered while Gracita prospered.

Raven ate the entire bowl, though her stomach clenched. She handed her bowl back to the innkeeper, hoping the older woman wouldn't notice how badly her hands were shaking.

"How are you holding up, dear?" asked the innkeeper. She glanced at Raven's hands, then at her eyes.

"My nerves," Raven whispered—her stepmother had often complained of her nerves.

Zander joined another table, the one in the thick of the talking. Raven excused herself. She entered the hall as the room exploded into drunken laughter. Zander began to spew a joke of his own, his words slurring.

He hadn't drunk near enough to be drunk. Then, she realized, he was pretending.

Raven tiptoed to the far room in the hall, the room with an iron number three nailed to the wood. As good of a place as any to start. She slid a steel hairpin from her hair—pins that Brent had gifted her—and easily picked the lock. She slowly let herself inside, eyes watching the room and the hall; she did not want to explain herself should the room's occupant come around the corner.

She didn't see the box in any obvious places. She went through the pockets of the smelly overcoat, the small leather bag, and every conceivable hiding place in the room. No iron box. With every moment that passed, every burst of laughter from the main room, her heart beat faster.

She locked the door from the inside and slid back into the hall. She looked through the other three rooms, but she found no iron box. She did find coin, both silver Gracitan tokens and copper Rhynwierian marks. Her hand clasped around the coins, and she fought a slither of greed to take them.

No. She had seen the people in the town and the people passing through. She couldn't steal from them. They needed their money more than she did. Not even the book of plants she found in the last room. If she stole it, she wouldn't have anywhere to put it.

She found many things among the possessions but no iron box. By the time she slipped back into her and Zander's room, a bawdy song about a bar wench had most of the tavern singing along, and her heart pounded deafeningly loud.

When Zander finally returned to the room, his voice was hoarse from singing and shouting. He cleared his throat and looked at her expectantly.

She shook her head. "Nothing."

Zander let out a sigh. "Then our thief's not here. He's moved on, I'd bet."

"Then, I suppose that means we should as well," she said.

He nodded.

That night, just as the sun began to set, they set out south, toward the old highway. Zander traded a few things for rations and first aid supplies, making Raven wish she had taken a few in her pilfering.

"Stay safe in your travels," said the innkeeper. "I wish you luck. Watch out for Cage Birds and Goliaths."

"Remember," said the innkeeper's husband, "the Goliaths might look tough, but they can't swim."

Raven and Zander headed out into the summer night. They followed the dirt path into the woods. She wanted to know what a Goliath looked like, what it sounded like, but she and Zander moved too quickly to talk. The forest slowly changed, and she spotted more and more maples and fewer pines. In the dark, she spotted things moving through the underbrush: coyotes, deer, and who knew what else. She took a small relief in knowing that Zander could shoot a deer between the eyes at a hundred yards. She'd seen him do it.

Finally, they stopped beside a lake to eat and drink. The moonlight reflected off the surface of the water, broken into constantly moving slivers.

In the quiet, Raven found her chance.

"What is a Goliath?" Raven asked, breaking her dried venison in smaller, easier to chew chunks.

"It's an automaton shaped like a man, only taller and wider and meaner. They have empty chest cavities to store people inside, but they more often kill on sight," Zander said flatly, eyes on the dried meat in his hands. He glanced around as if one might appear. "They are one of many automatons the Gray Elite used during the war."

Zander stared out over the water. The moonlight made his sapphire eyes glitter and his hair appear black. A shadow of stubble darkened his jaw. Beautiful, if she had to put a word to it. Handsome, without a doubt, even if she'd never admit it to him. It would only make him more arrogant. He turned his glittering eyes to her, and her heart skipped a beat.

She looked out over the water. "What if we don't find our thief?" she whispered. She didn't need to speak very loud. Aside from the animals scurrying and bugs chittering, there was little noise. Crickets sang from the rushes alongside the lake, as did a chorus of frogs.

"We'll find him," he said, his voice hard.

"You're awfully confident about it." She tossed another chunk of venison into her mouth.

A soft sigh escaped his lips. "You'd rather give up and sulk back home? Raven, we have to find that box, and we will." A shadow of desperation darkened his tone.

She believed him, but a part of her thought him mad to worry so much over a box whose contents he didn't know. "Do you think our thief knows its value?" she asked.

"He would have to." Zander leaned back on his elbows and stared up at the starry sky. "Either he knows, or he's guessed. It would have taken a good thief to sneak into the mines and out again, and any good thief wouldn't have come all this way unless there's a significant payout waiting for him."

Raven tossed a bit of fat from her dried venison into the shallows of the lake. The moonlight rippled. "I wonder what could be inside that's so valuable." The mystery of it tingled at the back of her mind.

An owl hooted in a nearby tree.

Zander sighed. "I don't know. I do know it's something the Gray Elite would pay a fortune for. It's powerful, priceless, and rare."

She whispered, "Is it magic?"

He didn't answer. After a long moment, he stood. "Come on, we're wasting time."

She nodded, regardless of her doubts and questions. Chasing a thief through the wooded countryside of Rhynwier trumped mashing blackberries into preserves and scrubbing the same pots and pans every night.

They topped off their canteens under a small waterfall and set off through the moonlit forest. Through the canopy, Raven spotted the endless stars. She watched for the moving shadows of airships, but she saw none.

12

Raven and Zander came to the old highway just after sunrise. Before the war, before the Gray Elite seized control of the kingdom, the old highway had been a main artery of transportation. It weaved through the major towns, leading all to the capital of Lenhala. Raven looked up and down the road, but she saw no other travelers. Way ahead of them, she thought she saw dots of something moving, but she couldn't tell.

She and Zander started south. The forest had grown closer to the highway, shading it from the sun. The years without care had left the road cracked, faded, and in some parts, fallen in. Weeds and bushes and trees ate at the edge of the road, crumbling it.

The highway ran beside a wide river, where fishing boats leisurely graced the water. Villages spotted the bank, and each one had the same rundown homes and lopsided fences, children playing in the shallows, jumping and splashing. It reminded Raven of the river near Silver Glen where, in the warmest days of summer, they had swam as children.

The water was safe. Automatons could not get wet.

"Down south, where the river is widest," said Zander, "there is a city built over the water."

"Over the water? Is it floating? Like a ship?"

"No. It's built over the river like a bridge. Ships pass underneath it."

She tried to picture such a place, but it looked ridiculously impractical in her mind. "What keeps it from falling into the water?"

"I don't know, another marvel of the Gray Elite's craftsmanship and desire to prove themselves above the laws of man and nature," Zander said bitterly.

Raven didn't ask any more about the floating city. Instead, she asked, "Have you ever seen a sky city?"

"I have."

"Have you been on one?" Curiosity bubbled in her stomach.

"Yes."

She bit her lip. "What was it like?"

He glanced at her, and when he beheld her childlike wide eyes, he smiled. "It's like being on a ship, only once it's in the air, it doesn't come back down. It's always moving, and it feels like it too. The turbines are always going, and the noise they make is deafening. Sleep is hard to come by."

She glanced into the cloud-speckled sky as if one might appear on the horizon. An entire city in the sky. Her heart ached to see such a sight!

"You want to see one that badly?" he asked. He knew of her desire; she had told him once, months ago.

"I want to live in one."

Zander frowned. "They're more confining than the mines."

"But they never stay in one place," she said in awe. "It would be marvelous to go to sleep in one city and wake up in another. Every day an adventure."

"Most sky cities have a path they follow," Zander said. "And the ship goes where the captain deems, which is greatly influenced by where the city's baron wants them to go, which is greatly influenced by where the Gray Elite wants them to go. It's not the freedom you think it is."

She pouted. "You're marring my dream."

"I'm adding reality to your dream," he said. "Sky cities are where barons and admirals hide their friends. They're more clubs than communities."

"I still think it would be thrilling to live in the sky," she said.

He chuckled. "You're just sick of living underground."

She did not disagree with him. His truths about the sky cities did not dampen her spirits entirely, and she refused to let them.

By midday, they came to the next town. It sat beside the river and had a number of rickety wooden docks and the near-overwhelming smell of fish. Raven didn't mind the smell; her feet ached, and her stomach begged for something other than venison jerky and water. The inn sat beside a blacksmith, and the whole inn smelled of white-hot iron, sweat, and smoke.

Zander paid for their room with Gracitan tokens. He acted the same as he had before; he played the role of the pitiful traveler weary from an escape of Cage Birds. This innkeeper did not whisper of Goliaths. He glared at Zander, at the coin, at Raven, but he slid them a key to one of the rooms, which Zander accepted with gratitude.

"I'd keep an eye out if I were you," Zander whispered, locking the door. "I don't like that innkeeper. He's suspicious."

Raven nodded, though she felt too exhausted to care much what the innkeeper thought.

Again, their room had a single bed. Neither said a word as they shed their outer layers and crawled under the musty-smelling blanket. Outside their narrow window, hammers beat iron and steel into submission. Over and over and over.

They slept until midafternoon. They washed up in the small bathroom, ate muddy-tasting fish at the tavern next door, and that evening, while Zander rolled the locals into a drunken song, Raven went through the rooms at the inn. After searching each one, she returned to their room without an iron box, but with a few Gracitan tokens, healing ointment, bandages, and a bag of almonds. She had taken things they could use, not things they would have to barter with; she didn't want the owner of the stolen item to recognize it.

45

She tucked the stolen items into their packs and then sat down on the bed. It surprised her how easy taking the things had been. She had assumed she would feel guilt, but she didn't. She reasoned with herself that she hadn't taken anything that would ruin a person or starve a family; she had taken small things. Things a person might not miss.

Raven waited, but still the drunks in the tavern sang. The sun set, the crowd in the tavern filtered out into the night, and Zander didn't return.

She began to pace. Had something happened? Had someone recognized him as Gray Elite? Had that innkeeper ratted him out?

Her heart beat faster with every passing moment.

Finally, she heard Zander's drunken voice drift down the hall of the inn. A pair of boots scuffed and shuffled; another pair walked steadily.

"This is great," Zander slurred. "I haven't had so much fun. I shouldn't go back to the city." He hiccupped. "You country folk know how to live."

"Aye," said a male voice. "That we do. You'd be welcome here if you're thinking of staying. Talk to me in the morning. There's always work for able-bodied men."

It took a moment to place his voice—the innkeeper. He spoke softer than he had when they'd arrived.

"Weren't there more people here?" Zander hiccupped. "I remember more people."

"We get people coming and going on the highway," said the innkeeper. "Not as much as we used to, though."

"What 'bout that fellow with the braids? Reminds me—" *hiccup* "—of my little brother."

"Oh, that one left before dinner. Odd fellow. A bit shifty. You're better off without talking to that one," said the innkeeper. Keys jingled. "Ah, here we are."

The door swung open. The innkeeper shuffled through, supporting a drunk Zander.

Raven didn't have to pretend to gawk. Fury bubbled. She jumped to her feet, hands knotted in her skirt. "What happened?" she demanded.

"What d'ya mean 'what happened'?" Zander hiccupped.

The innkeeper helped him over the threshold and then let go. Zander teetered, and Raven dashed forward to catch him. He leaned fully onto her, hot breath on her neck, and she grunted as she supported his weight to the bed. They made it to the bed, and Zander flopped. The metal frame squeaked.

Zander let out a sigh. "I drank a little bit," he mumbled.

"A little bit too much," laughed the innkeeper.

"Thank you for bringing him back," Raven said, patting Zander affectionately, though she felt like smacking him. While she had been looking for the box, he'd been drinking. Really drinking. She let her hand rest between his shoulder blades. The heat from his body soaked into her hand.

46

The door closed, and the innkeeper headed down the hall.

Zander hiccupped and rolled onto his back.

Raven stood and hissed, "You're useless."

"Useless?" he whispered, slur gone. He propped himself up with his elbows. "I can hold my ale better than that, Rae. Find it?"

She blinked. His eyes were no longer watery or unfocused. He looked at her with the alert intensity he always had. Of course. Pretending. She felt foolish for believing his act.

She fisted her hands in her skirt. "No."

She didn't tell him about the other things she'd taken. He would find out when he opened his pack; then she would explain.

Zander swung his legs to the floor. "Then, I'm willing to bet our thief left right after dinner."

She opened her mouth to question him, then realized. "The man you asked the innkeeper about."

He nodded. "I saw him at the last stop too. He's traveling alone and light."

She blinked, disbelieving that Zander could be that crafty. "And he's on the move," she said. "So, we'll be on the move. Good thing I've readied the packs."

Zander grabbed his jacket from the hook on the wall. "Right. We leave immediately."

"But you're drunk," she said. "Won't that look suspicious if you leave sober?"

"Drunk men make horrible decisions every night." Zander buttoned his jacket unevenly, slid his pack over his shoulders, and then sauntered with all the grace of a drunk man.

Raven grabbed her own pack. *Pretending.*

Zander had been right; though the innkeeper looked at him with heavy disapproval, he didn't force him to stay another night and sleep off the ale. He simply shook his head at Zander and gave a nod of sympathy to Raven.

As they left, she heard him mumble, "Poor woman. I'd hate to deal with that drunken bastard."

She let the door close behind her and followed Zander into the cloudy night with a smile on her face. She knew Zander had heard the innkeeper too.

They traveled through the night and into the morning. The stars faded one by one. The eastern horizon glowed blue-gray, then pink, then orange; then the golden-yellow sunlight spilled over the tops of the trees, burning away the pockets of lingering fog and dew. From a high point, she could see for miles. Villages and farms dotted the countryside, connected with dirt roads and circled with boundary fences.

They passed a field of golden wheat where automaton Harvesters worked. With scythes for hands and chests made for storing, the machines worked faster than humans could. Their bodies were silver against the golden wheat, their movements identical and monotonous. Steam hissed out at uneven intervals.

Raven stared—she had only ever heard of Harvesters.

"Another marvel of the Gray Elite," murmured Zander with distaste. "One Harvester replaces ten workers, and that's ten workers without a job and ten families without money or food."

She hadn't thought of that. Her marvel turned sour. Indeed, she didn't see a single human worker in the fields.

They continued on, skirting villages and fields in case humans or automatons spotted them. They kept to the forest paths that paralleled the highway when they needed, avoiding clumps of people and towns that sat on the highway. Zander explained that the towns that supplied better things for the Gray Elite received better supplies in turn.

"So the towns here have more incentive to turn in refugees," he whispered.

Still, they walked.

The sun neared the midpoint in the sky.

"My feet are killing me," Raven complained. They didn't hurt that bad, but she only wanted to take a short break. To rest, to breathe, to let the sweat along her spine dry.

"We're running out of time as it is," Zander said, though exhaustion underlined his eyes and snapped in his words.

Slowly, the sun reached the midpoint and started an impossibly slow slide to the west. Raven couldn't stand it anymore. Her stomach was grumbling, and her feet really did hurt.

"I'm exhausted," she said. "If we don't stop soon, I'm going to pass out in the middle of the road."

Zander growled and spat an insult under his breath. The next town they came to was larger than the others; several hundred people called it home. The lingering scent of freshly tilled fields tickled her nose as Zander led her to a shady inn off the main street, down a narrow side road with barely enough room for two people to walk side by side.

Raven hesitated outside the inn's lopsided, weathered, and discolored front door. It looked to have once been painted white, but the paint had streaked and peeled and flaked.

Zander rolled his eyes. "What? I thought you were tired," he growled.

"Yes, but, are you sure about this place?" She eyed a spiderweb in the corner of the roof. A fat spider sat waiting.

"Yes." He entered the inn without another word.

Raven hesitated but followed. She kept her eyes on the spider—she feared that if she took her eyes off him, he wouldn't be there when she looked back. The inn looked as questionable on the inside as it had on the outside. Smoke lingered against the ceiling, blown from a group of men with wood-and-copper pipes in their mouths. An odd smell lingered, sweet and warm and bitter all at once. Raven tried to place the smell, but she couldn't.

Zander approached the innkeeper, a hunched man with narrow, suspicious eyes. He took the silver token without question and handed them a bent room key. Zander dragged her to their room and quickly shut them inside. The room didn't look like it had been cleaned. The linens were stained, the floors needed sweeping, and instead of a bathroom, it had a water basin in the corner. A moth-eaten curtain the color of mildew hung against the wall, the only privacy for someone using the water basin. That strange smell lingered in the room, like it came from the very wood.

"It's disgusting," Raven said. "I think I'd rather sleep outside."

"If you were a thief, where would you stay?" Zander said. Exhaustion nipped at his words. He dropped his pack to the floor. "A thief trying to keep a low profile wouldn't stay at a decent inn. He'd go to one like this."

Zander pushed aside the ratty curtain over the window, the sunlight illuminating a strip down the middle of his face, and then he let the curtain flutter back into place. Dust swam through the dim air like snow.

She shrugged off her pack and set it by his. Sisters, how her shoulders ached. "What's that smell?" she asked, sniffing. "It's like sweet cloves and mint."

He half laughed. "Don't breathe it in too deep. That's opium."

She blinked. She'd only heard of the drug, but she'd never smelled it. She took another quick sniff of the air. "It smells like winter candy."

"It's laced with—" he stepped closer and dropped his voice "—magic."

Her heart thumped at the word.

"Oh," she said. Did that make it better? Worse?

"The men downstairs were smoking it, and I'm willing to bet the tavern next door is a den." Zander glanced again out the window. "And, if I had extra coin and a betting attitude, I would bet that our thief will stop by before he goes."

She tensed. "You want to visit an opium den?" A magic-opium den.

"They're illegal," he said. "So people who have no problem with illegal activities often visit them. Thieves, criminals, magicians. You can find them all in an opium den."

Her heart leaped. "Magicians?" she whispered.

He nodded. "With magic being illegal, the magicians left have had to find other ways to make a living. They can't exactly be farmers or fisherman. The automatons would find them," he whispered. He shot her a sideways glance.

She put the thoughts together. "They become criminals?"

"Drug dealers, back-alley healers, problem solvers," he said casually, waving his hand between them. He smirked, though his exhaustion pulled the humor from his eyes. "Consider it a lesson on culture."

They slept into the late afternoon, ate at the tavern, and after a few seedy conversations, Zander got them access to the opium den next door. There were no doors from the street. The only way in or out was through a secret door in the tavern, guarded by a man sitting on a barrel. He wore a dark cap low over his eyes, and at first glance, he looked asleep. But as Raven and Zander approached him, his dark, beady eyes took them in faster than she could blink.

The opium den was darkly lit and not much bigger than the tavern. Mismatched tables and chairs scattered the mezzanine and the sides of the main floor. A few dozen people lingered about the den, some inhaling from bowls, some smoking pipes. Most wore ratty clothes or dark cloaks; none looked like upstanding citizens. Their calm chatter resounded like the chittering of evening bugs, constant and natural.

Three lanterns hung from the ceiling and gave off a pale lilac light. Metal bowls of burning opium were scattered around the room, each producing a different color of smoke; the streams of smoke slithered up to the ceiling and mingled without mixing, creating an ever-moving rainbow. It hid the ceiling, and Raven had the strangest urge to drag her fingers along the smoke, but she withheld her urge and kept her arms at her sides.

The den smelled like cloves and mint, and underneath it, she detected a scent she could not identify. *Magic,* she whispered to herself. Magic smoke. What would happen if she touched it?

Zander ordered them drinks, and Raven tried her best not to cringe when the cheap ale touched her tongue. They took seats on the mezzanine, not too close to any opium smoke, and Zander joined a table of cards. Raven lingered beside him, sitting close enough that their hips touched. She pretended to be interested in his gambling and his easy talk with the others, but her eyes wandered. Her imagination went with them.

She spotted scantily clad women and men who wore vests with nothing under them and easy smiles on their faces. She spotted scrawny thugs and big thugs, beady eyes and watchful eyes. Could one of them be their thief? How many of these people were magicians forced into a life of crime?

In her mind, she invented magician criminals who thrived in the underbelly of the kingdom, breaking laws and serving their own kind of justice for the right price.

While Zander gambled and talked, a band appeared down below. They set up on a little stage and carried strange instruments of brass and strings and an assortment of drums. They began to play a haunting, somber tune; her eyes drifted to the smoking bowls, whose streams seemed to undulate with the music.

Were there more bowls than before? She didn't remember seeing the pink smoke or the pale blue or the sunrise orange—so many colors!

Her eyes met those of a blonde girl across the mezzanine. She sat on a man's lap with his arm draped over her thighs. The girl winked at Raven, and Raven winked back. She didn't see the harm in it.

She took another sip of her ale. It wasn't so bad after the first sip or two. She could barely feel the burn of it.

There *were* more bowls—the smoke rose thick in plumes of purple, pink, blue, orange, and red. It rose up and up, ever-changing, swirling, colliding into new colors she had never seen before nor imagined.

Zander was laughing, a low and steady sound. It reverberated in her chest, down her ribs, and into her hips. The drums were beating low. People danced on the main floor, over and under and all around. They looked to be having so much fun. She wanted to have fun too. Why shouldn't she be allowed to have fun? A flash of yellow caught her eye, and she met the golden eyes of the blonde on the other side of the mezzanine.

The brassy instruments began to play a rhythmic chime like she'd never heard, and those strings pulled her to the first floor. She joined the other dancers, clustered together, all dancing as one. The blonde girl from across the mezzanine joined her and wrapped her slender arms around Raven's waist.

The drums beat, the strings chimed, and Raven felt the music pulse through her veins just as the smoke filtered through her lungs. It made everything better. With the bodies clustered so close together, she felt the life beating around her. All hot skin, loose hair, colored smoke, and the beat.

The blonde tipped her mouth to Raven's ear, and her warm breath mumbled something that pushed a laugh from Raven's throat. The blonde smiled at her and pulled Raven closer.

Raven didn't know when Zander had arrived, only that he had. He pushed himself between her and the fun blonde, who vanished into the dancing crowd. Zander brushed Raven's hair away from her ear and spoke low, hot words; his breath tickled against her skin.

Whatever she told him hadn't been his desired answer, and his grip on her shoulders tightened. She tried to pull him into a dance, but he didn't budge. Why did he have to be such a stick-in-the-mud? He said something, but she couldn't hear him over the beat. She tried again to dance with him, but he pulled her flush against him and then pulled her off the dancefloor, away from the crowd. She stumbled, but he held her upright.

The smoke thinned, the music quieted, and then cool night air met her sweaty skin. She could still feel the beating of the drums in her blood.

Zander grumbled.

Raven caught sight of the stars; they were dancing, throwing themselves about the inky sky, and watching them, she fell backward into Zander's chest.

"Look!" She pointed to the dancing stars. "They're dancing too."

"I shouldn't have let you out of my sight," Zander growled. He sounded tired, why did he have to be tired? They could have danced all night.

She wobbled, but Zander's hands on her waist guided her forward, into the inn and into their room. His grip loosened, and she twirled to face him. A dizzy spell overtook her, and she latched her fists in Zander's vest to keep upright.

"Don't you puke on me," he warned.

She laughed, and the dizziness passed. Sisters, had he always been this handsome? Giggling, she ran a hand along his unshaven jaw, her fingertips over his lips. She caught his hot exhale on her fingers. She grabbed his shirt collar and brought those lips down to her own.

His hands on her waist twitched, then he pushed her away from him. She stumbled back and fell onto the bed. Zander stood above her, predatory gaze looking down at her. That gaze stirred the heat surging underneath her skin.

"Go to sleep," he growled.

"But I'm not tired." She tugged off her boots and started to pull at the ties of her corset. She yanked it off and tossed it over her boots. Dust whooshed from the floor. "You don't want to sleep either."

"Oh, I don't?"

"You want to have fun, don't you?" she asked, reaching for the laces on her dress.

Zander's eyes followed her hands.

"You love fun!" She worked the laces loose, to the bottom of her breast bone.

Zander's eyes widened.

He grabbed her wrists; his fingers brushed the material of her dress. Heat from his skin seeped through as easily as water. "Don't."

"Why not? I thought you wanted to? Aren't you always bragging about how talented you are with girls?" She tried again to pull at the laces, but Zander held her hands firmly. "Come on, Zander," she purred. "Show me."

He didn't answer. With a rough tug and a push, he tossed her to the other side of the bed. He growled, "Go to sleep."

She landed on the pillow, his pillow, that smelled of him. She hugged it to her face to smell it better. Oh, how soft! Had it always been so soft? Then, she couldn't let it go. Her limbs became unresponsive, and her mind shut down.

14

Raven woke with a pounding headache. She blinked several times before the world came into focus. She slept on her stomach. Zander slept on his back beside her. Zander inhaled like he might wake, but his eyes remained closed.

Why did her head hurt so much? She rolled onto her back and put her hands to her temples, and then the night before came speeding back at her with merciless guilt and shame.

The magic-opium den. The blonde. Zander.

Sisters, she'd tried to undress in front of him. She'd tried to seduce him. She'd *kissed* him.

Please, let it be a dream, she begged. *A horrible smoke dream, a fever dream, anything!*

But as she lay there, she knew it had been her own hands, her own mouth, her own want powering her ludicrous actions. But Zander had stopped her. He had grabbed her hands before she completely embarrassed herself. He hadn't jumped on her offer like she thought he would. He'd declined it, said no.

Face burning with embarrassment, she rolled onto her other side, away from him.

He had shoved her away last night, twice. He had been appalled, disgusted, and furious. She'd heard it in his voice. Why shouldn't he be? He had lived in the capital. He had met far more attractive and appealing girls than her, with refined manners and educations and gowns of silk and velvet and whatever else. She was the backwater girl, stupid enough to fall for the magic-opium. Plain. Forgettable. Useless.

Zander inhaled again; this time, his breathing changed. She heard the subtle shift of the pillow. She felt his stare on the back of her head, but she refused to acknowledge it. Zander shifted again. He got out of bed. His socked footsteps walked across the wooden floor, then stopped. With a twist of a creaky knob, water sputtered into the basin. The curtain swished along the track.

Raven rolled onto her back; Zander had shut himself behind the curtain. Sighing, she sat up and hugged her knees to her chest. Her head pounded like nothing else. She rested her forehead against her knees. The world tilted slightly around her, churning her stomach in unfriendly ways. She squeezed her eyes shut and sat like that until Zander pulled back the curtain.

"Wash up," he spat. He headed to the door. "We leave immediately."

He shut the door a little too hard. The sound thudded against her skull.

Great. Not only did she feel sick, Zander was mad. She couldn't blame him; she was mad at herself for letting the smoke get to me too. Mad and embarrassed that Zander had witnessed the whole thing.

Raven carefully peeled herself out of bed and washed her hands and face in the freezing water. She readied her pack and met Zander downstairs. He was leaning against the wall, glaring at the main door. He handed her a biscuit and then left the inn without another word. She followed, the biscuit feeling like sand in her mouth.

The sun had risen, and the world was slowly waking up. Bakeries were opening windows to let out the steam and the favorable aromas of their ovens to entice customers. Women and children flocked to the water pumps, buckets and pitchers in hand.

Zander didn't speak again until they'd left the little town behind.

"We lost a night of travel," he said. *Thanks to you*, is what he didn't add. He didn't need to. She hadn't gone through the other rooms either. Had Zander?

All around them, birds chittered away. Each tweet felt like a nail being driven into her skull. "Well, you could have warned me," Raven said in her defense. Or that it would feel like her brain was melting the next morning.

He spat, "I didn't realize you'd never encountered opium smoke."

"In Silver Glen?" She half laughed, and the shake of her lungs radiated into her head.

He huffed. "It wasn't entirely your fault. That girl you were dancing with, the blonde, she's what they call a Trance. She had you under her spell too."

A magician? Raven barely could remember the girl's face. She remembered her hair, bright yellow-gold.

"Trances work their magic to put people in trances, like their name suggests. They can then do with them whatever they want, sell them to brothels, rape and rob them, whatever," Zander said bitterly. "You're lucky I spotted you in time, or you might be halfway to a brothel by now."

She gripped the leather strap of her bag. Shame warmed her cheeks, but luckily, Zander walked in front of her. "I'm sorry," she mumbled.

Zander growled in annoyance. "Just pick up the pace. We don't have time to lose."

They returned to the highway. They didn't speak to one another until the sun had risen to the center of the sky, shortening shadows to puddles and lifting the temperature into a slightly uncomfortable warmth. Raven tugged at the collar of her dress and undid the top button. It helped but only slightly. The river rushed; she longed to strip herself of her cumbersome clothes and jump into the water, like they'd done as children. But the idea of Zander seeing her naked burned through her skin worse than the sun.

"Stop," warned Zander.

She tore her eyes from the glistening river. Zander had slowed his pace. It didn't take her but a moment to find out why. Up ahead, a monstrous automaton of dark bronze and steel stood on the roadside, checking the few travelers along the road. The automaton stood twice as tall as a man, its arms and legs jointed for elbows and knees, and steam hissed out at regular intervals from its thick neck. A man walking beside a donkey-pulled wagon loaded with barrels shrank from the automaton's red eyes. It watched the man pass.

"It's a Detector," Zander whispered. "It's looking for someone."

Her skin felt clammy, and the sweat turned cold. She whispered, "Who?"

Zander eyed the Detector warily. "I'd rather not find out. Let's avoid it. This way," he said, motioning her to the roadside.

They left the highway as the Detector turned its red-eyed gaze down the road toward them. They entered the safety of the forest and walked quickly, leaving the highway and the Detector behind. Zander guided her through the thickets and over tangled tree roots. Raven hadn't missed navigating through the brambles and bushes. Their quick scramble from the Detector tore her skirt in several places.

He guided them south, past the Detector, where they would walk parallel to the highway in the shallows of the forest.

"Was it looking for you?" she asked, fiddling with a large tear at her thigh. Luckily, the thorn hadn't reached her skin.

"I don't know," Zander said, but the hitch in his voice said otherwise. "I don't want to give it a reason to question us. The Detectors aren't regular automatons. They can detect faces."

Detect *faces*? Raven did not like the sound of that. "Do you think they would have recognized you?"

"Like I said, I'd rather not find out."

"I thought you were somebody in the capital," she taunted. "I thought you were one of the Gray Elite?"

"Who's been missing for six months. I'd rather not call attention to myself. That would call attention to where I've been, what I've been doing, and why I left."

And draw attention to that which he had been tasked with hiding. It made sense, although his answers seemed dodgy.

They were crossing over a dense trap of tree roots when Zander suddenly stopped. Raven nearly walked into him.

"What?" she spat.

He held up his hand to shush her. The predator's gaze returned to his face, and he scanned the forest before him.

Rolling her eyes, she turned to scan the direction he couldn't readily see. She saw the forest, sunlight through the shifting leaves, and then she noticed. The birds had gone silent. The bugs had too. The summer forest had gone deathly, unnaturally silent. She looked harder and listened.

There, through the rustling wind, she heard the clomping of metal feet, the clunking of gears inside a mechanical body, and the hissing of steam.

Her heart skipped a beat. In her mind, she pictured the Cage Bird, but the Cage Bird hummed. Whatever approached them walked—or stomped, rather—through the forest. Could it be another Detector?

Zander slowly pulled Birdie from the holster. He stepped closer to the thick tree, and she mimicked his stance. The tree hid them, but it narrowed her line of view too.

Cautiously, she started to climb the tree. Zander spat a whispered warning, but she ignored him. She climbed into the branches, high enough to see for a considerable distance. She spotted brass-colored movement, clomping through the trees, maybe a hundred yards away. The automaton walked on two legs. Four arms sprouted from its thick torso, and a monstrous, squat head sat upon its bulky shoulders. Red eyes scanned the forest before it.

"Goliath," Zander whispered from below.

Raven swallowed; the name fit the contraption. It stood twelve feet fall and thrice as thick as a large man. Its legs stomped through the underbrush, crushing roots, tearing weeds, and snapping saplings without faltering. It ripped through the thick roots of an oak, and at the ripping of the green wood, Raven felt her mouth go dry.

What could those feet and arms do to human flesh and bone?

"Move," warned Zander. "Slowly. It hasn't seen us."

She climbed down as quietly as she could. They made their way around the tree, heading the opposite direction of the Goliath. It stomped on, and they crept around it. Raven took the lead with Zander a step behind. He held Birdie, ready to defend.

Raven heaved a breath as she stepped around a thick three—and right into the path of a second Goliath.

The beam of its eyes found her and glared bright red, nearly blinding her, and all at once, steam hissed from its shoulders and hips, gears thrust into one another, and the machine came to life. It had been waiting, she thought with horror. The Goliath's four arms rose, each ending with three-pronged claws. The metal prongs twisted and clicked together.

"Stay where you are," said the harsh mechanical voice of the Goliath.

"Run!" screamed Zander.

Raven threw herself out of the way of its massive arms. She hit the forest floor as the hands came together where she had been standing. A bullet zinged off the metal, but the Goliath didn't stop. She staggered to her feet in time to see it stomping toward her, the bullets from Birdie bouncing off its metal hull with high-pitched dings.

"Raven, go!" Zander shouted at her.

The other Goliath ran toward them, red eyes coloring the forest in blood, each footfall an earthquake. Zander drew his unnamed gun and fired at the incoming

Goliath. The bullets bounced off the hull. One found purchase with a crack of metal, but the machine didn't stop.

"Zander!" Raven cried.

"*Go!*" he shouted.

One of the Goliaths started toward her, and she hoisted her skirts and started to run as fast as she could. She heard Zander do the same. She dodged trees, jumped over roots, and the Goliath ran after her, shaking the ground as it ran, too close for comfort. Nothing stopped the machine—it stomped through the bushes and knocked down saplings; it moved around the larger trees with stomach-flipping ease.

Its mechanical voice said, "Stay where you are. Do not resist."

Raven ran, ran, ran. Her side ached, and her breath turned ragged. She ran toward the sound of gushing water. Automatons hated water. The trees thinned, and she came to an old mill; a stone bridge arched over a wide river, where a similar mill sat on the other side. The Goliath stomped behind her, repeating, "Stay where you are. Do not resist."

Raven ran across the bridge. Halfway across, her boot caught on a loose stone. She fell and scrambled to her feet. Panting, her side aching to split open, sweat turning her clothes damp, she turned to see the Goliath; it stood on the bank, its metal feet an inch from the bridge's stone.

It can't cross, Raven thought hopefully.

And then, to her disappointment, the Goliath stepped onto the bridge.

She glanced down at the river. *The Goliaths might look tough, but they can't swim.* The Goliath was gaining with every heartbeat, its feet thundering on the old stones. As it reached the incline, the old stones began to crack and crumble under its weight.

She started toward the opposite bank, the bridge shuddering under her steps. She didn't make it. The bridge lurched downward with a vicious *crack*—the age-old mortar giving, the stone cracking apart. The lurch sent Raven careening into the stone railing.

Below, the water gushed at a good speed, but not too fast as to drown her.

The Goliath came closer. Its arms extended, steam hissed as the panels of its chest cavity began to open, and its hands turned to scoop her inside.

What choice did she have?

"Stay where you are. Do not resist."

As the bridge cracked underneath the Goliath's weight, Raven jumped into the river.

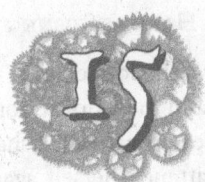

The cool water surged through her clothes, her nose, her mouth, her hair; it tugged her along faster than she had anticipated. The bridge collapsed, sending stones and the Goliath into the water below. The Goliath struggled, its voice a waterlogged croak, its steam chambers drowning, its gears gurgling. One of its eyes flickered out.

She fought to stay afloat, and soon, she stopped caring about the submerging Goliath and started to worry about her own survival. She tried to swim to the shore, but the water tugged her back in, under, and sideways. She heard the water gushing around her, but soon, that gush turned into a roar. A crashing roar that made her heart sink further into her soaked boots.

Raven found an old tree lost in the river and latched onto one of the thicker branches, scraping her arms against it, tearing through the sleeves of her dress. The Goliath approached, fixed its remaining red eye on her, and clamped onto the tree branch she held. The dead branch snapped, sending her and the Goliath back into the river's current.

The Goliath's metal hand clamped down on her arm, pulling her closer. Her already frightful panic turned white-hot. She twisted her feet up and slammed her heels into the automaton's chest with all the force she could muster. A shock zapped through her feet, up her legs, and into her hips, but her arm slipped out of the Goliath's grip, and she pushed herself out of its easy reach.

She and the Goliath surged downriver. The rushing came closer, fast.

A waterfall. She hadn't been able to see it from the bridge. As it neared, as the rushing and crashing water grew deafening, she knew she would not make it over. In her adventure books, waterfalls always ended in rocks, sharpened by water to deadly points.

She didn't have time to panic, time to wonder—over the falls they went.

Her descent ended nearly as quickly as it began; her back slammed into solid stone, knocking out what little breath she had left. Down below, a crash echoed above the roaring waters.

The automaton.

Water splattered her face, and she lifted a hand to shield herself from it. She had only fallen a few feet. Gasping for the breath she had lost, she turned onto her shaking hands and knees.

"Sisters," she gasped.

She had landed on a stone lip that jutted out from the waterfall at an upward angle, dividing the water without being submerged. Had she reached the falls anywhere else, she would have plummeted.

Cautiously, with limp fingers, she looked over the edge of the lip. The Goliath had fallen a considerable height, and pieces of it continued to float downriver. The majority of the automaton had been speared on a sharp rock, one of many that lined the bottom of the falls. Raven flattened herself against the stone. That could have been her. Should have been... She shook that thought and pushed it away. Not now.

Raven looked to either side. There was no way off the rock but to jump down, and that would be a death sentence. She couldn't go back up either.

Stuck. She might as well have fallen.

"Looks like you're stuck," came a girlish voice from behind her, shouting over the falls.

Raven started and whipped her head around. Behind her, standing halfway through the falls, was a head. Goggles blurred the eyes, and flaxen hair was plastered to the head.

The flaxen-haired stranger gave her a wide smile. "Come on this way. It's easier than going down."

The head vanished through the waterfall. Heart pounding, Raven inched her way to where the head had gone. She shut her eyes and crawled through the waterfall. To her amazement, she crawled through the water and found herself in a space large enough to stand up in. The sunlight filtered through the waterfall and lit the space in constantly moving shades of blue and silver.

The goggled girl stood waiting for her, no older than sixteen. She wore clothes fit for adventure; boots tucked with daggers, close-fitting trousers, a belt packed with daggers, tiny glass vials, and a canteen. She wrung water out of her shoulder-length hair.

Raven stood on shaky legs. "Thank you," she said over the roar of the falls.

The girl motioned for Raven to follow and started down the passage. Some of the rocks looked natural, but others looked to have been carved. Raven glanced over her shoulder; the passage connected the two banks. A secret, man-made tunnel.

They walked through and came out on a grassy patch a short distance from the waterfall.

"You're lucky to have landed there," said the girl. "I've seen what happens when someone goes over the falls. It's not pretty."

"Like the Goliath," Raven added.

The girl nodded. "Exactly, only much messier." She stuck out her gloved hand. The leather had scratches and nicks. "I'm Ivy, by the way."

"Raven." She shook the girl's hand. She had a surprising grip, or maybe Raven's hands shook too much.

"What are you doing out this far, Raven?" Ivy wiggled the goggles off her hazel eyes and looked Raven over. Freckles dotted her nose and cheekbones. "You lost?"

"I am now," Raven said. "I ran from the Goliath and ended up in the river."

"You mean you jumped to get away from it," Ivy corrected with a smile. She winked. "I saw you jump in. Smart move, considering it wouldn't have been worth a damn in the water, but dumb, considering you were so close to the falls. I saw it grab you. Normally, those things grab and don't let go, but the water saved you there."

"I was thinking about surviving the Goliath, not the falls," Raven said, her cheeks heating.

Ivy nodded, glancing toward the falls where the machine had met its end. The girl didn't look like Gray Elite or a threat, but could she be trusted? What other choice was there?

"Understandable," said Ivy. She set her hands on her hips and studied Raven. "But what are you doing out this far? You don't look like you belong out here. No offense, but..." Ivy gestured to Raven's soaked and tattered dress.

She decided to use Zander's sympathy card and said meekly, "We were...on the highway. We went into the forest, and the Goliaths found us."

"Us?" Ivy raised a brow.

Raven's heart squeezed. She nodded.

Ivy hummed and put her gloved hand to her chin. "Well, no one else went over the falls, and I didn't see anyone else. But, that's not saying your other half won't show up."

Raven's face burned at the wording. She started to correct Ivy but didn't. She and Zander *were* supposed to be lovers.

"Come on, Raven," Ivy said. She started up a beaten path that lead up to the top of the falls. "Your other half might be in trouble. Regardless, you'll need something dry, or your feet will start growing stuff."

Suddenly, her wet toes felt vulnerable.

She followed Ivy up the incline. They didn't go back to the mill. Instead, Ivy took her along a nearly invisible path through the forest. They walked and walked, and Raven's feet squished with every step. Ivy's hair dried into buttery blonde, wavy and dirty from the waterfall.

The trees grew thicker and thicker until some of the trunks had grown into one another, creating a monstrous tree whose branches twisted in every direction. The further they walked, the more ingrown trees she saw, until she saw nothing but them and the path wound between them.

"Here we are," Ivy said. They came to a twisted trunk with knots all along its bark. Ivy fingered a few of the knots, then pushed the one in the center. A trunk beside them opened with a hiss, revealing a wooden ladder inside a metal chute.

Ivy started up, and Raven staggered behind; her wet shoes slipped on the rungs. At the top, Ivy pushed open a wooden hatch, and sunlight spilled into the space.

"Hey, I brought a new friend back with me," said Ivy cheerfully as she crawled through the hatch.

"What?" came a male voice.

Raven neared the hatch, but before she could crawl out, a hand fastened around her upper arm. The grabber pulled her up and out, and her feet landed on solid flooring. Blinking, she saw the grabber—a large man in his thirties, brown-black beard and watery green eyes. He did not look happy to see her.

"You working for the Elite?" he demanded.

Raven blinked. "No."

He studied her, his piercing eyes looking deep into hers. He leaned away, arms crossed over his barrel chest.

"You a spy?" he asked.

"No," Raven answered, shaking her head.

"You a magician?"

Her heart thumped at the word. "No."

"Oh, don't be mean, Tay." Ivy stepped around the larger man. "She ran from a Goliath, got lost, fell in a river, and then almost went over the falls. I think she's earned a dry pair of boots and a snack or, at least, a place to nap while her boots dry out."

Tay glared daggers at Ivy, but he released Raven's arm. "Fine. But she's your charge, Ivy. You bring the strays home, you keep them in line. If she's led those machines to our doorstep, it's your fault."

"Noted," said Ivy, though she didn't sound worried.

Raven blinked and took stock of her surroundings. They'd climbed into a treehouse whose roof comprised of leafy branches woven so close together, they appeared solid; only small bluebirds and sunlight came through. The walls were wooden planks, metal sheets, and woven cloth and reeds, as were the floors.

Ivy slung her arm through Raven's and led her through the main room and down a hallway with an arched ceiling of tightly twisted tree branches. The ground gradually rose and fell, like they had built the floor from tree to tree. Ivy brought Raven into a hallway with a series of rooms with doors of multicolored cloth. "This is a guest room," Ivy said.

Raven wandered inside and sat down on a wicker chair.

"Yours for right now. I'll get you something dry to wear and something to eat. Then, we can find your other half."

The panic of the Goliath attack brought Raven to her feet again. "I have to find Zander." What if the Goliath had taken him? What if the Detector had found him?

"Zander?" Ivy blinked. Her brow furrowed.

"He's the guy I was traveling with. The Goliaths split us up."

Ivy leaned against the doorway, eyes looking at something far away. She blinked and asked, "What does he look like?"

Raven began to describe him, his dark hair, his blue eyes, his bronze skin, his lean and muscular build, his height and weight, his arrogant smirk and attitude. Ivy listened, eyes focused on the wall. She gently tugged her leather gloves off and tucked them into her back pocket.

When Raven had finished, Ivy said casually, "Don't worry about him. If he's out there, we'll find him. No one knows these woods like we do."

"Who are you?" Raven hadn't intended for it to come out so bluntly, but Ivy didn't balk.

"We've been called Forest People, but we call ourselves the Dwellers," Ivy said proudly. "Now, you need to get out of those wet clothes. I'll be right back with something dry. And I've got to tell Niall that there's a Goliath out there to be salvaged before the river takes it away."

With that, Ivy vanished back through the maze of tree branches. Raven sat down and removed her wet boots and socks. A bluebird chirped in the canopy, its black eyes flickering down at Raven.

Her stepmother's warnings about birds came to mind, but Raven shoved them aside. She unlaced her corset's slippery strings and dropped it to the floor. The thud frightened away the bluebird, and it fluttered away to find a quieter branch to sit on.

16

Raven unbuttoned her dress and let it flop onto the floor. The sun shining through the canopy warmed her bare, chilled skin like a blanket by the fire, and she relished the feeling. She pulled her wet chemise off her skin to stand fully in the sun. She rebraided her hair up into a bun to keep it off her neck.

By the time Ivy brought back a fresh set of clothes, Raven had nearly dried. She gladly dressed in the blousy shirt and close-fitting pants. Ivy brought her an old corset with new strings. It was shorter than her other and smelled vaguely of musty autumn leaves. It contained less boning, allowing her a wider range of movement. She liked the dark blue and handsome brass grommets.

Raven tucked her dagger through the loops on her pants. Ivy provided her a pair of slip-on shoes.

"Looks like it fits you well enough," said Ivy, eyeballing Raven's new clothes with a serious eye.

"It feels easier than a dress," Raven said, twirling in place and admiring the snug fit of the trousers. Moving through the forest would have been so much easier in pants.

Ivy nodded. "I've never been one for dresses myself. Too much weighty fabric going all over the place, getting caught on chair legs and bushes and tripping me."

"It's all I've worn," Raven told Ivy. She glanced at her soggy, discarded dress. The jaunt through the forest had cut and shredded the material and left the hem a tattered mess. Rags. "My father believes in tradition." As did the rest of the Silver Glen, but she kept that admission to herself.

Ivy shrugged then set her hands on her hips. "That's how the cities are too. Boring and stuffy. I prefer it out here in the wild. It's free."

That meant Ivy had been to the cities. Before Raven could ask, Ivy pulled her back into the hall. She followed Ivy through the Dwellers' camp and into what looked like a mess hall with mismatched wooden tables and chairs. A few of the chairs had legs made of tree branches—some still had bark on them. Ivy scrounged up a quick meal of nuts, berries, and a dried meat Raven didn't ask about.

"I sent for Niall and passed word along about your missing boy," Ivy said, gesturing to the open door of the mess hall.

"Did I hear my name?" asked a young man of eighteen or nineteen. He had tan skin and intelligent brown eyes; his shoulder-length hair had been braided and tied back in a thick bundle. He spoke fluently, his voice smooth and calm. A streak of grease ran along one cheekbone. His eyes fell on Raven, and he gave her a small but friendly smile.

"You did," Ivy said. "Raven, this is Niall, the best mechanic and tinker this side of the Himata River. Niall, this is Raven. I found her in the woods after she and a Goliath nearly went over the falls."

Niall chuckled, a soft sound. "Did she now?"

Niall sat at the table, and while Raven ate, Ivy told him about the Goliath and the falls. Niall listened patiently, his face schooled into calmness. When Ivy finished, he leaned back—his gaze turned to one of calculation and excitement.

"Sounds like a job for the Extractor," said Niall.

Raven didn't ask, and Ivy didn't provide an explanation; it sounded like a machine. After she ate, she followed Ivy and Niall to a lower section of the treehouse, one that looked less organic that the others. Wooden walls, floors, and ceilings had been hammered together with iron nails. The low lighting and musty smell told Raven they had gone underground. A cave.

It felt oddly familiar.

The narrow wooden walkway opened up to a cave, one with a mouth shaded by hanging moss and ivy. The sunlight slipped through in a misty green-gray. Within the cave, several machines lined the walls, their steam vents and engines quiet. A dock, she realized.

Niall walked over to one of the machines, a squat machine with a thick chest. The Extractor. One hand was pronged; the other was a drill. From the design of the arms, it looked like several more hands were hidden inside it, ready to be changed for whatever Niall needed. He climbed into the open driver's seat, and Ivy and Raven climbed in behind him, resting in the tight quarters, their legs stretched out on either side of his seat.

With the pulling of a few levers, the Extractor rumbled to life. The limbs shuddered, steam hissed through the pipes and vents, and with Niall's gentle touch at the controls, the Extractor took a step toward the moss-hidden cavern mouth, and when they approached, its thick hands parted the moss as easy as if it were human.

On the way to the waterfall, Niall quickly named off all the useful parts the Goliath would give him, all the upgrades and repairs he could make, the new inventions he had been thinking about. He talked the entire way to the waterfall, only being interrupted with comments and questions by Ivy.

Raven had little to say. Sitting in the Extractor, listening to Niall and Ivy, it reminded her of when she, Sweets, and Brent had more time to spend together, before her father deemed them old enough to work, before their friendship was interrupted by chores and duties.

The Extractor navigated the forest floor with surprising nimbleness, not unlike the Goliaths. Raven scanned the dense forest, but she didn't see any sign of people, and no sign of Zander.

At the thought of him, her heart squeezed.

Raven heard the roar of the falls before she saw them. The Extractor walked to the rocky shore, and Niall leaned over to see the Goliath better.

"Look at that," said Niall, his voice awestruck.

Ivy let out a whistle.

At the bottom of the waterfall, the Goliath had been impaled by a water-sharpened rock. It had gone through the softer metal between the breastplate and the collar, and it would have impaled anyone who had been inside the chest cavity.

Raven imagined Zander trapped inside the chest of the other Goliath, and her heart shuddered. The Goliath suddenly seemed a waste of time.

Raven and Ivy stood to the side while Niall used the Extractor to fish the Goliath's parts from the river. Like the Goliaths, its chest was empty. It lifted the parts with one hand, supported itself with the other, and swallowed the parts. They clanged inside of its chest, one after the other, until the largest parts of the Goliath remained. Then, the Extractor lifted the Goliath's hull in its arms.

Niall returned to the shore and looked expectantly at the girls.

"You go on ahead," Ivy called over the Extractor's engine. "We're going to do some manhunting."

Niall didn't question her. He gave them a parting wave and started back through the forest for the hidden cave. Ivy pulled Raven toward the rocky incline that led to the top of the waterfall.

"Manhunting?" Raven asked once they reached the top and the roar lessened somewhat.

"We're going to look for your other half," Ivy said. "Let's retrace your steps. We might find some clues."

Raven nodded and walked beside Ivy as they made their way upriver, past the broken bridge and rundown mill and into the forest. Raven walked back to where she thought the Goliaths had appeared—she wasn't sure. She had done a lot of running, and the forest looked the same in every direction.

They wandered through the forest without a sight or sound of Zander. With every glance through the trees, Raven's gut twisted. Had something happened to him? Had the Goliath gotten to him? She shivered at the thought of him crammed into the chest of the machine, on his way to slavery for the Gray Elite. Or worse. Sisters only knew what the Gray Elite did to their deserters.

Or he had left her behind and gone after the thief. He'd been mad that she'd cost them so much time, and he might have seen his chance to finally be rid of her—she'd done nothing but slow him down.

She didn't know which scenario made her feel worse.

"Hey, don't worry." Ivy snaked her arm around Raven's shoulders and gave her a squeeze. The warmth in her eyes pushed away Raven's hopelessness. "We'll find him."

Raven wished she felt as confident as Ivy sounded.

They made it to the highway, and by then, Ivy had begun to frown. The Detector still guarded the road, watching all travelers.

The machines had been looking for Zander, or Zander had suspected they were. That's why they had gone into the woods. The more she thought about it, the more it made sense. Her gut agreed too.

The sun started its downward fall into the west, and Ivy guided her back into the dense part of the forest. Raven walked in a daze. Her body felt separate from herself.

They hadn't found him. Zander was gone. Either he had gone on without her, or he had been captured. If he had gone on without her, she wouldn't be able to catch up to him. She wouldn't know which way to go or where he would have gone. If he had been captured, she couldn't go after him. She couldn't fight off a Goliath or go into Lenhala to find him.

She didn't know the way back to Silver Glen. Without Zander, she was on her own. Maybe...it wouldn't so bad. Ivy was friendly. Niall was nice.

By the time they reached the Dwellers' camp, the sun touched the west and painted the forest in golden hues and deep purples and rich blues, and while Raven would have liked to stay outside and watch the colors change, she couldn't bring herself to do it. Her body felt numb. She followed Ivy up the ladder.

Her stomach felt like upheaving itself with worry for Zander, whatever his fate. If only she'd been stronger against the opium smoke, they would have had the thief by now. It was her fault. Useless.

She lifted herself into the treehouse to the sound of male chatter. It came from a curtained-off room from the main space, and Raven paid little attention to it. She felt like lying down for a few weeks until the world felt right-side up again.

"Well, look at that," said Ivy, her voice cheery. She stopped, and Raven nearly ran into her. "We were scouring the forest for you, you know."

A familiar voice chuckled, though he didn't sound very humored. "Sorry, I got distracted when your friend here decided to blow up the Goliath and nearly me with it."

Raven snapped her attention up. There, sitting on the other side of the curtain that Ivy held back, was Zander. He looked worse for wear, with a cut on his chin and a split lip, but alive. Alive. Here.

The dark-headed young man sitting beside him laughed. He had what looked like grenades attached to his suspenders. He leaned forward and slapped Zander on the shoulder. "Sorry 'bout that, mate. I didn't think the boom would be *that* bad."

Laughter resounded from half a dozen people, but Raven didn't see them. She saw only Zander, there—alive. His stare met hers, and the floor tumbled out from under her feet. He looked her over, and his smile faltered. A hint of his anger returned.

She balled her fists. She saw the accusation on his face, the blame. How dare he blame her for this! She wasn't the one the Detectors had been looking for. And while she had been hunting him down, worried for his safety, he had been here, lounging about with the Dwellers like old friends. Her stomach twisted with jealousy and bitterness.

"Glad to see you're okay," he said flatly.

"You as well," she said as calmly as she could.

Ivy glanced between her and Zander, then cleared her throat. "Rae and I did quite the jog around the woods. We're famished. Bye." She let the curtain fall back across the doorway. She snaked her arm with Raven's and pulled her away from it. "Well, that solves that problem. Thirsty? Gab makes a mean cider from the Gompa fruit."

"The what?"

Ivy took her into the mess hall and pulled a dark bottle from one of the cabinets. She poured a yellow liquid into two steel goblets. Raven brought it to her lips and sniffed. It smelled sweet like juice but like something else too. Ivy took a sip, and Raven mimicked her. It tasted like...she didn't know, but she liked it. She drank mostly in silence, while Ivy talked about the mysterious fruit they'd stumbled across decades ago—Gab had perfected the cider recipe soon after.

Ivy tapped the side of her goblet. "So...you and Zander nearly got eaten by Goliaths."

Raven nodded. A part of her wished he had been. "I'm sure he would rather I had been."

"That's harsh, even for Zander."

"He's mad I keep slowing us down." Raven sighed. She didn't know how much to tell Ivy, though she seemed trustworthy enough. She had saved her from being stuck on that ledge, given her dry clothes, and shown her hospitality. She couldn't be that bad.

"You tired?" Ivy asked. "I've got a spare cot in my room if you'd rather not sleep alone in a strange place."

Her first thought went to Zander. "I'm not sure what Zander's plans are. I'm sure he'll want us to leave immediately."

"No," came Zander's voice from the doorway.

Raven glanced at him from over her shoulder. He leaned against the doorway and wore a grim expression. Niall and the boy with the grenades lingered in the room behind him. Waiting.

"We leave first thing tomorrow. Get your rest." Zander turned around and followed the other two down a hall and out of sight.

"Well, I guess that settles it," Ivy said. "Come on. I'll get you settled in."

Raven followed Ivy down another hall and into a part of the tree where stars peeked between the branches. She led her into a room with one well-used cot and one not-so-well-used cot. After finding some spare blankets, Ivy showed her to the women's privy. The pipework looked similar to that used in the towns, only better kept. A Goliath's claw arm had been made into a wall hook.

Raven returned to Ivy's room and sat on the edge of her cot. She glanced up at the twinkling stars between the branches. A night breeze fluttered by, brushing against the leaves.

"What do you do if it rains?" Raven asked.

"There's a shield that goes up," Ivy said. She pointed to the far side of the room where a brass cover curled—when unwound, it would cover the room like a roof. "The water runs into the network that feeds the trees and us."

"Incredible," Raven said. She undid her shoes and vest and laid back on the cot. She brought the blankets up to her chin. "It must be nice to sleep under the stars every night."

"Where do you usually sleep?"

"We live underground," Raven said. "I had nothing to look at but stone."

Ivy hummed. "Sounds stuffy. You're free to stay here, you know. We'd welcome another pair of hands to help out. Always something to do or fix." She quickly added, "You know, whenever you and Zander are done with whatever it is you're doing."

Raven thought about it. The Dwellers were not that different from her friends and family, however far away they were now. If she went back to Silver Glen, she would have a lecture and a half waiting for her, and a kitchen job. She might never see the sun again, or the stars. Lying here, looking up at the stars, she thought about living with the Dwellers instead, living in the freedom of the forest.

But she knew she couldn't. She couldn't leave her father and stepmother like that, or her sister. Silver Glen was her home, like it or not. She couldn't just forget about it.

Then again, a tug in her chest reminded her of the things she had stolen from strangers, how easy it had been. Would it be just as easy to leave Silver Glen and never look back?

17

Raven fell asleep dreaming of sky cities, their brass and copper hulls gleaming in the moonlight, their leathery balloons painted to match the gold of morning, the steam of the engine puffing out cloud after cloud. She dreamed that she had been invited to a ball aboard such a ship, a grand ball of gowns and suits and ice swans.

An automaton band played from a suspended stage above the dance floor, their brass limbs caressing finely crafted strings. Underneath them, a music box added a harmonious melody. She dreamed of the music, magical and heavenly, something that could only have been played in the sky cities, only this far above the world.

Raven danced with faceless men in fine suits of all manner of colors. The amber windows cast the dance floor in strips of gold that flashed by as she danced.

Oh, the colors! The music! She traded partners, one after the other, as women in beautiful dresses joined her on the dance floor. Around and around, she twirled to the sound.

Her new partner reached for her hand, and she set her other on his shoulder. He held her closer than the others and smelled of gunpowder and steel. His sapphire eyes met hers.

"Zander?" she asked him.

He lifted a brow in that cocky way of his. "What? Didn't think I could crash a party like this one?"

"You can't even dance," she said. "Why are you here?"

"What do you mean I can't dance? I've been dancing since I could walk." He led her through the steps and didn't miss a single one. He moved with effortless grace.

"Well, now you're just showing off," Raven said.

Zander laughed, that soft chuckle of his that sent a prickle along her skin and a warmth underneath it. At her blush, he gave her his charmer's smile. "What do you mean? You're supposed to like me, Rae. We're lovers, after all."

She let out a sigh and whispered, "We're just pretending, Zander. I don't like you like that." Suddenly, everyone in the ball was looking at the two of them. No one spoke. "Zander, keep dancing, everyone is looking."

He laughed. "What do you mean you don't like me like that? Come on, Rae, you know that's not true."

Her face burned, and she dropped his hand. She took a large step away from him. She wanted to run, but the crowd formed a fence around them, shoulder to shoulder, blank faces—all of them.

Zander puffed out his chest and gave her his arrogant smile. "Come on, Rae, stop ruining the party for everyone. We've already lost enough time as it is."

Something cool touched her face; one of the swans had started to melt. It tilted dangerously forward. She reached to shield herself from the falling beak, and—

Raven snapped awake to see Ivy standing over her. She held a cup in one hand, and several cool drops of water dripped from her fingers, which she suspended over Raven's forehead.

Ivy gave her a wicked smile of greeting. "There you are," she said. "I kept trying to wake you up the old fashioned way—you know, by talking—but you kept mumbling. Some dream, eh?"

Raven wiped her face on the blanket and sat up. "Yeah, I was in a sky city. At a party. The ice swan started melting on me."

Ivy glanced at her fingers and laughed. She patted them dry on her shirt. "Figured. Anyway, we've got breakfast ready for you and some supplies. Zander's eager to get going."

Raven washed up in the privy, then followed Ivy into a small mess hall. Zander was already seated. At the sight of him, her face heated. She kept her eyes off him and on the plate the cook placed in front of her.

She picked at her food and tried to eat most of it—she'd never been a big breakfast eater. She found the glass of warm tea much more satisfying. On her second cup, she chanced a glance at Zander. He hadn't eaten much better, and he kept his eyes on his plate. He had that intent stare again. A heartbeat and a half passed, and then Zander felt her gaze. He looked up; all of the dream came back to her.

But he didn't give her one of his charming smiles. He looked like he wished the Goliath had taken her, anxious, a little unsure, and frustrated. "We leave as soon as we're done. The Dwellers have been kind enough to give us supplies."

"That's good."

"Eat up," Zander said, pushing his food around his place. "You'll need your strength, and I can't guarantee a warm meal after this."

She didn't eat much more. Neither did he.

Fed, dressed in fresh clothes, and with a pack on each of their shoulders, Zander and Raven followed Ivy, Niall, and Thalame—the boy with the grenades—through the treehouse and down a second ladder inside a fake tree trunk. This one led deeper than the other and exited among thick tree roots. Niall held an old-fashioned lantern, and the five of them walked single file down a cylindrical metal tunnel—an old pipe. A layer of dirt and pine needles softened the bottom of the pipe and evened it out for easier walking.

Raven walked behind Zander. Thankfully, he couldn't see her eyes on the back of his head. He hadn't said a word since breakfast, and he had kept his face straight-lipped and unhappy. Still mad. How could he still be mad at her? Of course...this entire ordeal was her fault.

Guilt sank deep into her bones.

The tunnel led out into a cavernous platform. The ceiling and walls were mismatched hammered metal of varying shades of copper, bronze, steel, and iron. Several panels curved, some had windows, some doors—parts of old machines.

"Ah, here she is," said Niall, his voice proud and bright. "My little Hellcat."

Raven blinked. She had been looking at the walls and nearly missed the most obvious thing in the room—a metal monster resting upon tracks, its face pieced together from metal scraps to make it look like a predatory cat, only longer and narrower. She spotted bits of Goliaths and Cage Birds and automatons she didn't recognize in its body. The top half was open to the air, and three rows of differently colored leather seats rested inside it.

Raven stepped onto the base of the car's platform and glanced down the tracks. They vanished down a tunnel barely wide enough for it, its metal sides spotted with rocky walls. About a hundred yards down, the lights vanished into a circle of darkness.

"Where does it go?" she asked, her voice echoing off the walls.

"Where we're going," Zander snapped. He climbed into the first row of seats. Niall joined him, taking a seat at the commander's wheel. "Get in."

Raven climbed into the middle seat with Ivy, and Thalame sat behind them. Niall tucked his lantern underneath the control panel; its light illuminated the front of the car, shining through the metal bars, giving it fangs and fire-eyes. A Hellcat, indeed.

Thalame leaned forward between Ivy and Raven, a wicked grin on his face. "You're gonna want to put your belt on." His rough voice strained with anticipation.

She found a leather belt at the corner of the seat. A metal hook on the end fastened into a buckle on the other side of her hip. Thalame gave her a quick run-through of how to tighten the belt.

"Why, exactly, do I need to wear this?" Raven asked.

Thalame grinned wider. He winked. He leaned back and fastened his own belt. Ivy was fastening hers, as were Zander and Niall. Raven drummed her fingers on the leather seat.

Ivy gave her a knowing glance and whispered, "It's not that bad. I remember my first time. Screamed myself hoarse."

Raven shot a worried look at Ivy, but as her mouth opened, the car underneath her rumbled to life—gears vibrated against each other, belts hummed, and the engine pumped, gurgled, and spat—then purred like an automaton cat. Steam hissed out of from underneath the cat in quick white shoots.

"Here we go!" shouted Niall. He wore an unmistakable grin.

The car started forward, its feet hooked onto the tracks. A little faster. A little faster still; then—Ivy threw her hands into the air—steam burst out, metal screeched, and the car shot forward into the darkness.

Raven's back slammed into the leather seat. The impact stole the scream from her throat.

Ivy let out a whoop; Zander was laughing, the sounds of them both barely audible over the rush of air and rumble of the Hellcat. The Hellcat's light barely lit the tunnel walls; metal and rock and rust flashed past and gave the sickening impression that the tunnel was shrinking. Air rushed by at tearing speed, whipping Raven's hair from its braid, lashing the strands against her cheeks. She squeezed her eyes shut, but the darkness felt only a little better.

The tracks began to turn and tilted; the Hellcat leaned dangerously sideways. Raven gripped the leather seat, biting into it with her nails, hard enough to hurt.

"Yeah!" Ivy shouted, her voice moving too fast to echo.

The tracks leveled. The Hellcat rumbled down the tracks at feverish speed, never slowing, turning this way, that way, speeding along the dark tunnel with only the light from the Hellcat's metal monster face. After a time, the panic wore off. Talk was impossible over the roar of the engine and the whip of the wind. Only the occasional scream of joy and fit of laughter sounded, though none came from Raven.

Then, at last, a light at the end of the tunnel. Niall slowed the hellcat with the switching of levers. A screech of metal and a punch of steam, and the car jerked and jostled its way into the light.

It was a platform not unlike the one they had left, only smaller. The top of the cavern had holes that allowed the sunlight to filter in, along with incessant dripping and vines. The sunlight filtering through seemed impossibly bright. The walls of the platform were mostly carved rock and natural rock—it must have been a cavern once. It reeked of mildew and stagnant water.

The car came to a final halt, and Ivy undid her belt. Raven fumbled to undo hers; her hands shook.

Zander jumped out of the car and started at once for the bulkhead on the far side of the platform. Thalame appeared beside the car and held his hand out for Ivy and then for Raven. She took it; his hand felt considerably sturdier than her own.

Booth feet on solid ground, she mumbled, "Thank you."

Ivy beamed, hands on her hips, grin wide, hair wild. "Well?"

A creak—Zander was unlocking the bulkhead.

"It's not what I expected," Raven admitted. She swallowed. Her throat felt dry.

Ivy laughed. "Beats walking, don't it?"

Raven nodded, though she didn't know if she agreed or not. A nice calm walk through the woods sounded pleasant after that experience. Yet, at the same time, she wouldn't turn down another ride on the Hellcat.

"Well, this is where we leave you to it," said Thalame, a farewell mixed into his words. He climbed into the backseat and lounged against it, hands behind his head.

Ivy hopped into the front seat with Niall. She said, "It was nice to meet you, Raven, but Thalame's right. I hope you find your thief."

Thief? Raven blinked; Ivy knew about the thief?

Zander inhaled sharply. He stood with his body halfway through the bulkhead door, his face twisted in a grimace. "Enough talk," he growled. "Let's go. We're on a time limit."

"Bye," Raven said to the Dwellers. "Thank you for all your help."

Thalame brushed it off, Ivy grinned, and Niall gave her a nod. Zander then grabbed her arm and yanked her through the bulkhead. He shut the door and twisted the wheel into a locked position. The Hellcat roared on the other side, spitting to life. With a whoop that sounded like Ivy, it shot out of the tunnel.

How many more platforms did the Dwellers have scattered around the underground? She didn't have the chance to ask, for Zander stomped down the dimly lit tunnel. Raven jogged to catch up with him, leaving an arm's space between them.

"I would have liked to say a better goodbye," Raven said.

"Life's too short for goodbyes," Zander spat. "Now, come on."

She heaved a sigh of agitation. "Where are we going?"

"Niall's Hellcat saved us a day's travel," Zander said. "Our thief is staying in the town above us. This is our last chance to catch him, Rae. We can't afford any more *mistakes*."

She clenched her fists. She caught the emphasis he put on "mistakes." As in, *she* couldn't make any more mistakes.

"How do you know that he's staying there?" she asked.

"Because it's the quickest route to Lenhala," he said flatly. "I talked it over with the guys back in the Dwellers' camp. They agree. They...have smuggled the occasional person or object into and out of Lenhala, and this town is the best bet. Plenty of holes to hide in. Black market connections."

"But—"

"Stop talking," Zander snapped. "You walk slower when you're talking."

She huffed and stomped after him. He led them down a short tunnel, then up a ladder that rose into a fake tree similar to the one that led into the Dweller's treehouse. She climbed out after Zander, and he shut the tree; the fake tree blended in so well with the trees around it, if she hadn't been looking at it, she wouldn't have noticed it.

Zander led her into a town bigger than any of the others they had stayed in. The main streets were paved stone, not dirt or gravel, and the shops bore colorful window displays and welcome signs. People walked along the sidewalks, meandering through the shops and talking—a gentle hum lifted through the air.

Zander didn't stop or even pause; he kept moving through the alleys and streets, and with each street, the town grew less impressive and more questionable. The paved streets gave way to narrow dirt streets, the colorful displays became dingy glass storefronts, and the people were less inviting. They came to a narrow street with stalls instead of stores. Blankets and clothes had been strung over the rooftops, shading the street in shadowy shapes. People wore cloaks and scarves, most kept their heads covered, and Raven felt horribly exposed. The chatter became a low murmur, full of whispers and strange words she didn't understand.

They passed stalls that sold carved trinkets, stalls that sold bottles of liquid and bottles of smoke, stalls that sold shimmery cloth, stalls that sold leather-bound books without titles, and stalls that didn't have any merchandise at all—no signs announced store names, items for sale, or prices. They passed a stall whose vendor wore a head-to-toe black robe. The table before him held all manner of sickly looking blades that curved, hooked, split, and scooped. The handles, she realized with a pitting of her stomach, looked like bone.

The bone-knife vendor shifted, and in a drawling voice like dry grass, he said, "Fancy a test of my blades, lass?"

Beady black eyes settled on Raven, and she felt her skin go cold. Zander's arm appeared beside her, and his fingers fastened around her elbow. He pulled her away from the strange vendor, further down the shaded market, and onto a wider street. He didn't stop until he reached a dark weathered building with a single sign hanging from rusted hooks that advertised: *Inn*.

Zander pulled her onto the porch of the inn and pulled her closer to him. Startled, she flattened her hands against his chest, ready to shove him off. Before she could shove, he bent forward and pressed his mouth against her ear, his breath hot as he whispered, "Don't speak to anyone." His words tingled against her skin and sent a shiver down her spine. "Don't look at anyone. Don't take anything anyone offers you. Act like you know what you're doing, where you are, and that you belong here."

She thought of the strange vendors they had walked through, and embarrassment flushed over her skin; she must have looked like a startled deer. Stupid. Useless.

She couldn't formulate a response, but Zander didn't require one. He straightened, hooked his arm with hers, and led her into the inn. Inside, the stench of beer, human stink, and smoked meat cogged her throat. On the first floor, six or seven tables littered the dark space. Five cloaked men were playing a game of cards in the corner, each smoking; purple and pink smoke slithered up from their table. Two women were whispering to each other, sorting buttons like coins.

Raven looked away before she could make eye contact and held her chin high like she belonged there, though she held tight onto Zander's arm. She held her tongue while he paid for a room; he gave the innkeeper the name Hamilton rather than his own.

"All we've got open are the upstairs rooms," said the toothy innkeeper. "Downstairs is full."

Zander glanced to Raven and drawled, "Is an upstairs room all right with you, Linda?"

Raven nodded.

He paid with silver Gracitan tokens, and the innkeeper didn't bat an eye. He slid across a rusty key. Zander led Raven up a set of rickety stairs to their room. A dull, broken number six had been nailed to the warped wood. Inside, Raven set her pack on the dingy floor. It felt marvelous to have it off her shoulders.

Zander closed the door and then sat down on the bed. He lowered his head into his hands and let out a frustrated sigh. "That market was a black magic market," he whispered.

Her heart skipped a beat. She inhaled sharply. "A black magic market?" she repeated. A black market for magic, or a market for black magic? She supposed they were the same.

Zander kept his stare on the opposite wall. "Because magic is illegal, magic dealers and magicians have had to go to the black markets in order to make a living, and as you saw, most of them belong in the black market," he said, rubbing his temple. He pulled the tie out of his dark hair and raked his fingers through it, loosening it. It fell near to his shoulders. "That vendor who spoke to you, that was a bone-knife dealer; they make their blades from human bones."

She swallowed; she had thought those a myth.

Zander leaned forward, head in his hands, and groaned.

"I'm sorry," Raven said quietly.

Zander peeked through his fingers at her, blue eyes weary. He dropped his hands. "For not talking that long?" A slight smirk broke through his grimace. "I thought you'd be purple in the face by now."

She huffed. "For losing us so much time."

"It's fine." He looked away from her and to the small bathroom. "Can't do anything about it now. We're here, and we're close, and we'll get him."

"How do you know he's here?"

He fixed his stare on her, then looked away. He stood and walked into the bathroom. "I saw him walk in here. He's here." He turned on the water. "It's here. Tonight, I'll distract; you search."

He shut the bathroom door, and she couldn't voice her concerns about his plan. She hadn't seen anyone walk into the inn before them, but she hadn't been paying that close of attention. Maybe he had. Zander had seen him before, not her. She wasn't even sure what the thief looked like. Zander had mentioned a man with braids to one of the innkeepers, but braids were not uncommon.

She let out a sigh and unbuttoned her jacket. She hung it on the hook beside the door and picked Zander's up from where he'd thrown it on the bed and hung it beside hers.

It didn't matter how Zander knew the thief was here. She would find the box tonight, or they wouldn't find it at all. Not with Lenhala so close. No mistakes, she told herself.

No mistakes.

With Zander in the bathroom, Raven had time to collect her thoughts and rattled nerves enough that she dreaded the coming night. No mistakes.

Zander walked out of the bathroom with his hair down and the top three buttons of his shirt undone, exposing the hollow of his throat and his collarbone. He pushed the curtain from the small window, and his intent eyes scanned the street outside.

"What are you looking at?" Raven asked, picking at a stray string on the quilted bedspread. The square under her hand looked to have once held a button.

"Nothing," he said too quickly. She narrowed her eyes at the back of his head. He let the curtain fall back into place, shutting out the sunlight and letting the dingy shadows grow. He caught her stare and sighed through his nose. "This is our last chance."

He blinked, and underneath the agitation, the snarkiness, she saw something else, something she hadn't noticed: fear.

Zander took a deep breath and paced once from the window to the door. He ran his hand through his hair.

"We'll get it," she whispered, though she knew such a thing was outside of promises.

"I know the thief is here," he said quietly.

"But—"

He held his hand up to silence her. "I...know that the deal is going down tomorrow. Here. In town. And...I know that the thief is staying here."

"How?"

He fixed his eyes on her, bottom lip between his teeth—thinking. He knew, but he didn't want to tell her.

She pulled her legs up to her chest, easier in trousers than a skirt, and guessed, "Did the Dwellers know?"

His gaze sharpened; then he nodded. "They've got connections all over the kingdom, and some in the next. They're not just people who live in the woods; they're spies and scouts too."

"Do you know them? From before?" When he had lived in Lenhala as Gray Elite.

"Yeah," he said, barely audible. He looked again to the closed window. "Look, I'd rather not discuss this here," he said quietly. "We've got too much at risk, and I need to get down there and put on an act."

"Well, at least you won't have to pretend to be stressed," she said, trying to make him feel better, but the smile she faked didn't look like it worked.

"I'll go down there as the drunk husband whose wife"—he pointed at her—"is pissed off at him." She frowned, but he didn't let her speak. "People won't ask why you aren't down there with me or why you're okay with me getting smashed."

"Why are we fighting?" she asked, if only to further the story.

He thought for a second, then said, "Because I lost all our money gambling. That way, any thugs down there looking for a quick token won't look twice at us."

She let out a dark chuckle.

"Oh?" His brows rose. "Would you rather go down there and distract a tavern full of thieves, assassins, mercenaries, and other such lowlifes while I search through all the rooms?" He waited for her answer, and when she held her tongue, he said, "That's what I thought. I'll stick to what I'm good at, and you stick to what you're good at."

"You're good at being a drunk, and I'm good at going through other people's things?"

He frowned. "That's one way to put it."

He was good at *pretending*, she told herself. And she was good at going unnoticed.

They slept into the late afternoon. Raven woke up numerous times to strange sounds in the hall, creaking boards that sounded as though someone had entered their room, and she woke up in fear of seeing a black-cloaked figure standing at her bedside. In the narrow double bed, she felt Zander's heat against her back, and though she would never tell him so, his presence settled her nerves each time she woke.

She woke once more with finality and knew she would sleep no more. Her nerves returned in anticipation of the night to come, of what she would be doing in just a few hours. Beside her, Zander slept on.

The sun gradually lowered in the sky, and the town chittered with people and summer bugs as the evening arrived. The cicadas sang louder here than they had in Silver Glen, as though they sang right outside the window. Maybe they did. The sunlight seeping through the shutters turned from golden yellow to bronze. The black magic market a street over buzzed with activity, hushed and secret.

Zander rolled onto his back and let out a sigh. An awake sigh.

"What are you thinking about?" Raven whispered.

"How I'm going to be dead if we don't find that box," he whispered back.

Raven rolled onto her back and turned to face him. She hadn't taken off her locket, and it slid across her chest as she moved. The dim evening light warmed Zander's face but shadowed it at the same time. His eyes were closed.

"I'm sorry I've been short with you," he whispered. "I'm worried about what might happen if we don't get to the thief before he makes the deal. If that box slips into the capital, it'll be gone forever. If we don't find it tonight, then it's over. It'll be too late."

"It's not your fault he stole it," Raven admitted; it had been hers.

Zander's lips turned upward, a slight smile. He opened his sapphire eyes and sought hers. "Thanks for taking the burden of blame, Rae." His smile turned a shade brighter, truer. "I... Thank you for coming with me. This would have been harder without you."

His fingers graced the back of her hand, and then he laced his fingers with hers. Could he feel the heat that rose at his touch? Hear the lurch of her heart as it skipped a beat?

"I'm sorry about what happened at the opium den," she whispered. Shame and guilt warmed her face, but she couldn't look away from him.

Zander chuckled. "I wanted to dance in the street with you." His eyes glittered. "If we hadn't been running short on time, we would have."

"When this is over," she said, holding onto that warm gaze, "we can dance wherever we want."

His smile widened and warmed, and she melted at the sight. He squeezed her hand and brought it up to his lips. He placed a chaste kiss on her knuckles. His eyes turned mischievous, and the sight sent a hot tingle over her skin.

"When this is over," he said lowly, "I'll let you kiss me all you want."

Her face burned, and Zander laughed. He kissed her knuckles again and returned her hand to the bed but didn't let go of it.

"I'm so glad you remember that night in such detail," she said, her voice a pitch too high.

"Oh, I remember," Zander affirmed. "*Every* detail."

Her face burned hotter still, and she rolled away from him so he couldn't see it, slipping her hand out of his. Laughing, Zander propped himself up on his elbow and leaned over. He placed a warm kiss on her temple.

And her heart flip-flopped nearly out of her chest at the sensation of his lips against her skin.

"It's okay, Rae. I should have kept a better eye on you that night, warned you about what might happen. I forget you don't know all the things that I know." He set his hand on her shoulder. Its warmth seeped through her sleeve. "But I'll do better from now on. I'll keep you safe. I promise."

"How can you promise that?" she asked.

He raised a brow.

"If I throw myself headfirst into danger, you're going to throw yourself in after me?"

He smiled wickedly. "As the Sisters as my witness, I'll throw myself into the Underworld after you."

She rolled onto her back to see him better. He wore no humor, only sincerity, and by the Sisters, a light pink tinted his tan cheeks.

"That's quite possibly the sweetest and strangest thing anyone has ever said to me." She let her gaze fall from his eyes to his lips. Just once.

"Don't ever say I haven't been nice to you," he said, his voice lower. He started to lean toward her, and she knew she wouldn't stop him. He leaned closer, his breath on her lips, and then—

The dinner bell rang, a ghastly, intrusive sound that made them both jump. Just like that, the moment between them dissolved.

Zander leaned away, blinking rapidly. He cleared his throat. "Time to go."

"No mistakes," she said.

Zander got out of bed first. He slid on his boots and his vest. He stepped to the window and lifted the curtain an inch or so, just enough for him to see out without too many people seeing him do it. He let it fall back into place. Dust motes fluttered from the material.

"Okay," he said, buttoning his jacket. "Wait until I start singing 'Jim Goes Fishing.' That's the signal that our thief is downstairs, leaving his room exposed."

She nodded and sat on the bed. Zander left, and in a few long minutes, she heard him laughing with several other male voices. Within the hour, the crowd below had increased, and the drunken chatter began. She paced. She peeked on the street outside, where the evening crowd strolled about, arm in arm in their best dresses and clothes. Through the alleys, she spotted the nicer streets, nicer dresses, and funny hats.

What would it have been like to grow up in a place like this instead of Silver Glen? On the outskirts of the capital instead of north of nowhere? Where the automatons didn't hunt fugitives and refugees like game. Where people just lived. Where they didn't have to hunt for their food or make their homes in an old mine to protect themselves from turning into slaves.

If she had been born in Lenhala, rather than Silver Glen, would she have craved the wider world so much?

Zander had grown up in Lenhala, and he knew so much more about the world than she did. Zander knew about the Dwellers. He knew about the Gray Elite. He knew about all the automatons they'd encountered and more. Seeing the world for herself made her feel...small. She'd been hiding in a small corner of the world while all of this was happening, while places like this town existed with all its shops, people, and events.

And he had almost kissed her. She brought her fingertips to her lips, where a ghost of his breath lingered. And he hadn't been high on magic opium either.

Sighing, she walked into the bathroom and washed her face and hands in cool water. Her reflection in the dirty mirror was a blur of pale beige, unremarkable.

Wait. Why did she care what Zander thought of her? Why did she care if Zander thought her simple or stupid? She didn't! She shouldn't, yet deep down, she knew that it bothered more than she wanted it to. She'd fled Silver Glen with

Zander in hopes of an adventure, and here she was, worrying about what he thought of her.

She took a deep breath of the humid air in the bathroom, mixed with the opium-laced air vented from below, tinted with stale ale, smoked meat, and human stink.

They would find the thief, get back the box, and then head back to Silver Glen. All would return to normal. She would return to her new job in the kitchens, and Zander... What would her father do to him when he found out what he had done? That he had talked Raven into leaving with him? Of course, if this box was as important as Zander said it was, her father had to know about it. He knew about everything that happened in Silver Glen, above or below.

And...maybe Silver Glen wouldn't be so bad if Zander was with her.

Raven returned to the bedroom and ate from the rations, including the last of the almonds that Zander hadn't mentioned. When he had pulled the bag from his pack, he had blinked, then continued on as if they had always been there.

He knew she stole them, but he hadn't said a word about it.

She tossed a few almonds into her mouth and watched the sunlight sink deeper into orange, then purple. She lifted the curtain. The town was lit with lanterns, but to the east, a white glow warmed the horizon enough to black out the stars above it.

Lenhala, the capital and royal city of Rhynwier. Even from this distance, its sparkling towers of glass and steel glowed like gold and silver in the twilight. How amazing it must look at night, all lit up. She had heard through traders that Lenhala was always lit up, day and night; there were stadiums and parks that glowed as bright as day during the night.

Raven had loved the trips to the surface with her father to meet the traders, but when she had gotten old enough to ask questions, her father had refused her pleas to go with him.

He didn't want her asking questions. The mines were secret, he had told her. If the Gray Elite found out about Silver Glen, they would come charging in. As a child, she had accepted that story without a doubt, but as she grew older, she knew her father had made it up to keep her from talking to the traders. To keep the world and her separate.

The sun sank lower. Lenhala grew brighter. Bright enough that it outshone Wilyn's Star. The little town glowed too, with all its shop windows, apartments, stacked homes, and lanterns, but not like Lenhala. How must it be to live in a world that never goes dark?

The ruckus downstairs grew more drunken by the minute. She heard Zander's bawdy laugh, and every so often, a horde of male laughter would fill the entire inn, belly-shaking and beer-aided. Raven took a deep breath and sat on the bed.

Waiting.

Any moment, Zander would start singing.

Unless he didn't. Unless the thief didn't show. Unless the thief had gotten smart and stayed in his room.

A horrible thought struck—what if the thief kept the damn thing on his person?

That thought didn't stick too long, for it hadn't crossed her mind a moment before Zander's drunken slur drifted up the stairs:

> *Jim goes fishing every day.*
> *Jim goes fishing every night.*
> *Jim goes fishing.*
> *Boy what a sight!*

Raven was on her feet, treading lightly to the door. She fastened her hand around the handle.

A cacophony of voices sang with him:

> *Jim goes fishing to escape the wife.*
> *Jim goes fishing to forget his strife.*
> *Jim goes fishing,*
> *But forgets his knife!*

Raven crept into the lonely hall of the inn's room. "No mistakes," she repeated to herself. No mistakes.

20

Raven slipped into the hallway without a sound. She repeated her search of the upstairs rooms, picking the locks with her steel hairpin, sorting through the sparse belongings. Zander hadn't been kidding about the type of people staying at the inn. She found vials of strange liquid, bags of teeth that looked sickeningly human, runes carved in stones, and an old doll the size of her thumb, with black eyes.

She didn't dare take anything from the rooms; her gut warned her not to.

Three of the six upstairs rooms were occupied, and none contained the little metal box. Which meant she would have to go downstairs.

Raven started down the stairs one at a time. Zander led the drunken tavern through another bawdy bar song, this one of mermaids. She reached the second to last step as they began to sing a verse about the mermaid's peaked breasts. Raven's entire face burned. That Zander knew such a song infuriated and embarrassed her.

A man stepped out of the third room. Raven froze; she didn't have time to move—he stepped around the staircase. Their eyes met. He was of average height, lithe but thick with lean muscle. He had dark skin of the southern kingdom and eyes like coal. His black hair had been done in dozens of thin braids that fell halfway down his back. He wore close-fitting clothes, a lightweight leather cuirass and trousers adorned with knives and daggers. His sharp eyes did not gleam with ale or glint with malice.

He halted before the staircase, just out of sight to anyone on the main floor looking toward the back hall. He leaned onto the banister, his movements easy with grace. A stark aftershave wafted along with him. Closer, he didn't look that much older than her, maybe twenty.

"Judging by the disgusted look on your face, you must be that drunk's wife he keeps going on about," he said, his voice smooth and pleasant.

She swallowed. "I-I didn't know he knew such songs," she said meekly.

He looked Raven up and down. "How long you two been married?"

She bit her lip, withholding the answer. That wasn't something she and Zander had discussed. She hadn't planned on meeting anyone, explaining herself, or talking.

He shook his head, frowning. "I take it, it's not been very long, then."

She didn't answer.

His quick eyes darted to the doorway to the main floor, where another verse dedicated to women's body parts had all the men singing, and a few women by the voices. "I heard him say you hadn't known each other long." His eyes returned to Raven.

"Not long enough," she said quietly. She balled her fists on the knees of her trousers. She was starting to think she didn't know anything about the real Zander at all. All that he had done, the singing, the flirting, the lying, the pretending. "I'd known him to be a scoundrel and a braggart, but..."

"You thought you could change him?" He shook his head in pity. "Word of advice, little bird, men don't change. No matter how much yelling or pouting or withholding a woman does, men don't change." He pointed toward the door. "Women do, though. Not for worse, but they do change with age."

"Please, don't tell him you saw me here," she said quietly. "He'll only make a scene about it."

He considered her, his clever eyes searching her face. "How old are you, bird?" he asked.

"Seventeen."

He frowned. "Not old enough to marry. Some people got strange ideas about marriage. Especially the rich. They think it's like game pieces, marrying off children like they sell off property or stock. I lucked out by growing up poor."

"You're married?"

He shook his head. "I've got a girl back home, but we're not legal. Can't afford the wedding, the license, or the taxes that would come along after. But we don't need a piece of paper to tell us that we can be together. Love doesn't have to be certified."

She nodded. "That is a nice way of thinking about it. I wish more people thought that way."

He chuckled, and his black eyes glittered. A certain joy brightened his entire face, and it made Raven think of Lena. "You know, bird, you don't have to stay with that scoundrel. I've got connections. I could get you passage out, somewhere better. Somewhere you won't have to worry about pleasing that scum or how many kids you'll have. The south is still outside Gray Elite rule, and it's a good place to start over. My people could find you a job, a place to stay, maybe even some friends. Ever see the sunrise over the gulf? It's a beauty, let me tell you."

She looked at the man thoughtfully; though her marriage to Zander was a ruse, the proposal of a new life outside of Rhynwier, beyond the Gray Elite, was enticing. She could leave it all behind and start new somewhere else. She could leave Zander, the box, Silver Glen—start over with a new name, a new life.

But...she couldn't leave Zander.

"Tell you what." The man reached into his pocket and withdrew a coin. "If you ever change your mind, follow the stars to Wayward Point. Go to the white brick building, called the Destiny Show, and present this coin to the doorman. Tell them Conrad sent you. You'll find help inside."

He set the coin in her palm. It was not a silver Gracitan token or a copper Rhynwier mark; it was a wooden coin. Both sides had been carved with an elegant circle with a diamond inside of it.

"Thank you," she said, gazing up at the man.

He nodded. Without another word, he returned to the main room. The song never fluctuated.

Raven took a deep breath, tucked the coin into her pocket, and started down the hallway. She picked the lock on the closest room, let herself in, and quickly went through the personal effects. Nothing. She repeated with the second room, but still nothing. She hesitated at the third door, the door Conrad had come from. She skipped it and went to the fourth room, then the fifth. No box in either.

She stood in front of the third door. Conrad had been nice to her. Going through his things felt wrong.

Still...

No mistakes. This was their last chance.

She picked the lock and slipped inside. Like the others, the room was sparsely decorated. Water trickled in the bathroom. The same stark aftershave lingered in the air. Her panic rose; she had no defense if Conrad returned and caught her going through his things. She doubted he would be as friendly the second time.

The song shifted to another, and she began her search with trembling fingers. She looked in the obvious places first, under the pillow, in the small dresser, and finally, she turned to a shabby leather jacket. She started to search through the pockets—there were dozens of pockets inside it—more than any other coat she had ever seen.

Why did one man need so many pockets? Did he go around handing wooden coins to all the girls he met? She found all manner of things, tokens and marks, buttons, necklaces, rings. What in the world did—

Her thoughts slammed to a halt as her fingers closed around a cool metal box in one of the jackets's deeper pockets. Her heart slammed into her ribs, and she gently pulled it out.

A small iron box. No more than an inch wide. The metal had dulled with time and age and looked like something Brent would have thrown into his Scrapper.

This? *This* was what she had come all this way for?

And then she realized—the man who had given her the coin, the man who had been so pleasant and friendly—he was their thief. Conrad the Thief. A professional thief.

No sooner had that thought passed, than booted footsteps sounded in the hall. She quickly tucked the box into her pocket and rearranged the jacket. The footsteps stopped in front of the door, and a key shoved into the lock.

Her heart stopped—she hadn't the time to plan. She dropped to her knees as silently as she could and rolled underneath the bed. She covered her mouth to quiet her breathing, and the door to the room opened.

The thief's boots walked inside—the only part of him visible. It was Conrad, if that was indeed his name. He marched to his jacket and yanked it from its hook.

"Five tokens a night," he mumbled. "The whole inn's not worth five tokens."

Raven's heart threatened to beat its way out of her chest and expose her to the thief. What would he do if he found her under his bed? Nothing good.

The thief let out a sigh and something crunched—bread, she realized, as he began to chew. He reached down, and his dark fingers fastened around the strap of his satchel. Raven held her breath despite her thundering heart. He straightened, hauling the satchel out of her view. He left as quickly as he had entered.

Raven stayed under the bed until her heart slowed, then clawed out on shaky limbs. Dust clung to her clothes and hair, but she hadn't the time to worry about it. Out. She needed to get out and to the safety of her own room. Before anyone else came looking. She double-checked the box in her pocket and then let herself back into the hall.

The thief had gone. The only other person in the hall was a balding man who held onto the waist of a whore. Her eyes were horridly painted in red and black, and her dress dipped dangerously low in the front. Neither of them paid Raven any mind, and she skittered up the stairs and shut herself into her room. She twisted the lock, and as metal slid against metal and settled with a *thunk*, something like relief spread over her shoulders.

No one came thundering up the stairs after her. She took each breath as it came and pressed her forehead against the backside of the door. After a long moment, she shut herself into the small bathroom. She stripped herself, dusted off her clothes, and washed in cool water. She set the box on the basin, within sight.

The box didn't look worth hiring a thief over. It looked like junk. But the Gray Elite had hired someone like Conrad to find it, so it had to be worth something.

Raven turned off the water and stood to dry. Without the rushing of the water, she could hear a few people still singing downstairs. It sounded as though ale had gotten the better of a few of them. Outside, through the slatted vent above the water tank, a fight had started. She listened to the sound of fists colliding with flesh, the grunts and groans of injuries, the cheers of drunken onlookers. Her heart thumped, and she thought of Zander. She listened harder to the voices and picked his out of those still singing.

As dry as she cared to be, she dressed and braided her hair and carried the iron box into the bedroom. She sat on the bed and turned it over in her hands. It felt warm to the touch. She didn't see a way to open it. The metal was seamless. She rattled it; it was not empty. Something was inside, although it didn't move. It had weight but not more than a few ounces. What could be so valuable as to go to all the trouble of stealing it? And then stealing it back?

Or was it the mystery of the thing? No one knew what was inside, and the mystery made it valuable.

The singing downstairs faded with a final song, and Raven tucked the box into her pocket. Patrons were filing into their rooms in the inn, and others were meandering outside. The drowsy, drunken chaos drifted with them, sputtering out into the night. Footsteps sounded on the stairs, but the owner walked past her door. She released a breath. The door to the room next to hers opened and closed; then a body collapsed onto the metal frame bed with a heavy thump and creaking metal.

Another set of footsteps sounded on the stairs, sloppy and uneven. Drunk. The feet made it up the stairs and fell into her door, and she jumped at the sound. She drew her legs up and closed one hand around the dagger in her boot.

A key hit the wood around the handle, a drunken man's thrust, and after several attempts, the key slid into the lock. It turned slowly, and then Zander stumbled inside. He shut the door louder than he should have, then fumbled to lock it back.

He turned his drunken gaze on her, his eyes swimming. He swayed dangerously back and forth but somehow made it to the bed. He flopped with the grace of a stone, landing on his stomach. He released a deep, ale-laden breath. Raven leaned back onto her pillow. Zander opened his eyes and met hers. He couldn't stay focused.

"I drank a little too much," he said, slurring. Really slurring, not pretend-slurring. His breath reeked of ale, stout and too sweet.

"Then go to sleep," Raven whispered. She eased onto her side. "I'll tell you the good news in the morning."

He blinked several times; then he smiled wide. It lit up his drunken eyes. He let out a bark of a laugh and slung his arm over her side. "Really?"

"Really." She pushed his hair out of his face. He started to speak, but she pressed her finger against his lips. "Shh, you're drunk," she whispered. And his breath stank. "You're talking far too loud. Go to sleep."

He hugged her against his chest, warm and rhythmic with his heartbeats. His clothes had soaked in the smoky tavern stench, but Raven had no immediate desire to move.

Zander fell asleep quickly, his lips slightly parted, his ale-laden breath warm on her temple. When he had fallen deeper into sleep, she slithered out from underneath his arm and shut herself in the small dark bathroom. She washed her face in cool water.

She gripped either side of the metal basin, her hands shaking.

She had found the box. She should be happy. But her stomach twisted.

She reached into her pocket and fastened her hand around the iron box. Warm to the touch. Just iron, she told herself, but something deeper inside of her didn't believe that. Something else, something more.

Back in the bedroom, the moonlight gleamed through the holes in the curtain. She tiptoed to the window and pushed the curtain aside. Beyond the lights of the town, Lenhala glowed bright on the horizon. A man-made star.

She removed her boots and Zander's boots and slipped back underneath his arm. He didn't even stir. She took a deep breath, spiced with Zander's ale-laden exhales, and tried to find sleep.

Raven tossed and turned most of the night, waking up at every sound the inn made, fearing the thief would burst through the door, anger twisting his face. Would he get to wherever he was going, discover the box gone, and know she had taken it?

A hand touched her shoulder, and she jerked awake at once. Her fist collided with her assailant, and he let out a grunt.

"Shit," Zander spat.

She blinked

Zander sat back on his heels, rubbing his cheek. "What the hell was that for?"

"I-I'm sorry," she said, clutching her fist to her chest. "It was a reflex."

He glared like he didn't believe her. "Well? Do you have it or not?"

She reached her pocket and pulled out the little iron box. Zander's eyes widened, and his hand fell from his jaw. With a sharp inhale, he gently lifted the box from her hands and turned it over.

"Is this it?" she whispered.

He nodded without taking his eyes off the box. "Yeah." He closed his hand around it and met her gaze. His awestruck expression fell into a frown. "What's wrong?"

She blinked; had she made a face?

"Did something happen?" he whispered. He motioned to the box.

She bit her lip, then told him how she had met the thief on the stairs and how he had nearly caught her. Zander's brow crinkled. She left out the thief's name and the wooden coin he had given to her. She didn't feel like explaining it to Zander. Not right now.

After a moment of silence, Zander set the iron box back into her hands. "Hold onto it with your life." He scooted off the bed. "We should get out of here as quick as we can." He stood too quick and wobbled. He threw out a hand to catch the wall before he fell, then put a hand over his eyes and let out a groan. "Sisters," he mumbled.

"Well, that's what you get for drinking so much," Raven said.

Zander shot her a deadly glare as he walked into the bathroom. Raven pulled on her boots and readied the packs while Zander washed up. With them ready, she walked to the window and opened the curtains. The fresh morning sunlight burst in, warming her face while the cool breeze kissed her cheeks.

She took her turn in the bathroom while Zander stood outside the door, tapping his foot, munching on hard bread, murmuring for her to hurry. When they, at last, left the inn, Zander walked at a clipped pace, winding their way around the black magic market.

"Are we heading back through the tunnel?" Raven felt a jump in her chest at the thought of riding the Hellcat again.

"No."

"Why not?"

"Because there's no way of knowing where it is within the tunnels," Zander said, motioning toward the ground. "There's no way of contacting them with enough time for them to get here. We're on foot for a while."

Raven sighed. The idea of walking back to Silver Glen filled her with dread. "That's so far."

"We just need to get back to Oun. It's the town we skipped with the Hellcat," Zander said. "When we get there, we can send word to the Dwellers."

"Oh, that's not dreadfully far," Raven said, though she didn't know for certain.

"Now, hurry up," he grumbled.

They retreated through town and toward a path that led through the forests to Oun, rather than take the main road. According to Zander, too many people would see them on the main road. Zander led the way, and it left Raven able to look around. People were getting to work around the town, fixing homes, tending to animals, and opening shutters and shaking feather dusters. Somewhere, fresh-baked bread and sugary sweets wafted through the air, making her mouth water.

Zander paused, and she got a second look at a man sweeping dust from the stoop of a store—he wore plain clothes, and his hair had been shaved close to his scalp.

A slave, she realized. Bile rose in her throat.

At the sharp bark of a woman, the slave retreated back into the store, his face devoid of emotion. Zander started forward again, and Raven followed, feeling sick. She had never seen a slave before.

They crossed another street and wound through a narrow alley. Raven glanced down the street to see if other slaves were working, when her eyes met those of a young man standing at the open door of a nicer inn. His dark hair was short and slicked back, and he wore the yellow and gray uniform of the Gray Elite. He was speaking to a well-dressed innkeeper; behind the innkeeper, a slave stood silent, obedient.

She had never seen a Gray Elite before, at least, not in uniform.

Her stomach twisted into knots. She tore her eyes away from the Gray Elite and focused on Zander's back. He gave no indication that he had seen the young soldier. He wound through another alley, up a street, and through another alley.

They were passing a sheep farm on the outskirts when her stomach growled too loudly to ignore.

"We'll get something to eat when we get to Oun," he said.

"Why not now?"

He didn't answer immediately, then growled in frustration. "Because we need to get out of here while we can."

91

The knot in her stomach tightened. Had he seen the Gray Elite? Was he following them? Looking for them? Her thoughts churned her anxiety and fears, and her hunger got pushed to the side.

The sun vanished behind a cloud as they started down the winding forest path to Oun. The path rose and fell with the hilly terrain, far more than it had to the north. Rocks jutted out from the ground in some places, a few creating shadowed coves. The sun came and went between the clouds, dousing them in bright light and then shade and back again. The sun rose higher and higher, and the temperature rose with it.

By the time Oun came into view through the trees, her stomach had grown viciously empty, and sweat stuck her shirt to her back. Oun was set on a hill, and the final incline nearly did her in. Zander led the way through the simple wooden shacks and stone homes. She walked a step behind him, and he guided her around a larger stone home to a small clearing.

She lost her breath at the sight.

Because Oun sat on a hill, the land before it dipped downward and gave them an uncrowded view of Lenhala. It rose in the distance, gray and faded blue, its white and metal towers reaching for the sky. It almost sparkled in the light.

"I've never been so close," Raven whispered to Zander.

"And hopefully, it will be the closest you ever get," he said with distaste.

They walked into an open-air food counter, and Zander paid for a simple meal of smoked meat, sliced brown bread, and cheese. They took their late breakfast outside in the shade of a tall oak, and she ate without talking. She finished all of her food, but Zander picked at his. At her stare, he ate a little faster.

"Why are you so nervous?" Raven asked him as they filled their canteens at the bar. "We did what we needed to."

He nodded, though his eyes were elsewhere. Raven looked back to Lenhala. It looked like another world, where metal ruled over stone and dirt, where the machines weren't cobbled together with ancient parts, where girls didn't have to work in the kitchens because of their overprotective fathers.

A part of her wanted to run away to the capital, or to Wayward Point—wherever that was. She didn't want to drag her feet back to Silver Glen and give up the possibilities of the world before her, of adventure, of new people, of sights she'd never dreamed of. Of all the places she had seen, the inns and taverns and houses, Silver Glen was by far the shabbiest, smallest, and loneliest.

"What are you thinking?" Zander asked, tearing off pieces of bread.

"That it would better to be a slave in paradise than a king in hell," she said.

He frowned. "Lenhala looks nice, but it's a different kind of hell."

He continued his slow eating, and Raven glanced back at the little town. A flash of yellow and gray caught her eye, and her stomach dropped into her groin.

The same Gray Elite she had seen that morning now stood at the very food counter they had visited; the man at the counter pointed in Raven's direction, and the Gray Elite turned. Their eyes met. He gave her a warm smile, but something sinister lay beneath it.

"We're being followed," she whispered.

The Gray Elite started toward them, walking with the learned grace of one used to combat. A saber hung off his belt, and a fine leather holster hung off the opposite hip.

Zander glanced over his shoulder. His eyes settled on the stranger, and he jumped to his feet—food abandoned. His straight-line mouth fell into a grimace, and he looked ready to kill. His fingers twitched toward Birdie, and Raven pushed herself onto shaky legs.

The Gray Elite stopped in front of Zander, who'd gone a shade too pale. Raven studied the uniform. He wore dark green decorations on his shoulders, signifying him as an officer. Raven felt her own skin pale; an officer of the Gray Elite had followed them, looking for them. Raven thought to the box in her pocket and fought the urge to curl her fingers around it.

The officer's small smile stretched wide. He looked Zander up and down and then threw his arms out wide. "Zander, it is you! I half thought the reports to be false." He spoke elegantly. The officer's gaze slid over Raven. "And you're not alone. The reports were right on that account too."

Zander took a step closer to Raven, his fists clenched. "Hello, brother," he said, though he didn't sound happy about it.

Brother? Raven looked between the two. She saw resemblances: their jaws, their noses, their dark brown hair, the shape of their eyes; they looked like brothers, but where Zander had sapphire blue eyes and bronze skin, his brother had charming brown eyes and beige skin. Zander stood with a lethal grace, while his brother held himself like a soldier.

"Aren't you going to introduce me to your..." his brother motioned toward Raven, and she bristled at the subtle distaste in his tone. She knew at once, she didn't like him.

Zander turned to her, unhappy in every sense. "Raven, this is my older brother, Baxter. Baxter, this is Raven."

"Raven," said Baxter, her name a purr on his tongue. His eyes slid over her, and she felt his assessment happen before she could speak. He took in her disheveled clothes, her loose braid, her dirty boots—and gave her a small smile full of snobbish pity. Her cheeks burned. He held out his hand for hers, and she cautiously gave it to him. His fingers curled daintily around hers. He placed a quick kiss on the back of her hand. "It is a pleasure to meet you."

"The pleasure is mine." She had the urge to wipe her hand on her trousers. His fingers twitched as though he thought the same.

"Where have you been?" Baxter asked, clapping Zander on the shoulder. "I was worried you'd gone somewhere you shouldn't have, and someone got the better of you. I cringed every time the news came, fearing I'd hear your name in the passages."

While Baxter spoke elegantly, he spoke with a learned charm, a practiced insincerity. With every word he said, Raven liked him a little less.

"I've been fine," Zander said, his words clipped. He brushed off Baxter's hand. "I've been busy."

Baxter's gaze slid back to Raven. "I see. I never thought you would be the type to run off with a girl, but I'm not surprised. I daresay that Mother will be overjoyed." He started to say something else, but he hesitated. His eyes roamed over Raven's state of dress once more.

"While it's great to see you, we need to be going." Zander took Raven by the arm and tried to lead her around his brother, but Baxter sidestepped to block their path.

"Just like that?" Baxter's brown eyes widened, feigning insult. He put a hand over his heart. "You wound me, Brother, to just leave again. Please, come home first. You look like you could use a few good meals and a few good washes too."

"I'd rather not." Zander tried again to step aside, but Baxter blocked his path.

"You've been gone six months," Baxter said, a plead on his tongue. "Half the city thinks you're dead."

94

Raven swallowed. Half the city? Lenhala was *huge*. Was Zander that well known?

"It's not a good idea," Zander said. "It'll only cause a stir."

Baxter laughed. "Since when have you worried about causing a stir? I thought you loved stirring?"

Zander huffed.

"Just for a few days," Baxter said. "Show the world you're alive and well, and then you can be on your way. This way, the Gray Elite won't be shoveling resources into finding you."

Zander gritted his teeth, and his hand tightened on her arm. So the Detector *had* been looking for him.

"Fine," Zander spat.

Baxter's smile widened, and he led the way to the main road, where a fine horse-drawn coach sat. Raven blinked; the horse was not a horse at all, but an automaton. It had been built to resemble a horse, its metal coat a shined brass. Rather than a mane, glass globes of dark red lined its neck. A driver sat on the front of the coach in a red coat with brass buttons and slicked-backed hair. The inside of the coach was a rich black leather and buttoned beige velvet. Baxter sat across from Zander and Raven, and with a knock on the coach's wall, the automaton horse hissed and roared to life.

The coach started forward, and the Detectors guarding the road didn't give them a second glance.

Baxter leaned back into the leather seat, his posture lazy but alert. Beside her, Zander sat straight as an arrow, his hands digging into the leather. Baxter peppered them with questions of where they had been, who they had seen, and why; Zander answered each with a non-answer. It didn't seem to bother Baxter. If anything, he seemed amused. His overly sweet tone irritated her, and by the look on Zander's face, it irritated him too.

From the window, Raven watched the capital come closer as Zander dodged Baxter's nosy questioning. They started through the outskirts of dilapidated homes, shoddy farms, and lean-to shacks. A stone fence kept the road separate from the outskirts. No one seemed to notice or care about the coach passing by. Some of the workers had shaved heads; some did not. Slaves and working poor.

As the coach trotted closer to the city walls, Raven noticed dots above the city; the dots became steadily larger, and then, with no small amount of surprise, she realized what they were. Airships. Hundreds of them, darting back and forth, up and down, all over the sprawling city. There were airships of every shade of metal and design; some looked like dragonflies, others like bullets with balloons, and others were coaches with winged automaton horses.

They produced a gentle roar that blended together into one endless engine purr, fluctuating as the wind shifted, as the airships moved. Raven couldn't take her eyes off the airships—so many of them! The part of her that had carved airships and stars into her ceiling wanted to shout, but as she glanced back inside the coach to find Baxter watching her with interest, that desire faded into embarrassment. She calmed the smile that had stretched her lips wide and forced her attention away from Zander's brother.

The outskirts became ramshackle buildings of dirty stone, weathered wood, and rusted metal. Farms shrank. Homes grew taller and cleaner. Each street they passed grew a little sturdier, a little prettier, and a little richer. By the time they arrived at the outer wall of Lenhala, the houses were taller, grander, and of clean metal and washed stone.

The gates of the city halted their advance, but with one look at Baxter and a flash of his shiny bronze badge, the guardsmen bowed their heads and allowed them passage.

"Right away, Lieutenant," said the man at the window.

Raven glanced at Zander. His lips had gone pale and tight. His knuckles were white on the seat. He eyed the guardsmen like a cornered fox eyeing wolves.

The car passed through the iron gates and into Lenhala—indeed another world. The buildings were smooth stone, metal, and glass, in all manner of colors. This close, the city was not pale gray and white, but a rainbow of purples, reds, blues, and all colors in-between. Splotches of green burst between houses and on top of them—gardens and parks. An endless cacophony of sounds flooded through the coach's windows, of people, of automatons, of airships—engines, chatter, laughter, clanking hooves, shouting—all the rhythmic heartbeat of the city.

And the people! She'd never seen so many people at once, walking along the wide sidewalks, riding in coaches drawn by all manner of automaton animals. She spotted several beautiful horses, bears, cats, and a winged creature she'd never seen before. The automatons came in every color of metal she could imagine, more colorful than the city. The coaches themselves were encrusted with gems and jewels, bright and shined, open and closed.

It all came with a metallic scent, underlined with perfume and grease.

She glanced at Zander, and he gave her a small smile.

"I take it this is your first time in the city?" came Baxter's carefully worded question.

"Yes," Zander answered for her. He didn't elaborate. He met Baxter's eye, and the conversation ended.

Raven swallowed. Baxter had been watching. After that, she tried her best to hold in her glee at all the wonderful things she'd never seen before.

Baxter explained that Lenhala had been built on a hill, and each district rose higher than the one before it. The first district was unremarkable; the second district held smaller businesses; the third and final district, which rose the highest on the hillside, housed the military, the palace, and the Gray Elite.

She wanted to stick her head out of the window to see the tall buildings of steel and stone for herself, but she held it in. She sat firm in the seat and watched the first and second stories pass her window. The steel was shined to a gleam, giving it the sparkling nature, and white and gray marble had been engraved and carved with all manner of things to give each building a dozen things to look at.

The people dressed finer than she had ever seen or imagined. The women wore silks and hats and heels and corsets and walked like goddesses. The men wore fine suits and jackets and shined shoes. She spotted several women carrying fans; she saw one woman tuck the fan into her dress's sleeve, where it vanished.

Raven thought of her clothes. Her trousers had been slept in, her shirt wrinkled, and her vest suddenly felt cheap. Compared to these people, she was nothing but country trash, uneducated and un-pampered and stupid to the ways of the city.

The coach took them through the heart of the third district, past grand halls and buildings so high, they left much of the street in shadow, for which blue-white lanterns had been lit along the sidewalks. It felt so...otherworldly.

"Welcome to Lamp Light Way," said Baxter.

"Because it's in the sun for only an hour each day," added Zander. He motioned to the lamps. "The lamps are lit day and night."

"It's lovely," Raven said.

"Lamp Light Way is the main street in the third district," said Baxter, his tone light and airy. "Symphony Hall is here, as well as the more prominent residences toward the south end."

They passed what must have been Symphony Hall, a grand structure with stone and marble. A theater, she realized. A large theater.

They drove down Lamp Light Way, through the otherworldly shadows and blue-white light, to the south end Baxter had mentioned. Grand mansions and palace-like homes dotted the street, fenced in with stone and metal and wrought iron, with magnificent gardens and orchards.

It looked like a place for gods to live, she thought.

And then, the coach slowed. It turned into a gated drive. The property's black marble and wrought iron wall rose twenty feet, ending in sharp points. The wall was as beautiful as it was intimidating. The house beyond it stole her breath—a palace of pale red stone, white marble, and light wood. The front garden sprawled with apple trees, peach trees, and red maple.

Zander looked nearly sick. Raven nudged his hand with her small finger, but he didn't budge.

The coach pulled alongside the gatehouse so that the window of the coach and the window of the gatehouse were parallel. A well-dressed man in a uniform of pale red and gray stuck his head out.

"Ah, afternoon, Lieutenant," said the man.

"Afternoon," said Baxter's calm voice.

The gateman glanced at Zander, and his pleasant smile faded. He blinked several times. Baxter cleared his throat, and the gateman stumbled back to the gatehouse. With the pull of a lever, the gates began to open with a soft squeal of metal and the silent thumps of gears. The coach pulled through the open gates and down the drive to the looming mansion at the other end.

"Where are we?" Raven asked.

"Welcome," Zander said quietly, his voice rough, "to Winchester House. It's my home."

Her breath came out in a disbelieving gasp. Zander had said he came from the aristocracy, but she hadn't expected this. He lived in a house as big as the entire mining system of Silver Glen! He didn't look happy at all to be home; he looked nearly sick. The color had faded from his cheeks and neck.

The coach pulled into a steepled garage the size of a tavern. Though the stench of oil and cleaning polish lingered, the room was immaculate. The tiled floor was spotless, the wooden beams dust-free, and every tool and contraption had a place on the shelves. Four stalls lined one wall, three of which contained a coach and its automaton animal. One coach was solid black with a gleaming steel horse, another was a stunning sky blue and pulled by a white wolf, and the third was ivory and pulled by a golden cat. A servant stood on the far side. He stopped whatever he had been doing at the workbench and bent into a deep bow.

The coach pulled into the empty stall and hissed to silence; the driver opened the door. Baxter stepped out first and then held out his hand to Raven. Behind her, Zander hissed a curse. His brother didn't seem to notice.

Raven gently placed her hand into Baxter's and stepped out of the coach. Zander quickly appeared at her side, between her and Baxter. A subtle glare passed between brothers. Baxter led the way across the garage and to a set of brassy double doors.

"I'm sure you are both famished," Baxter said. "I'll call Demetri for—"

"I can do it myself," Zander interrupted.

"I only thought—"

"I'm not a guest," Zander spat. He curled his fingers to fists. "I know my way around. This is my house too."

Baxter looked like he wanted to argue that point, but didn't. He nodded. "I'll meet you in the Orange Lounge for lunch, then?"

"Fine." Zander didn't sound enthused.

Baxter walked through the double doors, and Zander slowed his pace as to not be right behind his brother. He then led Raven through the same doors, through a breezeway lined with floor-to-ceiling windows, flowering ferns, and bright gold and red tile, and then into the house.

The air darkened, despite the tall windows. Dark wood paneling and red walls made the space darker and somber.

They entered a parlor. The ceilings were twice as tall as Zander, half dark paneling and half elaborately painted red and a slightly darker red. Zander didn't give her time to gawk; he pulled her through a set of wide, dark wooden doors with massive bronze handles. He pulled her down the hall, without a word, and up a grand staircase to the second floor.

Everywhere she looked, she saw elaborate paintwork on the walls; metalwork on the chandeliers, door handles, and curtain rods; and woodwork on the banister, panels, and doors. She saw candlesticks of silver, bronze, and copper, each a masterpiece. She followed close behind Zander through the second floor, up another grand staircase to the third floor. She had never seen so many paintings and spindly tables!

Despite the house being as big as the mines, she saw only one person inside—a woman in the same uniform as the gateman and the garage attendant, cleaning the rosewood picture frame of a large woman in pink. She didn't look up when Zander and Raven walked past.

Servants. He had *servants*.

She caught glimpses of the grounds through the tall windows. She spotted leafy green fronds and bright flowers that angled around a gray stone and iron gazebo as well as a sparkling fountain the size of a small pond.

And he'd left all this for lonely Silver Glen?

Zander led her through a set of wide doors into what, at first, appeared to be a sitting room; then she saw the pocket doors on the left and right. A grand fireplace of marble looked like it hadn't been used in a while, though everything looked pristinely upkept. Zander shut the doors behind them and heaved a heavy breath.

"Sisters," he breathed, setting his head against the polished wood of the door.

Raven meandered into the spacious sitting area and ran her hand along the back of a red and gold chair. "You live here?"

"I *lived* here," he corrected. He leaned away from the door and rubbed the back of his neck. His sapphire eyes took in the room with disdain. "The bathroom is to the left. The bedroom to the right."

She blinked; then she realized. "Is this your room?"

"It was." He met her eyes and frowned at her expression. "What?"

She shrugged and motioned to the fancy chairs. "It's so unlike you." Unlike her too. She had never stood in a room so nice, and it made her feel beyond insignificant and unworthy. Especially in her dirty boots and wrinkled trousers.

"Exactly." He diverted his attention to the walls, which were painted in shades of blue rather than the red that prevailed in the rest of the house. "Clean up while I try to find something else for you to wear."

"What's wrong with this?" she asked, motioning to her slept-in trousers and blouse.

His eyes looked her up and down, his lips set in a straight line. He met her gaze; not even a shadow of humor lit his eyes.

She felt something deflate in her chest. "I'm kidding." She started toward the bathroom. "Find me something nice."

Zander sank into the chair closest to him and hung his head, running his fingers through his dirty hair. Raven meandered to the pocket doors, finely crafted of dark wood and elegantly carved with lines and panels. She tucked her fingers into the smooth brass handholds and pulled the doors apart.

The bathroom on the other side was as big as the sitting room. White and gray tiles covered the floor and walls. The ceiling had been painted a sky blue. A brassy chandelier hung from its center. A grand bathtub took up the same amount of space as her entire bedroom back home. A separate shower stood away from it. On the other side, a toilet sat behind a blue and white folding screen with delicate gold metalwork.

She turned the faucet on the bathtub for warm water, and it spilled from the waterfall spout halfway up the wall. She found soap in the cabinets that smelled like jasmine and shampoo that smelled like apples. The towels were soft beyond reason and wide as blankets. She readied the items on the table beside the tub, stripped herself of her clothes, and stepped into the hot water.

Oh! She had missed a good bath—the washings she'd had along the way hadn't done the body justice. To be submerged in the water, to let it soothe and pull out the aches and worries—nothing compared.

She washed and soaked until the water cooled, then wrapped herself in the soft towels. She combed her hair and left it down to dry. She started to reach for her dirty clothes to return to the sitting room, but she spotted a beige robe hanging beside the door. Silk. She pulled it around her shoulders—she had never felt material so soft! Like water woven into thread.

The bath put her in a much better mood. She returned to the sitting room and found Zander slouched in a different chair. His listlessness had faded, and he stared into the empty fireplace with that intensity of his—thinking.

"You could do with a bath too," she said.

"There are a few dresses for you in the bedroom," he said without looking at her. His eyes focused on something she could not see. "I didn't know what size to tell them, so there's an assortment."

She pulled the pocket doors to the bedroom open. Soft sunlight glowed from the other side of the closed curtains. The dark wooden floors and dark blue walls gave the room a somber, tomb-like feel, and it mimicked the underground well enough that she felt a shiver. The room held a curtained bed large enough for five people, and piled on the blue-and-gold blankets were dresses. Dozens of dresses.

A rush of excitement raced from the top of her head to her toes and back again. She had never had so many clothing options!

Raven shut the pocket doors and went to examine those options.

Beside the dresses were undergarments of beige silk. That Zander had ordered her underthings filled her with hot, hot air that pushed against the inside of her face and her chest. She dropped the robe and quickly dressed in drawers and pulled a soft silk chemise over her arms. She grabbed the closest dress and pulled it over her head. Too big. The next was too small, the next too big, the next a strange style, but then she tried on a sage dress that fit perfectly. She laced up a corset of dark gold.

On the floor were three pairs of the same brown leather shoes—different sizes. She found the pair that fit best and returned to the sitting room. Zander no longer sat. Instead, water ran in the bathroom. Raven stood for a moment in the sitting room, then meandered to the large windows that looked over the garden. A high wall separated the Winchesters' grounds from the neighbors' equally sprawling grounds.

What must it have been like to grow up in a place like this? With fine clothes and servants? With more rooms than people? Without fighting for hand-me-downs and leftovers?

A knock landed on the main door, and she froze. She glanced at the bathroom door, but Zander gave no indication that he'd heard. The knock came again, louder. Raven opened the doors.

Two servants stood in the hall. A young woman held a tray of tea and cookies. The other was an older man with slicked-back white hair. The young woman bowed, the teapot and cups gently rattling, but the old man stood still as a statue. His nose crinkled as though he had smelled something awful.

"Master Baxter ordered tea *for two*," said the older servant, his voice matching his distasteful look. Raven hadn't missed the emphasis.

"Oh." Raven stepped out of the way.

The young woman walked the tray into the sitting room and placed it on the low table in front of the fireplace.

"Thank you."

The young woman bowed once again, but the old man didn't budge. They started back down the hallway, and Raven shut the doors. Her heart pounded; someone didn't want her here.

Raven poured a cup of tea into one of the two delicate china cups, added a cube of sugar, and took a sip. She added a second cube of sugar. They rarely had sugar for tea in Silver Glen. They had what the traders brought, which was never much. On her second sip, she decided that one sugar cube had been plenty. Despite the too-sweet tea, it warmed her throat and her insides like the bath had warmed her outside.

Halfway through her first cinnamon cookie, Zander walked out of the bathroom, wearing nothing but a towel around his middle.

She almost choked. The upper half of his bronze body was sculpted and lean. His damp dark hair hung to his shoulders. Water shimmered on his chest and taut stomach, pulling the sparse hair at a downward angle. Thin scars crisscrossed his skin with no discernable pattern; they must have been from his days in the Gray Elite. She wanted to ask him about it, but her throat refused to form words.

"What?" Zander cocked a brow. "Someone stole my robe. You'd rather I walk out naked?"

Her face burned, and she yanked her eyes off him and focused on her shoes.

"Where'd that come from?" His bare feet appeared in her view. His legs were sculpted and strong. He plucked a cookie from the plate.

"Your servants brought it when you were washing," she said.

He tensed. "What did they say?"

"That Baxter ordered tea."

Zander sat down beside her, eyes intent on her face. The towel came open over his thigh, and she fought to keep her eyes on his face. "What exactly did they say?" he asked.

She blinked. "Uh...that Master Baxter ordered tea for two, I think is what he said."

"He?"

She briefly described the servant who'd spoken and the servant who'd held the tray.

"Demetri," he spat. "What did you say?"

"I said thank you."

He nodded, eyes on the tray.

"Why does it matter?" she asked.

He turned his gaze back on her. He wore the same look that he wore when he aimed Birdie. Focused. Intent. Predatory.

Zander took her hand in his. "Raven, listen to me, this is important. While you're here, don't speak to anyone without me there."

She frowned. "I am capable of speaking—"

"I know you can," he said, his words quick and desperate. He squeezed her hand. "That's not what I'm talking about. People here are vultures. They will pick apart anything you say and use it against you. I know you won't mean anything by it, but there are people here who live to destroy other people. Please, Rae, don't talk to anyone without me."

To monitor her. To make sure she didn't say anything stupid.

She nodded. "Okay."

Zander sighed, stood, and took his cookie into the bedroom. Raven dared a glance at his retreating back, and what she saw stole her breath. On the right side of his lower back was a sprawling circular tattoo of steely gray; the whorls looked like the runes she had seen from the black market. She blinked, and he walked into the bedroom and out of sight.

The towel plopped on the floor, and she took a loud sip of her tea. She didn't need to think about him without a towel.

Why would Zander have a rune tattooed on his back?

Zander led her to the Orange Lounge, which got its name from the blood-orange wallpaper. Tall windows let in plenty of light and overlooked the front lawn. Baxter stood at the windows, his back to them. He had traded his Gray Elite uniform for a housecoat of deep purple. At the sound of the door, he turned and greeted them with a warm, practiced smile.

"It's been too long," said Baxter.

Zander shrugged. "That makes one of us."

Baxter's smile never faltered. If anything, he looked amused.

Lunch was served at a small table within the light of the windows, big enough for four people, set for three. Baxter and Zander sat across from each other, leaving Raven to sit between them. No servants lingered in the room. Though birds chirped pleasantly outside, Raven had a dreadful feeling of being trapped.

"Father isn't here," Baxter said. "He and Mother are on business in the east."

Zander's shoulders relaxed, but only slightly. "And you've sent word that I've arrived, no doubt."

"No. Not yet. I wanted to speak with you first." Baxter looked to Raven, then back at Zander. "You had us all worried when you disappeared. Father turned the house upside down, thinking you'd hidden somewhere, and Mother had the patrols scouring the city for weeks."

Raven swallowed a gulp of cider. *Disappeared.*

"I sent a letter," Zander said bitterly.

"A month later," Baxter said, a ghost of a smirk on his face. "Mother had started to face the grim reality that she might have to plan your funeral."

Zander chuckled.

"You think I joke?" Baxter glared at his brother, humor gone. "She cried for weeks. Barely ate. Father sent her to the hospital twice for observation, concerned the grief was too much."

Guilt replaced Zander's smirk, and he looked down at the expertly folded napkin binding his silverware.

Baxter continued, "When your letter arrived, Mother had gone with Aunt Meryl to write your obituary."

"I'm sure it was heartfelt," murmured Zander.

"Since Mother wrote it, I'm sure it was," Baxter said bitterly. "And I wouldn't know of its contents; no one got to read it. When your letter arrived, she had the obituary burned."

"I'll leave her an apology before I leave," Zander said, his tone tense.

Baxter frowned. "You're leaving? Again?"

Zander sighed. His eyes flickered to Raven, then to the window where Lenhala sparkled in the sunlight. "This isn't my home anymore, Baxter."

Baxter turned his gaze shamelessly onto Raven. His brows rose. "Oh. I see." He pursed his lips. "You didn't mention a girl in your letter."

"I hadn't met her yet," Zander said.

"Where are you from?" Baxter asked Raven, but before she could open her mouth, Zander said, "Small village north of here."

Baxter leaned back in his chair and pinned his brown eyes on Zander. "Still keeping secrets, are you?"

"Isn't that part of being a Winchester?"

Baxter laughed. "I suppose it is. Still, I know I can't stop you from leaving or force you to wait until our parents return. Tomorrow night is the Summer Solstice Ball. All I ask is that you attend. Prove to the world that our mother isn't mad for thinking her *favorite* son is alive."

Raven didn't miss the spiteful emphasis on "favorite." She glanced between the brothers, neither looking enthused about the other. She felt a pin of remorse for what Lena might be thinking of her right now. Did her family think her dead? Or had Mel told them the truth?

Zander's laugh sliced through her thoughts, bitter and humorless. "Don't try to guilt me into staying." His smile vanished, and he glared at his brother. "We both know Mother thought more highly of you. Better marks at school, better business sense, more friends."

Baxter shrugged. He didn't argue with any of those things. He turned his gaze again to Raven. "And think how it would be for her to attend the event of the year. It would give her something to remember."

With both brothers looking at her, she flushed. A certain maliciousness underlined Baxter's stare, a soured judgment for the girl he thought had stolen his brother.

"I'd rather be on my way as soon as possible," Zander said to Baxter.

Baxter's gaze lingered a heartbeat too long on Raven; then he nodded and looked away.

Raven released a slow, calming breath.

"I'll make you a deal, Brother," said Baxter. "Stay until the ball, and leave the morning after. I promise not to send word to our parents that you are here."

"You'd lie to Mother?" Zander raised a brow.

"Oh, no, if she asks, I will tell her that you were here but that you left again. I will tell her honestly that I promised you not to tell her," Baxter said, adjusting his collar. "I would never lie to my own mother."

Zander considered the offer. "You promise this?"

Baxter put a hand over his heart. "On my honor as your brother, I promise you, I will not send word of your presence to our parents."

A heartbeat passed. "Fine," Zander said. "I accept. We leave in two days."

Zander and Baxter held a long, silent stare. Raven shifted in her seat, and both sets of eyes turned to her. Baxter smiled, and Zander frowned; she had the distinct feeling that both brothers held back what they wanted to say. As they began to eat, the silence thickened with what had been left unsaid, and she suspected it had everything to do with Zander's sudden disappearance six months earlier—*that had left his family worried.*

He had not left with his parents' blessing or their knowledge, which made the weight of the little iron box in her pocket like a hundred stones.

Winchesters and secrets, she thought—just as Zander had said.

After lunch, Zander took Raven for a walk of the house. He walked her through the formal dining room, which had an oak table capable of holding forty guests, a number of sitting rooms with distinctly colorful wallpaper, the kitchens, and the room where his mother did her painting. Canvases in varying states of completion scattered the room—most were stunning.

Wouldn't it be nice to live a life where she could paint rather than work? Raven didn't voice those thoughts to Zander, who took in the wiles of his home with distaste.

He showed her the library, a room of thousands of books, and told her to pick a few out for herself. He meandered to the windows while she ran her fingers along the spines. So many books! She'd never seen so many at once! Zander helped her choose a few that were adventures, not dull history. Books in hand, they started back toward his room.

"What is the Summer Solstice Ball?" she asked softly. She didn't like the way her voice echoed in the empty hall.

"A ball they hold during the solstice."

She rolled her eyes. "Thank you, I'm glad you clarified that part of it. I would have never figured it out on my own."

He smirked. "That's what I'm here for." They reached his room, and once on the other side, his smile vanished. "It's just a party."

"Your brother said it was the event of the year."

He sighed. "That's because it's the summer party. But it's just another party. There's fireworks, drinking, dancing, and all the backstabbing chitchat you could want."

"Fireworks?"

"They're these things that have fuses like candles, and when lit, they fly into the sky and burst into colors with an ear-splitting bang."

"Oh," she said, trying to imagine such a thing. She sat down on the couch and stacked the books beside her. "And you would rather not go?"

"I would rather have the stomach flu," he said dryly. He plopped down onto the couch beside her.

"You would rather leave immediately," she said.

He half laughed. "I'd rather not have been dragged back here at all."

She fingered the edge of one of the leather-bound books. It didn't have the frayed edges and withering pages that hers had. Someone had read it but not many times. She had never held such a book, and a part of her didn't want to defile it by opening it. "You didn't tell your parents that you left," she whispered.

Zander released a heavy sigh. He leaned forward, elbows on his knees. "I know. I was hoping to avoid this, but I guess I can't anymore."

She reached into her dress pocket and closed her hand around the box. She had kept it on her person at all times, like Zander had said.

"It's not the best of stories," he said quietly.

"Tell me anyway," she said.

He gave her a weak smile, nerves and guilt showing through. "The truth is, I stole the box. I wasn't given the task of hiding it."

The box suddenly felt twice has heavy as it had before. *Stolen.* The thief had stolen it back. She scooted closer to Zander and placed her hand atop his. He wrapped his fingers around hers and gave her a sheepish smile.

"Do you hate me for lying?" he asked.

"No more than I did before," she said.

His smile stretched his lips, but it did not reach his eyes. "I grew up privileged. I grew up admiring my father. I grew up thinking the Gray Elite had done right in slaying King Reginald and his family and inserting their rule instead, but I thought all that because that's what I had been taught. I'd been raised to think highly of the Gray Elite and lowly of the dead king. But, as I grew up, I saw the Gray Elite rule in motion. They stole infants who showed signs of magic, enslaved those who disagreed, and I decided that I didn't like them.

"And then, when I was nine, I discovered my father, a Gray Elite, had been working in a secret order against the Gray Elite since before I was born. They protected magicians and sent them beyond the Gray Elite's grasp. They wanted to reinstate the kingdom to its former glory. I'd always thought the rumors of a resistance were a joke, but it was real, and I jumped at the chance to be a part of it, just as my brother had done before me. My father welcomed me into the order's ranks with open arms, and for the first time, he was proud of me."

"Resistance?" Raven whispered. It sounded like a story, something parents would tell their children to explain why bad things happened. It sounded like the stories of the Revenant, a story to explain disaster and the unknowns.

Zander nodded. "They call themselves the Order of the Hawk. The hawk was the symbol of the king of Rhynwier. They say it was the symbol of the god whose name the Gray Elite have worked so hard to erase from history."

"The Sisters?"

"No, before them," Zander said. "It's one of the things the Gray Elite doesn't want people to talk about or know." He pointed toward the books on her other side. "They've spent hundreds of years destroying evidence that a god existed before the Sisters. Give them another hundred years or so, and they will have destroyed the Sisters too."

Raven felt a pitting in her stomach. Though she did not claim to be devout, the idea that the Gray Elite could just erase such a thing chilled her bones.

Zander leaned back into the couch and squeezed Raven's hand. "I was so happy to be a part of the Hawks. I was so happy to be involved in something bigger than myself, something that I thought could change the world."

"But...what could the Hawks do against the Gray Elite?" she asked.

"They smuggle magicians out of the city." A shadow passed over his face. "The Gray Elite want nothing more than to rid the world of magic, to make sure that their machines are more powerful, and we make sure that magic stays alive. We—"

Raven gripped his hand. "You take children away?"

"To save their lives," Zander said, frowning. "I know it's not a perfect situation. Even as the Hawks save them, every day, children are taken by the Gray Elite. They're never seen again. They never say what happens to the children, but we all know."

She paled. He didn't have to say it. *Killed.*

"The Hawks work in secret all over the city and the countryside. Protecting magicians we find is one thing, but we also work against the Gray Elite rule, taking out troublesome automatons, disrupting their functions, taking out figureheads, and making sure the Regent knows that he doesn't have complete control."

"Taking out figureheads," she repeated. She dropped her voice. "You kill them?"

His eyes became hard. "Just like they have killed thousands of magicians. The people the Hawks take out are people who ordered those deaths. We are killing the killers before they can hurt anyone else."

She swallowed. Dark logic but logic nonetheless.

Zander held her hand between both of his. "This is why I didn't want to come back. The underbelly of the city is vicious, but the topside is just as bad."

"What happened?"

"Hmm?"

"You didn't finish your story," she said. "Why you left."

His smile vanished. "Oh." He cleared his throat. "I went to my father's office one night. I don't remember the reason I went, but I overheard him and a few officers talking. They knew a coup would result in Gracita declaring war, and thousands would be slaughtered because of it. The Gray Elite has an army on the ground and in the air, and the Hawks were a small band of rebels. They had found something that they had been looking for, something they could use that would guarantee a victory against the Gray Elite, and they were planning on using it."

Raven breathed, "What?"

Zander's eyes grew dark. "Altair's Augur," he whispered.

She blanched. "That's just a legend," she said, her voice barely a breath.

He shook his head. "I thought so too. But it's not. I've seen it. It's underground, under the city. It's been there the whole time."

She caught her breath in her throat. Altair's Augur was a doomsday device named after the ancient philosopher and engineer who'd supposedly built it.

Legends said the augur produced a blinding white light that obliterated an enemy city in the blink of an eye. Hundreds of thousands of people, gone in a flash of light.

"It's folklore," she argued.

"It's history," Zander said. "It's another part of history that the Gray Elite want to erase. A few books about it remain, but they are kept in secret."

"By the Hawks?"

He nodded. "Another thing we do. Preserve the history before it's gone forever. Some say the augur was built by the old god, but no one knows." Zander leaned forward and rubbed his temples. "I couldn't believe it was real. I didn't want to. I couldn't believe my father would be involved in something so horrible, something that would kill so many people at once."

Raven couldn't either. Altair's Augur. Underneath her feet. The city felt substantially less sturdy.

"I stole a vital piece of the machine. It won't work without it." His eyes traveled to her pocket, where she held onto the box. "I ran for my life with it."

"And you ended up in Silver Glen," Raven finished, "on the edge of the world, where no one would think to look."

He nodded. "And that is where we have to go," he whispered. "Because that device cannot be used. By anyone."

She nodded. She understood, though she didn't want to believe it. To save people, to prevent unthinkable disaster, they would have to return to Silver Glen. It made sense, logically, although it left a terrible pitting in her stomach. "But, before that, your brother is right."

Zander frowned.

"You must allow me the privilege of attending the Summer Solstice Ball. If I'm going to live the rest of my life as kitchen help, I am going to enjoy what freedom I have left."

Zander laughed and brought her hand up to his lips. As he kissed her hand, a tingle zapped underneath and over her skin from her hand to her toes to her scalp like a shock. A pleasant shock.

"And, if you're going to the ball, you'll need something to wear," he said, leaning back and gazing up at the ceiling. "It's a fashion event. But, before that, we need to talk about our cover story."

"What do you have in mind?"

They decided to stick with the story that Zander had met her while traveling. They had gone to Oun on a journey through the countryside. She knew nothing of why he left or that he had been from Lenhala.

And, as Zander told her twice, they had to leave before his father returned. His father would know he took it, and his father would be furious enough to do anything to get it back.

27

Raven took one of the books and nestled into the cushioned seat below the large window in Zander's sitting room. She quickly lost herself in the story and didn't return to the real world until someone cleared their throat. Zander stood over her. He had pulled his dark hair back and wore simple trousers, a plain white silk shirt, and a clean vest. His black leather boots shined. He didn't wear his holsters; he looked thinner without his guns.

"Are you going somewhere?" she asked.

"I've got some people to see," he said quickly. She started to close her book, but he added, "Alone."

Her heart fluttered. Alone, without her.

"I won't be gone long, or at least, I hope not." He glanced nervously to the window.

"Why can't I go?" She would love to see more of Lenhala.

"Because..." He fought for words, huffed, and said, "Because I can move faster without you."

His words stung, and she leaned back against the seat's wooden wall. "Oh. It's that, then."

He let out a sigh. "I don't want the Hawks looking any closer at you than they need to. For all they know, you don't know anything about me or why I left or them. Do you still have it?"

She nodded, patting the box in her pocket.

"Good. Don't let it leave your person. Ever. I'm serious, Raven." He knelt down to look her in the eye. "Don't mention the Hawks to anyone. You think I'm Gray Elite; that's it. You're a simple girl from a simple town."

She nodded.

He squeezed her hand, then left. She waited until the doors closed, then slumped further into the pillows. A simple girl from a simple town. That's all she was. Too naïve to go with him to see anyone from the Order of the Hawk, too backwater to understand secrets, and too stupid to understand how his world worked.

She returned to her book with an attitude that had gone sour.

A knock sounded on the door, and Raven froze. Should she answer it? The knock came again, a quick two-toned knock. She shut her book and walked to the door. She straightened her shoulders, lifted her chin, and opened the door.

"Dresses, miss," said the servant on the other side.

Two servants brought in a rack of dresses—fine dresses, much finer than the ones she had tried on earlier. Dresses for the ball, she realized.

She said nothing as the servants pushed the rack into the bedroom or as they curtsied and left. She listened to their soft shoes in the hall; then she went to inspect the dresses for herself. They were lovely! Silk and velvet and shined buttons of gold and silver and pearl. She pulled a few from the rack.

They were all so revealing. All strappy shoulders or bare shoulders, low backs or no backs at all, with tight bodices and low necklines. She pulled out a dress of vivid royal purple. The shoulders and back were nothing but crisscrossing straps of gold velvet cord.

Raven glanced to the open door of the bedroom. With Zander not there to gawk or tease, she could try on as many as she liked! If he was hellbent on dragging her back to Silver Glen, she might as well pretend to be someone else for a while. Someone far more interesting and cultured than herself.

She unlaced her corset, pulled off her day dress and chemise—for where would a chemise go in these dresses? She didn't try on the purple one first; no, she went with a pink dress without shoulders. She opened his wardrobe to see herself in the mirror; the dress fit tight, hugging her chest and hips, while the skirt flared when she twirled.

She tried on a red dress with sheer panels for a torso, a bejeweled black dress, a sky-blue dress with no back and a barely-there bodice, and then a creamy yellow dress with a deep V that nearly reached her navel and left much of her breasts exposed. The sunlight-colored skirt twirled with her as she moved.

"That's not your color."

She stopped dead, losing her balance and careening into something solid and warm. She looked up to see Zander standing there, a smirk on his lips. Her face burned, and she pushed herself off his chest.

She cleared her throat. "I didn't hear you return."

"Good thing too, or I would have missed this." He motioned to all of her. He shamelessly glanced at the exposed skin between her breasts.

She flushed hotter and crossed her arms. "These are the dresses your servants brought up."

He scanned the rack, unimpressed. He fingered the skirt of a blue silk dress, his eyes elsewhere. Distracted.

"I like the purple one," she said. "I might wear it to the ball."

Zander blinked, then sought the purple dress from the rack. He fingered the straps, then let it flutter back into place. Unimpressed and unenthused.

Simple girl, simple town.

She swallowed, suddenly feeling foolish. He saw fine dresses all the time, on girls more attractive than her. Of course, he wouldn't think the dresses were special.

"Okay," was all he said. He went back into the sitting room and shut the bedroom door.

Raven stood there, staring at the back of the door. In a huff, she tore the yellow dress off and put her chemise and day dress back on. She busied herself with returning the gowns to the rack; she'd thrown them a bit haphazardly onto the bed.

She steadied herself, then returned to the sitting room. Zander was sitting, elbows on his knees, staring into the dark fireplace. He didn't so much as glance in her direction as she returned to her book, to her cushioned window seat. She found her place in the story and returned there. When she looked up again, Zander hadn't moved.

Where had he gone? Who had he seen? What had put him in such a strange mood? Then again, he had been in a strange mood since they'd met the Dwellers. Did it have something to do with the Gray Elite? The Hawks?

He's keeping secrets, said a mean little voice in her head. *Keeping secrets from you, from his brother, and from his father too. From everyone. He doesn't think you're smart enough to understand.*

A knock came to the door, and Zander stood with the fluid grace of a nobleman and trained soldier. A servant stood on the other side, his nose as high as any noble.

"Yes?" Zander asked as if he had been interrupted.

"Miss Ivaline Pemberton wishes to be received for dinner, sir," said the servant in a dry tone. "She is overjoyed to hear that Master Winchester has returned."

Zander sighed. "Fine. We'll receive her in the first-floor lounge."

"I will send word at once." The servant gave a slight bow and retreated into the hall.

Zander shut the door.

"A lady friend of yours?" Raven asked. *Miss* Pemberton.

"Of a sense," Zander said listlessly. "We went to the same school. Our fathers went to school together, joined the Gray Elite together, have had a weekly poker night since I can remember. So, yes, we know each other. I guess that makes us friends."

Miss Pemberton probably knew Zander better than Raven did, and the thought burned. Had he tried to kiss her too? She shoved that thought away. She had only known Zander for six months, and the people here had known him his entire life, eighteen years. It would be like Zander being jealous of Lena knowing Raven better. Nonsense.

Still, that bubble of bitterness and jealousy didn't recede. She returned her eyes to her book. "I suppose I will be dining in while you enjoy dinner with your lady friend," she said calmly.

"What? Oh. No, you can go." Zander sighed and stepped toward the bathroom. "Miss Pemberton isn't that bad." He stopped in the doorway. "She's a sickly girl, always on bedrest. She's spent the majority of her life indoors, away from people and stressful events. She rarely leaves her home. She's got a weak constitution."

"Ah," Raven said. "And your reappearance has spurred her to leave her home. She must think highly of you to attempt it."

Zander glanced at her over his shoulder, brows furrowed. She hadn't meant to snap at him like that, but she had. She wouldn't apologize for it. She turned her attention to her book, and a heartbeat later, the bathroom door closed.

For dinner, Zander donned a red housecoat and found Raven a simple shawl. Together, they walked to the first-floor lounge. Baxter had gone out for dinner, leaving them to dine with Miss Pemberton alone. Raven would be lying if she said she wasn't a bit relieved. Baxter would be one less person to lie to, to pretend for. A servant opened the lounge door for them, and Zander walked through first.

Miss Pemberton sat with her back to them, facing the window. A table had been set for three, the covered dishes ready to be served. Servants stood by to do just that. Miss Pemberton wore sky blue, and her blonde hair was done up in an elegant bun, secured with pearl-tipped pins. She sat straight, and a servant of hers—Raven assumed, for he wore different colors than the Winchester house servants—stood close by her.

At the sound of the door, her girlish, cultured voice rang out, "Is that dear Zander?"

Zander escorted Raven around the table to where the sickly Miss Pemberton could see them. A lady indeed, for she wore glittery dark kohl around her eyes and pale powder over her face and neck. Her eyes met Raven's, and a sweet, mildly bitter smile came across her lips.

"And this must be the darling girl who swept him off his feet," she said.

Raven started to speak, but Zander interrupted by pulling out her chair. She sat.

"Yes," Zander answered, his tone light. "I do apologize for leaving like I did. I didn't expect to be gone so long."

Miss Pemberton smiled. She cocked her head to the side and snapped, "Charles, leave us."

"Are you certain, miss?" drawled her servant.

"Yes, yes, I'll call if I feel uncertain," she said, waving a delicate, white-gloved hand toward him.

"As you wish, miss." Charles relocated to the hallway outside.

"Git is what he is," whispered Miss Pemberton in a tone that struck Raven. She pinned her eyes on Raven, and her lips quirked upward like she knew something Raven didn't.

Raven bristled. Miss Pemberton didn't relent her stare.

Zander leaned in closer, his humored voice in her ear, "Haven't figured it out yet?"

Miss Pemberton smiled at her—really smiled. Through the powder and kohl, Raven saw a face that she already knew. *Ivy.* Ivaline. Her mouth fell open.

Ivaline winked playfully.

Zander spoke to Ivaline, "I'm glad to see that you're doing well enough to pay me a visit. I do appreciate your company."

She's a sickly girl, spends a lot of her time indoors.

Raven felt struck; Ivaline spent a lot of time indoors so that Ivy could be a free girl out in the woods. But how had she gotten here so fast? There had to be a Hellcat tunnel that led into Lenhala.

Spies and scouts, Zander had called the Dwellers. All over the kingdom.

A servant served dinner, uncovering the dishes and pouring cider into cut crystal goblets. Zander and Ivy—*Ivaline*—spent much of it talking about people and places that Raven had never heard of, and she felt left out. She tried to pay attention to the names, but there were too many to keep track of.

"So tell me, Zander, how you met this darling of yours," Ivaline said with a coy smile at Raven.

Zander chuckled, and then he spun the fake tale of how he met Raven—for the listening ears at the door and to inform Ivaline of their cover. She soaked in the story, every word. At the mention of the Summer Solstice Ball, she let out a lady's gasp of surprise.

"You're attending the ball?" Ivaline clapped her hands together. "That is wonderful! I've planned to attend, but I've kept the option open in case my health takes a wrong turn. I am glad to know that you will be there, Raven. It will give me someone to talk to."

Raven nodded. She felt a small bubble of relief too. Ivy would be there, and she wouldn't be in a ball of total strangers.

"Do you know what you're wearing?" Ivaline asked casually, then she added in a drawling lady's simper, "I expect that you don't know many of the designers here in Lenhala. I wouldn't want you to be caught wearing something from last year or from one of the less tasteful designers."

She'd said it so convincingly, Raven felt a pitting of shame at not knowing those things. She reminded herself that Ivy sat across from her, not a simpering lady.

"Zander was kind enough to arrange a few gowns to be brought for me," Raven said as sweetly as she could, and Zander took in every word.

Because they were being listened to, and the charade of Ivaline needed to exist even behind closed doors, as well as whatever charade Zander was playing, Raven had, however much she hadn't agreed to it, been pulled into the charade.

"I must see them," Ivaline said. "After dinner. I refuse to allow my dear here to wander through the Summer Solstice Ball in anything less than perfect."

After dinner, Ivaline—and her attentive servant—followed Zander and Raven to his bedroom, to the dresses. Ivaline rummaged through the dresses one by one, whispering insults at each. Too bright, too low, too shimmery, wrong fabric, horrid color, too many straps, not enough coverage—the list went on through the entire rack.

"Where in Minerva's name did you get these, Zander?" Ivaline playfully struck him on the arm with her lace-and-pearl fan.

"I asked one of the servants. I gave them her size, and this is what I got."

Ivaline put a hand to her chest, gasping as though physically struck; her servant jerked a step toward her but, upon realizing the act had been an exaggerated response, returned to his passive pose.

"You relied on *the help* to find her something suitable to wear to the event of the summer?" Ivaline shook her head, her chin high. "That will not do." She snapped her fingers and said sharply, "Rora."

A mousy-haired servant girl stepped into the bedroom and gave a quick bow. She wore the colors of Pemberton House. "Yes, miss?"

"I need you to run down to Raffela's and ask for the Gold Star, the one that I liked. She'll know what I mean. Tell her it is a fashion emergency, and bring her and the dress here."

"Yes, miss." The servant vanished as quickly as she had appeared.

"Oh, that's not necessary—" Raven started.

"Nonsense," Ivaline said, waving away Raven's concern. "If you are to be seen with me, then you will be dressed in nothing less than the best. And I know the best." She put a hand over her heart. "Raffela is a dream with a dress. Just you wait and see."

They waited for Raffela in the downstairs lounge while drinking tea. Ivaline went on about the designers of the city, names that Raven would never remember, and their fashion choices and horrible dresses. Ivaline talked nearly nonstop, and it was hard for Raven to see Ivy behind all the glitter and glamour and chitchat.

Footsteps sounded in the corridor, and before a servant could move to answer the doors, they flew open. A tall, tan woman rushed inside, her flaming red hair a wave behind her. She wore a glittering blue scarf over her broad shoulders. The servant girl, Rora, carried a garment bag in her arms.

"I heard there was an emergency!" Raffela stopped in front of Ivaline, bent to one knee, and gently kissed her hand. "I am at your service."

They shooed out the servants and Zander, and the designer had no qualms about stripping Raven down to the bare nothings; Ivaline spoke constantly over the dresses that Zander had managed to find, and Raffela added small comments and agreements when helping Raven into a gown of blue and gold.

Compared to the others, the blue and gold dress looked a world better. With a few adjustments, it fit like a dream.

"That is much better," Ivaline said, nodding proudly.

Raffela kissed her fingertips and flourished them through the air. "Perfection."

Raven caught her reflection in the glass-front cabinet, and from the ghostly image she saw, the dress did look good. She did not get to see it fully, for Raffela stripped her, and she was left to dress herself in her day dress.

Raffela hung the gown in the bedroom and whisked the other dresses away to dispose of them properly, as she said, which Ivaline whispered meant she would sell them at a discount.

"Oh, the lighting is lovely for an evening stroll," Ivaline said longingly, her eyes looking out at the garden. "Come, Raven, walk through the garden with me."

She didn't have much of a choice, for Ivaline strung her arm through Raven's and guided her to the back door, then out into the glorious gardens of Winchester House. Zander stayed inside at Ivaline's behest, and she guided Raven toward the stone and iron gazebo surrounded by lavender shoots and tiny yellow flowers.

The twilight didn't last long, and the tiny yellow flowers started to glow—bioluminescence, Ivaline explained. A wonder of the city. Hundreds of bioluminescent flowers dotted the garden, yellows, purples, pinks, a rainbow of color. Not unlike the fungi in Silver Glen, Raven thought, though she didn't tell Ivy that. Still, the glowing flowers tugged on something in her chest, and for the first time in a while, she felt a little homesick.

"How has your stay been?" Ivaline asked softer, casually rather than simpering and dripping with fake politeness.

"Good," Raven said. "The capital's been more than I expected."

"You can speak freely," Ivaline said. "Just not very loud."

Raven released a sigh. "There's so much to keep track of, and I'm worried I'll say the wrong thing. Zander's got me on edge more than anything."

"He's terrified," Ivy said. Ivy, not Ivaline.

"His father?"

She nodded. "Zander made some hasty choices before he left, and I mean hasty as in not the best choices. There are a lot of people who are angry at him and confused, and his father is at the top of that list."

Raven nodded. Ivy knew more of Zander's past and disappearance than Raven did, but she didn't want the other girl to think her stupid on the matter, so she didn't ask for details. Nor did she know how much of Zander's past she knew regarding the Hawks or the iron box in her pocket.

"Everything is much more complicated than I imagined," Raven said.

Ivy chuckled. "Isn't it though? I wasn't kidding when I said I preferred the countryside over all this. Yes, it's sparkling and nice, and everything is just so dreamy, but it has a darker side. The price we pay for all this convenience and glamor is steep. Too steep for me."

The wind rustled through the trees in a haunting whisper.

Raven whispered, "Who are you?"

"That's a good question. I feel like two people sometimes." Ivy shifted and rested against Raven. "Did Zander tell you about the resistance?"

"Yes."

Ivy nodded. "I've spent most of my life in the resistance," she whispered. "My father is one of the officers spearheading it, along with Zander's father. I was a sickly child, and it was the perfect excuse for my parents to stay home more than others. As I grew up, the sickness went away, but it's still a good excuse for spending time away from the city or, as far as anyone here knows, locked away in a room at the house. I've spent more time with the Dwellers, and I come back here when I need to. Appearances, recon, that sort of thing." She gave Raven a sly smile. "Who'd ever suspect poor little Miss Pemberton of wrongdoing?"

"I surely wouldn't," Raven said. "The poor dear is pale as death."

"It's powder," Ivy whispered. "Works wonders."

The two girls sat in the gazebo until the sun finished setting, and Ivy's servant came to fetch her. Her mother had ordered her not to be out past a certain time, lest the cold of the night take her health in the wrong direction. Faking exhaustion, Ivy became Ivaline once again and allowed her servants to escort her to the waiting coach.

Raven returned to the house and to Zander's room, where he looked unenthused. He stood by the window, the perfect spot to have watched them from.

"What?" Raven asked, tossing the shawl over the back of the chair.

"What did you two talk about?" he asked.

"Just girl talk, nothing you'd be interested in."

He lifted a brow but didn't respond. Raven was to the bathroom door when he said, "Ivy's a good girl. But she can be reckless and a bit naïve at times."

"I like her." Raven shut the door. She didn't need Zander to tell her who she could be friends with. Ivy made her feel less alone in this strange world, and she needed someone like her.

Raven returned to her book; Zander paced. He remained on edge throughout the evening, barely speaking. He would halt his pacing now and again, and Raven would catch him staring out of the window, his eyes on something she couldn't see. What was he thinking about? His father? The Dwellers? The box in her pocket?

Her mind was still spinning. She could barely concentrate on her book. The box, the augur, Ivy and Ivaline. She had never had to take in so much information at once.

The sun had sunk in the sky, and the lights of Lenhala burned bright, hiding the stars from view. The lights of the airships dotted the sky instead. Even inside the house, she could hear the gentle rumble of the hundreds of engines.

The clock chimed ten, and not a moment after, a knock came to the door. Zander jumped to answer it first.

The servants had brought Raven toiletries and a pair of silk pajamas in a steel gray.

"Would the lady require a room of her own?" asked Demetri, the dreary old servant. Through his narrowed eyes, he glared at Raven with heavy and obvious disapproval.

"No," Zander said quickly. He closed the door in the servant's face. Raven started to speak, but Zander put a finger to his lips. He pointed to the door—Demetri hadn't yet walked away.

Several heartbeats passed. Still, Demetri stood. Waiting. Listening.

Raven slid off the window seat and took the pajamas from Zander. She ran her hand over the silk. "These are lovely," she said, not a lie. "And so soft!"

Demetri's boots started back down the hall, away from the door.

Raven looked to Zander, and her face warmed as she asked, "You wouldn't rather I sleep somewhere else?"

"No." He secured the deadbolt on the door and then started to unbutton his dress shirt.

Her face warmed, and her heart flipped; she turned her face away from him before he could notice.

"The servants would pester you, and I'd bet gold that Baxter would show up in the morning to see what information he could get out of you."

"Oh, I see," she said. It made sense.

She started toward the bathroom with her basket of girl-oriented toiletries. They had included a golden bottle of what looked like perfume.

120

From behind her, there came a swish of silk. Zander's shirt. Her thoughts drifted to the rune tattooed on his back. She wanted to ask him about it, but she held her tongue. Thinking about him without a shirt made her face burn.

"What's wrong?" Zander asked. "We've shared a smaller bed before."

She paused at the bathroom door and glanced into the open doors of the bedroom. True, his bed was twice the size of a normal bed, near triple the size of what any inn had had. Still, it was Zander's bed, his space, his house. She thought to the last night they'd spent at an inn; he had slept with his arm over her.

Zander crossed the room with silent footsteps. He still wore the silk shirt, but he had unbuttoned it, revealing the lean chest and stomach underneath. She tore her gaze from his chest and forced herself to meet his sapphire gaze. He wore an emotion she couldn't recognize, one she'd not seen on him but a few times.

"We're still pretending, Rae," he whispered. "Everyone here thinks I ran off with you. It would look strange if we slept in different rooms."

And everyone assumed the worst. Her face heated, and the word "whore" resounded in her mind. Her heart flip-flopped.

Pretending, she told herself.

"Raven?" He stepped closer.

She hugged the pajamas to her chest. "Of course."

She shut herself in the bathroom and took her time getting ready for bed. She left the toiletries on the counter and, wearing her silk pajamas, carried her dress back into the sitting room.

She held up the dress and started to ask, "Where—"

"Just throw it somewhere," Zander said from the bedroom, his voice tired. "The servants will pick it up when they fetch the laundry."

She blinked, confused. She glanced around the sitting room. Indeed, he had tossed his silk dress shirt into one of the armchairs, along with his pants and vest. Zander emerged from the bedroom in dark blue pajamas and took the dress from her arms. He then tossed it over one of the chairs.

"There," he said.

"Is that what the rich do with their dirty clothes?" She followed him into the bedroom. Without the sunlight to warm it up, the single candle beside the bed gave the room a very tomb-like feel. "Toss it aside like garbage for the lowly servants to deal with?"

"Yes," he said simply.

She crawled into the cushy bed, and Zander untied the bed-curtains. He pulled them closed on all but one side, his side, and then he blew out the candle. Bright moonlight—no, she realized—it wasn't moonlight streaming through the windows. It was city light and the glowing flowers.

Raven settled into her pillow and listened to Zander's soft footsteps. His weight pushed on the bed, and he crawled underneath the blankets beside her. He pulled the last curtain closed, shutting the space of his bed in near-total darkness. He settled into his pillow.

It had a very underground feel to it, and she didn't know if she liked it or not. While the dark mimicked the underground, it smelled too fresh, and the city was too loud.

"The servants don't come in my room that often because I don't want them to," he said quietly. "I can do things for myself." He inhaled and released a long sigh. "The city is nice, but I'd rather live outside it. I like the villages where everyone works, everyone pulls their weight, and everyone earns their supper, not like this, where it's a matter of how much money a person has or how powerful they are."

"This bed is nice, though," Raven said.

Zander laughed, a soft, tired sound. "Do you think they'll notice if we take it with us?"

"We could sleep outside instead, under the stars," she added.

"After we dance," he said, a near whisper.

She smiled; she couldn't help it. He hadn't forgotten about that. She hadn't either.

The morning came; Raven didn't have much time to herself. After breakfast, servants came in to help her get ready for the Summer Solstice Ball. They did her hair and makeup and helped her into the dress. A few hours after midday, Raven stepped out from behind the dressing screen and saw herself in the mirror. The blue and gold dress fit her splendidly, leaving her arms and back exposed, but showed little cleavage. According to Ivaline, cleavage was last year.

Her light brown hair had been done up with blue ribbons and gold beads that clicked as she moved. Her mother's locket rested on her chest. The servants had tried to remove it, but she refused.

The doors opened, footsteps entered, and then a low whistle sounded.

Blushing, she turned, thinking it was Zander who had entered.

Baxter stood in the doorway. He wore his Gray Elite dress uniform, dark gray jacket, and pressed trousers with yellow stripes and white threading. It complimented his tall, lean frame—the frame he and his brother shared. Baxter had combed his dark hair back and parted it to the side, the Gray Elite style.

"You look stunning," Baxter said, giving her a charming smile.

"Thank you," she said, giving him a small curtsy. "You clean up well yourself."

He smiled. "'Clean up'? Is that a saying where you're from? It's cute."

She blushed. Simple girl, simple town. "Yes, it is."

She would rather not be thought of as cute. Children were cute. Small animals were cute. She, nearly a grown woman, was not cute.

Footsteps sounded in the hall—boots. Zander appeared behind Baxter, and at the sight of his brother, he scowled.

122

"What are you doing here?" Zander demanded. "Don't you have your own date to bother?"

Baxter chuckled. "Yes, and I was on my way out when—"

"Then you should continue on your way," Zander said.

Baxter closed his mouth and glared at his younger brother. "Very well," he said in mock-politeness. "I will see you both this evening." He turned on his heel and walked out.

Zander shooed the servants, leaving him and Raven alone. He hadn't dressed as Gray Elite. Instead, he wore a lovely suit of dark blue that fit his strong shoulders and lean waist. His velvet vest had buttons of gold. Someone must have told him her dress was blue and gold, for they looked as though they had planned it.

"You also look nice," Raven said absently.

"What? Oh, yeah." Zander glared at the doors, after his brother. He rolled his shoulders. "You look nice."

"You're not even looking!" Raven set her hands on her hips. Zander's sharp blue eyes met hers and then rolled down her body and back. She turned to the side to show him her exposed back.

"You look nice, Raven," he said. This time, his words were genuine.

She nodded. "That's better."

His eyes lingered on her a heartbeat longer, then moved to the window behind her.

"How are we getting to the ball?" she asked casually.

"By coach," he said simply. He took a deep breath, then released it. He came over to her, eyes serious and nervous. "Raven, you're about to walk into the lion's den. People are going to ask you questions, the same question over and over, trying to get information out of you."

"What kind of information?" She didn't know anything of worth.

"Anything they can turn into gossip, about me, about you, about anything," he said, almost pleading. "Don't answer anything directly."

She frowned, but before she could protest the absurdity of that command, he added, "Think how Ivaline speaks. She doesn't say anything that means anything. It's all mindless chitchat, pointless; around and around it goes. Talk like that."

"You want me to be stupid on purpose?"

"Not stupid," he said quickly. He set his hands on her bare shoulders and took a step closer. "It's a safety mechanism. Information is power. The less these people know about you, the better. Right now, our plan is to get out of here as soon as possible. Ivy's here, and that means we've got the Hellcat."

Zander had gotten that out of Ivy's words, her presence, and Raven hadn't thought of that. In that moment, she did feel stupid.

"Raven," he whispered, stepping closer. She could feel his breath on her lips. "We cannot let that box fall into anyone else's hands. We cannot afford to have anyone trying to find you or anything about you that might put us in danger tomorrow."

She nodded. "Okay."

"Where is it?" he whispered.

Her cheeks reddening, she lifted a hand to her bodice and pointed to where she had tucked the box—between her breasts.

He raised a brow.

"What? I don't have pockets in this thing," she whispered back, her cheeks getting hotter by the second.

His thumb touched her collarbone. He stood there a moment, eyes pleading into hers. She didn't know what else to say to him, and she didn't have the words—that same tingly feeling fluttered up through her ribs. Was he about to kiss her? She blinked, he began to lean in, and her heart jumped into her throat.

A knock sounded at the door, followed by a servant's drawl, "The coach is ready, Master Zander."

He cleared his throat, eyes looking anywhere that wasn't her. "Right, well, we best get this over with," he said, his voice a pitch higher than normal.

He offered her his arm; she took it, willing her heart to slow before it burst from her chest.

She could pretend to be ditzy and stupid for a night. A dark little voice in the back of her mind told her that she wouldn't be pretending. No one expected a simple girl from a simple town to be smart or cunning, and she didn't particularly feel either of those things.

Regardless, she refused to let any of that spoil this once-in-a-lifetime chance. Ivy would be there; Zander would be there; she would not be alone.

She took a deep breath, held her shoulders straight and her chin high, and walked with Zander to the garage. A well-dressed driver stood beside the readied ivory coach, and Zander helped Raven into the red leather seats. The golden cat automaton hissed to life, and the coach started out of the garage, down the winding lane, through the iron gates, and onto Lamp Light Way.

The entire city seemed to be getting ready for the ball, with suns painted on windows and storefronts and carts and stalls set up along the main streets, selling candies, candles, woodwork, clockwork, and all manner of things.

"I forgot to mention," Zander said, his voice drawling—for the ears of the driver. "This is a military event."

"So I should expect old men in suits with war stories?" She tried to imitate Ivaline's bored, polite tone, and when Zander didn't blink and the driver didn't even glance back, she suspected she had gotten it right.

Zander gave her a wry smile. "There are those too."

She tried to pick out what that meant; was there something else under his words that he wanted her to understand? A hidden meaning? Did it mean she should be careful when speaking to the military personnel? Or did it mean that people like

Zander and Baxter would be there—sneaky and full of secrets? Ivaline's father was Gray Elite too, as was Zander's father; they were also part of the resistance. The Order of the Hawk.

She pieced together a meaning, unsure if it was the one Zander intended. There would be Gray Elite there who knew of the Hawks, those who were in the Hawks, and those who despised the Hawks. She would not know who was who without Zander or Ivy.

Raven, being the lovebird that she was, pulled Zander's arm a little closer to herself and gave him a warm smile, to let him know she had gotten his meaning. He gave her a warm smile in return, one that did not escape the driver's notice.

She could play a lady for a while, and she could play the game. Let them all think her simple and stupid. This time tomorrow, she and Zander would be far from Lenhala, and this ball would be a but a dream.

The Summer Solstice Ball was held at the old palace. It had once been the beating heart of the kingdom, the home of King Reginald; now, the Gray Elite used it as a play park for their social events. The Winchester coach trotted down the front drive, and Raven gasped at the grandeur. The palace was a masterpiece of ancient architecture. It rose three stories, all milky stone and pale marble. Each grand window held stained glass of gold and blue; each had an ironwork balcony. Dormers lined the roof, each arched with iron fashioned into the shape of a hawk in flight.

"It's beautiful," she whispered to Zander.

"It was even more beautiful before the Gray Elite moved in," he whispered back, low enough the driver couldn't hear. "See those platforms? Statues of the Sisters used to be there, but they tore them down."

Indeed, three stone platforms lay in the trimmed grass like river stones. In the center of the stones, a marvelous fountain spewed aquamarine water over a brassy automaton woman.

Their coach joined the procession to the front steps. One by one, the coaches paused, and their well-dressed occupants stepped out. Most of the men wore Gray Elite uniforms, and she spotted a few women who had opted for the uniform rather than a gown, although most of them wore gowns. The Winchester coach paused by the front steps, and a footman opened the door. He held his gloved hand out for Raven. She took it gently and stepped out, Zander on her heels.

They started up the sweeping stairs of white marble. Zander and Raven followed the example of the couple ahead of them and looped their arms together. Their coach moved on, and another took its place.

At the top of the stairs, a large set of dark wooden doors had been propped open, and three Gray Elite soldiers stood on duty on either side, faces impassive, and all armed with crossbows on their backs, a saber at one hip and a pistol on the other.

Raven whispered to Zander, "Why carry a crossbow and a pistol?"

He whispered back, "Crossbows are more ceremonial."

The soldiers paid little attention to the Gray Elite walking inside, but as Zander and Raven approached, every set of eyes followed him.

"It's good to see you back, Lieutenant," said the Gray Elite closest to the door. She nodded at Zander.

Zander nodded back as he guided Raven through the doors. They walked into a vestibule of amber walls and marble floors. An ironwork chandelier hung from the ceiling, lighting the room with a hundred burning glass globes. The ceiling had been painted in a dazzling display of copper and ivory—a scene of automatons and humans working together.

"Lieutenant?" Raven whispered.

Zander winked.

People lingered in the vestibule, talking and greeting; nearly every pair of eyes followed Zander. She didn't have to look. She felt them. She heard his name in whispers, curious and suspicious. He gave the whispers no mind, and she followed his example and held her chin high.

A lion's den, he'd called it.

And they were the fresh meat.

Zander guided her toward the other end of the vestibule, where golden curtains had been tied back from the doorway, and they walked into the ballroom.

Raven barely held in her gasp at the splendor before her. The copper and ivory of the vestibule continued into the ballroom. The floor had been shined to a near-perfect reflection; from the amber ceiling hung a dozen ironwork chandeliers; leaded glass made up an entire wall of arched windows, through which the sprawling gardens glowed in the afternoon light; and everywhere she looked, she saw carved amber, gleaming gold, and startling white.

Zander guided her along the mezzanine that stretched across the back of the ballroom, off which two wide staircases curved onto the ballroom floor. Two sets of dark wooden doors led off the mezzanine, but they were closed and corded off and guarded by Gray Elite.

Zander and Raven made it halfway across the mezzanine when a voice called out from behind them, "Zander?"

She felt him tense, but he turned to the speaker with a polite smile on his face.

A pleasant-faced young man strolled toward them. He wore the Gray Elite uniform with blue honors, and he had his blonde hair combed back in the formal style. A bored-looking girl with dark hair done up in a ruby comb hung off his arm. Her painted eyes ran over Raven, and in an instant, Raven knew she disliked her. Ivaline had pretended snobbishness, but this girl oozed it.

"It *is* you," said the young man. Relief and happiness warmed his face.

"Ezra," Zander said, neither relieved nor worried.

The two of them shook hands like old friends.

Ezra's golden brown eyes looked Raven over with friendly interest. "Is this the girl you ran off with?" His smile widened. "I can see why. She's lovely." The girl on his arm rolled her eyes and gave a small, quick sigh. Ezra's smile diminished as he looked at her. "Jasmine, I'll meet you in the ballroom," he said shortly.

Without a word, Jasmine slipped her arm out of his and glided down the steps to the dance floor. Ezra watched her go, frowning.

"I was secretly hoping she'd trip and fall," Ezra mused. He glanced at Zander. "Is that wrong of me?"

"You came to the ball with Jasmine Clemens?" Zander raised a brow at Ezra. "I thought you had better taste than that. Not to mention common sense."

Ezra shrugged. "I put off finding a date because I thought I'd be in Moorin, but here I am. And all the nice girls were taken." Ezra leaned against the brass railing. "But enough about me, what about you? Where have you been, Zander? And why haven't you introduced me to your new friend yet?"

"Where are my manners?" Zander put a hand to his heart, abashed. He chuckled. "Ezra, this is Raven Thane. Raven, this is Captain Ezra Deacon. He's a friend of mine."

Friend. Was Ezra also in the Hawks? She didn't ask. Instead, she gave him a warm smile and a curt bow of her head. "It's a pleasure to meet you, Captain."

"And she's polite," Ezra said with a smile. "You must tell me where you found her; I want a girl like her for myself."

The crowd thickened in the ballroom as more guests arrived. The chatter floated, the laughter lifted, and glasses chinked as toasts were made and cider and wine flowed freely. A servant passed by with flutes of cider, and Zander grabbed one for Raven. She sipped her cider as Zander told Ezra the cover story that they had created.

She paid partial attention; the ballroom was too stunning. Everywhere she looked, she saw something new. The dresses reflected in the floor, giving the impression that another party was happening below them. Ice sculptures dotted the tables. Her eyes found a graceful swan made of ice, and the long-ago dream came surging back to her. She'd dreamed that she and Zander had gone to a ball—and now they were at a ball. Maybe she had known all along that they would end up in the capital.

A band of humans played winds and strings, a gentle tune that swept more and more people onto the dance floor. The tall windows looked to the west; Raven imagined they would provide a stunning view of the sunset. Already, the afternoon sunlight shone off the amber and bathed the room in honey-gold. Come sunset, those colors would become molten.

"Ah, how well it is that her first time in Lenhala would be to the Summer Solstice," said Ezra, and Raven snapped her attention back to the two boys. Both were looking at her. Had she missed a cue? Had she already messed up the evening?

She gave Ezra a shy, embarrassed smile. Zander took the smallest of steps closer to her. "I'm sorry," she said, her voice tinny. "This place is beautifully distracting."

"You should see the Canterbury Theater," said Ezra. "It's a marvel in itself but not as bright."

"It's on my list of things to show her," Zander said. "But I'm in no hurry."

Ezra raised a brow, and this time, Raven got his meaning—he made it seem as though they were staying, to hide the fact that they were leaving so soon.

"Or the Balle Gardens," Ezra said. "They'll be blooming soon."

"Those too," Zander said, nodding. One song came to an end, and another began, and Zander glanced to the dance floor. "Oh, Jasmine is dancing with Benjamin Kilgore."

Ezra frowned but didn't look surprised. "That's to be expected. At least I won't have to dance with her. If I'm lucky, she'll find some poor soul to take her home instead of me."

Zander chuckled and guided Raven down the stairs toward the dance floor. Ezra quickly fell into conversation with a few other Gray Elite, all with blue honors. Captains.

Raven quickly discovered that her lack of knowledge about proper dancing didn't matter; many others missed steps and danced as they pleased. She and Zander danced in the sunlight, and it dazzled in his sapphire eyes and gave his dark hair a honey sheen.

All around her, the ball was a display of wealth. The ice sculptures didn't melt, automatons served cocktails and cider, dresses twirled with the dance, and chatter filled the air. It became another world. It had never occurred to her how many people watched her and Zander, how many people watched him, whispered about him, asked about him. She heard his name float by, heard talk of the rumors of where he'd gone, why, and how.

The song ended, and a slower song began. Zander pulled her closer.

Lovers, a voice in her head said.

They stood close enough to share breath. His hand rested on the bare skin of her back, and she set her hands on his shoulders. She found his eyes amid the golden room, two sapphires, and she found it hard to see anything else. They danced, and the rest of the room faded away. She heard no more whispering rumors of runaway lovers. She heard the music and the gentle thump-thump of Zander's heart underneath her palm.

The somber song ended sooner than she expected.

And just like that, Zander stepped away. He was leading her off the dance floor and toward where the drink flowed. He handed her a flute of sparkling cider.

Zander's eyes drifted over her shoulder, and she wanted to yank his attention back. At that moment, a voice said, "Ah, Zander, my boy."

A taller man with blond hair combed in the Gray Elite style approached. He wore many honors on his arm.

"Colonel Pemberton," Zander said at once. He extended his hand, and they shook.

Ivy's father, Raven realized. They had the same eyes.

"I'm glad to see you healthy and alive," said Colonel Pemberton. "I admit, I feared the worst when you vanished into thin air. How are you, my boy? Doing all right? Not gotten any of those nasty country diseases, have you? I hear there's a fever to the west that squeezes the life out of its victims in three moons."

Zander chuckled. "No, I haven't gotten any of those."

Colonel Pemberton glanced over Raven, and she had the impression that he already knew about her—then, she realized that if he, too, were in the Hawks, Ivy might have told him. However, she thought it best not to assume.

"This is Raven Thane," Zander said.

"It is a pleasure, Colonel Pemberton," she said, giving him a quick curtsy.

"Attractive *and* polite," Colonel Pemberton said. He chuckled. "Where did you find her? I should send my son there to find a girl too." He laughed, then dropped his voice back to a normal whisper. "Your mother was dreadfully worried about you, Zander. Your father too, although he held it in a bit better. I'm sure he's ripe with relief to know you're safe and sound. I know I am, and the news of your sudden reappearance has been the talk of the town."

Zander tensed. "I'm sure."

"Well, I must be off. People to see." Colonel Pemberton clapped Zander on the shoulder and then strode off into the crowd.

Zander held his face stoic as the next person demanded his attention, a man whose name Raven quickly forgot. She nodded and smiled when appropriate, but she unraveled Colonel Pemberton's words. She had felt the warning within them.

Your mother was dreadfully worried about you, Zander. Colonel Pemberton disapproved of how Zander's disappearance had put a toll on his mother. *Your father too, although he held it in a bit better. I'm sure he's ripe with relief to know you're safe and sound.* His father had been worried but not in the same way his mother had. He had known what Zander had taken. *I know I am, and the news of your sudden reappearance has been the talk of the town.* Everyone knew that Zander had returned, the Gray Elite and the Hawks—including his father.

His father knew.

That was why Zander had tensed. Because his father knew, and his father was surely on his way back from wherever he'd gone.

And they were running out of time to get out.

The ball went on with drinking, delicately arranged food, dancing, and endless chatter. Zander and Raven danced, and when they weren't dancing, Gray Elite surrounded them and peppered them with conversation and questions.

"Zander! Where have you been, boy?"

"Is this the girl you left us all for? My, she's a beauty."

"You're not wearing the uniform, Lieutenant. Is this a sign you've left us for good?"

"I'm glad you've returned. Your mother has been worried to death about you."

"I knew you were alive. You're too much of an ass to die like that."

The last one had Raven giggling. Zander frowned at her.

It was not just the officers who inquired about Zander. Their wives and dates eyed Raven with suspicion and interest.

Zander's disappearance had caused a stir among the aristocracy and the Gray Elite, and Raven understood why he had been hesitant to talk about it. Everyone seemed to know who he was the second they saw him, and everyone seemed eager to speak to him. They knew of his father. Many of them dropped his name, Brigadier General Winchester.

Raven didn't mind the sharp looks she received until she met the eye of a dark-haired girl in red who hung off the arm of a barrel-chested Gray Elite. The couple easily parted the crowd to Zander.

"Zander," said the girl in red. Her dress fit loosely. Strings at her shoulders held the dress together, letting the shimmery red silk flutter about her unrestrained chest. A braided leather belt hugged her hips, and the silk hung loosely to the floor. She fluttered her heavily lined eyes at Zander and then racked her gaze over Raven's frame. "So, this is the country girl who stole you from me."

Zander shrugged. "Nice to see you too."

Raven fought to keep her expression as masked as the other girl's. She'd *stolen* Zander from this girl? Raven glanced sideways at Zander, who didn't look the least bit bothered by this girl's presence or claim. Was she an ex-lover of his? The thought left a knot in her stomach.

The girl gave a warm, well-practiced laugh. "I can see why, though. She's a lovely little thing, and those eyes!" The girl's stare bore into Raven's, and she had the strange feeling of invasion. Her smile stretched. "Zander's always been a fool for a pair of brown eyes."

She fluttered her own brown eyes, as dark as her pupils.

"Raven, this is Marie Kenara," Zander said pleasantly, "a friend of mine. Marie, this is Raven Thane."

"And it is a pleasure to finally meet you," Marie said, extending her graceful hand. She wore a diamond ring on her middle finger and half a dozen silver bangles on each wrist.

"The pleasure is mine," Raven said as kindly as she could. They gently shook hands, and then the Gray Elite escorted Marie to the dance floor.

Raven didn't have the time to question him about his supposed ex-lover; another Gray Elite and her date appeared. Raven stood through several more introductions, none as exciting as Marie's, thank the Sisters.

Ivaline appeared in a fine dress of white and gray, making her look angelic against the gold around her. She had done her blonde hair up in an elegant twist, dotted her neck with diamonds and pearls, and walked on the arm of Ezra, who looked delighted by her presence. Ivaline's faithful servant walked not that far behind, one eye on his mistress at all times.

Ivaline spotted Raven and Zander and pushed her way toward them like she was the only person in the room, and by the awed stares as she glided by, others shared the notion.

"There you are," Ivaline said sweetly.

"I see you found yourself a date," Zander said, smirking.

Ivaline let out a lady's soft laugh. She patted Ezra's shoulder and batted her lashes at him. He blushed.

"I didn't bring a date," Ivaline said. "Can't make such promises to these young men with my health being the unpredictable beast that it is. And here, I walk through the doors and don't even make it to the ballroom before Ezra has found me and offered his arm for the night." Her eyes grazed over the dance floor. "And seeing as how his date has wandered off yet again"—she lowered her voice—"not surprising. If I had a token for every man in the room who's been with Jasmine Clemens, I'd have enough to open a new greenhouse in my name."

Ezra and Zander both chuckled; neither denied the claim. Raven looked between the two boys quickly, wondering if either of them had experienced Jasmine Clemens.

"And I see dear Marie has returned from her southern vacation," Ivaline said with mild distaste.

"Yes, she's been to see Raven and me," Zander said.

Ivaline glanced at Zander, and something unspoken passed between them. A heartbeat later, the glance had gone. Zander fell into a conversation with Ezra, and Ivaline snaked her arm from Ezra and stole Raven from Zander's. While the boys spoke of people she didn't know, Ivaline walked Raven around the dance floor and to the gardens on the other side of the ballroom.

Raven tried her best not to notice the stares that followed Ivaline as she walked—*glided*—through the room. They walked through the tall doors to the garden, and the chittering of the ball faded into the sound of a dozen fountains sprinkling water over automatons and stone. They walked toward the hedges and rosebushes and meandered through the shaded, evening-lit grounds. They passed countless couples hiding between topiaries and trees, underneath trellises, and in plain sight on wooden benches, hands and mouths in varying states of slow passion.

Ivaline led her around a towering rosebush and into an unoccupied gazebo designed for two people. The outer wall of the garden loomed on the other side of the hedge, gray stone and thick ironwork. They walked far enough that the sounds of the party dimmed; somewhere unseen, a fountain trickled and spewed. The sun had sunk enough to streak the sky in rich reds, oranges, and purples. The roses sweetened the air, and Raven felt the allure of such a romantic place.

"You didn't bring me all the way out here to frolic, did you?" Raven asked Ivaline playfully. "I must warn you in advance, I prefer men."

Ivaline gave a lady's chuckle and shot her a devious grin. "You prefer men, but that doesn't mean you won't give the other a try?" She raised a brow.

Raven's face burst into a fierce blush. Was she serious?

Ivaline sat on the gazebo's small wooden bench and patted the seat beside her. Raven sat, unsure of what it meant in Ivaline's eyes. Ivaline made her heart pound but not in the same way that Zander did.

"Whatever will people think?" Raven crooned.

Ivaline gave her a small wicked smile. She leaned in closer, slid her arms around Raven's shoulders, and whispered, "It's no small gossip that Ivaline prefers women, although Ivy does not."

Which was why men and women stared in awe as Ivaline walked past them. Another layer to her character, to her charade.

"Oh," Raven said, her voice a pitch higher.

"So no one will think twice when Ivaline steals Raven from Zander's arm for a few minutes of quiet fun," she said, winking. She leaned in, close enough that her breath puffed against Raven's lips. "How are you holding up?" she whispered.

If anyone caught them, they would think them locked at the lips, not whispering.

"We've danced most of the evening," Raven admitted; her breath bounced off Ivy's lips, tinted with cider. "Zander has done most of the talking, and anything that I've said has been simple and short."

"Good girl," Ivy whispered.

"I met your father."

"He's a great man. In truth, I couldn't have asked for a better father. He's both eager to see me independent and proud that I'm me." Ivy leaned in closer. "Did he mention that Zander's father is on the way back?"

"Yes," Raven said, glad that she had gleaned that much from his words.

"And, from what he said before we left, he is not in a good mood."

"I've gathered as much," Raven said, unsure of how much Ivy knew.

They fell silent, and as Ivy opened her mouth to speak, a scuffle came from somewhere behind them. Both girls whipped their heads to see, and to Raven's horror, half a dozen black-clad figures were inching toward the gazebo.

Ivy stood, a scream on her painted lips, but from the shadows, another black-clad figure approached. A gloved hand snaked around Ivy's mouth, and a dagger appeared at her throat a heartbeat before a black leather glove pressed against Raven's mouth, and something cool and sharp pressed against her throat.

"Look what we've found," whispered one of the black-clad figures. The speaker, like the rest, wore black from head to toe, leaving only his eyes visible. The speaker's blue eyes traveled the length of Raven and then did the same to Ivaline.

"That's Pemberton's brat," said one of the others. "We'd get a fortune for her."

Ivaline shuddered; her muffled whine seemed to agree with them. *Yes, my father will give you anything for my safe return.*

Raven remained still. The man holding his hand over her mouth and a dagger to her throat pressed his chest against her back, and she could feel how quickly his heart beat.

None of the men moved, and Raven had a terrible thought. Had they come looking for the box? She trembled, and the hand on her mouth flinched. Zander had told her to keep it on her person, and she had done just that; the small iron box currently rested between her breasts, held in place by the dress's built-in boning, softened with a velvet necktie she had found in his room.

The leader of the men looked between the two girls, thinking. Finally, he said, "We take the blonde. Leave the other as a message of what could happen to Miss Pemberton here."

Raven's heart sped, and Ivaline made a whine of protest.

The blade at her throat shifted, then began to press into her skin. Raven gave a muffled cry of protest—

And then the man's hand twitched, he let out a grunt of a sigh, and the dagger clattered to the gazebo's floor.

"Ralph?" asked the leader, blue eyes shifting over the thug.

The thug holding her let out a slow breath, a colorful curse, and then went limp. He tumbled down the gazebo's few steps and landed on his side. A bolt stuck out of his back—directly over his heart.

"I was wondering where you scampered off to," came a drawling voice.

Raven gasped.

Marie stepped out of the garden's shadows, a miniature crossbow aimed at the man holding a dagger to Ivaline's throat. "You're sneaking off with this little county scamp too."

"Get her!" hissed the leader.

The black-clad men dashed around the gazebo, and Marie shot one of them—but she couldn't reload her crossbow fast enough. They seized her arms and yanked the crossbow out of her hands; they smashed it against the stone wall.

Raven started forward, to do anything, but the thug holding Ivaline grunted. "No, no," he said, taunting by wiggling the dagger at Ivaline's throat. "Don't make no sudden moves, or you'll have a dead girl on your hands."

135

Raven balled her fists. If she bent for the dagger, he would kill Ivy.

The men surrounded Marie. They grabbed her arms and roughly yanked them behind her.

Blood pounded in Raven's ears. How had the night gone so wrong so fast? Where was Zander? Would he be worried when she and Ivy didn't come back? One scream, and the Gray Elite would come running, but they wouldn't get there fast enough to save Ivy or Marie.

And Raven was stuck. She could do nothing. She stared at the entrance to their secluded corner of the garden, willing Zander and Ezra to appear with a dozen armed Gray Elite behind them, but no one appeared. No one came rushing to their aid. Useless.

One of them struck Marie. Raven cringed at the sound his glove made when it collided with the skin of her cheek. The impact sent Marie careening to the side, held up by another man. She looked up at the man who had hit her, and then a wicked smile stretched her bloodred lips. And she laughed.

The leader spat an unsavory curse at her and pulled his fist back to hit her again. Marie's smile widened. The man let out a sudden gasp, stumbled backward, and let out a vicious howl of pain as he clutched his arm.

"Chief?" one of the men asked. He let go of Marie and ran to his boss's side.

With her free hand, Marie pulled the shoulder ties of her dress. The red silk loosened from one shoulder and then the other. It fluttered away from her torso and hung from the belt at her hips. As Raven had expected, she wore nothing underneath it. The sudden exposure of her breasts stumped the man holding her other arm, and she easily yanked it from his grip.

And then, in a blink of an eye, the men surrounding her let out a collective gasp of pain and collapsed to the ground.

Marie wore the face of a killer, determined and ruthless, and Raven sucked in her breath at the sight. She heard the man holding Ivy do the same. Marie's fiery dark eyes met Raven's, and a chill went down her spine.

Raven had seen that same look when Zander had taken on that Cage Bird. A predator.

"What...what are you?" gasped the man who held onto Ivaline.

"Come closer, and I'll tell you," she said sweetly. She ran her hand from her hip to her shoulder.

"Stay away," said the man, his voice shaking.

Marie took a step closer and wiggled her fingers at one of the men on the ground. He started to stand, his movement jerky and uncertain, unsettlingly puppet-like. The man stood. His eyes had gone entirely white—unconscious.

The man holding Ivy gasped.

"Run home, little boy," Marie said, her voice deadly. "Before I cleanse the earth of your presence."

He withdrew the dagger, shoved away from Ivaline, and scrambled toward the wall—he didn't make it. His fingertips grazed the stone of the wall, and then he went rigid. His arms snapped to his sides, and his legs stiffened. He took jerky steps back toward the gazebo. His eyes were wide with fear.

"I changed my mind," Marie said in her sweet, vicious tone. She sauntered toward the man, her hand extended toward him, her fingers moving slowly in his direction.

Marie walked past the gazebo, and Raven held in her gasp. There, on Marie's exposed back, was a sprawling rune tattoo. Just like Zander's. She walked to where the man stood, flinching and twitching and whining. With a wave of her hand, he collapsed on the ground. Marie set her heel on his chest. He begged, his words lost in his mumbling, and a second later, something snapped—the man gurgled and went limp.

Marie sauntered back to the gazebo, eyeing the other men.

"Are they..." Raven whispered.

"Dead," Marie confirmed, none too worried about it. "You all right?"

Ivaline put a hand to her unmarred throat. She nodded. "I've never been happier to have a stalker."

Marie gave her a wicked smile. She approached the gazebo and turned, pointing to her shoulder. "Help me tie this back."

Raven lifted the fallen back of the dress with shaky hands. Her knuckles grazed the tattoo, and to her surprise, the skin there was burning hot. Around the ink, the skin had reddened. Marie tied up the dress quickly and turned to fix Ivaline's hair.

"What did... What happened?" Raven gasped.

"An ambush," Ivy said. "Looks like the work of the Black Dogs."

Raven blinked.

"They're just a band of thugs," Marie explained. She finished with Ivaline and turned to Raven. She started to work on Raven's hair. "They're nothing to worry about. Sounded like they were looking to make a quick token by kidnapping a rich girl."

Raven stared at the ground, at the bodies. Dead. Without a wound. Without being touched.

"Magic," Raven breathed, her voice barely there.

Marie's hands paused on either side of Raven's head. Her dark eyes met Raven's, indifferent. "Does that bother you? Think before you answer. I just saved your ass. Oh, forgive me," Marie said, hand over her heart. "I forgot where we are. I meant, I saved you from these rapscallions and whatever nefarious deeds they might have committed, namely your murder."

Magic. Raven blinked, unable to believe it. "Thank you."

"We should get back to the party before someone wanders into this part of the garden," Ivaline whispered. "I'd rather not be here when these are discovered."

"I thought any press was good press?" Marie smirked.

"Being seen with a horde of dead bodies is not good press," Ivaline hissed.

The three girls left the secluded corner and, thankfully, didn't meet anyone on the garden path. They took the long way around the shrubbery, and when the brightly lit doors and windows of the ballroom came into view, Raven loosed a sigh of relief.

To the west, the sun had nearly set, shrouding the city in golds and purples. The color slowly leached from the sky, from the clouds, and from the city.

They stepped onto the main path to the doors, and Marie slipped her arm into Raven's.

"I'd appreciate if this night remained between the two of us," Marie said casually.

"I understand," Raven said. A magician, right in the center of the Gray Elite festivities. "You did me a great favor, and I will uphold your request."

"Such manners," Marie said, her grin wicked. "It's no wonder Zander snatched you up. I would have too."

Marie, Ivaline, and Raven returned to the ballroom, where the party continued as if nothing had happened. Marie vanished through the crowd, and Ivaline and Raven returned to where Ezra and Zander stood. They were speaking to a tall honey-eyed man who wore many honors on his sleeve. His silver-streaked blond hair had been combed aside. Ivaline took in a small hiss as they approached, but kept her face neutral and pleasant.

The honey-eyed Gray Elite spotted Ivaline and Raven, and his face broke into a wide smile. He smiled like Baxter, insincerely.

Ivaline made a show of handing Raven back to Zander, who held her a little closer than he had before.

"Thank you for keeping her entertained," Zander said to Ivaline, who took Ezra's offered arm.

Ivaline smirked. "It was no problem at all," she said sweetly. "But it wasn't in the way you're thinking of, naughty. Though, if you ever tire of him, Raven dear, feel free to seek me out."

"I will keep your offer in mind," Raven said, trying to mimic Ivaline's casual smile. Her heart still pounded from the garden, but she forced her face into bored neutrality.

With a small smile, Ivaline tugged Ezra to the dance floor.

"And this must be the girl you ran off with," said the Gray Elite, his smooth voice one used to giving commands.

"Yes." Zander cleared his throat. "This is Raven Thane. Raven, this is General Oliver Deacon. Ezra's father."

"It is a pleasure, General Deacon," Raven said with a short bow of her head.

General Deacon examined her through a clinical gaze, and she didn't like it. His eyes ran over her, head to toe. Assessing. She tried her best not to look like she felt it. To pretend that she had nothing to hide. To pretend that the little box was not nestled between her breasts. To pretend that she hadn't witnessed a magician slaughter a gang of thugs who had tried to kill her and Ivaline.

The talk with the general didn't last. Several others demanded the general's attention.

She met a few more Gray Elite, all of whom were delighted to see Zander and interested in the girl who had stolen him away. They retold their story enough times that Raven was starting to believe it, although she knew it untrue. She focused on the story, on Zander—to keep her mind off Marie and her magic. Off the dead thugs.

The drink flowed freely, and the music sped up as the crowd grew restless, drunken, and chaotic. The dancing became hectic and ungraceful. Several men and a few women gave Raven lascivious glares and offers to dance, but she declined them all, and she held Zander's arm a little closer.

"I would like to go," she whispered.

He nodded and immediately set his sparkling cider on the closest table. They started through the crowd, and Raven cast her eyes for Ivaline or Marie, but she didn't see either of them. The dancing crowd consisted mostly of adults—drunken adults.

Halfway up the stairs, a bloodied scream echoed from the garden. The Gray Elite guards jumped from their positions, alert and ready, while the drunken crowd barely noticed. A woman came screaming into the ballroom from the garden and latched onto the arm of the first Gray Elite, her sobs fluting up as a strange instrument among the music. Though her blubbering was gibberish, Raven knew what had happened.

They had found the bodies.

Raven gripped Zander's arm and urged him up the stairs. He obliged without a word or question, and the two of them were in the vestibule and out the doors and climbing into the coach.

"Did I hear screaming?" asked the driver, brows together.

"Yes," Zander said politely, concerned as anyone could be. "I'm not sure what happened. Something in the garden."

The driver asked no more, and the coach pulled away as the chaos unfolded in the ballroom. Raven reclined against Zander as the coach pulled through the palace's gates and started through the city, calm by comparison, though many commoners had taken to partying in the streets.

"You should see the other districts," Zander said in her ear. "There are some bars and taverns that stay open all night, and people dance in the street until they pass out from the wine or from exhaustion. It's quite the sight."

The driver was listening; she saw his head twitch to the side every few moments to hear them better.

They *had* left the ball at a very convenient time, a little voice reminded her.

"Zander," Raven asked lowly, as to make it seem as though she did not want to be overheard, "what do you think happened? Why was that woman screaming?"

"I don't know. With all the drinking, Sisters only know what happened. She might have slipped something else into the party. A few years ago, someone slipped hallucinogen into the cider." He chuckled. "I wasn't yet old enough to attend, but stories were flying like bats in the night."

The rest of the ride went by in silence, save for the clacking of the automaton's paws on the stone street. She held onto Zander's hand, wary of black-clad figures lurking in the shadows, waiting for their chance to strike. Finally, the coach trotted through the gates to Winchester House. Every window was dark.

As they pulled into the garage, Raven stifled a yawn. She didn't know what time it was. She would need to sleep well if Zander wanted to flee that morning.

Zander led her into the house and into the quiet kitchen. He poured them each a glass of water. She drank it slowly. She could feel the terror of the attack under her skin, the panic, the odd sense of satisfaction when Marie had slaughtered those men.

They tried to hurt me and Ivy, she thought. *They were bad men. They deserved a worse fate than what they received. They deserved to be hanged, a warning to the others.*

"We should leave tonight," Zander whispered. He set his empty glass on the counter. He unbuttoned his silk shirt down to his vest. "Without telling anyone. They all think I'll be here tomorrow, and no one will think otherwise. I'll leave a note for my mother. This is too important."

"Tonight?" she asked, only half listening. Each time she blinked, she saw bodies.

Why did they have to leave that night? Why did they have to leave at all? Why not hide out in his room for a few days? Why not sleep until this strange feeling went away?

"We have a few hours," Zander said. "It will give us time to get things together."

Raven set her half-drunk glass of water on the counter and drifted to the backdoor to the gardens. The flowers were blooming with pinks, yellows, purples, and blues—beckoning. Without permission, she let herself into the garden. She wandered over the stone path, her feet not entirely feeling like her own, to the other side, where a marble fountain sparkled in the glowing flowers' light.

Her blue and gold dress reflected in the fractured fountain. She lifted the skirts and twirled, watching the colors shift. In the glowing flowers and radiant city light, her dress glowed.

"I'm glad to see you're enjoying yourself." Zander came to stand beside her. His reflection fractured as hers did. He had undone his vest and a few more shirt buttons, leaving several inches of his chest exposed.

In that moment, she made a choice. She did not want to tell Zander about the murders or magic. She didn't want to think about those things; she didn't want to acknowledge that they had happened, so she pretended that they had not.

And, just like that, they hadn't happened.

"I thought balls would be stuffy and stiff," she said, picking up the skirts of her gown and twirling slowly. "But everyone was dancing and smiling. I didn't think they would be so lively."

Zander smiled, a lovely sight in the glowing light, a lovely sight anytime. He took a step closer to her, his boots clicking on the stone. "And that was a tame party too, all things considered." His eyes wandered into the sparkling water. A shadow passed over his features, but when he looked back up at her, it had passed. "Some of the dinners I've been to have gotten out of hand to the point that guards were called in."

"Out of hand? How?"

He chuckled, eyes never leaving hers.

You've got his attention, all of it.

"People drink too much," he said with a shrug. "Then they think that being naked in public is acceptable or that punching someone is fine. Most of them end with someone being arrested." He laughed, and a shiver ran down her back. "Rich or poor, a drunk man is a drunk man in every city in the world."

The idea of Zander being at one of those parties, having fun without her, sent a dislike shooting through her bones.

"I was never a fan of them," he said, stepping closer. "They were more for adults. They would typically lock us kids in one of the wings of the house and then come back in the morning to make sure we hadn't died."

"What did you do all night?"

"We snuck out." He shrugged. "No one missed us, and we'd go wander the city, causing trouble, destroying public property, and the like."

"We?"

"Ezra, Marie, sometimes Ivaline, and a few others," he said. "Baxter was always the prude and sometimes the tattletale. Of course, when I got old enough to hit him, he stopped tattling."

"Of course." She could imagine Baxter being the prude.

She imagined them all being together, friends, having fun, and then thought of herself wandering the woods around Silver Glen, alone. Jealousy burned. It wasn't fair.

Zander stood a little closer, close enough that she could feel his breath. And then, he lifted his hand to her. "May I have this dance, my lady?"

"It would be my honor, good sir." She placed her hand into his. The heat from his hand surged and spread through her body. He set his other on the small of her back, just as he had done at the ball, but without the music, without the other people around them, it felt different. Did he stand closer?

They began a slow dance to the sound of the trickling fountain, to the night birds in the atrium, to the sound of their footsteps. Her heart beat like a drum. Could he hear it?

For a few moments, the city light became moonlight, and the night had gone smoothly—no magic, no murder, no secret conversations in the garden, no hidden messages.

Zander paused his dancing but did not step away. "Raven," he said, his voice a warm whisper against her cheekbone.

"Yes?"

He leaned closer. Her heart thudded so loudly, she knew he heard it. Blood rushed in her ears, her stomach clenched, and the world around her fell away; the mansion disappeared, and she stood in a different plane with Zander. He came closer still—would he kiss her?

She felt his breath on her lips. She closed her eyes, but she never felt his mouth. She blinked her eyes open to find Zander looking at her, sorrow in his eyes.

"Did I do something wrong?" she whispered.

"No," he said, barely a whisper. His hands twitched, and he let her go in a sudden movement that made her jump back; he moved like he'd been burned.

"Zander?"

"I'm sorry," he said as he turned from her. He started toward the house without a glance back at her. "We need to get going. We're running out of time."

She stood in the garden, dazed, and all her delight turned to ice. Shame. Guilt.

Simple girl, simple town.

A means to an end for Zander.

Raven deeply inhaled all the scents of the garden, the strange bittersweetness of the bioluminescent flowers, the flowering fruit trees, the musk of the fountain. She gave the garden one last look, knowing she would never see such a sight again, and followed Zander's path into the house. She found him waiting just inside, and he guided her up to his room.

They changed into traveling clothes and packed in silence, adding a few things that could be easily sold at any trading post.

"The easiest way to get to the Hellcat tunnel is underneath Pemberton House," he whispered as he stuffed a silver candlestick into his bag.

Raven nodded, folding a few extra shirts and soap into her bag. She adjusted her ebony dagger in her boot, felt for the iron box still tucked between her breasts—it felt safer there than in her pocket. Harder to pilfer. Between the silken bandeau and the short corset, the box was secured. She felt for the thief's wooden coin in her pocket.

She didn't know why she still had it. A keepsake of her adventure. A reminder that a wider world still existed.

One that she'd likely not see.

Zander donned his holsters and tucked Birdie into one side, his unnamed pistol in the other, and extra ammo in his pouch. The familiar sight of him and his guns settled something in her chest. She watched him tie back his dark hair. He had freshly saved the bottom half.

"Let's go," he whispered, tugging his pack onto his shoulders. He led the way into the dark, quiet hall. "We can get to the tunnels through the cellar. No one will see us that way."

Meaning she wouldn't see Lenhala again. She took a breath and accepted it and followed Zander's silent steps through the house. They made it to the first floor, and Zander stopped so abruptly that she ran into his back, smashing herself against his pack.

She sidestepped to spit a curse at him, but when she saw what had stopped him, her stomach fell into her knees.

A tall dark-haired man stood in the foyer. He wore fine traveling clothes and was handing his cloak and cane to a servant. The servant scurried away, and the man turned his sapphire eyes onto Zander. A cold smile stretched his thin lips.

"There he is," said the man, his tone not surprised or glad, but cold.
Zander went rigid. "Hello, Father."

The air in the hall turned cold, the silence deadly. General Winchester and his son stared at one another with matching dislike, unease, and wariness. Raven swallowed; as often as she had infuriated her father, he had never looked at her like that.

Zander looked like his father, the same brown-black hair, bronze skin, and piercing sapphire eyes. They both stood tall and lean.

"Your mother is in the lounge," said General Winchester, his voice a drawl, airy and proper. "I suggest you show yourself to her before you flee." He motioned to the bag on Zander's shoulder.

Zander took a small step to the cellar door.

"I've stationed men down there," said General Winchester with annoyance. "You won't get out that way without my blessing. Unless you'd rather march down the street?" He unbuttoned the cuffs of his shirt and rolled his sleeves. "It would be foolish, considering what happened tonight at the ball."

Zander tensed. "Did I miss something?" he asked coolly. His tone so matched his father's that Raven felt a chill.

His father regarded him with mild interest. "It would seem that a few thugs crashed the Summer Solstice Ball," he drawled. "And wound up dead. No wounds. No injuries. Just dead."

Zander balled his fists.

"Strange murders." General Winchester undid the top button of his shirt. "And right under the Gray Elite's collective nose. Literally in their backyard." He smiled, but it did not show happiness. His smile teamed with cruelty. "They're saying the Hawks are to blame. Others say it's the Revenant's return."

"Are they?" Zander's words seethed.

"I should be asking you," said his father innocently. "I had just arrived back in the city when my people brought me the news. You were at the ball, were you not?"

Zander scoffed. "I wouldn't be so careless."

"These past six months might have softened your approach."

"They haven't," Zander whispered in a voice she hadn't heard before, deep and deadly—a threat.

"That is good to hear. Do see your mother, Zander. She's been in a tizzy since you left." His father walked down the corridor and vanished into his office—if Raven remembered the tour of the house correctly.

Zander stood still as stone. His eyes held a deadly glare, searing like fire. His fists were clenched, turning his knuckles white. Small sounds came from the first floor of the house, of people moving, as if until General Winchester had returned, the house had been sleeping.

145

"Zander?" Raven breathed.

He let out a long sigh, closed his eyes, and shifted the bag on his shoulder. He started toward the lounge on the other end of the hall. Toward his mother.

Raven hesitated on the stars. "Should I go upstairs?"

"No," he said at once. "Come with me."

They made it to the lounge, and Zander took a deep breath before letting himself inside.

A flaxen-haired woman sat on the chaise, her legs folded and her head tilted back. Her eyes were closed, and she held a hand against her forehead. She looked like a painting in her pale blue traveling dress, her hair slightly disheveled and feet bare. Her boots sat on the ground.

Raven saw the similarities between her and Zander, though Zander took after his father; Baxter took after their mother.

"Tea already? You have gotten fast," said Mrs. Winchester. "Best leave the sugar out, Margret, I don't think my stomach can handle it tonight. Not after the fish we ate. I'll be feeling ill for days, I'm afraid."

Zander set his pack on the floor and took a step closer. "Hello, Mother," he said flatly.

His mother's brown eyes shot open, and at once, they landed on Zander. She blinked once, twice, and then shot to her feet, disbelief turning into joy. She threw herself at Zander, wrapping her arms around his neck and pulling him as close as possible. A gasping sob left her throat.

"Oh, it's not a trick, is it? It's you! Not a ghost but my boy," she cried, kissing Zander's cheek and temple. She felt the shaved half of his head and frowned. "What is this strange hair you have? Is this one of those country things?" She pouted. "You always had such beautiful hair."

"I'm sorry," he said. "I thought my letter would get here a lot faster than it did."

Mrs. Winchester eyed her son a moment longer, taking it all in—the son she thought dead. Tears lined her eyes. She rested her hand on his cheek, and then her teary gaze settled on Raven. At once, the relief in her eyes turned to distaste. She released her son and folded her hands in front of her, shoulders back, nose high—a lady. She regarded Raven like something dirty stuck to the underside of her boot.

"So, it's true?" asked Mrs. Winchester. She looked Raven up and down, taking in her trousers and simple corset—disapproving. "You left me for...this?" She motioned to Raven with a delicate, enraged flourish of her beige hand.

Raven flushed; no doubt, his mother thought the worst. Zander started to speak, but the door opened. General Winchester marched through. He shut the door swiftly behind him.

"Well? Where is it?" he demanded.

"It's hidden," Zander said flatly.

General Winchester frowned, rage burning in his eyes. Raven had the urge to reach for the box, but she held her arms at her sides.

"That is not what I asked." General Winchester glided into the room like a cat about to pounce. He stopped before his son. "Where is it?"

Zander didn't answer.

His father looked about to burst from rage. When he spoke, his voice barely contained it. "Do you know what happened the night you left?"

Zander didn't move. He didn't flinch. Mrs. Winchester looked between her husband and son, worry deep in her eyes. Raven felt as though she had invaded something she ought not to, and she wanted desperately to be back in his room, away from all this. To be with Ivy, who would explain it all to her and make it less horrible than it seemed.

"Because of you," said General Winchester, "because you failed, your brother also failed, and because both of you failed to eliminate your targets, the Hawks were discovered. They did not get to Princess Rosaria in time."

Zander paled.

"If she is still alive, she is no longer in Lenhala," General Winchester said, each word drenched in rage and guilt.

Raven bit her lip to keep from gasping. Princess Rosaria? No, she had died in the coup that killed the king and queen when the Gray Elite seized control. She couldn't be alive... If she was, it would be a lever against the Gray Elite rule.

Of course the Hawks would go after her.

But they hadn't succeeded. Because of Zander. And he looked nearly sick about it—he hadn't known.

General Winchester took in the ghastly look on his son's face with pride, and he continued, "If you had done your part, if you had done what I told you, if you had only listened, we wouldn't be in this mess. We would have had the Regent begging for mercy by now. We would have won. If you had stayed—"

"If I had been your puppet?" Zander exclaimed. "If I had done everything you wanted me to do for your cause? If you would have had your way, Father, the world would be in shambles."

General Winchester clenched his fists. A moment later, his fist collided with Zander's jaw. Zander fell backward into the bookcase, sending one of the glass baubles to the floor. It landed with a sickening crunch, sending the bauble into pieces.

"Joseph!" shrieked Mrs. Winchester.

Zander rubbed his jaw but didn't get up at once. His mother fell to the floor beside him, pulling his hand away to inspect the damage.

General Winchester's furious gaze flashed to Raven, and the box between her breasts suddenly weighed more than a sky city. She feared he might strike her next, but he held his fists at his sides.

147

"And this is the whore you ran away with?" General Winchester took in Raven's trousers and vest with distaste. "Everyone's told me about the beautiful girl my son brought back with him, the lovely girl from the country." He took a step closer to Raven, and though she wanted to run the other way, she held her ground. "Tell me, Raven, did my son tell you what he does for a living?"

Raven glanced at Zander. He still sat on the floor, his wide gaze pinned on her. Genuine fear shone in his eyes. His mother held onto his shoulders, holding him where he sat.

General Winchester pinched her chin and brought her gaze back to him.

"He didn't?" General Winchester's lips curled upward into a sneer of a smile. "He didn't tell you why he left? Why he fled in the middle of the night like a coward?" His smile turned merciless. His grip on her chin tightened. "I'll tell you. I'll tell you who my son really is."

"Father," Zander said, fearful warning on his tongue.

His mother gripped his shoulders, and General Winchester went on as if he hadn't heard a thing. "My son works for the Hawks, a group working to unseat the Gray Elite in this country and restore power back to the rightful ruler," he said calmly.

Raven remained silent; she knew that.

"But my son is a special part of the Hawks. Tell me, girl, have you heard of the Wraiths?"

She shook her head, a difficult task with his fingers pinching her chin.

He smiled; he took pleasure in her discomfort. "The Wraiths are assassins," he hissed. "Not all Wraiths are assassins, but the ones the Hawks have recruited are. My son was one of the best. I was so proud of him, I gave him the most important job of his life, to assassinate a single target, which would allow a domino effect that would allow the other Hawks to rescue Princess Rosaria from the Gray Elite stronghold. With her, we would be one step closer to victory over the Gray Elite. But my son decided to change those plans. He failed to kill his target. The chain reaction didn't happen, and the entire mission failed." General Winchester took a step closer to Raven, and because she did not want to feel his breath on her face, she stepped back.

"But I could have forgiven him for failing. We all fail from time to time, but then, I learned why my son failed. While most of the Hawks were in position, he snuck off, and he stole something very, very valuable to the Hawks. Something the Gray Elite would pay dearly for."

The box hidden between her breasts, the box only a hand away from where General Winchester gripped her chin.

"I'm only going to ask you once, Raven Thane." He lowered his voice to a whisper. "Where is it?"

She shook; she didn't have to pretend to be frightened. General Winchester took in her trembling, her teary eyes, and he released her chin.

"I-I don't know," she said, her voice wet.

One word resounded in her mind. *Assassin.* Zander, a killer, a murderer. He could shoot so well because he had had practice. He had the glare of a killer because he was one.

Raven blinked and stole her eyes away from General Winchester. She found Zander's eyes, full of fear and worry. His mother sat beside him, eyes fixed on her husband. Raven blinked, and then something hard collided with her cheek. She staggered back and tumbled to the floor. Someone shrieked, a scuffle—and Raven sat up.

She put a hand to her cheek where General Winchester had struck her; her hand trembled worse than her cheek throbbed.

It had been Mrs. Winchester who'd shrieked and Zander who had jumped to his feet, rage hot in his eyes. His mother held him back.

"Don't touch her!" Zander screamed, his fists balled. "She knew nothing of what I'd done!"

General Winchester yanked the pack off Raven's shoulders and began to rifle through it. Looking for the iron box. He ignored Zander's outburst and spoke with indifferent calmness. "I set up the world for you, boy. I had the plans set in motion to put this kingdom right side up again, and you threw it aside." He tossed the items from her bag onto the floor, the shirts, the soaps, the rations. "We had the power at our fingertips, the final solution, and you decided to take matters into your own hands."

Raven touched her lip; it had split. She tasted copper. Blood.

Not finding the box in her pack, he started to go through Zander's. If the pilfered goods bothered him, he didn't show it.

"Father," Zander started, exasperated.

His mother shifted her hand to his chest.

Not finding it in the other pack, General Winchester stood and kicked the bag aside. He glared at his son. "I set up the world for you, boy," he spat at Zander. "I arranged your marriage to Rosaria. You could have been a king. You could have been sitting on the throne of Rhynwier, had you followed your orders. A *king*. Yet you spat in my face. You threw it away. And for what?" His rage flared at Raven, and she shrank against the wall. "A country whore?"

Raven ruffled at the insult, but she did not want to garner any more of his attention.

General Winchester tucked his hands into his pocket. "My thief recognized you," he said to his son. "When we met to discuss payment for his retrieved item, he suddenly couldn't find it; then, he remembered meeting a young man who resembled me, frighteningly so, traveling with a young woman."

His thief. The thief who had stolen the box in the first place. The thief she had met on the stairs. The thief from Wayward Point. Raven felt her skin clam. Her heart raced, and the wooden coin pressed against her leg.

"He mentioned meeting the young woman on the stairs, the very night he had last seen the item in question." General Winchester returned his burning gaze onto Raven. Zander's eyes widened.

General Winchester took slow, casual steps to where Raven couched against the wall and then bent down to look her in the eye. He whispered, "Where is it?"

When she didn't answer, his palm met her cheek and sent her sprawling to the floor.

"Where is it?" he asked again, his voice venomous.

"She gave it to me," Zander said quickly, and his father stood, intent on his son. Zander swallowed; his entire throat moved. "I don't have it anymore."

General Winchester's frown turned into a scowl. He grabbed his son by the front of his shirt, yanking him out of his mother's grip. She jumped back, hands fisted in her skirt, face ashen.

"What did you do with it?" General Winchester spat, each word clipped.

Zander didn't answer, and his father's eyes widened with his assumed answer; in his fury, he threw his son to the floor.

"I knew it," General Winchester spat, furious. "I knew it! I suspected it that night. You've been spying for the Gray Elite. Guards!"

The door burst open, and five guards rushed inside, all armed and armored in dark blue leather and gray metal. Hawks. They grabbed Zander by the arms and hauled him to his feet, and in a few blinks, they had him cuffed and gagged.

"Joseph!" cried Mrs. Winchester. She grabbed for her husband's arm. "He's your son."

"He's no son of mine." General Winchester pulled his arm from his wife and marched after the Hawks.

Fear held Raven in place. The Hawks dragged Zander from the lounge, and only when she could no longer see him did her thoughts snap—she crawled to her feet and stumbled to the door. The Hawks were dragging Zander toward the stairs, and General Winchester walked behind them.

"Wait," she cried. She started to run after them, but two strong hands on her shoulders pulled her to a halt. Mrs. Winchester stood beside her, holding her back.

"No," said the older woman.

Tears gathered along Raven's eyes. "Where are they taking him?" she cried.

"Below. To the dungeons," said Mrs. Winchester, her voice low. She didn't look happy about it either.

Tears began to roll down her cheeks. Zander's sapphire eyes met hers a moment before they hauled him through the cellar door. The Hawks vanished down the stairs, and General Winchester slammed the heavy wooden door back into its frame.

The silence in the hall made her sobs that much more apparent.

Mrs. Winchester guided Raven back into the lounge and to the sofa in front of the window. The world felt blurred at the edges, unreal. A servant brought in tea for two, and Mrs. Winchester made Raven a cup of tea. She set the tea in Raven's hands and then made her own.

"What are they going to do to him?" Raven asked, her voice small.

"Drink," Mrs. Winchester said, her voice softer than it had been before. "It'll warm you up."

Raven lifted the dainty cup to her lips. The bitter tea entered her mouth, along with a strange sweet taste. Her first thought went to poison; she turned to question the older woman, but her words fell short. Lady Winchester was pouring a clear liquid from a golden flask into her own tea. She then took a drink.

"They call it moonwater," Mrs. Winchester explained. "It's popular in the south. This batch was infused with jasmine." She took a sip of her tea.

Raven drank her tea slowly. Indeed, she felt a sort of calm come over her. The warmth of the tea, the sugar, the jasmine moonwater.

"By the look on your face, you didn't know a thing," said Mrs. Winchester.

Raven shook her head. *Pretend.*

"I'm sorry it happened like that. Joseph was furious at Zander, and that anger has been fuming ever since. He's been trying to recover from that night's failure. It's been hard. We lost people that night, more than we should have."

"He's an assassin?" Raven asked, her voice small.

The older woman nodded grimly, eyes on her tea. "The Hawks operate in the shadows. We have to. That night, Zander was very close to exposing us."

Raven had questions bursting through her mind too quick to catch them all. The Hawks, the Wraiths, the mission that Zander hadn't completed. She settled on, "And...you are all right with your son being an assassin? A...Wraith?"

Mrs. Winchester gave a quiet, gentle laugh. She met Raven's eye. "Yes and no. No, because it is a dangerous, ruthless job. Terrible hours. High risk. Yes, because I am proud that my son is willing to do such a job in order to restore this kingdom to its former, rightful glory."

"You're a Hawk too?" Raven asked.

Mrs. Winchester nodded. "I took a bolt to the thigh," she said, placing a hand against her leg. "I haven't been able to walk the same since, and my career as a nimble scout and assassin ended."

"Assassin? You were a Wraith too?"

"No," Mrs. Winchester said. "I was an assassin, but I wasn't a Wraith." Raven opened her mouth, but Mrs. Winchester continued, "The Wraiths are...separate.

Zander is one of the few who managed to gain entrance into their society of sorts. Don't ask me more about them. I don't know much more than that. It's a need-to-know type of society."

Raven blinked, trying to imagine the cultured woman before her as a ruthless assassin; but then she thought of Ivaline, of Marie. She swallowed a large gulp of tea. Zander had grown up among secrets, assassins, and rebels; and Raven had grown up in an underground mine. Simple girl, simple town.

"But enough about all this dreary business for tonight." Mrs. Winchester sighed through her nose. "I am exhausted, and you look like you've had a rough night as well. The ball, I take it?"

Raven had almost forgotten. She nodded.

"Tell me about it," Mrs. Winchester said, standing.

Mrs. Winchester escorted Raven upstairs. She walked with a limp, but had Raven not known it, she wouldn't have seen it. As they walked, Raven relived the splendor of the Summer Solstice Ball, minus the murders and magic.

"Did the Hawks murder those people?" Raven asked slyly, as if she knew she shouldn't ask.

Mrs. Winchester shrugged. "I can't say. The Gray Elite blame the Hawks for everything they can't readily explain. Any unsolved crime is blamed on the Hawks, to make them look like scoundrels and common street scum." She waved her hand between them. "Best not worry about it, dear. It could be something as simple as a fight gone wrong."

Raven nodded and hoped to the Sisters that guilt did not show on her face.

They paused in the third-floor corridor. "Which guest room are you staying in?" asked Mrs. Winchester.

Raven's cheeks got hot, and Mrs. Winchester frowned. "I've been staying in Zander's room," Raven admitted.

Mrs. Winchester's frown deepened. She let out a short sigh of disapproval. "Well, since Zander is occupied, I suppose it won't hurt for tonight. But tomorrow, I request that you relocate to another room. Another bed." She started toward Zander's room. "I know this isn't the same as what you're used to, wherever you're from—" she paused to let Raven fill in the answer, and when she didn't, Mrs. Winchester continued "—but here, we stick to tradition. Men in one room, women in another. When you are married, you can do whatever you wish."

She opened the door to Zander's room and held it open, her motherly glare burning.

"Yes, ma'am." Raven took a sheepish step into the room, then turned. "I'm sorry for all the trouble we've caused. A part of me thinks that if I would have stayed home... I don't know. Then maybe none of this would have happened."

Mrs. Winchester cupped Raven's cheek, the cheek her husband had slapped. Twice. "It's not your fault," she said firmly; she meant it. "My son, for all his good

152

qualities, has a few bad ones too. We all do. Best not dwell on what could have been, because it does nothing for the future." She stroked Raven's cheekbone, then released her. "Goodnight, Raven. I will see you in the morning."

Mrs. Winchester stepped into the hall and closed the door behind her. Raven let out a sigh, and then a sharp click resounded from within the door—her heart tightened. Heeled shoes retreated down the hallway, slightly uneven. Raven tried the door—locked. Mrs. Winchester had locked her inside. Trapped.

Raven sank onto the sofa. The Hawks had locked her in the house, and they had taken Zander to the dungeons. The *dungeons*. Doubtful he had a sofa to sit on or a bed to sleep in. But what could she do about it? What could she possibly do against the Hawks? They were armed and trained, and she was...she was a simple country girl with no training, no skills, no...anything. She slumped against the sofa and put a hand against the box General Winchester so desperately wanted.

So much worry over something so small.

Her heartbeat slowed, and all the exhaustion of the night came back to her. Too tired to wash, she went straight into the bedroom and changed into her silk pajamas. She tucked the little iron box underneath her pillow, kept her locket around her neck, and set her dagger on the pillow next to her—which would have been Zander's. After she had pulled the bed-curtains closed, she crawled under the blankets.

Even in the dark, the bed felt too large without Zander.

In a way, it felt like her room in Silver Glen. Dark. Secluded. Private.

She rolled onto her side; her locket moved against her skin. Rolling onto her back, Raven pulled her locket out of her pajamas. She ran her thumb over the gold, dull in the darkness. She had thought the engraved gold beautiful, but compared to the Winchester's finery, it held no worth. Like her.

She ran her finger along the seam of the locket.

Open it.

Raven pressed her fingernails into the seam, like she had done so many times, and tried to wedge the metal apart. She moved her nails closer together, closer to the locking mechanism, and then—

Click.

Her heart skipped at the sound. It opened. Fingers trembling, she opened the locket and—nothing. It was empty. No picture, no secret message from her mother, no well wishes for the daughter she had never known.

Her heart fell into her spine and stayed there.

As a child, she had imagined a secret message left from her mother that would lead her on an epic adventure like in her storybooks, to the stars, across the oceans, to the center of the world. All this time, the locket had been empty.

Raven pressed her finger into the locket's empty chambers. Her fingertip grazed something—grooves. An engraving in the metal.

She stumbled to free herself from the blankets and then tumbled through the bed-curtain. Raven half fell to the window and whisked back the curtains. Within the light of the garden, the engraving on the inside of the locket became visible.

A diamond within a circle.

The same image from the thief's wooden coin, the entrance to the Destiny Show in Wayward Point. A ticket to freedom. Raven blinked once, twice. Her hands shook; her mother had the Destiny Show emblem inside her locket?

A ticket to freedom.

What did it mean?

She closed the locket with a gentle snap and placed it beside her dagger. She didn't know what to think about the emblem, the locket, or the coin. She was too tired to think about anything tonight. She crawled back under the blankets and closed her hands around the iron box.

How could such a little thing cause so many problems? What was it?

A fine seam ran along the edges, as though the box had been perfectly designed to fit together. A box. Things went into boxes, so there must be something inside. The thing of great value, of immense stress and trouble. Whatever piece of the machine that Zander had stolen. A vital piece, he'd said.

Was it the Destiny Show emblem too?

Zander knew; he would have had to have known before he took it. A lever? A valve? The button that fired the machine? The password? The combination? Mrs. Winchester knew. General Winchester knew. Ivy might know too, as well as her father. Baxter too. Raven was the one left in the dark as to its purpose and function, as though they didn't trust her with the secret.

Because she was the simple girl.

Simple indeed yet smart enough to be holding the damn thing when everyone was looking for it.

The box grew warm under her touch.

Nothing she could do about any of her problems tonight. She released the box and tried to find sleep. Her exhaustion pulled her under quickly, but she slept terribly. Every little knock and creak woke her, fearful that the Hawks would burst into the room and tear it—and her—apart for the box.

Zander floated in and out of her dreams, beaten and tortured, bloodied and bruised. His father held the whip, asking over and over, "Where is it? Where is it? Where is it?"

Raven woke to blue-gray dawn light spilling through the narrow gaps in the bed-curtains. Sleep refused to return, and Raven pulled herself out of bed. She fastened her hand around the iron box and took it with her into the bathroom. She set it on the vanity, within her sight, and readied a bath for herself. She took her time soaking.

Clean and dried, she pulled Zander's silk robe around her and tucked the box into the pocket. She returned to the bedroom but stopped on the threshold.

The bed had been made. The curtains had been tied to the bedposts. Her boots had been straightened. Her dagger and locket had been set on the bedside table. Her traveling clothes had been taken. A blue dress had been delivered, along with a chemise and underthings and clean socks.

She hadn't even heard the door open. Someone had entered the room without her knowing it. Her skin crawled, and her stomach flipped.

Someone had gone through her things. Looking for the box in her pocket. Her hand tightened around the box; Zander had been right about keeping it on her person. It would seem that the Winchesters did not believe her innocence.

Raven dressed quickly, wrapped the box in velvet and tucked it between her breasts—secured by the lightweight corset. The hiding place had so far worked. Had it been in her pocket last night, General Winchester might have found it. This way, they would have to disrobe her to find it. That idea sent a wave of pinpricks down her spine and into her toes. She tucked her locket down the front of her dress, her dagger in her boot, and the wooden coin into her pocket.

The dress fit well enough. The blue-green material reminded her of a summer forest during a misty rain shower.

She tried the door handle—still locked. She returned to the couch. A heartbeat later, footsteps sounded in the hall.

"Is she awake?" came Mrs. Winchester's voice.

"Yes, ma'am," said a young servant girl.

Raven froze; a servant had been stationed outside the door. Listening.

The door unlocked, and Mrs. Winchester walked inside, followed by a servant carrying a silver tray. The servant set the tray on the table, tea for one and a letter.

"Thank you," Raven said.

"The letter is addressed to you," said Mrs. Winchester without kindness.

Raven blinked, then lifted the letter. Her name had been delicately written across the front. She turned it over; the wax seal had been broken. Mrs. Winchester had already read the letter. Raven pulled out the parchment.

A letter to her, requesting brunch, from Ivaline Pemberton.

A relief went through her bones, but she held herself steady, pretending that she did not care for the snobbish, sickly girl.

"It seems you've made an impression on the girl," Mrs. Winchester said bitterly. She knew who Ivy was.

"May I visit her?"

Mrs. Winchester's finely plucked brows rose. "I've arranged a coach for you," she said, her words clipped. "It will be ready shortly."

Raven nodded and asked quietly, "What about Zander?"

"The letter only mentions you," she snapped.

"Is he all right?" Raven asked, nearly pleading.

Mrs. Winchester met her eye—it looked as though the older woman had been crying. Raven thought of her dream. "He is fine." Mrs. Winchester didn't sound convinced. "Drink your tea. I'll return to fetch you when the coach is ready."

Raven nodded.

Mrs. Winchester's eyes wandered quickly about the room. Her stare lingered a heartbeat too long on the bathroom door—the only room they hadn't been able to search. Raven brought her tea to her lips and pretended not to notice. Mrs. Winchester then left, locked the door behind her, and marched down the hall.

Mrs. Winchester escorted Raven to the garage where the lesser of the coaches waited. A servant climbed into the coach with her, a middle-aged woman with a sour expression. She beheld Raven like a misbehaving child who had missed a punishment. A spy, no doubt.

"This is Miss Geraldine," said Mrs. Winchester. "She will accompany you."

"A pleasure," Raven said, though she did not smile at the woman.

Miss Geraldine gave a curt nod of her head.

Neither of them spoke on the ride to Pemberton House.

The coach trotted down Lamp Light Way and to a beautiful house of white stone and black shutters. Pillars lined the front of it, and a veranda lined both the first story and the second story and went all the way around the house.

A Pemberton servant met them at the door and led Raven and her servant-spy to the second floor. The room was full of tall windows, all letting in copious amounts of sunlight. Plants dotted the floor: ferns, bamboo, and lemongrass. Ivaline sat at a small table designed for intimate company. She wore a housecoat, and her blonde hair was loose. Little makeup touched up her face, other than the pale powder.

"Ah, there she is," Ivaline said, her voice softer than it had been. Less vibrant. Sickly, she realized. Ivaline motioned toward Raven, then to the chair beside her. "Sit, dear, sit. Come join me."

Raven sat beside Ivaline, and the other girl let out a soft sigh. "I intended to come visit you, dear, but my health took a turn this morning. I wanted to see you again, so I had the audacity to request this meeting of you."

"It's no trouble," Raven said politely. The servants, both Ivaline's and Winchester's, were listening. "I would have walked across the city to have brunch with you."

Ivaline beamed.

Brunch was served, fruit and nutty cookies and tea, and Ivaline shooed the servants away, including Miss Geraldine. The spy-servant obeyed but with a deep frown on her face. The door to the lounge shut, and Ivaline let out a short sigh. She scooted closer to Raven and motioned for her to do the same.

"What in Minerva's name happened?" Ivy asked, her whisper worried and thin. She searched Raven's eyes for answers. "I get home last night and everything is fine, but when I wake up this morning, I hear Zander's been imprisoned?"

Raven swallowed. She didn't know how much Ivy knew, how much anyone knew, and she didn't want to be the one to say something she shouldn't. Her fear must have shown. Ivy put her hand over Raven's.

"They think him a traitor to the Hawks," Ivy whispered.

157

Raven nodded. "I don't know what to do," she admitted. She felt helpless.

"I'm not sure if there is anything you can do," Ivy said, staring at the ceiling. "The rumors are all over the place too. I've got Thalame running back and forth, trying to find out what's going on. The Gray Elite blame the Hawks for the murders, and the Hawks think they're being framed, and everyone is in a tizzy. It's bad press for everyone. The Hawks look like murderers, and the Gray Elite look like fools for letting it happen in their backyard." She sighed. "I admit, the alternative was worse."

"Thalame is here too?"

Ivy nodded. She pulled a white lace fan from her sleeve and began to fan herself.

"He's not really a Hawk, but he's a Wr—" She paused, and her eyes widened.

"He's a Wraith?" Raven whispered.

Ivy's lips parted. She searched Raven for a brief moment and then nodded. "You know about them?"

Raven paled and leaned forward. Thalame was a Wraith but not a Hawk. That explained why he and Zander were so friendly back at the Dwellers' camp. They knew each other. "Is this the part where you tell me you're one too?"

Ivy shook her head. "No, that's not a line of work for me. I don't have the attributes for it."

Raven sighed and leaned against Ivy, the better to whisper. "Mrs. Winchester explained it to me last night. When they took Zander away."

They ate, though Raven didn't have much of an appetite. Ivy didn't eat much either. She kept glancing toward the doors. Was she waiting for Thalame? Her father? For news? Raven found herself nervous waiting for *anything* to happen.

"I'm worried about Zander," Raven said. She thought back to her dream, of his father holding a bloodied whip, of Zander bleeding and panting. "Would his own father do that to him?" Raven asked, her voice thin. "Hurt him?"

"Hurt him? I wouldn't put it past old Winchester. The man might be a Hawk, but he's got the ruthlessness of a Gray Elite. Maybe two. I'd like to tell you that he'd never kill his own son, but...I saw him that night," Ivy said, her voice quiet, her lips thin. "When Zander fled. People died, and they blamed Winchester for it because it had been his plan. It was chaos in the Hawks. He was beyond furious."

Had that been the last she would see of Zander? Cuffed and gagged and dragged into a cellar? Her chest squeezed. The tea in her hands shook.

"I fancy a walk through the garden," Ivaline said, hand over her forehead. "It's too stuffy in here."

She rang a brass bell, and the doors opened. Servants cleared the table and helped her to stand. They followed behind as Ivaline walked arm-in-arm with Raven to the gardens. Ivaline walked slowly, feigning her sickliness, and the two girls meandered about. While not as extensive as the Winchester gardens, it housed all manner of apple trees and roses.

The wind rustled through the leaves, sounding like voices, like footsteps. Raven didn't know how far the servants would follow them into the garden, but the more she listened, the more the wind sounded like footsteps.

In her mind, she pictured black-clad figures running toward them.

Behind them came the sound of two feet, one person.

Why would only one servant follow them? Raven's gut flinched. Ivy didn't speak. Her eyes were elsewhere, on the trees, on the blue sky between them.

Had someone come looking for the box? Had Zander broken down and told them where it was? Raven paused to pretend to adjust her boot, but she pulled out her ebony handled dagger. Ivy blinked, brow furrowed.

The footsteps behind them didn't stop. They quickened.

Raven turned, dagger at the ready—and the stranger lunged.

In a heartbeat, she saw his face, saw his vile intention, the coldness and hatred in his eyes, and she plunged the dagger into his throat. She felt the blade slide through tissue and muscle and scrape bone.

Ivaline let out a shriek, and a dozen footsteps came running.

The stranger's eyes met Raven's. She had never seen him before. The body thumped onto the stones. And then the light in his eyes faded. Raven yanked her dagger free just as a dozen Pemberton House guards and servants rushed into the scene. Some guards carried pistols; others held swords. At the sight of the body on the ground at Raven's feet, no one moved.

Blood dripped from the blade in her hand. It puddled on the stones, splashed on her boot.

"What happened?" demanded one of the guards.

"He attacked!" Ivaline shrieked, hand over her heart. Tears pushed against her eyes. "Raven pushed him off and attacked him back."

She had killed him. His blood was still warm on her dagger, on her fingers.

Raven felt the world wobble under her feet. She couldn't take her eyes off the dead man, the human being whose life had gone from his eyes—because of her.

"Take them inside," said one of the guards.

Raven felt hands on her shoulders, guiding her. She heard Ivaline's gentle sobs. But her body felt ages away. She didn't feel the sun on her face, or the breeze; she felt the blood on her hands and iron box hidden in her bodice.

The Pemberton servants took Raven into a guest room and provided her with a fresh dress. She washed off the blood in the bathroom. Word had been sent to Mrs. Winchester regarding the attack, explaining Raven's prolonged visit. Gray Elite arrived shortly to investigate the attack. Raven watched them from the guest room window. They stood around the body, talking and gesturing to the stones.

It felt like a dream. An absurd dream. Surely, she would wake in her room in Silver Glen. None of this had ever happened; she hadn't gone with Zander, there was no thief, and she had not killed a man in a garden.

She wanted it to be a dream, but at the same time, she didn't.

She heard the voices outside her door; the Gray Elite wanted to talk to her. Raven held her gaze on the dead man. She couldn't look away. The guest room door opened and closed, and calm footsteps walked toward her.

"I hear you've had one hell of an afternoon."

It took a moment to place the friendly voice. She turned. Ezra Deacon stood at arm's length. Captain Ezra Deacon. His honey-brown eyes met her own, and he gave her a weary smile—one that spoke of his exhaustion, not of the commotion.

Ezra held out his hand, and she took it. He led her to the couch. She sat, and he knelt on the floor in front of her.

"What's going on?" she asked, her voice meek. "First, the bodies at the ball, and now, this..." She withheld the question she wanted answers to: was someone following her?

"I'd like to know too." Ezra ran a hand through his short blond hair. He let out a sigh. "We are looking into the man who attacked you and Ivaline. Don't you worry about that. We will take care of it."

Ivaline, he said—not Ivy. They were alone in the room. If he knew who Ivaline was, he would have used her real name. Unless he didn't think Raven knew.

"The guards told me what happened," Ezra said. "You took care of him before he could do you or Ivaline harm. Do you have any idea why he attacked you?"

Raven shook her head. She knew, of course, but she pretended not to. For all she knew, the man from the garden might have been oblivious to the iron box and the Hawks.

He gave her a kind smile, and the gentleness of it reminded her of Lena. At the thought of her half-sister, her heart squeezed. The gentleness of a smile like that went straight through the core. Ezra meant no harm.

"And here, we all thought you were a quiet girl from the country. You've got a wild side, don't you? You'd have to be a little wild in order to survive out there. No wonder Zander couldn't come home without you. I'd have trouble too."

160

He gave her a charming smile, and she found herself smiling back. "That's kind of you to say," she said.

"It's only the truth as I see it." His smile faltered. "I'm surprised Zander isn't here. Is he all right?"

She blinked. Did he know? "I assume so. I didn't get the chance to speak with him this morning. I slept in, and Ivaline's invitation came early." Changing the subject, she asked, "Is she all right? Ivaline?"

Ezra nodded. "It gave her quite the shock. She's taken to bedrest. The doctor is on her way, but her maid assures us that she will be all right in time."

Guilt slumped on her shoulders. Though she knew Ivy's sickness to be an act, the sight of her wide, fearful eyes in the garden stained the back of her mind.

Ezra took her hand in both of his, his warmth seeping into her skin, and he looked her in the eye when he said, "You saved her life today, Raven. And your own. That alone is commendable. Already, word is spreading of the wild woman who defended herself against the madman." His smile warmed his entire face. "You are a hero this day, nothing less."

"It doesn't feel like it," she admitted.

"What do you mean?"

"I killed a man," she whispered.

Ezra gripped her hand tighter.

"He's dead." She looked down at her hand, the one that had thrust the dagger through his throat. "I felt it, the blade hitting bone and muscle and ripping through them, I felt the impact, the blood..." She shuddered.

Ezra let go of her hand and wrapped her in an embrace. She abandoned all other feelings beside the comfort he offered, and she collapsed into his arms. She buried her head on his shoulder, and the dam broke. She cried onto his Gray Elite uniform. He held her all the while.

When the worst of the tears had subsided, he whispered, "It is no easy feat to take a life. A soldier will kill within his career. I have. It...gets easier, but it is never something I enjoy or look forward to. That man would have killed you, or worse, had you not acted. You did not kill an innocent man. He had a criminal record, and had he been taken into custody alive, he would have faced execution."

That small fact made her a little happy, but only a little.

A knock came to the door, and Ezra released Raven. "Enter," he said.

A Gray Elite marched inside. He saluted Ezra, saying, "Captain."

Ezra stood. "Report."

"General Deacon requests your presence, along with Miss Raven Thane."

At the sound of her name, she tensed.

Ezra helped her stand and nodded to the Gray Elite. "We're on our way."

The soldier departed.

"Why would he want to see me?" Raven asked.

"I can't say," Ezra said, shrugging. "But best not to keep him waiting."

Although Miss Geraldine did not look happy about it, she set out to return to Winchester House without Raven. Ezra promised the servant Raven's safe return and escorted her to a Gray Elite coach, a simple white coach with golden yellow trim. The horse was plain and steel, made for function, not fashion.

Ezra sat in the back with Raven, and the silent driver took them down Lamp Light Way, away from the residences and into the military side. Towering buildings of steel, brass, stone, and glass rose so high, it made Raven dizzy.

They stopped at a building near the edge of the city. Ezra walked her around the building to the city's edge. A stone wall bordered the city. On the other side, the hillside dropped into a steep angle. Too steep to safely build upon. Beyond it, Raven could see to the horizon. Rolling hills, forests, and a winding stream, dotted with villages.

It was a breathtaking sight.

Ezra didn't linger. He guided her into a towering building of gold-tinted steel. Inside, the decorations were simple and clean, almost clinical. The white walls and steel floors were polished to a shine. Even the sparse wood accents shone. Everything was square and straight-edged, and it felt like walking into a maze of boxes.

Ezra personally escorted her to General Deacon's office. His father's office, she realized. The office was a modest space of footstep-softening blue carpet and brassy furniture. The general stood with his back to them, facing the floor-to-ceiling window that looked out over the countryside. He held his hands behind his back and made no notion that he had heard the door open.

"General Deacon." Ezra stood with his heels together, like a captain addressing his general, not a son addressing his father. "I've arrived with Miss Raven Thane, as requested."

General Deacon said, "Thank you, Captain. You are dismissed. Please wait in the hall to escort Miss Thane home afterward."

Ezra didn't move at once. He glanced sideways at Raven, then at his father. "Sir," he said curtly. He stepped toward the door, and Raven wanted to grab him and make him stay, but held herself still. The door closed, leaving her alone with General Deacon.

"Sit," said the general.

She sat in the chair closest to her, a brassy three-legged chair with a leather cushion. General Deacon took in a deep breath, then turned to face her. He wore no humor on his clean-shaven face, no glint of amusement. He peered down at Raven like a criminal.

She wanted to sink down, but she did not want him to sense guilt. She held her shoulders straight, her back firm.

"Lenhala is organized," he said lowly. "The Gray Elite keep that organization, that order, and it keeps the city moving. These so-called Hawks want to destroy that order and return the kingdom to the profanity of magic that ruined it in the first place."

At the mention of the Hawks, her skin turned clammy. At the mention of magic, her hands trembled.

"The Hawks are nothing but murderers and thieves, a haven for criminals. That boy of yours did everyone a favor when he fled the city," General Deacon said. "He saved people, more than he got killed." He waited for her reaction, but when she didn't speak, he continued, "I know this may seem complicated and new to you, or Zander might have told you everything. I don't know. It doesn't matter." He sighed, and the lines around his eyes deepened. "Raven, do you know what he stole? What it does?"

There—the answer to the question she had asked since they had left Silver Glen. Dangled in front of her.

She swallowed; she knew it to be a piece of Altair's Augur, but she couldn't tell Deacon that. No, her best chance would be to play dumb, be the simple girl from the simple town.

Gently, she shook her head.

General Deacon sat and laced his fingers over the bare surface of his desk. Paperwork had been neatly arranged in folders.

"The Hawks had been threatening Regent Dunel with Altair's Augur for years," he said darkly.

Her stomach fell into her seat. Pretending, she gasped in surprise. "But...that's a legend. It's not real," she whispered.

"It is a real device," he said. "It existed long along, built by the first people to settle in Rhynwier. It was used only once and destroyed an entire city. Altair then dismantled it. The pieces were buried and hidden. It has taken a century, but those Hawks have managed to assemble it once more."

She leaned forward, elbows on her knees. Breathing became hard.

"But it is useless without the last piece," General Deacon said. His honey-brown eyes bore into hers. "The piece that Zander stole is known as the centrum of the device. It's the magical core that fuels the machine."

Raven's breath hitched. Not a lever or a combination, but the *magical* core. Something irreplaceable. The centrum of the device; its power.

Whoever had the centrum, controlled the augur.

The very heart tucked inside her bodice.

General Deacon leaned toward her. The light from the window extended the shadows on his face, and for a frightening moment, she saw not him, but a black-clad figure.

"And I want it," General Deacon said, each word a command. He extended his hand toward her.

Raven didn't move. She looked at his large hand, then at him, and feigned confusion. He wiggled his fingers for emphasis, and she said, "I don't have it."

He didn't look convinced. "My sources tell me that the thief the Hawks hired mysteriously lost it when he spent a night in the same town as you and Zander. At the same inn, if I'm not mistaken."

He knew that too? Sisters.

Panic heated her skin. She swallowed. Innocence was her only card. She said, "I-I don't know. Zander didn't tell me his plan."

"This is a serious matter, Raven," said General Deacon. "The centrum you hold has the power to destroy cities, *this* city, in a blink of an eye. The Hawks would do anything, sacrifice as many people as they need to get rid of the Gray Elite, to attack Gracita. They are ruthless."

"Is the Gray Elite any better?" she whispered. They were the ones stomping through the kingdom with their automatons, slaughtering anyone with magic, snatching infants from their cribs, and erasing gods.

General Deacon tilted his head at her words, his eyes glinting with something between humor and pity, and she wished she hadn't spoken. "I will not use the machine," he said slowly. "We will keep the centrum away from the Hawks, destroy it if we can, so that the augur cannot be used by anyone, regardless of intent. There is never a reason to kill so many innocent people, even in war."

She agreed with him, but she didn't want to give him the centrum. She didn't want to give it to General Winchester either. She wanted to run back to Silver Glen and hide it among the Sisters' ancient relics and pretend that it didn't exist.

She understood why Zander had fled. Why he had taken the box. Why he had been nervous about returning.

"Raven," General Deacon said, his voice fatherly but commanding.

"I don't think anyone should have that kind of power," she said.

"Then we agree," he said. "The Hawks are desperate, and in the hands of desperate people, poor decisions are made. The Gray Elite have no need for such a device. We have armies of automatons and human soldiers." He squared his shoulders and his chin. "We have already won the war."

Then, why does he want it so badly? He is just as desperate as they are. Use it against him. Desperate men are easy to fool.

164

"I-I don't have it," she lied quickly. Another word formed on her lips, but she hesitated.

He leaned forward, his face slack, eager, greedy.

"With me," she added.

"Where?" he demanded.

"Winchester House."

And just like that, the eagerness and greed in Deacon's face turned to something sinister. He stood, marched around the table with the quick, efficient steps of a soldier, and opened the door. At once, heels snapped together. With a few quick orders in jargon she didn't understand, half a dozen feet marched down the hallway.

Raven leaned forward on her knees; she didn't need to feign anxiety. It permeated her bones like disease.

Ezra appeared at her side, eyes worried. "Raven?"

He offered her his hand, and she took it. He guided her out of the office and down the hall, but she barely paid attention to where they were going; she worked to keep her shaky legs moving and not to collapse. Sisters, she had no plan! She'd only bought herself time to think of something better. The moment the Gray Elite arrived at Winchester House, they would know she had lied and come storming back.

Ezra led her down a hall that opened up to a wide balcony that faced the countryside. A fresh summer breeze grazed her cheeks. Gauzy curtains fluttered in the breeze. They walked to the ironwork railing. Down below, a grate spewed water that cascaded down the rocky hillside to a lake far, far, below. The height made her dizzy.

"Thought you could use some fresh air," Ezra said. "I know my father can be intimidating."

Raven fastened her hands on the railing and glanced over the edge. The iron felt cold in her grip. Beyond the wall, beyond the hillside, freedom spread to the horizon. Above, the roar and hum of airships came and went as they flew over the city.

"I didn't realize we were so close to the edge of the city," she said.

"This building is older." Ezra leaned onto the railing. His fingers drummed on the stone. Did his father make him nervous too? "This used to be a dormitory for Gray Elite recruits until a hazing went wrong." He pointed to the underside of the balcony, where the ironwork continued in a twisting, turning pattern. A relic from the old kingdom. "The recruits would have to climb over the ledge and climb down the ironwork to the window below."

Her stomach turned, but she asked anyway, "What happened?"

"One of the recruits slipped."

"Did he..."

"Oh, he died," Ezra said. "The fall shattered him. They never found his body. It's a long way down."

Footsteps sounded in the corridor. She turned, and her already queasy stomach flipped. General Deacon and a dozen Gray Elite blocked the hall, trapping her on the balcony. By the blank look on General Deacon's face, he knew she had lied.

"Anything?" General Deacon asked.

"I haven't asked," said Ezra.

Raven gaped at Ezra, and he refused to meet her eye. When he finally looked back at her, his honey-brown eyes weighed heavy with guilt.

"I'm sorry," he said to Raven.

His father likely made him do it. What a father.

"Where is it?" demanded General Deacon of her.

"I don't have it—" Raven started.

"Winchester House has already been searched," he spat.

Her breath caught in her throat—it hadn't been Mrs. Winchester in her room. It had been the general's people. And the general had seen right through her lie. Then...the servants at Winchester House were not trustworthy. Zander had been right to push them away.

Zander had known. He had known all along. And she hadn't listened.

"Step aside, Captain," commanded the general.

Ezra hesitated but did as his father said. He stepped to the side of the balcony. He looked nearly sick.

"Ready," said General Deacon, and at once, a dozen pistols were readied.

Ezra gasped but didn't move. His eyes flashed from Raven to his father.

"Aim." Hammers were pulled. General Deacon's hard eyes bore into hers. "Will I find it on your body?"

She took a step back. One bullet could kill a person. Twelve wouldn't give her a chance. She took another step back, and her tailbone hit the solid stone of the ledge, her lower back brushing the ironwork railing.

Ezra looked at her, pleading.

Over the ledge, certain death by falling. Before her, certain death by a firing squad.

The recruits would have to climb over the ledge and climb down the ironwork to the window below.

She sucked in her breath; Ezra had known, and he had given her a way out.

A plan formed. A stupid, desperate plan.

Sisters help her. She spun and climbed onto the stone ledge of the wall.

"What are you doing?" General Deacon roared.

She turned, her feet unsteady on the stone, the iron rail not leaving much room to stand. She looked General Deacon in the face and said, "If you shoot me, you'll never find it." She lifted an unsteady hand and knocked on the iron box inside her bodice. General Deacon's gaze fixed on the box, and his brows rose.

166

For a moment, no one moved.

And then, something crashed in the corridor behind them; something burst—steam and boiling water flooded the corridor. Screams sounded, an alarm rang, and chaos ensued. The ledge shook; Raven fell backward. In the panic, one of the guns fired. She clawed at the railing and, by some grace of the Sisters, found purchase on the ironwork. Her weight landed on her fingers, and she nearly let go; a yelp escaped her throat.

Ezra's voice shouted from above, "Don't look down!"

That was solid advice.

Raven focused not on the death below her, but on the window a few feet away. She started across the ironwork, pretending she climbed through the trees instead, letting her feet dangle only a small fall from the ground. The trick didn't work; her mind knew exactly how far it was to the ground—too far.

She inched her way toward the window, her fingers cramping, her arms shaking, her mind thinking of the distance she would fall if she let go or slipped. The window came within distance, and she lunged all her weight toward it. She careened through it and landed on tile, her breath ragged.

She made it.

She would have to give a proper offering to the Sisters if she made it back to Silver Glen.

She allowed herself a few moments for her breath to return and her body to stop shaking. As she pushed herself onto her hands and knees, a searing pain tore through her arm. Her sleeve had been torn, and blood soaked into her dress. The bullet had grazed her. The wound didn't look dire, and the blood had already started to clot.

She stumbled to her feet. She had landed in a bathroom, the men's bathroom, by the equipment. She pressed her ear against the painted metal door. Panic sounded on the other side but farther away. Footsteps thundered on the floor above her; men were shouting, an alarm like a thousand bells was ringing, and someone was shouting orders above it all.

It wouldn't be long before someone came looking for her here. She slowly opened the door, and seeing no one in the narrow hall, she slipped out of the bathroom. The hall looked empty; the offices held paperwork and personal effects but no Gray Elite. By the mess, it looked like they had evacuated. Raven had made it to the end of the hall when another explosion sounded from somewhere above her, followed by a renewed sense of panic.

Pipes within the walls creaked dangerously. It sounded as though the building would tumble down any moment. The rumbling, the alarm, the pain in her arm—her heart beat faster and faster.

She turned down another hall, looking for anything that would lead outside. What she would do once she got outside, she didn't know. She would think about that when she got there.

"Hey!"

Raven spun; her heart jumped into her throat. Standing in a doorway was Ivy.

39

"Come on, before someone sees you!" Ivy whispered loudly. She had changed her dress for close-fitting trousers, a black blouse, and a charcoal corset. A thick leather belt on her waist held a number of knives and tools.

Raven ran to Ivy and through the door she held open. It led through a utility room, and on the far side of the room was an iron grate door that led to a narrow stairwell. Iron stairs and bare stone walls went up and down, connecting all the utility rooms in the building. Ivy started down. Raven didn't question her friend's direction and followed a step behind her.

On the other side of the walls, water gurgled and slushed; pipes clanked with water pressure. The stairwell smelled musty and dank, like stone that never dried. Dim yellow lights illuminated the stairwell, and shadows gathered in every corner. The farther down they went, the louder the water, the stronger the stench. At last, they reached the bottom of the stairwell. Ivy led her through an old metal door and into a dark tunnel; the yellow lights continued but left a horrid distance between them, leaving much of the space in shadow. They had come out onto a stone walkway barely wide enough for two people. Beside it ran a sluice channel thick with water and debris. The sewers. The stench was worse, the dank accompanied by something that Raven did not want to think about.

The sluice gushed toward a speck of daylight—the pipe that fed the waterfall underneath the balcony.

Ivy walked the opposite way of the waterfall. She led Raven down the walkway and through a series of crisscrossing tunnels. The further they walked, the less intense and rapid the sluice. Smaller pipes fed the main sluice channel, rainwater and drains trickling and dripping. They walked, walked, walked, and though the bleeding had stopped, Raven's arm throbbed. She could barely move it.

Between the pain in her arm, the stench of waste and mildew, and the incessant panic, Raven felt nauseated and lightheaded. She followed Ivy's blonde hair—a beacon in the dark.

And they walked.

Above them, people chattered, a siren wailed, and the clanking of automaton animals and their coaches beat against the stone street. The sound came and went as they walked, as they passed underneath streets and cellars.

Still, they walked.

Finally, Ivy came to a halt. They entered a side passage, then a room, then through a secret door in the stone into another room—a cellar of barrels and baskets and sacks. Ivy paused, and unable to hold her weight any longer, Raven collapsed to her knees. The stone between her fingers shifted in and out of focus.

"That doesn't look good," said a male voice. Thalame knelt in front of her, his face doubled and hazy.

A hand fastened on her wounded arm. She gasped.

"Not the worst I've seen," he said. "Coulda been sewn up a while ago."

"What? Don't give me that face, you know I'm not good with first aid," said Ivy.

Thalame laughed; then he ripped the sleeve off Raven's arm. Something cold touched her wound, something that stung, but Thalame held her still. She squeezed her eyes shut. It stung beyond words—surely, he was sawing her arm off, to ward off infection, to be rid of the blasted thing.

"Hand me those, will ya?"

Something else touched her arm, something warm; then she felt nothing between her shoulder and her elbow. She rested her forehead against Thalame's shoulder while he wrapped her arm. He smelled of leather and sweat and smoke.

"There we are," he said. "That'll hold you together for a while."

Raven lifted her head from his shoulder, and Thalame's face came into focus. Ivy stood behind him, her face a bit green. For a moment, Raven wished she were still at the Dwellers' camp and none of this had happened, but she knew it had. She had lived it.

"Think it's safe to take this one upstairs?" Thalame asked.

Ivy shrugged. "About as safe as ever, I'd say."

Raven leaned on Thalame as Ivy led the way through the cellar and into the first floor of Pemberton House. They walked to a small lounge where Thalame carefully set Raven down in a chaise.

"You'll be all right in a few hours," he said.

Raven blinked. Ivy wasn't there. She tried to get up, but Thalame pushed her back down. "You're woozy right now, girl. That'll wear off in a bit too. Ivy's gone to fetch you something to eat to settle your nerves. Maybe something to drink too. Sisters know I could use something strong."

Raven lay back on the chaise with Thalame's hand on her shoulder, the warmth of his skin soaking into hers. She closed her eyes and let it soothe her. Her arm stopped hurting. Her panic eased. She settled into the chaise; she'd not been so relaxed.

"Here we go," Ivy said.

A clank jerked Raven out of her daze. Ivy had brought a tray of tea and cookies.

"You all right?" Ivy asked.

Raven blinked, but Ivy wasn't looking at her. Thalame was sitting beside Raven on the chaise, leaning forward onto his knees, pain twisting his features. He'd taken his shirt off. One hand clutched his shirt; the other clutched his side.

"Yeah, I'm all right," he said.

"You don't sound all right." Raven blinked; every heartbeat brought her further out of the sleepy daze.

Thalame met her gaze and smirked. Sweat lined his brow. "Nah, it's nothing."

She thought of Marie, of how she had pulled the straps of her dress before she used her magic, of the tattoo that had felt hot to the touch.

"Do you have a tattoo too?" Raven whispered.

Thalame met her gaze once again, but this time, he didn't look happy. Ivy dropped her empty teacup, shattering it against the tray.

"What does that mean?" Raven asked softer.

Thalame's eyes widened, suspicious and worried; his lips fell into a frown. He swallowed, and his whole throat bobbed. He stood slowly and then turned. There, against his dark beige skin, in the same spot as Zander and Marie, was a tattoo.

"It's the same," Raven whispered.

Thalame turned. The knuckles holding onto his shirt had gone white. "The same?"

"You saw Marie's tattoo," Ivy said, absently picking up the pieces of the broken cup.

Thalame looked between Ivy and Raven and then sat back down. "She knows?" he asked Ivy.

"She was in the garden when Marie took care of the Black Dogs," Ivy told him.

He turned his gaze back to Raven, less angry than he had been.

"You can use magic," Raven whispered, understanding slamming into her chest like a bullet. "That's what it means. You're a magician."

"It's not the tattoo that gives me magic," Thalame said. He felt his back, felt the tattoo, and then pulled his shirt back over his head. "The tattoo is what keeps the automatons from sensing it. When I do use my magic, the tattoo burns, which is why I removed my shirt. It's a rune that burns off the magic essence or whatever it is that the automatons can sense."

Raven's heart beat faster and faster. Marie's tattoo meant she had magic. Zander's tattoo meant *he* had magic. The world wobbled, and Thalame's hand once again met her shoulder. Slowly, the world righted itself.

"I can heal," Thalame said quietly. He motioned to Raven's arm. "Physical wounds, and I can calm the wounds that don't bleed." He had calmed her just then with just a touch of his hand.

"Thank you," she said.

Ivy handed Raven a cup of tea, and she reached for it with both hands—the pain in her arm had lessened. She barely felt it.

She glanced at Thalame as Ivy handed him a cup. He had healed it. With magic.

Just like that, something had broken between them, a wall that she hadn't realized existed until it had gone. She felt closer to them. She also felt the fragility of it. The forbidden nature of speaking of magic and those who could use it.

Raven took a sip of tea. "What power does Marie have?"

"She's a blood binder," Thalame said. "She can control the blood in another person's body, make them act like puppets or turn it against them. That's what she did to those guys in the garden. A sudden, effortless death."

Raven didn't ask for details. She opened her mouth, but Ivy spoke first, "Don't ask what Zander's powers are. Ask him yourself."

Thalame nodded. "It don't feel right to tell you his secrets."

Raven nodded and took a long sip of her tea. The other two joined her around the tray. They ate mostly in silence. Thalame didn't drink tea; he drank something dark red and sweet-smelling.

Pemberton House stood quiet. Above, she could hear the thumping of turbines, the roar of the engines, and the hissing of great airship engines. Still, a siren wailed somewhere.

"What is happening out there?" Raven asked.

"Oh, it's hell out there right now," Thalame said, stuffing half a cookie into his mouth. He chewed and swallowed, and then said, "I heard that a crazy woman killed a thief, got taken into General Deacon's office, and then tried to assassinate him. They say she had this whole elaborate plan to sabotage the water filtration system and plunge the whole building into chaos."

"What?" Raven gasped. "That's not what happened! He tried to kill me!"

"We know that," said Ivy. "Deacon doesn't like losing, and he lost against you. He's pinned you as a criminal."

"Publicly," Thalame added. "And because someone threw out the Winchester's name,"—he looked suspiciously at Raven—"Gray Elite forces have stormed the property."

Her heart squeezed.

"I doubt they'll find the Hawks' cave, but you never know," Ivy said, looking into her tea. "My father left to see what he could do."

She didn't care what happened to General Winchester or his wife after what they had done to her, but if something happened to Zander...she wouldn't be able to forgive herself.

"I'm sorry," Raven said.

"You didn't do anything," Ivy said kindly. "Deacon is behind it. He probably sent that thief to either kill you or provide a way for his Gray Elite to slip in and bring you to him." Ivy held her gaze but said no more.

"If it weren't for little Ivy here and her steam trap, you might have gotten shot," Thalame said, pointing over his shoulder at Ivy.

She shrugged. "Those old pipes are easy to clog, easy to burst." Ivy gave Raven a wink. "The plan now is to get you out of Lenhala. We'll take you back to the treehouse and figure the rest from there. The Hellcat isn't too far. We can—"

"What about Zander?" Raven asked.

Ivy and Thalame exchanged a dark look. A bubble expanded in Raven's chest, then suddenly deflated as she realized—they were planning on leaving Zander.

"Raven—" Ivy tried to reason.

"No!" Raven shouted. "I'm not leaving him!"

Thalame frowned. "Zander's in the dungeons. I'm not sure if I could even get in there."

"But we can't..." Raven felt tears and anger and frustration pulse behind her eyes. Zander, bloodied and beaten, resurfaced in her mind. "I can't leave him."

The silence that fell thickened uncomfortably. At last, Thalame spoke, his voice grim. "I'm guessing you got something of a plan?"

Raven hung her head. "No. I don't have anything." She glanced at her boot's empty buckles. "I don't even have my dagger anymore."

The Gray Elite had taken it as evidence.

Ivy chuckled. "About that." She pulled Raven's dagger from her side. "I cleaned it off for you."

Raven blinked several times. The ebony handle sparkled in the light. The steel shone like a reflection. Shaking, she accepted her dagger. "Ivy...thank you."

"Don't mention it," she said, waving her hand. "Seriously, don't. I don't do well with the sentimental stuff. Just ask Thalame."

He chuckled, and a blush came over his cheeks.

Raven slid her dagger into her boot, and admittedly, she felt more prepared than she had before.

"Well, considering we're all a little beat up from today, I suggest we all think of a plan tonight and discuss it tomorrow morning over a pot of coffee." Thalame stood. Raven started to argue, but he held up a hand. "You're still injured, and I'm magically exhausted. We wouldn't stand a chance. And I come up with my best ideas when I'm 'bout to fall asleep."

The servants in Pemberton House were scarce. The three of them walked up to the second floor without meeting anyone. With the unease between the Gray Elite and the Hawks, Ivy refused to sleep in her room. Too obvious, she said, if someone came to kill her in her sleep. Ivy, Raven, and Thalame took over one of the smaller guest rooms. Thalame stole away to wash in another bathroom while Raven and Ivy shared the guest room's overly large bathroom. Raven opted for a bath, while Ivy took the shower.

Raven took care to peel the box in her bodice off with her clothes. Raven glanced—Ivy did not have the magic-blocking tattoo on her back.

All three of them fit into the guest room's large bed; Ivy insisted on sleeping in the middle. Bed-curtains closed, clean and in a fresh nightgown, Raven felt a strange sense of relaxation, even as she clutched the little iron box in her nightgown's pocket. The even breathing of the other two eased her panic; she was glad that Ivy had suggested they sleep in the same room. The thought of sleeping in an unfamiliar bed, alone, in a city hunting her down, gave her an anxious, lonesome shiver.

In the morning, Raven, Ivy, and Thalame retreated into the library lounge with a tray of fruit, crackers, and cheese. Pemberton House was eerily quiet. Ivy's father hadn't yet returned, and though she denied it, worry paled her face, and she frequently glanced out of the windows at the drive.

"A lot of Gray Elite coaches on the road," Ivy said absently.

"They're looking for someone," Thalame said, black coffee raised to his lips. He looked at Raven.

They were looking for her, he meant. She pulled a grape from the bunch and tossed it into her mouth, trying her best not to look worried about her newfound status as a criminal.

They ate, and after his coffee, Thalame explained the layout of the Hawks' lair. He had been there a few times with Zander, though he had never joined the group officially. According to Thalame, a lot of the Hawks didn't like having so many Wraiths in their numbers.

"Makes 'em nervous," Thalame said, "to have so many magicians."

The Hawks had built their headquarters in the tunnels underneath the city, an ancient branch of dungeons from a civilization long gone, complete with narrow halls, dark stone, and cramped cells far enough below the ground that no one could hear the prisoners scream.

The idea of Zander being locked and screaming in such a place made her breakfast turn in her stomach.

Thalame went over entries and exits, where the guards would be standing, and the most likely place they would have taken Zander.

"But, since Zander is a Hawk, a Wraith, and a Winchester on top of all that," Thalame said, "I'm betting that he'd be taken to the upper level. It makes it easier on us to find him and easier to get him out. However, the only problem is that there's guards everywhere."

"Leave those to me," Ivy said.

Thalame gave her a wary glance but didn't object. "If we enter the tunnels under Pemberton House, we'll enter the dungeons from the south." He pointed to his hand-drawn map. "From there, Ivy draws the guards away, and Raven and I get Zander out. Then, we get out. We reconvene underneath Pemberton, and if something happens and our rendezvous point is compromised, we reconvene at Star Point."

"Where?" Raven asked.

"You'll be with one of us," Ivy said. "We'll know the way. It's another access to the tunnels that will take us home. The northwest tunnels."

To the Dwellers' treehouse.

Thalame stood and walked to the windows. "Now, there's a lot of Gray Elite out there. And they're looking for Raven," he said grimly. He turned and fixed his stare on Raven. "No matter what, don't go up top, or you're a dead girl. Understood?"

Raven nodded. She'd rather not be dead.

"The Gray Elite will be on high alert, but so will the Hawks," Ivy said. "After the raid on Winchester, the other members will be bracing for the worst."

"And, I've got a surprise for you." Thalame walked to the mahogany cabinet and removed a false bottom. He pulled out a bag, and from that bag, he pulled out a smoky black outfit padded with leather and steel plates. It had plenty of places to hold daggers and throwing knives. Short dark blue robes covered the shoulders, robes made for combat and movement.

Thalame handed the outfit to Raven, who took it in both hands. She ran her fingers over the fine material, soft and durable. The leather was supple, the steel lightweight and strong.

"It's Wraith wear," he said. "It will not only hide your identity, but will give you an advantage of stealth. Wraiths are respected within the Hawks, and if you stick with me, no one will think otherwise."

Raven nodded, though the idea of parading around the Hawks as a Wraith set a strange fire inside her ribs. Excitement and nervousness.

Thalame turned his back while Ivy helped Raven into the Wraith's outfit. It fit snugly, but she could move more in it than in anything else she had worn—she could move as though she wore nothing at all. The cloak hid everything but her eyes, and she felt strangely powerful with the anonymity. She slid her ebony dagger into her boot, and Thalame nodded. He made a few small adjustments to the belts and buckles.

"There," he said, a grim smile on his face. "Hold yourself proud. Real proud. It takes a special person to break into the ranks of the Wraiths. Not just any magician can do it. You're hellbent on protecting other magicians from the Gray Elite, or anyone else who thinks magic's evil or worth an execution, and preserving magic itself. Got all that?"

Act like Zander. He'd always held himself proud and steady.

Thalame changed into his Wraith wear, and he looked at home in the leathers and steel. She tried to picture Zander inside those leathers, but the image was blurry.

Before they left, Raven visited the bathroom. After taking care of business, she stood in front of the floor-to-ceiling mirror. She looked nothing like herself. She looked powerful, mean, and someone to be leery of, not at all like the naïve girl from Silver Glen.

She had tucked the box in her pocket; it had been the easier place while Ivy helped her dress. Now, she set it on the countertop and undid the buckles of her cuirass. She ran her fingers along the nearly imperceptible seams in the box.

Such a tiny thing. So much trouble.

She heaved a sigh. Zander's life depended on her.
No mistakes.

Ivy remained in the house as Raven and Thalame returned to the tunnels underneath. He led the way and occasionally gave her pointers on her walk, her posture, and her manner.

Their entrance into the lair of the Hawks lay underneath Winchester house, and as expected, two Hawks stood guard on either side of the ancient iron doors. They eyed Thalame and Raven as they approached but said nothing as they entered. They made their way through the narrow, dark halls. Chatter echoed from side rooms. Hawks panicked over the raid of Winchester House, worried of the panic in the Gray Elite.

"Who will be next?" asked a man to another, gesturing to a map laid over a long wooden table.

They passed several rooms that looked like offices, quarters, and a medical bay, but Raven walked with disinterest, like Thalame had quickly taught her. She wasn't here to gawk at the new setting, but to see an old friend whose name had caused quite the stir within the ranks. She was here for personal gain, to tease and scold, not to rescue.

Thalame led her through the hold and to the iron door to the dungeons. A single Hawk guarded it.

As Thalame and Raven approached, the Hawk held out his gloved hand. "This area is restricted."

"Restricted?" Thalame drawled, his voice dripping with an assassin's murderous honey. "I know who's behind that door."

The Hawk glanced between the two Wraiths before him, nervousness obvious.

"I came all this way to see what the fool's done for myself. He's a Wraith, and the Wraiths will deal with him as they see fit."

"The general will have the final say," said the Hawk, though he didn't sound convinced.

"Yes, yes, whatever makes the old man feel important," drawled Thalame. "Let us through, Hawk."

The Hawk hesitated, then stepped aside. Thalame opened the door to the dungeons, and Raven walked through without a glance at the guard—superiority, Thalame had instructed her.

The dungeon felt worse than she'd expected. The low ceilings, low lighting, and dreary, dank air felt oppressing and hopeless. She casually scanned the cells that lined the walls, the thick iron bars hiding a few prisoners, none of whom seemed intent on making eye contact with a Wraith. The walls, floors, and ceiling were cold gray stone blocks. Iron brackets held torches—few were lit. Enough to leave much of the space in darkness.

It felt like a place assassins would retreat to. Dark, menacing, and forbidding.

"Wraiths who work for the Hawks are assassins," Thalame whispered. "Those Wraiths are the last thing people see; if you see one, it means you're gonna die. It's given the Wraiths a nasty name in the city."

Just like the stories of the Revenant, she thought.

"Not all Wraiths are like us, though," he whispered with a wink.

They walked through the first level of the dungeon but did not find Zander. Thalame casually guided her down a stairwell and onto the second level. The cells contained more people; one man in a tattered Gray Elite uniform, his hair shaggy and tangled, eyed them as they passed, almost pleading.

Despicable that anyone could do this to their fellow human beings.

The more she found out about the Hawks, the more she didn't trust them any more than the Gray Elite.

Zander wasn't on the second level either. They started down the stairs to the third level, and Raven's anxiety rose with each step. If Thalame showed any sign of anxiety, he hid it well in his saunter.

They strolled through the third level, and at the far end, came to a guarded iron door. At the sight of the Wraiths, the guard outside straightened.

"We've come to see the high security prisoner," Thalame said with a lilt in his voice, a playful cruelty.

"He's not allowed visitors," said the Hawk.

Thalame chuckled. "Do we look like visitors?"

"The general said no visitors," said the Hawk. Thalame stepped closer, and the Hawk twitched.

"We are not visitors," said Thalame, his voice venomous—a warning. "Wraiths deal with Wraiths, and we are here to see what our friend has done to warrant such foul treatment."

The guard swallowed. "Make it quick."

Thalame gave the guard a smile—it lit up his eyes in a menacing glint. The guard turned the wheel on the door, unlocking the heavy deadbolts on either side, and the thick iron door opened. Thalame walked inside with Raven on his heels.

A single torch lit the space. Zander slumped against the far wall, his hands chained. Her breath lodged in her throat—he had been beaten. His clothes were torn and bloodied. A cut ran from his temple to his chin, barely missing his eye. His hair had come loose and hung in dirty clumps.

Zander lifted his head and chuckled—his voice was dry—at the two Wraiths. "Here to finish me off, then? Make it quick; I don't think I've got that much longer to wait."

At his voice, her chest heaved relief.

Thalame motioned for Raven to take the lead, and she sauntered to where Zander sat. He watched her every move, his eyes dulled and glassy, but murderous. He hadn't recognized them.

Raven bent down and brushed his dirty hair from his face. "Looks like someone's had a rough night," she crooned.

Zander's eyes narrowed. Thalame chuckled. Zander looked from one Wraith to the other, his thoughts sluggish. Raven, feeling the rush of the cruel playfulness, tapped her finger gently underneath his chin, drawing his attention back to her.

Each breath came ragged, and Zander's eyes locked onto hers. Searching. Then, his sapphire eyes widened. His breath tumbled from his lips, a ghost of her name.

"Took you long enough," Thalame said, appearing at Raven's side.

"What are you doing?" Zander whispered, unable to look away from Raven. Genuine fear shone in his eyes.

"Getting you out, mate," Thalame said.

Zander shook his head. "What? No, you both need to get out of here while you can."

"Not without you," Raven said, and Zander met her gaze. She meant it. She wouldn't leave Lenhala, or this dungeon, without Zander.

"How?"

Thalame checked his timepiece. "We've got about...three minutes."

"Before wha—"

The answer came in a distant *crack*. An explosion. A second explosion rattled the very walls of the dungeon.

"Oh, that was closer than I expected." Thalame blinked. He pulled out a key and thrust it into the cuffs binding Zander. "Which means our time is shorter than I anticipated. Move."

The chaos erupted as they had planned. Ivy's blast had triggered the Hawks to scramble, abandoning their posts in the dungeon in fear they were under attack. Thalame walked ahead, while Raven supported Zander's weight. They walked as fast as they could toward their exit, not the one they had planned on, but the closest exit to them.

They made it through the exit and into the tunnel below, and then they heard the *clash* of steel against steel, the *thwang* of crossbows firing, the thunderous *blast* of pistols—bolts and bullets hitting steel, leather, and flesh.

"I thought you said it was a distraction?" spat Zander.

"It was," Thalame said, looking in the direction of the fighting.

"Which means something went wrong." Raven's heart tumbled into her stomach. No mistakes. She steeled herself. "We keep moving."

Thalame obeyed, and they made their way down the tunnel. All the while, the stone rattled and rumbled, and a few loose stones clattered to the ground. The majority of the fight seemed to be happening above them. They came to a crossroads; footsteps were rushing from the left. Somewhere, a deep voice shouted orders.

Thalame reached the corner and held up his hand. Raven lingered a step behind as Thalame peeked ahead.

He spat a curse. "Gray Elite."

"What?" Zander and Raven gasped at the same time.

Raven continued, "Here?"

Thalame curled his fist and thrust it into the stone wall. "What was she thinking?" Thalame spat. "She's exposed us!"

Whatever Ivy had done, it had drawn the Gray Elite into the underground lair of the Hawks. The panic on Thalame and Zander's faces stirred her own. An invasion.

Thalame led the way through the tunnel, away from the Gray Elite, down a shadowed access, and into another tunnel, a little farther from the main horde of fighting. The sluice that ran down the center shook with all the commotion. With a thunderous crash from above, the ground shook, the ceiling cracked, and the walls rumbled. The rushing water crested and waved with the uneven shockwaves.

"Move!" Thalame shouted.

And then, an ear-splitting crack opened the ceiling; debris and pipes and water came thundering down, blackening the air, dousing the pitiful lights. Thalame shrieked, and Zander grabbed Raven's arm and yanked her the opposite way. They crashed onto the walkway. Thalame's shriek ended with a splash—he'd fallen into the gushing waterway.

179

"Thalame?" Raven called, but no answer came.

"The water's moving too fast," came Zander's gasp. "He's already gone."

Raven scrambled to the edge of the walkway and gazed into the trembling waters. "No, he can't be!"

"I didn't say he was dead," Zander spat. "I said the water's already moved him on. It'll take more than a cave-in and a river to kill him off; don't fret."

She didn't have time to worry about Thalame. Raven scrambled to her feet and helped Zander stand. He winced and clutched at his side. Raven moved to examine a possible wound, but he waved her hands away.

"It's nothing bad," he said. His face said otherwise. "A broken rib, probably. Happened yesterday."

She frowned but knew there wasn't anything to be done right now for him. They had to get out and away. They would fix him up at the Dwellers' treehouse or at Ivy's house. Whichever came first.

They started down another tunnel in the near dark. Raven kept her hand along the wall, the other around Zander. The fighting faded with every step, with every junction. The air still smelled like old wet stones, tinted with mildew. Zander said little, and she didn't have the heart to start a conversation.

They made it to the hatch that took them into Pemberton's cellar, and Zander struggled to climb the ladder. Raven stayed on his heels, ready to catch him if he stumbled. He hoisted himself through the hatch and into the cellar with a painful groan. She pulled herself up after him, grateful to leave the dank sewer tunnel behind.

A sudden burst of light blinded her, and the hatch slammed closed behind her.

"Well, now, look who it is," said the drawling voice of General Deacon.

Her eyes adjusted to the light. General Deacon stood on the far side of the cellar, his uniform scratched with patches of dirt and blood. Gray Elite surrounded the cellar. Each had a crossbow or pistol aimed at Raven and Zander.

The general wore a vicious, victorious smile. "Two rats have come out of the sewers."

Her first thought went to Ivy, to her father. They had searched her house too. Raven didn't have time to dwell on that—a poke in her back urged her forward, the tip of a bolt. Hands ripped the hood of her cloak away from her face. A Gray Elite pushed her toward the center of the cellar, and another grabbed Zander by the hair and threw him at General Deacon's feet. Zander winced but then schooled his face into neutrality.

"No!" Raven took a step forward, but an unharmonious series of clicks halted her—several more crossbows aimed at her. She froze.

General Deacon glanced between Raven and Zander, and he laughed. He nodded to his men, one of whom grabbed Zander by the hair and yanked him to his knees. Zander gave her a withering look.

Trapped.

180

"You still have it," General Deacon said—not a question. His eyes wandered to her chest, to where she had knocked against the little box. Raven swallowed, her face warming, despite it being the hiding place of the box.

Zander frowned at her; he knew where she'd hidden it.

General Deacon said simply, "Give it to me."

Raven didn't move.

"Unless you don't think this traitorous scum's life is worth it," said General Deacon.

She clenched her fists. The stupid box had caused all of this.

General Deacon whistled, and one of the Gray Elite withdrew a pistol from his side—*Birdie*. Raven's skin prickled at the sight of the familiar gun, and her rage bubbled at the sight of Birdie in a stranger's hand. The Gray Elite poised the barrel against Zander's temple.

She tried not to flinch. "If you kill him, then I'll never give it to you," she said, her voice wavering.

"Yes, but he'd be dead," said General Deacon, like he didn't care either way. His grin turned menacing as he eyeballed her frame. "And you would be too. Or, we can end this without violence. We can all walk away."

She swallowed, and he noticed. His grin grew wider. The Gray Elite pushed the barrel against Zander's skin, forcing him to turn his head.

She met Zander's sapphire stare; he held no fear in his eyes, only stark defiance.

Don't give it to them.

Her stomach felt like it might upheave her breakfast.

The soldier cocked Birdie. His finger settled onto the trigger. He started to apply the pressure.

"Don't," she breathed, her voice a whisper of itself. He pulled Birdie away from Zander's temple.

With shaking hands, Raven started to undo the buckles on the leather covering her chest.

"Raven," Zander warned. The Gray Elite holding his hair yanked; Zander winced.

"I have it," she said weakly.

She unbuckled the front of her cuirass and unbuttoned her undershirt just enough to retrieve the velvet-wrapped box from its hiding place, without showing them any more skin than she had to. Though the Gray Elite eyed her hungrily, General Deacon looked only at the box. She unwrapped the velvet and held the little iron box in her palm.

General Deacon stepped closer to her, and she closed her fingers around it. "Let him go," she demanded.

General Deacon nodded, and the Gray Elite pulled back Birdie. They released Zander. He stood on shaky legs, gave the man holding Birdie an evil stare, and started toward where Raven was standing.

"You stole Birdie," she said to the Gray Elite. She tightened her fingers around the box.

Zander blinked, then stared at the man.

"Give him the bloody gun," General Deacon growled, desperation leaking into his voice.

Desperate. Foolish.

Another Gray Elite aimed a crossbow at Zander, finger hovering over the trigger. The Gray Elite unloaded Birdie, minus the bullet in the chamber, and handed her to Zander. He immediately pulled his crossbow from his shoulders. He aimed at Raven.

"Try anything, and you're both dead," said General Deacon. "You have him, the gun; now, give it to me before I take it."

She loosened her fingers around the box, and General Deacon lifted it like a precious gem, unworthy of his human touch. A mad grin spread over his face.

"Kill them both?" asked the Gray Elite who aimed at Zander.

Raven tensed, and she felt Zander tense beside her. He had Birdie and a single bullet; she had a few daggers and throwing knives. She counted four bolts and three bullets aimed at her, and at least that many at Zander. They were outnumbered, and she didn't know if whatever magic Zander had been hiding would be able to protect them.

"No." All of the general's attention rested on the box. Enough that he started to walk away, toward the stairs. "Give them a few days to enjoy each other. They will all be dead soon enough."

The Gray Elite held their aim, walking steadily backward. Then, they were gone, up the stairs, through the door. Outside, the whirl of an engine started. Fierce hisses signaled the rising of an airship. The beating of a propeller rose into the sky, higher and higher, quieter with each passing heartbeat.

Beside her, Zander sat down on a barrel of whiskey. He ran a shaky hand through his dirty hair and set Birdie down on the barrel beside him.

Raven heaved a sigh of relief and collapsed to the floor. "Sisters, that was stressful."

Zander's eyes snapped to her. "What?" His voice turned cold. "Do you realize what you just gave them? What you've done?"

The sound of Gray Elite in the Pemberton house stirred her panic anew, and she jumped to her feet. "We need to get out of here before someone comes looking for us. I don't trust General Deacon for a second." She turned and started toward the hatch to the tunnels.

Zander growled. "You just signed the death warrant of thousands of people. Innocent people. What is wrong with you?"

His tone and his words stung, but she bent down to open the hatch. Pemberton House had been compromised, and she didn't want to linger. She climbed down into the empty tunnels. Zander climbed down after her. She jumped the last few rungs and set off at a brisk pace, eyes ahead of her. She heard the hatch close, Zander's uneven steps on the ladder, his boots on the ground. Then he stormed after her.

"Where are you going?" he demanded, his voice venomous.

"To Star Point," she said.

He let out a gasp.

"That was where we were to meet if Pemberton House was compromised. And, by the sounds, it is. Do you know the way there?"

"Yeah."

"Good, because I don't," she said.

He jogged to walk beside her.

"And we need to get out of here before they figure it out. I don't know how much time we've got, and unless you want them storming down here looking for the both of us, I suggest you hurry up. We have to get to the Hellcat before the time's up, or they're leaving us."

Zander sidestepped in front of her. He threw one arm out to halt her. He kept the other at his side. His blue gaze pierced her, even in the shadowy tunnel. His breath heaved. "What the hell are you talking about?"

"I'm talking about the very narrow window we have to get out of Lenhala," she said, ducking underneath his arm. "We can discuss the next step in the plan later." He started to object, and she spat, "And then you can tell me what powers you've been hiding under your shirt."

That shut him up.

Raven and Zander walked the rest of the way to Star Point in silence. It felt like hours, and then the sewer tunnels opened into a natural cave. One side opened to the late afternoon sky, the clouds beginning to glow with the western-tilted sun. They were in the hillside on the other side of Lenhala, far below the city. The sluice joined an underground river that ran out of the cavern's mouth and cascaded down the mountainside. A stone bridge crossed over the wide river, and on the other side, a tunnel vanished into the rock—that tunnel would take them to the Hellcat.

From the tunnel, she could make out the voices of Ivy and Thalame. Raven's heart leaped; he had made it. Ivy had too. Sisters, she couldn't wait to get on the Hellcat and leave all this behind. She could almost feel the wind whipping against her cheeks.

Raven started over the bridge. Zander caught up with her, grabbed her arm, and pulled her to a halt. He sidestepped in front of her.

"Okay, we're here, we're safe. What did you do?" he demanded.

She met his eyes. They were at the Hellcat; they had made it. She saw no point in hiding it further. She glanced to make sure the others hadn't come out to see them, and then she reached for the chain around her neck. She pulled the locket from her collar. Zander's eyes followed, enraged and curious.

She hesitated, then snapped her locket open.

Inside, a red stone the size of her little fingernail glowed. Its red-yellow light reflected in Zander's eyes, which widened considerably. Heat radiated off the stone, a nauseating heat, and she snapped the locket shut, trapping it inside.

"What"—Zander blinked—"is that?"

"It was inside the box," Raven whispered. She tucked the locket underneath her collar.

He gasped. "You *opened* it?"

When she had been studying the box in the bathroom in Pemberton House, she'd had the mad thought to open it. She had employed one of the thinner, sturdier daggers on her Wraith's wear.

"The centrum," Zander breathed. "The core of Altair's Augur. I thought it was a legend. I-I heard my father mention it, years ago, but I didn't understand it. This... He was talking about this. And you..." Zander gawked at her, disbelief overriding any rage he felt. Then he laughed, and his frown bloomed into the widest grin she had seen on him since they arrived in Lenhala. "You are something else."

He started to lean in, and this time, before anyone else interrupted, she leaned in to meet him. He pressed his lips against hers and slid his hand around her neck and into her braided hair. She tightened her hands on the front of his dirty shirt, pulling him closer. Heat radiated from her toes to her fingers, shaking its way along her spine. Time crawled to a stop, and all she knew was Zander.

They broke apart, but Zander didn't step away from her.

"How did you get it out?" His eyes wandered to where the locket hid under her leathers.

"I didn't touch it with my hands," Raven said. "I used my hairpins to get it out and my sleeve to touch it."

"What did it feel like? Anything?"

"Warm," she said. "I could feel its warmth through the fabric. I suspect that if I had touched it, my skin would have burned."

Even then, she felt a tingle through the metal of the locket. But she decided against telling him about it. He might want to touch the locket, to wear it, and the very idea of parting with the only keepsake of her mother made her furious.

"A magic burn," Zander said. "I've heard about them. They're the worst."

They stood for a moment longer, neither speaking, only looking at one another. Underneath them, the stream gushed against the rocks, pouring from the mouth of the cave, tumbling down the mountain. In the tunnel, Ivy's sparkling laugh broke the silence.

"Zander," Raven breathed, and he took the smallest of steps closer.

His eyes flickered to her lips.

"Unless you're going to kiss me again, we really should get going."

His arrogant smirk returned, and with it, all the warmth in her heart. He leaned forward and placed a quick kiss on her lips and then took a step backward to the tunnel. "Let's get going, then."

The Hellcat didn't provide time to talk. They hurtled along the dark passageway for what felt like hours, up, down, side, side; it was a maddening ride that blurred the edges of Raven's falling panic. By the time the Hellcat came to a screeching halt at the familiar platform at the Dweller's treehouse, Raven heaved a heavy sigh.

None of them talked while they exited the car. Thalame was limping, she noticed, and he leaned on Ivy. Zander walked beside Raven, and though he held his face mostly neutral, every few steps, he would grimace in pain. He caught her noticing and tried to give her a charmed smirk, but it fell short of his eyes.

It wasn't until they climbed up into the leafy treehouse that Thalame let out a chuckle. They went into one of the sitting rooms, and Thalame collapsed into a wicker chair with plenty of cushions. Ivy sat beside him. Above them, the starry sky blinked between the leaves. Candles and lanterns burned low for the night.

"Well, that was some getaway," Thalame said bitterly.

"Those explosions didn't go the way I thought," Ivy said quietly. All eyes turned to her. Guilt pulled her lips downward. Dust spotted her hair and clothes. "The Gray Elite were on my doorstep, and I had to act fast."

Raven felt a pin poke her heart. She gasped out, "Your father?"

Ivy glanced back at her with wary eyes—she didn't know.

"It's hard to say anything." Zander leaned back with a hand resting on his side. "The Gray Elite know where the Hawks go. They've found the tunnels. It won't be safe there anymore, and the Hawks will be scattered."

"What do we do now?" Raven whispered to Zander.

He met her gaze, shrugged carefully, and then held out his hand to her. She took it.

"I don't know," he said. "The Hawks won't be enthused to see us; neither will the Gray Elite."

"We'll be wanted people on both sides." Thalame grimaced. "The Wraiths might be indifferent, knowing them."

"How many of them are there?" Raven asked. How many magicians were hiding in the shadows?

Zander gazed back at her. The low glow of the candles warmed his bronze skin. He gave her a tired, mischievous grin. "I can't say for sure."

"They're scattered," Thalame added.

"They're an ancient order," Ivy supplied, a wonder on her face. "They go back thousands of years and got their name because they wielded magic as deadly as their blades."

"You make 'em sound a lot more romantic than they are." Thalame chuckled.

The room went silent. Crickets and cicadas chirped through the trees.

Zander squeezed Raven's hand. His sapphire eyes were lined with sleeplessness, and she spotted dried blood in his hair. If he was upset that she had found out about the Wraiths, he didn't show it.

"Shadows," Zander whispered.

Raven blinked.

"My power. Shadows." He pointed to the shadow underneath her chair. At his command, the shadow moved of its own accord, a puddle of blackness, shifting along the floor. It shifted into shadow animals, then it flashed back to its original position underneath her. Then, in his palm, a blue-black shadow appeared like animated water, flowing at his will. Deep blue flowed into deepest black and bruised blue. Then vanished.

"A hundred years ago, the Wraiths were the first ones the Gray Elite went after," said Thalame. "The Wraiths fought back too, and the Gray Elite quickly learned not to mess with 'em." He sighed through his nose and put a hand over his ribs. Healing. "Of course, it won't be all of us on the wanted posters. You two," he pointed at Zander and Raven, "caused the majority of the mess."

Zander glanced sideways at Raven, curious. His mischievous grin tilted upward. "What did you do?"

"A few things," Raven said.

His curiosity only grew.

With Ivy's help, Raven explained what had happened in the garden at the ball and all that had happened since then.

"You honestly jumped off the balcony?" Thalame's eyes glittered with amusement. "I thought Ivy was making that part up."

"Clever move," said Zander, smiling—though worry shone in his eyes. He squeezed her hand. "Don't ever do that again."

Their return caused a stir within the Dwellers, and the four of them were whisked away to the infirmary. Folded shades blocked their cots from each other, but it didn't block the sounds. Zander had broken two ribs and bruised a few others. Thalame had a few fractures in his left leg; he had been hurt worse, but he had healed himself as much as he could without burning his skin off.

A few cuts and bruises, but no one had gotten horribly hurt.

That she knew of.

With all the fighting, the steel and the bullets and the bolts, people would have died. Both Hawks and Gray Elite. But she calmed herself with knowing that her friends had survived relatively unscathed.

Within the next several hours, they washed up, ate, and listened to the news trickle in from the surrounding towns. Dweller scouts brought back all sorts of news.

According to the scouts, General Deacon had survived assassination, naming Raven Thane as his attacker and Zander Winchester as a spy. The Gray Elite followed suspected Hawks to the Winchester House, where they had taken General Winchester and Mrs. Winchester captive; both were unscathed. With each scout, Ivy's eyes brightened. With each scout that did not bring news of her father, her eyes dimmed a little more.

Raven listened halfheartedly after a while. An assassin, her? General Deacon claimed that she had attacked him—making it impossible for her to return to the city without a disguise. Neither could Zander. Not that she was eager to go back so soon. Or ever.

You did sneak into the Hawks' lair as an assassin.

"So the Hawks managed to keep Winchester out of it?" Thalame said.

"My father is crafty," said Zander, eyes narrowed at a spot on the floor. "He would throw his lackeys in front of him if it meant saving his own life and reputation. I'm sure he threw his rank around until he got his way."

Raven swallowed. That man had bargained his own son for a chance at the throne, for a chance of power.

The night wore on, and news trickled in slower. Hawks were arrested; Hawks were executed in the street—although not all were Hawks. Scapegoats. Regent Dunel had spoken in defense of the Gray Elite and their violent actions, claiming that the scourge of the Hawks needed to be cut out before it grew to devour the city.

More people dead because of her.

Raven leaned her head back. Stars twinkled between the crisscrossing branches that roofed the lounge. Between the leaves, a night breeze rushed in with the scents of summer, of blooming flowers, of dirt, of tree bark, and haze.

Finally, a scout she knew came into the lounge.

"Niall?" Thalame said at once, his tired eyes zoning on the tinker.

Niall nodded once. A small team followed him. "Good news," he said. "the plan went without a hitch."

"What plan?" Zander said, eyes narrowed.

Niall smiled, and a blush came over his cheeks. Thalame spoke for him and said, "The other secret plan we had. That while the Gray Elite were busy with us, we'd sneak into the Capitol Building."

Zander blinked, then grinned wide. "And this plan of yours went without a hitch?"

Niall nodded. "Not everything I touch blows up."

Thalame chuckled. "Well? What news?"

Niall folded his arms over his chest. His face became triumphant and grim. "She's alive. She's been taken to Moorin."

Moorin, the capital city of Gracita, the heart of the Gray Elite empire. A city said to be swarming in automatons and machines, built with metal and stone, because the Gracitans had never been able to wield magic.

The air in the room thickened at the news.

"It gets better," said Niall. "She's in the Tombs."

Zander spat a curse, Ivy paled, and Thalame let out a rough gasp. Raven was the only one unaffected by the news, and when she met Niall's gaze, she asked, "Who?"

"Princess Rosaria," answered Zander, his voice hoarse.

Her skin prickled at the name, and it tugged on the back of her mind. Something someone had said that she couldn't quite remember.

Zander's hands curl into fists. "It's my fault she's locked up there," he said quietly. "I'll break her out."

The resolve in his voice unsettled Raven. The fierceness in his eyes unnerved her. All for this princess.

"It will be hard," said Niall. "No one has ever broken out of the Tombs."

"Few leave at all," said Thalame. "Unless it's in a casket or an urn."

Words shriveled up on Raven's tongue. A voice in the back of her mind whispered, *Maybe the princess should leave it in an urn too.* She pushed the horrible thought away. She should not think such things, especially about people she had never met.

"It doesn't matter," Zander said, standing. "Rosaria would never allow something like the augur to be used, let alone exist. With her on our side, my father and the others would have to see reason. They couldn't refuse an order from her, or they would become traitors. We can't wait around for the Gray Elite to..." He hesitated and glanced at Raven.

They couldn't wait for them to realize they didn't have the complete centrum. She resisted the urge to reach for the locket and hold it, to feel the dangerous warmth that gently touched her breastbone. A caress.

"So, I take it the stories that you stole a piece of the augur are true," said Ivy, frowning.

Zander nodded. "That's why I left in the first place, to hide it, but it doesn't matter now. Deacon has it."

Ivy and Thalame exchanged a dark glance.

"You could have told us, you know," Ivy said, her voice low, bitter. "We would have understood."

Zander sighed and rubbed the back of his neck. "I couldn't risk anyone else getting involved. The fewer who knew, the better."

Ivy didn't approve, but she didn't argue. Raven understood what Ivy felt—it was exclusion, and Raven had felt it plenty.

"We need to move soon," Zander said, fist curled. "We need to move faster than the Hawks, than the Gray Elite. We have to be ready."

"Aye," said Thalame. "We'll be ready. Don't you worry about that. We'll start planning first thing tomorrow morning."

"Right after you two tell us the real story of what happened," Ivy said, standing. "No more secrets."

Zander nodded, though as they filed out of the room, he glanced at Raven.

They would not tell them about the centrum dangling around Raven's neck. It was too powerful a secret to share. Again, she resisted the urge to reach for her locket, to the centrum she concealed. She curled her fingers into her palms.

It's better that way, whispered the voice, clear as if someone spoke beside her.

She glanced at Zander beside her to see if he had heard it, but he hadn't. No one else had. They continued on as if nothing had happened. She followed their lead. She was too exhausted to dwell on strange voices she couldn't explain, or anything.

They reached the corridor where they would part, and Zander gave her hand a squeeze before he let go, and they departed.

Tomorrow, they would plan their rescue of the princess.

Tomorrow, they would tell Ivy, Thalame, and Niall what had happened since Zander fled the capital.

She collapsed into the cot beside Ivy's without washing or taking her boots off.

Tomorrow.

Thick as Blood

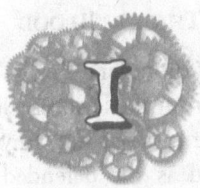

"Your stance is wrong," Thalame said, pointing his wooden practice dagger at Raven's legs. Sweat glistened along his dark hair and neck. "Your feet are too close together, and you need to bend your knees a little more."

Raven adjusted her stance.

Thalame considered it silently while catching his breath. "Not the best," he said at last, "but better."

Raven held in her irritation; she half wanted to throw her practice dagger at him. They had been practicing combat basics since dawn. Her stomach growled. Her head hurt. Her muscles ached from the strange new use. She had the beginnings of calluses from the wooden daggers and swords. But she couldn't quit. She had to be stronger.

So she adjusted her stance a bit more.

Thalame let her catch her breath while tossing his wooden dagger into the air. He caught it effortlessly, like he had been handling weapons since he could walk. Knowing him, he might have. He'd told her that he liked the stealth of a dagger but preferred the surprise of a well-timed grenade.

Of all the Dwellers Raven had come to know in the past two weeks, she knew the least about Thalame. He didn't talk about himself or his past, except in dodgy answers. According to Ivy, he had an unhappy past, but she didn't elaborate. Thalame didn't move like a soldier; he moved like an assassin, and his mysterious and unhappy past made him all the more interesting to Raven.

Despite his bulky build, he moved with grace and lethality. He had tawny skin, neither northern pale nor southern brown—a mixture, she had decided. When she had asked Thalame where he had come from, he had shrugged and said, "A town not worth mentioning."

All the Dwellers had come from somewhere else, and she loved the sheer diversity of them all. Some came from the north, some from the south, some from the far southern islands, and some from the far east. Everyone had different stories of how they had ended up with the Dwellers. It was so unlike her home of Silver Glen, where everyone looked the same and thought the same and knew the same stories.

She rolled her neck, and a few strands of her light brown hair fell into her face; her braid had loosened. She whisked the leather strap from the end and quickly braided it back. Raven had turned seventeen a few months prior, but she felt so much older than the little naïve girl who had left Silver Glen. She had seen and survived much. In those days of travel, her pale northern skin had turned a shade of peach. According to Ivy, she no longer looked as though she lived underground.

"Ready?" Thalame asked, catching his dagger by the hilt without looking.

She tossed her braid over her shoulder. "Ready."

Thalame shifted gracefully from his leisurely stance into a fighter's stance. She had only a heartbeat to see it—he came at her. Raven met his wooden dagger with her own, and the wood thunked as she defended and attacked. Thalame moved slower than he would have in a real fight, mostly for her benefit. She had gotten better, but Thalame met every attack she threw like he could sense her movements before she did.

He moved like he hadn't been injured a few weeks ago when part of a tunnel had collapsed on him. He healed remarkably fast thanks to his healing magic, bouncing back from that night faster than anyone else. Zander still winced from time to time, although with Thalame's magic, his injuries had healed remarkably fast too.

Raven ducked to dodge Thalame's attack that would have sliced her throat open in a real fight. She thought herself safe, aimed to counterattack, but his foot came around the back of her knee—down she went.

Thalame was on her in a blink, blade to her throat. "Gotcha," he said, a wicked smile stretching out his battle-serious grimace.

Raven released a sigh of defeat. Not that it bothered her; she hadn't defeated Thalame once.

"You lasted longer than you did last time." Thalame shifted the daggers into one hand and stood. He offered his free hand to her. She took it, and he hoisted her to her feet.

"I'm still horrible," she said.

Thalame shrugged, not denying it. "You won't learn years of combat training in a few weeks."

She rolled her neck and stretched her arms above her head. She adjusted the loose-fitting blouse she had borrowed from Ivy. Raven had accumulated a few basic articles of clothing from the nearby villages, but their stock was nothing impressive. A breeze fluttered through the ceiling of the training room, hot and humid with the sun-parched stench of summer.

The Dwellers lived in a treehouse; Raven didn't know where exactly it was, other than in the middle of a dense forest. She didn't have a clear grasp on the geography of Rhynwier, but she knew it was east of the capital city of Lenhala.

The Dwellers were outsiders, not part of the Gracitan military—the Gray Elite—that ruled both the Empire of Gracita and the Kingdom of Rhynwier, nor were they part of the resistance against the Gray Elite, known as the Order of the Hawks. The Dwellers were a group unto themselves, though from what Raven had gathered, they had ties to the Wraiths, an ancient society of magicians who worked all over the continent to smuggle magicians out of the Gray Elite's clutches so they could live peacefully.

The Gray Elite had decreed magic illegal, and anyone caught using it or helping those who could use it were executed.

The Dwellers were rebels.

Raven bent down to touch her toes, stretching the back of her legs. Her locket shifted under her blouse. She straightened and felt for it, tucked under her collar and out of sight. Her locket was special for two reasons: first, it was the only thing she had of her mother's; second, it contained the centrum of Altair's Augur, a doomsday device. The machine was useless without its magical core.

No one knew she concealed the centrum, except for Zander. Even now, the locket felt strangely warm against her chest.

Thalame got a drink of water, and Raven joined him. The earthenware cup felt warm to the touch, much like everything else in the treehouse. She drank the cool water eagerly; it surged down her throat but turned warm as it met her insides.

Sisters, she was burning up. Sweat coated her skin and lined her scalp. It shimmered against Thalame's brow. Summer's heat had permeated the entire treehouse. At the peak of midday, the heat became nearly unbearable.

The Dwellers' treehouse had been built into the thick branches of the ancient trees. Many of the walls and floors were made of timber or scrap metal. On the highest level of the treehouse, the ceilings opened to the canopy, to the sky. In other places, the branches twisted so tightly together that not even the rain could squeeze through. On the good side, birds and bugs were always chirping and singing. On the bad side, it was blasted hot.

"All right, one more go," said Thalame.

He and Raven returned to the center of the room, wooden daggers in hand. She fell into her stance. Thalame considered it but didn't offer her corrections; her pride swelled.

"Watch me," he said, like he did during every one of their training sessions.

He came at her. When he moved slower, she could see how his body moved as he began an attack or a block, how his muscles shifted, how his stance changed to support his shifting weight. They danced around the floor, and he even let her get a few jabs at him. Gradually, he sped up the combat. The faster he moved, the harder his movements were to predict. How could he predict hers so fast?

Around and around they fought. Sweat slid from her temple, down her face, and into the collar of her blouse. It covered her, thick as a wool blanket. Thalame stepped to the side, preparing for an attack, and she saw it—that small window of opportunity where his other side was left open.

She moved to strike, and then the air rushed out of her lungs of its own accord. A vicious, gasping cough knocked her to her knees. Her daggers clattered to the ground beside her. She gasped for breath—panic rose like bile in her throat, stealing what breath she managed to hang onto. Her skin went clammy.

"Sisters," Thalame gasped and knelt in front of her with the same lethal grace with which he fought, his own daggers laid forgotten on the floor. He pressed his bare hand against her collarbone, his calloused fingers against her throat. His face fell into a deep concentration—to detect any illness.

Gradually, her panic lessened, and her breath returned to normal. The sweat had chilled, but it came as a welcome relief in the heat.

"Hmm. Your fever is small but there," Thalame said, frowning. "I'm not feeling any obvious, known illness." And it worried him. She knew it did. She could see the frustration in his eyes.

She'd had a strange, mild fever since they'd returned from Lenhala. She hadn't said anything about it to the others. A fever was nothing serious, and most took care of themselves.

"The heat's not helping either." He frowned at the ceiling. The branches did not grow as tightly in the training room, and bits of pale blue sky peeked between the leaves. "Take it easy for the rest of the day, Raven. You've been training hard, and your body needs rest."

"I can do it." She jumped to her feet. The floor shifted—it took a moment to realize that *she* had shifted. She steadied herself.

Thalame stood and crossed his arms. "I have no doubt you can, but not today. You're trying too hard to learn too much in a very short time."

She started to argue, but a headache started somewhere behind her eyes. Thalame put his hand on her arm, and the headache dulled.

Pain flashed briefly across his face. He, like the magicians she had met, had evaded the Gray Elite's magic-hunting automatons by tattooing a rune on his back. When he used his magic, the rune burned off the magic that would normally escape into the air.

"Thank you," she said because she knew it hurt him a little to do so.

Healing the others had taken a lot out of him. He had used his magic enough in the past few weeks that Ivy had to hunt down aloe to ease the burns the rune caused to the skin around it.

"Your exhaustion is making you sicker," he said sternly. "You're pushing yourself too hard when you should be resting. You're running yourself ragged."

Raven heaved a sigh. She wanted to argue and keep going, but she also wanted to lie down for a while until her head stopped hurting. "Maybe you're right," she admitted.

Thalame snorted. "Go get yourself a cool drink and some rest." He returned the wooden daggers to the rack by the wall and glanced up at the bits of the pale blue sky. "Maybe the Sisters will grant us rain to take the edge off this heat."

The Sisters were Wilyn, Goddess of the Forest and Keeper of the Stars; Minerva, Goddess of the Sea and Wind; and Solen, Goddess of Stone and Steel. Legends told of how the Sisters had gifted magic to the people of Rhynwier, and the people of Gracita became jealous. That jealousy fueled their desire to conquer and to prove the superiority of their machines over magic.

Raven glanced up at the sky as if Wilyn might answer with a storm cloud. She didn't. Not even a slight breeze. Raven doubted the Sisters would do anything against the heat, just as they had done nothing when Gracita invaded Rhynwier and massacred their worshipers and demolished their temples.

Sweat smothered her in places she would rather it didn't, not to mention everywhere else, and she left the training room to cool down. Thalame was right; she was overheated and working herself too hard. Whatever fever she had picked up in Lenhala needed time to get out of her body.

And working herself to death wouldn't solve anything.

When Raven had glimpsed the treehouse for the first time, she hadn't realized how extensive it was. Ivy had given her a tour, and its sheer size astounded her. The Dwellers had built their treehouse high above the forest floor, hidden among the thick branches. They had rooms for everything: weaving, herbs, stargazing, reading, leatherworking. The treehouse wound around the thick tree trunks, connecting the rooms and halls with spiraling staircases made of tied-together branches and timber, ziplines, rope bridges, and ladders. The timber floors rose and fell with the branches, around the wide trunks, over and under branches thicker than a house.

Raven retreated to one of the bathrooms higher in the treehouse. Woven walls separated the water basins from the toilets and showers, with multicolored metal pipes connecting the basins to the tanks of gathered rainwater. Planks and woven reeds formed walls between the showers, and curtains looped over the branches of the ceiling for privacy.

Raven turned the knob over one of the basins, and rainwater flowed through the pipe. She washed her hands and face in lukewarm water. The burning underneath her skin eased a little. She held her hands and forearms under the water until she no longer felt as though she might combust. She glanced at herself in the shined brass that served as a mirror. Sisters, she looked terrible: sweaty, tired, and sick. Bags hung under her eyes, and sweat plastered her hair to her temples. Her entire face was flushed pink.

She placed her wet hands against her cheeks. Hot. Too hot.

Overheated—Thalame was right. These were the hottest days of summer, and with the open canopy of the treehouse, all the humidity and heat came right inside. It was nothing like Silver Glen, where the mines remained cool, regardless of whether the surface sizzled with summer or slept under piles of snow.

What she wouldn't give for a pile of snow to lay in...

She glanced up at the pieces of the pale blue sky. A few birds tweeted.

Rest. She needed rest. But how was she to rest when it was so ungodly hot?

Ivy had shown her a lagoon by the waterfall, half-tucked inside a shallow cave, half-shaded by towering oaks. The water stayed cool, perfect for an afternoon swim.

Raven let out a sigh. Her hot breath puffed against the shined brass mirror. Ivy had returned to Lenhala a week prior to assess the damage done. Raven hadn't heard a whisper or word about her friend, and each day tightened the ball of anxiety in her chest.

She let her face air dry, which didn't take long. She meandered back to her room—the room she shared with Ivy—mind on the rest that Thalame told her to get, but she found someone already inside. A younger girl, ten or eleven, was dropping a

198

leather satchel onto Ivy's made bed. A heavier satchel had been placed on the floor at the foot.

"Tara?" Raven asked.

The younger girl spun fast enough that her two long brown braids swung in an arc. Her sun-tanned cheeks spread in a wide smile. "Good news, Rae," said Tara. "Ivy's back. She asked me about you, and I said you were well, though I suspect she'll want to ask you herself." Raven inhaled, question poised, but Tara continued, "She's in the lounge upstairs, or she was when I saw her, waiting to discuss with the others."

Raven couldn't help the smile that stretched across her cheeks. "Thank you, Tara!" she said as she ran down the hallway and toward the lounge.

The Dwellers scattered themselves throughout the kingdom as informants, ambassadors, and spies. They bartered in information. Ivy wasn't a Hawk or Gray Elite or a magician; she was a spy. She lived two lives: one as Ivy, the free spirited girl in the woods—her true self—and one as Ivaline Pemberton, an uppercrust girl with a sickly disposition, who stayed inside for long periods of time. Ivaline was the cover while Ivy gathered information.

Raven stumbled through the doorway and found Ivy reclining on a wicker chaise. Thalame was sitting on a wooden stool beside her.

A fragment of movement, so quick she nearly missed it—and in Raven's mind she completed the image—Thalame and Ivy's interlaced hands quickly coming apart. Thalame glanced away, and Ivy's face brightened at Raven, though pink highlighted her pale cheeks. Raven decided not to mention it.

"Raven!" Ivy said cheerfully.

"Shouldn't you be resting?" Thalame asked, one brow higher than the other.

Ivy started to speak, then glanced at Thalame. Worry creased her brow. "Resting?" She turned her gaze to Raven. "Are you still feeling under the weather?"

"A little," Raven said. "But it's nothing I can't stand."

"That's good to hear," said Ivy. "But just in case, I'll hug you and kiss your cheek when you're feeling well again. I'd rather not catch whatever it is you've got."

Raven nodded, sitting in one of the wicker chairs that circled the lounge for meetings. "I will hold you to that."

Being in one of the highest points in the treehouse, they had an unobstructed view of the pale blue sky. Currently, a wispy cloud inched along.

"When did you get back?" Raven asked.

"Not long ago." Ivy still wore pigments of Ivaline's pale makeup and dark kohl, though it looked as though she'd tried to wash it off. She wore trousers and a blouse, rather than the dresses and corsets they wore in the city. Dust stuck to her boots. "I've just had time to grab a cup of tea and put my feet up."

Footsteps sounded outside the lounge, and Zander Winchester appeared. The sunlight had brought a healthy glow to his bronze skin, though standing in the shade of the doorway, he looked gaunt. He had left the top few buttons of his shirt undone, and sweat glistened along his collarbone. He wore knives on his suspenders and guns on his hips—he had named his favorite gun Birdie. Zander's sapphire eyes flickered between Ivy and Raven, and his straight-line mouth twisted into a scowl. "Ivy," Zander greeted. He sounded irritated, like he had been interrupted.

"Most people say 'hello' in a greeting," Ivy said playfully, "particularly when greeting a lady."

"Hello," he said through gritted teeth.

Ivy pretended not to notice and fanned herself with a piece of lace strung between wooden sticks.

Zander sulked into the lounge and sat beside Raven, though he didn't speak. He didn't even glance in her direction. She didn't have time to tease him about his mood before Niall—tinker, mechanic, spy—appeared. The dark braids that usually hung to his shoulders had been twisted up in a hasty yet somehow elaborate style. Sweat glistened along the brown of Niall's neck and face; the heat in the workshop, she figured.

Niall sank into the chair beside Zander, and the two boys shared a short, knowing glance. Raven frowned. Secrets had passed between them, she knew it. Zander met her gaze, and his frown deepened.

Zander and his many secrets, she thought bitterly. Had they not promised to be more honest with one another?

More Dwellers filed into the lounge; some she knew by name, and some she knew by face only. They all looked bogged by the heat. After a time, Ivy cleared her throat—a lady's signal to attention. The chatter silenced.

"Well?" asked Tay, the unspoken leader of the Dwellers. A hulking mass of a man, his intimidation contrasted greatly with his gentle demeanor—most of the time. He motioned toward Ivy. "Fill us in, girl, before winter sets in."

"Well..." Ivy started. With all eyes on her, she sat up a little straighter. If the attention bothered her, she didn't show it. "Lenhala is still in shock. Everyone is talking about the murders at the Summer Solstice Ball. The following attack on Deacon's life is fueling the Gray Elite's story that the Hawks were behind the whole thing. According to Father, they used the murders as their reasoning for storming the Hawks' headquarters. He told me that the Hawks are holding." Ivy looked to Zander. "Unfortunately, both the Hawks and the Gray Elite consider you a traitor. Father knows you're alive and well, but he's promised not to give your whereabouts away."

A few spat curses, including Zander.

Guilt weighed on Raven's shoulders. She knew, deeper down than she could think, that the murders and the attack on the Hawks hadn't been her fault, but it didn't stop her from feeling like it had been. The events of that night had been started by her, and so they felt like her fault. And as a result, Zander had been barred from his home by his own family.

"And," Ivy said, looking at Raven, "because General Deacon has framed Raven as his attempted assassin, she is the most wanted person in the city, possibly the kingdom. Regent Dunel has officially declared that the automatons are to seize you on sight. Alive."

A chill went through her bones at that word. Alive.

They wanted the centrum. Had Deacon figured out that the box she'd given him was empty? When he did, he would be furious. He would know that she'd lied.

"On the bright side, bards have already composed songs about you," Ivy said, waving her fan at Raven, her eyes glittering. "Some are rather endearing. Everyone loves a good antihero, you know."

Thalame scoffed. "That means the automatons will be looking for you with intent," he said to Raven.

"The general also claims Raven wrongly accused and planted evidence against Brigadier General Winchester," Ivy said dryly, looking at Zander with her head cocked to the side.

His brooding gaze widened.

"However, Deacon assures the public that Brigadier General Winchester and his wife are clean of dealings with the Hawks and that the accusation was a ruse."

Raven and Zander laughed, she scornfully and he bitterly.

"My father is a master of lies," Zander said, each word sharp as a dagger. "He's been spinning lies to the Gray Elite for years, and the general has fallen for it. My father has done well to make sure the public sees him campaign against the Hawks, and he's even staged fake missions with the Hawks so that the Gray Elite thinks he's on their side. He's a clever bastard, I'll give him that."

Raven held in her words. Had Zander inherited his father's knack for deception? He had fooled her and the people of Silver Glen. He had hidden his identity as Gray Elite, as a Hawk, and as a magician.

Zander leaned forward, elbows on his knees, the same look of disgust twisting his features that he wore whenever he spoke of his father—the father who had accused him of treason, thrown him in the dungeon, and tortured him for information. Raven wasn't fond of the man either. He had smacked her to the floor when she had refused him information.

Zander glanced at her as if he could sense her thoughts. A flurry of butterflies intertwined with her agitation, mixing into an uncomfortable anxiety. She averted her gaze from him and sought out Ivy instead.

"But," Ivy said, "the good news is that while Lenhala is ripe with petty politics, they aren't paying attention to us."

"Good," said Thalame. "There's a lot riding on this rescue mission. We can't afford to have any more Gray Elite attention than we've already got."

The air in the room tensed. For the past two weeks, they had been healing and training and planning, all in preparation for their upcoming mission: to rescue Princess Rosaria from her imprisonment in Moorin, the capital city of Gracita and center of the Gray Elite's military power. Rosaria was the rightful monarch of Rhynwier, and with her on their side, they could dismantle Altair's Augur for good.

"Speaking of that mission," piped up Tay, his booming voice taking up as much space as his shoulders, "how's that coming along?" He looked at Zander.

"Niall and I have been working on getting the maps together," said Zander. "We want one master map, not dozens of them. We've got maps of city streets, waterways, and surrounding villages, a few of the major buildings."

"I'm working on finding anything that might give us an advantage," added Niall.

"Good," said Tay. "Keep at it. We can't afford for this mission to go wrong or to let the Hawks or the Gray Elite know what we're up to."

Raven held her shoulders straighter. The mission was also why she had been training. She didn't want to be useless, not like she had been in Lenhala.

"I doubt the Gray Elite will be nice about it this time," said Zander, an edge to his voice—the same edge he got whenever they spoke about Rosaria. "If they think we're after her, they'll either get rid of her or put her somewhere we can't reach."

"They already think she's unreachable," Thalame reminded him. "And, generally speaking, anyone inside the Tombs is."

Thalame and Zander shared a prolonged glance. More secrets, more unsaid things.

Raven fought the urge to say something. Was she the only one in the treehouse who didn't have a mound of secrets? Even after she and Zander had told them everything—well, most things—everyone else still had secrets.

Sweat broke out over her skin, along her scalp, down her back, cold and hot all at once. The fever returned. Hot. Too hot. Burning. The edges of the world blurred; the lounge swayed. She gripped the arms of the wicker chair to remind herself that she had balance.

Thalame spoke, but his words were muffled. Zander spoke, muffled.

Neither were speaking to her.

Then, everyone stood—meeting adjourned. She stood too, and the blurriness faded enough that she could walk straight. It faded a little more with every step. She passed into the hall, and Zander brushed against her shoulder. His sapphire eyes briefly met hers, and then he continued down the hall and out of sight.

Raven kept walking. Her feet took her toward the cool lagoon where she could drown this burning fever.

Zander acted like he hadn't kissed her during their harrowing escape from the city. He talked only about Rosaria, about the mission, about the importance of saving the princess. She understood him being busy with all the preparations, but did he not have a spare breath for her? A heartbeat to spare for a good morning or a goodnight? He had said few words to her since their return. He'd been busy, she reasoned, as had she.

She would rather take his worry than his indifference. He likely didn't have room to think about her between his thoughts of Rosaria, his darling princess, the precious key to saving the kingdom.

The fever burned sudden and hot, blurring her vision. She careened into the wall, the side of a tree trunk, and rested against the bark until her legs could support her again. Luckily, she was alone in the hall. She didn't feel like listening to anyone else talk about resting or her health.

She heaved a slow breath. The lagoon. The cool water.

That was what she needed.

Raven meandered to a ladder concealed within a fake tree that led to the forest floor. She found purchase on the ladder's rungs and started to descend, already feeling a coolness from the shade of the tunnel. At the bottom, a door led to the forest floor. The door and the fake tree had been so cleverly hidden with bark and vines that if she hadn't already known where they were, she wouldn't have spotted the difference.

Between the treehouse and the impossibly thick tree trunks, the forest floor received little sunlight. Few plants grew in the thick shade, and it smelled strongly of tilled dirt and damp. It resembled a perpetual twilight—a nightmarish version of daytime—but it had a peacefulness to it. Birds chittered in the canopy, and cicadas sang incessantly.

Raven started toward the lagoon, and soon sunlight dappled through the canopy as she left the treehouse behind. The summer heat turned blistering in the direct sun, and by the time Raven came to the lagoon, the humidity had risen. It would rain soon.

She found the lagoon deserted, and she eagerly undressed and stepped into the cool water. It covered the overheated skin of her legs. She walked to the deeper end of the pool and submerged herself, staying under as long as her lungs would allow. The coolness of the water, the shade of the shallow cave—her fever relaxed. It did not relent, but it calmed. An underground river fed the lagoon, and the water continuously flowed to meet the aboveground river—the lagoon was always cool.

She closed her eyes and reclined against the water-smoothed side of the lagoon, a calm blue-gray stone. With the cooling, soothing, relaxing water, her mind didn't feel so cluttered. Her anxiety ebbed.

Why did it matter if Zander worried about Princess Rosaria? He was supposed to be on the princess's side in this war, the war their kingdom had lost. Raven should feel the same stubborn pride when it came to Rhynwier, but she didn't. Not really. She did want to see the Gray Elite fall. And, if they succeeded in this impossible mission, if they saved the princess, they would still have to put her on the throne and banish the Gray Elite from the kingdom.

That sounded more impossible than saving the princess.

"I thought you'd be here," came Ivy's chime.

Raven opened an eye to see the blonde girl walking toward the pool. She stopped by the rocks where Raven had left her clothes, and added her own to them. She joined Raven in the water. She dunked herself, coming up with a sigh of relief, her flaxen hair flattened against her head.

"I'm glad you're back," Raven said as Ivy settled against the stone beside her. "I missed you. The others aren't nearly as pleasant to talk to."

Ivy chuckled. "I don't suppose they would be. Everyone is all in a tizzy about this mission. They want to get it done as fast as possible but also as efficiently as possible, and I see those two things as counterintuitive. Personally, I vote we rest for a good two or three weeks more before plunging into something that could very well get us all killed."

"I second that," said Raven.

They rested for a while in silence. Raven had missed Ivy. She had missed having a friend to talk to.

"Zander is worried about the princess," Raven whispered at last, her words sharper than she intended.

"Does that bother you?"

Raven didn't answer. Her gaze drifted to the dark gray of the rocky ceiling. *Yes*, was the correct answer. "No," she said.

Ivy hummed in disbelief. She eyed Raven suspiciously, urging Raven to admit the truth.

Raven sighed through her nose. "A little," she whispered. "That's all he talks about, all he thinks about, and he hasn't said more than a few words to me since we've been back, and when he does, he glares. It's like he doesn't want me to be here." Saying it all out loud made it sound foolish. Raven's cheeks warmed.

Ivy didn't say anything for a moment. All the world was the trickling of the water through the rocks, the cascading of the underground river along the rockface and into the lagoon, and the thousands of birds chirping amidst the summer's heat.

Then Ivy said softly, "Zander feels responsible for Rosaria's capture. A few weeks before he fled, she was captured by the Gray Elite. It wasn't his fault, not entirely. Rosaria can be...willfully ignorant of risks. That's how my father put it. She and Zander went out one night, and, well, they got separated, and then she was captured. Zander knew only of his mission the night the Hawks were going to rescue her," Ivy said grimly.

An assassination, Raven remembered.

"He didn't know it was connected to Rosaria. When he didn't eliminate his target, the overall mission was exposed. No one knew what had happened. Zander was just gone."

Escaped. Zander had learned of his father's plan to use Altair's Augur. He'd stolen the centrum and fled as far from Lenhala as he could.

"The Gray Elite had Rosaria moved," Ivy said. "Until recently, we didn't know where. Zander didn't know about Rosaria until his father told him about it. Now he blames himself twice over."

Raven had seen his face when his father had told him. Shock, disbelief, shame. "And now Zander thinks it's his responsibility to get her back," Raven said.

"Yes."

Raven sighed. "He must care about her a great deal," she whispered. The words left a bitter taste on her tongue. Raven knew she was fishing for information—she had seen Ivy do it as Ivaline, and she had seen her own stepmother do it to her plenty, asking seemingly simple questions, only to dig through the answers.

"He does," Ivy said, her voice reserved. "But not in the way you're thinking. When the king and queen were killed, Brigadier General Winchester smuggled Rosaria out of the palace. He took her in, raised her in secret. She and Zander are the same age, and they grew up as siblings. So, yes, he cares about Rosaria, but not like he cares about you."

Raven let out a bitter laugh, guilt and anger and jealousy all mixed together.

"I'm being serious," said Ivy, smacking Raven's shoulder playfully.

"His father said he planned for Zander to marry Rosaria," Raven said. Which would make him king of Rhynwier, should they succeed and put Rosaria on the throne. *King*. Raven's stomach collapsed at the very thought.

Ivy didn't respond. Her silence and lack of comforting information confirmed that she had known. After a lengthy pause, she said, her voice full of its usual charm, "Well, Brigadier General Winchester isn't in charge of them now. If we get to Rosaria first, it will be her will against the Hawks, and I'm fairly certain her opinion outweighs theirs."

"And having her on our side will change things?" Raven asked.

"It will give us an advantage," said Ivy. "With Rosaria, we can start plotting the downfall of the Gray Elite and push them out of our kingdom. She's got a mind for political juggling, I've heard. And, she's royal by blood, so our chances of her having that royal magic is high."

"Royal magic?" Raven asked, turning her head to Ivy.

She nodded. The hair at her temples had begun to dry, and it curled like fishhooks around her face. "Yeah, they say that the royal magic was stronger than any other, passed down through the bloodlines, having been gifted from the gods to the first king of Rhynwier. Something about the ruler being tied to the land, or whatever. Who knows?"

So not only was Rosaria a princess and future queen, she was a powerful magician too.

"I only met her a few times. I'm not officially a Hawk," Ivy said, sighing through her nose, "but everyone tells me she's a clever girl with a good head on her shoulders. If only they said that about me." She chuckled.

Raven offered Ivy a smile and returned her stare to the rocky ceiling of the lagoon. Logically, she should want the best for her kingdom, her home, her princess, but where that sense of pride should have been, she felt a numb bitterness.

Even her sense of adventure had depleted.

Maybe Thalame had been right about the fever. It was making her sicker than she realized.

Ivy nudged her arm. "Don't worry about Zander. He's just being protective and vengeful. You'll see. We'll go on this mission, save our princess, and then you'll see how it is."

"Okay," Raven said because she could fathom no other response. "I'll take your word for it."

Because she wanted to believe Ivy.

A week passed, and Raven spent her days in a stupor. With all the planning, no one had much time for anything else. Raven's fever didn't recede. She slept sometimes for ten or twelve hours. The heat of the summer intensified, and it made her fever all the more prominent.

She kept her training sessions with Thalame light and short, her meals small and controlled, and her fluid intake high. Most of the Dwellers were too busy to notice anything amiss; only Ivy and Thalame seemed concerned.

When asked, Raven blamed the heat. Thalame didn't like that answer, but he never pushed for more information.

Raven escaped to the lagoon every day—sometimes with Ivy, sometimes without.

At the end of the week, the Dwellers gathered in one of the lower chambers. Bark and tight branches formed the ceiling and walls, and no natural sunlight lit the space. Instead, lanterns hung from the branches. Raven sank into a chair beside Ivy. The chamber was far too stuffy for her liking.

Niall and Zander stood beside a wooden table on which they had arranged a number of maps and diagrams. When everyone had gathered, Niall spoke first.

"We've gone over various ways we won't be able to get in," Niall said, motioning to a large map of Gracita. "Automaton patrols have increased on the main roads, waterways, and ports into Gracita. Air traffic is tighter than the roads."

"And there are no tunnels or cave systems leading under the border," Zander added. In the shadowy light, his exhaustion showed. Bruises hugged his eyes, and his skin looked pale. "That we know of, at least."

"We've few options for entry," said Niall. He pulled another map from the pile. It was an air traffic map; all the ports were marked by red and blue dots. "First, we can go by air. It's the quickest route, but also the riskiest. To avoid alarming Air Patrol, we would have to find a ship with clearance over the border. We would have to buy or threaten our way on board."

"And finding one that won't turn us in is going to be near impossible," said Zander, his distaste for the plan obvious. He pointed to the northern border of Gracita. The jagged edge of the mountains had been drawn with sharp points, like teeth. "There are a few uncharted airways into Gracita. They're to the far north and far west. Either would take us weeks to get to, although if we took the Hellcat north to Bell Falls, we could shave a few days off that."

Raven scanned the map for Bell Falls. It wasn't terribly far from Silver Glen—just to the southwest.

"It would take longer," Zander said, "but it would be safer."

"Either way, our chances of being caught or seen or reported are high," said Niall grimly.

Thalame shifted from his place against the wall. He uncrossed his arms to motion to the map. "What about to the south?"

"The south is heavily guarded," Niall said, looking as though he expected Thalame to have known that. "It's the main airway for the ports. Automatons and Gray Elite would be everywhere."

"Which would be the last place they'd expect us to come in through," said Thalame, raising a brow.

"Because it's near impossible," added Zander dryly.

"Maybe for us," Thalame said. "It wouldn't be hard to slip into Tinatun's western territory to see if our old friends won't help us out. If I remember right, Malik owes me a favor. He's got connections to the sky and to the Crusaders."

Silence drifted into the room and landed thickly. That silence quickly became uncomfortable. Thalame and Zander stared at one another, unsaid words passing between them.

"Who are the Crusaders?" Raven asked, her voice slicing through the silence.

"They're pirates," Zander spat. "They stayed out of the war and kept to themselves. They've made it clear they want nothing to do with our problems. What makes you think they would even hear us out?"

"Like I said, Malik owes me a favor," Thalame repeated. "And if he can't help us out, there's always the Wraiths."

Zander glared daggers. "No."

Raven glanced between the two boys. Zander's eyes were predatory, filled with warnings and threats. Thalame remained unfazed by it.

Thalame continued, ignoring Zander's silent but obvious objections, "The Crusaders will know every crack in the border patrols, and getting us through won't be a problem for them. Malik knows the ports; he might be able to get us on a cargo ship. Either way, we can slip into Gracita, maybe even into Moorin."

Zander heaved a sigh of displeasure. "We can find another way in."

"By trudging across the kingdom? By the time we get to Rosaria, we'll all be gray-haired," Thalame argued. "The Crusaders are the best chance we've got."

Niall rubbed the back of his neck, dark eyes moving cautiously between Thalame and Zander. "As much as I hate to admit it," he said, wincing as Zander turned his glare to him, "Thalame might be right."

A rumble of the room signified that most agreed with Niall. Zander released a long, agitated sigh.

"The only problem will be getting to Wayward Point without automaton interference," said Thalame. He strolled to the table and pointed to the southern border of Rhynwier where it met the kingdom of Tinatun. "While the borders aren't patrolled as heavily, they're still patrolled, and I'd rather not run into any wandering raiders."

Raven blinked at the mention of Wayward Point; she had met a thief who had told her to go there if she wanted out, and that thief had given her a wooden coin and instructions. Her lips parted, and as if hearing her thoughts, Zander shot her a steep warning glare not to interrupt.

She pulled her lips closed and met his glare with one of her own.

"If we take down an automaton, the Gray Elite will notice when it fails to return after its patrol," Niall said. "The Hellcat could take us most of the way, but we'd still have to get across the border."

"And because someone is the most wanted person in the kingdom," Thalame added, nudging his elbow toward Raven, "we'll have to be careful."

Raven felt a surge of gratefulness toward Thalame, but also the desire to kick him. He winked at her like he knew.

"Raven's not going," Zander said flatly.

Her heart jumped into her throat. "What?" she stammered. "What do you mean I'm not going?"

Zander looked up from the map and met her glare with his own. "It will be dangerous, and this mission is critical," he said, his tone low. "And you will only be a hindrance."

Thalame opened his mouth, but Raven cut him off, "A *hindrance*?" Her voice squeaked on the word. The fever burned underneath her skin, heating with the embarrassment that flooded her cheeks. "I would not."

Zander crossed his arms; he did not believe her.

She huffed. "Without me, you would still be rotting in the Hawk's dungeon."

Zander scoffed. "Even if you hadn't come to get me out, the Hawks wouldn't have killed me, and the Wraiths would have sent someone sooner or later."

She fumed. She opened her mouth to argue, but he spoke first.

"And, if it weren't for you, I wouldn't have been in that damned prison in the first place."

She balled her fists. If she had been paying attention during her watch duty, the thief wouldn't have slipped into the mines, wouldn't have stolen the centrum, and they wouldn't have had to chase him down. None of it would have happened.

Her fault. Her fault. Her fault.

Her cheeks burned, and she knew he was right. She held her tongue, and the subtle smirk that came over Zander's lips made her want to throw something hard and sharp at him.

Niall cleared his throat, and Raven became aware of the dozen other people in the room, all of whom had witnessed their disagreement, and her embarrassment turned to something poisonous. Her stomach weakened, her knees threatened to give, and she wanted nothing more than to be out of the meeting room and far away from them all, Zander especially.

"And...we will continue this discussion tomorrow." Niall started to gather his maps. "I'll have something on the borders of Tinatun and Gracita to present."

Raven stormed out of the meeting room first, pushing past Thalame to get out of there as quickly as possible. She headed straight for the outside, toward the lagoon, toward some semblance of peace between her uselessness and her fever. By the time she arrived at the mouth of the shallow cave, she was breathless, sweaty, and felt as though the fever would burn the skin off her body. She tore at her clothes to rid herself of them, and half fell and half jumped into the cool waters.

A *hindrance.*

How dare he! Why did he have to remind her how useless she was?

She submerged herself as long as she could, until her lungs felt like they might burst, and she let herself float to the surface.

A hindrance. That's what she was to him. A problem. She had let the thief slip into the mines; she had gotten them caught; she had gotten Zander accused and thrown into the Hawk's dungeons. Everything had been her fault! And he loved to remind her about it.

Without anyone in the lagoon to hear or see, she let her frustrations out—she screamed. It echoed off the cavern walls, frightened unsuspecting birds, and for a heartbeat, stilled the forest around her.

And then it felt like something had been lifted, removed. She sank against the lagoon's smooth sides. The birds resumed their chirping as if nothing had happened.

Raven soaked until the fever retreated. By then, the sun had sunk to the west and gilded the humid forest in blazing golds and pinks, setting the summer haze aflame. Cicadas sang, thousands of them, overshadowing the birds. She stood in the dying sunlight to dry, and in those fleeting moments, she felt something like peace.

A piece of a memory—she stood in the afternoon sun in the northernmost parts of Hammel Forest around Silver Glen. She was nine, and it was the first time she'd snuck out of the mine. Her father didn't know. Her stepmother didn't know. She'd kept out of sight from the lookout tower and slipped through the forest to the boundary fence. While she wouldn't have the guts to go beyond it that day, she stood at the fence and watched the forest fade from bright afternoon to hazy evening. At nine years old, the night forest still scared her.

An owl hooted. Raven blinked, and she stood again in the mouth of the lagoon, seventeen years old. Some days, she didn't feel any braver or smarter than she had back then.

Maybe she wasn't.

Maybe Zander was right in leaving her behind. She wasn't a spy or a magician. She had no skills that would get them out of a tight spot. She would only be a hindrance.

She dressed and left her hair loose and started back toward the treehouse. By the time she returned, the sun had gone entirely. With only the moonlight and sparse candlelight to go by, Raven guided herself with one hand on the wall as she made her way back to her room.

Her steps meandered, her mind for once restful. She needed a long sleep. She crossed an intersection of two halls, all shadowed in the clouded moonlight.

"...being overly protective," came Thalame's whispered voice from a lounge down the hall. "Her training has been going fine—well, considering."

"Fine enough to send her on this mission?" came Zander's whispered reply.

Raven stopped dead. Her heart skipped a beat. Her peace shattered like glass. They were talking about *her*.

"I wouldn't say that," Thalame said lowly.

"She doesn't need to go," Zander said, almost a plea. "It's too dangerous, and the Gray Elite will be looking for her. The automatons will be too. All the Detectors will have her face memorized. Not to mention the starving citizens who would gladly sell her or information about her to the Gray Elite for a few tokens. She doesn't know how to fight. She doesn't understand the gravity of this mission. She doesn't understand the finer elements that will be necessary in order to get in and out of Moorin without detection and without problem."

She felt her face burn with shame and embarrassment. Zander was right about those things, and though she knew it, his words stung like a sword through her chest.

Thalame scoffed. "I'm not sure If *I* have those things," he said, his words sharp. Zander started to speak, but Thalame cut him off. "And if you think you do, then you don't."

Zander grumbled something too low to hear.

"You said she did fine in Lenhala," came Niall's kind chime of a voice. "Moorin won't be much different."

"Except I don't know who to trust and who not to. In Lenhala, I had the advantage," said Zander.

Thalame mumbled something too low for her to hear. Niall's soft voice came after, but his words were lost to the blood gushing through her ears. She tiptoed closer to the door.

"...not well enough. She's nowhere near trained to survive a real fight," said Zander. "She will only slow us down or get herself killed. She's..." An exasperated sigh. "She needs to stay behind, where it's safe."

Raven heard the inflection on his tone, the half truth, the truth he wanted to tell them but couldn't. She touched the locket around her throat. The centrum, the core of Altair's Augur. Zander wanted her to stay behind and protect it, to keep it out of enemy reach, but he couldn't explain that to the others without telling them about the centrum. She and Zander had decided it would be better if no one else knew.

But she could leave it in the treehouse or bury it in the forest below.

Thalame let out a short sigh. "I know, mate. You're right on those accounts."

"But we can't just leave her here," Niall said, and Raven felt a surge of goodwill toward the tinker. "She will never speak to any of us again."

"She needs to go back to Silver Glen," said Zander. Firmly. "It's the safest place."

"That's why you wanted to go north," Niall said, at the same time as the thought passed through Raven's mind.

Her heart tumbled into her ankles. That was why Zander had been so adamant about going north; he wanted to send her back to Silver Glen.

Thalame made an argumentative sound.

"What?" asked Zander. "You don't think so?"

"Travel may not be the best thing for her right now," said Thalame. The silence thickened. "She's been fighting a fever since we got back from Lenhala."

Zander spat a curse. "Why did I not know about this sooner?"

"Because she asked me to keep quiet," said Thalame defensively. "I thought it'd go away on its own, but it hasn't." He dropped his voice. "A fever that lasts more than a week isn't a good sign; you know that. It's been three. She doesn't need to be traveling in this heat. It very well might do her in."

"But you've been training her?" Niall asked, and Raven could picture his face, one dark brow raised, his intelligent eyes searching Thalame for unspoken answers.

Thalame resigned a sigh. "Lightly. It's also how I've been monitoring her condition without her knowing. She gets defensive when I talk to her about it."

Silence fell between the boys.

"Fine," Zander said firmly, the final decision. "She stays in the treehouse for now. If she's ill, then she doesn't need to go on this mission."

No one disagreed, and Raven's lungs fell into her ankles beside her heart, yanking her breath with it.

"I'll leave it to you to break it to her, then," said Thalame.

Zander harrumphed.

The conversation ended, and before any of them could step out and see her, she tiptoed away, around the end of the hall, and darted away as quietly as she could. She didn't know what to think about first: that Thalame had told Zander about her fever, that they all wanted to leave her behind, or that she knew they were right.

She would only slow them down.

She was sick, untrained, and useless. Utterly useless.

A silent tear swelled at the corner of her eye, and with a blink, it ran down her cheek without her permission. She forced her chest calm, her breathing even, though it yearned to sob; if she started to cry, someone—everyone—would hear. It would be a scene. She couldn't handle that kind of humiliation and exposure.

The fever, the damn fever, burned like fire, and she broke out in a sweat. She walked past the hall to her bedroom. She couldn't face Ivy either. Not like this. Not until she got herself under control.

She stumbled down one of the secret ladders, her hands and feet shaking on the rungs, and half fell to the forest floor as her meager control broke. The first sob quaked through her chest, emitting a strangled cry from her throat.

They would leave her behind while they went to save the kingdom. They would leave her behind while they changed history, had an adventure, did the impossible, because she would be a hindrance.

Useless.

She meandered through the forest, away from the treehouse, and with no one to watch or listen, she let the tears fall. They rolled down her burning cheeks with vigor. Maybe the fever would burn her up, and then she wouldn't be in anyone's way. Zander could go save his precious princess and forget about her, the stupid, useless, simple girl that could do nothing and ruined everything.

A part of her hoped the princess would be dead before they got to her.

Another part of her knew how horrible of a thought it was.

Back in Silver Glen, Raven had a tree. She had carved her initials—RT—into its bark. It stood beyond the border, safe and unsafe, and had been a place where she could go without being found, without being chided for skipping chores, and just be. How many hours had she lounged in the tree's fork, daydreaming about sky cities and airships and all the adventure and romance and magic to be found in the sky?

Enough that her head had been without room for reality, it seemed. Strangely, Zander had been the only one to find her hiding place.

Raven wished she could run to that tree now and hide within its thick branches, imagine the world on the other side of the forest, and retain a fraction of the sense of wonder she'd felt when gazing at the horizon—of all the adventure she could imagine, there for the taking. Adventures just waiting to be had.

But there were no trees like that in this forest. She was far from Silver Glen, and she did not want to go back.

Raven walked and ran and ran and then walked. She didn't mind where she went, only that she moved. It helped, a little. She ran herself breathless and, when she could go no further, collapsed in a small clearing. The grassy, summer-baked earth barely gave under her knees. She had cried herself dry, but the trails on her cheeks felt fresh. The fever burned underneath her skin, pulsing with her heartbeat. Her vision blurred around the edges, each breath harder than the last.

She stayed a while on the forest floor, regaining her strength and breath. When she finally pushed herself to her feet, it felt as though she had been wrung out. A step—she lost her balance and leaned against a tree.

Sisters, she shouldn't have run so much. Everything hurt. She pushed sweaty hair out of her face and turned to go back to the treehouse. Sleep. She needed sleep. Her cot. Her room. Rest.

But...which way was the treehouse? She looked around the forest. The treehouse was at the thickest, oldest part of the forest. It wouldn't be too hard to find, right?

The fever pulsed, and she leaned against another tree. She closed her eyes, taking each breath as it came. All around, the night bugs and birds chirped and chittered. She willed her heart to slow, to calm; willed the fever to ease or just take her and be done with it.

It did none of those things.

Raven opened her eyes and looked up into the endless stars. Some glowed faintly blue, some yellow, some pink. Would those colors become more distinguishable if she were closer to them?

Her small reverie shattered with the sound of footsteps. Big, thunderous footsteps. Too big, too heavy, too wide a stride for a man. And then she heard the unnatural clicking of gears, the churning of belts and cogs, and the interval hissing of steam.

She froze and put her back flush against the tree. The footsteps came closer—to her left, on the other side of the tree.

Clomp, clomp, clomp.

It paused.

Raven held her breath and dared not move.

Pale red light flooded around the tree's trunk. It shone against the weeds and brush, on the stone and tree roots, throwing dangerous shadows. It was looking. Searching. *Hunting.*

The automaton took a step to the left, and she took a step to right—keeping the tree between them. It took a step; she took a step at the same time, hiding her footsteps within its. Soon, they had traded places. It took another step, and then another—away from her.

Raven dared peek around the tree. She saw the automaton's posterior, thick panels of steel, bronze, and iron. Its searching red eyes panned the forest, side to side. Its two arms ended in three prongs, made for grabbing. The thick chest resembled a barrel—a cage, she suspected. It moved further away from her, steam hissing from the shoulders. A second later, steam hissed from the hips.

Heart racing, fever pulsing, Raven let out a slow, steady breath. It hadn't seen her. She could already hear Zander's lecture of how dangerous the forest was, how she had recklessly thrown herself—and the centrum, by extension—into danger.

Raven started in the opposite direction of the automaton. She found a tall tree to climb and made it to the top easily. From the top, she spotted the thickest, tallest part of the forest with ease. That would be the treehouse. Raven climbed down and hopped to the forest floor. Before her knees straightened, pale red light flashed around her.

The light turned blood red.

"Do not resist," came the automaton's mechanical voice.

She didn't turn around. She didn't scream. She ran.

The automaton gave chase.

Raven dodged through the trees, around brushes, over tree roots, through weeds. Her breath became ragged quickly, her lungs heaved, her legs ached, the fever pulsed underneath a thick layer of sweat. Still, she ran.

Not fast enough.

The automaton closed in. Its large feet nimbly maneuvered over the forest floor, pushing weeds and bushes out of its way like they weren't there. Raven ran, ran, ran, but the fever blurred her senses. Unbalanced her.

She tripped. She fumbled along the forest floor, tree roots smacking into her arms and legs, and she fought to regain her unsure footing. She only made it a step

216

before thick metal hands clasped around her upper arms. The automaton yanked her backward, off her feet, and the gears clanked as its chest opened.

She did the only thing she could: scream.

She screamed as the automaton lifted her, as its chest cavity opened, as it pulled her inside. She screamed to let anyone hear her, to let anyone know she needed help. The doors of its chest closed, shutting her in near total darkness, muffling her screams. She beat her fists on the door, or what she thought was the door, but it did not open.

The automaton began to walk through the forest calmly, as though it hadn't just swallowed her.

Raven beat against the thing's chest until her arms fell limp against her sides. In her current state, it didn't take long. The automaton's chest became her personal oven; the fever burned worse than it had in days, burned with her exhaustion, her anxiety, her stress. Burned. Burned. Burned. It echoed off the metal insides of the automaton like sound.

She had room to sit, and she hugged her legs to her chest.

What would happen now? What would Ivy think when she never came to bed? What would they all think?

She'd messed up. Again. She only caused problems, and this time, she couldn't get herself out of it. Zander was right. If she were to go with them to Moorin, she would get them caught or worse.

Useless.

Why had she gone into the forest like that? She deserved whatever happened next.

She thought she'd cried all her tears, but as she sat there, a new wave pushed against her eyes. Before the first tear fell, a creak came from above her. Metal sliding against metal. A hiss—Raven felt something cool touch her skin, featherlight, like fog. Then she smelled it. Acidic and sweet. Sickly. She coughed and coughed and panicked as the strange odor coursed through her nose, down her throat, and into her lungs.

It pulled her down. She tried to fight it, but couldn't. The darkness came, and she went under.

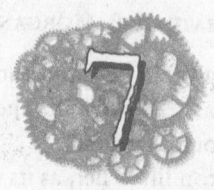

7

Raven woke to a thump and a crash, then stillness.

All around her, darkness and groaning gears. The automaton's insides clicked desperately, but with each hiss of steam, lost force. Her heart sped up as her mind woke, as the drug wore off, and the past several events returned to her. Captured. She'd been taken by an automaton.

Outside, she heard male voices, muffled and quiet. Her heart jumped—Zander had come before it was too late.

The two men continued to speak as the automaton groaned and creaked and hissed to silence. It had to be Zander and Thalame and Niall; they had wondered about her absence and come to find her.

Raven pressed her hands against the metal walls around her, willing her friends to stop talking and get her out faster. She didn't like this dark, cramped cage. She opened her mouth to scold them for dallying, but she stopped. Her heart fell into her stomach. What would they think of her after this? Zander's point about her being a hindrance had been proven—by her—and they would send her back to Silver Glen or lock her in one of the rooms in the Treehouse.

Something hard hit the automaton's head, and then metal creaked and groaned and slid, piece by piece. She had heard the sounds often enough when she'd meandered into the tinker shop of Silver Glen. They were taking the automaton apart.

"Niall?" Raven called. Her tongue slurred the word, making her acutely aware of how heavy and dry it was.

The tinkering stopped.

A male voice spoke, too low for her to hear the words or make out the speaker.

"Get me out!" Raven said. She gathered her strength and beat against the chest cavity, once, twice.

Silence came from the other side. The voices spoke lowly, and then something hit the chest cavity. Slowly, groaning and creaking, they wedged the doors open. Sunlight poured in, obnoxiously bright, and Raven shielded her eyes with her hand.

Two silhouettes stood over her.

Her eyes adjusted—but it was not Zander or Thalame or Niall.

She did not know the two men standing over her. They were tall and lean and had the dark hair and skin of Tinatun. They were looking down at her with a mixture of confusion and curiosity. One of them spoke to the other, his words lilted and quick, the syllables sharp. Tinatunian, she realized. She had only heard a few words of it from Niall.

The man speaking held a crowbar over his bare shoulders, sweat glistening on his dark skin. A talisman hung around his neck on a leather cord, a fishtail made of polished stone. Around his middle was a belt of tools that looked like something Niall would wear when scavenging. The second man wore a tattered vest; it hung open, and she saw the beginning of a dark tattoo on his chest. Both wore tattered and patched trousers.

The first man pointed the crowbar at Raven and spoke in Tinatunian. She shook her head, and he repeated himself, agitation on his words and on his face. He furled his brow at her and poked at her with his crowbar. "*Lin?*" He spat that word several times, *lin, lin, lin*. He jabbed at her with the crowbar.

She swatted the end away from her and growled, "I don't understand!"

The man in the vest twisted his head to the side and shouted, "Nia!"

Someone shouted back, a female by the sound, and the two men stepped aside as a third person approached. A woman with several years on Raven's seventeen stopped in front of her. She had the same dark skin as the men, and her hair had been cut short. Tattoos ran up and down both muscular arms.

The man with the crowbar said something else to the woman, the language quick and impossible to understand.

The woman nodded, and then gave a broad, welcoming smile to Raven. "Ah," she said. "We caught one with a catch of its own."

Raven's anxiety melted at the sound of her own tongue, even as curved as the woman's accent was.

The woman held her hand down to Raven. Her nails were short, filed not bitten, and a tattoo encircled her wrist, twining vines with small lotus flowers. Raven gingerly set her hand into the stranger's. The woman hoisted Raven to her feet and out of the automaton's chest.

The two men descended on the automaton, yanking it apart one panel at a time—not like Niall did, carefully and precisely with quick fingers.

Raven glanced around. The sun was shining, meaning she had been in the automaton's chest all night and into the morning. She felt it too. Stiff back, aching legs, pinched shoulders. The forest didn't look familiar, but it didn't look strange. Still the same forest. Hammel Forest stretched over most of Rhynwier; she'd seen that much on Niall's maps.

"Nia," said the woman, drawing Raven's attention.

"I'm sorry?" Raven said.

"Name. I am Nia."

"Oh!" Raven fumbled slightly with the woman's accent. The words were tilted and short. "My name is Raven."

The two men dissected the automaton with easy efficiency. They had taken the internal workings apart, scraping the gold, silver, brass, and steel. They piled the parts into a wooden cart. The Dwellers had mentioned automatons found in the woods, strung apart and stripped—by scavengers. These people must be some of those scavengers.

"Thank you," Raven said to Nia.

Nia nodded, then said something quick to the men. One of them spat something back.

Nia half laughed. "Good thing we came along," said Nia to Raven. "This one would have taken you somewhere far, far worse. This one is called a Retriever. They go out, find prey, and take it back to the Gray Elite hold in the west. The gas—" Nia pointed to the top of the chest cavity, to a small nozzle—"knocks the prey out cold."

They stood a moment in silence as the two men pulled bits and pieces from the automaton.

"Where are we?" Raven finally asked.

"We're about a day northeast of Gilini," answered Nia.

"And...that is where?" Raven asked, feeling foolish.

Nia blinked and looked at her with pity and humor. She said something in Tinatunian, then said to Raven, "Not the best with direction, eh? You one of those sheltered girls?"

Raven crossed her arms. The way Nia said *sheltered*, it felt like an insult. "I suppose I am."

"Gilini is in Tinatun," Nia explained. "We are about a day and a half north of the coast."

The blood drained from Raven's face. "That's far from where I started," she said quietly.

"Where did you start?"

Raven opened her mouth to answer, but then realized she didn't know where the treehouse was or even what it was close to. From the maps she had seen, she knew it to be somewhere in the middle of the eastern forest. But how to explain that? The Dwellers were supposed to be a secret. And now she was a day's journey from Tinatun? Her skin prickled. How long had she been inside the automaton's stomach knocked out by its gas? The automaton must have been running since her capture. It terrified her to think that a machine could move that fast. Then again, the Dwellers had the Hellcat which had taken them from Lenhala to Oun in a fraction of the time it would have taken on foot. Could automatons travel that fast?

"Not want to answer, then?" asked Nia, a friendly smile on her sun-warmed face.

Raven shook her head. "I don't have an answer. I don't know where I started. I was..." *Running through the forest like a fool.* "I was lost when it found me."

Nia's confusion and slight humor melted together into pity, and Raven looked away. She was smoothing the wrinkles in her blouse—or trying to—when a thought bloomed in her mind. A streak of hope in an otherwise bleak situation. A chance.

Feigning innocence, Raven hung one hand on her elbow, and asked, "How far is Gilini from Wayward Point?"

One of Nia's brows rose. "Wayward Point?" She said the name like a place she knew, and the hope in Raven's chest swelled.

Nia turned her head and said something to the other men, who were tossing the last bits of the Retriever into the cart. Raven heard what might have been Wayward Point pass her lips, but Nia spoke too quickly. The two men stopped working, both looking at Raven. Sweat dripped down their faces, shimmered on their brows and shoulders and cheekbones. Both wore varying expressions of interest.

Nia asked a question, and both men gave an affirmative answer.

Nia looked back at Raven, smiled, and said, "Good news, Raven, you can ride with us to Gilini. We'll get you to Wayward Point. But not for free."

Raven's heart sagged.

"You'll have to work for your passage."

"Okay," Raven said. Though she knew little about automatons, she knew about scavenging. She had done it plenty at Silver Glen, though the bounty had never been very good.

What, exactly, she would do in Wayward Point, she didn't know. Maybe she could use that blasted wooden coin or find someone who knew the Dwellers; Thalame said he knew people, that someone owed him a favor. Or the Crusaders might help them get over the border. She had options, she realized, and a dangerous bloom of hope-lined anxiety warmed her chest.

Raven joined the three strangers; they took turns pushing the cart over the forest floor, though Raven moved it much slower. The two men only spoke Tinatunian, and Nia didn't translate, so Raven spent much of the trek in the dark on their conversation.

Not that she minded. It saved her from having to be part of it.

They guided the cart to the bank of a wide, gentle river. Pockets of bugs swarmed over the still surface; fish swam underneath; and a mad cacophony of bugs chirped and chittered from the overgrown bushes along the banks. Trees grew wild on either side, looming over the water, some nearly halfway over the river. The muddy blue-green river ran as far as Raven could see either way, winding out of sight.

She tried to recall Niall's maps. There had been a river that ran down the southeastern side of Rhynwier, but she couldn't think of its name. Only that it passed through the eastern edge of Tinatun and ended in the ocean. The men unloaded the cart into a ramshackle skiff tied off on a stump. Raven helped Nia loosen the strange knot, and then—cargo loaded and people aboard—they were off down the river, toward the coast. The river naturally flowed south, Nia explained, and as long as they weren't in any hurry, they would go with the river.

Raven held her face into the breeze, ablaze with river mist and birdsong and the ripe scents of the river, as the two men and Nia chatted in Tinatunian. The two men lounged on the sides, looking like they had no place they'd rather be.

Had the Dwellers discovered her missing? Would they be worried? Relieved? Would Zander be glad that he didn't have to tell her that she had to stay behind?

A spiteful thought sprang. *She* had left *them* behind.

Not that she could find her way back to the Treehouse. She might as well go on to Wayward Point. Odds were, someone there knew the Dwellers. Or maybe she could take Conrad the Thief up on his offer of something new. She still had the wooden coin.

Raven had kept up the habit of keeping three things on her person at all times: her mother's locket, which held the centrum; her ebony-handled dagger; and the thief's wooden coin to freedom. She took a deep breath of the muggy river air, muddy and fishy and dank. A fresh start. Those words reverberated like a cold heartbeat, welcoming but dreadful.

She banished the worries of tomorrow. She would worry about what she would do when she got to Wayward Point. Until then, there was nothing she could do unless she planned to swim upriver until the forest looked familiar. Right now, sitting in the scavengers' boat, she had something of a plan. Get to Wayward Point, to the Destiny Show, and present her coin and see what happened. Conrad said he had friends, and she could only hope that he did.

R aven and her three new companions floated downriver toward the river city of Gilini. The two men rattled away in their tongue, and Nia offered no translation. Did everyone speak Tinatunian in Gilini? In Wayward Point? She hadn't thought of that. What if she got to Wayward Point and no one understood her?

Nia spoke to her occasionally, her grammar imperfect and her accent lilted with Tinatun's sharp syllables and quickness. She asked simple questions: where Raven had come from, how she had ended up in the forest, if she had done anything to upset the automaton.

Raven kept her answers simple. She had come from a village to the north; she had been wandering a while; she had been separated from her friends. Her non-answers caused the crease between Nia's brows to deepen.

One of the men said something, pointing to Raven, speaking to Nia. His black eyes glittered in the sunlight, his skin wrinkled from squinting and laughing.

"He wants to know why the automaton had you," said Nia flatly. "Retrievers go after people, he says, but not just anyone."

Fugitives, was what she didn't add. The two men were looking at her like they knew why, like they thought her a criminal, and Nia gazed at her with the same interest. Raven swallowed, unsure of what story to feed them, of what would appease them and not land her in trouble.

The second man spat a question at her, frowning.

"You are a magician?" Nia translated.

"No," Raven said quickly, too quickly, even though truthfully.

The men narrowed their eyes at her. They didn't believe her. Nia's steady, curious gaze never changed.

"I'm not a magician," Raven said, urging Nia to believe her. "If I were, I wouldn't have let that automaton get me. I would have blasted it to bits or something."

Nia gave a halfhearted smile.

One man said something to Nia, and she spoke back, her words low and threatening, and even though Raven couldn't understand, she knew they spoke about her. Nia exchanged a glance with the man, and he shied away. Nia obviously commanded the scavenging team.

"Take me to Wayward Point," Raven said to Nia. "Please. After that, I will be out of your hair forever."

Nia nodded, though she didn't speak.

✿

They crossed the border between Rhynwier and Tinatun without a fuss. Gilini came into view a little before nightfall. It was a port city of mismatched wooden planks, shanties, and shacks. The forest grew around its edges, giving the impression that the weeds and the people were in a constant state of battle for dominance. Shacks had been built in the trees, accessible by rope ladders and spiraling stairs bound by twine. Lanterns hung from storefronts, porches, and trees. It gave the village an eerie glow, like stars had fallen and landed haphazardly in the forest.

It reminded Raven of the treehouse, and she felt a pang in her chest.

The two men guided their skiff into the rickety docks that spanned the river side of Gilini. They spent the next hour haggling over automaton parts. Golden piks were exchanged, the currency of Tinatun. A pik was about the size of a Gray Elite token, stamped with the image of the crescent-shaped kingdom.

They stayed at an inn that smelled of damp wood and sweat, and Raven had barely fallen asleep when Nia shook her awake to leave. The first rays of dawn had barely streaked the inky sky in pale blues and pinks. She followed Nia back to the market, which bustled as it had the night before. Raven didn't ask questions as Nia handed her a plate of cooked fish and boiled roots. She ate it, though it tasted like muddy water. Food was food, and these people had bought it for her and had offered to take her to Wayward Point.

And she was grateful.

With the sun teetering over the edge of the world, they started back downriver. According to Nia, Gilini was a stepping stone, the first city on the river past the border, whereas Wayward Point was the last city on the river before the river emptied into the Linila Sea.

The Linila Sea, thought Raven. One of her favorite stories had taken place over the Linila Sea, a young stowaway named Leon Stark boarded a pirate ship by mistake. His adventure took him to see mermaids, sea monsters, cloud dragons, and a pirate lord. Raven kept her eyes on the river as it widened, as the trees changed from forest to jungle with lush ferns and fronds as long as their boat.

The change happened gradually. The dirt became light and sandy, the trees thinner, the leaves fronds, and the air stickier and wetter. The farther south they drifted, the stickier the air and the sweeter the smells, like salt and adventure.

Their skiff passed a dozen boats before midday, some heading south, some paddling upriver with giant wooden wheels painted an assortment of colors and a pillar of steam vanishing into the sky. Several boats chimed with laughter and song, picked lutes and swift drums.

Raven leaned forward to spy a school of tiny fish as they darted underneath the boat. They moved like glinting daggers, and the ease with which they moved as one marveled her. As she watched them pass, she leaned a little farther forward, and her locket shifted under her blouse.

One of the men said something, but she had gotten used to not understanding. She paid it little mind. The fish swam away and out of sight. She leaned back into the boat and jumped at the sudden proximity of one of the men. He had crouched forward while she had been looking at the fish. His dark eyes were focused on her neck—on the locket.

Her heart thudded in her chest.

The man's warm fingers brushed her throat; he started to pull on the locket's golden chain. As he started to lift it, he spoke, but Raven only stared at him, panic hot and fluid under her skin.

She didn't want him to see it, to touch it. Not her locket. Not her mother's locket. Not the centrum. It was *hers*.

Before he could form a grip on the chain, his face contorted in pain, and he wrenched his hand away, dropping the locket as if burned. The locket fell back against her blouse, and through the fabric, it was hot to the touch. She folded her fingers around her locket, and already, the heat faded. She tucked it back underneath her blouse where he couldn't see it.

The man was staring at her, trailing his fingers in the water—the fingers that had touched the locket. The other man spoke lowly, and the man who'd tried to take the locket spoke back without taking his eyes off Raven. His words were angry and disgusted—but his eyes were afraid.

In the moment between heartbeats, she felt a burning desire to make them all afraid, to make them see that she was no fool, but that desire faded as quickly as it had appeared.

Had the man been about to demand payment for their help? Raven refused to part with her mother's locket or the centrum inside it. She would rather swim to Wayward Point.

The man said something else, and she thought she heard Minerva's name—Goddess of the Sea and Wind—cross his lips. Raven looked to Nia for explanation, but the woman gave none. She was looking at Raven with a blank stare.

Raven steeled herself. She would have to be more careful around them. No more daydreaming. No more looking away. She wouldn't let them take it.

9

Wayward Point came into view as the sun began its downward descent. It looked a lot like Gilini and the smaller villages they had passed, with lopsided wooden shacks and ramshackle structures, all cobbled together with wooden planks, driftwood, rusting iron, and odd shaped metal sheets. The river had widened considerably, twice what it had been when she first boarded the skiff. Birds she had never heard before sang, cawed, and chirped; bugs she hadn't seen flew past in blurs of green, blue, and yellow.

They crossed into the outskirts, and docks lined both sides of the river. Bridges arched over the river, some held up with wooden poles, others with steel, and one with what looked like pink stone. As their skiff passed underneath, Raven saw that the pink stone was highly textured, almost like coral.

The sounds of the city hit them, the chattering of thousands of people—words she knew and words she didn't—singing, shouting, laughing; music made of drums, strings, and flutes; and vendors shouting prices in piks, tokens, and marks. It smelled like dead fish and the unmistakable stench of unwashed bodies.

They docked, tied off the skiff, and stepped onto the lopsided wooden dock. Raven spotted several men and women in similar armor. They wore crossbows on their backs and short swords at their sides. A few had pistols, but not all. They regarded the ships and the people lingering on the docks with matching looks of weary disdain. Raven followed Nia up a sandy stretch of beach and into the town.

Nia led the way through the busy docks. Men, women, and children worked, loading ships, unloading ships, scrubbing decks, hauling barrels and crates this way and that, shouting out wares and different fish and all manner of buyable things. She caught bits of her own tongue mixed with Tinatunian, and it created a strange harmony. They passed through a street where fisherman lined both sides, selling fish, gutting fish, selling parts of fish; the smell of fish and salt water made Raven want to hold her breath.

The gilded evening began to sink into the shadows of twilight as they started over the coral-looking bridge, the widest and grandest of the bridges. Lanterns hung from the ceiling, their light dim but enough to illuminate the timbers of the bridge and the faces of strangers.

In the center of the bridge, Raven glanced south. Through the palms and scraggy brush and sandy city that leaned over the river, the twilight gilded the Linila Sea. Raven's heart skipped a beat. It went on forever, as if the rest of the world were made of water.

Nia didn't pause, and Raven jogged a few steps to catch up to her. The streets on the other side of the bridge were only slightly more organized. They came to a vast market square of hundreds of stalls, twice as many people, and more things than

226

Raven had ever seen. She took in as much of it as she could in passing. She saw food, sweets, drinks, tools of all metal and size, baskets in every shape and weave, bolts of fabric, stacks of books—more than one person could ever want or need.

People meandered through the market in all manner of clothing, mismatched finery from all three kingdoms, silk and canvas, velvet and burlap, leather and cotton. She spotted the gray and yellow trousers of the Gray Elite uniform, and several gray coats—stolen Gray Elite uniforms. She spotted armor made to mimic automatons and some pieces that looked to have once been pieces of automatons. One man wore a Goliath's head as a helmet.

Everywhere she looked, she found a dozen things to see.

By the time they reached the other end of the market, the lanterns had become the main source of light. The sun had gone down, the moon had risen, and millions of stars spotted the sky, with the odd dark cloud passing by.

The two men started to talk to one another, lowly, cautiously.

They passed a building with scorch marks, the scars of a fire. The torches on either side of its door were hanging loosely. A small shake, and they would tumble. The wooden shack wouldn't stand a chance.

Jokingly, Raven asked Nia, "How many times has this place burned?"

"Several," Nia answered without pause.

Raven's brows rose.

Nia shrugged. "It is not a big deal when it burns. People do like they always do. They rebuild. The market used to be over there, but the last time it burned, they decided to build it over here. The old say it used to be by the beach, but a storm washed it away, so it moved inland."

Raven nodded. It made sense, though the idea of Wayward Point burning to the ground and being rebuilt left a strange taste in her mouth.

They left the crowded, bustling market behind and walked into a calmer side of Wayward Point. Stalls became shops and stores and smiths. They passed tavern after tavern, and even a place Raven suspected was a brothel. Still, they walked. She kept her eyes open for a white brick building, the Destiny Show, as Conrad had told her. She felt the wooden coin in her pocket, though she didn't reach for it. She didn't want the men to see it or think it valuable.

They came to a side of town with streets of cobblestone. The buildings were older and made of stone and wood. She spotted fewer and fewer scorch marks. The streets had no names, no signs, and they zigzagged and crisscrossed and ended abruptly, as though the buildings had been built wherever their owners wished. It left Raven feeling lost and confused; the darkness didn't help. This side of town had fewer torches too.

Finally, as a yawn worked its way up Raven's throat, they stopped at a large building of pale yellow stone. It took up half the block and held few windows, all of which were shuttered. The two men walked to the front door, illuminated by a lantern on either side, one of brass and one of iron. Nia stood beside Raven.

The shirtless man knocked. A grunt, and then a deep male voice replied in Tinatunian. The shirtless man opened the door. He walked in, the second man followed, and Nia set a hand on Raven's shoulder and guided her inside.

The room they entered had a single lantern hanging from the ceiling. The floor, the walls, the ceiling were stone. A circular rug adorned the floor, a swirl of red and yellow and white. A wooden counter stood at the far end of the room, and a barrel-chested man stood behind it. He leered over the counter on one elbow.

The shirtless man spoke to the big man but gestured to Raven.

Her skin pricked. The barrel-chested man's black eyes looked to her, first meeting her eyes and then running over her body with a fluid, cold indifference. She did not like the man; he looked at her like a butcher looked at meat.

Without looking at her, the barrel-chested man spoke to the two men. It took a moment to recognize, but the two men were bartering. But for what? Passage? Room and board?

Raven shifted on her feet, and she felt Nia's sure grip fasten around her elbow. Behind them, a large man stepped in front of the doorway. Blocking the exit. He leaned lazily against the wall beside the door, his wide face blank, his dark hair tied behind his head. Tattoos lined both hands, and scars dotted his knuckles.

Her gut twisted. *Wrong*, said something inside her. Wrong, like the silence of the forest when the birds go quiet.

A clanking brought her attention back to the counter, to the two men. A bag of coins had been dropped. The two men gathered and counted out the coins quicker than Raven could, but she saw a mixture of golden piks, silver tokens, and copper marks. A mixed currency for a city of mixed culture.

The man behind the counter looked at the two men, then at Raven.

Get out.

Raven tried to pull her arm free of Nia's grip, but the woman held on tight. The two men gathered the coins. Talking low, they started toward the door without a glance at Raven. Nia released her, speaking low to the two men, and started to follow them out. Raven felt a bruise forming from where Nia had gripped her.

She took a step toward the door, to get out of this place, but the man leaning by the door shoved her back.

"Hey!" Raven spat at him. "I'm with them. Let me out."

"No," he said, his voice deep, his accent rough.

"Excuse me?" Raven started, but the man behind the counter spoke up.

"You stay here," he said, his accent less rough but tilted. His appraising eyes met hers.

She felt relief that he spoke her tongue, but it did little against the coiling dread in her stomach. "What? No, I have somewhere else I need to be." She opened her mouth to tell him about the Destiny Show, but he held up a hand—his hand roughly the size of her head.

Then, the man stood.

Raven paled. She thought he had been standing. He was a tower of a man in height and width. Her words grumbled in her throat and fell silent.

"You stay here. You live here now," he said.

The man standing by the door shoved her another step forward, and she shot him a glare over her shoulder.

The man behind the counter grabbed her arm and yanked her against the counter. "You belong to me now."

Her gut twisted and squirmed at his words, their meaning, and the sound they made as they left his lips—a warning, a threat, something dreadful.

The man pulled her through a door behind the counter. It had blended in so well with the darkness, she hadn't seen it. He pulled her down a hallway lined with iron-cage doors—*cells*—each no bigger than a cot and narrow window. Most held people—sad, pitiful people.

He threw Raven into a cell near the end of the hall. She stumbled to the stone floor, and not a heartbeat later, the door slammed shut. A heavy click followed. Raven fumbled to her feet and turned in time to see the man standing on the other side, holding an iron key, one of a dozen on a heavy keyring.

"No," Raven gasped. She stumbled forward to the bars, folding her shaking fingers around them. "Please, there's been a mistake. I—I need to get out, I have people I need to see."

"Who?" he asked.

Her words froze; she knew no names. Stupidly, she said, "The Crusaders."

He laughed, a single burst of wind. "No mistake. You belong to me. Paid for in full."

She paled as realization hit her. The bag of coins. It had been payment. For her. Nia had *sold* her.

A cold thought went through her: how long had they planned on selling her?

From the start, said a little voice. *You should have known better,* said another voice that sounded like Zander's. She could see his scowl at the mess she had gotten herself in, hear the exasperation in his voice.

"You stay here until someone buys you." The man crossed his thick arms and looked her up and down. "It won't take too long. Pretty young things go fast." He returned to the other room, leaving her in her cell.

She stood there, hands clutching the iron bars, for what felt like a long time. The world went in and out of focus. A dream. It had to be a dream. A nightmare.

A nightmare she'd brought onto herself.

Raven stood at the door until her legs gave out. She collapsed to the stone floor, her hands sliding down the bars.

A single lantern hung in the hallway. The flickering light striped her cell with light and darkness.

She had been sold. And she would be sold again.

Her father's voice rang in her head, fresh from the repetition, his warnings of what happened to the people the automatons found and took back to the Gray Elite. The lucky ones became slaves. He never said what happened to the unlucky ones.

She had a feeling she was going to find out, and sooner rather than later.

In the quiet of the cell, the breathing of her fellow captives grew louder. Distant and muffled chatter filtered in through the narrow, barred window. Laughter. Music. Singing.

Raven pulled herself onto the cot, nothing more than taut canvas stretched over a wooden frame. She had never felt more alone, more helpless, more useless. No one knew where she had gone. No one knew where to look.

No one would be looking for her.

She lowered her head into her hands. What had she gotten herself into?

Thalame had seen a lot in nineteen years, more than a nineteen-year-old boy should. He stood by the window in his room in the treehouse, fingering his favorite dagger. He didn't have a need for it, but the leather grip was familiar, worn by his hand, and it was that familiarity that he craved.

From his window, the forest stretched on forever. It didn't go forever; he knew that. Eventually it hit the ocean, but the wilderness between the forest and the ocean was a nightmare and a half to cross. He'd only attempted it once and swore to the Sisters he'd never do it again.

He heard footsteps on the stairs, and as he turned, Zander stalked past the doorway, past his own bedroom, and to the lounge at the end of the hall. Grumbling too. Not a good sign.

Thalame sheathed his knife and meandered down the hall to where Zander stood in the lounge. He stood at the window, hands clutching the bark-covered sill, his shoulders hunched. Even without touching him, Thalame could sense Zander's unease, the turmoil, the panic.

"Anything?" Thalame asked anyway, leaning against the doorway.

Zander didn't answer. He hung his head and let out a quick sigh.

Thalame felt his own unease rise—that tiny sliver of hope quickly diminished—but he dispelled the unease. He had always been good at casting away his own emotions. Like stones, they sank to the bottom.

Zander heaved a breath and collapsed to the floor, back against the wall. He had dressed in dark clothes, armed and ready for a fight, and he nearly vanished in the shadows. Thalame wondered if any of those shadows were his own.

"I couldn't find her," Zander said quietly.

Thalame glanced out the window, at the endless treetops.

Zander buried his hands in his hair, shaking slightly. He looked a mess, unshaven, hair tangled and unwashed, bags under his eyes. Even the blue of his eyes seemed to have faded into a pale blue-gray. Maybe it was a trick of the dark.

Raven had been at the meeting, had been irritated with Zander's decision to leave her out of the mission, had stormed out, and then vanished. Not even Ivy knew where she had gone. The Dwellers had scoured the woods for the past few days, searching farther and farther out.

But Raven had vanished.

Thalame knew what he wanted to ask, to suggest. But he kept his dark thoughts to himself. "What now?" he asked instead.

Zander let out a woeful sound, a sigh, a whine, a plea. He gazed at the ceiling, the intertwined branches and leaves. "We move forward with the plan," he said, his voice stony.

Thalame didn't argue but added in a quiet voice, "You sure, mate?"

Zander closed his eyes and stood—wobbled but stood. He hung onto the window for support. He nodded once. He met Thalame's gaze, his eyes hard. "Yes. We have one chance. We will take it. Regardless of this, we have a job to do."

Zander started back toward his room. He brushed past Thalame, and then collapsed onto his cot, daggers and boots included. Thalame lingered in the doorway, waiting, hoping like a fool for a commotion to start downstairs, to signal that Raven had come back or that she had been found.

It didn't.

"Even if we're gone," Zander said, muffled by the pillow, "the others will keep looking."

Thalame nodded, though he kept his thoughts to himself.

Zander's breathing evened, his curled fists relaxed, and Thalame silently made his way into the room. He laid his hand on his friend's back, soothing the worry, easing the panic, and trying to give him a peaceful night's rest. He would need it for the journey ahead of them.

Thalame made his way back toward his room. A shadow stood at the end of the hall. It was Ivy; the moonlight glinted off her blonde hair, turning the outline silver. Thalame walked past his room and stopped a step from her.

"Anything?" she whispered.

Thalame shook his head.

"Shit," Ivy groaned. She rubbed her face. Thalame had always liked the sound of curses on her delicate mouth. "What are we going to do?"

"Keep looking," Thalame said.

Ivy rolled her eyes. She looked exhausted. Like Zander, she had been searching for Raven nearly nonstop. She had scouts with their ears to the ground, and she had pulled the strings of her spies tight. If something happened to Raven elsewhere, their spies would carry the news. Ivy knew that. Zander knew that. They all knew that, which made the prolonged silence all the more frightening.

"Thalame, if the Gray Elite had her, we would have heard about it," Ivy whispered fearfully.

"I know, mate."

"I'm scared." Her whisper quivered.

He stepped closer.

"I'm scared I'll find her at the bottom of some ravine or half-eaten by something or floating in a lake—"

"Stop." Thalame set his hands on her bare shoulders. He stole away her fear and panic in less than a heartbeat. In a slow breath, it felt as if it had never been there to begin with. Ivy had always been easy to calm. "We'll find her."

Ivy didn't argue or agree. She shut her eyes and sighed into her hands.

"You need rest." Thalame guided Ivy toward her room, the room she had briefly shared with Raven.

With Ivy tucked away for the night and Zander lightly snoring, Thalame returned to the window in his room. The forest stretched on forever, but nothing about it had changed since he'd been gone. Was Raven still out there somewhere? Did she even want to come back? Maybe she'd taken her chance to give them the finger and escape—he knew the feeling all too well.

They would find her. He knew they would; he just didn't know when or how. The sense of such things had come with his magic. He wouldn't call it premonition, but more of an intuition. He'd never told anyone about it, mostly because he didn't know how to. But he knew Raven was out there, somewhere, and likely alive.

He just didn't know how the hell to explain it to anyone else. So he didn't.

Raven woke to the sound of the hallway door opening. She didn't move from the cot. Water and a pitiful ration of stale bread had been passed to the prisoners that morning, sating her hunger a little above starvation.

Two sets of footsteps sounded on the stone floor. They paused. They started. They paused again. "No, no," said a male voice.

Raven's chest squeezed at being able to understand him.

"None of these will do. I need strong young men. These *yenti* wouldn't last a day."

She had heard that word several times from the people who'd walked by. She didn't know its exact meaning, only that it was an insult. By the way the man spoke, she guessed that Tinatunian wasn't his native tongue. *Yenti* didn't roll as sweetly off his tongue as it did others.

"May I interest you in my latest purchase?" came the deep, slithering voice of the man who had bought her—the slaver.

The two footsteps continued down the hall and stopped in front of Raven's cell. A man appeared on the other side of the bars, his skin lighter beige, tanned by the sun. Gray streaked his brown hair. "I asked for young, capable men," said the man, narrowing his eyes at Raven. "Not whores."

The slaver chuckled. "Whores always have their purpose," he said, and Raven's skin went clammy and cold. "This one came in two days ago. Fresh."

Two days? Raven blinked. The man came into better focus. He had wrinkles around his eyes and his mouth. The slaver stood to his side, two heads taller.

Had she been in his cell that long? She didn't know; time ran together. It slurred. Her fever came and went, and she found that if she thought about nothing at all, the fever didn't bother her so badly. But the notion of being bought as a whore agitated it, and she felt the burning course underneath her skin worse than it had in days.

The potential buyer sighed, then brought his attention back to Raven. She met his gaze with her own. If he bought her, she wouldn't have to sit in the cell anymore. She might be able to find a way out of here, away from him, and to the Destiny Show. If it even existed. For all she knew, this was the Destiny Show, and that thief had planned to sell her too.

Or it might be another hell entirely.

The man leaned closer to the bars. Raven refused to look away.

"I suppose she would make a nice gift to my son," said the potential buyer as if he had a thousand other things he could buy. "How much?"

"One hundred piks," said the slaver.

The man laughed. "For this skinny rat? I'll give you seventy."

"Ninety."

"Seventy-five."

The slaver frowned. "Eighty, and she's yours."

The man nodded. "Eighty."

And the deal was made. Sold, just like that, for eighty piks.

The two men retreated down the hall to the main room, their voices low. Sometime later—how much later Raven didn't know—the slaver returned with his keyring in hand. He unlocked Raven's door—wearing the face of a man eighty piks richer—and hauled Raven to her feet. He pulled her along the hallway a second time and back into the main room where the buyer stood.

A pile of coins sat on the counter. Piks. Her payment.

"Easy on the goods," snapped the man she now belonged to. He swatted the slaver's hand from her arm and then inspected the damage. Her owner—she cringed to think of him that way—led her by the arm to the door, his grip not any gentler than the slaver's.

The sunlight blinded her, bright and unforgiving, as if the sun were closer to Tinatun than anywhere else she had ever been. It might have been. It would explain the heat.

"Please," Raven begged once her eyes adjusted.

The man led her down the street, away from the market, away from the slaver's shop.

"There's been a mistake."

The man paid her no mind. She tugged on her arm, and he tugged her a step forward. "Keep your voice down," he commanded.

Raven tried to dig her heels in, but the cobblestone gave no resistance. "No! Let me go!"

No one on the street paid mind. A few quick stares, and then their gazes averted.

They took a few more steps, and then the man yanked her down a side street, narrower and less crowded. He grabbed her by the wrists and slammed her back against the stone wall. "No one is going to help you," he sneered. "Let me inform you how it works here. You are nothing. The Gray Elite aren't coming to save you. And I suggest, for your own benefit, to behave if you plan on eating for the next week."

Panic and rage pulsed underneath her skin. Tears pushed against her eyes.

"None of that," he said, his voice softer but no less comforting. His grip tightened on her arm, and he pulled her down the side street and onto another.

This side of Wayward Point felt subdued. People lounged in wide doorways, on porches, on benches. The flitting of music came and went: a harmonica, a guitar, winds that she couldn't name, strings she'd never heard before. It was beautiful; it was horrible. The buildings were made of stone, but none white.

Knowing her luck, the Destiny Show didn't exist.

Clouds were gathering overhead, shadowing the sky in grays and light blue. Somewhere in the distance, thunder rolled, low and lazy. The city went on as if nothing happened, as if she weren't walking to her life as a slave, as if she hadn't just been sold like a fish at market. No one met her eye either.

Like she truly didn't exist.

Like she was less than a person.

None of it seemed real. How could it?

She tried not to think about what would happen once this man—her owner—got to wherever he was taking her. She tried not to recount all of her father's warnings. Instead, she looked at the clouds, at the sky, at the sliver where blue met blue, where the world went on forever.

Finally, they came to a dark building on the edge of the old side of town. While mostly wooden, it had a stone foundation and several stone walls. It looked to have once been several buildings that had grown together like trees, growing upward rather than outward. Scorch marks licked along the stone foundation. Several wooden panels had been replaced recently, and several more needed to be.

Two men lounged outside a wide wooden door. As they approached, she realized that one of the men was a woman, a woman with shoulders made for crushing. She sat like a man and spoke like one, though her voice carried a feminine lilt.

Her *owner*—she cringed—spoke in Tinatunian to the two guarding the door. They snapped to attention. They nodded toward him, and the man swung forward to open the door. Raven had no choice but to follow the man through. The sudden darkness blinded her. The man pulled her forward, across what sounded like a stone floor. Distantly, she heard a roar of voices, cheering and shouting.

Her heart squeezed at the sound. Where had she been taken?

Her eyes adjusted, but she had but a moment to take in her surroundings: stone floor, stone walls, a single lantern on the ceiling, unlit. The man pulled her down a hallway wide enough for two. The cheering grew louder. They turned down a hall, and he pulled her down a staircase. The cheering grew quieter. He pulled her into a hallway—her heart sank—lined with cells. Half iron bars, half wooden panel.

Three lanterns hung from the ceiling, though only one was lit. He pushed her into one of the cells. It was twice as large as her previous one, with a bed, a table with an unlit candle, and a narrow barred window. Dulled sunlight streamed inside, catching the dust motes. The walls were stone; the ceiling, wood.

Thunder rumbled closer than it had been.

"This is your new home." The man pushed Raven a step further into the room and closed the door after her. He locked it. "You may call me Mr. Barrow."

"What?" she gasped. She turned to face him, her body feeling numb, disbelief like poison, the fever a drug.

"Your new home," Barrow repeated.

"What about your son?" Her words fell out of her mouth.

Barrow shrugged. "I haven't seen my son in ten months," he said as if it didn't matter. "He's out on the water most of the year. I'm lucky if I see him once a year. It suits me. The boy's a scumbag out for gold, just like his mother."

Her shoulders quaked, her knees gave out, and she fell back onto the bed. Softer than the cot. Not that it mattered.

"Why am I here?" she asked. Her knees twitched together.

He noticed and scoffed. "You think I bought you as a whore? I've got prettier women than you at home."

She wanted to laugh. She had never been more grateful to have a plain face.

Barrow leaned against the door, his face smug. "I've got something better in mind for you."

She swallowed, and a nervous twist stole whatever words she'd had on her tongue. "What?" she asked, though it came out as a whisper.

"You are going to win me back those eighty piks," he said, smirking.

"Win?" she repeated.

He laughed. "You think I don't know who you are?" he asked, narrowing his eyes.

She stared back at him blankly.

His smirk turned malicious. "I was in Lenhala when you tried to murder the general. Took me a week to get out. Your little face covered every bulletin board."

Oh. The blood drained from her face. Of all the horrible things she had thought about happening to her in the past few hours, being recognized hadn't been one of them.

"You're a wanted girl, you know," he said. "The bounty the Gray Elite put on your head is four times what I paid for you. That fool didn't know who you were. I'd love to see his face when he finds out." He laughed and slapped his hand against his side. "Maybe I'll invite him to the match."

"The match?" she managed to choke out.

He leaned against the bars of the door. "Yeah, the match. This is the *Chjelhu Tal*, the Kill Ring, little girl. Where anyone with guts comes to beat their opponent to a bloody pulp. Last one standing wins. Folks bet on the one they think will win. Winner gets half the coin. Since I own the place, I get the other half."

"You're going to let some pirate beat me into a bloody pulp for money?" she said, the words sounding ridiculous and dangerous. The fever pricked along her skin, behind her eyes, pulling at her mind.

"And when word spreads that I have the assassin who nearly killed General Deacon and threw the capital into chaos, these fools will pay anything to see you in action," he said, his words slithering, coiling around her throat, dampening her breath. "I'll make more than double your bounty in a single night."

"I-I'm no fighter," she said in a single breath.

"You don't have to be," he said. "One match, and you'll be paid for. If you die, you die. Besides, if you are the big bad assassin that the Gray Elite say you are, you'll have no problem fighting a few mangy pirates, right?" He grinned like he knew the truth about her.

Laughing, Barrow started back the way he came, keys jingling. Raven sank against the cool stone wall. It felt as though her heart had realized her fate; it fell silent for a long moment.

Admittedly, this was better than what she had feared would happen, but not by much.

R aven tried to sleep. She reclined on the bed, listening to the sounds of life pass
by her window. Chatter in Tinatunian, mostly, but she heard bits of her own
language mixed in.

A slave. Her stomach curled. Sisters, was this really what her life had come to?

Would Barrow tattle on her before he threw her into the *Chjelhu Tal*? Would
the Gray Elite come stomping across the border to find her and drag her back to
General Deacon? What would she do if they did?

She heaved a sigh. Her limbs ached. Her heart pounded, fever pulsing in time
with her heartbeat. She closed her eyes and listened to it, her heart, the fever,
beating. Behind her eyes, she saw red. She might have laid there too long, gone a
little mad in the seclusion and fever, but she thought she could feel it humming
through her blood, thrumming with its life-sucking force.

Why hadn't she just gone to bed that night? Why had she stopped to
eavesdrop? Maybe she could have argued with Zander's decision to send her home.
Now she would never see Silver Glen again.

The storm finally rolled in, shading her cell in stormy light. Lightning flashed;
thunder rolled a beat later. Soon, thunder and lightning fell into perfect sync.

In Leon Stark's story, storms happened when the cloud dragons flew.

If only.

Rain smacked against the stone outside her window. An awning prevented the
rain from coming inside, but stray drops streaked down the wall, leaving dark trails
behind on the stone. Soon, the rain beat with force. It sounded like a horde of
hooved animals parading through the streets, stomping over the cobblestones. People
ran by the window, children played and laughed, though, for the most part, it
sounded like Wayward Point had calmed.

The rain continued for hours, and somewhere within its blur of time, Raven
found sleep—only to be interrupted by a tray landing on the bedside table. She rolled
over in time to see a short woman shutting the door. The lock clicked back into
place.

The tray held a chunk of bread, hard cheese, nuts, and roasted fish. A canteen
rested on the table. Her stomach cramped just looking at it. She crawled out of bed
and pulled the tray onto her lap. She ate all of it and then took a large gulp of
water—and spit it back into the canteen.

Ale, not water.

Weak ale, but ale nonetheless.

She took another gulp, smaller this time, and then another.

Thunder rolled lazily overhead. The rain had lightened into a mist.

She returned the empty tray to the table and fiddled with the canteen's cap. Her father had kept a small flask in his desk drawer. He carried one with him too. When she was little, she had asked him once what he kept in it. He'd told her strong tea, and she had believed him. It wasn't until she saw Zander sipping a flask some years later that it dawned on her that he had lied.

Zander. What was he doing? Had he started out on his important mission to find his lost princess? Had he realized Raven's absence?

She heaved a sigh. No sense worrying about it now.

She laid an arm over her eyes; her skin felt hot to the touch. Why hadn't this sickness gone away? It worried Thalame, who had spent more time than any of the others with illnesses, and though she wouldn't admit it, because it worried him, it worried her. If he didn't know what it was, what was she to do?

As a child, she rarely got sick. Whenever the winter colds would blow into Silver Glen, she would evade them, while Lena caught ill. Raven's stepmother had said it was the difference in their constitutions. Had she somehow happened upon one of those diseases that slowly ate away at a person until they didn't know themselves or their friends and their brain gradually forgot how to breathe?

Thunder crashed into the sky, and Raven shut her eyes. She thought of Leon Stark, the brave boy who became a pirate captain. She imagined herself on the deck of an airship, sailing through the skies, looking for smaller ships to loot, empire ships to attack, and adventure within the clouds.

That daydream might have been the only thing keeping her sane.

Raven stayed in her cell that night, being led out only to use the bathroom by the same silent Tinatunian woman. If she understood Raven's questions, she didn't say anything. She didn't act like Raven had spoken at all. The next morning, the woman returned with a fresh set of clothes. Raven shut herself in the bathroom while the woman waited outside.

She washed quickly and dressed in the provided clothes—a pair of snug sand-colored pants and a sleeveless top that wrapped around her waist and tied behind her neck. It left much of her torso exposed. She secured her ebony dagger into her boot, her mother's locket around her neck, and the coin to the Destiny Show in her pants pocket.

When she returned to the cell, a tray of food had been delivered—smoked fish. While she ate, the woman combed a strange scented oil through her hair, smoothing it to a sheen. She then braided it tightly so that two identical braids started at her temples and wove together at the base of her neck.

Raven put a hand to her hair when the woman had finished.

The woman gave her a grin—she was missing several teeth—and said, "Better than shaved."

Raven nodded. Indeed, better than shaved. She thought of the slaves in Lenhala. They'd had shaved heads. Had they been tricked and sold like she had?

"You fight tonight," said the woman as she left, empty tray in hand. "You eat big meal later."

Raven nodded, though her stomach clenched. Tonight?

She sat on the bed. If she lost in the *Chjelhu Tal*, she would be dead or beaten near death. Neither of those sounded good. Or, when the truth of her came out, when they realized she was no assassin, what would happen to her then? Would her plain face be enough to save her from a life of whoring? Would they sell her half-dead to the Gray Elite?

The worry made her sick. The cell was barely big enough to pace, though she tried. The fever came in waves, and she rested for hours, hoping for it to die down, but it didn't. It ebbed but always returned. Fire under her skin. Burning.

She exhaled; her breath felt more like steam than air.

If she looked hard enough, she thought she could see white vapor leave her mouth, dissipating as it met the cooler air outside her body.

Nonsense, that logical part of her brain said.

Maybe I'm becoming an automaton, that illogical part of her brain added.

The woman returned with a hearty lunch: fish, cheese, berries, nuts, ale. Raven ate what she could.

And then, when the sun had lowered—according to the cloudy sunlight's shadow as it transitioned across the room—Barrow returned. He looked smug. "Your time to shine," he said, unlocking the door.

Barrow grabbed her by the arm and hauled her to her feet. He led her out of the basement prison, down an unfamiliar corridor, and up several narrow staircases. With each step, the roaring of a crowd grew louder. The stairs led into a windowless room with two sets of double doors, one leading forward and one leading back. The din of hundreds of restless voices came from the forward doors, talking, shouting, anticipating violence. The volume shook the wooden planks under her feet and vibrated in the walls like thunder.

Slimey anxiety and icy dread wormed underneath her skin, crawling from the base of her skull to the back of her knees. She would likely die tonight, and in front of a bloodthirsty crowd.

Barrow started toward the doors. Raven dug her heels in, but it did little. Barrow yanked her forward. He wrenched the doors open and threw her into the *Chjelhu Tal*.

It was a wooden arena built around a dirt-floored pit. Wooden benches rose all around the pit, and hundreds of people had packed into the stands. The ceiling above the pit opened, and clouded moonlight draped inside. A hundred torches lit the space in flickering yellow. She and Barrow stood on a small wooden balcony that overlooked the arena.

241

"They all came to see you." Barrow gripped her shoulder. "The biggest crowd we've had in years. All because they want to see the general's little assassin in action. They want to see this little girl who nearly killed one of the most powerful men in the Gray Elite."

Her hands trembled. She felt like she might burn alive before she took another step. The fever twisted the arena before her eyes, elongating it, turning it sideways. Had Barrow not been holding her shoulder, she would have fallen.

"See him?" he said, pointing to the other side of the arena. A man stood on a platform similar to the one under her feet. He wore no shirt, only dirty trousers. Scars crisscrossed over his dark chest. He was shouting, beating his chest, egging on the crowd. "He's been a crowd favorite, but the problem is, he's become unbeatable. Man's like a feral cat. He's your opponent."

She shuddered. She was going to die.

Barrow laughed like he already knew the outcome. He leaned down and said in her ear, his breath hot and rancid like cheap ale, "All you have to do is beat him. He's got to be either dead or out cold in order for you to win. If you win, you'll get your share of the winnings. If you die, then you'll be tossed to Minerva's court with the other losers."

Minerva's court lay at the deepest part of the sea. The goddess snatched the souls of those lost at sea and brought them to her underwater kingdom, a haven for sailors, pirates, and seafarers.

Raven swallowed. She tried to recount all the things that Thalame had taught her, her stance and how to read another in battle. All those sessions, but she had only learned to fight against someone moving slow, and against someone who didn't want to really hurt her. Suddenly, her sessions with him and the wooden daggers felt utterly useless.

At least, when they threw her body into the sea, she would forever protect the centrum.

But as Barrow pushed her toward a rickety metal lift in front of the platform, she realized she didn't want to die.

She wanted to live.

She wanted to see the treehouse again, to see her friends again, to see Zander's face when she returned. She wanted to tell Ivy about this strange adventure. She wanted to find those scavengers who had sold her and shove them into a pit to fend for their lives.

The lift started its descent, the gears shifting and twitching, causing the lift to sputter. Across the arena, her opponent entered an identical lift. He roared and swung his lift back and forth, much to the delight of the crowd. Raven wished for the chains of his lift to break, to fall and crush him before the fight had to begin.

But his lift made it safely to the floor, as did hers.

Her blood pounded, the fever twisted, and she felt like she might empty her stomach.

Barrow's voice boomed over the crowd. He spoke in Tinatunian, through a horn that magnified his voice a hundred times. From his safe balcony, he threw his arms out in welcome and wore a victorious grin. He pointed to her opponent, and the crowd cheered. He pointed to Raven—a pause of confusion—then the crowd erupted into a bloodthirsty roar.

People craned over heads and shoulders to see her better, and whispers churned into shouts. Fingers pointed at her. Faces turned doubtful. Barrow had announced her as the assassin.

"A lot of people don't like the Gray Elite," said a rough voice behind her.

She turned.

A tall and wide woman stood behind her, armed to the teeth, one of the arena's guards. She had one green eye and one brown eye; the difference was alarming. "Had you actually killed that Deacon bastard, you might have been a hero."

"Too bad," Raven managed to say.

"Too bad," echoed the guard.

With a final shout from Barrow, the crowd erupted. The guard opened Raven's lift at the same time another guard opened her opponent's. Raven stumbled onto the hard-packed dirt floor on wooden legs. She met her opponent's dark eyes, his stare wild and hungry. In a heartbeat, he was running toward her.

And the fight began.

Raven didn't have time to think. Her opponent came at her. She tried to dodge but couldn't. He slammed into her, knocking her to the ground. She stumbled back to her feet. The world tilted. His fist collided with her jaw. Stars burst across her vision. Another fist slammed into her stomach, knocking the air out of her lungs and almost her lunch with it.

The fever burned worse and worse, fire under her skin. Her heart sped to a frightening speed, trying to jump out of her chest and run from this.

Something hard—a foot—collided with her ribcage. She felt her insides give and threaten to snap with the impact. Her breath was already gone, and she couldn't draw another. Breathless, she collapsed to the dirt floor. Her hands and knees hit hard. The pain flared a heartbeat later: her chest, her stomach, her ribs, her entire body.

The fever's burn surged, eclipsing the pain, thrumming through her blood as fast as her heartbeat. Faster. The edges of her vision turned red.

She gasped; she would die here, either from her attacker or from the fever.

Boos and disapproving shouts sounded from the arena. She barely heard them over the pumping in her ears, the rushing, the surging, the pulsing.

She was no assassin, no fighter—simple girl, simple town, naïve enough to let herself get tricked and sold.

She wobbled to regain her footing, but something hard crashed into her side, sending her sprawling to the ground, gasping for breath. Pain seared through her middle like magma, liquid and spreading. The world blurred, the dirt shifted between her fingers. The fever burned like mad; she knew would catch fire any moment, burn up entirely.

But she wanted to live.

Her opponent appeared above her, his face doubled and hazy. He came closer, pinning her to the ground. His hands found her throat. Pressure from his hands closed her airways, silenced her gasps, pushed her into the dirt.

And something snapped.

Deeper than her bones, her breath, her heartbeat. Deeper than she thought possible. The thrum became a roar, the hum a song, the beat steady.

Somehow, she knew what to do.

Her opponent's face came into focus, and his dark eyes widened. A scar, she noticed, ran underneath his left eyebrow. She clamped down on his wrists, feeling the bones moving underneath as he tried to release her throat. His fingers loosened, but hers tightened. He let out a yelp of pain, of fear, pulling against her.

She released him. He yanked his hands away from her, stumbling back, clutching his hands to his chest.

244

Raven staggered to her feet. She didn't hear the fluctuation of the arena's crowd, the odd beat of silence. She heard the thrumming in her ears, the humming in her blood, and the pulsing of the fever. She saw only her opponent—the one standing in the way of her living.

He glared at her, eyes wide and furious and fearful.

Him. He tried to kill you, would have killed you, will still try.

"I won't let him," Raven whispered so faintly, no one but the man heard her.

Because she would live.

"*Aggi?*" the man spat. The fear did not vanish, but he grew enraged. He came at her again.

This time, she did not cower. She threw herself at him, grabbing at his neck like he had grabbed hers. He dodged, and her hands slid instead to his bulky arm.

Good enough—she gathered the fever and pushed it into him, as fast and hard as she could. She felt it leaving her body and flooding into his. The man let out a bloodied scream, shrill and piercing, painful—it filled the arena—and then silenced. His eyes dulled, his stance wobbled, his mouth fell open, and his dark skin turned gray.

He started to collapse. Before his body could hit the dirt, he disintegrated. His body and bones fell apart, crumbling into dark ashes at her feet. No bones, no clothes—just ash.

Burned.

Raven took a gasping breath as if she hadn't been breathing; the fever subsided. The red clouds on the edge of her vision shrank. The arena reappeared. The stench of ash reached her nose: burned cloth and hair and flesh. The stunned crowd erupted into wild cheers.

Her heart beat once, twice, and then—she stumbled backward away from the ash.

All around her was the roar of drunken applause, boots stomping on wooden floors, sloshing ale. Several wooden mugs crashed to the arena floor, spilling their contents onto the thirsty dirt.

Raven swallowed. Her senses returned.

She... She just killed him. *Killed* him. With her hands. With a touch. Dead. The man, her opponent, dead. Turned to ash.

Burned, she realized, by the fever. It had burned him alive from the inside out. She didn't even have a face to look into, no lightless eyes to save for her own guilt. She blinked and looked away. She didn't want to see the ash any more than a body. She looked into the crowd instead, the joyous, riotous, nearly hysterical crowd.

All cheered and shouted, except for one.

Near the middle of the stands stood a man in hooded robes. He did not cheer. He did not clap. He stood with his arms crossed, dark eyes gazing down at her—his straight-line mouth tilted to one side in a carefree smirk, but something dangerous lay beneath it.

Heavy footsteps sounded beside her. The guardswoman with one brown eye and one green eye appeared at her side, a broad grin on her face. She guided Raven back to the lift. Raven glanced back to where the hooded man had been, but he was gone. The lift started up, and she got a better look at the arena, but she still didn't see the hooded man.

The guardswoman guided her back onto the platform and back into the windowless room. Raven wanted nothing more than to sink to her knees and curl up somewhere dark and quiet.

"Assassin indeed," barked Barrow. He wore a vicious grin. He dabbed the sweat from his brow with a patterned handkerchief. "And you said you weren't a fighter. Ha! I'd say you earned yourself a warm meal and a cold drink."

The far door burst open, and a little woman with a dozen braids in her hair threw an accusative finger at Barrow. "What are you thinking?" snapped the woman. She glared at Raven. "You bring this *aggi* here?" She spat something in Tinatunian that made the guardswoman tighten her grip on Raven's elbow. "I don't want any freaks on my doorstep."

"It's fine," said Barrow. He spoke low and fast in Tinatunian, but the woman didn't look convinced. She kept glaring at Raven like she had insulted her.

Finally, the woman stormed back the way she'd come, and Barrow laughed halfheartedly.

"Freaks?" Raven asked, feeling a little insulted. Had the woman called her a freak? In truth, she felt a little like one. Was that what *aggi* meant? Her opponent had called her that too.

Barrow waved his hand toward the door. "Don't worry about what the old bat says, my little champion. She's superstitious. Nothing for you to worry about. Now, come on, let's see about that drink!"

Barrow guided Raven into another part of the arena, talking all the while about the match, how nervous he had been, how fantastic of an end—she tuned him out. Rather than underground, he took her up a staircase and to a room at the end. It had a single window that overlooked the street. She could see a sliver of midnight blue beyond the city and a smaller sliver of the Lanila Sea. At night, even under clouds, it shimmered as if made of diamonds and onyx.

The rest of the room was far better than her cell. A narrow bed had been pushed into one corner, a desk in the other, and a table in the middle with three chairs. The table held a tray of roasted fish, melon, hard cheese, and sliced bread. It smelled delicious, though she wasn't sure she could eat. She sat down at the table anyway; the green bottle of what she assumed to be ale called to her more than anything.

"I hope you like your new accommodations," said Barrow with a tone of parting.

"It's nice," Raven said absently.

She reached for the bottle, and Barrow left. He locked the door with an obvious click. She poured herself a glass. The deep red and sweet smell indicated it was wine, not ale. She took a drink. It didn't taste that different from the wines she'd tried at Silver Glen, tangy and a bit bitter but drinkable.

A heavy set of feet stopped outside her door—a guard.

Not a cell but still a prison. She stared down at her glass of wine. Now what? Would she have to fight someone every night?

She was far too exhausted for thinking. She drained her wine in a single gulp, then collapsed onto the bed.

Raven woke up to a scratchy female voice speaking Tinatunian. She pulled her groggy self off the bed and sat up just as the speaker left. The food of the night before had been cleared away, and a small porcelain teapot and a plate of buttered toast had replaced it. Raven scooted off the bed and gladly made herself a cup of tea. She relished the sweet, warm, and soothing taste.

The city had come alive with the morning. Laughter and playful chatter filtered in through the window. Gulls sang to each other, flaunting their freedom. Raven plopped into the chair. Sleep and food had cleared her mind, and the reality of the night before settled on her bones like lead.

She looked at her hands. It didn't seem real. How had she burned the man alive? There hadn't even been a fire, just...heat and then ash. The whole fight had a blurriness to it, like a dream, like she hadn't been herself. In truth, she didn't feel like herself.

Somehow, she had given her fever to him, and it had burned him alive like she thought it would do to her. She flattened her hands against the wooden tabletop. She tried to burn it, to turn it to ash, but nothing happened. It wasn't even warm.

Freak indeed.

She poured another cup of tea. She remembered wanting to live, and then...something happened—not a rage, but something feral, something not herself. It hurt her head to think about.

Footsteps sounded in the hall.

"Good morning, Guardswoman," came a charming, joyful male voice. He added something in Tinatunian. He spoke both tongues elegantly.

Her guard spat something in Tinatunian. Raven didn't have to understand it to feel the threat in her words.

"Off limits?" said the charmed voice. He scoffed.

Something about the voice sounded familiar, but she couldn't place it.

The guard said something in Tinatunian.

He answered with, "Well that's not very nice, is it?"

247

The guard grumbled and shifted. The next few moments happened fast: a scuffle, grunts, clothing swishing, blades colliding with flesh. A thump. A scoff.

"Let's see here," said the joyful man. He hummed a few notes of a song she had heard fluting through the city near dusk. "Ah, found you."

Raven set her cup to the side and slid to her feet. A key slid into the lock, turned, and the door swung open. She froze. Standing in the doorway was the hooded man from the arena. He had the dark, rich skin of Tinatun and coal-like eyes that quickly took her in. He wore dark blue robes made for adventure, with plenty of places for blades to hide. Several leather belts hugged his torso, holding all manner of things: a flask, a dagger, a compass. A saber hung from his waist.

He glided into the room with feline ease. "Well, well, what do we have here?" he said in a simpering, playful tone. He closed the door behind him. He sauntered a few steps closer, keeping the table between them. "A lost kitten?"

"What do you want?" Raven asked, trying to uphold an image of the strong girl who'd killed a man only hours ago.

Humor danced in his black eyes. "I saw what you did out there," he said, his velvet voice calm and sure. "And that poor bastard thought he stood a chance." His eyes narrowed slightly.

"So?" She straightened her shoulders. The woman's voice resounded: *freaks*. "Want me to do it to you?"

He chuckled and took a step around the table. "You could try, little bird, but I would rather talk first." He took another step, and then he stood on her side of the table. "What is a little bird like you doing all the way down here? Hmm?"

"I was kidnapped and sold," she spat. The spite came easy.

"Ah," he said, as though it explained everything. "Happens more often than it should."

A sound came from somewhere within the arena, a crash, a groan of wood, then a shout.

"Since we don't have much time before someone comes looking for you, I'll be quick." He stepped closer, close enough she could hit him, but she didn't.

She held her hand away from herself and tried to draw on the fever like she had before, but she couldn't. She couldn't feel the fever at all.

His eyes narrowed at her hand, then at her. "Can't use your magic now?"

"Magic?" she gasped, her heart skipping every other beat. "What are you talking about?"

He raised a brow. "What do you think you did out there? You turned a man to ash," he said, his lilting voice humorous but deadly serious. He took another step toward her, and all humor dropped from his words. "I am a seeker for a society that strives to keep magic alive as humanity and its machines insist on ending it. I'll give you a choice, little bird. Come with me, or stay here and live out however many days you have left before someone gets tired of you."

A choice: here or somewhere else.

248

The seeker extended his hand toward her, his dark skin laced with thin scars and calluses.

She swallowed. "What—"

Footsteps started down the hallway, toward her room. Whistling.

"Can you take me to the Crusaders?" she asked, her voice low.

The seeker's eyes widened a bit. "How do you know about them?"

Footsteps came closer.

The seeker glanced toward the door, then at her. He shook his head. "It doesn't matter," he said quickly. "Stay here, or leave with me." He wiggled the fingers of his extended hand.

The whistling stopped. A man shouted in Tinatunian. Footsteps stomped toward her door.

She slapped her hand into the seeker's.

14

The seeker twisted his body. In a single smooth motion, his heel came down on the door handle. With a crunch of metal and a crack of wood, the handle broke. A breath later, the person standing on the other side spat a curse, then threw his weight into the door. He shouted in Tinatunian.

The seeker wasted no time. He threw open the shutters and lifted Raven into his arms. She let out a shriek as he started toward the window. Her heart sank as she realized his mad plan. She curled her face into his neck, squeezing her eyes shut. He jumped, and for a sickening moment she felt nothing. Her heart skipped a beat and then jumped into her throat.

They landed, but she dared not open her eyes. He ran and jumped, his feet landing on something that sounded like wood. Another short run and a jump, and then they landed on solid ground. He started running, the cobblestone underneath his feet, and she dared to open her eyes.

They had landed on a narrow street between rows of red and gray stone buildings. People continued on their business, most of them. Some stopped to look to where the seeker had jumped from. Her heart sank a little—he'd jumped from roof to roof.

Shouting came from down the road, behind them. As the seeker slid down a side street, guards from the arena ran around the far corner. The crowd looked only mildly bewildered.

The seeker turned down an alley, down another side street, across a short bridge, and soon Raven had lost her sense of direction. Too many streets and alleys and bridges. The arena guards didn't seem to be following anymore either. He ducked into an alley and set her back on her own feet.

"How was that for a daring rescue?" he asked, a hum on his breath. Barely breathless. The morning sunlight darkened the hood's shadow over his face, but she caught the flash of his teeth. A wide smile curved, brightening his entire face.

"Thank you," Raven said because he had, however audaciously, gotten her out of the ring.

And now she was standing in Wayward Point, friendless and lost. The muggy air pressed in all around her, a second skin. Her sleeveless shirt now made sense. She would hate to wear the long-sleeve and high collared dresses she had worn in Silver Glen.

The seeker straightened, eyes on her. He adjusted his feet to take up more room in the alley, blocking her way past him while angling himself to see if anyone approached from the street.

"What?" she asked, as breathless as if she had run instead of him.

He tilted his head. He was looking at her, but not at *her*—all around her. "Interesting," he said.

And it hit her; she stood in an alley with a stranger. She had her dagger, but would it matter? She had one; he had at least five that she could see. He had proven his fitness with the rescue. She took a single step back. She might—if she were fast enough and lucky—outrun him.

The seeker pivoted toward her faster than she could move. The palm of his hand rested firmly against her cheek. She jumped at the contact.

"You're burning up." His smirk tilted downward.

She pulled her cheek away from his hand. "It's just...a fever," she said. And the thoughts came together. The fever had burned like fire with her panic, and after she had pushed it into the man, he had burned. Then the fever had gone. Now, it returned. It pulsed under her skin, though not as powerfully as it had before.

The seeker's hand hovered in the air for a heartbeat, then he returned it to his side. "A fever indeed."

A woman in a white shawl walked by the mouth of the ally. Two children, each no more than ten, held onto her hands. Raven met the eyes of the child closest to the ally. The boy pointed to the seeker and spoke in Tinatunian. The seeker casually rolled his head over his shoulder to look at the boy.

The woman looked once at the seeker, and her scowl vanished. Her mouth straightened, her dark eyes widened, and her skin paled to a sickly ashen gray. She forced her gaze away and started to walk faster, yanking the children with her. The boy spoke again, but the woman cut his words off.

The seeker looked lost between humor and distaste.

"Why did she look at you like that?" Raven stopped herself before she asked if he was one of the freaks she had heard about.

He shrugged. "I might have something of a reputation. Not all good."

"Clearly," Raven mumbled.

He glanced to the street. "It doesn't sound like we were followed. Good." He took a step onto the street. He motioned for her to follow.

She stayed still.

The seeker paused in the mouth of the alley. "Is something wrong with your feet?"

"Why should I follow you?" She wanted to reach down for her dagger, if only to show him that she was armed. "How do I know that you're not going to sell me to someone else or lead to somewhere worse than where I came from?"

He shrugged. If only she felt as calm as he looked. "You don't," he said. "That's one of the great mysteries of life. Trust is one of those fickle things that can hurt you far worse than it can help. But sometimes it's worth it." He extended his hand, not for her own, but for her trust.

A shout in Tinatunian came from the street, and the seeker's brows rose. His calm expression didn't crack. He leaned back to look and then leaned forward. "Well, I was wrong. Looks like your friends from the arena did follow us."

"What?"

"That doesn't leave much of a choice, does it?" The seeker stepped toward her, grabbed her hand, and pulled her down the alley.

They crisscrossed a dozen alleys, passed doors of wood and doors of cloth and doorways without doors.

He let go of her hand. "Follow me or make your own way. Pick fast." He didn't stop.

In the span of a single heartbeat, she had to choose. She didn't have the time! Face the strange city alone or with a stranger. She felt the tug, somewhere deeper than she understood, and she jogged after the seeker.

"This way," he whispered.

They walked through a building's backroom—a bakery. Barrels were stacked three high; crates of vegetables and fruit were stacked on the stone counters; bags of flour and sugar turned one corner into a white, powdery mess. From the front, the smell of fresh bread wafted through the air. Quick and silent as a breeze, she and the seeker were on the other side.

He led her through alleys and down streets and through a few more hidden passages that went behind and through businesses and homes. She noticed the way people—at least those who dared notice him—looked as the seeker's presence registered. Their faces paled, expressions turned to something between shock and fear. Everyone else pretended as though he didn't exist and, by extension, that she didn't exist.

She didn't mind, considering that the arena guards chased them, but she minded that she didn't know why.

Freaks.

They worked their way through the sprawling city. She heard the calls of the market square, the smells of sizzling fish and mystery meat, the vendors in their mixed languages, hagglers, and a dozen different songs. The cobblestone turned to dirty sand, packed by generations of feet. They passed barefoot children in scraggly clothes, who laughed as they played. It seemed to be mostly residential; older adults lounged on front steps and on porches, smoking or speaking to one another, sipping from coral-colored cups.

This part of Wayward Point felt older. The buildings were of a lighter stone, sun-bleached and well-used. The people didn't turn in fear of the seeker. Many waved, and he waved back without slowing down.

A ballgame played by older children stopped when the seeker walked onto the street, the children all gawking in mixtures of disbelief and awe. Several spoke in Tinatunian, at which the seeker answered. The children all smiled.

Revered.

On these streets, Raven did not go unnoticed. The people looked to her with the same revered awe as they looked at the seeker. It made her stomach plummet at the same time her heart skipped a beat. What did it mean?

When someone waved to her, she waved back.

A group of smaller children halted their walk and surrounded the seeker, dark eyes wide, faces brushed with sand and dirt. They all spoke rapidly, some looking to her, but most to the seeker.

He laughed, glanced at Raven, and spoke in Tinatunian to the children. They giggled.

"What did you say?" she asked when they had passed.

"That you didn't speak their language," he said. "It's true, isn't it?"

She nodded. They walked a little further in silence. She was about to say something else when they walked onto an old wooden bridge that stretched over a small canal. The water dribbled down the sandy stones and stretched out to—

She gasped at the view.

The beach stretched on from the bridge to the sea. The sea stretched endlessly to the horizon, glittering sapphire and aquamarine. She lingered a heartbeat too long. The seeker was waiting at the far end of the bridge, a curious smile on his face. She jogged to catch up.

He led her to a small clearing where palms and ferns grew between sandy shacks. They all seemed to be empty. Before them, the view of the ocean hadn't changed. He let out a sigh and leaned against one of the palms.

"Why are you helping me?" Raven blurted.

"Mostly because you needed helping," he said simply. "And because you have magic. Are you warded?"

"Warded? What does that mean?"

"I'll take that as a no." He cleared his throat. "I'll start from the top." He flattened his hand against his chest. "I am a seeker. I took an oath to protect magicians. You, a magician, were being held against your will. The rest is self-explanatory."

"I've never heard of a seeker."

"Not many have," he said, "seeing as how we're from a fairly private society—not to mention rare."

"What society is that?"

"It's a secret. I can't tell you out in the open, in case you scamper off and tell the world where we are. We wouldn't want the enemy to come flooding through the gates, now would we?" He tilted his head.

"The enemy? You mean the Gray Elite?"

He shrugged, a non-answer.

She sighed through her nose. "And I don't scamper."

He chuckled. He started to say something else, but she cut him off.

"Can you help me find the Crusaders?"

253

His expression didn't change. "Why do you want to find them?"

"They might know people that I know, and they might be able to contact them or help me get back to where I was," she said, avoiding all names.

"They're a rowdy bunch of pirates," he said. "I'm not sure they're in the market of helping strays." He looked her up and down. "Unless you've got a few hundred extra piks in that outfit."

She blushed and held her tongue.

"Hmm, broke?" he asked. When she didn't answer, he added, "That's what I thought."

If the Crusaders wouldn't help her, then... "Can you help me with something else?" She pulled out the wooden coin but held it in her fist. "I want to go to the Destiny Show."

The seeker's smile faded. "Why would you want to go there?"

"It's where I wanted to go in the first place," she said bitterly. She tightened her hand around the coin. "Before the people I thought were helping me sold me."

"Why," he said, not a question. His smile flattened into a straight line, and he studied her face with such an intensity that she wanted to take a step back.

She held her ground. She wouldn't let someone else push her around. "Someone told me to go there," she said, though the memory had fogged. She could remember the dark outline of the thief, the smell of the musty inn, and the feel of the wood coin as he'd pressed it into her hand.

"It's not a fun place to go," said the seeker. "Security is tight."

She opened her hand and showed him the coin. "He gave me a coin to get in."

He pushed off the tree with surprising lethality, and her body tensed. His dark eyes pierced her hand, the coin, then her eyes. "Who gave it to you? Do you remember?"

She swallowed; the sudden change in the seeker had stolen the breath from her throat.

"*Who?*" he whispered.

"He said his name was Conrad," she managed to say.

The seeker took a step back, and the predatorial gait fell away. He put a hand against his chest, over his heart, and looked at her as though he hadn't seen her before.

Had the name been a code? A message of passage?

The wind—cool from the sea—pushed against her, ticking her nose with salt and adventure. It smelled like Leon Stark had described it: dirty with silt, ripe with stone and sand that never dried, and full of the unknown, of endless horizons and bottomless seas.

Then the seeker laughed. He doubled over in laughter, and she felt her cheeks go hot, the sense of adventure from the sea breeze shattered. She turned to go, but he grabbed her arm. His eyes were shimmering with tears.

"Wait," he said, laughter still on his words.

"Why? So you can make fun of me some more?"

"No, no," he said, straightening. He cleared his throat and repeated firmly, "No. I'm not laughing at you, little bird. I'm laughing at fate."

She huffed, not in the mood. "What does that even mean? You think my situation funny?"

He let out a sound, half laugh, half groan. Then he leaned toward her. "You don't recognize me?"

She looked deeper into his coal-dark eyes, his plump cheekbones, his joyful smile. She shook her head. "Should I?"

He pulled back his dark blue hood. "I suppose not; it was dark, after all, and I didn't know you at first either."

She started to speak, but then she stopped. The seeker wasn't that much older than her. His black hair fell halfway to his waist, done in dozens of braids. Gold and bronze beads clicked together as his hair fell free of his hood. He smiled, and his entire face lit up. A gold bead studded one ear, and she spotted gold necklaces beneath his robes.

"You," she whispered, disbelief curving her words, her thoughts.

The seeker was the thief, the very thief who had given her the wooden coin.

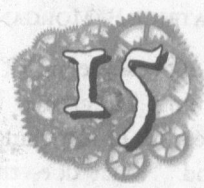

15

Conrad, thief and seeker, leaned against the palm. He kept his coal-dark eyes pinned on Raven, his smile wide. "Took you long enough," he said.

"You," Raven breathed.

"You," Conrad repeated, gesturing to her. "It looks like you took my advice to heart after all."

Conrad had been the one who had stolen the centrum from the Temple of the Three Sisters in Silver Glen. He had been the one she and Zander had chased to Lenhala. He had been the one Zander's father, Brigadier General Winchester, had hired to recover the centrum. He had been the one she had stolen the centrum back from.

She swallowed the urge to reach for her locket. Conrad knew how much the Hawks would be willing to pay for the centrum's return.

"So what happened, little bird?" Conrad asked. "You finally fly away from that windbag?"

He meant Zander. He and Raven had disguised themselves as traveling lovers. When they had met in that shabby inn, Zander had been distracting the people so that she could sneak into their rooms and search for the centrum. Conrad had found her on the stairs, listening while Zander sang lewd songs of mermaids, and had given her the coin. He had told her that if she wanted to leave Zander and start a new life, she should seek out the Destiny Show at Wayward Point.

Raven looked down at the wooden coin, the diamond and circle insignia engraved in its surface. The same insignia engraved on the inside of her mother's locket.

In a way, she had left Zander. Just not entirely on purpose.

"I..." She looked up to see Conrad patiently listening. "He was planning on going somewhere" —she twisted her fingers over the coin— "without me. He said I would be a hindrance. So I left him before he could leave me."

She decided to leave it at that because the truth of it would sound cowardly and stupid.

The slight humor in Conrad's face vanished. In its place, sincerity. "You did the right thing. I've met plenty of scoundrels in my life—trust me—and he was one of them. Men don't change, contrary to what some girls think. You are better off without that worthless excuse for a man."

She nodded. A part of her thought the same. Another part of her shuddered.

"If we're trading sob stories," said Conrad, bitterness in his words, "I'll offer you mine to make you feel better. I had a girl, and I loved her. I thought she loved me. I took a job that required time and travel—that's when I met you—and by the time I got back home, she'd already found someone to replace me."

Conrad let out a short, lighthearted sigh. He looked out toward the sea, toward the breeze of salt, mildew, and adventure. The bitterness in his eyes became a shadow of heartbreak, of betrayal. She thought she understood, but the grief in Conrad's eyes went deeper than his tone implied.

"I'm sorry to hear that." She meant every word.

He shrugged, and the bitterness fell away. His good humor returned, along with his grin. "Oh well. What's done is done, and my life has gotten easier to manage with just me to worry about." He laughed. "I had a mercenary threaten her life not a week ago, and I told him to go ahead and do it. He looked at me like I'd gone mad."

"Did he...?" Raven asked.

Conrad heaved a sigh. "No. Bitch is still alive." He took a step and clapped his hands together. "So, as I was saying earlier, before we were rudely interrupted, I am a seeker. You've got magic. It's my obligation to take you to see some people about that."

She tensed. "People? Who?"

"It's a secret."

She frowned. "Your secret society?"

"Yes."

"I refuse."

"Why?"

"Because I don't know who they are, what they are, or what their goals are. For all I know, they're slavers. And I have had enough of slavers," she said, her words sure and steady. She crossed her arms for emphasis.

"You won't even stop by and say hello?"

"The last people I said hello to sold me as a slave."

He nodded. "That is as fair a point as any," he said with a sigh. "In that case, the people I want to introduce you to are not slavers, on my honor, whatever it's worth these days. They are in the business of preserving magic. That includes people. Like you."

"They help magicians," she said.

Conrad nodded. "Most of the associates are magicians, and they are interested in finding more magicians before the Gray Elite gets to them."

Just like the Hawks, she thought. "What about the Destiny Show? You told me to go there."

"That is our first stop, should you agree," he said. "Even if you were not a magician, had you presented the coin and my name, someone would have offered something of help, be it a job at the docks or cleaning stalls."

"But..." She thought about it. "Is that where this society of yours is?"

"It's their office here in Wayward Point," he said. "I can't tell you where they are beyond that. That is a guarded secret. But I can take you to the Destiny Show. Do you still want to go?"

"Yes," she said without hesitation.

"Good." He nodded, his smile widening. "Then let's not waste any more time growing old."

Conrad started along a grassy path that hugged the beach, and Raven followed a step behind, the coin clutched in her hand.

Conrad guided her to the far side of Wayward Point, away from the arena, away from the market. He led her across the mouth of the river and across the coral bridge and past the fish-smelling docks. He weaved through sandy alleys and narrow streets of ancient cobble. The city gradually shrank to single-story wooden shacks and lean-tos, dotted with palms and scraggly bushes and leafy vines. They passed wooden shacks with fronds for roofs and doors, shells pressed into the stone around the doors and windows. The hard-packed dirt became loose sand, the houses vanished, and the wild nature took over. Palms clustered together, weeds and harsh grass grew in the sand, and dark gray rocks punctuated it like scattered bones.

The Destiny Show stood on the edge of Wayward Point, an old white stone building with no other discernible features. No sign announced its name. A vine had taken over a large portion of the roof, dangling off lazily and swaying in the breeze. Conrad stopped before a plain wooden door, the only entrance she could see.

He winked at her, then knocked three times.

No response came.

Conrad let out an agitated sigh and knocked three times more.

Heavy footsteps approached, and the door opened. The doorman stood tall and wide, built like a bodyguard, like the doorman of the arena. Raven caught the tendrils of thick gray smoke hovering near the ceiling behind the man, twirling slowly. It looked as though the smoke itself formed the ceiling.

The doorman grunted; he looked at Conrad, then at Raven.

"I've a client who would like to speak with Madam Mallori about the stars," said Conrad.

The doorman frowned, and Conrad repeated his words in Tinatunian—not without a bit of spite, Raven noticed.

The doorman spoke only a few words. His voice was deep and unsettling.

"Out?" Conrad snapped. He raised an eyebrow. "If Mallori is *out*, then who is *in*?"

The doorman frowned. Conrad repeated himself in Tinatunian. A heartbeat later, the doorman grumbled, "Malik."

Conrad sighed, no small amount of irritation on his breath. "Fine, we'll talk stars with dear Malik instead."

The doorman waited a beat, then stepped aside. Conrad guided Raven into the dark space, and when the doorman shut the door, what little sunlight had been with them vanished. Candles burned on a sidebar, each in a strange glass globe that funneled the smoke up, up, up, through a series of tubes, where it puddled on the ceiling in shades of gray and dark blue and green. The candles flickered and gave the room an eerie sense of shadows. Raven did not like it. It felt too small and cramped. The doorman showed them to the back of the room, where a curtain hung in place of a door, its edges frayed.

The doorman stepped halfway through the curtain and spoke in Tinatunian. A second voice answered him in the same language, a calm, smooth, tenor male voice.

Was she to have this conversation in Tinatunian? Would Conrad have to translate? Her skin prickled at the idea, at the memory of all the conversations the scavengers had had about her, right in front of her, about their plans for her.

The doorman stepped back, holding the curtain for them.

Conrad hesitated, and Raven wasn't about to walk into a new space first.

"Well?" came the voice from the room, with barely a hint of an accent. "Are you going to show your face?"

Raven tensed at the change of tone; where the voice had been somber a heartbeat before, it now spoke in maliciousness. Conrad clenched his fists, then relaxed. He inhaled, straightened his shoulders, and took the first step through the curtain. Raven followed a step behind. The curtain *whooshed* back behind her. The doorman's heavy steps retreated.

They stood in a dimly lit room. A few clouded globes flickered, blue and green and gray, all sitting on a small round table in the middle of the room. Cushions of different sizes and colors lay around the table, and resting on the largest pillow was a young man in dark robes. Undoubtedly, he was one of the most beautiful people she had ever seen. He had khaki skin, high cheekbones, and sharp eyes a honeyed shade of brown. He wore a dozen necklaces around his slender throat, beads, golden and silver chains, and three pendants at varying lengths. Raven counted three rings on each of his dark hands.

In the flickering candlelight, though Malik sat still, his jewelry glinted and shimmered.

Conrad took a step forward, opened his arms wide, and said happily, "Malik!"

Malik moved faster than she could blink. In less than a heartbeat, he pulled a knife from his billowing sleeves and hurled it straight at Conrad.

Raven gasped as the knife whisked through the air. Conrad dodged; the knife thunked into the wall behind him. She glanced over her shoulder to where the knife had embedded itself an inch into the wooden wall.

"Glad to see your aim has improved," Conrad said, hand on his cheek. He brought his hand away, and to Raven's surprise, red glimmered on his fingers. Not a lot, but enough to make her heart flip flop in her chest.

"I was aiming for your throat," growled Malik.

"Oh," said Conrad, wiping the blood off on his sleeve. "I suppose it gives you something else to work on, then."

"What do you want?" Malik sank back into the largest cushion with the grace of a bird landing on a branch. He draped one arm over the side and set the other on the table. The candlelight caught on his jeweled rings.

Conrad meandered to the table and sank into one of the smaller cushions, as calm as if Malik hadn't just tried to kill him. Raven tried to follow his calm lead, but her heart still thudded against her chest. She sat beside him, the cushion pulling her down. Getting up wouldn't be easy. Or graceful.

Malik looked between the two of them. His gaze lingered on Raven's.

"I've brought you a new friend," said Conrad, gesturing to her.

Malik's expression didn't change.

"I found her in the arena, of all places. Turned a pirate into a pile of ash with her bare hands."

Malik's brows rose. "This is her?" he asked, gesturing to her with a wave of his slender fingers. "I heard about the incident. The girl sucked the soul right out of the flesh, and the body withered in mere seconds."

"I don't recall soul-sucking," Raven said quietly.

Malik's gaze roamed over her. "I don't sense anything."

"I don't either, not right now," said Conrad. "But I saw it with my own eyes. I felt it then, strong as any, but by the time I got to her, it had vanished. That pirate didn't just wither away, he disintegrated to ash. No blood, no bones, no nothing. *Ash.*"

Malik looked again at Raven, his honey eyes searching hers like Conrad had done, looking at her, but not at *her*. Several long, slightly uncomfortable moments passed.

"What is this place?" she asked, looking at Malik, though she directed her question to Conrad.

"The Destiny Show," he said plainly. He motioned to Malik. "He's a seeker."

"You're both seekers?"

Conrad opened his mouth and inhaled to speak, but Malik spat, "This fool isn't a seeker. Not anymore." Malik's eyes narrowed. "His greed got the better of him. He's nothing but a scoundrel and a pirate."

Conrad shrugged, not denying it. "But, despite that, here I am, fulfilling my sacred obligation."

"You are bargaining for your redemption," countered Malik.

"Bargaining," Raven repeated. She turned her sharp glare onto Conrad. "I'm a bargaining chip?"

Conrad shifted, his joyful smile faltering into one of nervousness. A cat, cornered. "Yes and no. I did save you from the arena, and you wanted to go to the Destiny Show."

"But she doesn't have magic," said Malik, almost bored. "Is this another joke, Conrad?"

"No," Conrad said firmly. "I saw her turn that man to ash. I felt it in the air."

Malik leaned forward, eyes on Raven. "Why don't you explain what happened in the arena?"

She swallowed, and then she recounted being attacked by the Retriever, saved by the three scavengers, sold, and thrown into the arena. All the while, Malik's honey eyes never left hers. He barely blinked. When she finished with being broken out of the arena by Conrad, she felt winded and relieved.

"This fever," Malik said, "how long have you had it?"

How long had it been since they had left Lenhala? She didn't know. "About four weeks," she guessed. "Maybe more."

"Hmm. And you haven't shown signs of magic before it?"

Raven shook her head.

Malik leaned back in his cushion. "That is strange."

"What do you think it is?" Conrad asked. "I've never heard of magic coming and going like that."

"Because it doesn't," said Malik.

A strange weight of guilt fell on her shoulders. Raven tore her eyes from Malik and focused on the silk tablecloth. The threads frayed at the edges. Magic. She didn't have magic; she never had. Yet she felt the fever under her skin. It had been calm since she had killed that man. The fever had killed him, the fever that she had somehow pushed into him, through touch.

"What happened?" Malik asked, softer.

She glanced back at him.

Malik leaned onto the table. "When did this fever first appear? What were you doing when you first noticed? Did you meet anyone strange or go somewhere you hadn't been before? Had something strange happened in the days before it?"

The locket around her throat felt heavy and hot against her skin. Conrad and Malik both held their waiting stares on her. She couldn't tell them about Lenhala, the Hawks, or the centrum. Her skin prickled, she started to sweat, and her heart skipped every other beat.

"Is that when you left him?" Conrad asked.

Raven blinked.

"Left who?" Malik asked.

Lies, lies, lies. "My husband," Raven whispered.

Malik raised a brow.

"A rat of a man," Conrad said darkly. "A drunk and a bastard. Talked about women like a farmer talks about cuts of beef."

"You met him?" Malik glanced at Conrad.

"We stayed at the same inn not that long ago," Conrad said. "I met Raven, looking like a forlorn turtledove on the stairs while her husband sang unsavory songs about mermaids in the barroom. I told her about the Destiny Show."

"Hmm," hummed Malik. "Tell me about this fever."

She swallowed against the lump in her throat. She looked down at her hands, the hands she had latched onto her opponent with, the hands that had given him the fever, the hands that had held on when he crumbled to nothing.

"It's there," she said. "I can feel it. Not like it was. It feels like something squirming, like a second skin underneath mine." She ran a hand over her arm. "When I think about it, I can feel it more. I get overheated so easily now, breathless, like I'm burning up from the inside. And when I thought that man was going to kill me, I just...I don't know what happened. It's blurry. Like I wasn't myself."

Conrad and Malik both frowned.

"What?" she asked them.

"I've never heard of someone catching magic like a cold," Malik said.

"You think that's what it is?" her voice came out a wisp.

"What else could turn a man to ash?" came Conrad's voice.

Malik stared at her, his eyes hard. "Tell me about your husband, the one you bravely left."

"Scum," Conrad hissed under his breath. "The whole lot of them."

Malik didn't seem to hear, or if he had, he ignored it. But the word caught Raven's interest. She looked to Conrad and repeated, "The lot of them?"

Conrad's face went slack. Caught. He looked between Raven and Malik. He swallowed.

"Conrad?" Malik said, a warning.

"I may have come into contact with her husband's relation," Conrad said carefully.

Raven tensed. He *had* met Zander's father. It was a detail she hadn't considered until now.

"Our encounter was brief, but he was every bit as much of a pompous scumbag as his son. Shady fellow, but they looked strikingly similar."

Malik looked between Raven and Conrad, eyes searching.

"You know his father?" Raven asked. Her voice came out shakier than she anticipated. Conrad had met Zander at a tavern, though she didn't know how or to what extent that brief contact went.

Conrad scratched his chin, looking elsewhere. When no one else spoke, he let out a grievous sigh. "Fine, you caught me." He held up both hands. "His father hired me to find something. I lost it. That scumbag son probably stole it back." Conrad cast a wary gaze back to Raven.

She curled her fingers into her palms to keep from touching the centrum. Did he suspect her? She could cast the blame on Zander if she had to.

Malik released a resigned sigh.

"I didn't complete the contract," Conrad argued.

"It doesn't matter," Malik said, rubbing his temples.

Conrad glanced at Raven, his smile wide. "What can I say? I'm a pirate at heart."

"Raven," said Malik, "If you were staying at an inn, that implies travel. Were you and your husband going somewhere? Had you been somewhere odd? Sisters only know what affairs this fool is involved in." He gestured to Conrad, who took pretend offense.

"There's also the matter of how you ended up down here," Conrad added.

Malik didn't brush the comment off. He stared at her with curious intent.

She bit her lip. A lie. She needed a lie, a cover story. In a quick second, she chose a thin version of the truth. Under Malik's sharp gaze, she knew that a total lie wouldn't be good enough.

"My husband," she started. "He was—or he is—involved in plots to overthrow the Gray Elite."

A crease formed between Malik's brows. His lips moved, but no sound came out.

"He kept it secret from me," Raven said quickly. "He told me we were chasing a thief." She glanced at Conrad, who didn't look surprised. "But his brother found us. He talked us into going to the capital. His father knew that he had whatever it was that he'd wanted stolen, the thing that Conrad had been hired to find, and he wanted it. So did General Deacon."

Malik's eyes narrowed. "Wait. You...you're talking about the Hawks."

The blood rushed from her face at the mention.

Malik let out a groan. "And that means you're talking about Zander Winchester."

Her breath escaped her faster than she could think about keeping herself composed.

"Zander Winchester?" Conrad repeated. "Even his name sounds pompous."

Malik leaned onto the little table and rubbed his eyes. The candles flickered with the motion. "The bastard," he muttered. He looked to Raven again. "I heard he brought a girl back with him, but I didn't realize he had married."

Raven bit her lip, the truth written all over her face.

Malik noticed. His frown deepened, and he said, "You're not married."

She shook her head.

Conrad leaned forward, looking between the two of them. "Should this name ring a bell?" he asked.

"You'd already gotten kicked out by the time Zander came along," Malik said. "He was here less than two years, and he left to play the Hawks's game of resistance."

"You know Zander?" Raven asked Malik.

He looked back at her, and she saw the hesitation in his eyes. She put the pieces together herself. The mixed look that people gave Conrad, terror and awe, reverence and distrust. The woman's fear of freaks coming to the arena. The secret society that helped magicians.

"You're Wraiths," she whispered, and Malik's eyes narrowed.

264

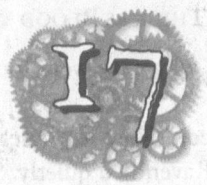

R aven's heart shuddered. Wraiths.

Conrad blinked. "You know about us?" He frowned at Malik. "Zander's a Wraith? He didn't look like one when I saw him."

"He's also a Hawk," Malik said with distaste. He looked to Raven. "You're not surprised. You knew he was a Wraith."

"It's one of the things I learned about him in the past few months," she said. Not a lie. "And you're a Wraith too?"

Malik held her stare for several breaths. "I am," he said at last. "Tell me, Raven, what he told you about the Wraiths."

"You're magicians," she said. "You smuggle other magicians out of the Gray Elite's clutches."

He nodded. "Those things are both true. We are not assassins, thieves," —he shot a pointed look in Conrad's direction— "or mercenaries. The Hawks have stolen Wraiths and turned them into assassins, sullying the name of the Wraiths."

"You saw how people looked at me out there," Conrad added. "People fear the Wraiths now. But the older neighborhoods, the people who have been here longer know better. They know what the Wraiths really are."

"Which is?" asked Raven.

"*Ulinta.* Protectors," said Malik. "We are a society dedicated to keeping the tradition of the Sisters alive. We protect magicians from their deaths, or worse, at the hands of Gray Elite."

"We also tend to be shadowy and sneaky," added Conrad with a smile. "So the jump to assassins and pirates isn't that far."

Malik glared at Conrad and said, "Indeed. As you would clearly know."

Conrad shrugged. "Some would prefer the name privateer."

Malik hummed his disapproval. He returned his gaze to Raven and said, "And you've left Zander because he's a bastard, and then you ended up down here."

"And I brought her straight to you," Conrad said.

"But as of right now, she is not a magician," Malik countered. "Raven, tell me what really happened."

"The rest of the story is exactly how I told you," she said. "I was in the woods, an automaton caught me, scavengers rescued me and then sold me. I thought the Destiny Show would help me get back there or something."

"Where is *there*?" Malik asked.

"That's also a problem," she said. "I don't really remember. But...I could find my way from the town of Oun." There was a Hellcat platform underneath it, and one of the Dweller scouts worked at the blacksmith.

"Ah," said Conrad. "Is that why you were looking for the Crusaders? A free lift?"

"The Crusaders?" Malik asked. "They're pirates. Who told you about them?"

"Zander mentioned them," Raven lied quietly. She didn't like how much Malik and Conrad already knew, and she didn't entirely trust either one.

Malik studied her a while longer. "He is still traveling," he said, never breaking his eye contact, "and...the Crusaders."

Raven's pulse beat harder.

Malik rapped his ringed fingers on the table. "Zander wants to get somewhere without anyone noticing. And the only place he would need to get without being noticed would be Gracita."

Raven didn't have a lie; she hadn't anticipated him figuring that out so quickly.

Conrad leaned onto the table, his eyes burning with curiosity.

"Why?" Malik whispered, more to himself than anyone else.

Raven didn't give him an answer.

Then his honey brown eyes blinked, softened. "He wants to get Rosaria out."

A pang of jealousy shot upward from her toes.

"The dead princess?" Conrad asked.

"There are rumors she is alive," Malik said. "It doesn't matter. It's a fool's errand. Even if Rosaria is alive, she has no military or political power. She is a figurehead. It would change nothing. That, and she would be well-guarded, or poised as a trap for any would-be rescuers. Even if she retains a fraction of the royal magic, she would not be able to take on an empire."

Raven didn't argue. A part of her thrived on Malik's distrust of the Dwellers' plan and his denouncement of the princess's importance. Another part of her worried for her friends' safety as they attempted that fool's errand.

The centrum hanging around her throat pulsed, and she fought the powerful urge to reach for it. Malik didn't know about Altair's Augur or its missing part. If he did, he held it in well. No one knew Zander's real mission had been to get the centrum far away from his father and the Hawks.

And it would stay that way.

Let everyone think the worst of Zander. Let them think him a deserting bastard. That way, no one would look any closer at his actions. The centrum would remain safe, Altair's Augur would remain silent, and no one would die from its use. It hurt to toss him to the vultures, but what choice did she have? She couldn't tell Malik and Conrad about the centrum, and if she tried to make light of Zander's actions, they would ask questions.

"But there's still the matter of our little bird," Conrad said, motioning with a graceful wave of his hand to Raven. "Magic or not, she turned a man to ash. Surely, that counts something toward my redemption."

"She's not a magician," Malik said with finality. "And your redemption lies with the Sisters, not with me. Of course, that doesn't mean you can't grovel at my feet."

Conrad heaved a dramatic sigh and turned to Raven. "I apologize for wasting your time."

"If you want help getting out of your mess, I will offer a hand," Malik said to Raven. "I can find you work if you are interested."

"What kind of work?" Raven asked. She hadn't intended to say it with as much bite as she did. Her first thoughts had gone to a job as a whore, then as a slave, and then as a fighter in the arena. "I'm not good at anything."

"Doesn't mean you can't learn," added Conrad lightheartedly.

"At the docks," Malik said.

"The docks?"

"He means air docks," said Conrad. "Not the sea docks."

Her heart skipped a beat. "Air docks? As in airships?"

Malik nodded.

Her thoughts scattered. "On an airship?"

"If that is what you want," he said. "I know a captain willing to accept a stranger onto his crew. You can work as long as you'd like. Seeing as you have no coin for boarding or food, I suggest taking a job."

Raven blinked at him. Her, work on an airship? The thought sent a nervous tremor down her spine and into her toes. She thought of her friends, of Zander and Ivy and Thalame. What would they think if she never returned? A mean little voice reminded her that her friends had wanted to send her back to Silver Glen. Zander hadn't wanted her along on his mission to save the princess; he had called her a hindrance.

Still, the idea of working on an airship in the meantime gave her a fluttery feeling. She couldn't tell if it was the good or bad kind of fluttery.

It took her a moment to realize Conrad and Malik were waiting for an answer. She swallowed and said as firmly as she could, "Yes. I'll work."

"It's hard work at times but better than fighting or whoring for your supper," Malik said. He shifted, and his beads shifted with him, clinking. He looked to Conrad and added, "And you."

Conrad waved off the concern. "I don't need a job, but I'm flattered you thought of me."

"If you're bent on redemption, our brothers and sisters in Moorin have had a string of bad luck. The Gray Elite are coming down hard on them. I'm sending you there to help."

Conrad let out a grunt of refusal.

"Moorin?" Raven asked without thinking.

"The capital of Gracita," explained Conrad. "The least friendly city to magicians. Filled with Gray Elite patrols and automaton soldiers."

"And," added Malik with a smirk, "I believe there is a ship leaving for Moorin tonight."

"Fantastic," Conrad mumbled, his humor gone.

Conrad led Raven back to the street. The sun seemed much too bright, and she shielded her eyes with her hands. The air felt just as sticky, though. She glanced to where the ocean met the horizon, the impossible blue on blue that stretched forever. How would it look from the deck of an airship? She imagined Zander's face when she told him about all of this. A rock fell into her stomach as a mean little voice reminded her that she might not see him or any of her friends again. If something happened to her or if something happened to them while they attempted the impossible... No, she couldn't think that way.

"A pik for your thoughts?" said Conrad. He was leaning against the white stone of the building.

She had no desire to talk about her growing mess of problems. "Malik said you were a pirate."

Conrad shrugged, but didn't deny it.

"How far have you gone?"

He followed her line of sight to the ocean. "Far but not that far. I've gone three days out in an airship. I've seen the southeastern half of Tinatun, the Islands of Ninulia, the Monilo Province. I've glimpsed the Gold Castle from the sky."

"The Gold Castle?" she asked. "It's real?"

"Oh, it's real," he said. "It's not as impressive as I thought. Spires of gold sure, and it gleams in the sun, but it's just a castle."

"Just a castle." She half laughed. "A castle is still a castle."

He nodded. They stood for a moment in silence. They were waiting on Malik to take them to the air docks. Raven hadn't gotten to stand still much since she had left the treehouse, and now that she had a moment, her thoughts churned, and her anxiety worsened until she thought she might be sick.

"So this friend of yours, Zander, was following me?" Conrad asked.

She nodded.

"And he took back that little box?"

She felt her skin prickle.

"And yet it was there when I left the room, and he was in the barroom the entire time, and you weren't. When I went to get it, it had mysteriously vanished."

He knew.

She swallowed and met his gaze.

"You stole it back, didn't you?"

She didn't deny it.

To her surprise and relief, Conrad laughed. "I'm lucky that old man of his didn't flay me on the spot for not having the damn thing. Tell me, little bird, what was in it that caused such a fuss?"

"I don't know. He never told me."

A lie, but not one that Conrad questioned. "The old man wouldn't tell me either. If you ask me, those Hawks are up to something."

"They're resistance," Raven said. "Of course they are."

Conrad chuckled.

The front door of the Destiny Show opened, and Malik walked out. He had left his dark robes in favor of leathers and robes similar to what Conrad wore. He had taken off his rings and necklaces, save for one ring and one silver chain with a pendant the color of the sun. He had a frightening number of knives and daggers. As he stepped toward them, he pulled his hood over his short brown hair.

"Let's be on our way." Malik fell into step beside Conrad.

Raven walked a step behind. She thought of Wayward Point—where would they have room for air docks? The air docks in Lenhala had been a towering structure of steel and glass with room for the hundreds of airships moving in and out. She surely would have seen such a building in Wayward Point.

They rounded the corner, and both Malik and Conrad halted. Raven nearly walked into them. Both stood still as stone. A feverish panic ran along her spine.

And then she saw what they had seen.

Men stood abreast in the street, armed with short swords, daggers, and clubs.

"There she is," one of the men drawled. Another man spoke in Tinatunian. A half dozen men spilled from an alley on their right, and more came from their left, surrounding them.

"Whatever do you gentlemen need?" asked Conrad. "There are nicer ways of asking for directions."

"The girl," said one of them, pointing his sword at Raven. "Boss is looking for her. He don't like you freaks stealing his things."

Raven tensed. Boss must be Barrow. The man who had bought her, from whom Conrad had stolen her.

"Ah," said Conrad. "He knows he lives in a city built on piracy, yes?"

"She belongs to him," another spat.

Another grumbled in Tinatunian.

"I belong to no one," Raven spat, earning herself a raised brow from Malik and an approving nod from Conrad.

"Nicely said, little bird," said Conrad. "I like the venom."

The thugs surged toward them, swords and clubs raised. Raven gasped, but Conrad stepped in front of her, and Malik stepped behind; both had drawn daggers. Conrad's blade found its mark on the first pirate's throat, and then a second and third. The two Wraiths moved with the lethal grace of a seasoned predator and a trained fighter, faster than wind, fierce as lightning.

And then the fight ended. The few wounded pirates who were left sulked and limped away. Most stayed on the ground, out cold or dead.

"Sisters," Raven breathed. She pressed a hand over her pounding heart.

Served them right.

Conrad cleaned his bloodied blades off on a dead pirate's shirt. Malik did the same and then slid the daggers back into their sheaths. One fit on a belt that hugged his torso; another vanished into his robes.

"Glad to see you're not rusty," Malik said to Conrad.

"Me?" Conrad gasped, hand on his chest in exaggerated shock. "Even the idea is absurd. If anything, I've improved."

"You're pale," Malik said to Raven. His honeyed eyes looked her up and down. "Are you all right?"

She nodded. She glanced around at the bodies. It was worse than looking into a pile of ash. The ash didn't bleed. These bodies slowly leaked onto the dirt street, staining it dark, seeping into the packed dirt and sand.

"They're dead," Malik confirmed. "And they would have done worse to you if we hadn't. This is a message to their boss that he no longer owns you, and if he wants to argue, he will have to take it up with the Wraiths. Few in this town are foolish enough, and those who are don't last long."

"One thing I always liked about the Wraiths," Conrad said to Raven with a nudge. "Not afraid to bully the bullies."

"I thought you weren't assassins," she said, her voice wobbly.

"We're not," Malik said. "We did not accept payment for these deaths. We were defending you. They attacked first. We reacted in defense."

It made sense, logically. Conrad nudged her arm again and offered her a calming smile. That he could be so calm after killing someone... She didn't know what to think about it.

"Come on," Malik said. He put a steady hand on Raven's back and guided her down the street, around and away from the dead pirates.

She didn't want to think about them or the man she had turned to ash or the stranger she had stabbed in Ivy's garden back in Lenhala. She turned her gaze to the ocean instead, the endless blue that whispered of adventure. What would it be like to sail on an airship toward the horizon? What would she find on the other side?

She trained her thoughts on adventure as Malik and Conrad walked with her toward the air docks. She imagined herself in one of her old storybooks, a world where the magical core of a deadly machine didn't hang around her neck.

The air docks of Wayward Point were cleverly hidden inside a large cavern that opened to the ocean. A rickety wooden staircase, half smothered in sand, led down to the rocky shore and to a small platform floating on pontoons made from heavy balloons that looked to have once been in use by an airship. As they walked across the platform, Raven thought she spotted a pirate insignia inked on the side of one of the pontoons, worn by time and the salt water.

The platform wrapped one side of the cavern's wide mouth and led into the shaded cove. Blue-green water rushed through the cavern mouth, between the teeth-like rocks that jutted upward from the shallows. A waterfall cascaded down one side of the cavern, echoing over the stone. The docks themselves started just above the waterline and rose all around the cavern—a clutter of steel, brass, and copper attached to the walls. Catwalks and ladders connected the ports to each other, all supported by steel cables. Laughter ricocheted off the cavern walls. The space had a strong stench of brine and fish. Underneath it all, she sniffed grease and the heat of engines.

Malik started up narrow metal stairs; they wrapped around the cavern, stuck into the rock with pitons and thick steel cables. With every step, the metal groaned like it might give way, yet it held. Without a rail to hold onto, Raven trailed her hand along the rocky wall.

"How high are my odds of these stairs collapsing and sending me to my death?" Raven asked casually, though her voice trembled.

"Low," Malik answered. He didn't even glance back. "Sailors come up and down these steps several times a day. They're worn, not rusty."

Raven glanced down; indeed, she didn't see a bit of rust. Magic? For in a cavern of humid air and saltwater, rust would be impossible to keep away.

They made it to the main platform of the air docks, a thick floor of steel that formed a semicircle around the cavern. Raven glanced down; the floor was not solid but a lattice, and she could see down to the water below. Malik paused beyond the door of what appeared to be a tavern. Laughter and unharmonious chatter flooded from within, voices harshened by years of breathing exhaust and shouting over the engines. Inside, men and women in working clothes drank and talked.

Malik led them not inside but to a patio beside it. Fewer people lingered there. One man had fallen asleep on a table, drool soaking into his beard, while two others were speaking quietly over a hand-drawn map.

"I've got to find my contacts," Malik said. "You two, wait out here. Don't get into any fights you can't win."

Raven blinked, then realized that Malik had spoken to Conrad, not to her. Malik walked away, toward a building on the other side of the platform.

"Do you often get into fights you can't win?" Raven asked.

"Trouble likes me," he said, stuffing his hands into his pockets.

Raven meandered to sit at one of the tables, and Conrad followed her. He sat where he could see the ocean beyond the cavern, and his dark eyes settled on the horizon. Raven thought she saw the thirst for adventure there, maybe a longing for what he once had seen, the desire to see it all again.

"I've heard that a man can sail the world until he's old and blind and deaf, and never see the same thing twice," she said.

"Who said that?"

"I read it in a book."

Conrad laughed. "Reading fairy tales?"

"They're not fairy tales," she said. "They're adventure novels."

He shrugged. "Life out there isn't always as neat and adventurous as people make it out to be. It's hard work, constant work, and if you're...not operating on a strictly legal account, you're paranoid." He let out a sigh of defeat.

Raven let her mind drift. She imagined Conrad as a Wraith, then as a pirate, then as the thief. He'd done more than she had, more than she might ever do. No, she told herself. She would do more than what she had. She would see what the horizon held.

And there, sitting outside the tavern in the hidden air docks of Wayward Point, she decided that she would have her own adventures. Yet, in her mind, when she imagined adventure, she also imagined a blue-eyed, dark-haired boy beside her. She reminded herself that he wanted to send her back to Silver Glen while he played hero; he clearly hadn't imagined the same of her.

Shaking off the surge of bitterness, she asked, "What are you going to do?"

Conrad let out another sigh, this one deliberate. "I suppose I could go to Moorin and see what adventure is to be had there. I've never been to the city itself, you know. I've been to smaller outlying cities around Moorin, but I've never been in the heart of the Gray Elite empire. Might be fun."

"You could leave now," she whispered.

Malik hadn't returned. The path to the stairs, to the town, to the ocean, was clear.

Conrad seemed to read her thoughts. "I could. But I would rather the Wraiths not be any madder at me than they already are."

"What did you do to make them mad?"

He shrugged and leaned onto the table. It tilted slightly. Resting his cheek on his hand, he said, "Like Malik said, I'm a greedy bastard. I like shiny things. I became a Wraith when I was eleven. Thought it was what magic folk like me were supposed to do. Turns out, I'm a pirate at heart. I found a map in the Wraiths' archives. I borrowed said map without permission, and they kicked me out not two years later."

"Did it lead anywhere?"

Conrad blinked as though that hadn't been the response he had expected. "It did. An island about three days from the southeastern Tinatunian coast, abandoned. Found good loot there." He sighed with longing and sank a little further onto the table. "The Wraiths didn't see it like that. They took the map and burned it, something about desecration or something sacrilegious."

"What did you do after?" Raven asked, building the story of Conrad in her head. Wraith, pirate, thief, seeking redemption for his crimes—she would read that book.

Conrad straightened. "Why so interested in my life?"

"Because it sounds like an adventure," she said.

Conrad gave her a half smile. "I suppose it does. Though isn't every life an adventure?" He looked toward the ships that lined the docks. There weren't very many, and most were small. "Besides, I could do with a vacation from this place. The beach is nice, and the people are entertaining, and I can sleep without worrying about my throat being sliced at night, but I've been here too long for my own liking. I'm starting to get anxious. And they say if you want to broaden your horizons, the best thing to do is go toward one."

She liked that advice. She liked it a lot.

"But what about you, little bird?" Conrad tilted his head toward her, dark eyes glinting in the lantern light. "I don't know if you know what you're getting into by jumping aboard one of these...fine vessels." He eyed the array of airships. None were shiny and none were new; most were patched and ramshackle. "You might fall in love with it and never want to get off."

"I don't know," she affirmed.

Conrad lifted his brows.

"I've never been on an airship or worked on one, but I've always wanted to." She looked into the sliver of sky she could see, where it met the sea. She felt a ping of longing, the urge to go toward it. Just to see. She thought of the airships and sky cities that she had carved into the stone ceiling of her bedroom in Silver Glen, of the dreams she had nurtured while trying to fall asleep. "I've always wanted to see the world from the sky, to just go wherever I wanted, see the world, see what's out there."

Conrad hummed. He set both elbows on the table and leaned toward her. His dark eyes searched hers.

"What?" she asked.

"I'm looking to see if there's a pirate in there somewhere," he said, looking down his nose at her, exaggerating a squint.

She let the comment roll off her shoulders. "I'm not a pirate."

"Yet," he said. "I wasn't a pirate either until I walked the gangplank onto the deck. Then I was."

"I wouldn't be good at it," she said. "Pillaging and stealing."

"Ah, got one of those pesky consciences?"

274

She nodded.

He let out a grievous sigh. "Well, I suppose someone in this world needs one. Thank the Sisters it's not me." He shifted in his chair. The wood groaned. "I sailed for a while, but I came back to Wayward Point because I had someone to come back to." Something dark passed over his eyes. "But, that string has been cut, and I can head toward whatever horizon I damn please. I don't have to come back here anytime soon—or ever."

She suspected he meant his lover, his girl, who had left him for another. She didn't know if the bitter pain she felt when she thought of Zander was the same or something different. Zander had not outright left her for someone else, though they hadn't been together in order for him to have left her in the first place. Yet it felt like it. A wound inside, as her stepmother had put it, that phantom pain of loss, grief, and heartbreak.

In a blink, that pain vanished from Conrad's face, and a smile replaced it. He glanced at Raven, then at the ocean. "I hear the west coast of Gracita is lined with white sand beaches," he said dreamily, "mermaid lagoons and sunken pirate ships, hundreds of islands waiting to be explored."

"Sounds exciting," she said.

"When I'm done in Moorin, I think I'll head west, see what's over there," Conrad said with certainty. "What about you, little bird?"

"I'd like to see as much of the world as possible before I'm blind and deaf and too old," she said. "I think I'll start with whatever Malik has lined up for me."

His grin widened, and he laughed—not a teasing laugh but one full of joy. Raven tried to picture him as a ruthless pirate, out there pillaging and sinking ships. He had made the decision to have adventure, and she had too.

While Zander was out rescuing his princess, Raven would have her own adventure. Maybe a job on an airship was what she really needed. She would only have been a bother to him and the others, a hindrance. Raven had always wanted to ride an airship and see the world, and now she had nothing stopping her.

Malik returned with good news; he had found a ship that would take Raven on as crew. It happened to be the same ship that would be taking Conrad to Moorin. Malik took them to the ship, docked on the first tier. It was a plain ship of dull steel and bronze, its bow and stern both pointed, its balloons a reddish brown. On the side, MARIANNE had been painted in a darling silver script.

Marianne, Raven quickly learned, was a cargo vessel that specialized in rum—a special rum only made in Vinitula, a city in the southern half of Tinatun, and according to Conrad, gold in a bottle.

"Goes down like liquid sunshine," he said with a coy smile and a wink at Malik, who scowled.

Raven sensed a story in that scowl, and she wanted to ask about it. Later, she told herself, when Malik couldn't frown.

Malik introduced them to Captain Warren, a narrow man with charcoal hair and a full beard to match. He wore a battered tricorn hat with a gold rim to signify him as captain.

"This the new meat?" asked Captain Warren in a gruff, jolly tone that sounded like it belonged to a much broader man. He looked Raven up and down. "She'll do. I've trained plenty of kids to sail. You won't be trouble, will ya?"

"No," Raven said. She quickly added, "Captain."

He nodded. Then he turned his attention to Conrad, who had been examining the lettering of *Marianne*.

"And you want me to transport this pirate into Moorin?" asked Warren. Every word dripped skepticism.

Conrad acted as though he hadn't heard.

"Yes," Malik said, drawing out the word, scowling at Conrad. "With full payment for passage."

Warren harrumphed. He looked none too enthused about Conrad.

"You have my permission to lock him in the cargo hold for the duration of the trip," Malik said.

That got Conrad's attention. He frowned at Malik.

"Keep him away from the rum and out of trouble."

"I'll consider it," said Warren, looking at Conrad like a piece of contraband that he didn't want aboard his ship. "Might make the crew feel more secure. And if we're stopped by the Gray Elite, we can claim him a stowaway, and then he'll be their problem."

Conrad's scowl deepened.

Raven swallowed. If they were stopped by the Gray Elite, they would recognize her. If they found her, she doubted they would care about a stowaway pirate.

276

Malik cleared his throat. "It would be best if the Gray Elite didn't know she was on board either."

Warren's eyes narrowed.

"It would be best if they didn't see her," Malik added lowly.

Warren frowned at Malik. "You're giving me some risk, boy," he said, though not maliciously. "You're going to owe me after this one."

"Of course," Malik said, nodding.

Conrad rolled his neck. "Don't worry about the Gray Elite, Captain," he said confidently. "They won't find me."

"Not if I tie you to the bow," Warren countered, his mouth a straight line.

Raven didn't know if the captain joked or not, and by the looks, neither did Conrad.

Warren turned back to Malik. "I forgot to mention," he said, his voice low. "There's no official word, but we heard rumors that Luckett's scouting ship went missing. They suspect it went down somewhere to the north. The crew's gone—captured, most likely."

Malik didn't respond, but his lips tilted downward. His fingers flinched like he wanted to make fists, but he didn't. He held himself remarkably still. "Thank you for the news, Captain," he said, his voice strained. "Keep me informed."

Warren nodded. "All right you two," he said to Raven and Conrad, "Let's get you settled in. We leave tomorrow at first light."

The captain led them up the gangplank and onto the *Marianne*. A U-shaped passageway went around the main deck, skipping over the back of the ship where the engines were. The interior mirrored the outside, all ramshackle steel and bronze, patched and welded, but it did not dull Raven's anticipation—a real airship!

He led them through a bulkhead and into the bridge. The pilot's raised seat faced an expanse of angled windows, giving the best view of the sky. Right now, those windows held a marvelous view of the cavernous air docks. The navigator sat to the left of the pilot, as noted by the mess of maps and charts, air traffic maps, patrol routes, no-fly zones; land, sea, city, and sky. The area to the right of the pilot held a number of gauges, speaking tubes, levers, and dials. Behind it all, a raised platform overlooked the entire bridge—the helm. Beside the brassy railing, a dozen speaking tubes surrounded the captain's chair.

From the bridge, Warren started the official tour of the ship. The passageways were barely wide enough for two average people to pass. Ladders connected the various decks: main deck, middeck, and the lower deck, also known as the cargo hold. The cargo hold took up the most space, though not much larger than a small tavern. The engine was a tangled mess of pipes, gears, gauges, and pots. It was silent now, but Raven could imagine all the parts moving with efficiency, just like an automaton.

The quarters were located on the middeck, along with the galley. The rooms weren't much bigger than her old room at Silver Glen. Rather than doors, sage green curtains hung in each doorway. Each room held four cots and four footlockers. There were two small washrooms at the end of the quarters—no bath, no shower, just a copper basin and a small toilet.

Warren led Raven to one of the rooms and pulled aside the curtain. "You'll be in here. You're sharing with two others, both women." He looked Raven dead in the eye, and all humor faded from his face. "If any of the men on my ship give you grief, you let me know. I don't tolerate such behavior."

Raven blinked, but the captain didn't relent his stare.

Conrad leaned closer to her and whispered, loud enough for the captain to hear, "I think he's serious."

"I am," said Warren. "When you meet Lewis, ask her what happened to the man who gave her grief."

Raven nodded. Where had Captain Warren's sense of justice been when she'd been in the arena?

"Do I get bunkmates?" asked Conrad.

"No," Warren said flatly. "I have a special room set aside for you."

Conrad's grin fell into a frown. "It's not a cell, is it?"

Warren chuckled, and Conrad's frown deepened.

"Can I stay in Raven's room?" Conrad whined. "I promise Raven will keep me in line."

It was Raven's turn to laugh. The bubble in her chest felt unnatural—when had she last laughed?

She thought of how easily Conrad and Malik had dispatched those pirates. Neither had gotten so much as a scratch. Conrad didn't need her, or anyone, to keep him in line. He knew it too, and Raven envied that about him. How easily he moved through life, knowing he could survive a fight. Then again, Malik seemed adept at keeping Conrad in line.

"No," Warren said firmly. "You want to sleep in that room, you ask the girls. If they say no, it's a no."

Conrad deflated a little.

Conrad's room turned out to be behind a secret door near the end of the quarters. A steel panel that blended in near perfectly with the rest of the wall—save for the natural-looking dent that served as a handle—turned out to be a door. The room beyond held a narrow cot, nothing more.

Conrad stuck his head in, examining the space. He hummed in disapproval. "I suppose it's not the worst. I was imagining something with a bit more footroom and color. Maybe a window."

"I'll inform the maintenance crew," Warren said dryly.

Raven glanced into another of the rooms. In the one across from Conrad's closet, each of the four bunks had a pillow. Every locker had a piece of fabric sticking out of it. One had a picture of a little girl taped to the front.

A crew. She would be in very close quarters with this crew. The rooms had barely enough room for one person to stand, let alone four. She imagined they had to get into bed one at a time and get up in the same manner.

Her gut trembled, but she didn't think it was from making a bad choice. No, it had the trademarks of newness, the anticipation of the unknown, of taking a risk.

"That's about it for right now," said Captain Warren. "The crew will help you learn the ropes. Best to learn by doing, in my opinion. Let's head back. Most of the crew is staying at the inn here, though a few have wandered into town for their dose of depravity, but we'll be meeting back here tonight to be ready to launch tomorrow."

With that, he led them back to the main deck and down the gangplank to the air docks. Warren headed to the inn—the tallest building in the cavern—while Conrad and Raven meandered to the tavern. Conrad went to buy himself an ale; he offered to buy one for her, but she declined. She had had enough ale for a while.

She leaned against the table and absently pulled the chain of her locket, pulling the locket into her fingers. The metal felt warm. She ran her thumb across the engraved front, thinking of the engraving inside. What did it mean that the Destiny Show's emblem was inside her mother's locket? Had her mother left her a message to go there? Had her mother been to the Destiny Show? To Wayward Point? Was there something here Raven was supposed to find? A clue in some scavenger hunt?

Or maybe the real answer was simple. Maybe her mother had bought the locket here—or stolen it, given the town's reputation—although the idea that her mother had stolen the locket didn't settle well. It took some of the magic of it away, and she didn't like it.

"That's a nice locket," came Malik's smooth voice.

Raven jumped and clutched the locket in her fist, hiding it from view. Malik stood a few feet away; she hadn't even heard him approach. Part of being a Wraith, she supposed. Malik's eyes were intent on her closed fist, the one that held the locket. He held a bundle of fabric in his arm.

"I haven't seen much jewelry like that around here." His eyes moved up to her face, searching. "Where did you get it?"

She thought for a moment to lie but, after a hesitation, didn't see the point. "It was my mother's," she told him.

She thought about asking him if the Destiny Show emblem had significance, but he might ask why. He might ask to see the emblem inside the locket. She couldn't open it. She couldn't let him see the centrum.

Malik wore an unreadable expression. "Your mother? She is..."

"Dead, I suppose," Raven said. "I never knew her. This locket is all I have of her."

"Oh," Malik said, with neither pity or sympathy. He handed her the bundle. "I found you a few changes of clothes. That outfit is fine here in the heat, but it's cooler inland, and you know how stingy people can be when it comes to skin."

The bundle looked to be a few simple shirts, a corset of brown leather and brass grommets, and simple trousers.

"Thank you," she said.

Malik started to say something else, but at that moment, Conrad sauntered around the corner. He wore a wide grin and held a tankard of ale. When he spotted Malik and Raven, his smile flickered into a frown, but quickly recovered. He walked up and threw an arm around Malik's slender shoulders.

"I could feel the seriousness ten feet away," Conrad said, mostly to Malik. "Has anyone ever told you to lighten up?"

"You have," Malik said, his mouth a straight line. "Several times."

"And you still don't take my advice to heart," said Conrad, sipping his ale loudly.

Malik gave a halfhearted chuckle and pushed Conrad's arm off his shoulders. With the distraction, Raven slipped the locket back under her shirt.

Raven spent her last moments in Wayward Point at the tavern. To keep her mind off her own anxiety, she picked Conrad's mind for stories, including the one that cast him out of the Wraiths' good graces.

"I'll find that island again," Conrad said, no doubt in his voice or in his eyes. "There was more to be found there, I know it."

After a meal at the tavern, they returned to the *Marianne*. As did the rest of the crew. They were fewer than she imagined, though on a ship as small as the *Marianne*, it wouldn't need that many hands. They all met in the galley—the only space big enough for all of them, minus the cargo hold, which was full—and Warren introduced Raven as the newest crew member, and Conrad as living cargo.

Lewis greeted her eagerly. She had olive skin and short dark hair. Lewis radiated warmth, and she reminded Raven of Lena—always happy, always smiling. Her other roommate, Jetta, stood a head taller than Lewis and held herself with authority. Jetta had dark red hair that she kept braided down her back, and a well-tanned complexion. Tattoos covered both arms, her neck, and most of the exposed skin Raven could see, mostly of tinker tools, blades, and fish. Lewis greeted Raven with a warm hug; Jetta greeted her with a handshake.

Conrad tried to say hello, but Jetta glared down her nose at him. "Cargo doesn't talk," Jetta said, her words accented with Tinatunian.

"The door locks from the outside, you know," Lewis added, winking at him.

Conrad frowned. "I will keep that in mind."

"See that you do," Jetta said, patting him on the shoulder. Conrad's knees buckled under the force, but he quickly recovered.

Night fell, and the lantern light of the docks and the reflection of moonlight on the bottom of the cavern combined to cast an eerie glow. Standing on the sundeck—the walkway on the top of the ship—Raven leaned over the railing to see the undulating reflection of moonlight, ever shifting, ever moving, casting a ghostly light over the cavern walls. The distance made her knees weak, and she tightened her hands around the railing.

A wild thought stuck: she could set sail and never come back. She could leave all her mess behind and start new in the skies. She could—

She couldn't walk away from her friends. She couldn't just leave Zander and Ivy, even if they might have done it to her.

A warm breeze blew into the cavern, brushing against her cheeks. It pulsed underneath her skin, and for a sickening moment, she stood in the arena, burning alive, fighting for her life—

She gasped, hands clutching the metal rail, and the vision faded.

But the heat did not. She put a hand against her neck. Warm. Too warm. Feverish.

Panic started at the base of her neck, along with a dull throb, and as she started back to her bunk, she convinced herself that it had been a long, stressful day. Pirates, escapes, and magic—too much for one girl. Too much for her. She needed to sleep it off.

Lewis reclined on the bottom bunk on the right, and Jetta had the bottom bunk on the left.

"There's the new kid," said Jetta, grinning. She fingered a dagger that had seen better days. "Don't be alarmed if you hear what sounds like a dragon trying to get in, that's just Lewis snoring."

"I don't sound that bad!"

"How would you know? You're asleep."

The comradery between the two women felt more welcoming than her introduction had. Raven tucked her boots into one of the empty footlockers beside her few articles of clothing and climbed onto the bunk over Jetta. Something about the woman's presence felt comforting.

"This is your last chance to jump ship and land on solid ground," Lewis said to Raven.

"I'm not giving up so soon," Raven said.

"Good," Jetta said. "You're going to need that spirit. The boys don't think they need to wash when they're in the sky."

"What's wrong with the privy?"

"Nothing," Lewis added. "But boys are boys, and whoever smells the worst gets bragging rights."

"That's disgusting."

"That's men for you," Jetta said, half laughing.

Raven rolled onto her side so that she could see Lewis. "The captain told me to ask you about the guy who gave you grief."

Lewis chuckled. Jetta snorted with bitter laughter.

"I hadn't been on the crew very long," Lewis said. "One of the crew kept making lewd comments to me, but I didn't take it seriously. I grew up in Wayward Point, so I'm used to stupid men and messy rules, you know? Then one afternoon, I was working the deck with a few others after a rainstorm, and the guy smacked my ass. Hard too. The guys all stopped like they'd been slapped, and the next thing I knew, they grabbed this guy and heaved him overboard."

"Oh," Raven said.

"We were over the ocean, a day out from the closest land," said Jetta. "The bastard either died on impact or drowned."

"I always imagined that he had survived the fall, floated on a piece of driftwood for days, dying of thirst, burning under the sun, going mad with hunger, and then, just when he thought he couldn't make it, he spots land, glorious land! And then a shark takes him under in a spreading pool of blood," said Lewis without a speck of malice in her voice.

Jetta laughed.

Raven offered her a smile. "That's a vivid picture."

Lewis grinned at her, the pale light from the window glinting off her eyes.

Raven didn't fall asleep immediately. She laid on her back, listening to the calm breathing of her bunkmates, breathing in the scents of steel, leather, and salt. An airship. All that daydreaming, and she had made it. It didn't feel real.

She lifted her hand to the cool metal of the ceiling. In the dim light, she could barely see the outline.

And she could feel it.

It might have been the humidity, the stale air of the airship, the stressful day, but she felt it. The fever, snaking underneath her skin like something alive. It wasn't as strong as it had been, a ghost of itself. Since she had burned that man in the arena, it had felt repressed, calmed.

Could Conrad be right? Had it been magic? But how?

She put a hand to her throat, where the chain of her locket rested. She hadn't taken it off; she didn't want anyone else to find it. The locket rested against her chest, warm.

Magic or fever—she didn't know which she would rather it be.

The next morning, Raven worked alongside Lewis. She gave Raven tips and advice almost constantly, but Raven didn't complain. She had never known how much work there was in readying an airship—tanks to check, supplies to organize and load, locks to secure, procedures to follow, and a tremendous amount of up and down ladders, shouting jargon, and checking things. And finally, finally, the engine rumbled to life.

Lewis took Raven to the sundeck, and from there, she watched the airship nimbly maneuver out of port, away from the dock, and through the cavern opening. The engines growled, then purred, and the *Marianne* started its ascension to the cloudy sky. The rocky shore fell away, the specks of Wayward Point shrank, and the ocean stretched on forever. Her eyes followed the gentle curve of Tinatun's coast, shrinking until it vanished into the horizon.

The ship rose through low clouds, and Raven held her breath—chilled mist graced her skin. She blinked, and the clouds were below them.

She had touched a cloud!

Lewis laughed. "It gets old after a while." She leaned onto the rail beside Raven. The wind rustled her short hair. "Or so they say. It hasn't for me yet." She winked. "And the view is always nice."

The view—Raven gasped. The *Marianne* rose high enough for her to see the expanse of Tinatun, beaches as far as she could see, spotted with cliffs and thatch-colored villages. The blue-gray of the sea became deep blue, light blues, and shadows, every bit of it glimmering. The ship started north, and they left the sea behind. Below, Tinatun passed at alarming speed, and soon they had crossed the border into Rhynwier.

"Should we go back inside?" Raven asked Lewis when the ocean was a speck on the horizon.

Lewis shrugged. "The captain said you might want to see the view your first time around. Says it keeps the new kids from wandering away from their work. This way, everyone knows you're up here and not down there, or assuming you're working when you're not. Clarity and communication are key to life. Keeps people alive."

Raven nodded, but a guilt settled on her shoulders.

"Don't worry about it," Lewis said. "The ship won't fall out of the sky because we're up here."

Raven meandered to the bow of the ship. The countryside stretched on forever to the north. The green became blue, then blurry blue-gray. What had happened in Silver Glen since she had left? Had her father cursed her out of his family? Had Mel told him what happened? What did they all think now that she and Zander had been gone all this time? Did her father assume her a failure, dead and enslaved in the city?

Maybe, if she got a chance, she would send him a letter, just to let him know she was alive and well.

And somewhere else, the treehouse stood hidden. Had they left to rescue the princess yet?

It didn't matter. She wouldn't worry about Zander or his princess. She had her own adventure to have, her own future to plan out. Raven turned her attention to the world as it passed below. The airship passed over numerous little villages and farms, so many people going about their days, doing chores, living.

Lewis came to stand beside her.

"Makes the world feel smaller," Raven said.

"Up here, yeah, it does." Lewis propped a thin leg on the lowest rung of the railing. "But once you're down there again, the world feels just as big as it did before."

"Does it?"

Lewis nodded. "I've been working for Captain Warren for seven years, and I haven't tired of it yet. I've seen places I never thought I'd see, places I didn't know existed, and met people whose lives were so different from mine, I thought I'd gone into another world. I didn't have any family to speak of when I joined, but the crew has become the family that I chose." Lewis turned to Raven. "It can be yours too, if you want. I'm not so sure about that friend of yours, but you are welcome."

Raven laughed, but the wind stole her breath. She coughed, and Lewis laughed.

Raven returned inside to work. With the minimal crew, something always needed to be watched or fixed. Raven spent the day with Lewis and Jetta. Lewis worked odd jobs. Jetta worked in the engine, the best damn pair of hands it had seen in a long time—according to Jetta. She spent the majority of her time in the engine room or in the tank room, shouting orders to the other mechanics, who listened without hesitation.

"That's the trick." Jetta nudged Raven's arm. "You got to let them know you're no pushover."

Raven nodded, though she doubted anyone would ever listen to her like they did Jetta.

The crew took meals in turns, and while Raven dreaded it being the slop she had read about in her books, the food turned out to be jerky, water, ale, and dried fruit and nuts. Conrad joined her for meals. He worked in the cargo hold, the least troublesome part of the ship.

Throughout the day, Raven kept busy, but she couldn't forget her fever.

When her attention slipped, when her mind wandered, she felt it, under her skin, burning a little hotter when she thought about it.

By sunset, she couldn't ignore it any longer. It burned when she thought about it; it burned when she didn't think about it. Lewis took her and Conrad to the sundeck to watch the day fade into night, and Raven relished the cool air on her face and neck, the mist of the low clouds, like tiny little drops of ice.

Raven glanced over the railing and spotted the mass of metal and glass behind them, sparking in the evening light, a blur on the horizon. In front of them, the countryside was green and speckled with small villages, rolling hills and curving rivers.

"We'll be crossing into Gracita around midday tomorrow," Lewis said, nodding toward the west. "We've got clearance, so they don't have a reason to search us at the border, but if they do, you know the signal."

So Conrad and Raven could hide.

Raven leaned against the cool railing of the bow, letting the chill leech some of the heat from her skin. It didn't last long. Soon, the metal under her hands was hot. She moved her body a little further down it, where the metal was still cool.

It didn't last long either.

"Raven?" purred Conrad. He appeared at her side without a sound. He tilted his head toward her, his eyes knowing more than he said. He searched her, around her, seeing more than most could.

She couldn't hide it anymore. She opened her mouth to tell him, to explain, but the words were lost. A sudden, violent upheaval of heat sent her sprawling onto the sundeck. She gasped for breath, the fever burning her alive, turning her to ash just like it had the pirate. She couldn't think, she couldn't breathe. The heat. Blinding, suffocating heat.

Conrad appeared and rolled her onto her back, but he quickly pulled his hands away, shaking them as if burned. His coal-dark eyes had gone wide. On her other side, Lewis bent over; she was speaking—her lips moved—but Raven couldn't hear her. All she heard was the rushing pulse of her blood; all she felt was the surge of heat through her skin.

Darkness ebbed on the edge of her vision.

Closer, farther. Closer, farther. Pulsing with the fever. Beating with her heart.

Every time she opened her eyes, Conrad met her gaze. She was still on the deck. Then stars blinked all around them, brighter and closer than she had ever seen them, almost close enough to touch. Were they made of mist too?

The darkness receded a little with every heartbeat.

"Sisters," Conrad breathed.

He sat beside her. Someone had put a pillow underneath her head. Something cold rested against her throat and her forehead. She tried to reach for them, but her leaden arms didn't respond.

"What happened?" she managed to ask, her voice hoarse, like someone who had been screaming.

"I was going to ask you," Conrad said, his smile gone. "Is this the fever you talked about?"

She tried to nod but couldn't. "Yes."

"I can feel it," he whispered. "The magic, it's there—unstable and violent, but it's there. No doubt about it now. It's unlike anything I've felt before." A crease formed between his brows. "Before, the magic was weak and fluctuating, but this... I don't know." He ran a hand through his braids, throwing them over his shoulder. The beads clinked. "The crew thinks you're sick, which is why you're still up here. That, and we couldn't touch you without burning ourselves."

"Am I?" she asked weakly. "Sick?"

Conrad met her gaze but didn't answer. His coal-dark eyes wore worry, and she didn't like it on him.

22

R aven slept on and off during the night. Clouds rolled in—cooling clouds and blessed mist—and blocked out the stars. The lantern on the deck went cold. Raven thought she had died, that she had crossed over to the other side or become something new entirely. The certainty of her death shattered when the first glow of dawn appeared, brightening the inky darkness with light blues and golds.

Conrad stayed with her. Lewis brought food and cold packs for Raven's head, though nothing worked. The fever consumed, and it would consume her. She knew it. Her bones knew it.

She closed her eyes, pushing away the thoughts of people she would never see again, the places she would never get to see. She didn't want to die, not yet, not until she had seen everything—

Conrad sat beside her—humming—and pulled her out of her sullen thoughts. He held an ink bottle and a fine-tipped brush.

"What's that?" she asked, her voice weak and wobbly.

"Protection." His lips formed a straight line that reminded her of Malik. "I'm worried you might attract the wrong sort of attention at the border. The automatons there can detect magic, and this is a temporary solution to get us into Gracita."

He uncorked the ink bottle, and the pungent smell carried more than simple ink.

She coughed. "What is that?"

"Tampered ink." He met her gaze. "I'm going to draw a rune on you. It will hide your magic from the automaton's detection. It won't last long, but it will be enough for a time."

"Like the tattoos?" She thought of the rune-like tattoo that Zander, Marie, and Thalame shared, for burning off the extra magic when they used their powers, to hide them from detection.

Conrad met her gaze. If he wondered how she knew, he didn't ask. "Yeah, like the tattoos."

With permission, he pulled up her loose fitting-shirt to reveal her stomach. Then the cool, wet stroke of ink brushed against her burning skin. The coolness lasted only a few seconds. The brush traced a complicated round whorl over her stomach. She tried to create the image in her mind as Conrad painted it, but she got lost in the sprawling, curving, spiderweb-like rune.

It relaxed her. The more of the rune he painted, the calmer the fever became. Something pulled the fever back, down and in, blocking it, sheltering it, hiding it somewhere deep within. Locking it away. A wet blanket over a smoldering fire.

Conrad set the ink bottle aside. "There. That ought to work for a while." He sighed and mumbled something in Tinatunian. Though she couldn't speak the language, it sounded something like a prayer or a mantra—practiced words.

"What did you say?" she asked.

He repeated himself in Tinatunian, "*Gua a ihignni ninun.* It's an old pirate saying: 'May the sea be kind,' or in this case, the sky. There's no word in your tongue for *ihiginni*, but it means the journey, the ride, the voyage. It's how we ask Minerva to guide the ship and keep it from crashing or capsizing or any those nasty things."

"I can feel it," she whispered.

"I can as well. The magic isn't as wild or tangled," he said. "The rune is old, far older than the Wraiths, one of the few things left over from the old world. It might be the only thing capable of hiding a magician these days."

"Old world?"

He shrugged. "No one knows much about the world before Gracita and Rhynwier, before magic and machines. It existed, but its ruins are scattered. I think of it like a mystery waiting to be solved." He looked down at her face and offered her a small smile. "You look better, less on the verge of death."

More like self-combustion, she thought. She said, "Zander has a tattoo."

"Most of the Wraiths who travel beyond Wayward Point do," Conrad said. "It's a safety precaution. If they didn't have it, the automatons would be able to detect them and hunt them down."

"It burns?"

He blinked, then nodded. "A side effect of the rune. It blocks detection, but it also blocks a bit of the magic, making it harder to use." He lifted a brow. "I take it you've seen Wraiths in action?"

"I have." She thought of Marie, the blood-binder, and Thalame, the healer. Their tattoos had burned when they used their magic.

"Ah, yes, my mysterious little bird," Conrad said, a smile in his words and in his eyes. "You've got quite the mystery behind you. Hawks, Wraiths, Gray Elite, and a bounty the size of a small bank vault." He hummed his approval. "Is this what you thought about when you wanted adventure?"

"I'd rather have mermaids and sunken treasure," she said.

Conrad laughed, a warming, heartful laugh. "I accept that answer. Though, in fair warning, mermaids are as temperamental as the sea: calm one minute; the next, a storm to rip unsuspecting vessels to shreds—not unlike a woman."

They sat for a while in silence. The sky warmed gradually, the clouds streaking with orange and purple and blue. The stars wavered, blinking out.

"Conrad," she whispered.

"Hmm?"

"What's happening to me?"

He didn't answer right away. "I can't say, little bird. I've never seen anything like what you've got. It's magic, that is for certain now, but it acts more like a sickness."

A magical sickness, which was why Thalame couldn't identify or heal it and why it hadn't gone away on its own. She wanted to ask if it would ever go away, if she would get better, but she feared his answer.

"I'm no expert when it comes to magic," he said darkly, "but when we get to Moorin, I know someone who is. The Wraiths there will be able to help. Because you're a magician, they are obligated by sacred oath to help you. I don't remember the exact words, but it's something about assisting the magically gifted regardless of risk to themselves."

She let out a long breath. A terrifying thought occurred—she had turned that pirate to ash, had burned him alive from the inside out. The fever had consumed him in a matter of seconds. What if it was consuming her, only slower? Would she fall asleep as a person and become a pile of ash in the night? Or wake up with her bottom half ash?

With that thought stuck in her mind, she couldn't find comfort. When sleep pulled, she fought it. Not even the cooling sensation of the rune could help.

When they came closer to the border, Conrad helped Raven into the ship and into the closet space. Her limbs were wobbly, her vision filled with shadows, her awareness numbed. She leaned heavily on Conrad. She didn't know how long they stayed hidden. She closed her eyes, and then Lewis stood in the doorway.

"All clear," she said, her voice distant, as though from underwater. "They didn't find reason to board."

"Good," came Conrad's voice from behind her.

And then Conrad half carried and half pulled her back to the sundeck where they wouldn't be in the way. As she sat down on the bow, a cloud passed over the ship and swathed her in cooling mist. Too soon, it left.

"Another day, and we'll be in Moorin," said Conrad, sitting beside her.

Raven didn't have it in her to respond. Would she make it another day?

The fever came and went in waves. She thought of rain. She imagined it would feel delightful against her skin, like the mist of the clouds, only better.

Conrad and Lewis exchanged positions beside her, one then the other, but always someone stood or sat nearby. Watching her, she realized. She felt guilty about not being able to work after Malik had gone through the trouble of securing this job for her. If she ever saw him again, she would have to apologize.

Gradually, the sky changed from bright blue to dim blue, and then streaks of yellow and orange made their way across the clouds. It was one of the most marvelous sights that Raven had ever seen, but the fever refused to allow her enjoyment. She could barely move, and so she had to witness the splendor while lying down.

Lewis left, and a second later, Conrad appeared.

He crouched with feline ease and folded his legs underneath him. He set the bottle of ink between them. "Let's see about that rune." He pulled up her shirt, and then gasped. "Sisters."

"What?" she asked, fear twisting her words in pleas.

"It's gone," he said, his dark eyes searching her stomach. "It's not been rubbed off or smeared. It's just gone."

"I haven't..." she started, but then she didn't really know. She might have moved too much and made the ink flake off.

"Not tempered ink." He frowned. His cool fingertips touched the skin just above her navel. "You're warm to the touch. Too warm. And the magic..." His gaze took her in, looking at her, but not at *her*. She realized then that he looked at the magic. "It's like the magic ate through the rune. I've never seen it happen that fast."

The color drained from his face, and her own panic flared at the sight.

Conrad painted another rune where the first had been. The initial strokes of the brush felt cool as ice, refreshing, but the feeling didn't last more than a few seconds. She could almost feel it working, feel the rune pushing down the magic, but at the same time, she could feel it working the opposite direction—the magic pushing back.

The sun sank lower as he worked, painting the delicate strokes and whorls. She set her sights on the changing colors of the clouds, from bright orange, to lush pink, to deep purple, to the stars as they blinked awake, one by one.

If she survived, she would come back to watch the sunset properly, standing with a mind ready to take in the beauty of it.

Only when the sun had gone completely did she notice that Conrad hadn't moved. He sat beside her, still as stone, his gaze on her stomach, on the rune. No emotion played across his face.

"That's what I thought," Conrad said after a long moment. "The magic is slowly pushing through the rune, devouring it, and it's dissolving. It's the same process that happens to the tattoos over time. The use of magic will deteriorate the rune. I've had mine done twice because of it."

She felt the cool touch of the brush, the coolness of the ink, as Conrad touched the rune up in places.

She released a slow breath, trying to keep her stomach steady as he worked.

With the rune fixed—for now—she sat up in her temporary lull to drink from a canteen. She hadn't eaten or drunk anything that day, and her thirst magnified at the sight of the canteen. She held the steel bottle with both hands, drinking eagerly, greedily.

Conrad held his hands over her, moving up and down her body. Searching the magic; he wore the same serious look. His hands hesitated over her chest. He frowned. "What's that?" he asked, his voice a rasp.

She pulled the canteen from her lips. Her hands shook as she twisted the cap back in place. His hand hovered above the locket.

When she didn't answer, he took the initiative and pulled it out of her shirt by the chain. Something in her bones snapped. The idea that someone else had their hands on her locket, her mother's locket, the centrum, turned her insides into something molten and furious. He turned it over in his hands, and then Raven yanked it out of his grasp.

"It's mine," she said firmly.

Conrad scowled, but underneath it, she saw something she hadn't yet seen in his features: fear. "What is in it?" he asked carefully.

"Nothing."

"Bullshit." Conrad grimaced. "I can feel it, Raven," he said, his whisper urgent. "There is something in there. I can see the magic around it. I couldn't see it before because it was cloaked in your own. Whatever is in that locket, it's the same magic that's killing you."

23

Raven spent the night slipping in and out of consciousness. Conrad repainted the rune on her stomach five times. He asked no more about the locket. He didn't speak much, but when he did, his words came out pleasant but forced. He was nervous about landing in Moorin—that much she could tell from the way his eyes flickered to the horizon, toward their destination, and the way his calm smile would fade into a straight line.

Moorin, capital city of Gracita, was the beating heart of the Gray Elite empire and the most dangerous place on the continent for a magician. She would be more worried about Moorin if she didn't feel like she might fall asleep and become a pile of ashes, never to wake up again.

Raven was somewhere between asleep and awake when she first heard the distant hum. She opened her eyes. From the sundeck of the *Marianne*, she could see airships in the distance. With every blink, they came closer. They glinted in the midmorning light, gold and silver and bronze and an array of other colors; balloons painted like clouds, like lightning, like bluebird eggs, like automaton heads; hulls sleek for speed, hulls wide for accommodating passengers and cargo.

Her breath tumbled from her lips.

"We're approaching Moorin," Conrad said, crouching beside her. "We need to get below before we land."

Though she knew Conrad was right, she wanted to stay and watch the airships fly. Conrad helped her to her feet and half carried her back into the airship. The buzz of the airships muffled into a dull roar. The commotion of their airship met them instead, the organized crew shouting jargon through the speaking tubes, preparing for landing, communicating with the air patrol in Moorin.

Conrad helped Raven to the galley instead of the closet. The cook put a canteen between her hands, and she drank the cool water eagerly.

"Attention," came Warren's voice over the speaking tubes, "prepare to land."

Relief and dread zapped through Raven. Relief to be off the ship, dread at what she might find waiting for her in the city of automatons and Gray Elite.

Lewis found her in the galley; she had assembled a disguise for her of men's clothes. Lewis helped her into their room to change; she didn't ask about the rune on her stomach. Raven quickly pulled the undershirt over her head to hide it. She didn't bother with a corset.

"It's all right," Lewis said softly. "You two aren't the first guests we've transported."

Lewis winked, and Raven got her meaning. If the captain and Malik knew one another, then this ship had likely smuggled magicians out of the city before.

Raven tucked her brown hair into a shipyard cap—a popular style in Moorin, according to Lewis, and thus inconspicuous. The brim extended along the front, shadowing her eyes. A loose-fitting vest hid her feminine frame, as did the trousers.

From the portholes in the galley, she and Conrad watched as they entered the city of Moorin, a sprawling metropolis of steel, bronze, and copper. The city sprawled farther than Lenhala. The buildings rose tall at the heart of the city, each building boasting a different color of metal, shining like a kaleidoscope in the sunlight, spotted with the vibrant greens of parks and gardens. The outskirts rose and fell along the rolling hills that surrounded the city. Several rivers intersected underneath grand bridges of white and beige stone, designed with gold and blue.

The *Marianne* approached the air docks, a massive stadium that rose above the shipyard, a dozen stories of docks arranged on a circular structure of steel and brick. Each dock opened with a copper-lined archway. Ships came and went from the air docks, the sounds a deafening roar of engines hissing and churning. Bigger ships docked on the highest levels, where the archways were wider and taller to accommodate size. The smaller ships docked on the lower levels. Raven craned her neck to see more as the ship slowed, as the engine purred lower and lower, but then the *Marianne* entered the air docks.

The crew busied themselves with docking; a Gray Elite met the first mate at the gangplank, a clipboard in his hand, asking for clearance permits; and Raven and Conrad slipped out of the cargo hold with the others and then into the air docks.

"Walk like a man," Conrad whispered to her.

Raven frowned but tried to mimic his saunter. She pictured how Zander walked, long legs first, hips still, shoulders tense.

"Better," Conrad whispered. "Might want to leer at a girl or two, for the ruse."

She didn't, mostly because the girls she saw on the dock were workers who looked like they could crush her throat with one fist.

Conrad guided her to the center of the air docks, where a dozen lifts carried cargo and crew and passengers up and down in gilded brass cages. Above, a glass dome protected them from the weather. Conrad chose a less crowded lift of passengers, and they started down to the street level.

Raven couldn't take in the sights fast enough. Every level buzzed with activity, boarding and unloading, people going every which way. The crowd was threaded with Gray Elite, but none paid any mind to her. Their lift landed on the street level, and she kept her eyes on Conrad as he weaved through the crowd toward the street.

Gray Elite guarded the exits, crossbows on their backs, pistols on one hip, a saber on the other. None of the guards looked enthused; most looked bored out of their minds.

They approached the gate, and one of the Gray Elite shifted. His green eyes met Raven's. Her heart thumped against her chest. She looked from him and to the city she approached. Across the street, a café declared the daily specials on a large blackboard, the letters neon and glittering. Beside it, a tavern advertised vacancies,

293

three tokens a night. Somewhere, a bard sang about the Tinatunian girls and white sand beaches.

She focused on her saunter, on Conrad's back, and on the archway that would lead them onto the street. And just like that, they walked through without trouble. Her feet hit the stone of the sidewalk, and she released a calming breath of relief. Conrad didn't slow, and she sped up her pace to keep up with him. The city blurred to shades of steel and copper and stone. The voices, the singing, the roaring and the airships—it all echoed.

Conrad turned down one street and then another and then turned into an alley. He caught Raven's arm and pulled her in with him. They walked down the alley and into another alley, blocking all view from the street.

"Are you doing all right?" he asked.

"A little flushed," she said. "But otherwise I'm...fine." Her breath left her. She felt the fever there, under her skin. She had been so focused on the arrival that she hadn't noticed it.

"Show me," Conrad said, motioning to her stomach. She lifted her shirt to the bottom of her ribs, and he clicked his tongue. "It's barely there. We don't have a lot of time before you'll need it redone. Come on."

Raven followed Conrad back onto the wide streets of Moorin. With every step, she felt the rune give a little more, felt the fever return a little hotter. She kept her eyes on Conrad, on the glints of sunlight off the beads in his braids.

They walked for a long time, or so it felt to her, with each step a chore, each breath a hammer in her lungs, each heartbeat a wave of burning heat. She stopped looking at the city around her. She stopped caring if someone recognized her.

"Hey," came Conrad's urgent voice. He appeared at her side.

She leaned on him; she had to. Her strength faded with each breath.

"Hold on," Conrad whispered. "It won't be long."

She forced her legs to move. To keep going.

Finally, when the darkness ebbed and flowed on the edges of her vision, when her legs no longer felt like her own, they arrived at a shoddy little inn tucked away on a side street. A plain wooden sign hanging above the door welcomed them to the Wooden Goblet Inn and Tavern. Conrad ushered her through the door and into the lantern-lit tavern.

"What can I get for you, gents?" came a pleasant woman's voice, though her words came out raspy and irritated. "Ah, drunk already?"

"No time for that," Conrad said. "I've got a problem for Engor. Immediately."

"He's in the back," said the woman, the irritation gone from her voice.

Conrad paused just long enough to hoist Raven into his arms. Relief swam through her limbs, and she gladly dropped her head against his shoulder. She heard the muttering of voices, quick and desperate; she felt the rumble of Conrad's chest as he spoke; she heard the telltale squeak of wooden stairs; and in the next moment, her back touched down on a hard mattress.

Through her swimming vision, she saw a room with dull plaster walls, no bigger than her room on the ship, just big enough for a narrow bed, a nightstand, and a washing basin.

Conrad stood at the bedside, and beside him stood a man with graying black hair and olive skin. His dark brown eyes beheld her with worry and jaded curiosity. The older man flattened the back of his hand against her cheek, her neck, her forehead. It took her a moment to register Conrad's voice—he was explaining the situation to the other man, the fever, the magic, the rune on her stomach.

"I didn't know what else to do with her," Conrad said. "I was hoping you would know something or someone who might."

"Caroline is your best bet," said the older man, his voice raspy and rough, not unlike his face. "Woman's got an eye for magical maladies, but getting to her is the problem. She doesn't leave her cave often. You might have to take this girl to her."

"Can we arrange a meeting?" Conrad asked, a bit of his joyful humor leaking into his words. "I would hate to drag Raven all the way there only to find she had stepped out for the evening."

The older man nodded. "I can arrange something. In the meantime, keep her cooled down. She's burning up. I'll find some iced cider or tea."

"I'll need ink," Conrad said.

"We've got plenty."

The older man left, and Conrad took his place beside the bed. He leaned against the wall and crossed his arms.

After a moment, he slid down the wall and folded his legs to his chest. He leaned forward on his knees and looked more like a child hiding than a grown man. "That's Engor. He's a retired Wraith. He no longer participates in the action, but he runs this little inn and tavern as a shelter and waypoint for magicians and Wraiths. It's something like a headquarters, though they have several other places like this in the city." He sighed. "I can't say what will happen now. You might have to stay here until the captain brings the ship back around."

Raven hadn't the space in her mind for such thoughts of her future. First she needed to survive. Then she could worry about Captain Warren and her job aboard his ship.

Engor returned with a pitcher of iced cider and a bottle of ink. He poured a small amount of the cider into a glass, and she drank it eagerly. Each sip cooled her, making it farther down her throat before her body heat warmed it. She drank three glasses of it before Engor set the pitcher and the glass on the nightstand.

Conrad took the bottle of ink and the brush and causally lifted Raven's shirt to show her stomach. He again drew the rune. This time, the ink felt like ice, and it took longer for the cooling sensation to fade.

"I was just telling Raven here how you are one of the few Wraiths who grow old in Moorin," Conrad said, a smile on his lips as he watched the older man's reaction.

Engor huffed. "Old? I hardly count forty-seven as old."

"For a Wraith living in Moorin, that's ancient," Conrad said.

"I won't argue that." Engor's gaze fell on Raven. "Life here is dangerous for magicians. One mistake means death. Like that Revenant. No one's heard from or seen him in months, which means he's probably dead."

Raven gasped. "The Revenant? He's real?"

Engor blinked in surprise; then the expression faded. "Of course he's real. He's a Wraith. Or was."

"I thought it was just a ghost story?"

"He's an assassin," Conrad added darkly in his storyteller's voice. "Deadly and accurate. The only people who see the Revenant are the ones he kills."

"If he kills anyone who sees him, then where do the stories come from?" Engor lifted an eyebrow, wrinkling his forehead even more so.

"That's an unimportant detail," Conrad said, his smile fading. He finished the rune, corked the ink bottle, and set it on the nightstand beside the pitcher.

"The Revenant is a Wraith, but he acts on his own," said Engor. "Some magicians do. He wore a copper mask when meeting with clients. That's how he kept himself hidden. I met him once. Creepy fellow. Silent. Still like stone. Let one of his fellows do the talking." Engor's frown deepened.

Raven pictured the Revenant in the dark blue and black robes like the Wraiths wore—the hidden daggers, belts and buckles, steel plates, and hardened leather. She imagined the copper mask, blank of expression, only the eyes visible, and the eyes her mind painted were entirely black, lid to lid.

She shivered.

Engor leaned against the wall, arms crossed. "But the real question is: what are we going to do with you? There's nothing more I can do without consulting Caroline. I've never heard of magic coming and going like this. Until we can get ahold of her, the only thing we can do is keep you alive."

Raven nodded as best she could. The rune helped to push down the burning fever and pull the darkness from her vision, from her mind.

Survive, she told herself.

Engor left, but Conrad lingered behind. When Raven glanced at him, she found his eyes pinned on the locket hidden beneath her shirt. Sensing her gaze, he looked up. A frown pulled his lips downward. She wished he would smile, tease, or joke, anything—he didn't.

Conrad touched up the rune—Raven had lost track of how many times he'd done it. The ink he used here lasted longer than the tempered ink on the ship, but even it succumbed to the fever. She drank continuously, iced cider, iced wine, near-frozen juice. It helped a little. She tried to sleep, but her worry of waking up as ash kept her awake.

Conrad vanished for periods of time, and she listened to the chatter coming from below. According to Conrad, the Wraiths met in the kitchen of the tavern. They talked about recon missions, interrupted automaton captures, and commandeered Moths, whatever that meant. They also shared patrol stories, jokes, and gossip. They spoke lowly, but with nothing else to listen to, Raven caught most of it.

"Hear anything more about Captain Luckett?" came one voice, and Raven's ears perked at that name. Warren had mentioned her to Malik.

"Captured," said another. "Found the reports. The Gray Elite wanted her alive, so she's not dead yet, but they're planning her trial and subsequent execution."

"Where's she being held?"

"The reports said East Wing in Doven Prison, but a guard we interrogated confirmed she's really being held in the Tombs."

"Then the reports about her being in Doven are a trap," said Engor.

"Most likely."

"We should do something if we can."

"The tombs won't be easy to get into or out of."

"Can we work her rescue into Project Demo? According to the maps, there's a way into the plant through the Tombs."

"It would be a suicide mission," said Engor. "The Tombs are impenetrable. No one escapes."

"So we let her sit down there until the Gray Elite execute her?" asked Conrad. "Or are you planning some daring rescue during that execution?"

Engor mumbled something under his breath.

"We've got scouts trying to pinpoint her exact location," came another voice.

"Project Demo is still being finalized, and we might be able to find a way in through the Tombs," said a mousy girl's voice. "Maps of the Tombs are harder to come by than maps of the emperor's house."

Raven took all the information in. What she would do with it, she didn't know. Captain Luckett had been taken into the Tombs, the prison where the Gray Elite had taken Princess Rosaria. If these Wraiths and the Dwellers could work together, they might be able to save them both.

What was Zander doing? Were he and the Dwellers on their way into Gracita right now looking for ways to save their princess?

Raven released a slow sigh.

The door to the room opened, and she sat up to see Conrad close it behind him.

"I hate meetings," he said as he sat on the floor beside the bed, back against the wall. He leaned his head against it. "So much talking, so little action. This is why I left. I hate all this waiting around and planning and talking and discussing and trying to keep everyone happy. It's a waste of time when I could be out there doing something. It's what I like about pirates, they're impatient. Never been the planning or debating kind."

The girl who ran the kitchens—Gretchen—brought up bread and hard cheese. "I made stew, but it's hot, and I didn't think you'd like it."

Raven accepted the plate of bread and cheese with gratitude. Gretchen was right—the idea of warm stew churned her stomach and agitated the fever under her skin.

She took a bite from the bread, despite her hunger's nonexistence. When Gretchen had left, Raven asked Conrad, "Who's Captain Luckett?"

"She's a retired Wraith. She does more piracy and smuggling nowadays," Conrad said. "She's been captured by the Gray Elite. The Wraiths here are working on getting her out, but they don't know how. It's a work in progress."

"Everyone is planning," Raven said more to herself.

"Are *you* planning?"

"It's hard to plan anything when I might not wake up tomorrow," she said grimly.

He frowned. "That's no way to look at things." He hummed, tilting his head. He lowered his voice. "Think about this instead: did you hear them talk about Project Demo?"

She nodded.

"It's an upcoming mission, bigger than anything they've done in ten years." Conrad's eyes glittered with mischief. "They are planning to blow up one of the automaton factories."

She blinked, unmoved by the plan.

Conrad leaned closer. "The big plant where they manufacture their magic hunters," he whispered. "It would put a serious dent in production, bruise the Gray Elite's ego, and make it easier to sneak a large number of magicians that the Wraiths have been hiding for months out of the city."

"That sounds more exciting," she said. She noted his frown. "You don't like the plan?"

Conrad waved away her concern. "I don't have a problem with the plan. It's big and dangerous. I love both those things, though I'd rather be on the beach somewhere or on a ship bound for an island I've never been to, but if this will grant me redemption with the Wraiths and the Sisters, then I'm here to help."

And he didn't like it. Conrad the pirate needed wide open skies and never ending seas, not the planning and scheming of the Wraiths. Raven would rather be elsewhere too.

He let out a sigh and leaned back against the wall. "In other news, Engor secured a visit with Caroline for you tomorrow night."

"Who?"

"Caroline," Conrad said. "I don't know if she has a last name or not. Never asked. She's not a Wraith, but the woman knows more about magic than anyone else alive today. It will be a harrowing trip across town, but the Wraiths are also planning a surprise on the Gray Elite to draw their attention elsewhere. That way, no one will pay attention to us. And we might have our answer as to what is happening to you."

She hoped so.

He stood and dusted off his trousers. "Now, if you will excuse me, I've got to see about a payment. Caroline won't be free. I could ask the Wraiths, but I'd rather not be in their debt."

Instead, she would be in his debt. She already was, more than she could repay. "Payment? How are you going to... You're going to steal it."

Conrad didn't deny it. "I won't be back until late. I've got a friend I want to stop and see. Don't you worry, little bird. I'll see if Gretchen won't sit up here with you." He flashed her a grin, then left.

Raven reclined. She draped an arm over her eyes, dousing her world in darkness. Even the shadows on the backs of her eyelids were tinted crimson.

The fever worsened. Raven drifted in and out of awareness. She drank cold teas and ciders and herbal water. Someone set ice wrapped in cloth against her face and throat and chest.

Despite the rune, she felt herself deteriorating, turning to ash.

People came and went from the room: Engor, the barmaid who never stayed too long, Gretchen the cook, and Conrad. He drew the rune anew every few hours.

Even now, the Wraith's ink wasn't enough.

No one wanted to say it, but she knew. She heard it in their calm, soothing words, the false hope. She would die. Raven focused on her breathing. In, out. In, out.

Between it all, the fever burned constant and harsh, stealing her breath, pulling on nerves. It wove vicious daydreams of her father's anger at her disappearance, her stepmother's frown of disapproval, Zander's scowl that she had gotten herself into so much trouble, and a man in a copper mask, blades drawn, gazing at her through blackened eyes.

She woke with a hand on her shoulder; the daydreams dissolved into the plaster room at the Wooden Goblet.

Conrad knelt by the bed. "Good morning, sunshine. You've slept the day away," he said, his smile undermined by worry. "You think you're up for a trip to see Caroline?"

She didn't think so, but she didn't want to tell him. Instead, she nodded. She tried to sit up, but her arms and legs refused to move. Her back felt leaden, and her stomach clenched. Conrad grabbed her hands and pulled her up; the world spun. Her muscles protested as if they had already turned to ash. Her bones felt like water.

Slowly, carefully, she sat her feet on the floor. The barmaid came and helped her wash her face and hands, helped her dress in dark clothes, and then Conrad carried her down the stairs. He carried her through the backroom and into the alley. The balmy air brushed against her cheeks. All around, the city settled for the night, with evening fading to inky gold in the low western horizon. Twilight stained the world in golden shadows.

Three Wraiths were making the journey to Caroline's with her and Conrad, and they had procured four automaton horses. Conrad helped her onto the back of one, and he climbed up after her. He secured one arm around her waist. The Wraiths set out down the alley, toward Caroline's, and Raven had a seed of hope that this mysterious woman would be able to stop the spread of the fever.

"She'll ask you about that locket," Conrad whispered. "She can see magic like I can, and she'll know that you're hiding something."

Raven tensed. She started to protest, to lie, but her words faded on a gasp—the fever stole her breath.

How could she explain the centrum to anyone? If anyone found out she carried the centrum of Altair's Augur, they would want it. They might sell the information to the Gray Elite. Anyone else who knew about it would be a liability.

But...if the centrum was poisoning her like Conrad had said, what option did she have?

She should have buried it in the woods when she had the chance.

As if tuned to her thoughts, the centrum's heat pulsed through the locket and against her chest.

No, she silently told it.

And it listened; the heat lessened but did not go away. The fever remained, wild and untamed, pulsing under her skin. She felt it burning through the rune on her stomach, burning the ink away. The steel horse she rode on blurred. Conrad's arm tightened around her, and she leaned into him.

"Just a little further," Conrad whispered. "Don't die on me now."

Zander wouldn't know what happened. Ivy wouldn't know what happened. Her father and stepmother wouldn't know what happened. They would wonder for the rest of their lives where Raven had gone, never knowing the full truth. Never knowing that she had turned to ash in the backstreets of Moorin, lost to the wind.

Maybe, if she were ashes, she could travel the world on the wind.

She didn't want to die. Not in Moorin. Not for a long while. Not until she had seen it all. So she fought against the magical fever, fought to keep her body alive, fought to keep it from swallowing her whole like it had the pirate, like it did the ink.

No, she told it.

Maybe Caroline would help her. Maybe she would know how the centrum was doing whatever it was doing to her and be able to stop it. Caroline might also tell her she only had a few days to live.

Raven closed her eyes. She missed her bed back at the inn. She missed the cool tea, the still air that smelled of cooking dinner, the feeling of the cool ink across her skin. The air of Moorin felt too balmy and warm, suffocating.

Someone ahead of them hissed; Conrad stilled and brought their horse to a halt.

Raven kept her eyes closed.

And then the night air shook with a violent wave of hot wind and bright light. Conrad's grip on her tightened; he gasped and curled his body around hers, shielding her eyes from the bright blast that lit the night like day. Then she heard the explosion. Thunder on the ground, shattering the air.

The automaton horses did not kick and nicker. They remained perfectly still.

The light faded, and Conrad shifted.

Raven opened her eyes. A plume of red and orange rose into the night several streets away, consuming the shadows with flickering, vengeful light. Fire.

"Sisters," Conrad breathed.

Two of the Wraiths in their procession jumped to stand on the backs of their automaton horses, and then jumped in unison onto the nearest building, effortlessly making their way to the rooftop. They moved like water given form, like shadows.

"What is it?" the Wraith ahead of Raven called up, his voice a loud whisper.

The Wraiths didn't get the chance to answer—the screaming started. Steel hit steel. Automaton gears hissed. Bullets seared through the air. Automation feet clomped against the stone street.

"Raid!" one of the Wraiths shouted.

"Gray Elite," spat another.

The screams grew louder, and several of them ended abruptly. A siren started—a vicious, high-pitched undulating wail.

"Get her out of here," said the first wraith, but Conrad was already directing his horse in the opposite direction of the flames.

Over his shoulder, she saw the chaos behind them. The flames grew. More sirens joined the first. Raven saw shadows running through the night, over rooftops, silent. She saw people on the other side of the alleys, shadowed by the flames, running.

A raid, one of the Wraiths had warned.

A man stumbled into the alley, screaming, pleading, his clothes on fire. An automaton chased him, its slender body twice as tall as a human, each of its arms ending in a blade. The flames flickered off the bronze and steel plating, its too-human-like face, and its glowing red eyes. Steam hissed from its shoulders and elbows as its arms moved in an effortless arc—slicing through the burning man. The two halves thumped to the alley's floor.

The automaton lifted its eyes to Conrad's fleeting back.

Raven grasped his sleeve. "It sees us," she gasped.

The automaton started for them, its long legs sprinting, gears silent, steam hissing out from its hips. Conrad urged the horse into a gallop. The automaton gained on them, its legs moving it twice the distance that the horse could.

It's slender arms stretched toward them, one blade bloodied, the other clean.

The blades came down.

Raven screamed.

A shadow appeared between them, landing on the automaton's shoulders. A Wraith. In a shower of sparks, the Wraith ripped the head from the automaton—a flash of lightning crashed through the automaton's body, electrifying the metal and overpowering the machine. It staggered and jerked, and then the Wraith dropped something into the body and vanished as quickly as he had appeared.

The automaton horse carried her and Conrad away. They turned down an alley, and a heartbeat later, an explosion shook the alley they had just left. Pieces of the slender automaton scattered the alley, raining down on the rooftops, the stone ground, clattering and clanking.

Raven wanted to bury her head in Conrad's shoulder, but her fear kept her alert. She watched their backs for any other automaton threat. In the distance, the raging fire grew smaller and smaller.

Conrad abandoned the horse in an alley and carried Raven the rest of the way to the Wooden Goblet. He entered through the kitchen and paused on the other side. Engor and a handful of others stood around the meeting table, looking devastated, anxious, and angry.

"What in Minerva's name happened out there?" asked one of the cooks—he wore a stained apron.

"A raid," Conrad said, his voice thin with panic. "On Caroline's street."

"Barely made it out," said a Wraith entering the kitchen. She whisked off her hood. It was Gretchen, the cook. In the better light, she didn't look much older than Raven. Her dark brown hair had been elaborately braided, and a faint scar crossed one of her pale golden cheeks. "They were waiting for us. Caroline's cave is gone. Smithereens." She demonstrated an explosion with her hands. "There's nothing left. Half of each building on either side is gone too. Those Gray Elite weren't messing around with this one. They wanted it gone, and it's gone. Pulled out half a dozen Slenders too."

Slenders must have been those automatons. The name fit.

"They would have been planning this for a while," Engor said grimly. "The Gray Elite don't blow up buildings on a whim."

"We didn't have time or the people to take care of it," reported Gretchen. "We barely made it out ourselves."

"I don't like it," Conrad said, frowning deeply. He looked to Engor and motioned to Raven with a nod. "They knew she would be there."

Engor frowned. "Why?"

"Don't you recognize her?" Conrad asked, a playful lilt in his voice. Engor's frown deepened. Gretchen put her hands on her hips. "She's the assassin General Deacon's so worried about."

Engor spat a curse. Gretchen spat a dirtier one.

"And she's got a bounty to kill for," said Engor.

"A bounty worth betrayal," said Gretchen, her tone like a blade ready to slice through flesh. She turned her deadly gaze onto the other cook. "Where's Merril?"

"She's been gone since this morning," said the cook.

"She's been bitching about money for months," said Gretchen. "My token's on her slipping information to the Gray Elite in exchange for a slice of the bounty."

Engor growled under his breath, though he didn't object.

Raven squeezed her eyes shut and flattened her palms against her eyes to block out as much light as possible. Her fault. Her fault. Someone had been looking for her, and they had blown up Caroline's cave—likely Caroline with it. All in an effort to find her.

Entirely, inexcusably, her fault.

She thought of the man on fire whom the automaton had cut down without hesitation. His death had also been her fault, along with anyone else hurt tonight.

"We will wait on word before we assume Caroline's fate," said Engor. "The old woman isn't a pushover."

His tone said what he didn't—Caroline was missing, and she couldn't help Raven.

Conrad carried her back upstairs. He sat her on the bed, and he sat against the wall, resignation on his face. She wanted to apologize, to take the blame for the failure, to tell him that it would be all right, but she couldn't form the words.

She trembled. The seed of hope of finding help shriveled and died, and she would likely follow.

The following day went by in a heavy blur. The crease between Conrad's brows never went away. The Wraiths didn't know what else to do for her, beyond iced cider and the rune. Conrad drew a new rune every hour. Ice melted against her skin.

Raven had the thought to ask Engor to keep a message for Zander, to use the Wraiths to somehow get it to him, so that he knew what had happened. Maybe Zander would tell her father and stepmother. But thinking about leaving a final message pitted her stomach, and she didn't want to think about it.

The door to her room opened, and by the time she worked her eyelids to move, Conrad sat on the edge of the bed. He held a few large splinters of wood. Fire kindling.

"I have an idea." Conrad set a splinter on her palm. "You had this fever, and then you used it to turn that pirate to ash, and then you were fine for a few days before the fever came back. So, I want you to try and turn these slivers of wood to ash."

She closed her fingers around the splinter as much as she could. Her fingers didn't want to grip; she hadn't the strength.

Raven tried to turn the splinter to ash, but she didn't know how. She didn't understand how she had given the pirate her fever. She tried to push the fever into the splinter, but it didn't move. It stayed with her. The wood remained wood.

Conrad held his face neutral. He watched her hand, the wood, waiting. After a while, he took the splinter from her.

"Warm," he said. "But not ash." He let out a grievous sigh.

"I'm trying," she said weakly.

"I know," he said. *Not enough*, was what he didn't say.

That evening, Conrad came to her room. He wore common clothes, a thin summer tunic the color of spring leaves and beige trousers. He redrew the rune, then sat on the bedside.

304

"The Wraiths are planning a counterattack on the Gray Elite." His coal-dark eyes were on the wall ahead of him. "I volunteered to stay behind with you. If Merril did sell information about you to the Gray Elite, then the Wooden Goblet isn't safe anymore."

She didn't know what to say, so she said, "Thank you."

Conrad looked down at his hands. "I don't know what to do about your condition. The magic you've got is beyond what I know or anything I've seen. Sooner or later, the Gray Elite will find you if you stay here." His words sank in, but he refused to look at her.

"Conrad?" she asked, the trembling in her stomach working its way through her limbs. "What—"

Conrad took a deep breath and released it; then he fixed his gaze on her. Nothing of his humor remained. "I have a friend here in the city. He might be our last hope at saving your life. The Wraiths don't know about him."

Raven stared back at him, unsure of what to say. She didn't have much of a choice. She could barely move on her own. So she nodded. "Okay."

Conrad didn't say who, and Raven wasn't sure she cared enough to ask.

"When they go," he whispered, "we'll sneak out. If my friend doesn't know what to do, then at least he can provide us a safe location where the automatons won't be a threat."

She nodded. She had reached the point where nothing mattered. Anything that might offer a sliver of hope, of help, she would take. Risk or not.

The air in the Wooden Goblet was tense. Whispers echoed through the floor, low enough that Raven couldn't make out what they said. They worried about a traitor. Conrad slipped into the meetings, but he didn't tell her their plans.

No one had caught up with Merril either. Her tiny apartment was empty—she'd fled in a hurry. None of her neighbors knew a thing.

The evening fell into night, as signified by the sounds of the kitchen, of the pots and pans being cleaned. Raven slept a few minutes at a time; the fever never let her rest long.

Conrad came to her room dressed in dark clothes not of the Wraiths. His braids were pulled behind his head by a black ribbon. He wore a dark half-cloak with a silver brooch over his heart that caught the candlelight. He held a second half-cloak over his arm.

"Come on," he whispered urgently. He pulled her into a sitting position and quickly fastened the cloak over her shoulders. He fastened a silver brooch—identical to his own—over her heart. He pulled the hood over her head. He then lifted her into his arms and carried her down the stairs.

The Wooden Goblet had gone frighteningly quiet.

Raven leaned against him as if part of her body had already died. He darted through the kitchen's side door, and the night banished the light. An automaton horse waited for them. The horse pulled forward at a trot, and she closed her eyes. The repetitive motion of the horse lulled her into a calmness, the balmy air kissed her cheeks, and the warmth outside mixed with the warmth inside. They trotted through the dark streets. Lights passed by on the other side of her eyelids.

She took one breath at a time.

The city buzzed around her, a metronomic beat underneath it all, like the city itself ran on gears. She heard the mechanical steps of automatons, their movements fluid and graceful. She heard the canter of automaton-drawn coaches.

The horse slowed. Its hooves beat against the stone, and then they didn't; the sounds softened like it walked on grass. The air became warm and humid. She smelled dankness, like soil and stone that never dried, and the ripeness of vegetation. The horse stopped, and Conrad lifted her from it.

"Good," breathed Conrad. "I didn't know if you'd gotten my message."

Her back met something cool and hard.

"This is her? She doesn't look good," whispered someone to her right.

"I know she doesn't," said Conrad on her left.

A sharp inhale. "Sisters," the person to the right gasped. "Raven?"

That voice. She fought to open her eyes, and through the blurry, dark daze, she spotted a pleasant face and blond hair. She knew him.

Her breath came out ragged, "Ezra?"

Captain Ezra Deacon blinked at her and brought a pale hand to his hair. He wore it down and loose, not slicked back in the Gray Elite fashion as the last time she had seen him. Rather than his Gray Elite uniform, he wore a dark tunic and trousers.

Her heart sped at his presence—Ezra was the son of General Deacon, the man who had claimed her an assassin and demanded her head.

"What happened?" Ezra asked.

It took a moment to realize Ezra directed his question at Conrad, not her. The pieces came together slowly: his friend, the one the Wraiths didn't know about, the one who could provide a safe place from the automatons—Ezra.

The fever flared, and she closed her eyes. She hadn't the energy to ponder the connection between Ezra and Conrad. If she made it through the night without burning alive, maybe she would ask one of them.

"The runes fade within an hour," Conrad said.

Somewhere close by, a bird chirped. She opened her eyes; she glimpsed darkness and green. Leaves and potted plants. Flowers and budding fruit. She blinked. She lay on a worktable inside a greenhouse. Tinted glass shielded them from the city beyond. A hand lifted her shirt to reveal her stomach. The rune. Ezra and Conrad stood on either side of her, eyeing her flesh, and the vulnerability sent a tremor down her spine. Neither man wore hunger or lust. They looked at her with clinical astonishment.

"I drew this one with Wraiths' ink this evening."

Ezra gaped. "It looks months old."

"But it's not."

"The magic is eating through it that fast?" Ezra ran a hand through his hair, confused and worried.

"Every hour," Conrad said darkly.

"Sisters," Ezra breathed. "I've never heard of magic working so fast."

"Neither have I, nor have the Wraiths." Conrad replaced Raven's shirt. "The only one who might have got blown up by the Gray Elite."

Ezra flushed. "I had no hand in it; you know that."

"Still, you're the only one I could think of who might be able to do something about it."

Ezra met Raven's gaze. He doubled in her vision, became one again, and then doubled. "I have a solution," Ezra said. "But you might not approve."

Conrad chuckled. "I'm a pirate, friend. There's little that I turn my nose up at." He cracked a smile, and Raven's spirit lifted slightly. Right now, she would try anything.

"Ruby powder," Ezra said.

Conrad's brow rose. "You want to drug her?"

Ezra shook his head. "No, ruby powder gives regular humans a high, but in a magician, it will eat through the magic. It's why magicians can't get high off it, because their magic prevents it. For Raven, it might eat through the magic that's eating through her. A counterattack."

"It's better than letting her die," Conrad said. "I assume you have a plan on getting ahold of ruby powder?"

Ezra turned sheepish. He reached into the satchel at his side and withdrew a canteen. "I came prepared."

"You carry some around with you all the time?" Conrad asked, not judging, but surprised. "And here I thought you more straightlaced."

Ezra blushed and frowned. "You mentioned out of control magic, so I came prepared."

The fever surged; Raven released a low sigh. Everything hurt.

Ezra pressed the mouth of the canteen to her lips, the metal cool and then not. "Drink, Raven," he said softly.

She parted her lips, and a tangy liquid flowed into her mouth. It tasted like flowers and too-strong tea. It registered in her mind as something red—the color red, as if it had a flavor.

The drink flowed down her throat, into her stomach, and, by the Sisters, it *worked*. She felt it tug the fever back, devour it, cooling her body, pulling the darkness from her vision, and coursing through the magic that had been about to devour her whole.

She drank until Ezra pulled the canteen away.

"That should do for now," he said, corking it.

The relief spread through her bones, through her blood. Hope surged in her chest and spread her lips in a smile. In the place where that incessant worry and panic and fear had been for so long, an exhaustion stole into her. Conrad and Ezra started talking, but she didn't listen. She wouldn't burn up in her sleep. She wouldn't turn into a pile of ash in the night.

With that sweet hope on her mind, she drifted into sleep, the first peaceful sleep she had gotten for weeks.

When Raven came to, she found herself in a strange room. It was not the wooden-walled room at the Wooden Goblet. In her sleepy haze, she saw scores of white, vivid sky blue, and shades of gold. The more she woke, the more she saw.

She was lying in a four-poster bed as soft as a cloud and four times her size. The posts were copper; sheer blue and gold silk draped from post to post and formed a canopy. The copper ceiling had been carved with a masterpiece of whorls and diamonds. The room beyond was white with golden trim. A handful of scenery paintings hung on the walls, sunrises and sunsets over countryside rivers and lakes. High, narrow windows of leaded glass let in copious sunlight. The curtains matched the bed drapes, shades of gold and blue. Leaded-glass doors led out onto a balcony, to a bright blue sky. She could see the tops of buildings on the other side. A fern hung from the ceiling on either side of the balcony doors, the chain bright and glittering gold in the daylight. The fronds nearly touched the floor. On the far other side of the room, a set of oak doors—meticulously carved—led elsewhere.

It was perhaps the most beautiful room she had ever seen. But...where was she?

She continued to breathe, so she lived. That she knew for certain—unless she had woken up in the Underworld, but it looked surprisingly like the living world, but then again, who would know what the Underworld looked like?

She continued to breathe—in, out.

Raven sat up, and an aching pain seared through her body. A yelp escaped her throat, and she collapsed back onto the silken sheets.

Not the Underworld. There wasn't supposed to be pain in the Underworld.

She gasped for breath; her lungs felt like she had inhaled fire. Burning. The fever. It raged through her blood like teeth, razor sharp and everywhere.

The oak doors opened, and quick footsteps approached. "I take that scream to mean you're alive?"

That voice, joyful and tinted with laughter—she rolled onto her side to see Conrad smiling at her. He no longer wore his dark cloak and clothes. He wore a bright yellow tunic with ivory trim and trousers of gray. Half a dozen gold bangles hung off his wrists, and he wore several gold chains around his neck. He stood proudly, like he belonged in this godly house.

"Where are we?" Her voice came out hoarse, and her throat felt dry.

"Well," Conrad started, plopping down on the bed. "Do you remember meeting my friend?"

It took her a moment to remember. "Ezra Deacon is your friend?" she asked with no small amount of disbelief.

Conrad nodded. "It's a long story to explain, but I take it that you two have met?"

She nodded. She didn't feel like explaining that meeting to him. She didn't feel like explaining anything to anyone. She closed her eyes, and the rest of that night came back to her. The counterattack. The dark greenhouse. The bitter drink. The relief.

"What did he give me?" she asked.

"Ruby powder," he whispered.

"What is that?" She'd never heard of it before.

"It's one of the magic-infused illegal drugs that the Gray Elite fight hard to purge from the city," Conrad said. "It's made by magic and gives non-magicians a decent high, but in your case, it consumed the magic in your system and gave you a relatively smaller high."

"And Ezra had some?" She couldn't imagine Ezra, the general's son, the perfect Gray Elite soldier, breaking the law for her favor.

Conrad's smile widened. "Ezra has access to the confiscated stores, as well as a few magic dealers," he whispered. "And he did save your life, so I wouldn't question his methods or means too much."

She released a breath.

The door opened again, and this time, Ezra appeared at the bedside. He, too, had discarded his dark clothes for those of a noble. In his hands, he held a canteen. "I'm glad to see you're awake. I had a fear you'd not wake up at all. How do you feel?"

She groaned in response.

Ezra gave her a small smile. He gently jostled the canteen. "Time for another dose, I'd say. Fresh batch too."

Raven didn't ask where or when he had had the new batch of ruby powder made. Conrad helped her to sit up, and Ezra handed her the uncorked canteen. She took it in both hands. The metal felt smooth and cool, and the drink had a faint scent of flowers and that undeniably *red* scent. She lifted it to her lips and took several long drinks under Ezra's watchful eye. It tasted much the same as it had, only less bitter and more floral—and *red*.

She could feel the fever retreat with every drink, with every gulp that flooded down her throat and into her bones, her blood, her muscles.

Ezra pulled the canteen away, and she smiled at the boys. "It's working," she said.

Conrad nodded like he hadn't doubted it for a second. His eyes were looking at her but not at her—her magic, the fever. Ezra kept his stare on her, worried and intent.

"What happened, Raven?" Ezra sat down on the bed, corking the canteen. He set it on the bedside table and leaned forward onto his knees. "Is that even your real name?"

Conrad's dark brows shot upward.

"Yes," she said.

Ezra didn't look convinced. He looked...betrayed.

Guilt pulled her heart into her stomach. Sisters, she'd really made a mess for herself. She inhaled, unsure of what to tell him and what not to, of what Conrad knew and what he suspected. "Raven is my real name."

Conrad shifted. "I have a better idea. How about we discuss our secrets over lunch and a tasty beverage? Hmm? Breakfast has worn off."

Ezra took a moment to think about it, then nodded. "I'll send the order." He stood. "Raven, do you feel well enough to eat in the lounge?"

"There's a lounge?" She glanced to the doors where Conrad and Ezra had come from. "Where am I?"

"My family's estate," Ezra answered. "It's in the heart of Moorin, and it's the last place the automatons will look for you."

The Deacon Estate, General Deacon's home. She felt the color leave her face.

"My father isn't here," Ezra said, his voice quiet. "He is still in Lenhala. He won't be back for a while. *Someone* left the city in a state of chaos."

He meant her, she realized. Her face warmed but not from the fever.

Ezra met her gaze, his face serious. "Raven, did you try to kill my father?"

"No," she said without hesitation.

Ezra blinked, and relief replaced his worry.

"On the contrary, he tried to kill me. Twice." Her bravery returned, buffed by the ruby powder, and she added, "He was just mad that I got away."

Ezra chuckled. "Sounds like him." He motioned to the canteen on her nightstand. "You'll need to keep a regimen of ruby powder—a drink every hour or so, most likely." He glanced toward the door. "Stay in this room for right now. I don't want any of the servants to get suspicious. They know I have friends staying here, but I would rather them not see you up close. I'll come when the meal is ready."

"You've got wanted posters," Conrad added playfully. "They're not a bad rendering, though they make you look more vicious than you are."

Raven sighed and reclined back into the pillows. Wanted posters. Just what she needed.

"I'll see if I can't snag one for you," Conrad said.

Ezra cleared his throat in farewell, to give the order for lunch to his servants. He left, and Conrad released a sigh. He leaned back on the bed, propping himself up with his elbows.

"You're full of surprises, aren't you?" he said.

She sighed dramatically. The ruby powder made her feel significantly better. Was this how she felt before the fever? It didn't seem possible. "I remember when I wished for adventure. Now I wish I had a little bit less."

Conrad laughed, an easy rumble. "It does seem to happen that way, doesn't it?"

"How did you meet Ezra?"

He considered her for a moment. In the daylight flooding the room, his dark skin shone with golden tones. His coal-dark eyes glittered—thinking. "I'll trade you secrets," he said, grinning. "I'll tell you where I met him, if you tell me where *you* met him."

"In Lenhala," she said.

That part Conrad already knew, and he motioned for her to continue.

"You said *where*, not *how*."

He laughed, rolled his eyes, and said, "Correction, I'll tell you *how* I met him, if you tell me *how* you met him."

"Zander took me to the Summer Solstice Ball," she said. "I met Ezra there. Then, the next day, I was walking through a garden with a friend when a thief attacked. I defended myself and her and killed him. When the Gray Elite came to investigate, Ezra came with them. He brought me to his father's office, and because he knew his father would likely kill me, he gave me hints as to a secret way out, which worked. After that, I haven't seen him until now."

Conrad hummed. After a beat, he said, "I met him when I attempted to burgle him. He caught me but not before I found that he was trying to smuggle a few magicians out of the city. I offered him help in exchange for not turning me in; he accepted because he's the kind of soul to trust blindly. It worked in his favor, though."

She blinked. "Ezra smuggles magicians out of the city?"

Captain Ezra Deacon of the Gray Elite, son of General Deacon—a magician smuggler? Collaborating with a pirate?

Conrad's smile grew wider and a shade more wicked. "We help each other out now and then. We've become something shy of accomplices."

She laughed, the feeling foreign in her body, which had grown used to the constant burn. She ran a hand through her hair and then cringed at the oily feeling it left on her fingers. When had she last washed it?

"The bathroom is down the hall," Conrad said. "Second door on your left."

She nodded. Her stomach felt viciously empty, as empty as her scalp felt dirty. And yet she found herself in a cloud of carelessness. She glanced at the canteen of ruby powder on the nightstand. She could feel it working, dulling the fever into nonexistence, replacing it with something joyful, something bright and happy.

"I have a few things to take care of before this evening," Conrad said. "I will see you shortly for lunch. Do try to stay out of trouble."

"Only if you do," she said.

He winked, then left, leaving her alone in her strange new room.

She wiggled her arms and legs, no longer numbed and burning and useless. She easily pushed herself to the edge of the bed and set her bare feet on the floor. The floor was tile, alternating blue and white and gold, patterned in a lovely mosaic. Unlike the boys, she still wore her dark clothes, as soiled as her hair.

She took laps around the room to regain her balance. The ruby powder altered her balance, and it took a few moments to get used to the wobbly feeling. She meandered to the leaded-glass doors. She didn't open them. Beyond, the garden of the Deacon Estate formed a green square around the house, protecting it from the wide streets beyond. All around, similar estates grew like palaces and castles, some bigger and some smaller, but all grand. She spotted the heart of the city a short distance away, rising like needles toward the endless blue sky.

Would Ezra report her presence to Zander? Did they even know of each other's secrets? The thoughts passed through her mind quickly, and she pushed the worries aside. Compared to the fever that tore her apart, splintered her bones, and clawed at her skin, the high filled her with a sense of floating, carelessness, and peace. She preferred the high, despite the minor fluctuation in her balance.

She caught a whiff of human stink and grimy hair. Sisters, was that *her*? She tiptoed into the corridor. Ivory carpet softened her footsteps. The walls were pale wood and smooth white stone. Brass sconces dotted the walls, but no light flickered. The only light came from a window at the far end. Along with hers, she counted five sets of oak doors. All were closed. It gave the hall a lonely feeling.

The bathroom was a masterpiece of ivory and gold tile, deep purple walls, and pale wood accents. The center of the room held two wide sinks and a floor-to-ceiling mirror. Sisters, she looked awful! Grime darkened her hair and clumped the roots. On either side of the vanity was a pale wooden door that led into a separate toilet and shower. Brass pipes ran along the walls to the ivory fixtures. A narrow wicker cabinet held rolled towels and soaps.

She helped herself to the soaps, stripped off the dirty men's clothes, and stepped into the shower. It was a mosaic of gold and white tiles. She turned one of two matching brass knobs. The pipes creaked, a gush, and then cool water flowed from the showerhead and doused her. She played with the knobs until the water turned lukewarm. The soap smelled unlike anything she had used before, not floral, not sweet.

Only after she had scrubbed the grime and dirt from her skin and hair did she return to her room. She wore only a towel. She didn't feel like putting on her dirty clothes so soon. She had seen a wardrobe in the bedroom. She would look to see if she had any other options first. Sure enough, the wardrobe contained a few basic articles. She pulled a loose white cotton day dress over her head and tied the simple gray corset herself. She left her feet bare.

She meandered to the balcony doors and stared at the city beyond as she lazily braided her damp hair. Oh, how she had missed being clean! Her spirits had lifted tenfold.

The oak doors opened, and Conrad sauntered in. "Ezra had to step out. It will just be the two of us for lunch."

"I'm starved," she said and meant it. She meandered to the door, not minding her bare feet or state of dress, and Conrad didn't reprimand her.

They ate in a small, comfy lounge with purple walls and golden wainscoting. The heavy gray drapes over the leaded windows gave it a cozy, sleepy feel. The food wasn't anything special: sliced bread, soft cheese, fruit, and spiced nuts. As they ate, Raven talked Conrad into telling her one of his pirating stories, one where he wasn't yet a man but had a fierce thirst for the world.

"I thought I wouldn't return to the shore again," Conrad said dreamily, his hands moving with the story like ocean waves. He sighed and looked Raven in the eye, "But I was destined to return to Wayward Point, for I had already left a piece of my heart behind."

"The girl?" Raven asked, the girl whom he had loved, the girl who had left him behind for another, the girl who had broken his heart.

"Before her," Conrad said. Something calm came over his face. "It started bright and warm, but even then, when we met after that voyage, a part of me knew it wouldn't last. He was afraid of drowning, and I had a love of the sea."

"What happened?"

"We grew apart as people do," Conrad said, the longing in his voice turning bittersweet. "But my first love is the sea, and she always will be. He knows that." He took a drink of his tea and frowned, wishing it were something much stronger.

When Raven returned to her room, the fever had started to crawl back. She reached first for the ruby powder and took a large drink. At once, she realized her mistake. The sudden influx surged against the fever, making her dizzy. She corked the canteen and fell onto the bed, barely making it under the covers before it stole her into the darkness of a nap.

That night, Raven woke to a low rumble of thunder. She rolled her sluggish body onto her side, facing the balcony doors. Darkness pressed against the leaded-glass doors and the windows. The light in the room was dim—dark but unnaturally illuminated.

Raven fought to keep her eyes open; her eyelids were heavy. So tired. She leaned back into the silken sheets and let her eyes close.

A sigh, a creak—barely a sound against the gathering storm.

A breeze, she told herself.

A sigh, a creak—more than the breeze. Wood moving. Hinges giving.

She opened her eyes.

The doors stood open. The darkness beyond the doorway thickened, blacker than the night, undulating like stirred ink.

Wrong, her body screamed a heartbeat before her mind echoed, *wrong*!

Raven sat up. Every muscle, bone, and thread of her body protested. Sisters, what had happened to her? Why did she feel as though she had been beaten?

The storm rattled on the other side of the darkness. Those doors should be closed! Heart pounding, she tried to reason. *The wind*, she told herself. The wind had opened the doors. The darkness shifted, churning like fog, defying nature with every movement. It pressed against the windows. Tendrils of darkness searched the seams, the sill—for entry.

She tried to get up, but her legs had turned leaden, thick and useless.

Don't move.

A voice caressed her mind, cold as winter's darkest night, fearless and vengeful. A terror like she had never known gripped her bones.

Through the darkness, something stepped—something a shade lighter than the darkness around it. A figure emerged from the darkness. As it moved, though, it became humanoid and male. He stepped over the threshold and into her room. He wore dark leathers and robes made for silent movement, for shadows. Belts of daggers crisscrossed his lean torso. A hood hid his face in shadow. Tendrils of darkness clung to his frame, slipping into the room with him.

Raven trembled. Without thinking, she grabbed for the silver candlestick from her bedside table and held it like a sword. The burned wick angled like a tiny hook.

He took a graceful, lethal step toward her. She lifted the candlestick higher.

He tilted his face to the side, lifting his chin, and the shadow over his face receded. He wore a dulled copper mask.

Do you think that will stop me?

Somehow she knew it wouldn't, but she didn't lower the candlestick. She wouldn't go down without a fight.

315

Don't you know who I am?

The mask, the predatory gait—she knew. The Revenant.

Yes, that's right.

She trembled. The candlestick shook. No one saw the Revenant without dying. Wraith. Assassin. Deadly.

The Revenant reached to his sides and withdrew two daggers, sharpened to deadly edges. He took a predator's step closer. Ready to end her. The Wraiths had sent him to kill her for ruining their plans, for causing the death of Caroline and the destruction of her cave. For the Wraiths to have found and sent the Revenant, they must have been furious—enough to want her dead.

The Revenant stalked toward her the way a cat corners a wounded mouse. His shoulders and knees bent for easy movement, his entire body lithe with controlled grace. He came within reach of the bed, and she couldn't bring her arms to move. He knocked the candlestick from her grip. The darkness grabbed it before it hit the floor, swallowing it whole—it never made a sound. The shadows trailing the Revenant swallowed the room, the tiles, the doors, the walls, the ceiling, edging closer.

The Revenant climbed onto the bed, daggers gleaming in unnatural light. She couldn't move. She started to beg, her words a tremor of pleas, but a thunderous crash sounded from the storm. The thunder shook the estate, the room, tearing apart the floor, the ceiling, the doors—the room shattered.

Raven jerked upward—awake.

She gasped for breath. Cold sweat covered her skin. Nothing pinned her. She had fallen asleep in her corset. With every moment, her heartbeat slowed. She released her white-knuckle grip on the sheets. Outside the closed leaded-glass doors, thunder rolled low and lazy just like it had in her dream. Lightning flashed several beats after.

On the other side of the doors, despite the storm, Moorin glowed. Streetlights and lanterns illuminated the towering heart of the city in gold and silver.

A dream.

It had been a dream.

No assassin had come for her; no unnatural darkness had unlocked the balcony doors. The Revenant hadn't been sent to kill her. Still, her heart hammered madly. She could still see the Revenant's violent stance in the balcony doors, his dark robes and copper mask.

She put a shaky hand over her heart. She hoped Engor was right in thinking the Revenant's silence meant he had been killed.

She pulled her knees up to her chest, content to sit and listen to the storm while her heart returned to normal.

With the rough awakening of her nightmare, Raven didn't at once notice the fever. It came back slowly but still too fast. It raged like it knew she had dampened it, and the resurgence made her heart spin and bones ache. A fraction of the terror she had felt in her dream returned, and she fumbled for the canteen of ruby powder. Her shaking hands fought with the cork, but after a desperate time, she won.

She took a long, generous drink. And then a second.

Thunder rolled. She took a third.

She set the canteen on the bedside table and sat up while the drug worked, calming the raging fire, dampening the violent magic. She brought her hand up to the centrum. Such a silly thing to have caused so much trouble. If she told Conrad and Ezra what it really was, what would they say?

Conrad would be thrilled at the story, at the secrecy. Ezra would frown. Would he want to tell his father about it? Would Conrad say to give it to the highest bidder?

No. She wouldn't tell them about the centrum. No one could know.

Thunder rolled. Lightning flashed a heartbeat sooner. The air smelled like rain, wet and warm and fresh. She struggled to free her limp self of the blankets. Her legs felt like wooden sticks and sand. With every step toward the balcony doors, the ruby powder worked its magic, freeing, soothing, lifting.

She threw open the balcony doors just as a clap of thunder shook the sky. The air was heavy with impending rain, thick with moisture; it sounded like a cool drink of water to her retreating fever. She half fell onto the balcony and latched her hands around the ivory railing.

The humidity sank through her dress, sticking the thin material to her skin. The lightning flashed through the thick bubbling clouds of dark gray and blues. To the far distance, on the other side of the city, lightning flashed continuously between the clouds, a stream of light over the horizon.

She could feel the rain coming. The magic under her skin, be it her own, the centrum's, or the ruby powder, yearned for it. Craved it. She waited on the balcony, watching the lightning come closer, closer, closer, until the thunder and the lightning clashed together. She could hear the rain smacking into the steel and copper and iron and glass, each drop crashing to the earth from the boiling sky, cooling the air, the ground, and everything in between.

The wall of rain surged over the city. The sound grew and grew, overwhelming all else. The lines of rain grew distinct. The rain hit the edge of the Deacon Estate as lightning flashed, making each drop glow bright as a tiny moon. The drops crashed onto the well-kept lawn, the flower beds, the marble walkways, the foundation, and the edge of the balcony.

The rain hit her skin like drops of ice, cooling the fever, quenching the burn, aiding the ruby powder. The first drops turned to steam on impact. Raven held her hands palm up, watching as the rain hit and vanished into vapor.

She lifted her chin to the rain as it became a downpour, soaking through her dress, soaking her to the bone, banishing the last of the fever. It soaked through her hair and pulled it down her shoulders and back. It reminded of her diving into the cool lagoon at the treehouse.

"That's a good way to find a cold," came Conrad's voice from behind her.

She turned. He stood in her room, just outside of where the rain pitter-pattered the tile. He still wore his fine clothes, and he regarded her with a mixture of curiosity and concern.

When she didn't answer, he tilted his head. His loose braids fell over his shoulder, the beads clinking together. "Raven?"

"The rain feels nice." She stretched her arms out on either side of her.

"I'm sure it does," Conrad said, motioning for her to come inside. "But, seeing as it's nearly two in the morning, come back inside before someone calls the Gray Elite about the crazy girl on the balcony."

She didn't want to. "Why don't you come out here?"

"Because I don't want to get wet," he said simply. He motioned again. "Come on, before you get sick."

She let the rain soak her a heartbeat longer, let out a dramatic sigh, and walked back into the bedroom. Her bare feet slapped against the tile. Conrad shut the balcony doors, and once inside, her wetness became a hindrance to her movement.

"And you're leaving a mess," Conrad said with a mock sigh, head tilted at the puddle growing at her feet. "Wait here."

Conrad sauntered to the pale wooden armoire and rifled through the contents until he pulled out a simple robe of soft gray. He tossed it onto the bed. He held up his finger to her, vanished through the main door and returned a few moments later with a yellow towel as wide as a blanket.

He tossed the towel to her and turned his back while she disrobed and dried.

"Maybe you drank a little too much," he said. "No more than a sip at a time of your medicine."

"Yes, doctor," she said, her voice childish.

He laughed.

She grabbed the gray robe from the bed and slipped it on. Odd how standing in the rain had renewed her spirit. She took a quick swig of the ruby powder, a swig monitored by Conrad, and then collapsed back into the bed.

Had the bed always been this comfortable?

She never heard Conrad lock the balcony doors, gather her wet clothes, or let himself out. And this time, her dreams were pleasant.

They arrived in Moorin during the storm, after midnight but before dawn;
Thalame couldn't tell. He'd never been the best at telling the time. He'd met a
Wraith once who could spot the time of the day by the scent of the air.

The city lay quiet around them. Most of the automatons had been withdrawn
into whatever hiding holes they went to when it rained. Only the most resilient ones
marched up and down the streets, their copper and steel hulls blurred and dulled by
the rain. Zander walked a step in front of him, hood up, stolen clothes soaked.

Lucky resounded in Thalame's mind. He didn't like *lucky*; he liked it better
when he got through on his own skill, rather than luck, because luck was fickle.

The whole blasted trip into Gracita had been lucky. They had managed to
stowaway on a cargo ship and somehow evaded the Gray Elite air patrol, and the
Sisters must have been watching out for them when they slipped out at the docks in
the bleakest hours of the night.

But they were here, and that was what mattered.

Zander cracked his head to one side, the movement agitated. He easily
sidestepped into another alley; Thalame followed. He glanced down the alley they
had been going down—the shadow of one of the few automatons loomed closer.

The rain came down a little harder. Making their way through the streets of
Moorin came easier in the rain. The rain thickened the shadows and blanketed
footsteps. People stayed inside unless they had to go out, and even then, they hurried
with hoods over their heads or umbrellas blocking their view of the two darkly clad
men fleeting from alley to alley. The heavy rain dissuaded the patrols from a chase
should they be seen.

Thalame would've been lying if he said he hadn't dreaded this part. When Ivy
had questioned him about it, he'd played tough. She hadn't bought it. She'd gotten
that twitch in her upper lip, the one she got when she wanted to argue but didn't.

Zander led the way. Their directions to the inn were years old, but the odds of
it having moved were slim. Zander led; Thalame watched his back. Just like the old
days. Days long gone.

They paused to let a coach roll by. The automaton goat pulling it wore a
poncho. The rain smacked against the slick material, sounding like a thousand
needles hammering against steel. Thalame rolled his neck. Sisters, he could use a
solid night of rest. He hadn't slept through the night in weeks.

The coach passed, and Zander darted across the street. Thalame followed on his
heels. Neither made more than a whisper.

The alleys grew narrower. The streets became dirtier and less illuminated. The
automations became fewer and far between. Finally, they found the Wooden Goblet,
one of several cobbled-together buildings on one of many nameless side streets.

Without losing his threatening gait, Zander marched through the front door. Thalame followed.

The tavern was empty, save for a girl arranging tankards over the counter. She wore simple clothes and a stained apron.

"Welcome," she said halfheartedly. She eyed the two of them with careful suspicion, taking in their stolen clothes in a few quick blinks. Her eyes shifted to the clock, likely taking note of the late hour. "Breakfast isn't for a while, but we have beds available. One room or two?"

Thalame started to speak—

Zander barked, "Where's Engor?"

Thalame closed his mouth. Still in a bad mood, then.

The girl looked Zander up and down without surprise. She knew who—and what—they were. She held Zander's gaze for a moment, then said, "He's in the kitchen." She nodded toward the wooden door that led behind the bar.

Zander took two steps toward the door when it opened, and the graying man Thalame barely remembered marched through.

"You got friends," said the girl.

Engor eyed the two of them with callused suspicion, his scowl deepening. He sighed through his nose and turned back into the kitchen. The kitchen doubled as a meeting room. Several maps had been sprawled out on an oak table. It smelled like a kitchen; a thousand dinners had soaked into the stone and the pots and pans hanging from the ceiling. Herbs were drying, tied by hemp from the ceiling. The kitchen was empty, save for the three of them, so Thalame tossed his wet hood back. Zander hesitated, then mirrored his actions. His wet hair flopped to his shoulders in scraggly strands.

"The wind rushes from the stars," said Thalame.

"The sea reaches for the sky," added Zander.

"And the stone carries us," finished Engor grimly. "Welcome to the Wooden Goblet, Wraiths. You're just in time. We're going to need all the hands we've got."

"What do you mean?" Thalame asked before Zander could growl at the man like he'd done at every other person they'd come across.

Engor leaned onto the table and let out a groan. The table groaned too.

"What happened?" Zander demanded.

"There was a raid," Engor said. He looked down at the map where they had placed a red X over a building. "Unexpected. It was a doctor's place. Killed a few magicians. We don't know what happened to the doctor. She's still unaccounted for. Gray Elite blew the whole clinic to rubble. We didn't have the time or people to combat it. We retaliated the next night, a silent raid on the patrol station closest to where the raid happened. Poisoned the water tank. If we're lucky, it will kill a handful and put the others out of work for a while. We also got a few magicians they'd detained."

"Good," said Zander. "And they're safe?"

Engor nodded. "As safe as magicians can be in this place." He frowned; the lines on his face seemed deeper. "But we've got another situation."

Thalame stood still as stone, keeping his face neutral. He didn't like Engor's tone, like it had been their fault.

"Such as?" Zander asked.

"Conrad showed up a few days ago with a sick girl with him, half dead from magic eating her alive," Engor said gravely. "We tried our best to do what we could for her, but the magic was too strong, unlike anything we'd ever seen. I was going to write a letter to Deikun about it after our counterattack, but when I got back afterward, they were both gone."

"What do you mean sick?" Thalame asked first, before Zander could jump on the question. He felt Zander look at him, felt the accusation and fear in it, but Thalame ignored it.

"Sick like a fever," Engor said, and Thalame bit back his own surprise.

Zander cursed.

"We painted runes with Wraith ink, but the magic ate through it like nothing I've seen before. It was ravaging, starving. Conrad was painting a new rune every hour."

"And they're gone?" Zander spat, leaning on the table. He looked livid at the news, his eyes feral and his face grimacing. With his damp hair, he looked like a madman.

"Gone," Engor confirmed, nodding.

Thalame let out a short sigh, and he dared to meet Zander's gaze. A silent message passed between the two long time friends. A silent agreement and shared suspicion. Thalame had more to say, but he didn't want to say anything more in front of Engor. Wraith or no, Thalame didn't know enough about the man to trust him.

Magical sickness. Thalame had pondered the idea, but Raven wasn't a magician. Unless she somehow contracted it when they were in Lenhala, and her non-magical blood reacted poorly to magical exposure. He had heard of those. She had grown up in a small town, Zander said, with little to no magical contact.

"Why did Conrad leave?" Thalame asked.

"Sisters only know," Engor said. "We left for the counterattack, and Conrad volunteered to stay behind with her. I thought he was being a nice guy for once, but when we got back and saw them both gone, no one had any idea. I've got a few of my people trying to track them down as we speak."

"What did this girl look like?" Zander asked, his voice angry but resigned; caution underlined his words.

Engor opened his mouth, but he never got the chance to speak. The backdoor to the kitchen opened, and two darkly clad figures walked inside. By the looks of the robes and leathers, they were Wraiths. They wore fewer daggers than Thalame or Zander did.

321

"Report," barked Engor.

"We found them," said one of the Wraiths, a female, her voice sharp as a razor's edge. She threw back her hood. She fixed her eyes on Zander and Thalame. "Who are they?"

"Friends," Engor said. "Extended family."

She nodded once, then she turned her full attention to Engor. "Like I said, we found them."

"Where?" Engor said.

Thalame felt Zander tense beside him, fighting the urge to clench his fist, every nerve in his body fighting to stay calm and composed. Thalame reached out and casually set a hand on his friend's shoulders. It took little effort to still the warring emotions, and Zander released a calming sigh. Zander glanced at Thalame, a silent *thank you* in his eyes.

To anyone else, it would have looked like Thalame had stopped him from speaking rudely when, in truth, Thalame had used his powers to calm him. Same endgame.

The girl with the sharp voice took a step toward Engor. "You'll never believe where they went," she said, dark glee shining in her eyes. She leaned forward and placed one of her fingertips on the map of the city.

R aven took a swig of ruby powder first thing the next morning. Sisters, what had gotten into her last night? Had she drunk too much of the potion? She remembered the stiffness of her fever and then the ecstasy of the rain. Thank the Sisters Conrad had come when he did, or she might have spent the rest of the night on the balcony.

The storm lingered, the clouds pale and gray. The rain was light and misty, the wind a gentle pressure against the walls and windows. Raven sat up in bed while the ruby powder worked on her fever, and when she felt better, she got up. She walked a lap around the stately room. Its sparse and clean style reminded her of the Gray Elite.

She hunted through the armoire and found only an extra set of bedclothes and a simple robe like the one she wore, only in white.

Footsteps sounded outside, boots, and then a gentle knock came to her door.

She paused, unsure of what to say. She saw the shadow of two feet standing on the other side. She cleared her throat. "Yes?"

Ezra let himself inside. He wore a fine housecoat with a stylized D over the heart. "I'm glad to see you're awake." He shifted a parcel in his hands as he looked between Raven and the open wardrobe. "I didn't have time to stock much, only the essentials, but I managed to procure you something else to wear in the meantime." He set the parcel on the bed.

"Thank you." Raven had never been overly sentimental, but the feeling overwhelmed her. "For everything you've done. You didn't have to help me, but you did. Twice now. I owe you a great deal."

Ezra nodded and tucked his hands into his pockets. He seemed as uncomfortable with her gratitude as she did.

She shut the wardrobe doors. "Why did you help?" she asked, her voice soft. "Not that I'm not grateful. I am, very much so."

"That is something I planned to discuss over breakfast." Ezra swallowed and glanced at the leaded-glass doors. "Which is why I came to see if you were awake. It's a casual meal, just the few of us."

His tone—he wasn't telling her something.

"The few of us?" she repeated.

Ezra nodded, still not meeting her gaze. "Conrad, you, myself, and maybe another, but I'm unsure if the fourth guest will be able to attend." He cleared his throat. "Breakfast will be in the lounge down the hall. It's not ready just yet. If you should need something else, let me or Conrad know."

"Thank you," she said.

How much would she owe Ezra by the end of her stay?

Ezra gave her a quick, polite bow and left. It wasn't until the door shut that she realized his words—she could ask him or Conrad for things she needed, meaning Conrad could walk freely around the house and outside it in order to fetch those things. She couldn't. She was to stay within these few rooms.

A prisoner. Again.

Irritation heated her blood and her cheeks. The fever surged past the effects of the ruby powder, only instead of a numbing, painful heat, she felt a pleasant rush—not unlike the sensation of falling.

Then she reminded herself that Conrad wasn't the most wanted person in two kingdoms. If she left, she might be recognized. Then she and Ezra would be in trouble. Ezra was right to keep her inside.

She inhaled, filling her lungs to capacity, and released her breath slowly. Then she unwrapped the parcel that Ezra had brought. Inside was a dress of blue and copper, and underthings. She didn't pause to consider if it would fit. It had been a gift, and she would make it work. She gathered the parcel and returned to the bathing room. One of the showers was in use; running water rattled through the pipes and smacked against tile. A male voice was humming a lively tune. She blushed, the heat traveling from the top of her head to her toes.

"I assume that's Raven," came Conrad's voice from the shower to her right.

"It's me," she said, her voice awkward and a pitch too high.

Conrad laughed. The sound rumbled against the water. "Don't worry, little bird. I don't bite—unless you ask, but even then I reserve my right to refuse. I have to be in the right mood for that."

Her blush heated even more. She shut herself in the other shower. It didn't bother her to share a bathing room. She had shared one with the other girls in Silver Glen and with the Dwellers. She'd never not shared a bathing room. She washed; all the while, Conrad continued to hum a tune that made her think of seaside shacks and the endless ocean, of mermaids and deserted islands.

Raven took her time washing, drying, and dressing. The dress Ezra had chosen was a simple sleeveless summer gown with bright blue silk skirts and corset bodice of copper. It fit as fine as anything. The silk around her legs felt like water woven into fabric. She returned to the vanity. Conrad—dressed in beige silk trousers and matching tunic—stood at the sink, running a fragrant oil over his braids.

She joined him at the sinks and found a comb in one of the drawers. She combed and tossed her damp hair over her shoulder.

Conrad extended his arm to her like a gentleman, and she threaded her arm through his. They walked into the hall and into the lounge, where Ezra stood by the windows, alone. The eyes of his reflection glanced toward them, then back outside.

With the storm, the windows let in only dreary light, and the chandelier had been lit. A dozen glass globes flickered with light, brightening the space.

On the round table, tea had been served—four cups set around the teapot. Four place settings had been arranged. Covered dishes lined the table, and Raven could

324

smell bacon and ham and eggs; her mouth watered. She didn't even know how hungry she had been.

Conrad and Raven sat at the table, but neither moved. The settings, the room—it all felt so formal and stiff.

"Help yourself," Ezra said, eyes on something out of the window. "No need for excessive manners."

Conrad made himself a cup of tea, and after a moment, Raven followed his lead. She took several sips before Ezra joined them. He looked bothered. Raven glanced to the fourth place sitting. Did his nervousness have to do with the lack of the fourth guest?

Conrad lumped a large amount of everything onto his plate. Raven took nearly as much, eager to sate her wild hunger. Ezra sipped his tea and waited until they had filled their plates before adding small servings to his own. Raven didn't ask or question it; her hunger didn't allow space for her mind to think such thoughts. They began to eat, silently.

Ezra picked at his food. Conrad and Raven devoured theirs.

"I owe you an explanation, Raven," Ezra said after a while, a bit reluctantly, his fork pushing eggs around his plate. He met her gaze. "And I believe you owe me one as well."

The food in her mouth soured. She paused mid-chew, her throat suddenly tight. She forced her food down and took a large drink of tea. Beside her, Conrad's brows rose. Ezra held her gaze, patiently waiting.

She nodded, her face warming. "You're right."

"Oh," said Conrad, leaning onto the table, "I do love a good story. And I get two? The Sisters must not hate me after all."

Raven pushed the remaining food around her plate while Ezra and Conrad recounted their first meeting. Ezra, the strapping young Gray Elite eager to please his father, and Conrad, the Wraith-turned-pirate looking for an easy token. Either could have blown the whistle on the other. Ezra could have turned Conrad in for what he was—a magician. Conrad could have turned Ezra in for treason, for aiding magicians.

Their alliance had been sporadic at first but had grown steady in the past few years. Ezra kept his father off the map. Conrad helped the magicians once they crossed the border into Tinatun. They settled deeper into the kingdom, he told Raven, and pockets of magicians dotted the central parts of the kingdom.

"The Wraiths aren't the only ones capable of helping," Conrad added a bit darkly. "Despite what some people think, pirates aren't all murderous madmen."

Ezra's grimace softened. He looked like he had something else to say, but with Raven present, he held his tongue. Raven wondered if it had something to do with the boy Conrad had left to be a pirate.

"You don't help the Hawks?" Raven asked carefully, not wanting to throw suspicion onto herself.

Ezra shook his head. "I've had little contact with the Hawks," he admitted. "They're not the most...understanding—at least, not in my experience. They're more worried about starting a revolution than they are righting things."

Raven took a sip of her tea. Did he know about Zander?

"You have a look that wants to say something else," Conrad said, curious stare on Ezra.

Ezra frowned. "Why must you notice things?"

Conrad shrugged. "Observant men last longer."

Ezra released a heavy sigh. Keeping his eyes on his plate, he said, "I distrust the Hawks because they sent the Revenant to kill my mother."

Raven gasped. "Did she..."

"I saw it happen," Ezra said lowly.

Raven's breath caught in her throat.

Conrad's eyes widened, his humor gone. "You *saw* him?" Conrad asked, awestruck.

"I wasn't supposed to," Ezra said. "It was four years ago. My father had gone on a tirade, and I didn't want to be in his crosshairs. So I hid. Yes, I know, it was a moment of cowardice on my part. My mother came into the room after having argued with my father. She paused at the window, and I saw living shadows surging toward her. She didn't have time to scream before the shadows took her. I saw...a figure in the shadows. I closed my eyes, and when I opened them again, the shadows were gone, and my mother was dead."

Assassinated.

Raven remembered her dream, the living shadows thick enough to block out the light, that never stopped moving. How could she dream of someone she had never met? She had only heard the stories. Her mind invented them, she told herself, had invented the Revenant in her dream. Her nightmare. Thinking about it made her nearly sick.

"Why did he kill her?" Conrad asked. He had the grace not to be smirking.

"She was Gray Elite," Ezra said. "The real reason was never made clear, although I assume it had everything to do with my father. They tried to kill my father that same day, but that assassin failed. They've tried several times since, with no luck. The Hawks are determined to see me orphaned, it seems."

Heavy silence fell over the table. As if in sympathy, the thunder rolled.

Ezra released a sigh—even his sighs were dignified—and leaned back in his chair.

Conrad broke the silence, his perpetual grin breaking through the grimness. He looked between Ezra and Raven. "I hear that our little bird tried to assassinate your father," Conrad said, shaking his fork at Ezra.

"He framed me," Raven said.

"I believe you," Ezra said. The story of his mother had taken its toll; he looked exhausted. "I was there during this supposed assassination attempt, remember. I had a feeling he was planning something."

"You told me how to get off the balcony," Raven said. Which had saved her life.

Ezra chuckled. "I honestly didn't think you'd have to use it. I was worried. I hadn't slept since the ball, and then my father started this..." He rolled his hand through the air, gesticulating for words he couldn't find. "He has always been hungry for power, but it was like he had started to go mad. He would do anything to gain Regent Dunel's favor, and since Dunel despised the Hawks, and he thought you were involved with the Hawks, he despised you. And you got the better of him, which he couldn't stand, and he had to make it look like he had been taken by surprise."

"I would like to say I planned it all," Raven said, "but I'm not nearly that conniving."

Ezra offered her a small smile that did not reach his eyes. It faded quickly. "It started about seven months ago. Suddenly, my father was agitated, angry, and shouting at everyone. I thought it had something to do with Zander's disappearance. My father was blaming the Hawks for it, saying they had killed him. His obsession with the Hawks grew into something unseemly."

Raven felt the color drain from her face—seven months ago, when Zander had stolen the centrum from the Hawks.

But...how had General Deacon known that? Raven dismissed that worry. She knew only a fraction of what had happened that night.

"Raven?"

She blinked; Ezra and Conrad were both looking at her. Both wore curiosity, though Ezra's mixed with worry, and Conrad's mixed with his special type of madness.

Ezra leaned onto the table. "Did it have something to do with Zander?" he whispered.

"I...don't know." She couldn't tell him about the centrum, and despite her assumptions, she didn't really know—so it wasn't a lie.

Ezra held her gaze for a long heartbeat, then he whispered, "I know about Altair's Augur."

Conrad dropped his fork and spat a curse that fell somewhere between a hiss and a laugh. He bent to retrieve his fork from the floor.

Raven's lack of surprise didn't faze Ezra. He held her gaze, and she knew that he knew.

"The senior staff of the Gray Elite have known about it for a while," Ezra explained. "To the rest of us, it was just a myth. Something to joke about. I started looking into the subject on my own, and I discovered that not only did the thing exist, but the Gray Elite had been actively seeking to rebuild it for years. And then the threats started. The Hawks had rebuilt it and claimed it was functional.

"So, the Hawks who wanted a revolution had Altair's Augur, but the Gray Elite wanted it too. They traded threats back and forth, each a little more menacing than the last. Then, the Hawks threatened to use the augur on the old palace, saying that seeing it in pieces was better than seeing the Gray Elite profane it." Ezra sighed and poured himself another cup of tea.

Raven held her hands under the table to hide how they trembled. She worked hard to keep her face calm.

"Zander was sent by the Hawks to kill my father," Ezra said. He spoke the words evenly, but his eyes told a different story—that his friend had been sent bothered him. "But my father caught him. I was in the next room. I overheard him tell Zander that he would spare him if he brought him the centrum of Altair's Augur." He ran a hand through his hair, leaving it a mess. Even ruffled, he looked regal. "And then Zander vanished."

Ezra's knowing, suspicious gaze fell on Raven. Conrad remained stone still, eyes wide and lips slightly parted—like a child waiting for the next part of the story.

She swallowed. She reached for her tea for something to do with her hands. In her shaky grip, tea sloshed over the sides. She set it down on the saucer with a sharp clank.

The silence thickened, awaiting her addition to the story.

"He stole it," Raven whispered.

Conrad's lips quirked into a pirate's grin. He approved.

Ezra held her gaze. The truth settled, and relief washed over his face. "My father was furious when he heard the news. He threw things, shouted at the servants, and beat one for serving his tea too hot. He took over the search for Zander, claiming it to be out of worry, but I knew the truth. He sent his men all over the country, but no one could find him."

"Both the Hawks and Gray Elite knew that the centrum had been taken," Raven said. To say the word out loud sent a prickle of dread along her skin.

"And the Hawks hired me to fetch it back," Conrad said. Understanding had washed the humor off his face. He knew the true value of what he'd stolen, what he had briefly held. He let out a grievous sigh. "This is why I'm not a fan of the city. So much squabbling and backstabbing."

"You didn't know what it was?" Ezra asked, brow raised.

"No," Conrad said, shaking his head. "The man who hired me gave me a rough description of Zander and of the item I was to retrieve. He conveniently left out his name."

"You didn't find that strange?"

"He offered me a hundred thousand marks, tokens, or piks. Said I could have any currency I wanted," Conrad said. "To a poor man like me, that kind of money could set me up for decades."

"You could have sold it for whatever price you wanted," Raven said.

Conrad groaned. "Hindsight has perfect vision, I know."

"Zander didn't tell me until he had to," she said.

"You knew?" Ezra asked, though it didn't come out as a surprise. He motioned to her, and said, "Seems like it's your turn to tell us a story."

The locket around her neck seared against her skin.

"Zander showed up in the village where I grew up." She could still see him, that first time she laid eyes on him: terrified, ragged, a refugee. "He told everyone he had escaped the capital. We welcomed him. We believed his story. He came to hide the centrum, I realize now. Then a thief snuck in while I was on watch." She glanced at Conrad, who wiggled his eyebrows. "And Zander and I went after him. We chased this thief nearly to Lenhala. Zander's brother showed up and took us into the city. We got mixed up in the Hawks and the Gray Elite, and that's when Zander told me about everything."

"Oh, tell the story of how you got sold in Wayward Point." Conrad waved his hands at her.

"You *what*?" Ezra said, frowning.

Raven half laughed. "I was in the woods, avoiding Zander, actually, and this automaton got me. Scavengers found me and sold me as a slave."

"To a fighting arena," Conrad added excitedly. "She turned her opponent to ash."

Ezra didn't look enthused.

Raven shrugged. In a few more breaths, she told him how Conrad had gotten her out. Conrad explained how the Wraiths helped her find a job onboard a small smuggler's ship.

"And then she got sick," Conrad added last.

"Where is the centrum now?" Ezra asked.

Raven paused. She pulled her lip between her teeth and averted her eyes from Ezra. What should she say? Did Ezra know she had given the empty box to his father? Had his father kept it from him?

"I had it," Raven said. The lie came smooth, "I don't anymore. Zander does. He wanted to hide it where no one would find it ever again."

"The bottom of the ocean is a good hiding place," Conrad said matter-of-factly. His tone came light, but his eyes stared hard at Raven. He glanced to the locket—her skin went clammy.

She waited for him to ask, to expose her, but he didn't. He sipped his tea.

Ezra considered her but didn't push the issue. "As long as it stays gone, it doesn't matter where it is." He leaned back and took a sip of tea. "I don't blame Zander for what he did. I would have done the same in his position. No one should have that kind of power. That's why the ancient people dismantled it. If I were regent, I would take the damn thing apart again and destroy the pieces. If the Hawks had their way, they would destroy Moorin. If the Gray Elite had their way, they would destroy Lenhala."

Just like they tried to do with magic, she thought bitterly. Raven pushed her cold eggs around on her plate. So much information to take in at once.

"The best we can do is continue to help magicians out of the Gray Elite's wrath until a better solution is found," said Ezra.

"Or until the world tears itself apart and the little things are no longer problems," Conrad said lightheartedly.

Ezra tipped his tea to Conrad.

Raven stared at her mostly empty plate. All this talk of Hawks and Gray Elites and Altair's Augur and its missing centrum—she thought she left it all behind when she left the Dwellers, but it had found her again.

Considering she held the centrum, she supposed she understood why.

The doors to the lounge opened. From where Raven sat, she couldn't see who had entered. Ezra and Conrad both could. Ezra quickly stood—a nervousness came over his features that made him look like a boy. His cheeks reddened, and his eyes brightened.

"I'm glad you were able to join us," Ezra said.

A sweet-sounding female voice laughed, gentle and beautiful. "You mentioned tea and biscuits. How could I say no to that? Are these your guests?"

Conrad watched the girl with interest, his coal eyes bright as stars.

Raven started to turn her head, but the fourth guest walked around the table and to the last place setting. Ezra eagerly pulled the chair out for her.

"Thank you," said the girl. She sat.

She looked to be around Raven's age, maybe a year or two older. She had olive skin and a healthy amount of weight on her slender frame. Her black hair shone like wet jet. She wore a simple, elegant summer dress of sky blue and yellow. She carried herself with regal intimidation and polite grace, her back straight, her neck poised. Her honey-hazel gaze settled on Raven, as watchful as a hawk's and gentle as a deer's.

Ezra cleared his throat. "This is Raven Thane and Conrad," he said, motioning to them in turn. "Friends of mine."

The girl kept her eyes on Raven.

"Raven, Conrad, this is Rosaria Whisehunt, Princess and rightful ruler of Rhynwier."

R aven gawked at Rosaria. Princess Rosaria. The very princess that the Dwellers were bent on rescuing, right here, in front of her, only an arm's length away, looking at her.

Rosaria lifted a well-groomed brow. She wore no makeup, though she looked achingly beautiful. Subtle bags darkened the skin under her eyes, the evidence of sleeplessness being her only imperfection.

"Are you all right?" asked Rosaria.

"I'm fine," Raven stammered. "I thought... You're here."

Rosaria blinked; then understanding washed across her face. "Ah, you thought me dead like the rest of the kingdom."

"I thought you imprisoned in the Tombs," Raven admitted.

Rosaria nodded. "I was, or I still am—technically speaking, of course."

Raven glanced around the room. "The Tombs do not uphold the horror the name suggests."

Rosaria smiled. "If only that were true." She glanced at Ezra, and a strange softness came over her face, soothing the subtle emotion that had been there before.

"My home," started Ezra, "like many of the old estates, is connected to a network of tunnels. They were once a way for military leaders to meet in secret, but I have been using them to sneak Rosaria into the estate."

"The estate is much roomier than a cell, and I assure you, the Tombs lives up to its name," Rosaria said, tipping her tea toward Raven.

"Dark, forbidding, and underground?" Conrad asked.

"All three of those," Rosaria said, nodding. A darkness came over her face, though she tried to speak lightly.

Ezra and Rosaria shared a long look, and the same softness came over his face that she wore on hers. Conrad winked at Raven.

"I am no more a prisoner here than I was in Lenhala," Rosaria said. She brought her attention back to Raven. "I am no closer to my throne. I am watched. No matter how many times I tell the Gray Elite I won't ask for the throne if they would just let me out. I'll become a citizen, I've said countless times, but still they refuse. You are from Rhynwier?"

"I am."

"I apologize for being useless and powerless." Rosaria's eyes softened with sadness and regret.

"It's not your fault," Raven said, and she meant it. "You didn't willingly give up your throne. They stole it."

That admission smoothed the crease in Rosaria's brow. "However, my time here and there has given me much time to think on how things should be, how I could change things. The only way from this mess is forward."

"Things change and will always be changing," Ezra said. "Power changes hands. Kingdoms shift, and borders shrink and expand."

"And this war between Gracita and Rhynwier will destroy us both in the end," Rosaria said grimly.

"Rosaria and I share many political views," Ezra said to Raven. "I didn't expect it, and neither did she. We started to talk more and more, and then I started sneaking her upstairs to the estate." He looked almost giddy. "Did Zander tell you about her?"

"Zander?" Rosaria focused on Raven. "Winchester? You know him?"

Raven nodded. "He mentioned you."

Rosaria's eyes brightened. "Is he well?"

Raven bit her lip. "I can't say. He was the last time I saw him." How long ago had that been? Two weeks? Three? "He blames himself for your capture."

The princess's eyes darkened with guilt. She took a deep breath and slumped in her chair. "Sisters...all that seems like ages ago. It wasn't his fault. Or, even if it was, I don't blame him. I convinced him to go out that night because I was feeling stuffy. He didn't want to go, but I talked him into it. I'm to blame, not him."

"Am I the only person who doesn't know this Zander fellow?" Conrad asked, brow cocked.

Raven ignored him and said to Rosaria, "Zander told me you grew up together."

The princess nodded, a faint smile curving her lips. "I grew up thinking my last name was Winchester. I was thirteen when his father told me the truth of my heritage. I went to bed in tears that night, and Zander snuck into my room to tell me that I'd always be his sister, and he would still beat up people for me if I asked him to."

Raven half laughed. That sounded like Zander.

Underneath it, she felt a pinch of jealousy.

"How did the princess end up here, I wonder?" Conrad asked.

"Well, I suppose it started after General Winchester told me who I was. Zander and I got swept away in the Hawks," Rosaria said. "I thought the idea of rebels taking back the city was thrilling at the time. I wanted to be queen as much as any little girl, but as I grew older, I realized that what I imagined was a game of dress up, and that being queen was no game. The Gray Elite caught rumors of my existence, and the Hawks treated me like a glass doll that would shatter if left unattended—it drove me mad. I convinced Zander to sneak out of the house with me, like we used to do before, and...we ended up separated, and I was captured by Gray Elite. They locked me in the palace for a while, and then they sent me to the Tombs several months ago. And now here I am."

Rosaria had a storyteller's smooth voice, one that drew the ear to her words, one that never hurried or hesitated. Even her words were regal, sharpened with cleverness and intelligence, softened with kindness and empathy. Both Ezra and Conrad were listening intently.

"Those were a few hard months for the city," Ezra added. "The Gray Elite and the Hawks were trading punches in broad daylight. Every day, back and forth." He cleared his throat. "But there is something else I wanted to ask you about," he said to Rosaria. "What do you know about magical sickness?"

Rosaria blinked. "Not much. Why? Is someone sick?" She glanced at Conrad, who pointed at Raven. Rosaria's brow furrowed. "You're sick? Magically sick?"

Raven hesitated, lip between her teeth.

Conrad leaned onto the table, and said, "She turned a pirate to ash."

Rosaria's eyes widened. "Ash?"

Raven retold her story to Rosaria, starting with the slavers. She didn't know why she told the princess so much or what compelled her to speak so freely. Conrad and Ezra already knew the story—something in Rosaria's eyes softened at the story and encouraged Raven to continue, no matter how foolish the story made her look. Rosaria listened, and just her expression made Raven feel as though she hadn't done everything wrong, as if the whole mess weren't her fault.

Finished, Raven slumped onto the table and reached for the teapot.

"I haven't heard of anything quite like that," Rosaria said. "I haven't heard of someone catching magic like a cold. Magic is..." She struggled for the right word. "...deeper than that. It's not just in the blood. It's in the spirit, the soul. It is a person."

"I don't understand it either," Raven said. She didn't want to think about the mess she had made: the magic, the fever, the Hawks, the Gray Elite—everything had been turned upside down several times, and now her head hurt when she tried to sort it all out.

Rosaria's eyes lingered on Raven. "What do you know of the folklore of magic?"

"Little," Raven admitted. "Only that the Sisters gifted magic to the people of Rhynwier a long time ago."

Rosaria nodded. "I remember hearing the stories from my nurse when I was little. Some scholars thought the Sisters gifted the magic; others thought humans stole it. Either way, it was my ancestors who either accepted the gift or stole it. They used the magic to unite the people and form the Kingdom of Rhynwier, named after Rhyn, the first king. As more children were born with the gift of magic, entire schools were built to teach them about the Sisters and how to use their magic.

"But somewhere, it began to change. Our neighbors did not have our magic, and they grew to hate and fear magicians. To prove that they did not need magic, they developed technology, including Altair's Augur. Altair himself studied magic, intent on learning it. He could not, and it made him bitter. He built the augur to be able to use magic."

At the mention, Raven's skin prickled.

Somewhere deep in her bones, she felt a spike of doubt. The story seemed to be lacking, but because she didn't understand the feeling, she didn't tell Rosaria about it.

"I don't know the stories that well," Rosaria said, her eyes going misty. "The Gray Elite slaughtered the scholars in their takeover, and the few who escaped were hunted down. An older scholar lived at Winchester House, and much of what I know came from him. He died not a month after I learned of my heritage."

Ezra took Rosaria's hand in his own—a small gesture, but it's effect on the princess was immediate. She brightened, smiled, and that softness returned to her features.

Raven understood. Rosaria's parents, the king and queen, had been murdered by the Gray Elite, assassinated. Their servants, the magic scholars, the magicians—anyone with magic had been purged from the city on that day. Books of magic and history had been burned. Entire libraries and schools were destroyed.

"And the Gray Elite did all of that," Raven said, "because they feared magic?"

"Fear gets the best of us," Conrad said. "Even grown, educated men."

"I admit," Ezra said, still holding onto Rosaria's hand, "I fear magic. I used to have nightmares about the Wraiths coming for me; my father told me stories of the assassins, shadow-men, he said. Looking back now, I know he wanted me to be afraid of them, to see the Hawks as monsters to be eradicated. Still, I didn't entirely believe him, then..."

"You mentioned you are on a routine of ruby powder," Rosaria said to Raven, breaking the tension.

She nodded. "It's helping considerably."

"I'm no scholar, but I would like to speak with you after breakfast about this magical fever of yours," said the princess.

"I would have to move around a few appointments, but I'm sure I could make room," Raven said. "Maybe if I move my hour of pacing after my hour of counting the floor tiles, I could make room."

Rosaria smiled. "I will be there."

After they finished breakfast, Raven sat with Rosaria on the floor of her room. The sunlight had broken through the stormy clouds, glowing bright gray and yellow through the balcony doors, brightening the floor around the two girls.

"This is an old trick." Rosaria held her hands between them, palms up. She motioned for Raven to do the same, their fingertips barely touching.

Raven felt a shift, barely there, like someone had opened a window in the room, allowing the air to move in a different direction, only *inside*. Rosaria wore deep concentration, her eyes focused on their hands, on the space between them. After a long moment of silence, Rosaria curled her fingers around Raven's.

The feeling came gradually, a subtle shift within her. It came from somewhere deep. The fever, she realized. It obeyed Rosaria's summons, coming gently toward the surface.

Rosaria's brow creased.

And the feeling subsided. Rosaria released her hands.

"What was that?" Raven asked.

The fever crept back to where it hid underneath the ruby powder.

"I summoned your magic," Rosaria said. At Raven's blank face, she added, "It is an old trick the magicians used to see if children were gifted. The scholars taught it to me when I was young. They knew who I was, even when I didn't. Later, Brigadier General Winchester told me it's part of being royal. He said I should know how to summon forth magic in others."

"You have magic," Raven said.

Rosaria nodded. "It's part of the royal bloodline, I was told. A king or queen is tied to the kingdom in ways we can't understand. We are connected to the magic, somehow. I've always thought that's why the Gray Elite needed me alive, because the kingdom and its magic need me."

"Then..." Raven looked down at her hands. "You summoned magic. From me. That means I do have magic?"

Rosaria nodded. "It is there. It responded, but it's not like magic I've felt before. It's tangled, wild, and...raw. It's not throughout your body; it's clustered. I've not felt anything like it before. It's different. It's..."

"Wrong?" Raven supplied.

"Unnatural," Rosaria whispered.

Raven's heart sank. She didn't see the difference in those words.

"Magic lives within the person, a force that compliments the magician in personality and heart," she explained. "This magic, your magic... It doesn't ebb and flow with you like it should. It's violent, aggressive. Did something happen while you were in Lenhala? Something strange? Did you come into contact with anything odd or unusual?"

If she took the centrum off, would the fever go away?

Rosaria studied her face, her hazel eyes penetrating. She stared, unblinking, for what felt like too long, until Raven thought her heart would burst out of her chest.

"Something did happen," Rosaria said softly, her voice velvet. She tilted her head and blinked once—deliberately. "It isn't just the magic that is tangled. You're tangled. You've been through a lot in a short amount of time. Change is hard on most people, and you've had a large dose."

Raven nodded. "That's an understatement."

"Tell me about it."

"Which part?"

"All of it."

Raven blinked at the princess. "All of it? I don't know where to start."

"The beginning."

Raven swallowed. She didn't even know if she could recount the entire disaster, but she knew where it started.

"I grew up in a small village to the far north of the kingdom," Raven said. "Nothing ever happened. I wanted out. I wanted adventure like those I'd read about. I wanted to see the rest of the world. I feared that I would live out my years in that place and die without ever stepping foot beyond it." She half laughed.

"You are a very long way from there now," Rosaria said, smiling.

"And I often wonder if I will ever see it again."

"Do you have family there?"

"My father and stepmother and my half-sister."

"Do you miss them?"

Raven hesitated to answer, and her own silence surprised her. She did miss them, but she did not miss being in Silver Glen. She wouldn't mind seeing them, if only to visit and then continue her adventure. She nodded. "Yes."

Rosaria's eyes drifted to Raven's throat, to the locket her dress did not hide.

"It was my mother's," Raven said, covering the simple locket with her hand. "It's the only thing I have of hers."

Rosaria gave her a small smile, one that understood loss. "I had hairpins that belonged to my mother. They were in my hair the day my parents were killed. Those hairpins were the only thing I had of that life, but I left them in the Winchester house. Speaking of, how did you and Zander meet?"

At the mention of his name, a different warmth surged under her skin. Raven told Rosaria what she had told Conrad and Ezra, how Zander had ended up in Silver Glen, pretending to be a refugee. "We went after the thief," Raven said, "who ended up being Conrad, but I didn't meet him until later." Raven told Rosaria everything—to get it all off her shoulders felt incredible.

Rosaria said nothing with words or by expression. She simply listened.

"And now all of this is happening," Raven said with a sigh. "Are the Hawks and Gray Elite really trying to start a war?"

Rosaria sighed before she answered. "From what I have gathered, tension is rising steadily on both sides. I'm afraid that a terrifying and costly end may be in sight."

Raven pulled her legs to her chest. War. "I sometimes wish I'd never left home. I wanted adventure, but... Sisters, I don't know much more I can handle."

A soft, motherly smile stretched across the princess's lips. It spoke of a deeper understanding that reminded Raven of her stepmother. "There was a saying inscribed on the wall of the royal library," Rosaria said. "It had always been there, written in the old language. The scholars translated it to say, 'Fate throws us where we need to go, not where we want to go, and sometimes we fail; sometimes we change the world.'"

"The old language?" Raven asked. Like the old god, the one the Gray Elite tried so hard to erase.

Rosaria nodded. Her peaceful expression turned into a grim one. "So much knowledge has been lost over the past one hundred years, and it scares me. How will we ever get it all back?" Her voice thinned. "There are books and scrolls scattered around the kingdom, kept safe by loyalists to the crown, but even if we could take back our kingdom, how would I be able to make that knowledge public again?"

The faint emotions traveled over Rosaria's fine features, fear and uncertainty. Solemn sincerity shaded her eyes. She worried over her kingdom's future, a future that she might not have a part in shaping. Her kingdom—Raven couldn't imagine the guilt she felt.

"Zander worries about you," Raven said, and Rosaria's eyes drifted back to her own. "He blames himself and wants to help you get out of here. He thinks you're being held prisoner."

"I am, but I don't see how freeing me would do anything other than upset the Gray Elite," she said, hugging herself. "And that isn't something the Hawks need to do. And it's not terrible here. I like it better here than in Lenhala."

"Is it because of Ezra?" Raven whispered, mischief on her tongue.

Rosaria smiled, a secret smile. "We have gotten along rather well." A spark appeared behind her eyes. "His visits have made these months in the Tombs much more pleasant and endurable. He sneaks me out like this now and then when his friends in the guard are on duty. That way, I won't be counted as missing."

Friends in the guard. Ezra had people in the Gray Elite, as did his father. The webs grew and grew.

"Do the servants not suspect?"

"Many of them are in the dark, along with the general," Rosaria said. "There are several secret entrances to the tunnels below, and one of them is in my room.

That way, I can get out easily should the general or his men make a surprise visit. That hasn't happened, but I like to be prepared."

"Ezra must care about you a great deal to take that risk," Raven said. Should either of them get caught, both would face treason and Sisters knew what else.

Rosaria nodded. "Ezra has the bravery of ten men; he just doesn't know it. Don't tell him, because I don't want him to know. I like him better that way." A blush warmed her cheeks. "And now he's taken you in as a prisoner too. He tells me you're a wanted woman for attempting to assassinate the general. Don't worry, I don't believe a word that comes out of that horrid man's mouth, if he's a man at all and not some demon in human skin. I'll never understand where Ezra came from. But, if it comes down to it, the secret entrance to the tunnels is through the wardrobe in my room. There is a notch in the wood, on the upper right corner. Press it to release the false panel."

Raven quickly committed that to memory. "I hope it doesn't come to that."

"As do I." Rosaria stood and held a hand out for Raven. "Tell me, have you ever played chess?"

"A few times with my sister."

"Are you any good?"

"I can't say. My sister never took the game seriously. She let me win."

Rosaria smiled. "I love the game, but Ezra does the same to me. He lets me win. I know he does it, but still he continues. I have a set in my room. Come, let's play and give each other a real challenge."

Raven walked with the princess toward the doors, going over the rules in her mind. It had been a while since she had played chess, but the idea of not sitting alone in her room, waiting for her next hourly dose of ruby powder, sounded pleasant.

Raven was smoothing the clean linens over the bed when she heard the gentle rustle of a breath. She whirled around; her breath caught in her throat. A figure stood against the twilight of the balcony. The doors stood open, letting in the sprinkle of the fountain down below, the gentle chatter of a garden party an estate away.

The figure leaned casually against the doorframe, his lean body easy and his posture nonthreatening. The glow of twilight hid his face.

"Don't look so surprised, little bird," came Conrad's voice from the figure, and relief spread over her limbs. "There are few places in this city I can't get into. A locked door is no match for me."

"I will send word to the locksmith of his folly." She tossed the sheet over the bed a bit haphazardly. She didn't care if they were tucked in. She preferred them not.

Conrad chuckled and stepped into the room. She could hear the gentle tinkling of the beads in his braids. He shut the balcony doors behind him and locked them.

"Did you go out into the city?" Raven asked.

"I did." He offered no other explanation. "Your balcony was closer, and a few servants were clustered underneath mine. I thought I'd be cautious. Don't want to make the help think I'm breaking in."

"You are, technically."

He shrugged. "Details." He sauntered to the door, then paused. He leaned against the side of it like he had nowhere else in the world to be. The softening twilight glittered against the knives along his torso, attached to a thick leather belt. "It might be in poor taste, but I overheard you and the princess talking."

"Eavesdropping?"

He didn't deny it. "She said your magic was unnatural and clustered."

Raven busied herself with straightening the wrinkles in the sheet.

"Kind of like it's not supposed to be there. Kind of like your body isn't used to it being there, like it was thrust upon your body suddenly." His words were not cold, only curious.

Raven glanced up; Conrad's eyes were pinned on her locket. She put a hand over it, hiding it from his view.

"You have it, don't you?" he asked, his voice low and whispering, threatening but playful. His coal-dark eyes glinted.

She didn't answer.

"It's all right, little bird," Conrad said, pushing off the door. He turned to go. "I'd rather not dive headfirst into a war either. Your secret is safe with me; however," —he paused with his hand on the knob— "what happens when the ruby powder no longer works? Are you going to let it eat you alive until you're nothing but ash?"

"If it keeps the kingdom safe," she said.

"Then they will steal the stone from your ashes," he said darkly.

The sunlight had been fading imperceptibly, growing darker with every passing heartbeat, until she and Conrad stood in darkness. The lights flickered on in the garden, shining blue like light through ice.

She closed her hand around the locket. "Then, I suppose I won't care if there's a war."

He chuckled, his grin turning feline. "If that is the case, I'll take it first and hide it somewhere no man will ever find it."

"Better than Zander did?"

"Oh, much better," Conrad said. "I once visited an island full of lost things. It's where people go to forget things, and once an item is there, anyone looking for it will never be able to find it. However, if one isn't looking for anything, they find everything. Quite a mystery."

Raven had the thought to ask him where this island was but held her tongue. Conrad hesitated a moment more, then left himself into the hallway. His ghost-like footsteps trailed into the hall.

Raven finished making her bed, mind on the centrum and the augur and the island where things could be hidden forever.

It would be better for all if the centrum could be lost forever.

34

The storm had blown out, and without the clouds, Moorin lay beneath a sky of stars. The lights blanketed all but the brightest, but Thalame could imagine a sea of stars up there. He'd spent enough nights staring at the sky above the treehouse.

Sisters, he wished he was there now, with a cup of berry wine and Ivy's company. Maybe two cups of berry wine. Or three.

Thalame and Zander stood in full Wraith gear on the darkened edge of some fancy house. Engor called them estates, which in his opinion was just a fancy word for house—big houses but houses nonetheless.

The Deacon Estate stood proud among the oldest and grandest estates. It's garden sprawled and ended in an iron-spiked wall. Few rooms in the estate held light, not surprising for this time of night. According to Engor's spies, General Deacon was still in Lenhala. There should be few lights in his house, yet there were four rooms in use—in the guest wing.

Zander couldn't keep still. He clenched and unclenched his fists; he paced; he tapped his feet. Poor bloke. He'd barely said a word since they'd left the Wooden Goblet, other than muttering curses to no one and everyone. Thalame understood without having to touch him. He'd tried to calm the raging emotions, but Zander had shrugged off his hand.

"We don't have to do this," Thalame said quietly.

Zander didn't say anything. He didn't acknowledge that Thalame had spoken. He held his stare on the lit windows of the Deacon Estate.

They had told Engor they would look into Conrad and the girl's disappearance and reappearance at the Deacon Estate. Neither had implied they knew or suspected any more than what Engor did.

"Yes we do," Zander said, almost too quiet to hear. Fury painted his face. "If nothing else, we need answers."

Thalame understood; Zander wanted to know why she had snuck away, where she had gone, and how she ended up in Moorin—with Conrad, of all people. Blasted thief. In Thalame's opinion, the Wraiths should have strung him up as an example to anyone else feeling greedy.

Thalame had his suspicions. Had she found out that Zander wanted to send her home? Wanted to keep her safe at the treehouse? Girls were smart like that. And Conrad—Sisters only knew what that madman was scheming.

"She needs to be held accountable," Zander said. Thalame thought he spoke more to himself than to him. "She needs to explain why she's here, why she's *there*, and smacked for making herself so hard to get to."

342

Thalame didn't agree with the last one, not entirely. Though the girl had put a wrench in their plans, she'd kickstarted them at the same time. He'd known Zander for a long time. He'd like to think Zander wouldn't actually hurt her, not even after all she'd put him through with her disappearance, but if she had committed treason against the Wraiths? Thalame didn't know if Zander would follow through or not.

"Zander," Thalame said. "Do you think the general's people got to her first?"

"I don't know. It might be another of Conrad's games," Zander spat with distaste. "Malik warned us not to trust a word he said."

Thalame hesitated; he knew what he needed to say, what needed to be said before they set foot on the Deacon Estate. "Zander, if she has spilled any of our secrets, Hawk, Wraith, or Dweller—"

"Then she will receive the punishment fitting of that crime," Zander said, his voice flat, empty, emotionless. He lifted his chin. "The punishment for treason within the Wraiths is death. If she has betrayed us, then she deserves no less."

Thalame held his breath. Zander had wiped the emotion from his voice, his face, locking it up wherever he put it when he didn't want to feel it. His eyes blanked, cold as starlight.

"There's still a chance it's not her," Thalame said.

"I know," Zander said. "But who else could it be?"

"Anyone, really," Thalame said. "Do you want it to be her?"

"Yes and no," Zander said, emotion slipping back into his voice. "I want it to be her because that means she's alive. I don't want it to be her because I might have to kill her for treason."

And if Zander flinched, he would have to kill the girl. He hated the thought of it, but he knew that Zander never flinched, never missed.

And, the girl wasn't their only objective. Engor had given them another, one more pressing. Tonight, the Wraiths launched Project Demo, and everyone had to be on their toes. All across the city, Wraiths waited, prowled like Zander.

All they had to do was wait for the signal, and then the fun would begin. Fun for them, not for the Gray Elite. They would have a long, long night.

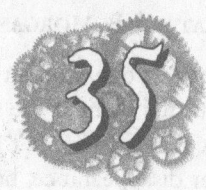

Ezra came to fetch Raven for tea. He did not take her to the lounge down the hall, but to another lounge in a different wing of the house. The lounge was larger, the circular table capable of sitting ten. Heavy blue drapes hung on either side of the windows. Sconces brightened the room in shades of pale yellow.

"It has the better view," Ezra explained, motioning to the window.

He was right. From the leaded-glass windows, she could see the sprawling gardens, dark for the night, and in the distance, the glittering heart of Moorin glowed like barely-contained sunlight, pale yellow and blue spilling from every window. The spires and towers looked like something from a dream, whimsical and beautiful and dangerous.

Rosaria already sat at the table, her ankles crossed, her shoulders straight. Even as a prisoner, she sat like a princess. Raven sat beside her and helped herself to a cup of tea—a sweet tea infused with fruit and herbs to rest both body and mind, Rosaria explained.

Ezra cleared his throat—two guards stood on either side of him. Raven blinked; had she walked right past them? She hadn't heard them enter the lounge. Both guards wore a Gray Elite uniform. They stood like soldiers, ready for action, armed with a pistol, a saber, and a crossbow. Neither looked older than Ezra.

"These are two of my trusted men," said Ezra. He introduced Warrant Officer Bertrand, the taller of the two, built like a wall. He had a full but trimmed sandy beard. Next to Bertrand, Warrant Officer James—the other guard—looked small, though he stood as tall as Ezra.

Both men gave respectful bows to Raven.

She stared blankly. Did they not know who she was? Who Rosaria was? Then she remembered Ezra's words. His men. Trusted men. Like the guards who reported Rosaria in her cell when she was not.

"This is Raven," Ezra said, motioning to her. "She is a guest of mine."

"Is it a pleasure to meet you, Miss," said Bertrand, his voice deep and strong.

"A pleasure, indeed," said James, his voice reedy and lyrical.

"Likewise," Raven said.

"Word on the street is I've invited my friends over for tea," Ezra said.

The two guards joined them at the table. Conrad remained absent. Ezra didn't mention him, so neither did Raven. Being the pirate that he was, he had likely gone snooping for loot in the city. With all these towering estates, she doubted he had to look far. Or he might have been busy with Wraith business. And she reminded herself that Conrad's business was his own, not hers.

Bertrand and James shared a casual and respectful greeting with Rosaria—they had met before.

Raven sipped her tea while Ezra told Rosaria about meetings he had attended that afternoon. One had been with Gray Elite; the other, with smugglers. Rosaria listened intently. Bertrand and James had been on patrol that afternoon. Not as exciting as a meeting with magician smugglers.

"Patrol is always boring," Bertrand told Raven. "Reported robberies, fights, drunken brawls, civil complaints, that sort of thing. The automatons handle the dangerous stuff. We get stuck with the paperwork."

James had gone to a suspected home invasion in a wealthier district, though he doubted the homeowner because Slenders had been patrolling, and nothing got past a Slender.

"Some people just crave the attention," said James. "They can't find something; they immediately call the patrol and cry burglary. I told the guy to question anyone else living in the house. He didn't like that suggestion."

"Oh, you mean suggest that they're idiots?" Bertrand said, laughing.

James began to tell another story of his patrol, and Ezra leaned toward Raven. He hid his mouth with his teacup. "You all right?" he whispered.

"Yes," she whispered back, hiding her mouth with her teacup as he did. "Where is our other friend? The one with sticky fingers?"

"He doesn't tell me where he goes," Ezra said. "He's always kept his agenda close to the chest, if he's got one at all. I wouldn't put it past him to make it up as he goes. He comes and goes, and as long as he doesn't cause a stir out there or bring a horde of angry patrollers to my door, I'm content."

The story came to an end, and Bertrand and Rosaria laughed. Ezra smiled, as did Raven, and she found her eyes flickering to the windows to see if a shadowy figure lurked beyond. She admired Conrad, his cunning, his fearlessness, his ambition. Without his assistance, she would still be fighting for her life in that pirate arena. If she hadn't been killed. If she hadn't escaped on her own.

The conversation flitted around with a casualness that Raven hadn't felt in a while. For the past couple weeks, it had been a constant sense of panic, of scheming, of rushing. This newfound peace—she liked it. The ruby powder helped too.

As it turned out, Ezra had an inner circle of Gray Elite like Bertrand and James who reported to him and occasionally brought him magicians or gave him their location. James worked in the emperor's office and gave Ezra access to high-tier reports and files. He had, more than once, hidden reports on magicians or added notes to deter the Gray Elite.

When she had first met Ezra, he hadn't seemed nearly so treasonous. She liked this other side of him. Beneath the regal stance and soldier's smile, he rebelled.

Raven didn't add much to the dwindling conversation. Between the tea and the ruby powder, her thoughts drifted like clouds, pretty and hard to grasp. Her body felt airy, her feelings indifferent.

Ezra and James were discussing a theater uptown that they had been using as a safehouse for magicians when a distant commotion sounded from somewhere in the house, a crash like something had fallen, something heavy.

The lounge fell silent. Ezra stood, as did Bertrand and James, each wearing a soldier's mask—ready for anything. Rosaria tensed.

"What was that?" Bertrand asked.

"I don't know." Ezra pushed his chair out and started toward the door. "I will find out. Escort our guests back to their rooms. Quickly."

Bertrand and James nodded. Ezra left, his steps quick, steady—the march of an officer.

Raven met Rosaria's eyes. Though the princess held herself calm, her eyes gave away her unease, and that unease matched Raven's. Neither knew what had happened. Had a servant dropped something or fallen? She hadn't seen servants, but Ezra had mentioned them, so they must have existed somewhere else in the vast house. Her gut, however, dismissed that logical answer.

Bertrand and James silently escorted Rosaria and Raven out of the lounge. Bertrand walked with Rosaria, and James walked closer to Raven. In the corridor, they headed in opposite directions. Raven glanced over her shoulder at the princess, who walked steady, despite the fear in her eyes. Raven tried to mimic her.

Why would Bertrand lead Rosaria the wrong way? Unless he planned on taking her a different route or, more likely, underground. They would be walking to the closest entrance to the Tunnels and returning her to her cell in the Tombs.

Which meant they suspected something other than a bumbling servant.

Raven's gut twisted—what did they think it was?

James turned through a narrow passage between corridors, a servant's passage, and he hastened down an unlit hall. Raven sped up to walk with him. His nerves did nothing for her own. Thunder boomed, but it sounded off. Too close, contained.

"What's that?" she whispered.

James didn't answer. He gripped the hilt of his saber.

They turned down a corridor that looked familiar. She and Ezra had walked through it on the way to the lounge. Not far from her room, where she could indulge in the sleepiness of the tea for the rest of the night, and—

"What?" James gasped and stopped.

It did not take long for her to see why.

Moonlight and city light glowed through the high windows that lined one side of the corridor, but something was very wrong. Raven stumbled forward as her eyes focused on that wrongness.

Moorin's white-light brightness had changed. During the time it had taken her to leave the lounge and walk into this corridor, dozens of fires raged across the city, red-orange and angry, consuming. She couldn't take her eyes off the flames, bright as daylight, red-hot, deadly. Moorin was burning.

The coolness of the window shocked her—she had unknowingly pressed her hands flat against the leaded glass; her nose was an inch from her wide-eyed reflection. Her breath fogged the glass.

"Miss?" came James's quiet command, an order, not a question.

She stepped back from the window, her breath a heartbeat behind. The fires had grown bigger, their plumes of black and gray smoke billowing out of control toward the stars. As they stood there, another burst of light came from another part of the city. The sound of it reached them seconds later—like contained thunder.

"An explosion," James breathed. "Sisters."

Sirens began to wail, a thousand undulating screams. Raven could almost hear the muffled screams of thousands and thousands of people, waking from their sleep to panic and chaos. She could imagine it, people rushing into the streets in their night clothes, unsure what to make of the smoke and fire, only to be rocked by another explosion, sending fear rushing as high as the smoke.

She gasped, feeling a mimicry of that fear.

Panic, fear, rage—it lined the smoky air, rising with the plumes, staining the night sky in shades of black, gray, and red, blanketing even the brightest of stars.

James's eyes searched the horizon. He spat a curse as realization turned his uncertainty into rage. "Sisters. Those are the patrol stations. The locations are right for them. They've blown them up!"

"But who would—" She stopped herself from finishing the question. She knew exactly who. The Wraiths. "Why would they do this?" Didn't they know how many innocent people would be caught in the middle?

"Revenge," James answered grimly.

She shook her head in disbelief.

"I know, but I will say this for the Wraiths. They're not careless. If I had to guess, they evacuated the homes around the explosions. I've heard they go in and tell the people to get out, and if they listen, they live, but if they refuse and remain, well then, Sisters had better be watching over them."

It made her feel only a little better.

"We need to move." James put his hand on her shoulder, guiding her away from the window. She allowed it. He was right.

She tore her attention from the burning city. The corridor had darkened. The tint of the flames and smoke dimmed the light, turning it smoky. With every step she took toward the other end, the smoky light dimmed; the corridor darkened.

And darkened.

And—*wrong*, something inside her screamed.

Raven looked to the high windows; they had gone dark, blackish. She couldn't see the fires or smoke or anything—a blackout. Her panic surged, and her heart raced, threatening to jump up her throat and out of her body.

James pulled his saber free. "What's this?" he gasped. He maintained a fierce countenance, but his voice shook.

Raven felt something, but her thoughts hit a wall. Blurred. She knew...something, had felt something before. Had she forgotten it? Something important. Something... It was an infuriating feeling. Had the ruby powder affected her memory?

And then, within the dimmed light, shadows jumped from the ceiling. Quiet and nimble as ghosts. One landed behind James; the other landed in front of Raven, blocking her view. It took less than a heartbeat for the shadow to become a figure. Dark robes and leathers and dark steel plating. They were Wraiths.

Wraiths. Her heart skipped a beat. The Wraith in front of her held his ground; he had his gloved fingers wrapped around the hilts of two daggers at his waist. James let out a war cry—and was abruptly silenced. He fell to the ground, blood seeping from a wound on his throat. His eyes went dark.

Dead.

And, like that, she stood between two masked Wraiths. James's killer advanced a step toward them but hesitated. James's killer wore a dark silver mask; the other wore a mask of dulled copper.

Raven trembled. They had been sent for her, hadn't they? They knew that she had gone to Ezra, and here they were, hunting her down. She had become a traitor, and these Wraiths had come to kill her for it.

She fumbled a step back. The Wraith in front of her didn't move; the second Wraith took another step closer.

She turned and ran. The closer Wraith grabbed her arm. She didn't hesitate; she balled her fist and slammed her knuckles into the Wraith's jaw. Her knuckles hit the edge of the copper mask, but she didn't feel the pain.

The Wraith spat a colorful curse, and his grip loosened. She yanked her hand out of his and ran.

She made it to the door—her fingertips brushed the handle.

Faster than lightning, tendrils of shadows slithered up from the floor and down from the ceiling, locking together like teeth across the door, locking her in. She wrenched her hand from the handle before the shadows covered it. She stumbled back but hadn't anywhere to go—black and blue shadows crawled up the walls faster than she could blink, slithering and converging. They surged underneath her, and all in the matter of a few seconds, the shadows submerged her, the corridor—everything. She stood encased in a tunnel—with the Wraith.

He stood at the other end of the shadow tomb. The shadows moved like light through water, constant and beautifully deadly, alternating shades of deepest black, blue, and gray.

Shadows, these shadows—she had seen them before. They had entered her dreams, haunted her for hours after waking.

And the mask, the copper mask.

The Revenant.

He stalked toward her with the grace of a seasoned killer, a predator ready to tear her throat out. Raven scrambled back until her back hit the smooth wall of the shadows. The shadows gave a little with her weight but held. She could feel the shadows moving, undulating, slithering, an oddly sizzling texture—magic, she realized. Powerful magic.

He came at her. She screamed but it did little; the sound itself seemed to be trapped inside with them, muffled and distant. She tried to strike him again, but he caught her wrist. In a few quick moves, he pinned her to the ground. He held her wrists on either side of her head, opening his robes and exposing his middle; daggers lined the leather belts strapped around his torso. He hadn't pulled any of them.

She squeezed her eyes shut. No. No. No. A gasp escaped her throat. A feeble plea for her life. She felt tears of panic and fear push against her eyes. If he hadn't drawn a knife, how did he plan on ending her? Crush her throat with his bare hands? Craft a dagger out of shadow? Force his shadows down her throat and tear her apart from the inside?

She shuddered. She tried to pull herself out of his grip, out from underneath him, but he wouldn't budge.

She stopped struggling.

The shadows made the smallest of sounds, like the muffled chitter of a thousand cicadas underwater. Was that what the underworld sounded like?

And breathing. Soft, agitated breath hitting the other side of the Revenant's mask.

Raven opened her eyes. The Revenant had lowered his head until he hovered a hand above hers. His copper mask had been carved with lines that curved around each other, never meeting, never crossing. It looked like a design from the Temple of the Three Sisters.

She slid her gaze along the copper and into the eyes of her killer, the only part of him visible. The Revenant met her gaze. He had sapphire eyes—her breath caught in her throat. Her heart skipped too many beats. Everything stopped.

She knew those eyes. She would know them anywhere.

Her breath tumbled out in a gasp, "Zander?" Her voice choked on the tears she had yet to cry.

He shuddered. Hot breath hit the other side of his mask. The shudder traveled down his arms and into her wrists, down his torso and into his legs.

"Zander," she repeated, a little louder. It was him. Zander had been sent to kill her by the Wraiths; Zander was the Revenant.

Zander's sapphire eyes searched hers, wide and disbelieving, caught between regret and relief. She couldn't hold it back. Her chest heaved, and tears began to fall—her fear and panic got the better of her.

He shuddered again, his breath heaving. He gasped—the shadows around him faltered, loosening their seams. Raven glimpsed the white of the walls between the tendrils. The second Wraith stood in the corridor, waiting. He made no move to intervene.

Zander shifted, releasing her arms, but he did not get up. He leaned forward onto his hands, one hand on either side of her head. His breaths came out strained, pained. It mirrored in his eyes.

Raven lifted her shaking hands to his mask. Her fingertips grazed the smooth metal, along the cheekbones, the carved edges, and to where it tied around his head. She pulled the leather ties and lifted the mask off his face.

Zander's bronze skin had gotten a few shades darker since she had last seen him. He had pulled the top half of his hair back, and the bottom half had grown out. She clutched his mask to her chest; the emotion in his eyes shifted to something she hadn't seen on him before—regret and joy mixed together.

She found the same emotions tangling inside of her. Joy at seeing Zander again, regret because of what she had likely caused.

"What are you doing here?" Zander whispered, his voice shaky, not at all like the arrogant cadence she remembered. He blinked; wetness smeared across his eyes, glistening along his lashes. "What did you tell them? How could you turn on us? Don't you realize what this means? The Wraiths think you've betrayed them to the Gray Elite, Raven." His voice shook on her name. "The punishment for betrayal is death."

He *had* come to kill her. On the Wraiths' orders. She had suspected it, but hearing his admission tore through her.

"Is that why you're here?" Her voice came out just as weak as his. She couldn't take her eyes off his. If she blinked, would he finish the job? All that time thinking she would never see him again. Even after all this time, her heart still jumped when he looked at her. "To finally be rid of me?"

Zander choked on a gasp.

He had. He had come here to kill her, nothing more. Suddenly, the relief at his presence and the fear at his magic turned to fiery rage. She gripped the mask hard enough that it shook; her knuckles turned white.

"That's what you came for?" she asked. "To get rid of me? Fine. Do it."

His eyes widened.

"Then you won't have to worry about me being a *hindrance* in all your plans."

"Raven—"

"You just want me gone!" She thrust the mask up and smacked it against his chest.

He yelped as the air rushed out of his lungs, but didn't relent.

She beat it against him. "You were going to leave me behind! You wanted to send me back to Silver Glen!" Tears started to roll down her cheeks. Furious that he had both caused her to cry and witnessed it, she beat the mask against him harder.

He didn't move.

"You didn't want me there. I was just a problem, a hindrance, an obstacle. A means! All you cared about was yourself and your princess, and she's not even in trouble!"

His brows came together at those words. Of course he would want to hear about Rosaria, his princess. All about his princess.

She beat the mask against his chest one last time and then threw it. It hit something, but she didn't look. The words had left her hollow. All her rage, gone. Ashes. She wiped the tears from her face.

Zander parted his lips, but rather than speaking, he winced. His shadows sputtered. He let out a gasp of a grunt, slumped onto one elbow, and the magic around them dissolved. His hot breath hit her ear, gasping.

"Raven—"

Raven put her hand on his shoulder, then shoved him hard. He fell off her and onto the floor, and she rose to her feet. She straightened her dress and smoothed her skirt while he fumbled to his feet.

The other Wraith leaned against the wall, his arms crossed. Another boy stood by him, wearing dark robes and leathers, not that much different from the Wraith's wear Zander wore. It took Raven a moment to realize that this third Wraith did not wear a mask; it was Conrad. At the sight of his familiar face, relief spread through her limbs. His braids were tucked underneath his hood, but his eyes shone with his casual mischief.

He looked very much like the stranger she had met at the arena.

Zander grumbled a curse under his breath while glaring at her and rubbing his chest. He took a shaky step, and as his eyes slid to the windows, exhaustion wiped any other emotion from his face. His magic, the rune—it took a heartbeat for Raven to realize he had used his magic, and the rune on his back likely burned. His steps evened out with each one he took, and he grabbed his copper mask from the floor.

The other Wraith laughed—she knew that laugh. Through the dark mask, familiar eyes met hers. Thalame.

"Long time, no see," said Thalame, his voice muffled by the mask. "Glad to see you're not automaton chum."

"Who're you?" Zander spat, pointing at Conrad with his mask. He swiftly attached it to his shoulder so that the face looked at Raven.

"Zander, this is Conrad," Thalame said before Raven could speak. "Conrad, this is Zander."

"Oh," Conrad said in exaggerated understanding, his eyes wider than they should have been. He looked Zander up and down. "You're the one everyone keeps talking about. Yes, you do look familiar. Hmm?" He tilted his head at Zander, studying him. "That is an interesting mask. I haven't seen many quite that color."

Zander shifted his shoulder. "And I'd prefer it stay that way," he said lowly.

"Gotcha," said Conrad, winking at Zander. "Wraith's honor or something like that, right?"

Conrad glanced at Raven, and something like sympathy and curiosity shone in his eyes. Zander glanced between the two of them, a crease between his brows. Raven saw the assumption in his eyes, and she made no assertion to correct him. Let him think whatever he wanted.

A beat of silence, and then Zander spat at Conrad, "What are you doing here? I didn't think you were a Wraith anymore."

Raven frowned at the bitterness in his tone, but Conrad let the comment roll off his shoulders. He sauntered a step forward. "I would love to stand here and trade insults, but we don't have that kind of time. The Gray Elite are searching the house."

Raven tensed; Zander spat a curse. Thalame didn't look surprised. Conrad must have already told him.

"And we need to get out before they find us," added Thalame. He closed the space between him and Raven and pulled a dagger from his side—he pressed the blade against Raven's throat.

Zander balled his fists and stared at the blade. Conrad scowled. Neither moved.

Thalame met her eye with a grim seriousness. "Have you betrayed us?"

"No," she said. As she spoke, her skin graced the sharp edge of the blade.

Thalame's expression didn't change. "Yet we find you here, a guest in the enemy's house, wearing clothes of the enemy."

"Ezra isn't the enemy," she said.

Thalame's eyes narrowed.

"I didn't tell him anything he didn't already know."

The dagger at her throat didn't scare her, though she knew it should have. Thalame's empty stare did. She turned her eyes to Zander, whose skin had turned a shade ashen.

"He knows more than you think he does," she said. "The Hawks, the Wraiths, the magicians. But he's not your enemy."

Conrad sighed dramatically. "She's right, but let's do this later. Like I said, we don't have—"

A blast shook the floor, the walls, and rattled the windows. A flurry of voices followed, shouting orders; booted feet thundered on the tile, then the carpet. They were on the floor below them.

"—time," Conrad added.

Thalame spat a colorful curse and pulled the blade away from Raven's throat. With deft fingers, the blade vanished back into its sheath.

"This way's a dead end," Zander spat, pointing to the end of the corridor where Raven had come from. "We'll have to hide and wait it out or fight."

"Neither of those sound promising," said Thalame.

Conrad glanced at Raven with a knowing glance. His eyebrows wiggled.

Her thoughts clicked together.

"Rosaria's room," Raven breathed.

All eyes turned to her. At the sound of the princess's name, Zander's eyes focused hard, and her anger flared. Ignoring it as best she could, she started toward the other end of the corridor, toward Rosaria's room.

Raven said calmly, "There's a passage that leads underground."

She walked down the corridor, Conrad on her heels. Thalame and Zander followed. Conrad fell into step beside her and slipped her an encouraging smirk. It annoyed her at first, but then she realized he had armed himself. She had nothing, only her ebony dagger, but she would fumble before she could get to it. If a Gray Elite squadron surprised them, she would need his daggers and his skill.

Raven led them to Rosaria's room, just a door down from her own. By the sounds, the Gray Elite had started their search of the floor. Her heart thumped like a drum, so loud she knew everyone had to hear it.

Rosaria's room was dark, though the blaze of Moorin glowed behind the gossamer curtains. It cast the room in a ghostly light. The room didn't look in use, aside from a few books stacked on the desk and the lingering perfume in the air.

Raven walked straight to the wardrobe, a carved masterpiece of oak. Little moons had been carved along the doors, repeating the moon's phases over and over. Raven pulled open the doors and pushed aside the simple linen and day dresses. She ran her hand along the upper right side until she found the notch; she pressed it. A series of clicks sounded from within the wall, gears connecting and turning, a belt clicking, unlocking—the back panel of the wardrobe swung out like a door to reveal a spiraling stone staircase. Pale orange lights hung from the walls in wide intervals, just enough to illuminate the edges of the steps.

"Would you look at that," came Thalame's nonplussed tone behind her.

Raven started to go first, but then Conrad set a hand on her elbow.

"Allow me," Conrad said, gently pulling her aside and stepping into the wardrobe, "considering I am armed and you are not."

She didn't argue. Conrad started down first, Thalame followed, and Raven moved next. She didn't want to have to stare at the back of Zander's head. His sure footsteps came after her, and she heard the panel slide close with the same clicking gears.

The pitiful light from above diminished with each click until the light from Rosaria's room vanished. She trailed one hand along the stone wall and held her dress away from her feet with the other; she did not want to trip. Zander walked a step behind her, closer than she thought he ought to, but she didn't complain. She wouldn't give him the satisfaction.

Several long moments passed in silence. The sounds of the Gray Elite faded; the sound of the chaos and fires diminished. A stale, muffled silence replaced it. Raven knew the feeling well—underground. She had lived seventeen years underground.

It didn't have the sense of comfort she thought it might. Instead, it felt stifling.

At last, they reached the end of the spiraling stairs. A hallway stretched out before them. Other tunnels connected to the hall, archways leading into near complete shadow. The lights buzzed, a muffled chittering that put Raven on edge. The pale orange lights left generous shadows between them.

Conrad paused at the bottom and gave her a smirk.

"Do you think Ezra made it out?" she asked.

"He has rank in the Gray Elite," Conrad said. "They wouldn't kill him on sight, especially in his own house like some common criminal. He is well liked by the people, and his murder would cause quite the stir."

"Why would the Gray Elite storm the estate?" Zander asked.

Conrad shrugged, gesturing to Raven and himself. "You knew we were there. It wouldn't be a stretch to assume Gray Elite spies figured it out or suspected it."

"They were looking for us?" Raven asked, voice dry.

"Most likely, they were looking for *you*," Conrad corrected.

Because of the centrum. She fought the urge to reach for the locket. She caught Zander's eye and turned her gaze away before he could say something, either out loud or silently.

That meant that if anything happened to Ezra, it would be her fault. Her fault for leading the Gray Elite to his door. Would General Deacon charge his own son with treason? She would like to think he wouldn't, but she remembered the coldness in his eyes when he had taken the iron box from her, like nothing else in the world mattered.

"Where are we?" Thalame asked, running his hand along the stone wall. "Please tell me it's not the sewer."

"Tunnels that run underneath the city," Conrad said. "They connect the upper crust Gray Elite to the secret places they feel the need to know about without the public knowing about them."

Zander grunted, a scowl on his face. The tunnels under Moorin likely reminded him of the sewers under Lenhala the Hawks had used. These smelled better, at least.

Thalame set his gaze on Raven. "You said Rosaria was in the house."

"She has a cell in the Tombs, but she goes up to the house," Raven said. Zander started to speak, but she added bitterly, "Yes, the tunnels lead into the Tombs."

Zander's lips came together. He looked like he wanted to say something else, but didn't. He swallowed. "Do you know the way?"

She shook her head.

"I do," Conrad said casually.

Raven raised a brow at him. He shrugged. Of course, being a pirate and a thief and a Wraith, she shouldn't be surprised that Conrad knew his way around the secret tunnels of Moorin or how to get to the high security prison.

"Why? Do you need to find a cozy cell for yourself?" Conrad asked Zander.

"We volunteered for the route that goes through the Tombs," Thalame said.

"Oh, risky," Conrad said.

"Volunteered for what?" Raven asked.

"Project Demo," Zander said, meeting her eye. "The Wraiths' plan to destroy an automaton factory, and—"

"I've heard about it," Raven interrupted.

Zander's lips pursed before he continued, "We volunteered for the route that goes through the Tombs. We had planned to go in through the entrance a few blocks from here after we'd dealt with you."

"Our plan was to rescue Rosaria and do our part for the Wraiths in one go," said Thalame.

"Ah," Conrad said. "Interestingly enough, we have similar goals. This way. Don't dally."

Conrad started down the long hall without further explanation. Raven started after him. Zander fell into step beside her, and Thalame a step behind. She didn't look at Zander. She didn't acknowledge his presence. They followed Conrad in silence down a side passage, down a flight of stone stairs, and into a long hall that looked similar to the other, except the lights had a yellowish cast, not orange.

No one said a word. Raven suspected that, like her, they were listening for footsteps. These tunnels would not be an ideal place to be ambushed by Gray Elite.

They came at last to the end. A picture of a dreary old general on a fat automaton horse had been mounted on the stone wall. Beside it, an iron panel held a lever. Conrad closed his fingers around the lever and pulled it down. A series of clicks and clanks sounded behind the painting, gears and cogs and belts churning to life. The painting swung inward.

Another secret door. How many more existed within the city?

The painting opened into a broom closet. A globe hung from the ceiling, sputtering pale yellow light over stacks of barrels, dusty crates, broken picture frames, toolboxes, brooms, and mops. A single door stood on the other side, made of plain iron.

Conrad walked toward it. He turned sideways and put his finger to his lips. He pressed his ear against the seam. He listened, an intensity took over his eyes, and then he stepped back and pulled the door open.

Artificial light flooded through the doorway, enough that Raven shielded her eyes. It took a few heartbeats for her eyes to adjust to the light. Blinking, she saw Conrad step through, followed by Zander. Thalame motioned for her to go next, and she did. Wraiths on all sides.

They stood in a hallway. The walls and ceiling were stone, painted white. One wall held nothing but stone. The other held equally spaced iron-barred doors. Pipes ran along the ceiling: some went to the lights; others never stopped. The lights buzzed incessantly. The gentle rumble of human moans and whispers gave Raven a chill. It smelled stale, unwashed bodies and sterile cleaning solution and starched linens.

A prison. The Tombs.

No sooner had the thought crossed her mind than a voice asked, "Raven?"

In the cell closest to the secret entrance, an olive skinned girl with dark hair appeared between the iron bars. Rosaria still wore her simple dress. Behind her, the commodities of her cell were above the average prisoner. She had a real bed, not a prison cot like the empty cell next to hers, and a red and gold rug on which sat a little table. A teapot sat there, a thin line of steam twisting into the air. A folding screen shielded a toilet and sink, decorated with an ocean scene, complete with pirate ships and sea dragons. A bookshelf stood just out of view, thick with colorful spines. A cushy chair sat beside it.

"Is something wrong?" Rosaria whispered. "What happened?"

"The Gray Elite stormed the house," Raven said. "We just barely made it out, thanks to you."

Rosaria gave her a small smile. Then her gaze slid from Raven to the three Wraiths. Her smile fell into a frown, and she took a step back from the door.

Zander appeared beside Raven at the door. "Ros? You're okay?"

Rosaria looked him up and down and studied his face. That she hadn't recognized him immediately gave Raven a burst of sadistic enjoyment. Rosaria's eyes widened. "Zander," she said in disbelief. "I'm fine, but what are you doing here?"

"We came to get you out," he said like it was obvious. He looked down at the sturdy iron lock. "Stand back." He stepped back and readied his hips; he would kick the lock.

"Don't," Rosaria warned. She rushed to the door and slapped her hand over the lock.

Zander gaped at her.

"A guard patrol will come through at any time to check on the prisoners, and if they see me gone or the door broken, they will sound the alarm. Something has happened up top, and it won't be the same guard as normal. The Tombs have a very strict kill-on-sight policy when it comes to prison breaks."

Raven caught her meaning—it wouldn't be Ezra's men coming to check on her.

Zander wanted to argue, but he gave in. "Fine, but I'm coming back for you. I promise."

Rosaria held his gaze, nodding.

Footsteps sounded from the far end—boots.

"That's the patrol," Rosaria whispered. "You need to go."

357

Zander hesitated.

"Go," she insisted. "I'll be fine. They have orders not to harm me."

The patrol came closer. By the muttering, they were not happy. Thalame put his hand on Zander's shoulder and guided him away. They skirted the end of the cellblock as the patrol came around the other.

"We're on the south end of the Tombs," Thalame said, urgency on every word. "We need to get to the north end with as little fuss as possible."

Zander's gaze settled on Raven, and she bristled—as if she would be the one to cause the fuss. She met his stare and glared back, daring him to say something. He didn't.

They started north. The prison was a grid pattern, long corridors of cellblocks, halls on either side, and meandering patrols. Sneaking past the patrols was easier than Raven thought it would be. With the panic stirred by the unknown chaos above, four extra sets of footsteps didn't stand out.

By the muttering she heard from the patrols, they were performing a routine inspection as per protocol during an emergency. They had to make sure all prisoners were where they were supposed to be. Rosaria had been right. If she had been discovered as missing, an alarm would have been raised. Sneaking would not have been an option.

They made it through twenty corridors without a problem. On the twenty-first corridor, as Raven sprinted across the corridor, a Gray Elite patrolman turned the far corner.

"What's that?" the patrol spat. He stomped down the corridor.

Zander cursed under his breath.

Conrad stood on the other side of the cellblock—if he crossed, the patrolman would see him.

"Show yourself," spat the Gray Elite. Several more boots joined the first. A gun cocked. A saber unsheathed. "This is your only warning before we fire."

Conrad met Raven's gaze, then winked. A mischievous smile stretched across his lips. He started to move, and once she realized his intention, her heart jumped into her throat. She started to protest, but Zander pulled her back.

Conrad leaned out from the corner. "Who? Me?" he asked innocently, pointing to himself.

"Stop!" The patrol ran toward him.

Laughing, Conrad ran back the other way, leading the patrol south.

Zander grabbed Raven's arm and yanked her north. She watched the patrol dash around the corner without looking at them. They chased Conrad down another cellblock.

Raven sucked in her breath. Conrad had bought them time.

"Come on," Zander said, pulling her forward. "Make it worth it."

Gunshots echoed down the corridor, and her chest tightened. She quickened her pace, following Thalame. With the distraction that Conrad had started, the patrols ran toward him, toward the south end, leaving the path to the north end clear.

A second gunshot, then a third. She didn't look back.

Thalame, Zander, and Raven paused for breath at the north end of the Tombs. Like the south end, it ended at a stone wall, painted a sterile white. Thalame started along the wall, and Raven followed. Her entire body shook. Her breath came in gasps. Her heart felt as though it had crumpled.

"He'll be fine," Zander whispered. He walked behind her. "He's survived our attempts to kill him; he'll survive a horde of Gray Elite."

Horde. She didn't like that word. The gunfire had stopped. She desperately wanted to believe Zander, believe that the silence wasn't because the target had been hit, but because the target had vanished.

Conrad had bought them time by luring the patrols away from them and where they needed to go. He had used himself as bait. If something happened to him...she couldn't take it. He had done so much to help her. If it hadn't been for him, she would have died long ago, either from being beaten to death in the arena or burning alive in her sleep.

Thalame led them into a workroom. An iron grate floor hid a mess of pipes and pumps, all hissing and gurgling. Pipes jutted up through the grate, dividing the room into sections, and joined pipes on the ceiling. Some pipes vanished into tanks and pumps as large as small houses; others vanished into the stone walls. The entire room rumbled, the sound blanketing their footsteps.

On the far side of the workroom, a worker stood with his back to them, watching a dashboard of dials and gauges. Thalame snuck up behind the worker, and in a blink, he had the man on the floor, unconscious. Thalame then led them to the far side of the room, to a series of four giant tanks behind a web of pipes. The smallest pipes were no bigger than her arm; the largest looked big enough for her to stand in.

"This is our way in." Thalame started to climb the web of pipes, moving quickly and efficiently, reminding Raven of a spider. He climbed to the top of the pipes and dropped onto the farthest tank.

"Through a pipe?" Raven asked.

"Yes," Zander said, jumping onto the pipes. He started to climb.

Thalame twisted the hatch on the tank, pulled it open, and dropped down inside. Raven sucked in her breath as he vanished. No splash followed.

"It's empty," Zander said, looking down at her. "The Wraiths were thorough in their planning. Come on."

Raven hesitated.

Zander raised a brow. "Unless you'd rather stay here and wait for someone to come by and ask why you're here?" The cadence of his voice, playful and arrogant, reminded her of Silver Glen, back when the world was wide and full of adventure, not ravaging fever magic and automatons. Zander's lips twitched into a smirk, curious and watchful.

She bit back an insult and started up the pipes—a feat in a dress. She climbed slow, and Zander matched her pace. He made it to the top a hand before she did.

Raven dropped onto the tank and glanced into the dark inside.

"Thalame's fine." Zander crouched by the hatch and jumped down. His boots landed on the bottom of the tank. He looked up at her, his sapphire eyes catching the light, as did the copper mask on his shoulder. "I'll catch you." He lifted his arms and motioned for her.

His words hit something deep, but she pushed it back down. Not now. Instead, she gathered her blue skirts, inhaled, and jumped. For a thrilling heartbeat, she felt nothing but air. Then Zander's strong hands caught her waist, softening her landing. For a moment, they stood so close, she could smell the sweat and leather and the sour scent of ale on his breath. She met his sapphire eyes, and the trembling in her stomach settled.

Crack—a glow appeared in Thalame's hands, glinting off the metals scattered Zander's torso. Raven jumped out of Zander's hands, breaking the small moment. She smoothed her skirt and cleared her throat. Thalame held a small clear cylinder with brass-capped ends. Inside, blue-green smoke swirled, glowing bright enough to see by.

"A new trick of Niall's," Thalame explained, twirling the cylinder through his fingers. "It's a reaction of something to something else. Don't ask me questions about it; I don't know the answers."

The blue-green glow illuminated the rusty inside of the water tank. Hundreds of pipes led off it. Thalame started toward the largest of the pipes, just wide enough for him to crouch inside it. The light moved with him, leaving the big tank in an inching darkness.

"We're crawling through that?" Raven asked, her distaste echoing off the tank.

Thalame chuckled but kept going. "It's not so bad." The pipe dampened his voice.

"Easy for you," Raven said, motioning at her skirts. "You're not wearing a dress."

"You're welcome to take it off," Zander said, smile stretching his lips.

At the sight of it, she realized how long it had been since she had seen it. Something tight loosened in her chest, and it was just like old times. "I wouldn't want to distract you," she said, gathering her skirts in preparation to follow Thalame and the fading light. "You need all the focus you can get."

Thalame laughed; Zander gave her a smirk.

She crouched into the pipe, her hair brushing the top. Zander crouched behind her. She moved slower than Thalame, but he didn't comment on it.

"You're helping them blow up the factory?" Raven whispered as casually as she could.

"Yeah," Zander said. "It's part of the oath we swore when we became Wraiths. We have to help each other against those who oppose magic, and help our fellow Wraiths. It's not worded like that, but that's the point. And, when we saw that one of the routes into the factory went through the Tombs, we took it without question."

"The Wraiths aren't going to help you rescue her?"

"We didn't mention it," Zander said. "The fewer who know, the better."

"Most people here don't know she's alive," added Thalame, "including most of the Gray Elite and the Wraiths."

Zander knew she lived because of the Hawks, and because he had grown up with her. Because he'd gotten her kidnapped.

"And it just happened that the Deacon Estate was on the way to the entrance of the Tombs," Zander added, his voice light but underlined with something darker.

"The Wraiths are concerned about Conrad and the sick girl vanishing," Thalame said. "We didn't ask, but we thought old Engor might be talking about you."

"We asked what she looked like," Zander said. She heard the desperation in his voice. "Description fit."

"And besides that, Conrad had been seen consorting with Ezra, a Gray Elite, and they assumed treason," Thalame said. "We were to investigate that too."

"Did you try to kill him too?" Raven asked, failing to hide the bitterness.

"Yes," said Thalame, a half laugh on the word. "But he caught on, told me the Gray Elite were coming and we needed to get out if we wanted to finish Project Demo without being dead."

"Rae," Zander asked, her name a breath. "What happened?"

"That's really too long of a story to explain in this setting," Raven said. "If we survive, I'll tell you about it."

"Okay." He started to say something else but stopped. He cleared his throat. "You met Rosaria?"

"I did," Raven said. "She's nice. I like her. Ezra has taken care of her since she's been here. I think they like each other."

Zander scoffed.

"What?" she asked. Did he not believe her? That old feeling burned through her chest, but she pushed it down. "Oh? Jealous that Ezra's been taking all her time?" It came out more bitter than she intended.

"No, I'm not jealous," Zander said quickly. A beat passed before he added, "Ezra is like a cousin to me. Why would I be upset that he wants to spend time with other people? I'd rather know more about you and Conrad. You two seem to be getting along."

His words were strained, and it brought a shameless smile to her face. Thankfully, he couldn't see it.

The pipe widened and ended at another tank similar to the other, ending their conversation. Raven straightened and stretched the tension out of her back and legs. Behind her, Zander did the same. Water lingered in the bottom, evidence that the tanks hadn't been emptied that long ago. It would seem the Wraiths had people on the inside, either to inform them when pipes would go dry or to make sure the pipes dried. Thalame stuck the glowing glass between his teeth and climbed up to the hatch. He hung off the sides like a spider and worked to open the hatch.

Zander stepped close to her, close enough that his breath warmed her cheek. He whispered, low enough for Thalame not to hear, "It's not like that between me and Ros. I'm not... She's not you." His voice came out husky and raw, and it sent a warm tingle up her spine.

She dared a glance at him; his eyes were soft, nothing like the killer's eyes she had looked into at the estate.

"Ros's like my sister," he said.

Thalame opened the hatch, bathing them all in in dull, artificial light. The sudden brightness startled her. Taking advantage of it, Zander leaned in and planted a kiss on Raven's cheek and then jumped up to follow Thalame out of the tank. For a moment, she stood alone in the tank's shadows. The kiss had turned her bones to lead, her blood to fire, and kindled the fever the ruby powder had dampened. Her mind replayed his words over and over until they sounded nothing like him and she doubted he had even said them.

Then Zander appeared in the hatch. He reached his hand down for her. Raven jumped and latched onto his hand, and he heaved her out. They were in a workroom similar to the one in the prison, only smaller. Tanks and pipes gurgled, hissed, and steamed, pumping water through and taking it back. In a short few heartbeats, Thalame and Zander knocked out the two workers, and hauled their unconscious bodies near the tank. Out of sight.

"Okay." Thalame threw his glowing glass back into the empty tank, where it smashed against the bottom. The smoky insides let out a sigh of release, then fell silent. "Here's the plan. We're making our way into the factory's basement. From there, we plant explosives—" he patted a small canvas bag hidden under his cloak "—set the timer, and get out as fast as we can. With luck, we can be on the surface with Rosaria before these things blow."

"We were all given a portion of compact explosive powder," Zander explained to Raven. "We set the timer for two hours. If all goes well, all the Wraiths will have planted theirs, and by the time they go off, we'll all be clear."

"What about anyone inside?" Raven asked.

"They should be evacuated," Thalame said. "The sources on the inside said the place would be empty tonight."

"We're all placing the explosives at different locations, so that the effect will be total and catastrophic," said Zander.

Raven blinked between them. "That's it? You're just going to plant explosives and get out?"

Thalame raised a brow.

"I expected something more...elaborate."

Thalame shrugged. "Sometimes the simple solution is the most effective. We're going for effect and result, nothing more."

"And, when one explosive goes off, it will ignite any close by," Zander said. "So it doesn't matter who gets there first."

Zander met her eye—he didn't like this plan either. She could think of too many things that might go wrong, too many people who might get hurt because of revenge on the Gray Elite.

"You wouldn't think it harsh if you witnessed the public executions the Gray Elite put on," Thalame said, scowling. "They hang magicians where all can see. It's south of the city and set up like a theater so everyone's got a good view. The Gray Elite have done more than enough damage to magicians and non-magic users in the pursuit of stomping out magic from the world."

Raven's stomach turned over. "I didn't know."

Thalame shrugged. "Sometimes, it's not even magicians they execute but people they just don't like and want to be rid of. Accuse someone of consorting with magic, and the Gray Elite storm in. Can't prove someone's not a magician as easily as you can prove they are."

She swallowed, feeling foolish.

"We're going to show them magic isn't something they can push around forever," Zander said, his voice firm. "If a few people get caught in the crossfire tonight, it will be nothing compared to the number of people the Gray Elite have killed."

"Okay." She summoned what courage she had left. She could feel the ruby powder wearing off; she should have taken a drink right after tea.

"We plant the explosives, we get out, we get Ros, and we all hightail it out of Gracita." Zander's eyes fell to the locket around her throat. "Do you still have it?"

She blinked, put a hand over the locket, and glanced at Thalame.

"He knows," Zander whispered. His voice fell. "He, Ivy, and Niall. I had to explain it after...you vanished."

Her stomach turned over with guilt. She wanted to correct him, *after I ran away*, but she didn't. "Yes," she said instead. "I have it."

Relief washed over his face. Thalame's gaze flickered to her locket, just once. Zander hadn't wanted to tell anyone about the centrum. The fewer who knew, the better. And she had forced him to confess to his friends.

"I'm sorry," she said before she could stop herself. "I didn't mean..."

"We'll talk about this over tea or rum," Thalame interrupted. "Later, when we're all alive and well. Right now, we've got a job to do, and I don't want to keep these explosives strapped to my chest any longer than I have to."

Raven nodded, shaking herself out of her guilt. "You're right," she said, voice stronger. "Lead the way."

Thalame started through the workroom. The iron grate floor held them above a tangled web of metal pipes, much like the other room. Everything hissed and steamed at the joints. If Ivy were here, she would have been able to rig one of her steam traps and blow the factory up in minutes.

They started up an iron-grated stairwell, through a dingy hall with ghastly orange globes for lights, and through a series of halls and iron doors—all underground, all stale and muffled. Finally, Thalame took them through a door and into a vast room filled with thousands of pipes of different metals and sizes, tanks of varying shape and use.

"The subbasement," Thalame whispered.

Raven gawked as they walked. The subbasement of the factory seemed to go on for several city blocks. Pipes vanished into the ceiling and ran into bigger pipes and pumps and tanks. On every side, machines rumbled and pumped and gurgled and clanked. Giant machinery, belts and arms, rotating and humming—the purpose for most impossible to guess. The air stank of grease, oil, and the tang of metal. She followed Thalame, hoping he had a better sense of direction in this place than she did. Hundreds of glass globes illuminated the basement in pale yellow. Every other globe had been turned off, leaving puddles of shadows between each one.

Thalame led them to an iron-grated stairwell and into the basement, a less jumbled version of the subbasement. The pipes seemed to be more organized, most running from the subbasement, and fewer tanks. Narrow, horizontal windows lined the top of the basement wall, letting in light from the street level.

They moved through the basement, and halfway around a thicket of copper pipes, a vicious, unearthly *crack* sounded above. Raven gasped, ducking involuntarily. Neither Zander nor Thalame jumped. Through the narrow windows, a blinding white flash lit up the night. Sparks surged through the globes and the wires connecting them together—the lights burst. Globes shattered, raining glass onto the iron floor. Luckily, they had been standing between two globes.

The factory fell into darkness. Faint emergency lights, spaced farther apart, remained on, shading the basement in a dangerous shade of red-orange. The machines rumbled and then halted, and all at once, the basement felt like a tomb. Too dark, too quiet.

"That's the signal," Thalame said.

"For what?" Raven whispered. A retreat?

"Gretchen's shut off the main power by shorting the factory's circuits," Zander explained. "Her magic is lightning."

For less than a heartbeat, Raven wondered what it felt like to command lightning.

"We're on a timer now," Thalame said, picking up the pace. "We've got to get to the boiler before it's up."

Thalame made barely a sound as he moved, darting between the machines. He navigated a path away from the main aisle that ran through the basement, away from the emergency lights, leaving a shadow of himself for Raven to follow. Zander stayed behind her, no matter how slow she moved up and under and over the obstacles that Thalame seemed to have phased through.

She wiggled between two pipes, hands on the floor, and slithered out the other side. She took a brief moment to see if Zander had the same trouble she did—he did—when she caught movement—a humanoid figure, no more than a shadow, walking along the aisle parallel to them.

Zander crawled between the pipes and stood beside her.

"I thought you said the workers weren't here?" she whispered, eyes on where the figure had been.

"They shouldn't be," Zander said. "And when the emergency lights kick on, that means they have to head to the surface. Anyone left inside will leave."

Raven hadn't taken her eyes off the sliver of the aisle. Zander frowned and followed her line of sight.

"I saw someone," she said.

"Hopefully, they were heading out." Zander gave her a little push.

"Keep moving," Thalame whispered, just far enough ahead for them to still hear him. "No time for stragglers."

Someone leaving, Raven told herself. She followed Thalame through the machinery, Zander on her heels, but she kept one eye on the aisle. More than once, she thought she saw someone move. They were not in a hurry. It made the hair on the back of her neck stand.

And, worse yet, she felt the ruby powder's effects fading even more. The fever crept upward from wherever it slept.

She caught up with Thalame—no, Thalame had stopped. He held up his hand to them for silence.

"Is someone there?" asked a voice, human and not human at all. The cadence came too melodic, too calm.

Raven's heart skipped several beats, and she reached out to a pipe to steady herself.

"Shit," Zander spat, his whispered voice as panicked as she felt.

Footsteps sounded in the aisle, soft and even. Then, ahead of them, walking across a smaller aisle toward the main one, came the pale red glow of an automaton's searching eyes. The glow came closer, the beams growing brighter, sweeping across the aisle, looking.

The automaton appeared between two thick pipes. It paused.

None of them moved. Raven dared not even breathe.

The automaton had the shape of a man, its sleek metal body formed nearly perfectly, the metallic skin a sickening beige. It wore no clothes, but it didn't need them. The skin over its legs and middle was smooth like metal, seemingly seamless, and it had *ears*. In the shadow, Raven couldn't see its face but didn't think she wanted to.

"I detect magic within the vicinity," said the automaton man, the voice in the same calm, melodic tone.

Zander's breath came out in slow, strained puffs. Thalame breathed the same.

Slowly, the automaton's pale red eyes started to look their way. If it saw all of them, the mission would be lost. Raven bit her lip. It detected magic. Thalame and Zander had runes tattooed on their backs to hide their magic from detection. The automaton could only be detecting her surfacing magic as the ruby powder wore off. And if she ran, it would follow her. Not them.

Foolish, stupid, and desperate.

She thought of Conrad, how he had led the Gray Elite patrols away so they would have a chance to succeed. He had thought of them, not himself.

She had to think of them too.

She knew what she had to do. As the pale red lights inched closer, she darted to the side of the passage. The beams followed her movement.

"Halt," said the automaton.

"Raven," Zander hissed.

She crawled underneath a set of pipes and toward the main aisle. Her feet hit the iron floor with force enough to signal her presence to the automaton. She stood, bathed in the red-orange glow of an emergency light. The automaton came around the corner, slim body moving with mechanical pace, unlike a human. Its pale red beams found her immediately.

In the red-orange of the emergency light, she could see its face. It wore a human's face like a mask, its skin waxy and dull.

"Halt, civilian. This is a restricted area," said the automaton. Its waxy lips didn't move. A high-pitched whirl of machinery sounded, and then its eyes turned blood red. "Magic detected."

She ran. The automaton ran after her, its sculpted legs carrying it just as fast as hers. It wouldn't tire. It would outrun her. She dashed around a corner and grabbed hold of a wire shelving unit, yanked as hard as she could while running, and sent it and the dozens of tools and toolboxes clattering to the floor. The unit itself lodged across the aisle.

She didn't look back. She didn't stop to look where she ran. She didn't slow down or pause. Half a dozen automatons joined the pursuit, their eyes going from pale red to blood red, their metal feet thundering against the iron-grated floor.

"Magic detected," chorused around her, in time with, "Intruder alert."

What would they do if they caught her? She didn't dwell on the thought. Maybe Ezra would get to her before the Gray Elite hanged her. Or would she be sent straight to General Deacon?

She ran around a corner and down a narrow aisle. Right into the path of a waiting automaton man. She tried to stop but couldn't. She careened into its chest, and with the automaton's human-sized legs and human-sized balance, they both crashed into the floor. Raven landed on top; the metal did not give as flesh would. Rather than a heartbeat, gears churned, and steam hissed with its chest.

Its pale red eyes turned blood red. As she scrambled to her feet, a cold metal hand fastened around her arm and yanked her to her feet. It held her arm high, forcing her to stand on her tiptoes. Blood red eyes surrounded her, bathing her in their light.

"Magic detained," said the automaton.

Detained. She did not like the sound of that word.

As it pulled her arm a little higher, stretching her in ways she shouldn't be stretched, a shadow jumped from the ceiling. Dark robes and leather and steel and a dark silver mask—a Wraith. The Wraith landed on the automaton's shoulders and, with a deft movement, slid a dagger into the automaton's waxy neck. The eyes sputtered.

The Wraith let out a cackle of laughter—a feminine crackle—and with a sickening twist, she popped the automaton's head off its shoulders. Steam hissed out in a shoot, wires sparked, and a tiny gear rattled from the broken neck to the floor. Its arm fell, releasing Raven's.

The Wraith jumped from the automaton as it began to fall and landed on another before it could move. A second head popped off as the first automaton crashed into the floor with a thud.

"Move!" shouted a second Wraith. He joined the other in popping heads, and Raven didn't stay to watch. She listened and ran.

Wraiths descended from the shadows, and head after head smacked the iron floor. More humanoid automatons appeared, but they gave Raven little mind; they ran to the fight. Raven ran and ran and ran until she couldn't breathe, then collapsed to her hands and knees, gasping for breath. Underneath her skin, the fever crawled. It picked at her bones, warming and tearing and searing.

It stole the very breath from her throat.

Not here, not now.

If the fever came back and took her, she would be a dead girl.

Raven slowly caught her breath. It did not want to be caught. The fever kept it at bay, just outside of her reach.

"Raven?" Zander appeared at her side, eyes wide with worry. Several daggers from his belts were missing. "What was that? You could have gotten yourself killed." He wasn't yelling. He sounded afraid.

She didn't have the breath to tell him she had done it to give them more time. He didn't ask. He closed his fingers around her arms and hoisted her back to her feet.

"Thalame?" she managed to ask.

"Probably in the fight," he said. He looked over his shoulder. The fight continued. Knives and heads and blood red eyes. Metal on metal, yelps and grunts and shouts.

As he spoke, an automaton darted out from a side path, one of its arms missing. Its blood-red eyes sputtered but found them. Zander hurled a dagger at the automaton. The dagger sank into the slit of the automaton's mouth, and as it reeled backward, Zander jumped. He grabbed the hilt of the dagger, twisted, and with another dagger, popped the automaton's head from its shoulders.

Another automaton appeared, and a Wraith appeared from above and took it down.

Raven turned and ran. Zander followed.

"There wasn't supposed to be anyone down here," Zander said between breaths. "We didn't know about the security automatons."

"What now?"

"We go ahead with the plan," Zander said. "This only complicates things. The Gray Elite will know without a doubt that it was the Wraiths. They might be on the way right now."

Zander slid around a corner and pulled her with him, and they ran down a narrow side aisle. She imagined the sirens, running throughout the night, and the people. First the explosions and fires, now the factory. Zander guided her through countless aisles, away from the fight. How many Wraiths would die tonight because of her? She had tried to help, had wanted to help, even by putting herself in danger, and she had only made it worse.

"That's the boiler," Zander said, breathless.

It was hard to miss. The boiler was a massive tank that stretched from the ceiling of the basement to the floor of the subbasment. Metal railings circled it. Water gurgled and rushed through the hundreds of pipes that led into the tank. The pipes ran through the ceiling, through the floor, and every which way. A raised platform before the boiler held numerous dials that measured temperature and pressure. The needles on each twitched continuously. Smaller tanks surrounded the bottom of the boiler, catching runoff and holding any surplus.

Raven circled the boiler. She didn't see any explosives.

"Shit," spat Zander, kicking a nearby pipe out of frustration. He'd noticed the lack of explosives too.

No one had arrived, because they had all rushed to help her.

"I'm sorry," Raven breathed. "It's my fault."

Zander didn't jump to argue, and she knew it was true. She doubled over, shame heating what the fever hadn't already. She released a pitiful sigh of frustration. Again, she had messed up their plans. First the princess, now the factory.

Maybe the fever should eat her alive.

And it felt like it might.

Zander turned around, unsheathing two daggers in a single deft twist of his body.

An automaton approached. "Unauthorized personnel. Magic detected. Emergency Protocol Initiated." The automaton raised its hand, palm first. Its fingers stretched, moving backward to reveal the metallic insides. The barrel of a pistol emerged from its shifting palm.

Raven sucked in a breath, and in a flash of black and gray and blue, Zander moved. He jumped faster than the gun fired, smothering the automaton in shadows. The gun fired; the bullet tore through the shadows—not without resistance—and landed in a nearby tank. The shadows dissolved. The automaton's head hit the floor; the body followed.

"Scrap metal," Zander muttered. He kicked the automaton's head.

Raven turned her attention back to the boiler. She circled it, then walked up to the platform. The dials remained constant. Her blurry reflection looked back at her from the largest dial.

"What now?" she asked, more to herself than anyone else.

Zander climbed the few steps to the platform, a dagger in each hand, not unlike her dream version of his assassin self, the Revenant. The sounds of fighting hadn't died down. It had attracted more attention, more automatons.

"Sisters," Zander breathed, leaning on the railing. "This isn't working. We need to get out of here while we can, before the Gray Elite storm the place and we're all dead."

One of the larger pipes creaked. The water within the boiler gurgled, hot water surging up and pushing steam through the factory and cold water surging back into the boiler. Water that ran through the entire plant. Through every floor, every sink and toilet. Between the floors, the walls, the ceilings.

Ivy would have done something clever by now to have the whole thing explode.

And Raven knew what she could do.

The fever had returned. The magic had returned—the automaton had detected it in her. The magic that had turned a man to ash in the blink of an eye. The magic that boiled under her skin like fire.

A strange calm came over her. She focused, searched for the fever, and pressed her hands flat against the steel of the boiler. She felt the water inside, felt the energy of it, felt it feeding the boiler—gushing through pipes like the veins of a creature. And she had her hands on the heart, the source of its life.

"Raven?" Zander asked, but she barely heard him. He took a step closer. His hand touched her shoulder. "We need to go."

"No," she said, firmly. "Let me do this."

He hesitated but pulled his hand back—as if burned. Did he feel the fever?

She called on the fever, urged it to her command, and it listened. She pushed the fever into the boiler, into the water. At first, nothing happened. Then, the temperature gauge began to shift toward the red side. Higher and higher it twitched. Beside it, the pressure gauge did the same.

A warning bell sounded on the boiler, a pitiful bell compared to the war raging between the pipes.

"Sisters," Zander gasped. He stepped closer to Raven, daggers at the ready. "Keep doing whatever you're doing. I've got your back."

She fed her fever into the boiler, into the water. The steel under her hands warmed considerably, but the heat didn't burn her. The water overheated, the steam too much for the pipes, overloading the machines it ran. Above them, all around them, pipes began to groan, whine, and creak.

More. More. More.

She forced her magic into the pipes in the subbasement. The subbasement filled with the creaking, clanking, and banging of pipes as the pressure rose faster than the machines could handle. The first pipe burst. Steam hissed from the break, and water splattered onto the subbasement floor. A second burst, and then a third. Boiling water poured from the broken pipes, and steam thickened the air with heavy humidity. One after another, the pipes in the subbasement burst.

Raven stumbled backward. Her fever remained, but it had been sated, just as it had been with the pirate. A dizzy spell knocked her into the railing.

Zander appeared at her side. "How?" he gasped, looking between her and the boiler with wide eyes.

Her breath came in gasps, and he didn't push her to answer.

They didn't have the time. Water poured into the subbasement. Already, the water reached the first step of the stairs, and the steam made the air horridly heavy. Sweat stuck her dress to her skin, and it sank into her scalp. Zander pulled her away from the boiler and into the basement. The air was less heavy, but the steam was seeping through the vents. As they ran, water gurgled unpleasantly in the walls, and several machines had flashing red lights.

"This way!" Zander slid around a corner.

How he knew his way around, she didn't have time to question. They had known their way in, and it made sense for them to have an escape route planned.

An automaton man tried to stop them, but Thalame appeared from nowhere, digging a dagger into the machine's neck, twisting, and throwing its head into the rising water. He had a split lip, and a Wraith who followed him had a black eye. Sweat glistened on their faces. Water splashed under the floor, rising far too quickly for comfort. Thalame and the other Wraith joined the dash for the exit. They reached the stairwell just as the steaming water splashed over the top stair of those leading down into the subbasement. Pieces of machines and forgotten tools floated in the rising tide.

"The others?" Raven gasped as she made it to the main floor, a step behind Zander. He had paused to look behind him.

"There's a dozen ways out of the basement," Zander said. "They'll get out."

"I don't know what you did," Thalame said to Raven, chuckling. "But I'm glad you did it. You used Ivy's trick, eh?"

Raven winked at him. She didn't feel able to explain what she had done. Not now, at least.

"Let's move!" said the other Wraith. He kicked open the stairwell doors and they ran onto the factory floor. An alarm wailed, and red lights flashed. Through the tall windows that lined the main floor, the city still burned in shades of frightening orange and red. Shadows darted from doors across the room, jumping to lose sections of the windows, climbing up the massive machinery to skylights, and fading into nothing at all—Wraiths escaping.

"Come on," Zander said, urging her forward. He took her hand, and they ran toward the closest door.

From behind them, a door crashed open. A man shouted, "Pull the emergency vents before it ruins the whole batch!"

Thalame and the other Wraith threw their combined weight against the doors. The lock cracked and burst, and the doors swung out. They ran out into the smoke-stained night. Behind them came a dangerous *creak, creak, creak*, and then—*crash*. Something heavy fell from somewhere high and smashed something else.

They had destroyed the automaton factory. Not the smoothest mission, but a success.

Moorin was in chaos.

Smoke covered the sky, and not even the brightest stars shone through. The smoke drifted upward, fast from some fires and slow from others, clouding over the city like fog. The fires reflected off the smoke, making it seem as though the sky itself burned. The smell—Raven coughed as it racked against her throat—smoke, fear, ash, and dust.

The street outside the factory was crowded with worried Gray Elite and panicked civilians, and no one noticed Zander, Raven, and Thalame slip out. Too much fire, too much smoke, too many people shouting and yelling and crying. Too much distraction. Fires raged from the patrol stations, and the factory creaked and groaned like it might collapse at any moment.

Thalame and Zander slowed, making their way through the wide-eyed crowd. So many people stood on the streets, watching, waiting for the next fire, the next explosion. It didn't take long to realize why; streets had been shut down, and the blocks surrounding the burning patrol stations had been evacuated. People in sleeping gowns, dressing robes, and slippers clung to one another, children sobbed, and they all looked terrified.

Raven's stomach squeezed. How many people had been hurt? The Wraiths had evacuated the people they could, but what about their homes? Their possessions? True, their lives mattered more, but to lose everything—she hated the thought.

A part of her thought it justice. The Gracitans had caused her kingdom nothing but suffering and loss for one hundred years: killed thousands of magicians. Destroyed history. Erased culture. They deserved it...didn't they?

Raven shook her head. She wouldn't think about that. Not right now. They had to get out of this mess first. Then she could wallow all she wanted.

She kept her eyes on Zander's back. Thalame walked a step in front of him. The farther they went from the factory, the less chaotic the streets. Thalame led them from the chaos, and it took a few streets for her to realize they were winding back to the Deacon Estate.

For Rosaria.

Even though she knew it shouldn't, a twinge of jealousy stung her chest. *Stupid*, she thought. She cared for Rosaria too. She wanted Rosaria to come back with them.

Thalame led the way through the crowded street without trouble. Too many people stood around, looking lost and helpless, begging the Gray Elite for help, complaining about not being able to go home, asking for help looking for loved ones. The Gray Elite were far too busy handling the fires, the factory, and the chaos of people to pay attention to the two Wraiths and a wanted girl slipping between shadows.

Getting to the Deacon Estate proved easy. Thalame and Zander took Raven through the unlocked gate near the servants' door, through the empty kitchens, and through a series of servant passages to the floor where they had ambushed her. The lights had been extinguished, leaving the corridors in shadow.

"That guard," whispered Thalame to Raven. He glanced over his shoulder at her. "Did you know him?"

It took her a heartbeat to realize he meant James, the Gray Elite who had been charged with escorting her back to her rooms. The Gray Elite whom Thalame had killed. Her stomach somersaulted; she hadn't thought of him since. His body had vanished from the corridor.

"I knew only his name," Raven said. "I met him at tea."

Thalame grunted, and they fell again into silence.

Raven led them first to her room, intent on another drink of ruby powder. Since she had steamed the factory, the fever felt slaked. It hadn't vanished, and with every heartbeat, she felt it gather, growing. She pushed open the door to her room but stumbled to a halt on the threshold.

Her room had been trashed: the blankets on the bed, thrown off; the mattress, upturned; the wardrobe, strung about; the ruby powder, gone.

"It's been searched," Thalame said, toeing one of the silken sheets on the floor.

"They were looking for something," Zander confirmed, eyes drifting to her locket.

Raven put a hand to her locket. Looking for her or it?

"No time to dwell on it," said Thalame.

Rosaria's room had been searched too. The clothes were strung over the floor, the curtains had been rifled, and the drawers of the desk had been pulled out and emptied. An inkwell, turned on its side, slowly leaked from its corked top. A puddle of black stained the tile and the wooden handle of a pen unlucky enough to have fallen into the ink's grasp. The wardrobe had been emptied, but the secret door hadn't been opened.

They slipped into the tunnels through the hidden panel and started toward the Tombs. It took Thalame a few tries to recount the path Conrad had taken them on, but they finally came to the portrait and the broom closet on the other side. Thalame listened at the seam of the door. After a pause, he led them into the Tombs. Thalame and Zander walked with cat-like steps; Raven's footsteps echoed.

Like the factory, the main lights had gone out. The stone halls were lit with the same red-orange emergency lights, spaced to leave each cell in a ghostly glow. The inmates howled and laughed at the chaos.

Rosaria met them at the door, panic-stricken. She had tied her black hair into a braid and pulled a cardigan over her dress. The red-orange light striped her cell. A series of lumps under the blankets on her bed mimicked a human body, and for a moment, Raven felt sickened. Then she realized—a decoy to buy them time.

"What happened?" asked the princess.

"No time," Zander said.

He stepped back to kick open the cell door, but Rosaria held up her hand. She pulled a simple iron key from her pocket. She easily slipped her small hand through the bars and stuck the key into the lock. With a gentle turn of her wrist, the door unlocked, and she stepped out of her cell. She locked it back and tucked the key into her pocket.

"I have my own key," Rosaria whispered. She winked at Raven, and the last remaining ill-will she felt toward the princess vanished.

Raven took a step back toward the secret door, to find their way back up through the Deacon Estate, and get out of Moorin, when a whisper of a voice drifted from somewhere else in the Tombs—a voice she knew. A voice that hammered in her chest with its mischievous familiarity.

Thalame opened the broom closet's door, and Raven took off down the hall. Zander hissed her name, but she didn't stop. She careened around the end of the cell block and into the next.

And there, leaning casually against the bars of one of the cells, stood a tall, lean young man with dark skin and dark braids nearly to his waist. He looked ghastly and full of shadows in the red-orange light, but that intimidating illusion vanished when his eyes met hers and his lips spread into a wide grin.

"Conrad," she breathed, starting toward him. He was alive!

"Look who's alive after all," he said, his tone light and playful. He turned his attention to the cell he stood beside. "This is the girl I told you about."

Raven came to a stop just outside the cell, leaving a little more than arm's reach between her and it. A tall, slender woman stood within the cell. The harsh light aged her, but at second glance, she didn't look older than forty. Unwashed brown hair hung past her shoulders. She wore the uniform of the Tombs, brown trousers and shirt. Her eyes appeared dark in the light, though the shadows couldn't mask the cleverness within them. The prisoner took Raven in from head to toe with an objective appraisal.

"Hmm," said the woman. "I'm glad to see she's dressed for tea, not adventure." She spoke in a lighthearted, authoritative tone.

Raven blushed; the stranger's words felt like a scolding. "I wasn't prepared for adventure," Raven said, glancing down at her blue silk skirt. It had been torn, stained, and soaked with only Sisters knew what.

"One should always be prepared for adventure," said the woman. She had a mild accent that Raven couldn't place.

Footsteps approached from the other end, quick and quiet.

"Raven? What are you doing?" came Zander's voice. He stopped a hand's distance from her. His eyes fell onto Conrad, then the woman.

"Raven, this is Captain Bailey Luckett," said Conrad, as if Zander hadn't appeared. "She's a friend of mine."

"Captain Luckett," Raven repeated. The captain Warren had told Malik about, a retired Wraith, Conrad's friend—and the pieces clicked together. Captain Luckett was a pirate captain, *his* captain. She looked a bit ragged and worn around the edges, but she looked far too clever to be lumped in with the typical pirate scum, as did Conrad.

"I found her. Now all I've got to do is get her out," Conrad said. "Gather any master keys on your travels through the Tombs?"

Zander said something under his breath that Raven didn't wish to repeat. No, she didn't have any keys, but she did have a solution. She stepped up to the bars and set her hands on the lock of Luckett's cell. Conrad raised a brow, and once he realized her plan, he took a large step back. Luckett looked at Conrad with a raised brow, then mirrored his step back.

Raven pushed her fever into the lock. The metal warmed, warmed, warmed, and started to soften. A little more.

"What are—" Luckett started to ask.

The lock melted like hot clay and landed on the floor in a red-hot pile of goo.

"Sisters," Conrad and Zander breathed in unison. Zander looked worried; Conrad looked thrilled.

"Sisters, indeed," said Captain Luckett, mouth tilted in a smirk. She carefully touched the bars of her cell, testing for heat, and finding them suitable for touch, pushed the door open. Luckett stepped out, skipped over the goo, and then looked at Raven. "I like you, kid."

Conrad and Luckett started the other way.

"We've got a way out," Raven said.

"Don't worry," said Luckett, throwing a smirk at Raven over her shoulder. She walked like a captain too, sure of her every step. "We've got one too."

"Come on." Zander pulled her away from the cell. "Before a patrol wanders through and finds the door melted."

Zander pulled Raven by the hand, and they slipped into the broom closet to find Thalame and Rosaria waiting inside. Thalame pulled the hidden lever, the painting swung open, and they clamored through.

"Want to explain how you did that?" Zander asked her as they started down the stone corridor.

"What did you do?" Thalame asked.

She told them, and neither Thalame nor Rosaria looked surprised.

"But...how?" Zander gawked at her hands.

"I don't know." She put her hand up to the locket. His eyes followed. She knew now that the centrum had somehow infected her, and she had somehow used it, but she hadn't the slightest idea of *how* or *why*.

"When we have time to sit and talk," Rosaria said, "we will."

Spoken like a queen. No one objected or disagreed. Raven didn't feel like talking or trying to think about the locket or the centrum or her strange new powers. Right now, they had to slip out of Moorin while the chaos distracted the Gray Elite.

None of them spoke on the way back to Rosaria's room. It looked as disheveled as it had the last time. The fiery light of the city hadn't diminished, and it bathed the room in a sickly glow. However, the Deacon Estate was quiet, and they took this moment to take a collective breath.

Zander muttered a curse and bent over, hands on his knees. Thalame slumped against the wall. Rosaria took a lap of the room, taking in the damage. Her stare lingered on the spilled ink, her face not betraying any emotion or thought. She held her shoulders back, her chin up, proud but thoughtful.

"What now?" Thalame asked. "Should we stay here a while? Might be the safest place in the city night now. Right under the Gray Elite's nose. They've already searched it so they might not come back for a while."

Zander shook his head. "No," he said, looking toward the windows. The fiery light cast his face in grimness. "We need to get out of here while the city's a mess. Besides, the Gray Elite have shown their true thoughts on Ezra. They don't trust him if they searched his house like this."

"For all we know, the general could have ordered it," Thalame added.

Zander agreed.

Raven thought about suggesting they wait for Ezra. He could give them a good plan of escape, a sneaky way out of the city, but a twinge of fear held her lips closed. The fever swirled under her skin, ever present, waiting for the time to strike.

"The Gray Elite would not have searched this house without the general's approval or knowledge," Rosaria said, her voice calm. "They've not bothered Ezra in these six months, so something has changed." Rosaria's eyes drifted to Raven, knowing.

Raven felt Zander and Thalame look at her too. They all knew.

"I suppose we all know what that was," she muttered, but in the quiet of the room, she might as well have shouted. The Gray Elite were looking for her. They had stormed the Deacon Estate for her, trashed the rooms looking for her.

Whatever fate Ezra found, it would be her doing. Raven met Rosaria's stare again, but the princess didn't smile or offer encouragement, as though she knew it too.

"And if the general gets word that I am gone, he might come back to the house," Rosaria said.

"We need to leave soon," Raven added, and Rosaria nodded.

"Ros," Zander started, but she held up her hand.

"Later," she said. "When we're not in danger."

Zander gazed at Raven—he had more he wanted to say, but Rosaria was right. Now was not the time. He stood between Raven and Rosaria, looking a bit lost between them, two bits of his world that had found each other without him. Raven felt a bit delighted that she had a connection with the princess that he didn't. Shameful thoughts, but her thoughts regardless.

"We could go back to the inn," Zander suggested. "Engor's got connections to get magicians out of the city. We could use him."

"The Gray Elite will be looking at the Wraiths," Thalame said. "They know that we attacked the factory and are smart enough to assume that we also attacked the patrol stations. The Gray Elite will be unorganized but no less ruthless."

"And the air docks are likely shut down," Zander said. "That eliminates the sky."

"Don's," Rosaria said.

The other three looked at her.

"Who?" asked Raven.

"Don's place," Rosaria said. Something dangerously like hope brightened her face. "Ezra told me about it. It's a pub he told me to go to if I ever needed to get out of the city. He said to ask for the barkeep's special and say that Ezra sent me."

Thalame and Zander glanced at each other. Neither had heard of Don or his place, but they wouldn't question Rosaria.

"Sounds as good a plan as any," said Thalame. "Do you know the way?"

"No, but I know the address," Rosaria said. "He told me in case I ever had to escape." She rattled off the address.

"That's not far," Thalame said, glancing toward the windows. "We'd be out of the city just after dawn."

Before they set out for Don's Place, they washed the grit and grime off their faces and hands and brushed it off their clothes as best they could. Zander and Thalame found summer cloaks in a spare bedroom, and Rosaria pulled cloaks for herself and Raven from the pile of discarded clothes in her room. They returned to the tunnels, following Rosaria as she melodically recalled Ezra's instructions on how to navigate the tunnels; she had turned it into a sort of song. Rosaria did not have a singer's voice, but if her song got them out of the tunnels, Raven didn't care.

At last, they came to a dull iron ladder. It took them into an alley between two shops, both closed for the night. They had put distance between themselves and the old estates, as well as between them and the burning city center. The chaos sounded farther away, and the smoke and fire glowed in the distance. The air still smelled of smoke.

Rosaria took Raven's arm in her own, two casual girls walking to destress from the horrors of the night or to look for someone lost. They trotted out of the alley, the boys behind, into the darkened street.

They had entered a shopping district. To Raven's horror, looters and thieves were having their way along the street, smashing storefronts and grabbing whatever they could. Some seemed to only be in it for the smashing and breaking. Rosaria held on tighter to Raven's arm and led them away from the worst of the looting.

It all made Raven's stomach turn. Chaos on every side.

And she felt the fever clawing at her insides, feeding off her panic and fear.

They continued on their way, avoiding looters and the few automaton patrollers who remained beyond the city center. Gunfire peppered the air, both nearby and distantly. Had all the Wraiths made it clear?

How many people would be dead once the sun rose? How much of it would be her fault? If she had never gotten on that airship, if she had stayed in Wayward Point—if she had stayed in the treehouse—how much of this would not have happened?

A part of her didn't want to know the answer, and another part didn't care. She could hear her stepmother's voice: *What's done is done.* Raven banished all thoughts other than survival from her mind. Later, as Rosaria had said. Right now, she wanted to get out. She did not want to be anywhere near Moorin when the sun rose.

Don's Place glowed on a street corner, brassy doors facing either street, with glass globes burning inside despite the hour and chaos. Through the windows, Raven spotted maybe a dozen or so patrons sitting around the dark tables. Most were drinking, but no one looked happy. She could feel the tension in the air, the panic, the fear.

A man stood just outside the doors, hands in his jacket, cigarette between his teeth. He stared blankly down the street, but as they approached, his dulled eyes sharpened on them. Exhaustion pulled his face down, aging him ten years. He took a puff on his cigarette, making the end glow bright red-orange.

The red-orange of the emergency lights, of alert, of panic.

Rosaria's hand tightened on Raven's. *Wrong*, she seemed to say.

And within the same heartbeat, the wrongness became clear. From the alley behind Don's, a dozen Gray Elite swarmed onto the street, pistols drawn. They came from an alley across the street, and then one adjacent—blocking them in.

Rosaria sucked in a breath as the word tumbled from Raven's lips, "Cornered."

"They were waiting for us," Rosaria breathed.

The guns were cocked in disharmony.

"Halt," shouted a voice through the silence.

Raven suppressed a shudder. The Gray Elite had been waiting for them at Don's. They knew they would come here. Someone had told them, tipped them off. Her fear for Ezra's life had churned her stomach; her doubt of his loyalty burned. Either he had told them willingly, or they had forced it out of him. Neither settled well.

Thalame let out a low, quick whistle. A warning. Raven followed his line of sight, and her heart fell. Gray Elite lined the rooftops all around them, guns and crossbows aimed.

They had come prepared.

A spotlight flared to life, bathing the four of them in harsh white light. Another joined it, and another. Three spotlights marked their location, shrinking the shadows to puddles beneath their feet.

"Do not move," shouted a Gray Elite from the street. "You are under arrest by order of the Gray Elite. Do not resist, or we will open fire."

The Gray Elite on the street began to creep toward them.

"You got the cover?" Thalame asked lowly.

Zander let out a quick sigh, and in the blink of an eye, shadows rose like walls around them, the tendrils tightening together and curving over them. Bullets peppered the shadows, but none made it in. They made the softest ding against the shadows, dozens of them, like water against hot iron. Zander gritted his teeth like he felt every single one.

"Zander?" Raven asked.

"I'm fine," he spat back, his voice strained with concentration.

"Start moving," Thalame commanded. "He'll follow."

"Where?" Raven asked. "We are surrounded."

"Don's?" Rosaria asked. "We can still get away. We get in and block the tunnel after us. It will give us time."

"And if the Gray Elite get in?" Raven asked.

"We can fight better if they're coming at us one at a time," Thalame said, his voice strained. "Now move. I don't know how much longer Zander can—"

"Just go!" Zander growled.

They started to move toward Don's. The shadow globe moved with them, undulating as it rolled around them. It reminded her of a bubble moving through water. The spotlights hit the sides, dancing across the thinner shadows. Footsteps thundered on the other side. Gray Elite were coming closer.

"They're blocking us," Zander said.

"I got it," Thalame said immediately. He drew two daggers from his person and handed one to Raven and the other to Rosaria. He drew two more for himself.

The shadows widened, and then in the blink of an eye, swallowed the Gray Elite in their way. The shock of being inside the shadows gave them a disadvantage. Thalame attacked in a fluid motion; Zander's shadows smacked and distracted. Rosaria disarmed and took down a Gray Elite. It all happened so fast. One of the Gray Elite came at Raven, and as a tendril of shadow smacked his head to the side, her dagger found a place in the Gray Elite's neck.

Another came at her. Raven didn't think, didn't hesitate, only acted.

And just like that, the Gray Elite patrol was dead. Three. She had killed three Gray Elite. Their bodies lay bleeding at her feet. She grabbed the pistol from the closest, cocked it, like she had seen Zander do a hundred times with Birdie.

Shouting came from outside the shadows, commands, orders, warnings. The sound moved through the shadows like water, turning distorted and heavy.

"What now?" Raven asked, breathless. "We're just drawing attention to ourselves."

Zander winced. His shoulders flinched inward. Pain, she realized, from the rune that burned when he used his magic. As if reading her thoughts, he grunted; a part of their shadow globe dissolved, but Zander flexed another tendril in its place.

Rosaria opened her mouth, but a massive roar of an airship's engine stopped her words cold. The engine crackled and hissed. Machinery cranked and clanked, and something hit the street with a thunderous bang, shaking the stone under their feet—something large. An engine roared to life, gears smashing against one another, cogs groaning, belts whining, steam hissing—louder than she had ever heard them. It sounded as loud as an airship, only bigger and meaner and closer.

In her mind, she saw an army of automatons, red eyes glaring brighter than the city on fire.

"Sisters," Zander gasped. He reached out with his hand, and the shadows parted enough for them to see the commotion.

Raven gasped, but she wasn't the only one.

It was not an army of automatons, but just one. A massive automaton. It crouched on the ground, its arms and legs folded together. The Gray Elite transporter that had dropped it onto the street was flying into the smoky night. The automaton rumbled and clicked. Steam hissed from its shoulders and hips and back, and its limbs began to unfurl. Creaking and hissing, it rose to a height of forty feet.

Gleaming red eyes focused on the shadow orb. It started toward them. As it moved, thunderous and heavy gears crashed together, clicking and clanking in a dangerous, mechanical harmony. It had feet the size of small houses, and each footstep cracked the pavement. The brass and copper and steel plates left few vulnerable spots, and the steam from its shoulders shot twenty feet into the air.

Zander tightened his shadows. He and Thalame readied themselves, daggers in each hand. Sweat ran down Zander's temple, and exhaustion muddied his stare.

"Zander," Raven started. "You can't fight that thing. Look at it! It's a death sentence."

He grimaced at her. He knew. He would still fight.

Panic, hot and slippery, worked its way into every limb, every thought. She shook her head. Her grip on Thalame's dagger shook. Her aim with the pistol wavered.

They should escape, give themselves up, anything other than fight that monster. But if they gave themselves up, they would surely face execution. All of them, magicians. If the Gray Elite didn't shoot them on sight first.

No, their odds were not good.

Surrounded on every side. Guns aimed at them. A colossus coming for them.

Raven pulled back a sob. She didn't want to die, especially not like this, cornered and exposed and vulnerable and helpless.

Are you helpless?

The voice spoke as clear as it ever had. She glanced to see if anyone else had heard it—no one had. The voice felt as close as if the speaker stood beside her and yet closer still and yet from nowhere.

The thunderous automaton came closer. It raised its balled fists. Zander spat a curse and tightened his shadows. A whirl sounded—something struck the top of the shadow orb. Zander screamed, the shadows flashed, and then the entire orb shattered like glass. Zander collapsed onto his hands and knees, panting.

And they were fully exposed, but the bullets did not fly.

The Gray Elite watched from the sidewalks and rooftops—watching the colossus.

The colossus straightened. On the bottom of its closed first was a glowing rune. As it retracted, the glow faded.

"That's a disrupting rune," Thalame spat. He crouched beside Zander and set a hand on his shoulder. "You all right, mate?"

Zander spat a curse and wobbled to his feet. He pulled two daggers from his waist, and he and Thalame jumped into the fight.

At first, the size of the colossus worked against it. The boys dashed between its legs, around its ankles, looking for a way up to the neck—the most obvious place for a weakness, like in most automatons. Every time they found a foothold, the colossus would shake its leg or swat them off, or one of the Gray Elite would shoot at them.

The colossus was too fast for them, the metal too slick, too thick to pierce. With every passing heartbeat, Raven felt something tug at her stomach, not panic, not fear, but a knowing. A nudge.

You are not helpless.

Zander had made it to the colossus's waist, his dagger between his teeth, when the top half swiveled. Zander lost his grip and started to fall; the colossus swatted at him, but rather than hit him with the flat palm of its hand, as the hand moved, the fingers extended. From the index finger of the colossus, a sword slid out.

Raven screamed the same moment that Zander's painful cry pierced the air—the sword had gone through his upper arm. The colossus thrust toward the ground, pinning Zander to the pavement. A beat passed, then the colossus yanked the sword free.

Zander's blood, fresh and bright and red, splattered the ground at Raven's feet.

See what it did? It shouldn't exist. Erase it.

Zander whimpered, and the sound shattered something in Raven's chest. She ran to him, regardless of the Gray Elite, of the colossus, regardless of his blood spilling out too fast. She collapsed beside him, his name on her lips. His arm had been cut through, nearly severed. The bones were crushed, splintered, the muscles torn, and everything else in the way had been obliterated. Pain paled his face to a deathly white.

All else went quiet. The wet thwack of his body hitting the ground sounded again and again in her mind.

Zander. His trembling body at her knees. His limp arm and paling hand. His blood, soaking into the knees of her dress and hem of her cloak.

All she knew was Zander and the automaton monster that had hurt him, that would hurt them all.

You're not helpless.

The fever, the panic, the fear—it became white hot fury. She felt it in her hands, in her blood, in her body—the magic that had boiled the water in the factory, that had melted the lock, that had turned a man to ash.

Do it.

She knew what to do.

She stood.

The colossus loomed over her, bloodied sword still protruding from his finger. Despite Thalame's efforts, he hadn't done any damage. He stood on the other side, shaking his head at her. He said something, but she didn't hear him.

The automaton lifted its sword to finish the job.

"No," Raven said to the colossus. She stepped over Zander, stood in front of him, his blood wet and warm on her clothes.

The colossus's red eyes refocused on her, nearly blinding her, but she didn't need to see.

"Raven," Zander hissed, her name a gasp on his pain-laced breath.

The colossus retracted the sword and started to reach for her with both of its hands. To capture, not to kill.

It never touched her.

The colossus's red eyes flickered. Its gears jerked. Its engine sputtered. It straightened, its movements slowed, jerky. An alarm rang from within its metal body, the high-pitched warning bells muffled by the steel plating.

Raven did not let her focus fade. She had more, and she would give more.

A Gray Elite officer shouted commands, and as his words met the air, blue-white flame erupted around the colossus, bright as daylight, blinding the officers, stunning the civilians who had gathered at the commotion. Screams echoed, panicked and fearful and trembling.

They should be afraid.

Raven felt the flames consume the colossus, melting the metal gears and cogs and belts and screws and plates, turning them to liquid, to gas, to nothing at all. The water in the machine's innards boiled and burst and evaporated; the gears malfunctioned and sputtered against each other; the brass and bronze and steel armor bled into the others.

She felt it consume everything, burning it out of existence.

Raven released her hold over what remained of the automaton. The fever—the magic, her magic—returned to her without fuss, sated with the burning. As it returned to her, she stumbled backward; a wave of dizziness and nausea hit her hard, and she collapsed to her knees. She tried hard not to empty her stomach.

Where the colossus had stood, a pile of molten white-hot goo remained. The pavement it touched hissed and steamed.

She had done it.

She had tried to turn it to ash, not goo, but she supposed she would accept that. Maybe metal didn't become ash.

Pride filled her, not entirely her own, but the magic's too.

She heaved a breath, unaware of having held it. With it, the heat of the colossus flooded her lungs.

"Raven?" came Rosaria's uncertain voice.

The street came back into focus. People in their robes and housecoats gawked and stared and pointed from alleys and side streets. The bewildered Gray Elite looked too, wide-eyed, open-mouthed, and unsure. It didn't last long. The Gray Elite quickly recovered from the shock and reorganized themselves. Those on the street began to close ranks around her.

She could... No, her magic dwindled with the use. She couldn't do anything. Even if she could, she couldn't burn these people. They were people, not machines.

Her stomach upheaved, and she bent over on her hands and knees. The pavement beneath her palms was hot, but the heat didn't hurt her. Her stomach turned over. She squeezed her eyes shut.

Feet on the pavement. Scrambling. Gray Elite shouting orders.

The world shifted under her hands, and she felt the cold, clamminess of unconsciousness slithering across her skin and through her mind.

The Gray Elite would certainly kill them now.

The worst of the feeling subsided. The pavement blurred between her fingers. Gray Elite boots came into her view, dirty with dust and debris. A strong stench of smoke wafted with the soldiers.

She took a breath, unready to meet whatever fate the Gray Elite had for her.

A second pair of boots appeared. Orders were spat, but as the words met the air, a roar sounded in the sky. An engine—and then dozens of them—roared above them. The two officers stumbled backward, eyes on the sky.

Raven managed to look up, craning her neck and stretching her dizziness to do so. Airships raced through the smoky sky and toward the city, faster than any other airship she had seen. The buzzing of the engine chittered like bugs, like wasps.

The airship flew closer. Rockets screamed through the air with a piercing howl, spitting sparks from the ends. The rockets exploded over the crowd with an otherworldly bang, spitting too-bright colors in every direction in a dazzling display of light. A few pistols shot, but the sound of the rockets' swallowed the sound of the bullets.

Hands grabbed Raven's shoulders and hoisted her to her feet. The world wobbled. She didn't have the energy to resist.

"Let's go," came Rosaria's strong voice. The voice of a queen giving an order.

Raven fell against the princess, and Rosaria lifted Raven's arm over her shoulder. Raven blinked at the scene as it unfolded; Thalame lifted Zander's limp body from the street, pulling his good arm over his shoulders. Zander's limp arm hung awkwardly as his side, dripping blood. Ladders dangled from above, and Rosaria pulled Raven onto the closest one.

"Hold on," Rosaria breathed in Raven's ear.

She folded her arms around the wooden rung. Rosaria did too, keeping Raven between her arms, securing her body with her own. Thalame did the same to Zander, only he strung a belt between Zander and the ladder.

"*Go!*" Rosaria screamed.

An airship whirled, the high-pitched screech deafening, and then a second airship joined it. The ladders lifted them away from the ground, flying higher and higher. Raven glanced up—the ladders were attached to smaller airships. Two ships carried the four of them away while a small army of them blasted the air with light and sound—a distraction. The airships moved in a chaotic pattern, organized but frenzied.

Raven rested her head against the rung of the ladder. She didn't have the mind to question this rescue. The vibrations of the airship carried through her hands and into her head. It took all of her failing concentration to hold on.

The airship carried them away from Moorin, away from the automaton and the Gray Elite, away from the smoking patrol stations and collapsing factory. They flew higher and higher, through the clouds, through the smoke, and to a massive airship waiting on the other side.

What little breath Raven had vanished at the sight.

The engines purred like thunder. The balloons were painted gold and white, flecked with stars of blue and silver. A promenade deck shone like crimson. On this side of the clouds, the first rays of dawn highlighted the edges of the airship with liquid gold. The hull was shaped like a boat, the bow pointed, the stern curved, and masts held up rigging between the balloons and steam vents.

Raven tried to count the decks, but they moved too fast and her mind moved too slow. But she didn't need an exact number to know they approached not just an airship, but a sky city.

The smaller airships flew underneath the sky city, to air docks tucked safety underneath. Her attention wobbled and darkened as their airship did not fly underneath but hovered over an extended platform. Rosaria and a stranger helped Raven down from the ladder.

Between her unsteady feet, through the iron lattice floor, she could see the clouds below them. The clouds swirled where the airships had punched through. The dawn glowed against the clouds in shades of lavender.

Several strangers helped Thalame with Zander. They lifted his unconscious body between them. Blood dripped from his arm.

All the commotion formed a buzzing in her head. Too much.

"Hey there, little bird," came a familiar voice. Conrad appeared beside her. The pale morning light caught the gold beads in his hair. He tilted his head at her. "Welcome to the *Orion*. Looks like someone else needs a medic."

Rosaria said something, but Raven didn't hear her. The world closed in, darkening the corners of her vision, tunneling. She put her head into her hands.

The *Orion*—a sky city.

With that thought, with the gold and white sails unfurling with snaps and whips, with the sunlight waxing into daylight, Raven's world faded to black.

Raven came to in a room of plain oak walls. A brass lantern hung from the ceiling, gently swaying. Dividers of white linen and oak blocked two sides of her view. It smelled clean, coldly so. Every heartbeat, every blink, brought her closer to reality.

A hospital or a clinic. She sat up, despite her achy body. She was in a narrow corridor lined on both sides with cots, each divided by folding screens of stark white linen. A figure lay sleeping in the cot across from her, an arm thrown over his face.

It took a long moment to adjust; exhaustion tugged on her shoulder blades, urging her to return to the cot, to the warm blankets, to the pillow.

She rubbed her face. What had happened?

And then she remembered.

Moorin. The patrol stations, the Wraiths, the factory, and the colossus automaton she had reduced to glowing goo. She drew up her legs and rested her head on her knees. She had been exhausted after turning that pirate to ash too.

Magic. She hadn't believed it at first, but now she did. She had magic, like it or not.

The hospital ward sounded with the moans of several patients and snores of others still. After a long moment of gathering herself, she pushed her feet toward the floor. Someone had taken the time to remove her filthy dress. She wore instead a simple gown of off-white that ended above her knees. Her boots sat on the floor beside the bed, and a cloak had been thrown over the foot of the bed.

At the commotion of her movement, a man appeared around the partition. He wore a short-sleeve off-white shirt and brown trousers. His small satchel held clean bandages, pills, and bottles. A tattoo of a cat stretched up his right arm.

"There you are," he said kindly in a Tinatunian accent. His golden brown face stretched into a welcoming, friendly smile. "How are you feeling?"

She groaned. Like she had been dropped from the airship and picked back up.

"That's expected," he said. "I'm Corin. I run the hospital ward, particularly the magicians. I hear you had quite the expenditure on the ground. Melted a whole building of an automaton." He pulled a green bottle out of his satchel. "Drink this. You'll feel much better."

She took the bottle and held it against her lips. It tasted cool and refreshing. Only after it ran down her throat did she think that it might have been wise to ask before drinking. She drank all of it, the few gulps the bottle held.

"What was that?" she asked, handing him back the bottle.

"Rejuvenation Potion," he said. "It's a blessing for magicians. Takes away that bite of running on empty."

Raven nodded. She didn't feel like asking questions or listening to an explanation of how it worked. She could feel the potion working, warming through her bones, waking her up, bringing a small amount of energy back to her body. She moved her arms and legs about. While the potion did not erase her sluggishness, she no longer felt as though she might collapse.

Corin watched her with a knowing smile. "Better?" he asked.

"Better," she said. Then, her heart squeezed. "What about the others? My friends. Zander, what about Zander? His arm—"

"Slow down," he said, holding a long-fingered hand in front of him. "They are all fine. Well, they're all alive."

She choked on that word.

His smile flickered into a frown of sympathy. "Can you stand? I'll take you to see them. They've been asking about you every hour."

"Zander—"

"We will see him first," he said, his words calming and soothing. "But let's make sure you're capable before we head out anywhere."

Corin moved to the bedside, arms waiting to catch her in case she fell. Raven worked her way to the edge of the bed, set her bare feet on the floor, and stood. The world wobbled once, then righted itself. She quickly slipped on her boots and the cloak. Corin led her down the corridor.

She could feel the gentle movement of the sky city, the vibration through the shined metal floor and the rosewood walls, humming and buzzing. The engines rumbled, a distant but constant roar. It thrilled her to be in a sky city, enough that a part of her hadn't yet accepted its reality. She wanted nothing more in that moment than to see Zander and make sure he had made it.

They came to the end of the corridor. Double doors led to the hall outside, to the rest of the airship, and four single doors led into the intensive care rooms. Two were occupied. Through the clouded glass, the first patient was a stranger, but the second—Raven caught her breath in her throat. She knew the dark hair, the bronze skin.

Corin let her into the room.

Zander's chest steadily rose and fell. He lived. A tube and a mask pumped air into and out of his lungs. They had removed his bloodied clothes; a linen blanket covered him from his ankles to his navel. Bandages lined his chest, thickest around his left shoulder. His left arm was gone. Nothing but a stump remained.

Raven stood at the bedside. His right arm lay exposed, unmoving. She gripped the bedsheet hard enough to turn her knuckles white. His arm—he had lost his arm. Tears gathered in her eyes. It felt like her fault. She should've been the one lying there, missing a piece, not him. She had been the stupid girl alone in the woods that day.

She hung her head. She didn't want Corin to see her shame and guilt.

Standing there, she heard the faint rumble of engines, the creak and groan of metal and leather and wood, the hissing of steam. An airship. A sky city. A dream realized. She would give it all up to make Zander whole again.

"The blade went completely through," said Corin. "Amputation was our only choice. It severed the nerves."

Raven bit her lip as the first tear slipped out of her eye. It drew a wet line down her face.

"But," said Corin, stepping into her view. He stood on Zander's left side. "We have other options now that the arm is gone. Mechanics. An automaton replacement."

She blinked at him. "A mechanical arm?"

He nodded. "It's not a new idea. But, this is something we will talk to him about when he wakes up."

When, not *if*.

Raven swallowed what tears she hadn't yet cried and braced herself. Zander would wake up; the medic said so. She looked down at Zander's still face. Her life had been a constant of ups and downs and unknowns since she had left that day with Zander on what she had thought would be her only adventure—that felt like a lifetime ago.

"There's a room set up for you," said Corin. "When you're ready, I can call someone to take you there."

Raven took a long look at Zander. Would he blame her for his missing arm? Would he agree to a mechanical replacement? She would have to wait for him to wake up. She took a deep breath, gave Zander's warm hand a squeeze, and let go.

A young boy led Raven out of the hospital and through a maze of hallways and staircases; she tried to keep her bearings, but within a few turns, she felt lost. The hospital was in the lower deck, said the boy. The lower deck looked like it had been cobbled together from a dozen other ships: some metal, some wood, some with curved doors, some with rectangular doors. Finally, he led her up a spiral staircase of iron lattice and into a corridor of rosewood paneling, shined brass grating, and polished steel—the upper deck.

The upper deck looked as romantic and beautiful as Raven had imagined airships being, only with a bit of pirate flare that she found quite endearing. He led her up a wide staircase and into an identical corridor to the one below. Rosewood doors lined the corridor, equally spaced. Each had a creature emblazoned on the wood in gold. He led her to the lion's door.

He knocked.

"Enter," came Rosaria's voice, and Raven's heart jumped into her throat as the boy opened the door. Raven stepped over the threshold, and her eyes at once fell on the princess. A relieved smile stretched over Rosaria's lips as she pulled Raven into an embrace. "Thank the Sisters."

Beyond Rosaria, the little room held the necessities. Not unlike an inn, only much nicer. Two beds were stacked on one side, fastened to the wall to keep them from toppling. One corner held a wash basin; the other held a small wardrobe and bookshelf.

"I can handle her from here," Rosaria told the boy, and he bowed and left without another word. Rosaria closed the door and let out a sigh of contentment. "I rather like the crew here. I feared at first they would be pirates and no good, but they have been beyond accommodating and pleasant."

Raven washed up and changed into clean, simple clothes—trousers, blouse, and plain corset with minimal boning. Though she could nap, she wanted to see the others first. Rosaria didn't object. She hooked her arm with Raven's and led the way to a lounge a floor above with a gorgeous view of the blue afternoon sky. Clouds floated in the distance, fluffy and unmoving as mountains, while wispy clouds raced by.

Thalame, Conrad, and a few others she didn't know sat around an oval rosewood table. Leather-padded chairs circled it. Three teapots had been scattered along it, none matching, set into a swiveling stand that moved with the ship so that the teapot remained steady. Cups hung off the stands, each a different pattern and color.

She met Thalame's eyes; he looked utterly exhausted, but he tipped his head to her in silent greeting.

Captain Luckett sat at the head of the table, looking like a pirate queen in her ornate chair. She slung one leg over the arm of her chair and sat with her arm draped over the other. Her brown hair had been washed, untangled, and braided back. Her drab prison clothes had been replaced with dark trousers, black leather boots, a beige blouse and dark blue corset, and a red coat with gleaming brass buttons and black trim—every bit a captain.

"There she is," said Luckett, motioning to Raven. In the light, her eyes appeared light brown but no less clever. "I hoped I would get the chance to thank you for getting me out of the Tombs and for giving me the chance to show off my new fleet to the Gray Elite. Those bastards won't be forgetting that defeat anytime soon." She laughed, and the hearty sound filled the room. She motioned to the empty chair to her left. "Sit."

Rosaria slipped her arm from Raven's and sat beside Conrad, who watched the exchange with curious eyes. Raven made her way to the captain's side, every pair of eyes in the room on her. She sat, and her gaze fell on the young man sitting across from her, on the captain's right. It took a moment to place his brown eyes and skin and assortment of rings.

Malik.

"Glad to see you're alive," said Malik, leaning in his chair like he had somewhere else he would rather be.

Raven made herself a cup of tea while the conversations along the table resumed. Luckett and Malik returned to a conversation of what in the ship had been repaired while she had been away, how many of the crew had died or left, anyone new who had joined, engine room gossip, and what news of the empire since they had made their dramatic escape.

She gathered that their majority of losses had been on the Gracitan side of the fight, while the rebels—as Malik called them—got away relatively unscathed.

According to Malik's gossip, more than just Wraiths had taken the opportunity to rebel against the Gray Elite.

Raven listened halfheartedly. Something about Luckett bugged her. She had dark brown hair and light brown eyes with streaks of gold like lightning. She and Malik shared several facial features—the straight nose, the shape of the lips, their ears—too many similarities for coincidence. They had to be related. Mother and son, if Raven had to guess. By Malik's beige-brown skin, his father had been Tinatunian.

"I hear my medics think your friend might be a good fit for one of their mechanical limbs," Luckett said to Raven.

One of—so there were others? Raven swallowed a large gulp of tea. "I suppose so."

"It's not as scary as it sounds," Malik explained. "Corin has a mechanical leg."

Raven blinked. "I hadn't noticed."

Malik nodded, confirming his point. "It's hard to notice when you're not looking."

Tea time passed casually, and as the others trickled out, Luckett invited Raven to come with her—by her tone, it was not a suggestion. Luckett sauntered beside Raven at a leisurely pace; Malik walked a step behind. Luckett led Raven through a verbal tour of the *Orion*: the engines, tanks, uppers and lowers, the barracks, the village, the cargo hold, the bridge. Raven hadn't the mind to keep track of all the jargon. It sounded familiar from her books, but she didn't want to admit that to Luckett.

Luckett led Raven into a room with cushy chairs and a beautiful rosewood desk and matching high-backed chair—the captain's office. One wall was entirely glass and held a fantastic view of the bridge. Raven approached the window. Down on the bridge, the pilot stood at the helm. To the right of the pilot, the navigation stations boasted more maps than Raven had ever seen, charts and more compasses than she thought necessary, even for a large ship. To the left of the pilot was a station packed with speaking tubes, dials, and gauges. It looked like the bridge from the *Marianne*, only larger and more complex.

At the bow, a glass front showed a marvelous view of the sky as the *Orion* parted the clouds around it.

"She's a beauty," said Luckett with a sigh. She sauntered to a mass of speaking tubes behind her desk. She flipped one open and said into it, "How are we doing, Bear?"

"Steady on course, Captain," said a hoarse female voice.

"That's what I like to hear," said Luckett, and she closed the speaking tube.

Down on the bridge, Raven spotted the woman called Bear—she manned the station of speaking tubes and gauges. She did not look like a bear, nor did her hoarse voice suit her small frame and tidy bun of dark hair.

The wall behind Luckett's desk held the largest map Raven had ever seen. It showed Gracita, Rhynwier, and Tinatun, but also the expanse of ocean on either side, and a large landmass on the far western side, an ocean away. Raven gravitated toward it without realizing it.

"Where is this?" Raven asked.

"That is known as the Untamed Lands," Luckett said. "It's a wild kingdom with nature as its ruler. Some say that dragons lurk in the dense jungles and wide desserts and that ghosts haunt the ruins of the people who came long before us."

"Have you been there?"

"Only once." Luckett came to stand beside Raven. She put her finger on the eastern side of the Untamed Lands, on a gulf surrounded by jungle. "Spent a week trying to navigate the coast, but it's like the land itself doesn't want you there. We would make maps, and then the land would change on us, and our maps were useless."

Raven's stomach turned over, but not in fear. It sounded like an adventure from a book.

"But I asked you here to speak about something different than the Untamed Land's impossibilities." Luckett sat in her captain's chair.

Raven walked back around the desk, only then realizing how she might have been disrespectful by going to the map. Luckett's map. One thing she knew for certain—do not disrespect the captain. She laced her hands together. Luckett and Malik both eyed her as though they had never met her before.

"Is there something in particular you require of me?" Raven asked, her voice reflecting her unease.

Luckett continued to study her.

Raven added, "I thank you for your timely rescue. We would have been dead if not for you and your crew."

"Do you still have the locket?" Malik asked.

Raven blinked at him but nodded. She put a hand to the chain around her neck and pulled it out of her blouse. Did Malik know about the centrum too? Thalame and the rest of the Dwellers did, and Conrad had figured it out on his own. She didn't think it extreme for Malik to have discovered it.

It didn't matter; she wouldn't let them have it either. She wouldn't let anyone use the centrum like she had done. She would keep it safe.

Luckett's eyes fell on the locket, and her gaze shifted into something between disbelief and remorse. She blinked, and dampness smothered her lashes. She brought a hand to her mouth, but it didn't hide her discomfort.

"Is something wrong?" Raven asked.

"You got that from your mother," Luckett said. Not a question.

"I did. It's all I have of her. She died when I was little."

"She died?" Luckett asked, eyebrows raised. The mistiness of her eyes cleared, and she fixed her piercing gaze on Raven. "*That's* what your father told you?" She scoffed.

Raven started at Luckett's insensitivity, but then her words clicked. "How did you know my father told me?"

Luckett sauntered around the desk and stopped in front of Raven. She took the locket in one hand and ran her thumb over the engraved gold. "I won this locket in a game of dice when I was twelve years old," Luckett said. "I cheated, but that's not the point. I carried it with me always until I met Samuel."

The implication smacked the breath from Raven's throat. Her words came out weak, "You gave it to him?"

"Not to him," Luckett said. "But to our daughter."

Raven took a closer look at Luckett, her light brown eyes, her peachy skin, her heart-shaped face. All thoughts ceased. Luckett cupped Raven's cheek and tilted her face up. Raven's heart trembled over and over—her *mother*.

"You look like me at your age," Luckett said. The mistiness returned to her eyes. "My mother's name was Raven. When I had to name a baby girl, that's the first name I thought of."

Raven couldn't speak, couldn't breathe. She had imagined her mother a hundred different ways, but never had she been a pirate captain of a sky city. Reality had always come at the end of any daydreams involving her mother, reminding her that her mother was dead.

But she wasn't.

As it sank in, Raven found her voice. She murmured, "What happened?"

"Samuel was a mechanic; I was a navigator. One thing led to another, and then I was pregnant. The war was raging, and the world was in a state of change and uncertainty. He insisted we go back to that little town of his to get away from the world for a while," Luckett said, her touch ginger on Raven's chin. "I agreed because few captains want a pregnant girl working. You were born, and I couldn't sit still. Samuel settled well, but I hated it. I couldn't live underground. The walls felt like they were pushing in on me. I wasn't old yet, and I couldn't stand the slow life of retirement, not when I had so many years of my life yet." Luckett blinked, and the moisture along her eyelashes thickened. "When my baby girl was old enough to drink cow's milk, I left. Samuel refused to let me take my girl with me. He stayed on the ground; I returned to the sky."

"You left me," Raven managed to say. The weight of those words hit Luckett as hard as the realization hit Raven. She flinched as though struck.

"I wanted to take you with me," said Luckett, her voice thinning. "But your father refused me. He knew I lived dangerously, and he said I wouldn't be able to take care of a baby like he would, and I wouldn't find a nursemaid who would love her like he would. He seemed to think I'd let her wander right off the edge of the ship." She tried to laugh, but it faded. "He...made a good argument, and I...I left you with him."

Malik shifted. Raven glanced at him; he looked guilty.

"You knew about this?" Raven asked him.

Malik averted his gaze and nodded. "Your locket gave it away," he said quietly. "I remember playing with it when I was little. I knew where it had gone. When I saw it with you, and you said your mother gave it to you, I knew who you were."

"Malik is your brother," Luckett said. "Half-brother, but a brother still."

"Did you leave his father too?" Raven asked. The words left her mouth with a bitterness.

Luckett sighed through her nose. "Yes, but it's a different story. Malik's father was a nice man for a while, but underneath his handsome face was a violent drunk. He hit me once, and I didn't give him another chance. I took Malik with me because I knew I could raise him better."

Raven wiggled her locket out of Luckett's grasp and fell into one of the cushy chairs. She leaned forward, elbows on her knees. Her mother, alive and well, a captain of an airship. If she had known, she might have left Silver Glen sooner. Her father had known, and he had withheld the information from her all these years.

So much information, so many thoughts, rattling without course.

"And it seems you've inherited my sense of adventure," Luckett said with a sigh. She leaned against her rosewood desk. "I'm not sure if it's a blessing or a curse. Could be either. Runs in the family, I'm told. I had an uncle who sailed to the Untamed Lands and never returned. Who knows; he might be living in the wild out there."

Raven inhaled, held it, and slowly released it. So many secrets. So much, so fast. She met Luckett's gaze; it had softened.

"I guess I can't be that mad at you," Raven said to her mother. "You did rescue us, after all."

"You broke me out of prison," Luckett added. She tipped her head toward Raven. "Conrad's been telling me all about you. Really riled up the Gray Elite in Lenhala, and now we've nearly burned Moorin to the ground. The Gray Elite will be after blood this time—yours, to be specific—especially after that automaton meltdown." She let out a low whistle. "Magic also runs in the family." She motioned between her and Malik. "Likely another thing you picked up from me."

"You were a Wraith," Raven breathed as she remembered.

Luckett nodded. She closed her fist tight and then unfurled her fingers like a flower blooming. Something dark as midnight hovered in the air above her palm. It wiggled like water but thicker.

"What is that?" Raven said, pushing herself into the chair.

"Ink," Luckett said. "Stains like a bitch, though it helped me be one hell of a mapmaker."

"It's the same ink that we use to tattoo the runes," Malik added.

Luckett turned her hand over. The ink spilled out her hand and onto a piece of parchment. Rather than go everywhere like regular ink would have, it listened to Luckett's silent command and painted a rune onto the paper, perfect lines and curves, the rune the Wraiths tattooed on themselves, the rune Conrad had painted on her.

Raven glanced at the map behind the desk. It had been drawn with ink, the lines too perfect to have been brushed or stenciled, Luckett's map.

Luckett awaited Raven's response, but she didn't give her one. Raven didn't feel like explaining the mess of her magic to Luckett or Malik. She flattened her hands against her trousers, letting the heat from her palms soak into her thighs.

"Another time," Luckett said, her voice soft. She stood and sauntered to the map behind her desk, hands folded behind her back. When she spoke, she spoke with the strength of a captain. "We head north for now, away from Moorin. The news will spread, and the Gray Elite will be furious and hungry for revenge. They will be on the hunt. They might even see this as a declaration of war. It's hard to tell from this distance. We'll have to wait and see what happens. I've got ears on the ground in Moorin and Lenhala. Either way, we are getting out of the line of fire."

Raven nodded. War. At least Altair's Augur couldn't be activated, not without the centrum.

Luckett promised a hearty dinner, and Malik offered to walk Raven back to her cabin.

"Would you like a proper tour of the ship?" Malik asked.

"Not right now," Raven said. She didn't feel like walking. She wanted to lie down for a while and rest. Until dinner, or maybe until dinner the following day. She didn't know.

They paused outside her door. No one else stood in the corridor.

"It's okay," Malik said softly. He laced his graceful fingers together in front of him. "Do you want something to drink to take the edge off?"

She considered it but shook her head. She met his eyes. "I've never had a brother before."

"I've never had a sister." He gave her a sympathetic smile. "We will both be learning something new."

He hesitated, then drew Raven into an awkward hug, a man not used to hugging anyone. With an equally awkward parting, he left and she let herself into the room. Rosaria hadn't returned, leaving the room empty. Raven took a steadying breath—she'd had so few moments alone to think. She took off her boots and corset and meandered to the bunk beds. A few dark hairs clung to the bottom bunk's pillow, so Raven climbed to the top. A cloth panel hung along the side of the bed to prevent her from rolling out or being thrown should the ship tilt. The cloth was faded blue and stitched with clouds and stars.

Raven flopped onto her back and released an exhausted breath.

Before she slept, she had to see for herself—she pulled her locket from under her shirt and then unhooked it. She lifted it off her skin and held it up. She pressed her nails into the seam, and the mechanism gave—her heart stopped and tumbled into the back of her ribcage.

The glowing red centrum was gone. In its place was a clear crystal. Raven dumped the crystal into her palm. Cool to the touch.

Empty.

Then she knew without a doubt that her suspicions had been right. The iron box had kept the centrum contained and safe. Her locket had not. The centrum had slowly seeped through the metal and into her, infecting her with the fever. She had survived the fever, she had conquered it, and she had won the centrum's magic.

She returned the empty crystal to her locket and snapped it shut. She would explain herself to Zander and Thalame and the others. Later.

A strange calm came over her, one she hadn't felt in months. Without the centrum to keep safe, to hide and guard, she didn't have anything to lose in telling them about it. With the centrum gone, Altair's Augur could never be used. She had inadvertently prevented it.

She had stopped the worst from happening.

She tucked the locket under her pillow and reclined. The bed was soft, the blanket was warm, and she fell into a dreamless, peaceful sleep, unlike she'd had in months.

Raven woke to Rosaria's head peeking over the side of the bunk. Raven blinked rapidly to clear the intoxicating drowsiness from her eyes.

"Zander's awake," Rosaria said. "He's asking for you."

Raven bolted up and fumbled down the ladder. She quickly laced up her corset and pulled on her boots and ran into the corridor. Rosaria ran with her to the hospital and into the intensive care room. Zander was sitting up in bed, reclining on a mound of pillows, his sapphire eyes glassy but open. They fell at once onto Raven, and a sleepy smile stretched over his face. Fresh bandages wrapped his shoulder and his left arm's stump.

He lifted his right hand for her, and she grabbed it with both of hers. He tugged without force, trying to pull her closer. He hadn't the strength.

"I'm sorry," she said, collapsing into the chair beside the bed. She clutched his hand tighter. She pressed the back of his hand against her forehead. "I'm sorry."

"For what?" he asked. He spoke slow and sleepy.

"For everything," she said, her voice a plea. She met his eyes, her own wet with tears. "For running away, for getting caught, for messing up your plans over and over. I thought...I thought you didn't want me there. And now I..." She glanced at the stump of his arm. "I'm sorry for what happened to you."

"It's not your fault, Rae." Her nickname on his lips sent a wild surge down her spine. She wanted to curl up beside him on the hospital bed. "You didn't stab me. If not for you, that thing would have finished me off."

"If not for me, that thing wouldn't have hurt you in the first place," she said lowly, a mirror of what he had said to her not that long ago.

Zander frowned. "No. I shouldn't have tried to keep you safe like that. I was doing the opposite of what I wanted. I thought...I thought you'd be safer if you stayed, so I could focus on the mission instead of worrying about you. I didn't want anything to happen to you. I should have just told you. I thought I'd get another chance when it was all over. And then you were gone...just gone." His sapphire eyes searched hers. "I looked for you. I didn't know what to do. I looked and looked, but you were gone."

She blinked. Warm tears smothered her eyelashes, and one traitorous tear trailed down her cheek.

"I should never have let you out of my sight," he whispered. "Not even for a second. No matter what."

"Zander," she started, but didn't know how to say what she wanted to say.

"I love you," he said. The words came out shaky, but they struck through her. She gaped at him, sure she misheard.

"I love you," he said again, softer.

Raven gripped his hand tighter; her own shook. Everything inside of her seemed to have stopped at his words. She tried to form her own, but her throat refused to cooperate.

"I have for a while," he whispered. "I didn't know how to tell you. I thought..." He sighed, and a sad smile came over his face. "I asked your father for your hand, you know."

"You did *what*?" Raven's brows shot up, and her voice croaked.

"He said no," Zander said, smile widening. "He said he didn't trust me enough, and if I wanted his daughter, I had best prove myself. He said to ask again in a year. I'm sure this will count against me."

Raven laughed, and it unclogged whatever had closed her throat. She couldn't imagine Zander asking that of her father, but she could imagine her father resisting the urge to punch Zander. And her father's behavior in regards to Zander, the glances in her direction, looks exchanged with her stepmother, the odd look when Raven mentioned him—it made more sense.

"That's why I wanted you to come with me," he said. "I thought I would find the time to tell you."

She returned his sleepy smile. "If you had said those words to me at any other point than right now, I might have hit you."

"Ah," he said. "The invalid thing works for you, huh?"

She blushed but laughed. She leaned toward him and kissed him. Her lips met the soft wax of balm. She lingered a breath above his lips.

"Again," he whispered.

She leaned away. He pouted.

"You will get another one when you're better," she promised.

"I will hold you to that."

"You better."

He grinned, and that old arrogant mischief shone in his eyes. She brushed his dark hair out of his face. He would need a haircut too. The bottom half of his hair had grown out and gave him a shaggy look that she didn't like.

"What do you think about an automaton arm?" she said.

Zander's smile widened. "I told them I'd do it."

Her eyes widened.

"I can already picture it." He looked to where his left arm should have been. "Brass and steel, strong enough to shatter bones and deflect bullets and blades."

Raven smiled. Zander would get better. He would get a mechanical replacement for the arm that he had lost. The panic in the city would die down. She would explain her story to the others. They no longer needed to keep the centrum safe, and maybe she and Zander could join her mother in the skies, away from the Gray Elite, the automatons, the Hawks, the Wraiths, and everything else. They could find their own adventure in another part of the world, maybe Tinatun or the Untamed Lands or find somewhere entirely new.

She had no plan, and the world felt wide open for the first time in a long while.

General Oliver Deacon hated flying. He liked the convenience of flying, but he preferred his boots on solid ground.

His private airship had landed in Lenhala in the middle of the afternoon, and among the dozens of other airships coming and going from the docks, no one paid him any mind. He kept his face calm on the way to the house, but once past the servants and staff and safely in his study, he let his fury show.

Bested again by wicked magicians.

Wicked as sin, the lot of them. Mistakes of nature. They thought themselves gods among men, but he would prove no such thing existed.

But how was he supposed to know the Wraiths were planning an assault on the Gray Elite the same night he had planned to slip into the city unnoticed? His spies had seen the girl at his house—his own damn house—but by the time he had arrived, the city had been burning, sirens had been wailing, and the streets had been clogged with panicked masses and looters. The air docks had been shut down, and he'd had no choice but to return to Lenhala.

Someone among the workers at his estate had hidden the girl and her friend there, in a wing rarely used, right under his son's nose. He'd already reprimanded the boy for being narrow-sighted. It didn't matter; he would discover the traitor, even if he had to torture his entire staff to death. No one played him for a fool and lived. He knew from experience that someone would crack. He just had to keep pressing.

But it would have to wait.

Deacon sighed through his nose. No sense in worrying about it now. The girl had fled—on an airship, no less. Tracking her down again wouldn't be easy, but it could wait until she showed her face again. He had more important things to worry about.

Like a meeting he didn't want to be late for.

Deacon walked to the far side of his study, one shadowed by monstrous bookshelves. He pulled a heavy tome, pulling the lever hidden inside, and the far bookshelf swung open. A lantern waited just inside the passage. The small flame within the dusty globe flickered brighter and brighter as he made his way down the winding iron staircase. The door shut automatically after a few moments, though he paused to make sure it closed completely. He didn't want any snooping servants to find it again.

The stairs led deep into the hillside. It had originally been a bunker, an ancient meeting room used by the dead king and his generals before the Gray Elite had taken it over. Deacon had made a few minor adjustments, but overall, he had found the secret bunker a marvel for discreet meetings and uninterrupted naps. He paused at the large oak table in the center of the room to make sure nothing had been moved since he had last been inside. Seeing that nothing had, he started toward an iron door on the far side—one of his minor adjustments.

The door led down a stone hall with no lighting other than the lantern he held. The stone had been carved with magic. The smooth walls and ceiling and floor showed no signs of tools. It irked him that magic could simply bypass the tools of humanity.

The hall led into a cavernous chamber far below Lenhala and directly underneath the old palace. Another door led up into the palace's library, but Deacon kept that door locked at all times. He didn't want some Gray Elite to wander down and find his treasure. The room was an ancient structure of glass-smooth stone walls with decorative arches around the domed ceiling. It had come from a kingdom before Rhynwier, in the days of rampant and unchecked magic, a time of utter chaos.

And, as per their meeting agreement, the chamber had a single occupant. He stood on the far side, mostly in shadow. He had brought a lantern too, but it burned low. He drank from a short glass of amber. His dark suit blended in with the shadows around him.

"How is Moorin?" asked the man.

"The devastation is remarkable," Deacon said lightheartedly. "The Wraiths planned their attack well, striking hard to distract, and then striking harder. They've done enough damage that Moorin will be feeling it for years, maybe decades."

"They acted out of desperation," the other man drawled.

Deacon shrugged and waved away the talk. He walked to the table and set his lantern down. Maps of Moorin, Lenhala, and cities in between littered the table. He put a hand on his lower back and stretched. Blasted airship seats.

"I hear some are calling this a declaration of war," said the man, his tone lazy and bored. "I hear that the Gray Elite's prototype automaton was *melted*."

Deacon snorted his answer. His spies had brought him the news, fear wide in their eyes. He wished he had seen it, but he was glad he hadn't. Magic like that shouldn't exist. "I can't comment on that nonsense," he said. "Regardless, Gracita would still be victorious in war."

"Not if you can't see your enemy," said the man. "The Wraiths are everywhere and nowhere. They have support throughout the kingdom."

Deacon grunted. He hated the entire idea of there being a society of magicians out there, consorting on all the wicked things they could do with their magic, the evil they could create.

The man in the shadows chuckled, a sinister sound that grated on Deacon's ears, like he had planned the whole thing from start to finish, right under Deacon's nose. "I think this is a prime time to test our project," the other man said darkly. "Remind any lingering rebels who is in charge and who is not."

"I agree," said Deacon.

Both men turned their attention to the structure that took up the majority of the chamber, a monstrous network of obsidian pillars, crystal veins, and limestone. It took up the space of a large house, reaching nearly to the top of the cavern. Altair's Augur. Horrible, mysterious, and beautiful.

The two men walked side by side to the platform that served as the control panel for the device. The user stood on an obsidian platform, before a limestone ring. Inside the ring were alternating crystal and obsidian spikes, leaving enough room between their points for the centrum.

Standing beside the augur, Deacon felt small, and he loved the feeling of having control over such a thing. Godly, even. No one knew how it worked, only that it did. The magical laws and logic that the device followed went beyond what anyone knew; even the dead scholars hadn't a clue of its workings. Deacon had read every book those fools had had on magic before tossing them into the fire, but he found nothing on how the machine worked, only that it existed. It didn't matter. The machine worked, and that was good enough for him.

Like Altair, Deacon didn't need magic to be powerful. Magic would bow to him.

Deacon reached into his suit jacket and retrieved the little iron box—the centrum. At the touch of smooth metal against his fingers, his heart skipped a beat. He restrained himself. Not too eager. He held the little box on his palm, offered it toward the other man, and asked, "Would you like to do the honors, Brigadier General Winchester?"

General Winchester gave him a small, lazy smile as he took the little box. "It would be my pleasure."

Deacon stood still while Winchester stepped up to the limestone ring, his shined shoes clicking against the stone, the lantern light sliding down his slicked-back hair. His sapphire eyes glittered in anticipation, despite his calm face.

This way, he could say without lying that Winchester had started the augur. His hands were clean.

Winchester set the box in the middle of the limestone ring. It hung there between the spikes without touching any of them, another feat of lost technology. Winchester placed his hand on the limestone pad underneath, and a gentle hum started. It sounded like a thousand children humming the same note, and it gave Deacon a horrible sense of being watched. The humming grew louder and louder as the device woke.

The crystals began to glow a faint yellow, then a glorious orange, and finally a violent red. A pulse surged through the crystal, toward the centrum. The energy would surge into the centrum, where it would be magnified tenfold, and from there, it would surge up the obsidian covered crystal tower of the device and into the Gray Elite watchtower, the tallest point in Lenhala, where the blast could be aimed and fired.

Right now, the canon was aimed at a small town east of Lenhala, a known hideout of magicians fleeing into Tinatun. That little town and its traitorous sheep farmers would be the first to see the true power of the Gray Elite.

Deacon felt a shiver in the bottom of his stomach just thinking about it.

Altair's Augur hummed louder and louder, the ancient magic working, and then—all at once, it silenced. The red magic flowed into the centrum and stopped.

Neither Winchester nor Deacon moved. Both looked at the centrum. Winchester removed his hand, and before he could try it again, Deacon pushed him aside. He put his own hand on the panel. The device whirled to life, humming and humming, glowing brighter and brighter. The red light surged into the centrum once again—and again stopped dead.

"Something is wrong," Winchester spat.

Deacon stared at his hand, then at the box. The box. The box. The box! He grabbed it and forced a dagger into the seam of it, wrenching the iron open.

The box was empty.

Deacon swore. That's why that little harlot had given it up so easily. She knew. She had taken it out before he could. She had tricked him, fooled him. Again.

"Well," Winchester said calmly, though his eyes burned. "This complicates things."

Deacon set the empty box on the table. "Yes, it does." The empty box. The melted automaton. A wicked smile stretched his lips. "But don't worry, old friend. I know exactly how to get it back."

Strong

as Steel

Raven Thane held a soft orange flame in her palm. It flickered in the humid breeze.

"A storm is brewing." Conrad's coal dark eyes were on the horizon, nostrils flaring as he inhaled the incoming breeze. "Smell that?"

"Smell what?"

"The rain in the air."

Raven inhaled. "It smells wet," she said flatly, focusing on the flame. It hadn't been easy at first to keep it stable and the same height, but she had gotten better in the last seven days.

"That's the perfume of a storm," Conrad said. "But we've got time before it blows in."

Raven glanced away from her flame and to the horizon. She hadn't quite gotten used to being in a sky city, or being able to see from horizon to horizon, or being able to look down on a floor of clouds, or having an endless sky of brilliant blue above her. Today, however, gray clouds bubbled below them and to the east. Not that the bubbling storm bothered her. Of all the things about the *Orion*, she loved the view the most.

She had almost gotten used to the fire she held in her palm. The blue base of the flame licked against her skin but did not burn her. She felt the warmth of it, but it didn't feel like real fire.

That's because it wasn't real fire. It was magic. Her magic. It felt unreal to think of it as magic, let alone her own. Her, plain Raven, a magician.

For the majority of her seventeen years, she'd had no magic, but thanks to her own naivety about the nature of magical items, she had unknowingly allowed the magic from the centrum of Altair's Augur to seep into her body. It had started as a fever, making her sicker and sicker, but she had conquered it. The magic had become hers.

Her friends had been helping her control it. Today, Conrad accompanied her on her morning trip to the Belt—the promenade deck of the *Orion*—to burn off the excess magic before it could build up and make her sick. It had been Princess Rosaria Whisehunt's theory, and so far it had worked.

The magic contained within the centrum had not been normal magic. It was wild and untamed, as Conrad said. He had the ability to see and sense magic in others, and sometimes she caught him looking at her, but not at *her*—at her magic.

She had asked him once what it looked like.

"It's not something I can really see," Conrad had said, tilting his head. "It's more of something I can sense...like how the heat radiates off stone or how the air blurs right before it rains."

She didn't really understand, but she hadn't asked further questions.

Every morning for the past seven days, Raven had gone to the Belt to burn off her magic. The first day had been trial and error, trying to bring the magic forth. Every day since then, she had held the flame in her hand. She felt it happening too. She felt it stemming the tide of the fever, calming it, sating it.

And without the fever threatening to burn her alive, she could feel the magic with a clearer mind. She could feel it working under her skin, within her bones.

"Are you nervous?" Conrad asked.

Raven glanced from the fire to him. His eyes held his usual mischievous glint, but also something else. She'd come to think of it as his form of worry.

"If I said no, would you believe me?" she asked.

"Not even a little."

"Then, there is your answer." Her magic fluctuated, and she shrank her flame in response.

"You're doing remarkably better." Conrad leaned against the brassy railing of the Belt. He tilted his head back and inhaled the storm-scented breeze. It fluttered through his long braids, clinking the golden beads together in disharmony.

"I've had several remarkable teachers."

"Oh," Conrad said, pretending to be embarrassed.

"Did you learn to smell storms as a pirate?" she asked, mostly to guide the conversation away from her and her magic. And she loved his pirate stories.

"I did," he said with a sigh. "That's one of the things about the ocean. You have maps, but they aren't as reliable as the stars. Maps are good if you know where you are. Stars will tell you where you are, what season it is, and where you are headed. The smell of the air will warn you of a storm before your eyes see it, and the smell of the crew will keep track of how long you've been on the sea."

Raven chuckled, and her flame responded with a flicker.

"Remember," Conrad said, stifling a yawn, "when you feel your magic start to pull, stop before it really pulls."

"Yes, sir." Raven let her flame shrink a little more. "I'm not there yet."

Conrad hummed but didn't respond. He'd done that several times in regards to her magic, that non-answer of curiosity. He knew a lot more about magic than she did, and she took every opportunity to pick his brain. She also took every chance to pry a pirate story from him.

"What about you, little bird?" Conrad hummed a note. "Word is, you've been avoiding the captain."

"I have not," Raven lied. "I've just...continually been in different parts of the ship than her."

He harrumphed.

Raven's conversations with Captain Bailey Luckett had been short and few. The air had turned awkward between them since Luckett confessed to being Raven's mother, who had abandoned her as a child to fly in the sky. Everything about the story made Raven's stomach churn—being abandoned, growing up thinking her mother dead, and finding out her mother had been flying around in the sky the entire time while Raven had grown up underground with nothing but daydreams.

And, if she were to be honest, a part of her was jealous and bitter that her mother hadn't taken her with her. How different would her life have been if she had grown up in the sky rather than a stuffy old silver mine with her overprotective father?

"You can't avoid her forever," Conrad said, a rehearsed line. "And she asked me to inform you that she would like to be friends."

Raven glanced at him over the flame.

Conrad shrugged. "Yes, she asked me to speak to you, and so I have."

"I will make sure to mention it."

"But onto more important things." Conrad pushed off the railing. "I'd say it's just about time to head inside if you want to see Zander before he goes under."

Her heart thudded at the reminder, and her flame flickered in response. It had been a long week for her, but a longer one for Zander. He had lost his left arm in their flight from Moorin, and today he would undergo the surgery to replace it with a mechanical one. Raven let her flame die out.

"Finished?" Conrad asked, eyes on the horizon.

"Good enough." She hadn't felt the gentle tug of depletion, and she suspected Conrad knew that, but he didn't argue.

They started toward the doors that would lead them down into the corridors of the *Orion*. As Raven followed Conrad inside, thunder rolled low and lazy in the distance.

2

Conrad and Raven parted ways, and she made her way to the hospital ward several decks below. Corin, the medic in charge of the magicians, greeted her with a smile.

"We were just getting settled in," Corin said. "Come on in."

He led her into the surgery room, all clean walls and bolted steel cabinets. Zander Winchester sat up in his hospital bed. The top half of his dark brown hair was tied into a topknot, the bottom half having been shaved that morning. A week of healthy meals had brought color back to his bronze skin. His sapphire eyes fell onto Raven, and a grin spread over his otherwise grim face.

Thalame stood at the bedside, arms crossed over his white medic's smock. He would be using his healing magic in the surgery, just in case. Thalame's eyes shifted to Raven, and then he went to the other side of the room to assist the medics. Raven took his place at the bedside.

"He's nervous," Zander admitted to Raven, his voice lowered so Thalame wouldn't hear him. "He plays tough, but he's been twitching all morning."

"Can you blame him?" Raven glanced to where Thalame stood with the medics, his back to them, his foot tapping on the steel floor.

Zander shrugged. "I guess not."

"How are you feeling?" Raven's gaze drifted over the clean bandages across his bare chest and the stump of his left arm.

He noticed her stare and shrugged. "I'm fine." He flashed her a crooked grin, though unease threaded his words. He swallowed, and that grin fell into a straight line. He motioned to his left shoulder and said, "Next time you see me, I'll have a new arm."

One of the medics appeared at the bedside, holding a glass of pale purple liquid. "Here she is." The medic motioned to the glass. "One order of knock-out juice."

"Looks delicious," Zander deadpanned. He accepted the glass and sniffed it. His nose wrinkled, he coughed, and the medic laughed.

Raven caught a whiff—it did not smell like anything a human should ingest.

"Drink it slow, like a fine scotch," the medic said. "Drink it too fast, and you'll wake up sooner than you want to. It's strong enough to knock you out and keep you out during the surgery and most of the day. Maybe tomorrow too."

Zander grimaced at the glass. He took a drink. "Bleh, that's disgusting. If I die during this, I want it on record how horrible the last meal was."

"I'll note it," said the medic.

Zander smirked at Raven, but she couldn't find the strength to smile back. Not with his surgery hanging over their heads. Zander was trying to make it easier on everyone, but her nerves refused to be helped.

"It's not funny," Raven said.

Zander's smirk flattened. He opened his mouth but then closed it. He glanced at the medics. Whatever he wanted to say, he didn't want the medics to hear it. He sipped the tonic instead, then sat the empty glass on the narrow table beside the bed. Already, his eyes looked glassy.

He reached across the bed and held his right hand out to Raven, palm up. Raven wrapped her fingers around his. The feeling of his warm callused hand against hers unsettled her nerves in an entirely different way—a pleasant way.

"I'll be fine," he whispered. "Thalame's here."

Raven nodded. Thalame wouldn't willingly let anything happen to Zander. But what if it was too much for him?

The medic team wheeled a tray to the other side of the bed. They had gathered what looked like torture devices, all sleek steel and sterile, made for slicing, prodding, and pinning flesh and human innards. The assortment made her skin crawl, and the feeling worsened when she imagined what Zander must have felt.

Whatever he felt, he held it in well. When his eyes gazed over the tools, his face calmed and hardened. Ready.

"Raven," Zander said.

She tore her eyes from the tools and met his. He squeezed her hand and gave her his typical smirk, but it lacked humor. He knew the risks of the surgery. He had known from the moment he'd agreed to it.

He blinked, and it took a moment longer for his eyes to open again. When they did open, his eyes had to refocus on her. "I loved you," he breathed.

The words slammed into her. She started to form her response, but they lumped up in her throat. The medical team circled the bed, hands gloved, faces masked.

The moment was gone, and it was time for her to go.

"I'll see you on the other side." Only after the words left her mouth did she realize he could have thought she meant the other side of death, so she quickly added, "of the surgery."

Zander chuckled. His grip on her hand slackened. He fought to keep his eyes open, and he held his unfocused gaze on her. As the tonic finally pulled him under, his breath came out in a whisper. He went under. His body relaxed: his eyes closed, the crease between his brows smoothed, his head slumped to the side, and his fingers released hers.

"Don't worry," said one of the medics, her voice muffled by the mask. "He'll be fine. We've done more complicated surgeries than this."

Thalame stood beside the medic, masked and gloved like the others. Raven left them to do their job and took up a post outside the surgery room. She took a moment to collect herself. She did feel better about having Thalame in the surgery. She had felt his healing magic firsthand. On the other side of the doors, the medical team mumbled to one another, and tools clinked against the tray—the surgery began. With nothing else to occupy her thoughts, Raven started to pace.

And she paced.

And paced.

⚙

The storm blew up, and Raven could no longer hear the sounds of surgery coming from the other side. Wind howled against the ship, whistling through the rigging and whipping against the thick leather balloons—the sound had startled her at first, as if the entire ship would tumble from the sky, but it held. She doubted the average storm could do any real damage to the *Orion*.

Rain beat against the hull, clinking against the metal parts and thumping against the wooden. Thunder quaked across the sky, the crack vicious and close, more violent than she had ever heard it. Each clap resounded through the ship and through her chest, making her heart skip a beat with each one.

Each clap reverberated within her magic too. It pulsed with the thunder.

But she hadn't the time to worry about her magic right now.

She paused in front of the hospital doors and pressed her ear against the seam. She heard the *click-click* of metal tools, the rustle of the medical team's sterile smocks, and the beeping, humming, and clanking of the dozen machines that kept Zander alive during his surgery.

Her legs itched to move again, her nerves already rattling with the lack of motion. She returned to her pacing.

Even now, hours after the surgery had started, she couldn't shake the look of Zander's face as the tonic had pulled him under. It was the look of someone trying to memorize a face he didn't think he'd see again.

There was a chance, the medics had said—as there was always a chance—that the worst could happen. Zander might not wake up. His body might reject the new hardware or see it as infection, causing his body to attack itself. Raven pushed those unhappy thoughts as far away as she could, though they persisted like an itch she couldn't reach.

"You're wearing a groove in the floor," came a soft female voice.

Raven halted her pacing. Princess Rosaria stood in the doorway, a cup of steaming tea in her hands.

Her short tangerine cloak looked marvelous against her olive skin. Her tightly braided dark hair hung over her shoulder. She wore a dress of silver and indigo underneath. Despite the simple dress, Rosaria held herself like a princess, shoulders poised, back arrow-straight, chin high but not arrogant. She stood like a queen before her court.

It came naturally, Raven supposed.

"Here," Rosaria said, handing Raven the tea. "You need this. And you also need a break from your worrying. Come on, walk with me."

412

Raven thought about protesting, but she knew her pacing wouldn't change Zander's fate. His life was in the hands of the surgery team. Raven accepted the tea and followed the princess into the corridor. Warmth seeped into her fingers. Not that she was cold; her nerves had been on edge since Zander's eyes had closed.

"Thank you," Raven said. The first sip of tea warmed the whole way down. Herbs, she guessed. Conrad had mentioned an herbalist on board and a greenhouse somewhere. It would have to be high to catch the sunlight.

The glass globes that lined the corridor glowed yellowish white, warming the rosewood and brass panels. The two girls walked down the corridor. Without the tea to hold, Rosaria laced her fingers together and held them over her stomach. The light glinted off steel pins tucked in her black hair. Raven had told her about the steel pins in her own hair, and Rosaria had taken to doing the same.

A girl uses every talent she has, the princess had told her.

"How long?" Rosaria finally asked.

"It's been five hours." Raven had kept count. Every minute. Every hour. Five hours of her standing outside, unable to help, unable to do anything but wait and hope and pray to the Three Sisters that Zander pulled through.

Rosaria glanced over her shoulder at the hospital doors, her eyes moving through her own worries and apprehensions. She and Zander had been raised together; she thought of him as her brother. Raven wanted to know what else the princess thought, but she worried her own fears would come pouring out of her mouth instead. So she kept it closed.

When her thoughts slipped into those fears, Raven felt the squeezing in her chest—a ghost of the loss she would feel if Zander didn't wake up. The feeling started in her chest and worked its way into every limb until she didn't think she could stand.

To stem her dark thoughts, Raven took a drink of tea. The herbal effects warmed her throat, soaking deeper than her skin, into her bones and tissues, soothing her. She knew the feeling—she had taken several tonics in the past seven days, either to calm the wild magic or to help her sleep.

"They said it would take five to seven hours," Raven said, though she knew Rosaria knew. She had been there for the meeting—they all had. Raven took another drink. If she asked the bartender in the cafeteria for something stronger, would he give it to her? Most of the crew had been or were pirates, so she didn't think he would mind. Most on board carried their own flasks.

"He will be fine," Rosaria said, her voice calming and reassuring. "He's Zander."

Raven gave her a smile, though it felt weak. By the look on Rosaria's face, it looked as weak as it felt.

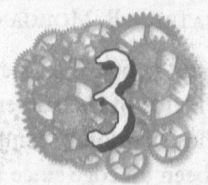

Rosaria led Raven down the corridor, the rain clattering, the thunder rolling, the wind howling. She led her up the wide stairs to the corridor above and to the stairs that would lead to the Belt. Rosaria tugged her up the stairs to the landing, but the double doors leading onto the Belt were closed for the storm.

Thunder cracked too close. Raven felt a tingle in the air as the lightning sizzled somewhere in the clouds.

Captain Luckett had assured Raven that the *Orion* had lightning rods to which the bolts were attracted and then redirected harmlessly. Rather than strike the ship and electrify the metal or burn through the leather or wood, the ship funneled the lightning to a coil, where the ship used what they could of it for power. What they couldn't use zapped into the air behind the ship, leaving a literal trail of lightning.

Rosaria, despite the storm, unlatched and opened the doors to the Belt. Unlike that morning when she had burned away her excess magic with Conrad, shutters had been drawn over the Belt to protect it from the storm. Scrolling wooden shutters arched over the Belt in sections, grayed with weather and time, secured together with small metal casings and hinges. The shutters shook in the wind; they rattled and trembled but held.

Every fifth shutter held thick glass though which the eerie stormy light flooded in, striping the Belt in dark blues and grays. Water dripped through the seams, hitting the lattice floor and vanishing, lost through the maze of tubes and pipes that gathered rain water and recycled it for whatever the ship or its crew needed.

Rosaria started through, walking underneath the center panel in the ceiling to avoid being dripped on. Raven walked with her, despite the tremor in her stomach that came with being on the Belt during a storm. Another part of her thrilled at how close the thunder sounded, how vicious the wind howled, and how angry the rain beat against the shutters.

On the other side of the portholes, thunderheads bubbled in dangerous shades of purple and gray and blue. The wind lashed through the rain, sending the rain in torrents. The lightning flashed between clouds, a constant barrage of light.

They walked along the Belt for a while, and then Rosaria asked, "What's on your mind?"

It occurred to Raven that Rosaria had brought her to the Belt, of all places, so that they wouldn't be easily overheard—granting her privacy, which hadn't been very easy to come by on the *Orion*.

"Too much to be healthy," Raven said with a sigh.

"Give me a few of your thoughts," Rosaria said.

Raven didn't want to start out talking about Zander, so she chose the second most occurring thought. "I don't know what to think about Luckett."

The princess gave a soft hum of acknowledgment, encouraging Raven to continue.

"I..." She sighed. She didn't know where to start. "I used to make up stories about who my mother was, who she had been. My father would never tell me anything, only that I had her eyes. I didn't grow up without a mother. I had my stepmother, and I love her like a mother. She raised me, treated me like her own." The words kept pouring out, faster and faster. "And now Luckett is here, my actual mother, who left me as a baby so she could go play pirate in the sky."

"You are bitter," Rosaria said softly.

"Of course I'm bitter," Raven snapped. "She left me to grow up underground, knowing that I would live the rest of my life there, washing dishes and making soap while she was flying around...doing whatever she does. I..." Raven sighed, releasing the pressure in her chest. "I wish she had taken me with her. I wish I had grown up in the skies."

"And you would be a different person." Rosaria nudged her arm. "Everything that has happened to you, your childhood, the mine, meeting Zander, everything that's happened in the past few months, it is all part of who you are today. If you had been raised in the skies, then you wouldn't have met Zander, you wouldn't have met me, and Sisters only know where you'd be. Maybe we wouldn't have met at all. You have made a difference in the future of both the kingdom and the empire."

Raven hadn't thought of it like that. "Still, Luckett wants me to just forget what she did? She wants to be my mother now, after all this time, and she wants to pretend like nothing happened?"

Rosaria paused by a porthole. On either side of them, the Belt stretched on. It went around the entire airship, and it didn't look like anyone else had come there to walk. According to the crew, a storm made for precarious flying. The crew stood alert, ready for anything, all hands on deck. No one had time to lollygag, as Luckett had said.

Despite her flaws, Raven admired Luckett's readiness and fearlessness. If she had grown up in the sky, would she be both of those things?

"I can't say I have advice for your situation," Rosaria said. "I'm not a parent either, so I can't help you understand what the captain is thinking or feeling." She sighed through her nose. "I don't remember my mother. I grew up with a caretaker and Mrs. Winchester. I used to think that since I had survived, and people thought I was dead, that maybe my parents had survived too. As I grew older, I started to realize the silliness of that."

Raven swallowed. Her problems suddenly felt childish. "You think I should give her a chance?"

"I think," Rosaria said slowly, "I think you should let her be herself. Maybe she isn't the world's best mother, but maybe she is trying to be a mother in the only way she knows how?"

Raven glanced at Rosaria. The princess gave her a sympathetic smile.

"Maybe one day I'll have better advice for daughters and mothers," Rosaria said.

Raven thought about mentioning Ezra Deacon, the Gray Elite captain whose estate Rosaria had been staying at. The two of them had gotten close during her imprisonment in Moorin. However, with Ezra's fate still unknown, Raven held in the thought.

They had left Moorin in a state of chaos. As the airships had sailed upward through plumes of smoke, Raven saw the destruction of that night. She hadn't forgotten the sight: fires everywhere, smoke trailing into the red, gray, and orange sky. The colossus automaton she had reduced to a pile of molten metal, the remains a speck of white-hot goo on the street.

And everyone had seen her do it too. The Gray Elite would have it out for her now.

Gossip from the city had been less and less. With the Gray Elite on high alert, their spies couldn't get into or out of the city easily, and with the *Orion* flying away from Moorin, they had fewer chances to gather information.

"And you're worried about Zander too," said Rosaria.

Raven didn't have to respond. Everyone knew how worried she was. She had gone to Zander's hospital room every day the past week, sharing meals, explaining all that had happened, and just spending time with him.

"When Zander was ten, he and Baxter and I were playing in one of the parlors," Rosaria began. "Zander climbed one of the bookshelves almost to the ceiling. He fell. Sliced his leg open. He started to cry, but then he saw how worried Baxter and I were, and suddenly he was too tough to cry. He didn't want us to worry about him, so he played it off as no big deal. That is what he is doing now. He knows we're worried about him, and he's trying to be a tough guy so we won't worry. Namely you."

Raven blushed.

Zander's voice resounded in her head with the last words he'd breathed before he'd gone under, *I love you.*

Twice he had said those words to her—when he woke up the first time, and now again before his surgery. She hadn't said the words back to him the first time. She had been too stunned, too relieved to see him awake.

And if he didn't wake up...

"It will be okay," Rosaria said, giving Raven's hand a squeeze.

She desperately wanted to believe Rosaria, but it did not calm the quiver in her gut.

They walked in silence while the storm banged and rolled. Tea long gone, Raven swung the empty cup in her free hand. She was thinking about Luckett and her father when she heard footsteps thudding behind them. She reached for the ebony-handled dagger she had always kept in her boot, which she now kept openly strapped to her middle. Rosaria tensed. Raven closed her hand around the hilt of her dagger and unsheathed it as she twirled to face—

Thalame ran toward them. He stopped just out of dagger distance, bent over on his hands and knees, and gasped for breath. Sweat shimmered on his brow and neck. His white smock was spotted with blood.

Raven's heart and lungs fell into her ankles, yanking her breath with it. "What happened?" she gasped, knuckles turning white.

Thalame waved off her concern. He caught some of his breath and then leaned against the railing. He wore no panic on his face, no fear or worry. "He's fine," he said, voice croaky. "He's awake. He's groggy as hell but awake."

Her heart jumped into her throat, swelling twice its size.

Thalame motioned to the dagger. "Planning on using that?"

"I heard footsteps, and I panicked," Raven admitted. She sheathed the dagger.

"Better prepared than sorry," Thalame said. "I ran up here to tell you that Zander's asking for you, mate."

Raven took off down the Belt.

Raven ran. She didn't look back to see if Rosaria or Thalame followed. Zander was awake! By the time she reached the recovery room, her lungs heaved for breath, and a stitch in her side threatened to rip open. Sweat stuck her shirt to her back.

Corin met her at the door. Blood spotted his smock, more than Thalame's. A lot more.

"There you are." He gave her a tired smile. "Come on in."

Raven tried to ball her fists in her skirt, an old nervous habit, but she wore trousers. Instead, she steeled herself, leveled her shoulders, and walked into the recovery room. It smelled like blood, metal, and antiseptic. The mixture churned her stomach. The medics stood on the far side of the room, cleaning the bloodied tools in a wide basin. By the sterile stench, they used more than just soap and water.

Zander had been moved behind a white curtain on the other side of the room. Raven tiptoed closer. He lay on his back amid clean gray linens. His bronze skin had paled with the surgery. A fresh blanket covered everything below his navel, and looking at him like this, she could tell he had lost weight in the past week. His stomach flattened, and the bottoms of his ribs showed. Most of the bandages on his chest were gone. Zander's new left arm lay on a special table beside the bed. It had the shape of a human arm, only instead of skin, it had panels of shined brass and steel, and rather than bones, it had gears and wires. It was jointed at the elbow and wrist to mimic the human range of motion, and complicated little joints made up the five fingers. A salve had been heavily applied where the metal met the skin of his shoulder.

She traced the arm with her eyes several times, then met Zander's stare. His sapphire eyes focused on her, as focused as he could be—a film covered his awareness.

"Your name was the first thing on his lips," said Corin as he stepped around the curtain. He inspected the salve on Zander's shoulder.

Zander didn't look at Corin. He didn't acknowledge that he knew he was there. His eyes remained on Raven.

"The surgery went remarkably well." After applying another layer of the salve, Corin vanished around the curtain.

Raven stepped up to the bedside.

Zander's sleepy eyes searched her, and a lazy smile stretched over his chapped lips. "Hey," he said, his voice dry and weak.

"Hey," she said. The fingers of his limp right hand twitched, and she gently curled her fingers around his. "How are you feeling?"

"Like I'm a floating head." A crease formed between his brows. "I've got legs, right?"

418

She tilted her head toward his legs. "Yeah, I'm pretty sure that's what those are."

"Are you sure? You might be looking at something else." Zander chuckled, a one-note huff of air through his intoxicated lungs.

Heat rushed to her face, but the retort rolled off her tongue—maybe it came from all the time she'd spent around Conrad in the past week— "No, I'm certain those are your legs. I doubt you're that big."

Zander's sleepy smile widened, and his eyes wore a mischievous glint.

Her face heated more. She cleared her throat, and before he could add to the lewd joke, she nodded toward his mechanical arm. "Does it hurt?"

Zander slowly turned his head toward his left arm. For a long moment, his eyes scanned the metal, his shoulders to his fingers. "It's nice," he said at last. "I can't move right now. Not for a few days, they said. It will take a while for my body to figure out what happened or something like that." He turned back to her and smiled. "The engineer that built this baby said there's a blade hidden in the wrist, a compass in the palm, and a place for bullets in the bicep."

She scanned the metal panels. None seemed like they opened, but she didn't know what to look for. "Convenient," she said. "Does it have a snack compartment?"

Zander studied it a moment longer, an appraising look on his face. Even in the short time since she'd arrived, the glassiness of his eyes had ebbed. "I don't know," he said. "Maybe."

"Are you sure it doesn't hurt? Not even a little?" Raven asked, skeptical of his answer. It looked like it would be painful. Thalame had told her a little of how the procedure worked, attaching nerves and bolting bones and... It gave her a chill to think about.

"No," he said. "They gave me a shot of something after I woke up. I can't feel anything right now. That's why I asked about my legs. I can't see them or feel them."

She looked to his metal fingers. When the shot wore off, would he be in pain?

"Rae?" Zander's brow furrowed.

She blinked, and water smeared across her eyelashes. She quickly wiped at her eyes—she hadn't realized she'd teared up. "I'm fine," she whispered. "I'm glad you're okay."

"Thalame said you were pacing in the hall." Zander ran his thumb along hers.

She nodded. She squeezed his hand. Seeing Zander awake and alive opened something in her chest, something that had been coiled tight far longer than a week. He would live. Everything would be fine.

"What are your plans tomorrow night?" Zander asked, grin tilting to the side.

"I...uh, dinner? Maybe train a bit with Thalame. Why?"

His grin widened. "Want to grab something to eat? Maybe eat together somewhere?"

She blinked. "Like a date?"

"Exactly like a date," he said. "Only you know, there's likely going to be other people around, and it won't be as romantic as one of those hideously uptight and expensive restaurants in the city. It'll be a little more pirate-themed."

"I do have a soft spot for airships," she said, smiling back at him. "And I think I know the perfect place."

His brows rose in question.

"I'm not telling you. You'll have to wait and find out."

His smile widened. "I'm looking forward to it."

With shaky, limp fingers, he brought her hand to his lips. It wasn't the most graceful maneuver, but she blushed all the same.

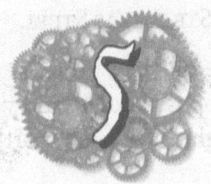

Raven returned to the hospital the next morning to see Zander sitting on the edge of his bed. His mechanical arm hung in a sling, the hand and fingers limp. Zander's eyes found Raven immediately, and his bored face stretched into a grin.

"Come here," he said.

She came to stand at the bedside. Zander motioned to his mechanical pinky—it twitched. He flashed her a triumphant smirk.

"Did you do that?"

He nodded.

"The rest of the arm will take time," Corin said from the other side of the room. He walked over and set a jar of taupe salve beside Zander. "If the skin on your shoulder gets irritated, rub this on it. The skin touching the metal will eventually callus, but until then, there's salve."

"Thanks," Zander said. He took the jar and tucked it into the pocket of his trousers.

"You know," Corin said lightly, "a night of observation might be in your best interest."

Zander glared at the medic. "No. Everything went fine, and I'm sick of this place."

Corin chuckled. "I'm kidding. You're free to go. If you start feeling like something's not right, come back and see us."

"Yeah, yeah." Zander scooted closer to the edge of the bed.

Raven stood on one side and Corin stood on the other. Zander set his socked feet on the floor. He wobbled once, gained his balance, and took the first step toward the hospital doors. A few steps into the corridor, and Thalame appeared at his other side. They walked first to the room Thalame had been staying in, which Zander would now be sharing with him. Raven stood outside while Zander changed and washed—when the boys reappeared, Zander had clean hair, fresh trousers, boots, and a simple shirt with baggy sleeves that hung halfway down his arm.

"I've got some things to take care of," Thalame said, walking down the corridor with a nonchalant wave of his hand. "He's your problem now, Raven."

"Feel better?" Raven asked Zander.

"It's a wonder what a bath does for the soul," he said.

He let out a content sigh and ran his right hand through his loose hair. He held his hand out to her, and she took it. Water from his hair clung to his hand and squished between their fingers. Despite it, a tingle ran up her arm at his touch.

"Would have been better without Thalame waiting on the other side of the shower curtain," he added lowly.

"You'd rather have to figure out how to dress yourself with one arm?" Raven eyed his mechanical fingers. "I suppose I could find you a dress to wear instead."

Zander sighed. "A dress might have been worth not having another man help me put on my pants."

She chuckled and said, "I'm sure Conrad would have helped."

Zander frowned. "No."

Raven wanted to tell him that she would have helped, if only to make him blush, but even the thought of saying the words aloud brought a mild blush to her cheeks. If she were to say them, her face would burn. And Zander might take her up on the offer when he needed to change.

"The others have prepared a little surprise brunch for you," Raven said.

"Thalame may have let it slip," Zander said. "He knows I hate surprises."

She knew too, but it hadn't stopped her. "Just remember to act surprised. I'm supposed to be bringing you."

"Lead the way." Zander glanced down both sides of the corridor. "You know your way around better than I do."

Raven guided him down the corridor at a leisurely pace. Zander hadn't been out of the hospital since they'd boarded the *Orion*, but she had told him all about the ship. In the first few days, it was all she had talked about. Zander hadn't shushed her, letting her go on and on about the corridors and decks and tangled maze of ladders and lifts and catwalks.

Zander paused by one of the portholes. Dark gray clouds whisked by. The worst of the storm had blown away and left streaks of brilliant blue between the straggling clouds. Far, far below, the world stretched on in blurry greens, grays, and blues. In the far distance, mountains rose in shades of purple and grayish blue.

"Is being in a sky city everything you thought it would be?" Zander asked, taking his eyes from the clouds and looking at her.

"It has been so far," Raven said. "I've heard all manner of sky pirate stories from the crew." She frowned. "Except flying through the storm. That was a little lackluster."

"No cloud dragon attacks?"

She blushed. In one of her favorite books—one she had left in Silver Glen—storms were caused by illusive cloud dragons. To fly through a storm could provoke an attack, and only the toughest, bravest, or foolish pirates flew through storms.

"No," she said. "None of those. But I suppose I'd rather not be attacked by ancient magical beasts while hovering miles over the earth."

The sun broke through the clouds, dappling over the lower clouds and dashing them in gold and yellow.

Raven cleared her throat. "I don't know if you have heard," she started.

Zander's brow rose.

"But Captain Luckett is my mother."

Zander's brows shot to his hairline. "What? You're kidding."

She shook her head. "No. My locket used to be her locket." She lifted it from under her blouse. The gold shone in the sunlight. "That's how she knew who I was. Malik saw me with the locket and told her. Luckett won it in a game of dice when she was twelve, a game in which she cheated."

Zander whistled his astonishment.

"And Malik is apparently my half-brother," Raven added.

Zander shook his head in disbelief. "Sisters. I've known Malik since I became a Wraith. He's your brother?"

"What's he like?" Raven slipped the locket back under her blouse. It no longer held the centrum, but wearing it hidden had become habit. She liked feeling the metal against her chest. "I haven't spent much time with him. I...might have been avoiding him and Luckett."

"He's a seeker for the Wraiths." Zander leaned against the rosewood paneling. "That means he can detect magic in others. I didn't think he left Wayward Point. He's the one with connections. He knows people everywhere, has spies all over. He's something like the Wraiths' spymaster."

"Spies?" Raven asked.

"Contacts, friends, pirates, smugglers," Zander explained. "When I was training, he was the one I asked questions. I always thought of him as the one who knew everything, or knew where to find the answer. He's also serious as death, ridiculously smart, quiet, and a bit, uh, sensitive. The opposite of Conrad."

At that, she laughed. "Is being sensitive a bad thing?"

"No," Zander said quickly. He cleared his throat. "Just a thing. But let's get back to the important topic. Luckett is your *mother*? Your mother is a pirate captain?" He laughed. "That explains where you got your stubborn streak and your bizarre interest in airships."

The conversation dwindled. Raven met Zander's eye, and she felt three words rise in her throat. Three words she needed to say.

She swallowed and said instead, "The others will start to wonder what's taking so long."

She tugged him down the corridor, and he didn't object. Those three words jumbled in her throat. The timing didn't feel right. She had never said those three words to anyone other than her father, stepmother, and her half-sister, Lena.

Raven had grown up hearing her father and stepmother reciting those words to each other every day—Raven had grown up with love. She thought she understood it and how it worked, but then Zander had said those words to her. Now, the very concept of love felt like something unreal and impossible. Since those words, every time she thought of Zander, it felt like ribbons tightening on her ribcage.

How could he say those words to her after all the problems she had caused? If it weren't for her, he would still have two arms.

They walked down the corridor and started down the next and the next, and then familiar voices drifted out of the lounge at the end of the corridor. Their friends.

Zander pulled her to a stop. "Raven," he breathed.

"I'm sorry," she blurted, though she had said those two words over and over to him in the past week. Her eyes fell onto his mechanical arm. "I should haven't acted like a child."

"Raven," he said, his voice deep and velvet soft. "It's okay. We're here now, and everything's going to be fine. There's nothing we can do about the past. It's done."

She blinked at him. She motioned to his mechanical arm. "Is this your idea of okay?" she said, her voice high and squeaky. "Moorin all but burned to the ground, and Sisters only know what the Gray Elite think of us now, and then there's the Wraiths, who probably think—"

Zander's lips met hers. His kiss was chaste, just enough to silence her worries.

"It's fine," he breathed, his lips hovering a hair's breadth away from hers. "It's not a perfect situation, but it is what it is. There's nothing we can do to change what happened. We deal with it. We move on. We punch through walls with our new metal arm."

She frowned. "Is that your plan?"

"It's one of my plans." He smirked, hooking his right arm around her waist. He couldn't pull her too close with his metal arm in a sling. "But we will be okay. I won't push you away again. It's obvious that you don't need me to protect you anymore."

She sought solace in his eyes and found it. Steadiness. Forgiveness. "I did save your ass this time," she whispered.

His smile returned, wider than before. Something in her chest broke apart at the sight, broke into a thousand pieces of white-hot ooze.

Rosaria's voice fluted through the corridor, followed by Thalame's. Zander and Raven both jumped. His metal arm jostled. They stepped apart just as the door to the lounge opened and Thalame stepped out. He had words on his tongue, then spotted Zander and Raven.

"Don't tell me you broke it already, mate," Thalame said, grinning.

Zander blinked and looked at his limp left arm. "I have to be able to use it in order to break it," he quipped.

Rosaria and Conrad stuck their heads out of the doorway.

"There you are," Rosaria said, giving them a cheerful wave.

Sensing the moment gone, Raven pulled Zander to the lounge. Rosaria patted the couch she sat on, and Raven and Zander joined her. The others had gathered for tea, cookies, and sandwiches. Like the rest of the upper deck, the lounge had rosewood and brass paneling, hardwood floors, and brassy glass globes shining with yellowish light. The rosewood furniture had been bolted to the floor and angled around a large coffee table.

424

It had been a while since they had gathered in one place without planning or scheming. The change of pace was nice.

"Look who's up and walking," Rosaria said to Zander.

"Give me a week," Zander said.

"And you'll be jogging?" Raven asked.

Zander shrugged and accepted a cup of tea from Rosaria. "What have I missed?"

They took turns telling Zander stories from the past week on the ship and what news they managed to get from Moorin and Lenhala. The Crusaders were mostly pirates and smugglers, but the Wraiths had spies all over the continent. They didn't have solid news. They could only speculate on the movements of the Gray Elite since the dramatic retrieval and subsequent escape—as Conrad called it.

"It's not every day the most wanted person in the empire flies away while the Gray Elite are scratching their heads," Conrad said, winking at Raven.

Conrad's version of that night sounded more like a fantastic adventure, full of whizzing rockets, bursts of colored sparks, and purring airships. Due to his injury, Zander had missed that part. Raven had been mostly out of it, but as Conrad told the story of that night, she started to doubt whether they had experienced the same night. She didn't ask; Conrad's version of the night made her sound dangerous and exciting, as if she had cleverly planned her escape and remained a step ahead of the Gray Elite.

"We've got the entire city talking about us," Conrad said, grinning wide. He leaned forward and plucked a cookie from the tray. "The girl who melted an automaton already has bards composing songs of her outlaw life and pirate associates. Some say she could swoop down at any time and set the world on fire."

"Swooping makes it sound..." Raven hummed her disapproval.

"They've also upped your bounty," added Thalame. He tipped his tea to Raven. "That makes you twice the wanted girl you were. They've thrown Zander and me into the heat too." He glanced at Conrad, who awaited Thalame's next words eagerly. "Turns out, Conrad here already had one on his head."

Conrad didn't look surprised. "Piracy does have its drawbacks."

"I've sent word to the treehouse," Thalame said to Zander. "Ivy will've heard about the mess by now, and I don't want them thinking we're dead."

Raven tapped the side of her teacup. She hadn't seen Ivy in what felt like forever—she had so much to tell her. Ivy maintained a healthy chain of spies for the Dwellers—freedom fighters who lived in the forest of Rhynwier. Thalame was a Dweller too, and he would know how to get word to her.

"Here's the next question." Thalame bent forward, shoulders hunched. He looked ready to pounce. "Do we use the Gray Elite's confusion to rest up and plan our next move, or do we use their confusion against them and use this time to hit them again while they're weak?"

"Trouble is, we're weak right now too." Conrad tipped his half-eaten cookie toward Zander. "As much as I'd love to march in and kick the dragon while it's down, I think the more intelligent move would be to wait."

Zander glanced down at his mechanical hand. A shadow passed over his face.

Raven raised her brows at Conrad. "That sounds like a reasonable decision." She put a hand to her heart in pretend worry. "Are you feeling all right?"

"It could be the thin air up here." Zander tore his eyes from his hand and looked clinically at Conrad. "I've heard it does strange things to the head."

Conrad grinned wider. "Then, we're all snorting the thin air."

Zander laughed and opened his mouth to speak—a series of bells pierced the air. An alarm. The bells started somewhere in the belly of the ship and rang through the speaking tubes that traveled to every room and office and mechanical closet.

Since their escape, Raven had heard a dozen different bells. A bell for dinner. A bell for incoming weather. A bell to signal the start or stop of an engine. A bell to signal the need for a medic, and another bell to signal where the need is. A bell to signal the officers to the captain's office. But these bells hadn't yet rang through the ship.

"What does that one mean?" Raven asked.

Conrad stood. All humor faded from his face. "An enemy ship is approaching."

R aven, Zander, Rosaria, and Thalame followed Conrad through the Orion and toward the air docks tucked underneath the ship. The rosewood and brass of the upper decks became the oak and steel of the lower decks, and then they came to a wide set of iron double doors. Wind whistled through the seams. Conrad pulled the crank, and the heavy doors opened.

At once, chilled wind rushed up to meet them, a residual beat of the storm. The doors opened onto a sturdy mezzanine of thick steel that circled the perimeter of the air docks. Steel walkways, held aloft by thick cables and rigging from the roof of the air docks, connected the mezzanine to the maze of the air docks—hundreds of narrow catwalks, rope bridges, and ladders connected the leveled berths.

Hundreds of air ships docked, varying in size and function. Some were small and painted sky blue, others were thick and equipped with multiple guns, and some were large and windowless. The air docks gave off a gentle rumble, a mixture of the wind, engines, and commotion of the docks themselves—from the engineers and mechanics in varying states of repairing and cleaning, and from the constant creaking of the rigging.

They weren't the only ones that had come to see the incoming ship; it seemed most of the free crew had come.

Conrad navigated through the air docks, and the others followed. Raven tried to copy his fearless posture, but the view left a wobbly feeling in her stomach. The clouds formed a floor far below them, but she knew her body would fall right through. The steel railing only helped a little. Zander's presence behind her helped a little too.

A strong wind blew into the docks, rattling the rigging and shaking the catwalk. Raven gasped and grabbed both sides of the railing. The wind passed, and the catwalk stilled. Raven's heart continued to pound.

"It's okay," Zander said in her ear. He held onto the railing too.

Raven blew out a breath—Conrad hadn't hesitated, and she jogged the several steps the wind had cost her.

"We've got procedures in place in case of a man overboard." Conrad glanced over his shoulder at her. "Don't worry, little bird. If you fall, we'll dive to catch you."

"And then we'll both be falling."

Conrad waved off her concern. "For a little while, but then we will be back on the ship."

"But—"

"We've got pilots standing by at all hours, waiting for deployment," Conrad explained. "See those ships over there?" He pointed to the small single-passenger ship painted sky blue. "They're the nimblest machines in the air. If you jumped right now, they'd catch you before you hit the clouds."

"And you know this for certain?" Raven asked.

"I am one hundred percent certain." Conrad paused at the uneven intersection of three catwalks and leaned against the railing. "I've both fallen and piloted to save someone from falling." He winked. "Yes, it is terrifying. For both parties. A little more so for the pilot."

Raven blinked at him. "Saving someone is more terrifying than falling to your death?"

"Yes." Conrad nodded. "When you are falling, it is your life you are going to lose, and the feeling of falling is a bit exhilarating. But when you are diving to save someone from falling, it is someone else's life you stand to lose. When you are the one who is going to die, you won't have to live with the guilt of failing."

"Oh. I hadn't thought of it like that." She looked down at the clouds. She had trouble envisioning it.

"I understand." Zander glanced at Raven, guilt darkening his face. "Saving someone else is more stressful than being the one who needs saving."

She frowned. He was clearly talking about her. She started to say something, but her words fell short. Being trapped in an automaton's chest had been stressful; being thrown into the *Chjelhu Tal* and fighting for her life had been stressful; not knowing if the fever would burn her alive in the night had been stressful; but witnessing the colossus strike Zander had been worse. Standing outside the surgery room, knowing she could do nothing, had been worse.

Had he felt the same panic when she had vanished from the treehouse? She met his eyes and saw a ghost of that panic, the worry.

She started to apologize again, but Conrad interrupted, "See?" Snapping his wrist toward Zander, he winked at Raven. "You just need more experience saving Zander."

Zander frowned, and Raven offered Conrad a laugh.

"I'd rather not be either," Raven admitted.

Zander nodded. "As would I."

More Crusaders made their way into the air docks. Even with all the extra bodies and footsteps, the catwalks barely swayed. Crusaders lounged on the rope bridges, looking comfortable standing so far above the ground with so little keeping them from falling.

"What's happening?" Raven whispered to Conrad.

"I don't know," Conrad whispered back. In a normal tone, he added, "The alarm signaled an enemy ship approaching, yet no further signal has come. The enemy ship has not yet posed an obvious threat."

"We're just waiting to see what happens?" Zander asked.

"Oh, don't you worry." Conrad grinned at Zander. "You can bet there are at least three Vultures circling, ready to take down the enemy ship." He motioned to where vicious-looking airships rested—spiked and painted black and red, made for offense.

Over the whistle of the wind, the buzzing of an airship sounded. The chatter around the air dock silenced, and more than a few Crusaders drew pistols. Many on the lower walkways held daggers and short swords—ready for a fight. Raven felt oddly unprepared, but then she remembered her magic. She would never be without a weapon or unprepared for a fight again. That knowledge settled her rattling nerves.

The heavy iron doors to the *Orion* opened, and Malik hurried into the air docks. Despite his quickened steps, he moved like a prince about to greet a visitor, but with the caution of a lion stalking prey. The Crusaders parted to let him pass. As the captain's son and a seeker for the Wraiths, he warranted their silent respect.

Malik hurried onto the catwalk on which they stood. As he passed Zander, he said, "Follow me."

Zander didn't hesitate. His gaze turned predatory, and he followed Malik toward an empty berth. Conrad grabbed Raven's hand, and they fell into step behind them. Malik didn't acknowledge them. Rosaria and Thalame remained on the catwalk.

"What news?" Zander asked Malik.

"It's a Gray Elite Buzzer," Malik said quickly, lowly. "Its pilot has asked permission to dock. He says he's got magicians on board seeking asylum and that he's been shot."

Raven tensed; beside her, Conrad did the same.

"What's the plan?" Conrad asked.

"Captain's given permission to dock." Malik cast a glance around the docks at all the crew armed and ready. "And she's given permission to shoot at the first sign of trouble."

Conrad sighed. "I love when she gives the shoot-first order. Makes life easier."

"We're not shooting first," Malik corrected. He gave Conrad a stern glare. "We're asking questions first, and depending on the answers, we shoot second."

They turned onto a downward angled catwalk toward the empty berth, and as they turned onto another, Raven glimpsed steel at Malik's waist. A pistol.

The buzzing grew louder. From below the *Orion*, an airship of white steel appeared through the clouds. It didn't fly as smooth as the others—gunfire had peppered its starboard side, and the front window had been cracked. As it came into the berth, it swayed, and its engines sputtered. Malik stood stone still as the air dock crew rushed to tie the ship off and hook it into the rigging. Crusaders moved into position, pistols and crossbows aimed at every side of the Gray Elite ship.

Malik stood in clear view of the door, stoic as a king greeting his enemy. Raven tried to stand like him. If they shared half of their blood, could she muster that same regal grace? Or had he inherited it from his father?

The airship's engine died, and the door opened with a hiss. Crusaders stood firm. A gangplank shifted into position, and a young man stepped out of the ship

429

with his empty hands stretched in front of him. Blood spotted his shirt and trousers—the wound on his shoulder still bled.

"Don't shoot," he said, voice hoarse. Behind him, several other faces appeared. None were armed, all were wide-eyed and afraid. They wore dirty, tattered clothes of refugees. One small girl hugged the waist of an older girl, tears glistening in her eyes.

Malik stepped forward. "You're a magician." It wasn't a question.

Raven understood then why Malik had hurried to greet the ship. As a seeker, he could sense the magic in other people. She glanced sideways at Conrad, who had the same ability. He too, was staring into the ship with an intensity she'd come to recognize as his seeker abilities at work.

The young man nodded. "Yes."

"You seek asylum from the Gray Elite?"

"Yes, please, sir."

Malik looked the man over. He glanced once at Conrad—something passed between them, an agreement. Malik looked back to the young man. "Exit the ship," he said. "My friends here will escort you to a safe place."

"Thank you," he breathed as he limped down the gangplank.

The young man was not the only one wounded. Most others had cuts and bruises and poorly wrapped wounds. They carefully exited the ship one at a time, under the watchful eyes of the Crusaders, none of whom had lowered their weapons.

"What in Minerva's name happened?" Conrad asked, his tone not as serious as Malik's. Malik glared at him, but Conrad pretended not to notice.

"We were attacked when we tried to escape," said another of the magicians, who wore a bandage around his head and his right eye. The bandage looked to have once been part of a shirt.

"The pilot's been shot," said one of the magicians, pointing toward the cockpit.

As the magicians crossed onto the docks, the first young man started back in for the pilot, but Malik put a hand to his shoulder.

"We will get him," Malik said.

The magician didn't argue. A handful of Crusaders escorted him and the others up the catwalks and into the lower deck of the *Orion*.

After all the magicians had disembarked, Conrad walked up the gangplank and into the ship. Malik stood by the gangplank, watching his every move. Conrad turned toward the cockpit, hand on a dagger. He vanished from sight. Raven stood close enough to Malik to hear his sharp intake of breath.

"Well, I'll be damned." Conrad's voice echoed off the steel insides of the airship, a laugh on his words.

"Conrad," Malik said, a warning.

Conrad stepped back into view, a second person leaning heavily on his shoulders. The young man had indeed been shot. Blood had soaked through the left breast of his Gray Elite uniform. His blond hair was dirty and specked with blood, the knees of his pants torn, and his head hung. He looked ready to collapse.

430

"Looks like we've got ourselves a defector," Conrad said as he and the officer started down the gangplank.

"Or a spy," said someone behind Raven.

They made it to the docks, and a team of Crusaders made their way into the airship. The officer gasped and looked up, and Raven felt her breath leave her throat the same time Zander's did.

It was Ezra Deacon.

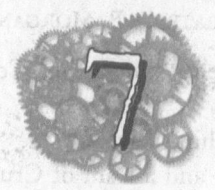

Raven couldn't believe her eyes. Ezra Deacon had defected? Rosaria, a catwalk above them, let out a fearsome shout—her voice silenced the muttering of spy and defector and throw him overboard. Rosaria started down the catwalk—the Crusaders parted for her. She marched, fearsome as a queen, determined as a general.

Halfway to Conrad, she shouted, "Ezra!"

At the sound of his name on her voice, he looked up. Ezra's bleary eyes sought her through the crowd, but he couldn't focus. Rosaria grabbed his face in her hands and forced his gaze to hers.

"Ezra?" Rosaria asked, her voice softer than it had been a moment before. "You're okay?"

He tried to give Rosaria a smile. With every passing moment, he looked closer to fainting. His peachy skin had faded to a frightening white, his hands shook, and his breath shuddered.

"Define *okay*," Conrad said. "Considering there is a bullet lodged somewhere in his chest, I'm not sure he would agree with you. I certainly don't."

Rosaria paled.

"Get out of the way," came Thalame's sandpaper voice. He shouldered his way down the catwalk and pressed his hand against Ezra's bleeding chest. Ezra didn't seem to register his presence. "Yup, bullet wound. Didn't hit anything vital, but he's lost an unhealthy amount of blood."

"And he still managed to pilot a Buzzer," said Conrad.

Ezra mumbled something too low for Raven to hear—Conrad chuckled.

"Boy's got a point," Conrad said. "Either fix him up or throw him overboard. End his suffering."

Mumbles surfaced on the surrounding catwalks. Several murmured to throw him overboard. Raven's heart hammered, and Rosaria frowned. Luckily, those who knew Ezra stood closest to him.

"Take him to the hospital," Rosaria ordered. The sound of her voice silenced the mumbling. "At once!"

"You want to take in this traitor?" came a pirate's objection.

Rosaria whipped her head around to see the pirate who'd spoken. "Yes," she said, any indication of doubt or fear gone from her voice. A queen spoke, not a dethroned princess.

All eyes in the air dock looked to her, and Raven felt a warm jealousy for Rosaria—she would have crumbled under all the stares. Her knees felt weak just standing this close to the center of attention.

Rosaria continued, "This young man is no traitor to us, but to the Gray Elite. Because of him, hundreds of magicians have escaped execution and imprisonment at the hands of the empire. Because of this young man, I am standing here." She turned her head to Conrad, her shoulders straight, her spine rigid, her chin up. "Take him to the hospital, and make sure his injuries are tended to."

"Yes, Your Majesty," said Conrad with a graceful dip of his head. His coal eyes glittered. He had said her title a little louder than he normally would have, to remind those around them who she was and who she would become.

Conrad and Thalame hoisted Ezra between them and started up the catwalks. Rosaria walked behind them, determination unmistakable on her face. Raven and Zander backed into the railing to let them pass, and Ezra's glossy eyes glanced up—his eyes met Zander's. Confusion, relief, and surprise passed over his pained expression, and the same mirrored on Zander's. As the procession passed, Zander and Raven fell into step behind the princess.

When they passed through the doors and into the lower deck, Zander whispered to Raven, "What just happened? What don't I know?"

"Ezra's been helping magicians escape the Gray Elite for years," Raven whispered back. "He smuggles them out."

Zander's surprise lifted his eyebrows nearly to his hairline. "He's done what?"

"He's been working alongside several turncoats within the Gray Elite ranks as well as a few smugglers and pirates," Conrad added.

Ezra grunted unintelligibly.

"We'll get more answers out of him when he's not dying," Thalame said pointedly.

The walk to the hospital seemed longer than it should have, and once again, Raven waited in the corridor. This time, however, Zander and Conrad waited with her. Thalame had gone into the surgery with Ezra. Rosaria paced in front of the closed surgery doors.

"I didn't realize how stressful it is to be locked outside and waiting," Rosaria said, her voice small and rushed. She stared at the floor as she paced, fingers fidgeting with the end of her braid. "I apologize for not being well prepared to handle it."

"You did just fine." Raven grabbed Rosaria's hands and pulled her to a stop, forcing the princess to meet her gaze. "Ezra has a gunshot wound, and Thalame had a decent meal earlier. He'll be fine."

"It's not like he's missing a limb," Conrad quipped.

Raven glared at him over her shoulder.

"This whole time," Zander said, hand to his temple, "Ezra has been helping magicians?"

"Yes," Conrad, Rosaria, and Raven said together.

Zander sighed, the information not fully wrapping around his mind. "I didn't know," he mumbled. "I could have helped him. We could have helped each other."

"He suspected you were a Hawk, but he didn't know you were a Wraith," Raven told him. "As far as either of you knew, you were on opposite sides."

"When in reality, they were on the same side." Conrad's smile turned up. "Funny how these things happen."

Malik came through the doors of the ward where the magicians had been taken, wearing his usual frown. The bangles on his left wrist clinked as he shut the door behind him.

"Anyone die on the way up?" Conrad asked lightly.

Malik's frown deepened, and he let out a quick, agitated sigh.

Raven, standing between Malik and Conrad, noted the glance that lingered between them, unspoken and unreadable. She had the worst feeling of having intruded on something private.

"According to the magicians' story," Malik started, "Ezra Deacon was planning their escape when the Gray Elite raided the safehouse where they were hiding. They barely made it out. Originally, Ezra was supposed to merely see them off, not to go with them, but those plans changed when the Gray Elite opened fire."

"They're all magicians?" Zander asked.

Malik nodded. "Every one. I've placed them under care for now. When they have rested, I will speak to them again. They also bring disturbing gossip that the Gray Elite have been shipping magicians south rather than executing them, though there are no records of this."

"The Gray Elite are saying they're executing magicians, but they're sending them south instead," Zander said grimly. "That sounds bad."

"South, as in...?" Conrad let his words trail off and waved his hand through the air.

Malik met Conrad's stare. "South, as in the magicians didn't know exactly. Somewhere in Tinatun. A few of the refugees claim to have overheard Gray Elite whispering about shipping magicians south."

"Why ship them south to kill them?" A fearsome chord struck Raven's chest. . "Unless...they aren't killing them. Could they be hiding them somewhere?"

"It's hard to tell," Malik said. "Those who go south never return."

"Magic isn't common in Tinatun," Conrad added. "The farther south you go, the rarer it is. Some of the far southern islands think magic is a myth."

"Then why...?" Zander rubbed his face with his good hand. "It doesn't make sense. We need more information."

"I agree," Malik said. "It doesn't make sense, but it doesn't matter. Whatever the Gray Elite are doing, the Wraiths will protect magicians. It's our sacred duty as Wraiths."

Conrad and Zander nodded in agreement, none too enthused.

Footsteps approached, and the surgery door opened. Thalame leaned out. His skin had paled with the use of his healing magic—he must have done more to Ezra than he had to Zander.

"He's awake and talking," Thalame said, his rough voice reflecting his exhaustion.

Rosaria didn't wait for permission; she rushed in first. Malik calmly followed.

Conrad meandered to the door and leaned to whisper to Raven, "This is going to be interesting."

The recovery room hadn't been designed for so many visitors, and Raven stood with her arm flush against Zander's. Ezra was sitting up in the hospital bed, bandages wrapped around his bare torso. Rosaria claimed her seat at the bedside and took Ezra's hand in both of hers. As Malik came around the other side of the bed, she held his hand tighter.

"He's not done anything wrong," Rosaria said to Malik.

Malik met her regal gaze with his own, his expression hidden behind a stoic mask. A beat passed between them. "I understand your concern," Malik said to the princess, every word careful, elegant, and vicious. "But I reminded you: you are not my princess. Your commands mean nothing to me or the majority of this crew."

Rosaria glared; Malik glared back.

Conrad leaned closer to Raven and mumbled loud enough to everyone to hear, "Pirates."

Malik broke his glare with the princess to glare at Conrad, who then winked.

"Ezra," interrupted Zander, who grasped the railing at the foot of the hospital bed. "What the hell happened?"

Ezra exhaled, the breath stable but stalled. "I could ask the same of you," he said, his words hesitant. He pointed toward Zander's mechanical arm.

"You first," said Zander.

"Fair enough." Ezra nodded. "I went to prepare another shuttle of magicians out of the city. Since your escape" —he glanced at Raven— "the Gray Elite have been in a frenzy. There have been several rebellions, not just in Moorin but in Lenhala, of magicians and magic-sympathizers. The Gray Elite ordered a block-by-block search for magicians. I tried to get them out before they were found, but...my father found out. I don't know how. Someone on the house staff, I think. Father tried to keep me from leaving, and that's when I knew something was wrong. I managed to get away, but as they were loading into the airship, Gray Elite stormed the safehouse. They opened fire. The pilot panicked and ran, and I took his place. I was shot in the process. After getting through the clouds, it was smooth sailing."

"I was expecting a shootout with the Gray Elite," Conrad added. "A bit more drama."

Ezra shook his head. "But my father will know that I've defected," he said, glumness overcoming his face.

"You turned traitor years ago," Conrad reminded Ezra. "This just means you're officially one of us. Wanted outlaws—saving magicians and making sure the Gray Elite stay on their collective toes."

Ezra's eyes fell on Zander's new arm, and a crease formed between his brows. "I'm not sure that's a comfort right now."

"Oh, this?" Zander twitched the little finger of his new arm. "I got this because that Colossus of yours nearly sliced my arm off."

Ezra winced. "It wasn't my Colossus," he said darkly. He glanced to the trashcan where his bloodied Gray Elite uniform had been thrown. A yellow striped sleeve hung over the edge, spotted with red. "I'm not Gray Elite anymore."

"Ah, the gloomy look of one recently thrown into the outcasts," Conrad said with a dramatic sigh. "I remember those gloomy days. Don't worry, it goes away with time and a few strong drinks."

Ezra offered Conrad a smile. "Good to know." His gaze shifted to Raven, then Zander. His smile faded. "There is something else. Something I overheard my father say. I didn't think I'd get the chance to tell you, but I guess the Sisters had other ideas."

"What?" Zander and Raven said together.

"My father," Ezra started, "he's planning—"

The doors burst open, and Captain Luckett stormed into the room. She wore her pristine crimson coat with black cuffs and brass buttons, a white blouse, and a black corset with golden strings. Her tricorn hat perched to the side. She had clearly dressed to impress. She marched into the room, fierce light brown eyes pinned on Ezra. She stopped beside Malik and looked down at Ezra like something rotten.

"This is Deacon's brat?" Luckett demanded.

Ezra reddened. "That would be me, ma'am."

Luckett blinked, then let out a bark of a laugh. "Ma'am," she repeated. Her smile vanished. "It's *Captain*, boy."

"Yes, Captain," Ezra said without hesitation.

"I see he's got that Gray Elite etiquette," Luckett said. "A bit refreshing after dealing with pirates and their attitudes." Her glare passed over Conrad, who looked sheepishly behind him. Finding no one, he turned back around, surprised, and pointed to himself. Luckett ignored him and returned her stare to Ezra. "What's the urgency, boy?"

"My father is planning something, an assault." Ezra looked again at Raven. "He knows now that you were in Moorin. Everyone knows about the Colossus you turned into molten metal."

Raven bit her lip. She'd been worrying about that. Would Deacon put the pieces together himself? She glanced sideways at Zander. He wore the same worry in his eyes.

"Something went wrong," Ezra said, a crease between his eyes. "I-I don't know what, he flew in from Lenhala a few days ago in a strange calm. He didn't seem upset by the Colossus, he seemed...fascinated. The emperor is calling the attack on Moorin an act of war by Rhynwierian rebels."

A stone fell into Raven's stomach.

"I overheard my father talking in his study. They are planning retaliation in the north," Ezra continued, "but I don't know exactly where. One of the servants came up the stairs, and I couldn't listen in without being seen."

Ezra continued to talk, but Raven had stopped listening. Her skin went cold, the floor wobbled beneath her feet, and she latched onto Zander's arm to keep from tumbling over.

"Retaliation in the north," she breathed, halting whatever Ezra had been saying. She met Ezra's gaze.

Understanding widened Zander's eyes.

Words tumbled from Raven's lips. "Could he be talking about Silver Glen?"

"Full steam ahead," Captain Luckett bellowed into the speaking tubes tucked into the corner of her office.

"Aye, Captain!" came the response.

A heartbeat later, the engines roared, and the *Orion* pushed faster through the clouds. Raven stood in front of the window that overlooked the bridge. Clouds rushed by the bow, fluffy white and wispy gray. The storm had moved on, a bubbling mass of purple clouds in the distance. The crew worked in seamless harmony; the pilot steered from his raised seat, the navigator pinned a map of northern Rhynwier to her wall, and the engineer sat on the other side, watching gauges and dials and levels of power that Raven didn't understand.

Raven had gone with Luckett to the bridge. Thalame and Zander had gone to see a mechanic about Zander's arm—something about a checkup. Thalame implied the mechanics expected the arm to have broken somehow in the first few hours, and Raven had chuckled at Zander's frown.

"We'll be in Silver Glen by tomorrow evening," Luckett said. "Luckily, we've been heading north anyway. If the weather holds, we might make it there by tomorrow afternoon."

Raven's stomach trembled. If the Gray Elite attacked Silver Glen... The little village wouldn't stand a chance. They had little defense aside from old pistols and a few hobbled-together crossbows. All the people she'd grown up with, her father, stepmother, Lena... She didn't want to think about what might happen to them if the Gray Elite attacked.

Raven jumped when a hand touched her shoulder. Luckett stood beside her—in their translucent reflections in the window, their similarities showed. They had the same eyes and heart-shaped face. The weight of her mother's hand felt strange and sudden, intrusive but oddly comforting.

"Don't worry," Luckett said in that motherly tone she used when she spoke to Raven, softer than her captain's bark but not as soft as Raven's stepmother's voice. "The Gray Elite might have some powerful ships, but none can outpower the *Orion*."

"I will take your word for it," Raven said.

They stood a while in silence, or in as much silence as the bridge allowed. The wind whistled against the window, the engines rumbled, and the maddening networks of pipes and speaking tubes hummed, hissed, and clanked—the airship continually thrummed.

It felt strange to stand here with her mother, as if this is what Raven should have been doing her entire life. Is this how things would have been if Raven had been raised on the *Orion*?

438

"What are you thinking about?" asked Luckett.

"What would be different about me if I had been raised here with you rather than in Silver Glen with my father," Raven said plainly.

Luckett hesitated. The hand on her shoulder twitched. Raven turned toward her, expecting her words to have found a sensitive mark, but Luckett didn't look at all aghast by the question. If anything, she looked curious.

"Hmm," Luckett hummed. "I wouldn't have kept you up here as a child. The *Orion* isn't child-safe, and small children would just get in the way."

Raven blinked. "What? You would have left me anyway?"

That struck something in Luckett, and for a brief moment, her eyes softened. It vanished as fast as a lightning strike. "You would have been under better care in Wayward Point," she said. "That's where Malik stayed until he could take orders and take care of himself. He was nine when I allowed him on the *Orion*, and even then, I had him working with others.

"Nine?" Raven hadn't been a very cautious nine-year-old. She had been in constant trouble with her father for skipping chores or sleeping during lessons or wandering into parts of the mine without worry of falling down lost shafts or getting lost.

"Malik has always been a very serious boy, and he took orders to heart. Never joked or tried funny business. Not until he met that Conrad." Luckett made a disapproving sound.

"You don't like Conrad?" Raven prepared to defend him; she had grown fond of him.

"Oh, don't get me wrong," Luckett said quickly, "the boy is a great pirate and an asset to the Crusaders. He's intelligent and clever, and he's got a mind for the seas, but..." Luckett inhaled, pulling whatever words she had to say back in.

"...but what?" Raven asked.

Luckett looked at Raven with many unsaid things behind her eyes.

Raven had her own suspicions about what those things were. "They had something, didn't they? Between them."

Luckett sighed, and her shoulders slumped. "They did," she admitted. "Malik told me about it." She chuckled halfheartedly. "I used to worry about Malik bringing back these airheaded floozies who couldn't string a sentence together. Instead, he comes back with that scoundrel. I'm afraid he got that from me. I never had good taste in men. Until your father, of course. The best man I've ever met, even if we didn't get along. Had a good heart and a good head. I just hope you got some of that. My list of good qualities isn't very long."

"You changed the subject," Raven said. Not that she had minded the compliment.

Luckett's brows rose. She looked at Raven, a beat passed, and then she let out a sigh. "Caught me," she said. "You're not as easy to distract as these pirates. A few compliments go a long way."

"Don't try it twice." Raven frowned.

Luckett chuckled; then her face became serious. "Fine, though I don't know how much of it is mine to tell. Conrad has a heart that belongs to the sea and to himself, and he broke Malik's more than once. I've told him to move on, but that's easier said than done. And I know how—"

The office door opened, and Malik strolled inside. At the sudden silence, he stilled, looking between his mother and his half-sister. His straight-line mouth fell into a frown. "What?"

For a long moment, neither of them spoke. Malik's frown deepened.

"How's Ezra?" Raven asked.

"Better." He came to stand beside Raven at the window. He stood straight, shoulders back and feet firmly planted. He crossed his arms over his narrow chest, and the daylight glinted off his rings.

There, standing between Luckett and Malik at the window, seeing their reflections side by side, Raven spotted the similarities. They all shared a nose.

Raven took a step back, eager to leave the awkwardness. "Well... If there isn't anything else, I should be going. I promised Zander we'd have lunch," she lied.

Luckett laughed. "I think you got that from me too."

"Got what?" Malik asked.

"A horrible taste in men," Luckett said plainly.

Malik's frown deepened. "You *were* talking about me!"

Luckett shrugged.

Malik's entire face turned a shade of pink. "Mother!"

"What? She's your sister," Luckett said dismissively, and Malik glanced at Raven.

She felt her own face redden.

"It's not like she'll think any less of you for having piss-poor tastes. If anything, I think she'd understand."

Raven let herself out of the office and hurried down the corridor before Luckett could embarrass either one of them again, though she couldn't help the smile that stretched across her face.

A corridor below, Raven nearly walked into Rosaria. The princess carried a tray of tea and cookies—for two.

"I thought Ezra could use a pick-me-up," Rosaria explained.

"Like a date?" Raven asked.

Rosaria didn't blush. Instead, she considered it. "No, I'd rather save dating for more romantic settings, like beaches or ballrooms or rose gardens. This is simply lunch. What about you? Any lunch plans?"

By the way she said lunch, Raven knew she meant dates.

"No," Raven said. "But I'm going to see what Thalame and Zander are doing. They went to see a mechanic."

The girls walked together until they could no longer. Rosaria headed toward the hospital, and Raven headed toward Zander and Thalame's shared room. She knocked on the rosewood door—inscribed with the symbol of a lizard—and on a verbal note of approval, she let herself in. The two boys sat in the little seating area, examining Zander's metal fingers. His arm rested on the table between them. His little finger moved a fraction farther than it had that morning.

Raven sat on the couch beside Zander. "Does it hurt?"

"I wouldn't say it hurts," Zander said thoughtfully. "It feels more like it's numb. You know when you sleep on your arm and it's numb when you wake up? The feeling is slowly coming back with pins and needles and this strange... I don't know how to explain it."

"Give it your best shot, mate," said Thalame.

Zander inhaled. "It feels like my arm is made of metal."

Raven and Thalame glanced at each other. After a beat, Raven said, "It is."

"I'm aware. I told you I didn't know how to explain it." Zander touched the little metal finger. "I can *feel* the metal, like it's a part of me."

"Magic works in its own way," said Thalame.

"Magic?"

"Magicians have a better time adapting to mechanical limbs than anyone else," he explained. "I'm sure someone could have explained it perfectly about two hundred years ago."

Before the Gray Elite began their purge of magic and magicians. Raven sighed and looked down at the little finger of Zander's mechanical arm. How much knowledge of magic had they lost? How much would they be able to retrieve? The entire task felt impossible in a way that nothing else had.

"Speaking of magic," —Thalame leaned forward— "how is yours coming along, Raven?"

"Fine," she said. Thalame held his piercing gaze on her. Zander took his eyes off his hand and looked at her. "Why?"

"You're pale," Thalame said. "If I were to put my hand against your cheek, would you feel warm?"

She put her hands to her cheeks. Indeed she felt warm, but she didn't know if it was due to the magic or Luckett's embarrassing remarks.

Zander and Thalame both gave her curious, knowing looks.

"I might not have gone to the Belt this morning," Raven admitted. Thalame frowned, started to speak, and Raven quickly motioned to Zander. "I was busy, and then Ezra showed up, and now we're rushing to Silver Glen to save it from unknown destruction. I haven't had time."

She could feel the fever worming its way through her skin.

"Well," Zander said, standing, "we've got time before we get there. Come on, show me what you can do."

Thalame stood. "Oh, it's a sight."

Raven felt a pitting of excitement and dread. She had the feeling of having been ganged up on, but she stood and slid her hand into Zander's outstretched hand, and the three of them started toward the Belt.

442

On the Belt, Thalame and Zander stood back while Raven summoned her magic—it burst from her palm in a bright yellow flame. As the flame burned, the bright yellow faded into red-orange, and the intensity of her fever diminished. The breeze whisked the top of the flame, curling it.

This high, the breeze felt cool, not the balmy breeze of summer as it would have on the world below.

"Will it always be like this?" she asked.

"Can't say," Thalame said, shrugging. "Normal magic doesn't build up like yours, at least not that I know of. And your magic is far from normal."

Zander appeared at her side. The red-orange flame reflected in his sapphire eyes and glinted off his arm. "This is what nearly killed you?" he asked, his voice soft but lined with guilt.

The flame sputtered.

Zander opened his mouth but closed it again. He looked at the flame in her hand, brows furrowed, eyes unreadable.

"It wasn't that bad," Raven said.

"Conrad told me how he had to paint the rune on your skin to keep the magic from eating you alive." Zander lifted his eyes from the flame and met hers. He wore no arrogant smirk.

She knew he would see through any lie, so she didn't bother to. "There were moments when I thought I was going to die," she said.

Zander flinched at those words.

"There were times when I didn't think I would wake up. I thought I would burn alive in my sleep. I didn't. I woke up every time. If it hadn't been for Conrad... I owe him a lot."

"So do I." Zander put his hand underneath hers. His calloused fingers brushed against hers, and with a feather-light sensation, tendrils of shadow drifted up her hand and intertwined with her flame. The red-orange of her flame and the deep plum, indigo, and black of his shadow combined into an unearthly sight; the two stems of magic burned together in a ghostly charcoal flame.

Raven couldn't describe the sensation—Zander's magic against hers felt like a cool breeze, like stepping into a shaded lagoon. The flame didn't feel hot or cold; it just existed.

"I didn't know you could do that," she said.

"It's not unheard of." Thalame appeared on her other side, eyes on the flame. "Sometimes magicians can combine their magic. Some combine better than others."

"It depends on the magicians," Zander added. "They need to trust each other."

443

She glanced away from the flame and met his eye. Trust. She hadn't flinched when he put his hand under hers. She hadn't worried about him being so close or about his magic spilling over her. She did trust him. And he trusted her, it seemed. Even after they had spent a considerable amount of time not trusting each other.

She burned through her magic with Zander's shadows surrounding it. When she let her flame die out, his shadows vanished as well. Rather than remove his hand, his fingers folded over hers.

She started to speak, but noticed the painful grimace on his face.

"The tattoo?" Raven asked.

He nodded and let go of her hand. "Mine's nearly gone." Zander turned and lifted his shirt. On the taut skin of his lower back, the swirling rune tattoo had faded to a pale gray. The skin around it had reddened.

Most Wraiths had the same tattoo. It burned off the extra magic that would otherwise attract the magic-detecting automatons. Unfortunately, the rune also burned the skin around it. The more magic, the worse the burn. Zander and Thalame both had been using their magic more, and by the look on Thalame's face, his own rune had paled.

"There's plenty of tattoo artists on board," said Thalame.

"No." Zander shook his head, letting his shirt fall back. "If we're going into war with the Gray Elite, I want all my magic. You should too. We'll need quick healing out there."

Thalame frowned. "I'd rather stay out of the fighting, mate."

"Oh, come on." Raven felt much better now that her wild magic had been defused. She hadn't even realized how much pressure had built up. "Don't you want a little excitement?"

Zander chuckled. "You're spending too much time with Conrad."

"That's bad for your health," said Thalame. "And ours."

Raven laughed as they headed back into the upper deck for lunch. Truthfully, she would rather stay out of war too. But the thought that they—a team of outcasts and magicians and pirates—could overthrow the Gray Elite empire and restore the kingdom tingled in her stomach. They could change the world if they wanted to, and she wanted to.

There were risks, but she would rather risk everything trying to change the world than cower for the rest of her life.

The *Orion* raced through the clouds and through the night. Raven found it hard to sleep, knowing she would be in Silver Glen soon, knowing she would face those she had left. Anxiety needled against her mind—she felt a glimmer of what her mother must have felt when she saw Raven for the first time.

The next morning, the air had changed. It had lost the summer heat and gained an ice-brimmed breeze—the cooler air from the mountains. The early morning sunlight stained the clouds bright blue and gold. Raven could see the distant peaks, bruised purples and faint blues and grays. It reminded her of when she used to stare at the southern horizon and pretend the clouds were far away mountains, full of adventure and mystery and magic.

Raven stood on the Belt, her magic flame flickering against the breeze, and gazed down at Hammel Forest. It stretched so far. It hadn't seemed so big when she and Zander traveled through it. How many times had she climbed her tree to gaze at the endless forest and dream of what lay beyond it? How many times had she stared at the sky, looking for airships and sky cities?

She felt a squeeze in her chest—she silenced her flame immediately. Wooziness overtook her senses, and she grasped onto the railing to steady herself. She hadn't been paying attention to her magic; she had gotten lost in a daydream. Luckily, no one else had come with her to the Belt. She didn't feel like listening to Thalame's scolding or Conrad's teasing or Zander's worry. The woozy spell passed. Her lack of sleep the night before likely had something to do with it too. Conrad had briefly mentioned how sleep rejuvenated magic better and faster than any potion or tonic.

"What are you doing up here?" came Zander's voice through the wind. He appeared beside her. He had tied his hair behind his head, and the wind whipped the loose strands behind him.

"Trying not to lose my mind," Raven said halfheartedly.

"Nervous?"

"Oh, no, not at all," Raven said, her voice light. "Why should I be nervous about seeing my father, who I left without a word?"

Zander shrugged, though his eyes trailed to the north. He couldn't hide his nervousness either.

"Going through your magic?" he asked.

"I'm already finished."

His brow raised.

"I've been here since just past dawn."

Zander whistled. "Let's go back inside." He nodded toward the doors and flashed her a wolfish grin. "I know something that might take your mind off it."

She glared.

He laughed. "Not that. Something else."

He took a step toward the doors, and she heaved a sigh and followed.

Something else turned out to be a long cargo hold in the lower decks that Zander and Thalame had set up like a shooting range. Three portholes allowed in the buttery morning light, tinting the discolored metal walls. The floor looked to be made of several different types of metal—steel and bronze and a strange bluish metal she'd never seen before.

Zander pulled Birdie from the holster—an awkward motion with his left arm in a sling.

"Is it going to affect your aim?" Raven asked.

"I don't know." Zander aimed Birdie at the targets on the far side of the room, set up at different lengths. He pulled the hammer back. "Give me the count."

She blinked; she'd nearly forgotten about that. She stepped into his peripheral and raised her fist into the air, splaying her fingers.

"Five," she said, and lowered her thumb. She counted down—putting down a finger each time—until only her index finger remained in the air. She hesitated before she put down her finger, mostly to annoy him, but he did not complain. She closed her fingers into a tight fist—the first bullet exploded from the barrel.

Bang! Bang! Bang!

Three targets, three bullet holes.

"Oh, I guess it hasn't affected my aim," Zander said haughtily.

Raven scoffed. "How is watching your target practice supposed to help me?"

"Because you're next," he said. "Come here."

She blinked—he had removed his hand from the trigger and held Birdie out to her. She gawked. "You're letting me touch her?"

Zander sighed. "I know, strange how things happen. Now, come here before I change my mind."

Raven took cautious steps to where Zander stood. He never let anyone else shoot Birdie. She was a beauty of a pistol, dark steel and red leather. Raven gently folded her hand around the grip. Zander stood behind and adjusted her fingers.

"Don't put your finger on the trigger until you're ready to shoot," Zander said in her ear. "Be careful not to get pinched by the hammer. Hurts like hell."

He adjusted her stance, talked her through aiming, and then released his guiding hand from hers. Raven looked at Birdie. The pistol had always been a strange extension of Zander, the prized possession he never went anywhere without, and he had let Raven hold her. It had demolished a wall between them she hadn't realized existed, and a different form of intimacy grew in its place.

"Ready?" Zander stepped into her peripheral, a safe distance away. He held up five fingers.

"Yes."

"Five." Zander started the countdown, and when he held his fist in the air, she pulled the trigger.

The kickback surprised her, and the bullet flew wide. It landed in one of the crates against the back wall.

"Try again," Zander said, no teasing in his voice.

She did—her second bullet missed, so did her third and fourth. Her fifth struck the edge of the target. Her sixth hit.

Zander laughed. "See? Practice."

"I'm glad to know it's not a natural talent of yours," she said, gazing sideways at him.

He smirked, and as he showed her how to reload Birdie, he told her about his time in the Gray Elite Academy. They trained for years to learn how to shoot with deadly accuracy, how to clean a multitude of guns, and how to handle aiming in combat.

"By the time a cadet graduates, they can hit a bullseye in the dark," Zander said. "Or so that's the plan."

"Can you?" Raven asked.

With a precise jerk of his wrist, the chamber slammed back into place. He shrugged. "Can't say. I've never tried. Seemed like a waste of bullets."

He set Birdie back in her hand, and this time, she only missed once. Granted, she took a lot longer to aim than he did. When she had emptied the chamber, she glanced at Zander—he was looking back at her with an expression of longing, of pride. He blinked, and the expression vanished.

"Hmm? See something you like?" Raven placed her free hand on her hip.

"I see several things I like," Zander said, sauntering over. "But it would take too long to list them all."

He slid Birdie from her grip and leaned his mouth toward hers. She leaned in to meet him—the door to the cargo hold creaked open.

"Ah, there you two are," came Thalame's dry rasp.

Zander sighed and straightened. He flicked his wrist and started to reload Birdie. "Great timing."

"No problem, mate." Thalame grinned like he knew. He carried two wooden practice swords over his shoulders. "I thought we'd see how much you learned while you've been gone. Feeling up to a combat lesson?"

Raven shrugged and held her hand out for the sword.

"Oh, and new rule," Thalame started, "no magic allowed."

Raven hadn't learned anything new since she had last trained with Thalame, and it showed. He didn't comment on it. Zander stood to the side—the medics and mechanics forbade him from any activities that might endanger his new arm. He focused instead on cleaning Birdie.

The morning went by in a blur. Raven tired herself out—but it didn't alleviate the anxiety tugging on her lungs and pushing on her ribs.

They shared lunch with Conrad and Rosaria, who then joined them in their practice room. Rosaria sparred with Raven—and won. Growing up with the Hawks, Rosaria had been trained in combat—she whispered to Raven how she had beaten Zander when they were younger, much to his fury.

"That's because I went easy on you," Zander said, having overheard. "I didn't want to hit you."

Raven half laughed as she slumped against the wall underneath the portholes. The sunlight had grown brighter in the afternoon.

Rosaria snorted. "So you say."

"That sounds like a fine excuse." Raven shared a knowing glance with the princess.

Zander scowled. "Just give me a few weeks. I'll show you."

Rosaria glanced down at his mechanical arm. Sympathy shadowed her eyes for a moment, then the brightness returned. "I doubt you'll be any better this time around."

Raven didn't see much of Malik, and she assumed he either didn't want to be around them or had other duties. According to Thalame, he had been spending a lot of time with the refugees, going over their options.

"He knows people," Zander chimed in. He took a long drink from his canteen. "All over the continent. He can get people to either end without the Gray Elite catching wind."

Conrad dropped his voice, adding, "Rumor has it, he's on the hill to becoming the next grand master."

"I wouldn't doubt it," Thalame said. "The Wraiths trust Malik. He'd be a good leader."

Raven sat on the floor, catching her breath; she didn't have the energy to ask them what they were talking about. Raven didn't know what all a seeker did, but Malik always seemed busy.

As the sun sank toward the west, a series of bells sounded. Raven's heart jumped into her throat.

Destination sighted.

Raven followed Conrad to the air docks. Standing on the catwalks, she watched Silver Glen appear through the thick forest, a spotting of wooden roofs and dirt paths. Her village rested at the base of the mountains, ramshackle and half-reclaimed by nature. She couldn't see the entrance to the mines from the air docks, but she could see the fake tree that served as their Lookout Tower. The bell would have been rung by now, and everyone in Silver Glen would know about the approaching sky city.

The *Orion* slowed. Its engine calmed, and the fans kicked on, allowing the sky city to hover.

Luckett wanted Raven to be the first to make contact. Silver Glen knew her, and her father would be less likely to shoot her on sight than a stranger. So Raven followed Conrad along the catwalks to a medium-sized airship of pale steel and yellow wings. Zander followed a step behind.

Conrad climbed into the cockpit of the airship, and Raven stepped into the hull. Zander gave her an encouraging nod—he offered no words of comfort. He looked as nervous as she felt.

"I'm sure it'll be fine," Conrad said as he started the engine.

Raven didn't have it in her to speak. Her nerves rattled like she'd swallowed crickets. She slumped into the passenger seat behind Conrad, where she could see through the front window.

A team of Crusaders unhooked the airship from the rigging. The ship swayed to the side, and then fell. Raven gasped—the sensation of falling fizzed from her toes, along her bones and skin, and to her scalp in a few short seconds—and then the ship's engine roared and started forward. Conrad steered them on a gentle downward slope, wearing a wide grin.

"You could have warned me about the drop," Raven said, breathless. The sensation ghosted over her skin.

"But then your reaction wouldn't have been genuine," Conrad whined.

The airship descended, and with every passing moment, her heart thudded harder. Silver Glen grew larger. Raven spotted a gathering outside the lopsided wooden structure that served as an inn and trading post. Among the villagers stood her father, tall and wide and imposing. He stood with his arms crossed, and he wore a deep frown. He and the others watched the airship land on a stretch of dirt and grass that had once been a sheep pen. The engines blew dust and old leaves into the air behind it.

Conrad idled the engine, and the lack of sound only made her thudding heart that much louder. Raven stared at her father through the window. He took a step

449

toward the airship, the others held strong behind him. None of them looked happy or welcoming. They looked threatened and ready to defend their home.

"Feeling good?"

"I feel like I might vomit," she said.

"Do that outside, please." Conrad frowned. "It takes weeks for the smell to go away. Seriously, puke outside."

She fumbled with the door's latch. It finally came open, and she took a deep breath as she took the first step outside.

Her father was walking toward the ship, hand on his pistol, ready to shoot. As his eyes fell on her, he stopped. Their eyes met. The angry, suspicious frown fell away from his face, and disbelief replaced it. Her heart stopped and sped up at the same time. He looked the same: short brown hair, strong jaw, and imposing stature. Raven took a shaky step toward her father, and then another. She stopped in front of him, and for a long moment, neither moved nor spoke.

And then her father dropped his pistol and wrapped his arms around her. The embrace knocked the air from her lungs. Her feet left the ground, and he spun her—just like he had when she'd been small. Her feet met solid ground again, and her father held her tight for a long moment before he released her.

"Raven," he breathed. He cupped her cheek. Tears lined his eyes—Raven blinked twice. She had never seen her father, the strongest man in the village, cry. "You're alive."

She had no response. Any words she'd had vanished at the sight of her father's watery eyes.

He embraced her again. One hand cradled the back of her head as he let those tears fall into her hair.

"Dad," Raven started. She didn't know how to continue. She'd expected him to shout, to scold, to point out all the things she had done wrong. She'd expected guilt, and she felt it—tremendously so—even more so than had he yelled. She returned his embrace, albeit awkwardly, and managed to say, "I'm sorry."

"I'm sorry," said her father. He said it twice more before he released her. He set his hands on her shoulders and held her at arm's length, his grip gentle as if he feared she would vanish again. His eyes were puffy and red. "Where the hell have you been? Mel told me she sent you out, but we assumed you'd be back in a few days. No one heard a word. I thought you'd been taken. I thought you'd been killed. I didn't know what happened. I..." He sighed. His eyes hardened into the look she had expected. His grip on her shoulders tightened. "Then we got word the Gray Elite had put a price on your head and that they were hunting you down."

"They are still hunting her down," said Conrad. He stood beside Raven, just outside of her father's reach. His familiar lilted words felt so strange in Silver Glen, beside her father's harsh tongue and calloused words.

Her father frowned at Conrad. He took in Conrad's assortment of daggers, his tunic and trousers, his dirty leather boots, his waist-long braids, and golden necklaces. Raven knew what her father likely wanted to say—something about men and long hair—but he held in his words.

"Who are you?" her father asked.

"No time for that." Conrad looked to Raven, motioning for her to continue.

Her father started to argue, but Raven cleared her throat, stealing his attention back. "Right," she started, clapping her hands together. "Do you have a minute? I need to talk to you about a few things."

"What?" Samuel Thane asked his daughter, eyes wide and brows high.

"We need to evacuate," Raven repeated, holding firm under her father's gaze. In her mind, she pictured herself like her mother, shoulders back and head proud.

Her father stared at her, the news of the Gray Elite's impending attack still processing. They had gone to the trading post, and Raven told her father the quickest explanation of her adventure, boiling it down to the essentials. Her father sat back in the chair, watered-down ale in hand, listening with a blank face.

"We've received intelligence that the Gray Elite could be on their way here, right now," Conrad added onto the heels of her story. He stood behind Raven's chair, foot resting on the bottom rung. "And unless you don't mind them stomping around your home and bullying you for information, you need to come with us."

"I can't just leave my—"

"*All* of you," Conrad clarified.

Her father glared at Conrad. He hated being interrupted. "And where would we go? This is our home." He motioned to the shoddy trading post.

"I know," Raven said, a plea on her words. "It's not permanent. It's to protect you from whatever horrible fate the Gray Elite have in mind. They know I'm from here, and they would hurt you to hurt me, or hold you captive and torture you all to spite me."

Her father's frown deepened. "You've really gotten yourself into trouble."

"I'm eyeball deep in trouble." Raven shrugged. "There's nothing I can do about it right now. Like it or not, you are in danger, and I'd rather the empire not find any of you."

"Or this all might be a simple mistaken rumor," Conrad said, his tone light. "But it's better to be on the safe side, don't you think?"

Her father let out a grievous sigh and ran a hand through his hair. "Fine." He looked to the other villagers. "We evacuate, but we will return when it's safe."

Raven nodded. A weight lifted from her shoulders. Her family would be safe.

"All right, now that that's settled," Conrad started. "Tell your people to bring only the essentials. The *Orion* is stocked with the basics and food."

Conrad returned to the airship, and Raven went with her father to start the evacuation. Returning to the mines felt strange after all that had happened, and given the current situation, her presence did not go unnoticed. She caught more than a few odd stares and whispers on the way to her father's office—not unlike the days when they whispered of her rule-breaking. This time, she did not shy away from their stares. She held herself tall and strong, like her mother, like Rosaria, like Ivy.

Her father delivered his orders of evacuation into the speaking tubes in his office; they connected with every other important part of the mines—the workshops and smiths, the kitchens, the foundry. He didn't explain why Silver Glen had to evacuate; he promised to explain after the evacuation.

Standing in her father's office felt stranger still. The last time she'd been here, he took her off scavenging duty and put her on kitchen duty. She'd left in tears. That was the last time she had seen her father, and likewise the last night he had seen her. Guilt tightened in her chest.

Her eyes settled on a ticking bauble—the one he had knocked off in his rage that day. It's tail stick ticked.

"Raven?" came her father's commanding tone.

She snapped out of her daze.

He stood on the other side of his desk, looking at her. He opened his mouth to speak, but then closed it again. "Come on. We've got people to look after."

The next hour passed in a blur of confused faces, unhappy children, and worried whispers and questions. Everyone carried bags and satchels—bare essentials and prized possessions. Raven stood with Conrad on the surface as an airship ferried load after load of people from Silver Glen to the *Orion*. While they managed the evacuation on the surface, her father managed it from within the mines. Her father allowed only a few people out of the mines at once, as to not draw attention. From *whom*, he didn't say.

The people passed Raven and Conrad as they boarded the airship. Most gave her an odd stare of recognition; most blinked twice at Conrad.

Raven kept one eye on the sky as the airship came and went, carrying Silver Glen to safety. The empty skies made her nervous. How far behind were the Gray Elite? Were they on their way? Would there be a Silver Glen to return to?

"Raven?"

It was a voice she knew, and it took less than a heartbeat to find the familiar face and flaxen hair.

Raven's smile stretched. "Sweets!"

Sweets pushed through the crowd and wrapped her arms around Raven. It felt like ages since she had seen the other girl. They had been inseparable as children, and Raven hadn't realized how her absence had felt until she embraced her again. Sweets's blonde hair had grown out a bit, and she wore it in two braids on either side of her head. Goggles sat on top of her head, the lenses framed with decorative brass.

"Those are new?" Raven asked.

"That's right. You missed it." Sweets grinned and blush warmed her cheeks. "These were an engagement gift from Brent."

"Really?" Raven clapped her hands together. She had long suspected something more than friendship between her two friends, and the confirmation warmed something deep in her chest.

"We were worried like hell, you know." Sweets frowned at Raven, then looked up to the *Orion*-shaped shadow on the clouds. "I was starting to think you'd found somewhere more exciting to live. I guess I was sort of right. Your father was a mess. He tried to hide it, but we all knew how worried he was. We kept expecting you and Zander to show up one day."

The guilt that had somewhat unraveled tightened again. Raven tried to keep her face neutral, but Sweets nudged her. "I feel guilty as hell, don't worry."

Above, the airship ferry pushed through the clouds and steadily descended to the ground. The engine buzzed louder and louder.

"Oh, well, that's good." Sweets had to yell to be heard over the airship's buzzing. "And it's good to see you alive and well. I expect the full story."

"You'll get it," Raven said.

The airship landed, sending waves of wind through the tall grass and weeds all around it. Her father's booming voice commanded, "Let's move, move."

Sweets gave Raven's arm a gentle squeeze and then climbed into the waiting airship. Brent followed—he gave Raven a nod in silent greeting.

"All right," came her father's voice. "This is the last. The mines are empty."

"Are you sure?" Conrad asked. "I'd hate to come up a few people short."

Her father scowled. "Yes, I'm sure. I checked every room, as did my wife. There's no one left inside."

Raven had noticed but not registered the few people following her father out of the mines. Her stepmother and half-sister, Lena, were among the last out. Her stepmother was fussing over something, and then Lena's eyes shifted and met Raven's. Lena's eyes widened; she dropped her bag and threw her arms around Raven.

"Raven!" Lena started to cry. Raven hugged her tighter. "Dad didn't say you were here!"

"I'll tell you the whole story," Raven promised, "but later."

"We are running out of time." The casual humor on Conrad's face had faded with every ferry, edging on a seriousness that made Raven uneasy. He kept glancing at the sky too.

Lena shouldered her bag and accepted Conrad's hand as she stepped into the airship. Her stepmother followed—pausing long enough to give Raven a motherly stroke on the cheek. Her father boarded last. Raven took one last look at shabby structures and hidden mine of Silver Glen, then turned to climb into the airship—then she heard it.

A humming from the sky. A new, high-pitched humming.

She glanced at Conrad. His lips turned downward, and his brows creased.

"Hurry," he said to the pilot. "We're not alone in the skies."

The engine whirled. Raven climbed inside as the airship started to rise, and Conrad jumped on board with feline ease. He pulled the steel door closed and latched it. An uneasy mumbling came from the final passengers. Most had never left Silver Glen or seen an airship. The airship rose above the treeline; through the pothole, Silver Glen shrank and then vanished.

Raven leaned against the welded metal wall and released a breath.

"What's that?" asked her father.

"Shit," Conrad hissed.

Raven wrenched her eyes open. Her father and Conrad were looking through the front window. She pushed her way between them.

Her breath vanished from her throat.

Black dots spotted the southeast horizon, and they were growing large with every passing second.

"Sisters," her father breathed.

The dots multiplied. The closest had doubled in size. Raven swallowed.

"We're not alone," said the pilot, worry on every word. "Company from the southeast. And they're moving fast."

"I doubt the captain missed them," Conrad said.

"You got guns on this thing?" her father barked.

"It's a transporter," Conrad drawled. At her father's glare, he added, "That means no."

Her father growled. "What use is a ship without firepower?"

Halfway to the *Orion*, the distant dots became white and yellow airships.

"Buzzers," said the pilot.

"The Gray Elite were on the way." Conrad's voice lacked its usual humor.

Their airship pushed through the clouds. For a moment, the skies were clear, and then a dozen Buzzers burst through the clouds to the southeast. This close, the Gray Elite crest on the hulls gleamed in the sunlight.

"Hold on," spat the pilot.

Gunfire peppered the air. It echoed like broken thunder, and for a terrifying moment, Raven's world went gray. Bits of metal clattered against the transporter, her stepmother gasped and latched onto her father's arm, and Raven started to fall. Conrad grabbed her and held her upright.

Holes in the airship—daylight came through in beams.

Airships fell from the belly of the *Orion*. Engines roared to life and raced toward the incoming Gray Elite, streaks of bronze and steel against the clouds. Shrieking engines and gunfire shook the sky.

"We're hit," came the pilot's distant voice. "We've got injured."

Conrad leaned over the pilot's seat. "How bad?"

"We'll hold." The pilot gave it more speed.

Conrad pulled Raven toward him, and another pair of hands rested on her shoulders.

"You'll be fine," Conrad said.

Raven blinked. Blood smeared on her hands. Had she been hit? She didn't feel anything. They raced over the clouds, leaving the firefight behind. The engine under her feet whirled and choked; a tremor raved through Raven's chest.

Then she felt it—a sharp, hot pain on her abdomen.

"You'll be fine," came her father's voice this time.

She began to shake, and the color and sound returned to the world. It moved too fast, too loud. The ship docked in the *Orion*. A team hooked it into the rigging, the engines quit, and a Crusader opened the door.

"Medic," called Conrad. "Where's Thalame?"

Raven fell into the arms of a waiting Crusader. She could feel the blood leaving her body.

"Single file. Don't look down," said the pirate to the others, well-practiced words.

"My daughter—"

"Will be fine."

Raven felt the darkness on the edge of her vision, cold and clammy and breathless. It pulled and pulled. Her stomach turned over. A cold sweat broke out over her skin.

She fell under.

Raven came in and out. She felt warmth, like the midday sun on her bare skin. She heard the distant call of gulls. She heard chimes, sweet and gentle and low-toned. She heard voices, muffled by walls. She opened her eyes and found herself on the catwalks of the Orion. She blinked. The warmth remained, but it faded with every second.

Thalame knelt at her side, his eyes focused, healing her.

The catwalks buzzed with activity. The chaos of the gun fight raged below, popping and blasting.

"There we go," Thalame said. "Can you stand?"

Raven nodded. Thalame helped her to her feet. The pain had lessened considerably, though she felt the slick of fresh blood on her shirt and pants, and she felt it clotting in the threads.

The strange comfort of the dream faded, and the organized chaos and panic of the air docks returned. Her father and the others stood around her—they hadn't gone into the ship. They had waited for her. With her back on her feet, the procession continued into the *Orion*.

Raven leaned on Conrad as her family and the last of Silver Glen's people followed a Crusader along the catwalks, each looking down, except for her father. He cast his eyes around the air docks, nothing of surprise showing on his face. Of course, according to her mother, he had worked on an airship before. He'd be familiar with it all.

The Crusader led them into the lower deck. Inside the *Orion*, the gunfire sounded distant, but no less threatening.

"You were shot," Conrad whispered to Raven, low enough her father couldn't hear.

"I'm aware." The blood had begun to dry, and it pulled at her skin with every step.

Conrad smirked. "No, I mean you were shot a few minutes ago and bleeding profusely, and now you're walking like it didn't happen."

"Thalame's a skilled healer."

Conrad's smirk widened.

"What?" she hissed.

"I've never seen Thalame heal someone that fast, especially not with a wound like that one. It might have killed anyone else."

She opened her mouth, the words *I'm not anyone else* on the tip of her tongue at the same time a foreign bitterness clamped around her chest—she bit the words back. A strange sensation oozed through her skin, and she hadn't the words to describe it. The words and bitterness had not been her own—they had pulsed from somewhere else. She swallowed the words and the feeling.

"My magic, I guess," she whispered back.

Your magic?

Conrad gave her a suspicious, knowing smile.

The Crusader led them into the mess hall—the only place on the ship big enough to hold all the people of Silver Glen, aside from the cargo hold. People sat around the mismatched wooden tables. A few of the kitchen crew had brought out a cask of ale. As Samuel entered, the frightful murmuring calmed. Raven followed her father toward the front of the mess hall. She felt eyes shift to her, as they had in the mine. She held herself like Rosaria, regal and confident, despite the quaky feeling of intrusion in her stomach and the blood clotting on her clothes.

"What's going on outside?" one of the smiths asked. "We heard gunfire. A voice came over the air, saying something about enemy ships. What does it mean?"

Conrad leaned in to Raven and whispered, "It means we were none too early."

"Is Silver Glen under attack? Why?" asked someone else.

The panic returned, a fraction softer than it had been before.

Samuel held up his hand, quieting the panic in their voices but not their eyes. All in the room looked to her father. Raven spotted Sweets and Brent standing together, the girls from the kitchen, and the elders. Mel stood among them, looking solemn as ever.

"The Gray Elite have come to Silver Glen." Samuel's booming voice reached every part of the mess hall. "It was not a friendly visit. They came armed, as you've heard. We barely made it out in time. If not for my daughter and her friends, we would have been on the receiving end of that gunfire."

A murmur sounded at those words, and many eyes looked to Raven and Conrad. Conrad waved.

"But why?" asked her stepmother, her voice soft but strong. "What have we done to invoke the empire's wrath?"

Samuel hesitated, his eyes hard. He turned his attention to Raven, and within a few long heartbeats, all eyes were on her. Waiting for the explanation.

She swallowed, and with a nudge from Conrad, stepped up beside her father. "War is brewing." Disquiet met her words. She did not command the room like her father, but within the silence, it did not matter. "Silver Glen was likely only the first."

She felt gazes on her bloodied trousers and blouse and the dagger visible at her waist. Most women in Silver Glen wore dresses and corsets and did not arm themselves. They cooked, cleaned, and raised the children. Raven had grown up with disapproving glances and pitied stares, but it did not make it easier.

She couldn't admit that the attack had been revenge on her, that she had caused this, that she was to blame for their displacement. Yet she suspected they already knew.

She was saved from any more awkward talking by a knock. Malik entered the mess hall, rings catching the lantern light. Malik glanced to Samuel; Samuel glanced at him. Recognition passed over both their faces.

"The captain requests an audience," Malik said to Raven.

"Captain?" Samuel asked, the word venomous on his tongue. He looked between Malik and Raven, knowing. He rubbed his face and let out a groan of realization. "Son of a bitch."

Conrad smirked; Malik shot him a glare.

"What is it?" asked her stepmother, touching her husband's elbow. She looked between Malik, Conrad, and Raven.

Samuel looked around the mess hall. "I knew this hunk of junk looked familiar."

"You've been here?" she asked.

Samuel took a deep breath. "The captain is an old friend of mine."

Friend. Raven recognized that tone. Disgruntled and surprised—and by the look on her stepmother's face, she recognized that tone too.

"I'm coming with you to this meeting," Samuel said to Raven.

She nodded. "Okay."

Malik looked like he wanted to protest but didn't.

"Make sure everyone's all right," Samuel said to his wife. "I'll be back soon."

She nodded. "I'll take care of things here."

Malik led Raven, Samuel, and Conrad to Luckett's office above the bridge. No one spoke. Conrad looked delighted by the awkward air, and Malik looked like he would rather be anywhere else. By the time they had entered, the gunfire had ended, and the *Orion* had started to move again.

Luckett stood by the speaking tubes, shoulders back, face calm in concentration. Her red coat had been thrown over the back of her chair. Her dark blue corset hugged her narrow waist, and a pistol and dagger hung off her hips. Voices were coming through the tubes, from all parts of the ship, reporting in.

"...all ships returned. A few casualties. Nothing major. No dead. Mostly minor repairs."

"...engines on full steam."

"Keep south," Luckett barked into the tubes.

"Aye, Captain!"

"What of the Gray Elite Buzzers?" Luckett asked into yet another tube.

"Scrap metal, Captain."

"Good." She leaned onto her desk. "Keep the ships ready in case the Gray Elite make a surprise visit."

"Aye, Captain."

"Captain," Malik said from the other side of the room.

"Ah, you're here," Luckett said, striding around her desk. If she looked surprised to see them all there, she held it in well. Her gaze settled on Samuel, then

Raven. She leaned against the rosewood, arms crossed. "The Gray Elite followed us. We led them right to Silver Glen."

Raven's heart tumbled through her ribs. "What?" she gasped.

"You did what?" Samuel stormed toward the desk and slammed his fist onto the rosewood. "You led them to my doorstep?"

Luckett didn't look the least bit intimidated.

"We led them?" Raven asked, her voice a whisper. She had led the Gray Elite to her family's door. She might as well have introduced them.

Malik stepped closer to her. "It's not your fault."

Raven swallowed and added, "How?"

"Deacon's boy," Luckett said, annoyed. "He didn't do it on purpose, but the Buzzers followed him. I went to him first and accused him of lying. The boy looked about ready to pass out on me. He's a terrible liar. I'd bet gold that father of his knew he'd end up a turncoat and planted the information as a failsafe, knowing his son would turn to us."

General Deacon had again delivered a blow, and he had used his own son to do it.

"I suggest you not yell at him," Luckett said to Samuel, her words a warning. "I already have. Boy nearly cried."

Conrad failed to conceal a chuckle, earning him a glare from Malik.

"So," Luckett said, straightening. "Sam, how have you been?"

Raven's father looked like he might burst, caught between anger and disbelief.

"I've been damn swell, Bailey," Luckett said in a deep voice, an imitation of Samuel's. "Thanks for saving our asses back there and taking care of our daughter. You're the best." Her voice returned to her own cadence, and she said, "Oh, you're still the dashing type."

Samuel groaned and pushed away from the desk, from Luckett. He made a lap around the office, glaring through the window to the bridge, to the clouds parted by the bow. "This is your ship?" he asked without looking at her.

"She sure is," Luckett said. "Renamed her *Orion*. I thought it had a better ring to it, and besides, a new captain means a new name for the ship. It's tradition."

"What happened to Captain Elbert?"

"Dead."

"How?"

Luckett scoffed. "What do you mean 'how'? The man was ninety years old and drank a barrel of rum a week. I'm surprised he lived as long as he did."

Samuel heaved a sigh and stalked to the chairs in front of the desk. He sat without grace. "What happened?"

"Quite a lot," said Luckett as she meandered around her desk. She plopped into her ornate chair. She propped her boots on the corner and glanced at Raven. "It's quite the tale too. I struck a bad deal a few months back and landed in the Tombs. I thought I'd die down there when one day Raven shows up, melts the lock right off my cell door, and I make a quiet escape. Thanks to the madness on the surface, I was able to get back to the sky relatively unscathed."

Samuel sat in silence for a long moment. Then, he turned his gaze to Raven. "You melted a lock?" Each word was careful and unsure.

Raven sat in the chair beside his. "It's more complicated than that," she said. "But yes, I did. I, uh, might have left a few things out of the story I told you earlier. We were pressed for time."

"We have time now," said her father.

"I'll call for tea." Luckett jumped to her feet and delivered the order to the speaking tubes, her tone calm and pleasant, as if they hadn't just survived a gunfire storm, evacuated an entire village, and were hiding from an angry and vengeful empire.

Over tea, Raven explained everything, starting with the Cage Birds that had attacked her and Zander months before. She told him about the centrum and Altair's Augur and Zander's true intentions for coming to Silver Glen. She told him everything.

Her father did not speak. He listened—for the first time she could remember, he actually listened to her. His fingers were curled into white-knuckles fists, but he listened.

Of course, Conrad added his own tidbits into the story, flourishing his appearances, particularly at the arena in Wayward Point. Luckett stayed quiet, as did Malik. Both listened with the same intensity.

Telling the story, the whole story, felt easier than lying. She didn't have to stop and think of what she was saying or what she shouldn't say. It felt...alleviating to have everything in the open, and yet vulnerable at the same time.

When Raven's story came to an end, she took a drink of the tea she had made some time ago. It had cooled but still soothed her dry throat. She didn't think she had ever talked so much in her life.

"You're a magician now?" Her father hadn't touched his tea. He had leaned forward onto his knees, hands together, fingers laced. Raven had seen the expression plenty—it was his thinking face.

Raven summoned a flame to the palm of her hand. Samuel grimaced.

"And now the entire Gray Elite empire is hunting her for it," Conrad said lightly, perching on the edge of the desk.

"Thank you for reminding me," Raven muttered. She released her flame but held her warm hand against the teacup, heating the contents.

"You need to go into hiding," Samuel said sternly. Disapproval hung on each word. "Silver Glen would have been the best place."

"Not anymore," Luckett said. "It's been compromised."

"Thanks to you." Samuel glared at Luckett.

"Thanks to a clever son of a bitch in Moorin," Luckett snapped, glaring back at him. "The sky is the safest place. She's protected up here."

"She would have been protected on the ground."

"Nonsense. There's more firepower up here, not including her own."

"Raven doesn't need to fight."

"She might not have a choice. If she's attacked, she'll have to defend herself."

"If she's well protected, she won't have to fight."

"Some girls don't need protection. Some are very capable of protecting themselves."

"This isn't some pirate den, Bailey, we're talking about the Gray Elite. An empire."

"I'm well aware of the danger."

"Then start acting like it."

Raven cleared her throat loudly, bringing her parents' argument to an awkward end. Both pairs of burning eyes turned toward her. She knew then why her parents had not ended up together. They were both stubborn and looked in opposing directions.

"Raven left out the part where she melted a Colossus automaton into a pile of molten goo," added Conrad, a wicked smile tugging at his lips. "Turned the Gray Elite speechless!"

"You *what*?" Samuel asked, eyes wide and angry.

Raven turned a seething glare onto Conrad. He winked back at her. She had purposefully downplayed their dramatic escape from Moorin.

462

To her father, she said, "It was that or die."

"See?" Luckett motioned to Raven. "She is her own protection. She doesn't need a village of old-fashioned ninnies with clubs."

"That's not the point!" Samuel seethed.

"She's not a child, Sam. You can't lock her in a safe like some porcelain teapot."

"Stop!" Raven jumped to her feet. She slammed the teacup back onto the tray with enough force to slosh most of it out.

As she stood, the fever rushed from her feet to her head. The world wobbled. She felt herself tilt and grabbed onto the desk. She took several shaky breaths, and the world slowly righted itself, and the fever retreated. She blinked; Conrad's hand held her shoulder. Concern flashed in his eyes—eyes that were looking around her, not at her. At her magic.

"Raven—" her father started.

"Stop fighting about me like I'm not here." Raven looked between her father and her mother.

Luckett cleared her throat. "What do you think?" Samuel started to speak, but she held up her hand. "Let Raven speak for herself."

Spoken like a captain.

Samuel glared at Luckett before turning his attention to Raven.

Slowly, the fever receded to wherever it slept nowadays. Raven straightened, and Conrad pulled his hand from her shoulder.

Raven cleared her throat. "We can't change what's happened. The Gray Elite can't hunt us as easily up here as they could on the ground. Right now, I think it's best we stay above the clouds. And I can fight for myself."

Luckett grinned. Samuel frowned.

"I've been learning how to fight," Raven told her father. "I'm not as useless with a sword as I used to be."

Her father's frown deepened. "Sword? You've been sword fighting?"

"Considering she can shoot fire from her hands, a sword seems a bit nonessential, doesn't it?" asked Conrad.

Luckett nodded.

Samuel sighed deeply and hung his head. He ran his hand through his short brown hair and sighed again. "Fine."

"I know it's hard when you're not in charge anymore," Luckett said absently. "But try to be on your best behavior, Sam."

He inhaled like he had a lot he wanted to say, but he held it. He glared instead.

Luckett stood up and grabbed her red coat. "I've got to check on things below decks. Come on, I'll walk you back to the mess hall." She tugged on her coat and marched to the doors.

They followed Luckett into the corridor. Raven's stomach quivered, though having Conrad's effortless confidence on one side and Malik's silent strength on her other, she felt better.

"I aim to have proper rooms set up by tonight, but there'll be some crowding. Five or so to a room," said Luckett.

"That's fine," Samuel said. "We're safe. That's what matters most."

"Correct," Luckett said. "However, until we can restock, I'll have to place some rations on food and water."

"Understood," Samuel said.

The list of things went on, but Raven didn't entirely listen. She focused on the magic, the fever. Her parents' argument had caused it to spike, but it had since returned to its semi-calm state deep inside of her. She felt a ghost of that spike under her skin, pulsing against her, waiting to lash out. It felt...wild and violent, and she didn't know what to do about it. Conrad and Malik, both being seekers, would have sensed it too. Which is why, she assumed, they walked on either side of her.

They approached the mess hall, and her father let out a grunt of disapproval—a sound she knew by heart. She looked up to see what had caused it.

Rosaria and Zander stood in the corridor, talking to her stepmother and Lena. At the sight of Samuel, relief came over her stepmother's face. Rosaria and Zander both turned, and Raven felt the change. He stiffened, his fists curled, and his shoulders strained.

Within a heartbeat no one could have stopped, Zander and Samuel exchanged a heated glance; Luckett and Samuel's wife sized one another up with a shrewdness Raven had never seen in her stepmother; and Rosaria and Conrad observed it all with clever eyes. Both of them must have known the awkwardness of it all.

"You're alive and well," Samuel said to Zander, his eyes blazing. "Mostly."

Zander shrugged, jostling the fingers of his limp metal arm. "Mostly."

"I hear you're the reason my daughter up and left in the middle of the night and now has an empire hunting her down."

Zander started to spit something back, but Luckett held up her hand.

"Do your revenge shouting later," said Luckett, an order. She turned to Samuel's wife and added, "We'll have rooms for you all by tonight. I've given Sam the details, but I'll have more in an hour."

"That is good to hear." Raven's stepmother smiled, but she looked exhausted. "I think sleeping on the floor up here sounds much better than sleeping in a prison cell down there or dead."

"As would any sane person," Luckett said, her words aimed at Samuel.

Samuel huffed and started toward the mess hall. "Let me know when more details are available," he sharply said to Luckett.

"Will do." Luckett crossed her arms.

Raven's father, stepmother, and sister vanished back into the mess hall, but not without a sweet goodbye from Lena to Rosaria. The doors to the mess hall closed, and Samuel's booming voice could be heard reassuring his people.

"Your sister is a sweetheart," Rosaria said.

"Sister?" Luckett asked, brow raised.

"Lena is my half-sister," Raven explained.

Luckett let out a breath of relief and let her shoulder slump and her chin fall.

"Stressed, Captain?" asked Conrad.

Luckett rolled her neck over her shoulders. "Malik, my love, see how those rooms are coming along. Why don't you two help him out?" She waved her hand toward Zander and Rosaria. "Conrad, I'm sure there's something you need to do somewhere else. Raven, with me."

Her friends went one direction down the corridor, and Raven followed Luckett down the other.

They had gone a few steps when Luckett said, "Your father and I fought all the time, even when we were crazy about each other. I know it would have never worked out, but there's always that little bit of jealousy when you see an old beau with another."

Raven nodded.

"Was she good to you?" Luckett asked. "Your stepmother?"

"Yes."

"I'm glad to hear that," Luckett said, a different note in her voice. She paused in the corridor, and Raven paused with her. The portholes tinted the space in creamy daylight. "I know you are bitter at me for leaving you like I did, but believe me when I say you were raised much better than you would have been by me. I barely raised Malik. Sisters only know what would have happened to you. Knowing my luck, you'd have become some pirate heathen—given you survived to adulthood."

It took Raven a moment to recognize the strange lilt to her mother's words and the new look in her eye—it was remorse. Luckett met Raven's eyes—the light brown eyes they shared.

"Do you regret leaving?" Raven asked.

A beat passed.

"No," Luckett said, her voice soft. "I would have been miserable underground, and I've had some incredible adventures in the past sixteen years. I regret not being there for you, not being there when you became a woman or needed someone to tell you that life isn't always fair. I...regret not being the mother I should have been, to both you and Malik." She sighed deeply, and without the stern expression, she looked like a young woman. She absently toyed with the cuff of her coat. "I wanted to take you with me. I wanted to raise you. But I knew what kind of life you'd most likely have with me, and I knew what kind of life you'd have with your father. I thought by leaving you, I was making the right choice for you."

"Why not stay?" Raven asked, though she knew why.

Luckett half laughed. "I'd be useless in that kind of domestic setting. My spirit was meant for the skies. Not unlike yours, if what I've heard about you is true."

"There might be truth to that," Raven said.

"I'm sorry for what I've done, Raven." Luckett turned to her and extended her hand. "Can you forgive me?"

Raven knew she already had. Her grudge against her mother hadn't been deep to begin with. She pretended to consider it anyway. "I suppose I could." Raven gripped her mother's hand. "I do."

Luckett's remorseful expression turned into a grateful smile. "Then we've got a lot of time to make up for."

"And seventeen years of birthday presents," Raven added.

Luckett laughed, a deep and warming sound. "That's my side of the family coming out. Come on, why don't you come with me to see how those rooms are coming?"

Raven spent the afternoon with her mother as she coordinated her Crusaders. They organized rooms for the people of Silver Glen, made sure they had blankets and water, and Raven was glad for the work. It gave her something to do with her hands that didn't involve combat practice. Zander helped too, as much as he could with one arm, though he avoided her father.

By the time evening arrived and the clouds gave way to a starry sky, everyone from Silver Glen had a bedroll and something to eat. Raven was exhausted. Somewhere after midnight, she collapsed onto the couch in the room she shared with Rosaria.

Zander and Thalame had given up their room, and the two of them had brought bedrolls into the girls' room. They spread the bedrolls on the other side, both looking exhausted. Rosaria sat on the bottom bunk, chin resting in her hands. The globes burned low for the late hour, tinting them all in a shadowy yellow.

Thalame yawned. "We should sleep good tonight."

Raven felt the strain in her body, in every muscle and tissue and bone, pulling her toward the bed, toward the rejuvenating abyss.

"But before we crash," Thalame started. He came to sit beside Raven. "Zander and I have been talking."

"About you," Zander clarified. He sat in the chair opposite Raven. He wore no humor on his face. He started to lean forward, but his limp mechanical arm offset his weight, and he leaned back. "It's no secret the centrum gave you its power. Since we don't know what that means, we think it's best if we go see the Wraiths."

"The Wraiths?" Raven repeated, the word tumbling from her lips. The Wraiths, the mythical order of magicians that stretched back thousands of years, of which Thalame and Zander were part.

"They know more about magic than anyone else," Thalame said. "If anyone has an answer for what's happening to you, it'd be them. It's possible they might have some insight that we haven't thought of yet."

"Grand Master Deikun is a wise man," Zander added. "He knows magic like a sailor knows the sea. And because of your stunt in Moorin, I'd say it's only a matter of time until Deacon figures it out. For all we know, he might already have. All he'd have to do is open the box."

Raven nodded. The idea of meeting the grand master of the Wraiths made her stomach turn over, and going back to Wayward Point didn't sound very appealing.

But Zander and Thalame were watching her, waiting for her answer.

"You think the grand master could help me with my magic?" she asked.

Neither nodded, but neither declined the idea. Because they didn't know. She bit her lip. It offered a sliver of hope that she might not have to burn off her magic every morning or worry about the fever returning.

She inhaled deeply and said, "Okay. I'll go."

"I'm glad you agree," Thalame said. "Malik went to inform Luckett about the new course earlier this evening."

"You knew I'd agree?" Raven asked.

"No," Zander said. "We needed to get away from Silver Glen. We couldn't go north into the mountains. We couldn't stray into Gracita's airspace to the west. There's a Gray Elite stronghold to the east. So south was the most logical direction to go."

She frowned but gave up. She was too tired to argue about it. She was tired enough that she didn't know if there was anything to argue. "Fine," she said. "I need to get some sleep. I'll yell at you both in the morning."

"I've got the lights," said Zander.

Raven trudged to the top bunk, Thalame collapsed onto his bedroll, and Zander stood by the light switch. A few moments after Raven had pulled the blankets to her chin, the room went dark. The glass globes hissed out, leaving tiny pinpricks of light for a few seconds afterward. Zander's calm, steady footsteps retreated to his bedroll. As her eyes adjusted to the dark, she found two sapphires looking back at her from the other side of the room.

Zander woke up before the others. He'd never been one to lie awake, so he got up and slipped into the corridor. Portholes allowed generous sunlight, splashing the rosewood and brass. He stretched as much as he could with his new arm. He twitched his little finger—it moved a little more. Or maybe he just thought it did because he wanted it to.

He adjusted the sling around his neck and pushed the hair away from his face. He itched to move, so he started walking.

His feet took him to the hospital.

Zander let out a sigh. He knew what he should do, but he didn't want to. He cursed himself and walked into the hospital. There were few people in the hospital, mostly pilots who'd gotten roughed up during the fight. Zander made his way to the bed on the far side.

Ezra Deacon was awake, and his tired brown eyes focused on Zander.

The two friends stared at one another.

"You're a turncoat," Zander whispered.

"You're a Hawk and a Wraith," Ezra whispered back.

Zander shrugged.

Ezra half laughed. "Looks like we're both traitors now."

"Seems that way."

Ezra's sleepy smile faded, and he set a hard gaze on Zander. "I hear you're also something else."

Zander's heart squeezed. He knew what Ezra meant, but he couldn't bring himself to say it.

"You're the Revenant," Ezra whispered, not hiding his distaste.

A tense moment passed, and Zander didn't deny it.

Ezra gripped the sheets. His grip turned white-knuckled. "You killed my mother."

Zander couldn't deny that either.

Ezra wore hatred—a look Zander had never seen on the otherwise good-natured boy. Everyone had always loved Ezra, how kind he was, how friendly, how charismatic. Few had ever said such things of Zander.

"I'm sorry," Zander whispered. "I know an apology isn't going to fix anything, but it's out there."

"Why?"

"Because I felt like apologizing," Zander said. "Believe it or not, I feel bad about it."

"No, why did you kill her?"

Zander heaved a breath. "My father sent me to do it." He met Ezra's eyes as he said it. "According to the Hawks, she had been hiring mercenaries from Tinatun to bring back escaping magicians, the magicians the Hawks had smuggled out. They wanted it to stop, but the tipping point came when she hired assassins to attack Major General Taylor."

"I remember him," Ezra said. "They said he was smuggling drugs over the border."

"He was smuggling magicians out for the Hawks," Zander corrected.

Ezra sighed—understanding darkened his face. "Do you...remember it? That night?"

"I've tried my best not to remember details," Zander said. "I made sure anyone I went after was alone and that they died quickly."

"I was in the room, you know," Ezra said.

Zander tensed, though he held himself calm.

"When you killed her. I saw the Revenant, and I was too afraid to do anything to stop him." Ezra lifted his gaze to the ceiling. "If I would have, would you have killed me too?"

"I don't know." Zander didn't want to think about that question, and he didn't want to have to give an answer. "I'm not that person anymore."

"I'm glad." Ezra closed his eyes. "He was kind of a jerk."

"I've heard." Zander dared a step closer to the bed. "Are we still friends?"

"I'll have to think about it." Ezra sighed. "I've never been one to harbor grudges. It's too hard. It's so much easier just to be friends with people. But I've never found out that one of my friends killed my mother."

Zander nodded. Another of the patients started to wake. "I'll see you when you're out."

Ezra waved halfheartedly, and Zander let himself out of the hospital. Standing in the corridor, he didn't feel any better about the situation than he had before. Life was easier without everyone knowing about the Revenant.

He'd heard of magicians with power over memory. He'd considered hunting one down just to be rid of the horrible memories of the Revenant. Then again, if he didn't have those memories, he might make the same mistakes over again. Might as well live with the guilt and shame.

He started walking. He had no direction or end goal. He only needed to move.

On the lower decks, a familiar voice called his name. He turned, banishing the dark thoughts, to see Brent strolling down the corridor. A streak of grease ran from his cheekbone to his chin, and his magnifying goggles rested atop his head. His eyes settled at once on Zander's mechanical arm.

"I saw you earlier, and I couldn't help but notice this." Brent motioned to the arm.

"Stop fondling my arm with your eyes," Zander deadpanned. "What are you doing up so early?"

"I volunteered to help with the engine. It's incredible." Brent reached for Zander's mechanical hand, then realized that it was a part of him, and then asked, "Can I?"

Zander shrugged.

Brent examined Zander's metal hand. "I've heard about mechanical limbs, but I've never seen one," Brent said, his voice distant. "This is amazing, so intricate and artfully built... Can you move it?"

Zander twitched his little finger.

"Fascinating."

"There's a medic with a mechanical leg, and a pirate with two mechanical arms," Zander said.

Brent's eyes widened.

Zander jerked his chin toward the other end of the corridor. "Come on. I'll introduce you."

Brent's joy oozed into the air around him, and Zander did his best to soak some of it. They had a long few days ahead of them, and he would need all the optimism he could find.

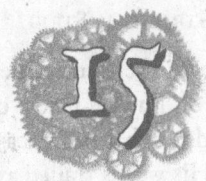

Every morning, Raven went up to the Belt to burn off her extra magic. Zander stood with her, using his magic alongside hers, trying to burn away his tattoo. Without the rune's restraint, his magic would be stronger and faster, he said. According to Thalame, several of the other Wraiths were doing the same. They all felt the dawning of a war.

War. The word sent a shiver down Raven's back and shuddered through her flame.

With her magic stabilized, she worked with Conrad and Thalame, learning how to fight with daggers, swords, and her fists. Zander stood to the side in those sessions, and though he held a steady expression, his tapping foot gave away his impatience. Rosaria came and went. Like Zander, she had trouble staying still with so much commotion going on around them.

Malik spent as much time as possible with the new magicians, learning about their powers and helping them understand the gifts they had been forced to hide for so long. He had tasked himself with finding places for them to go before they arrived at Wayward Point.

Raven spent her afternoons with her mother, playing a game of catch-up. Raven told her about life in the mines, and Luckett told her about her years in the sky—all the places she had gone, the near-misses with authority, and how she came to be the captain of the *Orion*.

The evening meal happened wherever it could. With so many people needing to eat, the mess hall wasn't big enough. Raven, Zander, Rosaria, Thalame, and Conrad ate where they found room. Raven's favorite place was the Belt, if the weather held.

Two days into their flight south, Zander took his metal arm out of the sling. He didn't have full mobility, and it hung limp at his side, but Raven caught him wiggling his metal fingers near constantly. At his current rate, Thalame thought he would have near full control by the time they reached Wayward Point.

At night, he flexed his shadows.

"There are more of them at night," Zander told her on the night of the second day, after their dinner on the Belt. Dusk was quickly fading into twilight, streaking the sky gold and pink and indigo.

"I don't understand," Raven said, looking at the inky puddles at Zander's command. "These look different from what you did in Moorin."

"They are different," Zander whispered. He glanced around them. Thalame and Rosaria had gone to see Ezra. "I can command natural shadows, but I have my own shadows I can use."

The natural shadows jumped back into their proper places, and Zander summoned a miniature version of Raven, made of the undulating grays, blues, purples, and blacks—the same shadows that had encased her in Moorin.

"I only use these when I..." His words trailed away, and his eyes hardened. The little shadow figure vanished.

"When you were the Revenant?" Raven whispered.

"Yeah," Zander said. "It was my father's idea. As a stupid kid, I believed him. I thought my father could do no wrong. I thought he was one of the good guys, and I wanted him to be proud of me." He scoffed. "I didn't know how wrong I was until I met your old man. I started to wonder how my life would have been different had I been raised by a father like him."

"He would have made you cut your hair," Raven said, a laugh on her tongue. "He hates that haircut."

Zander pushed a hand through his dark hair. He kept the bottom half shaved and the top half to his shoulders. Raven had tied it up for him; he couldn't with one hand, and if he left it down, the wind on the Belt would tangle it.

"Well, lucky it doesn't matter what your father thinks." Zander leaned closer to her. "What do you think?"

She bit her lip. She took a long moment to stare at his hair. At her prolonged silence, he deflated.

"I can shave the rest and start over, I mean," he started, fingering the barely-there hair on the bottom half.

"Don't do that," she said at once, earning his surprise. Her face flushed. "I mean...it's not that I don't like it...it's just..."

"What?"

Her face heated. "Fine, I kind of like it."

Laughing, Zander pecked a chaste kiss on her cheek.

The next few days went by in a blur of preparations and activities. The *Orion* made a few stops, that is to say the main ship hovered above the clouds while smaller ships visited trading posts on the ground. They couldn't do all their trading at once, so they sent a ship down every few hours to trade at a different little town. Among them returned a familiar face—Niall, the Dweller's tinker and mechanic. He had gotten word from a scout, and he had been in Oun to greet the Crusaders.

Niall's eyes went wide at Zander's new arm. He asked technical questions about calibrations and adjustments and nerve conduits, but Zander blinked at him.

Niall had laughed. "That's a fair answer. Can you tell me where I can find the mastermind who built this beauty?"

"You know, I have a friend that I think you would get along with," Zander said. He shared a knowing look with Raven.

While Raven burned away her extra magic, Zander wiggled his fingers. While Raven and Thalame practiced hand-to-hand, Zander wiggled his wrist. Soon, he could lift his wrist halfway up his chest and move all five fingers.

"Can you use your magic with that hand too?" Conrad asked during lunch, eyeballing the mechanical arm with curious eyes.

And as it turned out, he could. Zander's mechanical arm guided Conrad's shadow away from him and formed a smaller version of him on the railing of the Belt.

A week into the flight, Raven woke up earlier than the others. The room was still dark, and the three sets of lungs puffed sleepy breaths into the cabin. Raven crept down from her bunk, grabbed her boots, her dagger, and her jacket, and slipped into the corridor. At the stairs leading to the next corridor, she sat down and slipped on her boots, slung the dagger around her middle, and tugged on her jacket. This time of morning, the Belt was empty. Most of the night crew was tending to the engines, the tanks, and the weather patterns.

Raven started along the Belt. The cool morning air whisked her hair against her cheeks. Wispy clouds glided along the Belt and through the riggings like ghosts. Dawn glowed an innocent blue, framing the spiky treetops of the eastern horizon. Most of the stars remained—the world caught between night and day, between this world and the next. The air smelled like rain but sweeter. She could smell the scents of the forest underneath them, soil and vegetation and faint perfume of wildflowers.

A ghostly cloud slid past her, grazing her with cool pinpricks of moisture. The cloud did not register her presence; it continued its way along the Belt.

Raven couldn't help the smile on her face. Never, not once, did she think she would get to touch the clouds. She brought her flame to life. The yellow light glistened off the passing clouds, burning through those that drifted too close.

The door to the Belt opened, and steady footsteps sounded against the metal.

"Getting some alone time?" Zander asked.

"I didn't want to wake anyone up," Raven said. Zander's presence felt as comforting as the heat of her flame, only deeper.

Zander sauntered to where she stood, hands tucked in his pockets. The wind pushed his loose hair around his face and shook the flaps of his jacket. Her flame reflected in his sapphire eyes, turning them shades of yellow.

"I'm getting better," she said. "Look." At her command, the flame grew brighter, hotter, and taller—then smaller and pale. She repeated in time with her breaths—she had discovered her breathing had a special rhythm with her magic a few days before, and she'd been practicing.

Zander smiled. "You know, when we left Silver Glen, I was worried about protecting you. Every time I turned around and didn't see you, I panicked. If something happened to you, it would be my fault." He chuckled. "And now you're the one protecting me."

She grinned, though her cheeks warmed. "When my father took me off scavenging duty and stuck me in the kitchens, I knew that I'd never get out of there. I'd never see the daylight again, or leave that little village, or ride on an airship or see a sky city." She let out a sigh, then laughed as she looked up at the sea of stars. "I knew the ground would be as close to the stars as I would ever get."

She reached out with her flame-free hand and touched a passing cloud. The mist touched her skin like a cool breath.

Zander smiled. "And here you are."

"And here I am," she repeated. She set her free hand onto the railing.

"The whole time you were gone, I felt like everything had been torn apart," Zander said. "I thought you'd somehow been tracked down and captured or killed, and I didn't even know where to start looking. I...had this nightmare where you'd fallen and broken something and couldn't walk, and no matter how hard I searched or how fast, I couldn't get to you."

Guilt tore through her chest. "I..."

"You what?"

"After those slavers saved me, I remember wishing that you'd feel bad about it," she whispered, looking at the flame in her hand. Guilt squeezed her heart. "I was mad. I didn't feel good. Those weren't my best moments. I... I'm sorry."

Zander stepped closer. "It's fine," he started.

"No, it's not fine." She turned toward him and doused her flame. "Zander, if we don't trust each other, how can we be together?" His eyes widened, and her heart jumped into her throat. "I want to trust you. I want to know I can come to you with anything and not be yelled at or thought stupid or dumb or useless. I want you to feel the same with me. No more secrets."

Zander swallowed. He wore nothing of his arrogance. He wore vulnerability, an exposure she had so rarely seen. "Okay." He nodded. "No more secrets. No more scheming without the other. You tell me what you're thinking, and I'll do the same." He tilted her chin up. "What do you want to know about me?"

"Everything," she said and meant it.

"That's a lot of information. Where do you want me to start?"

"I don't know." Suddenly, the six months she had known Zander in Silver Glen felt like nothing.

"I'm sorry I didn't tell you about being the Revenant," he whispered. "It's not something I want to think about. Looking back, I wish I'd told my father no. I wish I'd have just been a regular Hawk and a Wraith. The Revenant was something else I was running from when I ran away from Lenhala. I had planned on staying in Silver Glen. I wanted to leave all the nonsense about the Hawks and Wraiths behind. Until Thalame and I arrived in Moorin, I had planned to never be the Revenant again."

"How did it happen? Becoming the Revenant?"

"It was my father's idea," Zander said. "He pushed me to seek out the Wraiths. Because of him, I thought only of the Hawks and rebellion. I was young and reckless and arrogant, and I wanted to please my father. He dangled the idea of being a king in front of me, and I took the bait. I wanted to be the one who saved Rhynwier from the empire. I wanted my name etched into history." He leaned onto the railing and looked down at the passing forest. "I thought I was ready for it. I thought I was tough enough. After my first assassination, I cried myself to sleep. I had nightmares for weeks."

Darkness passed over Zander's face—he looked haunted. Raven felt horrible for bringing it those memories.

"I started to regret that part of my life, but I was in too deep with the Hawks. I didn't know how to get out," Zander said. "I thought stealing the centrum would prevent war. I thought I'd be somehow making up for all the horrible things I did."

"What's done is done," Raven said. "It's a part of you, and regardless, I..." *I love you. Say it. Just say it!* "And I accept all of you, Zander."

He gave her a ghost of his usual smile. She tried again to form the words she wanted to say, but they wouldn't come. A beat, and then Zander's metal hand cupped her cheek. She felt the cool metal plates of his palm, the subtle movements of the gears within his wrist and fingers, the adjusting of the joints.

"I can almost feel it," he whispered. He lifted his flesh and bone hand to cup her other cheek. "It doesn't feel the same, but..." His flesh and bone thumb ran over her cheekbone.

She reached for him, just to touch him, to feel him. She grabbed fistfuls of his shirt collar and pulled until her nose grazed the skin of his throat. He adjusted his hands to rest on her shoulders, hugging her loosely.

"Is there anything you want to tell me?" Zander asked, his breath warm on her temple. "I know you told me the story, but is there anything you left out?"

"I honestly don't remember," Raven said. "I've had to go over the story so many times now, I don't know who I told what or what I left out. It's all a blur."

"Then tell me again," Zander whispered. "Don't leave out anything. Not a single detail."

She tightened her grip on his collar. Underneath her hand, she felt his heart thumping.

The blue dawn had steadily grown brighter. As they stood there, the first rays of golden sunlight spilled over the horizon. The wispy clouds glowed yellow, each drop of moisture illuminated from within—glowing gold, everywhere. A heavenly otherworld. It warmed Zander's sapphire eyes and bronze skin. She met those eyes, and he hugged her closer.

He leaned in, and she met his lips with her own. This kiss was unlike any other. He had opened himself fully to her, and his kiss reflected it. He held her close, hand of flesh and its metal twin mapping the contours of her back. She hadn't bothered with a corset that morning. She wore only the blouse she'd slept in and her jacket.

When their lips and tongues broke apart, the sun had burned away a portion of the wispy clouds, leaving the sky a crystalline blue. Raven released her hold on his collar and flattened her hands against his chest. She started to talk. She told him everything he wanted to know—why she had left, where she had gone, and her thoughts during the entire ordeal, many of which she now contributed to her feverish state of mind.

Zander held her as she spoke, occasionally nipping at her ear and leaving small, tender kisses on her cheek and jaw, stealing her concentration and focus.

She told him how she had been sold by the scavengers and how terrified she'd been. She told him how Conrad had gotten her out and taken her to see Malik, how she had gotten a job aboard the *Marianne*, how she had thought she would die, how Conrad took her to see the Wraiths and then Ezra. When she told him about the dream she'd had about the Revenant, his lips on her jaw hesitated.

"You dreamed about me?" His voice drifted along her skin, hesitant and fearful.

"It was the night before you tackled me," Raven said. "I know it sounds strange. I hadn't seen the Revenant or your magic before, but I dreamed about it."

Zander smirked. "How close was the dream to reality?"

"Frighteningly so."

His grin faded. His brow creased, lips parted in thoughtful curiosity.

"Is it strange to dream about things and then have those things happen?"

Zander didn't answer for a long moment. He stared at her, thinking. "Magic does strange things," he said at last. "The Wraiths might know more about dreams and premonitions. But it wouldn't hurt to get examined." He spoke seriously, but his eyes roamed up and down her body. "It might be a sign of a deeper issue. I could examine you. There might be a physical marking of a magical curse."

She blushed, heat flooding over her skin. "I think I would have seen it by now," she said. "I do bathe frequently, you know."

"What if it's somewhere you can't easily see?" Zander's brows rose. The sunlight illuminated the pink blush that warmed his own cheeks. "Like your back."

She smacked him playfully on his good arm. "You just want to see me naked."

"Any human being with an interest in girls would want to see you naked," he said plainly.

She steeled herself. "Well then, you'd better be prepared to return the favor." Even as the words left her lips, her face burned like the fever had returned.

Zander grinned mischievously at her. "Oh, I would let you examine me any day of the week."

He leaned in, and she met him. Her tongue grazed his bottom lip when a male voice shouted from somewhere in the rigging. Another called back. A third sounded.

Zander sighed against her lips. Another day had begun on the *Orion*. Crusaders were climbing into the rigging, some strapped into harnesses and others not, doing their daily inspection of the balloons and the mechanics that kept the ship flying.

Seeing Crusaders without harnesses made Raven's stomach turn over. They leaped from rigging to balloon like cats, never stumbling or hesitating.

The doors to the Belt opened, and passengers looking for fresh air further diminished the moment. Raven's slice of quiet now rang with murmurs.

Zander released a sigh, and his hot breath bounced against her lips. "Might as well go see what they've drummed up for breakfast today."

"I could use a cup of tea," she said, though she'd rather have his lips than a drink.

16

Halfway to the mess hall, someone cleared their throat. Raven and Zander paused and turned—Samuel stood in the middle of the corridor. He scowled at their linked hands.

"Morning, Raven, Zander," said Samuel tersely.

"Morning, Dad," Raven said. "Sleep well?"

"I've had better nights," Samuel said. "How about you, Zander? Sleep well?"

"I did." Zander cleared his throat. "All night, sir. Slept, I mean. In my own bed."

Samuel closed the space between them. He stopped within reach of Zander. He crossed his thick arms. "I heard a story, a wild story, that you and that other boy gave up your room and moved into Raven's room."

Raven felt Zander tense. Her father stood several inches taller than Zander and twice as wide.

"That is true," Zander said, speaking faster than normal. "Though there are four of us in the room, including Princess Rosaria. Between you and me, she's a bit of a prude. She wouldn't let anything unsavory happen on her watch."

"He's right," Raven agreed, though she lied. Rosaria had been the one to suggest the bed was big enough for two, insinuating Raven and Zander share one. Then she'd winked at Raven.

"Where I come from" —Samuel clenched his fists—"we marry the girls we fancy."

Raven laughed. She couldn't help it. It bubbled out of her throat without a second thought. Her father and Zander both looked as if she'd lost her mind.

"Is that true, Dad?" Raven asked. "Is that what you told my mother?"

Samuel blinked, and his gaze turned sheepish. "I meant—"

"You weren't married when I was born," Raven reminded him.

Her father blinked. Zander didn't dare speak.

"Raven," Samuel said, a different sort of terror on his face. "Please don't tell me you've already..." He hesitated, color draining from his face, and glared at Zander.

Something deep within gave her a boost of steely confidence she had never felt before, and she added, "No. I tried to jump him, but I was high on magic opium smoke, and Zander said no."

Her father inhaled sharply and pinched the bridge of his nose. "Sisters," he mumbled.

"I know," Raven said, softer. "Surprised me too. Turns out, Zander's not the arrogant, bumbling fool we all thought he was."

Zander scoffed. "Excuse me?"

"What? That's what I thought of you, so I only assumed other people thought the same."

"I'm not...those things," Zander said, brow furrowed.

"A little bit." Raven held up her index finger and thumb a hair's breadth apart. "You're a lot of things."

Zander frowned.

"Not all of them are bad," Raven added.

"Raven," said her father, a stern note back in his voice. "Relationships are serious, and trust me, babies are a hefty responsibility."

Raven blushed, and the confidence vanished from her voice. "I don't plan on bringing home grandchildren," she said. "Not for a very long time, at least."

Samuel cleared his throat. "Good. There are, uh, certain...precautions that can be taken to prevent—"

"Dad." Raven waved her hands between them. Her face burned red hot. "I would really rather not have this conversation with you."

Samuel cleared his throat. "Then, promise me you'll speak to your stepmother."

"I promise I will seek out my stepmother's counsel on the matter of contraceptives." Raven took equal parts embarrassment and glee at the twinge in her father's face at *contraceptives*.

"Good." Samuel cleared his throat and once again became the stern commander. "I'm glad we had this talk. I will see you later. And you" —he pointed at Zander— "mind yourself."

"Yes, sir," said Zander.

"Bye, Dad."

Samuel glared at Zander, a warning and a threat, and then continued down the corridor toward the mess hall. Raven lingered a few moments, wishing to put as much distance between her father and herself. At least for right now.

When her father had vanished from sight, Zander let out a breath and doubled over, hands on his knees. "Sisters," he gasped. "I thought he was going to hit me."

Raven chuckled. "I thought he was too." She looped her arm with Zander's and tugged him down the corridor. "But he didn't. Come on, I'm hungry. And now I've got to find my stepmother at breakfast so my father sees us talking."

At that, Zander's face turned a shade of pink. He gave a halfhearted, uncomfortable chuckle and said, "Remember, whatever bedroom advice your stepmother gives you, she's likely referring to your father."

Raven groaned; Zander laughed. She punched his good shoulder and said, "Just for that, you get to be my first opponent in training."

"Like you could actually hit me."

"I've got better motivation this time."

They continued into the mess hall to find it crowded, but not as crowded as it would have been for lunch or dinner. Zander sat with Thalame and Conrad, while Raven purposefully joined Lena and her stepmother—making sure her father saw them talking. Raven sheepishly brought up the subject of contraceptives, and her stepmother chuckled and gave her a motherly smile.

The conversation that followed was not nearly as awkward as Raven feared it might be; her stepmother gave her a list of herbal potions and mixtures, most commonly ginger and thistle, and Raven promised to stop by the ship's herbalist.

"Thanks," Raven said. "And make sure to tell Dad you told me."

Her stepmother chuckled; so did Lena—who had taken on a pink blush during the entire conversation and had taken much more interest in her tea.

After breakfast, Raven, Zander, Thalame, and Conrad headed to the lower decks for combat practice. Conrad had secured them a small cargo hold near the air docks. Crates and barrels lined the walls but left plenty of room for them. Due to the proximity with the engines, the air was hot and humid and loud. They kept the three portholes along the north wall open, but it didn't help. The only light came from the dull lanterns along the ceiling and the sunlight.

"All right." Thalame cracked his neck to the side. He motioned toward Raven. "Let's see what you've got today."

"Actually," Raven said, stepping to the middle of the room, "I told Zander he could try his hand today. He's been aching for a good beating."

Zander scoffed. He wiggled his mechanical fingers and flexed his arms. His mechanical arms moved slower than his real arm, but he had gained substantial range of motion.

Thalame chuckled and stepped to the side of the room. "Have at it, then."

"You're getting better," Conrad commented. "Must be the magic."

Zander stretched his metal hand toward Conrad and made a fist. His metal fingers clicked against his palm. He grinned. "Every day, I'm a little faster, a little stronger."

"Soon you'll learn to fly," Conrad said, unamused with Zander's dramatics.

"Stop talking, and start moving." Raven readied her stance. "Or are you just wasting time? Trying to get your bearings? Afraid to lose?"

Zander smirked. He sauntered into the middle of the room while Thalame hung back with Conrad. Raven took up a pair of practice daggers, as did Zander. She moved first—she flung herself at Zander, and he met her attack. Their wooden daggers clacked together, and they moved about the room. Raven had the feeling that Zander went easy on her. Thalame did, and Conrad did most of the time. They had trained for years to fight, but she could feel herself getting stronger, quicker, and more capable.

Luckett was right—she didn't need protecting anymore. She could fight for herself. Not just herself—she could protect her friends. Zander. Thalame. Rosaria.

Conrad. Her family. The people of Silver Glen. The crew of the *Orion* who had risked their lives to bring her out of Moorin and then had raced to protect her family from the Gray Elite.

She would fight for them all, and she would protect them.

Ivaline Pemberton reclined on the cream-colored chaise. She propped her bare feet on a pillow to watch the fresh crimson paint on her toes dry. Her black heels sat on the floor, spotless as the day she'd bought them. She corked the bottle of crimson paint and set it beside her empty teacup.

Sisters, what a long day. Ivaline had attended brunch with the ladies of society in Lenhala, but her poor health had taken a turn—she'd left early to rest. None of the ladies questioned why Ivaline suddenly fell short of breath or lethargic, or batted an eye of suspicion when she requested to be taken home.

The first thing Ivaline had done upon returning home was rid herself of the damned corset and velvet dress and the stupid heels.

In truth, Ivy needed a break. She could only handle so much petty gossip and fruitless chitchat, and she neared her limit. She wore a simple day dress and had left the corset behind. Ivy felt marvelously better. Ivaline needed her rest—and Ivy needed several deep breaths—before she attempted Darlene's bridal shower in the Rose Gardens that evening. As much as she didn't want to, Darlene's husband-to-be worked directly under General Deacon, and Darlene had always had loose lips.

Ivy leaned back and stretched her arms above her head. A few more days of this drivel, and Ivaline would come down with a fever and a cough. She'd remain inside, resting, and Ivy would escape the city for the open countryside and rejoin her real friends, the Dwellers.

Even if the treehouse would be missing a few key players.

Through the windows of the lounge, the partly sunny sky made the towers of Lenhala glitter and shine, all steel and brass and colored metal. It was beautiful on the outside, but Ivy knew the ugliness on the inside. Backstabbing and lies and power-grabbing. She hated it. She missed the countryside. She missed her friends.

She leaned her head back. The sunlight glittered against the inlaid gold in the ceiling tiles.

What must it be like to see the open sky in every direction? She huffed out a quick breath. She was stuck playing the ninny while Thalame and Zander got to fly around the kingdom on a sky city. At least they'd found Rosaria and Raven. At least they had gotten out of Moorin. At least they remained safe.

Everyone was talking about Moorin and the girl who'd melted a prototype Colossus. Ivaline had been dining at the Twain estate that night, so she knew as little as everyone else, and she felt the same thirst for gossip. Ivy, on the other hand, had heard the truth from the scouts. Raven had melted the Colossus. Raven had magic now. Powerful magic too. It had something to do with the centrum, she knew it, but her scouts didn't know about the centrum or the augur.

And then her friends had vanished into the sky.

Ivy blew out a long sigh and inhaled the peppermint oil recommended by the healer. Another magician. Another member of the team to be more important than her. Of course, it didn't take much to be more important than Ivy. She spied, spread rumors and gathered intelligence, while the others could shoot lightning from their fingertips or walk through walls or command water.

And when the dam broke, a spy would be no good in the flood.

Not that she did much good. Spying kept her busy, kept the Dwellers current on rumors. Niall didn't need her bothering him in his workshop; Thalame and Zander didn't need her bothering them on their important mission to rescue the princess. She had thought—hoped—that she and Raven would stay behind while the others went to save Rosaria.

And Raven had left too.

Ivy didn't blame Raven. Not really. Raven had been miserable, but that misery had been something of a comfort to Ivy. She had been able to ease that misery, fix what Thalame's magic couldn't. But Raven had gone anyway. Ivy hadn't been enough. Again.

Footsteps sounded in the corridor. Ivaline didn't move; she didn't feel like it. Besides, she was supposed to be feverish and tired. For kicks, she coughed into her embroidered handkerchief.

A quick two-note knock hit the lounge door.

"A visitor, Miss Ivaline," drawled a servant.

"Who?" Ivy crooned softly.

"Miss Marie Kenara."

Ivy sighed dramatically and pulled a lacey fan from the side table. "I'll see her."

The door opened with a soft swish, and a pair of heels entered. The door shut. Marie's heels made their way through the room, sauntered around the chaise. Her dark hair had been done up in an elegant bun, her dark brown eyes lined with glittery kohl. She sat in the chair closest to Ivy, looking like a dream in black and gold silk. She leaned back and crossed her legs, flashing a strip of golden flesh that went nearly to her hip.

"You look like you have somewhere fancier to be," Ivy said.

"I had a brunch date." Marie smoothed her skirt. "But he's one of those 'all about me' types. I don't care how much he makes in a year. It's not worth putting up with that for the rest of my life. Or, his life."

Ivy shrugged. "They can't all be winners."

Marie grinned. "That's true. If every guy was like Ezra, well, the world would be a little better off."

Ivy schooled her emotions. Marie had dealings with the Hawks, but she was a Wraith first. For Marie to mention Ezra—she had news. Ezra had been involved in something. The Gray Elite claimed he had been caught up in the wrong crowd and dragged into one of the riots. Her scouts hadn't been able to bring her anything on him.

"I'm not sure Ezra still likes me." Ivy pouted. "I haven't heard from him since he went to Moorin. I hope he's not gotten hurt in the Riots."

Marie shrugged. "I hear he's gone north."

Ivy swallowed. North? The Gray Elite suspected the rebels had gone north. They'd dispatched Buzzers a few days ago. But, If Ezra had gone north—had he been on a Buzzer? Had he gotten out of Moorin?

Ivy let out a bored sigh. "That's fine, I suppose. We never went beyond friends, anyway." Not that she wanted to.

"I hear you tuckered yourself out this morning," Marie said, drawling her words. "Poor baby, socializing is such hard work."

"It is!" Ivy pouted. "All the talking and remembering things and planning." The pleasantries, nimble words, and crafted replies. "I don't know how girls do this all day!"

Sisters knew Ivy couldn't. She didn't know if Ivaline could handle it anymore. Spying had started out fun, but lately it had become exhausting.

"We take breaks. It's called cocktail hour." Marie laughed—a sound as graceful as the rest of her. "I've been thinking of relocating permanently to the south. Have you ever been to the southern coast? It's divine this time of year."

Ivy hummed thoughtfully. The southern coast—Wayward Point, home of the Wraiths. Outside of the Gray Elite's power struggle. Safe. Ivy caught the hidden meaning—a warning to get out of Lenhala, to get to safety.

Were the rumors of war true?

"I haven't," Ivy said.

"Oh!" Marie put a hand over her heart as if stricken. "The white sand beaches, the fruit, the free flowing music that never stops, the barely-dressed people. I don't know about you, but I could stand to be half naked for the rest of my life. And to drink from a coconut!"

Ivy thought about it. She wouldn't mind wearing one of those wispy dresses of cotton or just a swatch tied at her waist. Or nothing at all. She wouldn't mind feeling the sun over all of her.

"I think I could stand living on a beach," Ivy said with a sigh. She could do with a few months of peace and silence.

Marie scooted forward and joined Ivy on the chaise. "Come with me," Marie purred. She tugged on the loose ties of Ivy's day dress. "We can lie on the beach together, swim in the ocean, bathe in the hot springs."

Marie—like Thalame, Zander, and now Raven—was a magician. As a Wraith, she had spent time in the south. She knew of the Dwellers, but Thalame didn't trust her. He thought her shifty. Ivy did too, but she liked Marie—she had an unpredictable side. She knew of the Hawks too, but she hadn't openly chosen a side. Marie was loyal to herself first, and anyone else depended on her mood.

Marie leaned in to say something else, but as her lips formed the words, a swift two-tone knock sounded on the lounge door. Their tryst ended before it began.

"A visitor, Miss," said the servant.

"Who?" Ivy asked, her voice reflecting her irritation.

"General Oliver Deacon."

Her blood ran cold. Marie's eyes widened, and a fraction of her panic came through her painted mask. Ivy steeled herself quickly.

"Just a moment," Ivy called.

Marie slid to the end of the chaise, and Ivy quickly smoothed the bodice of her dress. She pulled a throw over her shoulders to hide her lack of a corset. Ivy leaned back into the chaise as any ill-feeling rich girl would do. She tried her best to hide her nerves. The general had never called on her before. He had come to speak with her father, but never her.

Something had changed. Something had happened.

And she would be the one to discover it and relay the information to the others. Lightning coursed through her nerves.

"Send him in," Ivy chimed.

The door opened. Heavy-booted steps signaled his approach. Ivy held herself still, but her heart thumped with each footstep. General Deacon stepped around the chaise, a fake smile on his face. He sat in the chair across from her. He looked so much like Ezra. Same chin, nose, and ears, but where Ezra's eyes were soft and sympathetic, the general's eyes were cold.

His cold eyes passed over Marie and settled on Ivy. "I'm sorry to hear you're unwell."

Ivy gave a curt nod. "Thank you for your concern, General," she said softly. "I'm sorry to say that I'm used to it by now."

Deacon glanced at Marie, his glare intent.

Marie cleared her throat and stood. "Pardon me, General. Ivaline, love, I will take my leave." She swept around the chaise and pressed a chaste kiss on Ivy's temple before she left. The gesture brought a wry smile to Deacon's mouth.

"Ah, young love," he said. "It's always beautiful to watch."

Ivy returned his smile with one of her own. She'd heard rumors of the sort of beauties he liked to watch. Men like him were the reason whorehouses had peepholes. The game between Marie and Ivy had never been anything more. Marie had a lover; Ivy had never met them. The game between Ivy and Marie was the smokescreen that hid anyone else.

"What do I owe the pleasure of this surprise visit, General?" Ivy asked. "My father would likely be more suitable company."

"Yes, yes, I have a meeting with him shortly, which is why I'm here," said Deacon. "But, as it is, he is running late. I thought I would come and see how his favorite child is faring."

"You flatter me." Ivy grinned anyway.

Likely, Deacon came digging for information. However, Ivy had never had an opportunity to dig Deacon for information. She could use this chance meeting to make this blasted trip into the city worth it.

Painting panic on her features, she said, "I've heard dreadful things from Moorin, General. Marcy's brother had the worst time getting across the border, and he spoke of riots and looting. It sounds terrible."

Deacon nodded grimly. He folded his hands together. "Moorin is in chaos right now. Rebels started a series of attacks against the Gray Elite. A group of magicians attacked one of the automaton factories, and with all the rioting, there is a shortage of automatons. The Gray Elite have apprehended several rebels, but there are many more out there." He offered her a kindly smile and added, "But don't you worry, Miss Pemberton. These are things soldiers worry about, not young ladies like yourself."

"It's hard not to worry when there are riots happening," Ivaline said, her voice quivering. She drew her arms up and loosely crossed them over her chest, making herself smaller, vulnerable. "I heard...I heard Ezra was there."

Deacon's kindly smile became a flat line. Anger pulsed behind his eyes.

So the rumors were true. She gasped and covered her mouth. "No," she whispered. "Tell me it's not true, General. Tell me what I've heard is lies."

Deacon looked down at his hands. "My son is a criminal, Miss Pemberton. He chose to save a group of murderous rebels over his own people. He has deserted the Gray Elite."

Her heart flip-flopped. She deflated into the chaise, letting her breaths go shallow. "Why would he... I don't understand."

"Neither do I," Deacon said, his voice strong. "Ivaline, I need to ask you a few questions. This is a serious matter. Do you feel up to it?"

Ivaline pretended to consider this strange request. He had questions for her, and she had questions for him, though hers would not be so blatant. She calmed herself, took several deep breaths, and quickly found that girl deep inside that could lie and charm.

"Yes, General," Ivaline said, hand resting over her heart. "I will help in any way I can."

"I'm glad to hear it," Deacon said, his grin wolfish.

R aven stood on the Belt as they crossed the border from Rhynwier into
Tinatun. They flew above the clouds, and a dome of endless blue stretched
above them. Below was a sea of puffy white clouds. Through the occasional gap in
the clouds, Raven spotted the thick green of the forest, the serpentine aquamarine
river, and thatch villages. She couldn't see the ocean, but she could imagine it.
Endless blue-green, sparkling in the sun.

The *Orion* traveled into the mountainous coast of Wayward Point, tucking
between a cluster of spiky peaks.

Raven, Zander, Thalame, and Malik climbed onto a smaller airship that would
take them down to the coastal air docks. Conrad followed a step behind, but as he
started to step over the gangplank, Malik barred his passage.

"What? I'm not invited?" Conrad asked, looking between Malik's ringed fingers
and to his stoic expression.

"Not to the stronghold," Malik said firmly. "You have been barred from the
Wraiths until you can prove yourself with your patron Sister."

Conrad's grin fell, and his shoulders deflated. Malik's glare did not lessen, and
Conrad took careful steps backward on the gangplank, until he stood on the berth.
He held Malik's glare the entire time, casual mischief twisted into something serious
and unreadable. Malik closed the door and snapped orders at the pilot. The engines
rumbled to life.

Raven met Malik's stare, and she suspected he had other reasons for not
wanting Conrad to come. Within his glare, he wore a severe warning not to say
anything.

She didn't.

The ship dropped out of the air docks and into a gorge underneath. Raven's
stomach, heart, and lungs dropped with it, only to lurch back into place as the ship
started to fly. The airship nimbly navigated through the mountains and over the
forests and villages.

Raven tried to hold herself steady. She would be meeting with the Wraiths, an
order older than the kingdom, an order full of magicians and secrets. Raven wished
Rosaria had come with them, but she'd stayed behind to keep Ezra company.
Luckett had him placed in a holding cell belowdecks, because she didn't want the
risk of having a Gray Elite wandering about her ship.

And for Ezra's safety, Zander had added. Plenty of Crusaders had ill feelings
toward the Gray Elite. Rosaria would make sure none of them took out those ill
feelings on Ezra.

The pilot navigated them through the rocky opening to the hidden air docks of
Wayward Point. The air docks had been built inside a cavern, catwalks and berths

secured over the ocean by thick steel cables and pitons thicker than a grown man's arm. It felt strange to come back, Raven thought as she stepped onto the gangplank. It felt like a lifetime ago she and Conrad had departed from these docks, bound for Moorin. It still smelled like seaweed, mildew, and cheap ale.

Malik led them through the network of catwalks and out of the air docks. The path led down the cavern wall and wound around it—just above high tide—and out of the cavern mouth and to the rocky beach on the other side. The path led up along the beach and to a fork divided by palms. Raven vaguely remembered this. One path would take them into the outskirts of Wayward Point. It had been the path Malik had taken to bring her to the air docks. He did not take that path now. He chose the second.

The second path wound through the jungle of palms, scraggly bushes, and squat trees. The path narrowed and in some places, became as steep as stairs. Raven slid on the sandy rocks several times, and each time, Zander's hands flattened against her back to steady her. He didn't tell her to be careful, to watch her step, or to walk slower. He only prevented her from falling.

The path wound through cliffs, between cliff sides so close together, Raven had to walk sideways, underneath skinny waterfalls that splattered her face with drops of cool water, underneath vine-strung bluffs, and through the roots of one massive tree. Finally, after an hour of hiking, the path opened up to a small gulf. Cliffs rose on all sides, save for the narrow opening that led to the sea. A village of thatch and jungle wood nestled into the cove. Some houses had been built over buoyed docks, others had been built into the branches of the ancient trees, and others had been built onto the rocks.

The chittering of birds echoed through the cove. More than one waterfall cascaded from the top of the cliffs, and into the cove, the sound echoed until it sounded like a gentle roar.

As Malik led them through the village, Raven's stomach tightened; the village was empty. She heard no voices, saw no people. But fresh footsteps remained in the sand, several sets of them. The air smelled of roasted fish, overripe fruit, and smoke. People lived here, but where had they gone? It gave Raven the impression that she had disturbed something, like she had intruded upon something sacred.

"They've added more huts since the last time I was here," Zander said, his voice low, cautious.

"We've had more magicians in the past ten years than we've ever had," Malik said. "Thanks to the Gray Elite, magicians are desperately trying to get out and survive. Some choose to stay here and fight with us."

Malik led them toward the cliff at the back of the cove. The moment they crossed underneath the shadow of the cliff's ledge, the temperature dropped. Raven felt something else, something within the air, as if the world had fallen away from beneath her feet and she had walked into another world. The sensation sent every hair on her body standing on end.

488

As they continued, the shadow revealed the massive structure at the back of the cove, a stone temple carved from the cliff itself. Three stone dragons perched on three stone gables, each with vicious eyes and wings poised for flight. Pillars lined the front of the temple, each pillar carved with elegant depictions of trees, stars, sea life, and people. As they approached the temple's wide front steps, Raven could see that every inch of the stone had been carved. Whorls, runes, and stories had been etched into every surface.

Malik started up the steps without hesitation and then paused at the massive stone doors. No handle, no knocker, not even a peephole, but they were clearly doors. Of course, she reminded herself, Wraiths had magic.

Everything about this place—the otherness, the strangeness—it had to be magic. It radiated from the sand and stone, from the very air. Despite the chill working its way through her body, despite how her legs trembled and her knees felt like sand, despite how much she wanted to turn around and run back to the sunlight, Raven followed Malik up the stairs.

Her brother wore dire seriousness as he asked, "Are you ready?"

Raven took a deep breath. No. "Yes. I'm ready." For what, she didn't know, but she hadn't come all this way just to stand at the door like a coward.

Malik didn't knock. He didn't even touch the doors. The doors opened on their own, swinging inward, revealing a darkness as thick as ink.

Her unease doubled.

Malik walked inside first, his form vanishing into the darkness. Thalame set a reassuring hand on her shoulder and then followed Malik inside. He vanished too. He did not remove her fear and unease.

Steeling herself, she stepped across the threshold. Her boots echoed on the stone floor. Soon, the darkness swallowed her too. She couldn't see Malik or Thalame. She couldn't hear them. She heard footsteps behind her—Zander.

The massive stone doors shut, and the darkness was complete.

She heard only silence. Raven's heart hammered hard in her chest, once, twice—torches burst to life, flooding the chamber with bright gold light. Raven flinched at the brightness and shielded her eyes with her arm. She stood in a large square room of stone. The torches hung on iron brackets. In the middle of the ceiling, chains held a circular dish aloft. From that dish, gold flames flickered and danced, illuminating more than regular fire. Magic, she realized.

The chamber rose two floors. The second floor was a veranda that stretched around the chamber, and standing on that veranda were at least thirty people. Some were dressed in dark clothes like Wraiths, others wore simple clothes, and others looked as though they belonged on the beach. The people from the village.

A bronze-skinned old man stood on the other side of the first floor, his charcoal beard and matching hair braided with gold and silver beads. He wore gray robes tied loosely with a golden sash. His feet were bare. His black eyes took them in under an unreadable expression.

"Grand Master Deikun," Malik said with reverence. He bowed deeply.

Zander and Thalame stood on either side of Raven, and as they mirrored Malik's bow, she quickly mirrored theirs.

A beat passed, and Raven's heart tried again to escape up her throat.

"Three of our own, come home," said Deikun, his voice deep, harsh, and lilting with a sharp accent Raven had never heard. "And you have brought a guest."

Zander and Thalame straightened, and Raven copied. She found Deikun staring at her.

"I bring fresh blood," Malik said.

Raven bristled.

"Ah." Deikun did not have to speak loud; his voice carried. His dark eyes took in Raven. At first, his gaze merely searched, but then it sharpened. "Interesting blood you've brought before me, seeker."

Whispering came from the veranda, the gentle murmur echoing delicately off the stone, and it made Raven glance up. Indeed, most looked down at her. She swallowed, steeled herself, and met Deikun's gaze.

The grand master stepped closer, his bare feet silent on the stone, his hands folded behind his back. "You hold magic I have rarely felt before," he said to Raven. He halted in front of her, bringing with him the smells of the sea. His dark eyes studied her again, and then he held out his hands. "Your hands."

She cautiously set her hands into his. His were bony, age-spotted, and wrinkled, but sturdy. He closed his callused fingers around hers. Her magic responded, like blood rushing to her head. It brought a sudden wave of nausea, and then it stopped. Her magic settled back into its safe place, as did the sense that she might empty her stomach on the grand master's robes.

"Interesting, indeed." Deikun beheld her with a new curiosity. "Your magic is strong, but wild and untamed. Ferocious but precarious." His eyes narrowed. "Unnaturally obtained."

Panic, quick and hot, surged through her bones. The grand master could tell all of that from a touch?

The panic and fear must have shown on her face, for Deikun said, "It is not a crime, magician. Do not worry. There are no repercussions waiting for you here. This is not a trial, nor am I a judge."

Deikun released her hands and folded his behind his back. The whispers along the veranda silenced.

"You have passed the first test," said Deikun, his voice soft but loud. "You have found us, come of your own freewill, and have proven your magic. However, the next test is not as simple."

Malik took a step forward, and the words on Deikun's tongue vanished. By the shift in whispers along the veranda, Raven gathered that Deikun was not supposed to be interrupted.

490

"Grand Master," Malik started, his panic subtle but present. "We didn't bring her here to become a Wraith, we—"

"I know why you have come," said Deikun, his voice strong and steady, speaking over Malik easily.

Malik bowed again.

"You have come here for answers. You have come here, thinking that I have those answers. I will save you the trouble, seeker. I do not have the answers this magician seeks."

Raven felt the wind go out of her. Malik tensed. Zander let out the faintest of gasps. Only Thalame seemed to be holding himself steady.

"The Sisters know far more than I," Deikun said. "And it is in this magician's best interest to seek out that wisdom on her own."

"Seek it out on my own?" Raven repeated.

"Become a Wraith," Deikun answered. Zander started to speak, but Deikun held up a hand. "This is a decision she must make on her own."

Without confiding in her friends first, all three of whom were Wraiths.

But if she could find answers to her power, to controlling it, by becoming a Wraith? Several long beats passed. Malik glanced over his shoulder at her, urgency in his eyes. She blinked. He then nodded toward Deikun—it took her a moment to realize Deikun waited for her to speak. For her answer.

"I'll do it," Raven said. "I'll become a Wraith."

Malik's urgency faded into calm. On either side of her, Thalame and Zander stood still as stone.

"Are you ready?" asked Deikun.

Raven nodded. "I am ready," she said, her voice quiet in the vast space.

"And confident." A small smile tugged at Deikun lips. Winkles stretched from ear to ear. "Even if it is only in words."

He knew her fear too, then.

"To be afraid is not a shameful thing," Deikun said. "Fear keeps us humble. Fear keeps us alert. It reminds us of our own limitations and vulnerabilities." He cleared his throat. "The Trial begins immediately."

Zander, Thalame, and Malik all gasped; the sharpness of the sound stirred her own panic anew. Along the veranda, nervous whispers surged and rattled Raven's resolve. Had she chosen the wrong answer?

Zander met her gaze, worried and panicked. Thalame didn't look any better. Malik looked as though he had swallowed something too hot.

Had she known what the grand master had meant by the Trial, she would have felt the same. Likely more.

Every Wraith had gone through the Trial, alone and without guidance, as would Raven. Deikun and Malik escorted Raven out of the temple at once, to a rowboat tied to a dock. Zander and Thalame could not come, mostly because of the rowboat's size. Raven sat with her back to the stern, Malik sat beside her, Deikun sat at the bow, and Elizi—a young woman with rich brown skin and emerald eyes—sat in the middle.

The boat held no oars, and before Raven could ask how they planned to row a rowboat without them, Elizi held her hands over the sides of the boat. The water rolled beneath the boat, and they glided across the cove. Raven's gasp brought a smile to Elizi's face. Magic—she controlled the water underneath them, making oars obsolete. They glided through the cliffs and into the sea, smooth as glass. Gulls flew across the opening, wings white in the sun, calls bright. The briny sea breeze felt cool against her cheeks, even as the sun warmed her.

"Minerva's gulls are a symbol of protection against bad weather." Deikun watched the birds fly out of sight. His eyes settled on Raven.

"I hope so," Raven said.

Elizi steered the rowboat farther and farther from the mainland, and as it shrank, a nervousness set Raven's bones on fire. Her magic mixed with her fear, but she banished it as best she could. She could do this. She had done so much already. She could handle the Trial of the Wraiths. Whatever it was. She had her magic, her wits, and her will to survive.

They rowed farther out to sea, and then at last, she heard the crashing of waves against sand and stone. She turned her head, holding onto the stern for fear of falling into the water. They approached an island no bigger than a small village, on which sat the ruins of an ancient fort. As Malik brought them closer, the derelict state of the fort became clearer. Once, it might have been as grand as a castle, its towers and turrets and battlements made for protection. But over time, walls had collapsed, towers leaned, and battlements crumbled. Moss and ivy had taken over much of the outside. Despite the ruined state, a good portion of the fort still stood, windows dark and empty.

"This is what remains of Fort Agnar," said Deikun. "It belongs to no kingdom or country. Its origins are beyond our history. It comes from a time long before, another kingdom, another war. Within its walls are hidden treasures. You must retrieve one of these treasures and then explain its value to me. You have one week's time to complete this task. No outside help is allowed. No tools. No advice. You have your magic and your mind."

"Good thing I ate a full breakfast this morning," Raven said.

Malik frowned, but a small smile twisted the corners of the grand master's lips.

492

The rowboat approached a wooden dock that had seen much better days. Several of the planks had rotted away or fallen into the shallow water below. Elizi glided them closer and angled Raven's side of the boat against the studier part of the dock.

"This is where we part," said Deikun. "In one week, we will return to this spot to fetch you. If you do not return, we will assume you dead. No one will fetch your body from the ruins."

A chill ran through her at those words. She glanced at Malik; worry had wormed through his stoic mask. Now, she understood why they had been nervous at her answer—she might die. She glanced at Deikun, but his expression betrayed no emotion. Raven swallowed her fears, gathered her wits, and climbed out of the boat. The weathered boards of the docks creaked viciously under her boots. She took another step, testing the board before she put her weight fully upon it.

"Do you understand, magician?" asked Deikun.

"Find the treasure, don't die, and be back here in a week." Speaking her mission aloud made it sound simpler, and she felt a sprig of hope. She could do this.

She turned back to Deikun and Malik, both looking serious and dire. Elizi, at least, didn't look so grim.

Raven gave them a confident grin. "I'll be fine. What if I finish before the week is up?"

"You have a week," Deikun repeated. "No more, no less."

She nodded. "Yes, I understand."

Deikun nodded, his lips a straight line. "May the Sisters look upon you with favor, magician."

The boat glided away from the dock and started back to the mass of greenish blue mainland.

"I'll see you in a week!" Raven called from the dock, waving. She stood there a while, watching, but neither the grand master or Malik turned around or waved. Elizi was busy with the water.

Every Wraith had taken this Trial. Of course, Raven had no idea how many magicians had taken this test and failed. That would not be her. She could do this. She could become a Wraith.

A week. She had a week to find treasure hidden somewhere within the fort, figure out its value, and not die in the process. She had a week to survive on this island with no help.

She could handle a week. She had her magic, her ebony-handled dagger, and a will to survive. Her mother had said a will does incredible things if strong enough. The grand master had said no tools, but he hadn't told her to leave her dagger, and she wore it proudly on her waist. Weapons must not count, then. Even if they did, she might not even need a dagger with her magic.

Raven steeled her will and straightened her shoulders. She marched along the sandy path to the fort. She followed the winding path with her eye first, the overgrowth, the gravel, the loose pale sand, to what had been the front doors of the fort—grand wooden doors reinforced with iron bars that had long since fallen from the hinges. A wall had fallen on the other side. She wouldn't be getting in through the front doors. She trekked around the weedy island until she came to a hole—it looked like a pillar had fallen on the other side, knocking a sizable chunk out of the wall.

Raven waded through the weeds and climbed onto the fallen stones. The sunlight illuminated the room beyond, but darkness prevailed farther in. Raven climbed through the hole. Inside, the darkness lingering under forsaken furniture and crumbling stone looked thicker, heavier. This chamber had been subject to the elements for a long time. Vines had squeezed between stones, mold and moss grew along the walls, and water had streaked the stones.

It wouldn't do for shelter. Summoning a flame in her hand, she started for the dark corridor on the other side. The crashing of the waves became distant. Her footsteps echoed. She heard scurrying, rats likely. The mildew and moss turned the air dank and humid.

Beyond the exterior walls, the fort looked relatively sturdy. The thick stone ceilings and walls held and didn't look as though they would collapse if she breathed too hard or stomped too close. The chambers without windows had remained unscathed, only musty and damp and dusty with disuse. Rugs and tapestries had been eaten away by mildew and time to the barest of discolorations on the stone floor. Iron torch brackets had thick knots of rust. Paintings had molded, the colors leeched and frames rotting.

Raven wandered through several rooms and chambers and corridors until she came to what looked to have been the base of a tower. The roof was intact, the walls stood straight, and it had a hole that had once been a window that overlooked a stretch of sandy beach and the endless ocean. Thanks to a fallen pillar on the outside that angled over the window, rain hadn't fallen inside. With the natural light streaming in from the window, she didn't need her flame—she let it go.

If Raven had to spend a week here, she would need a base of operations. This chamber looked as good as any. A quick trip of the chamber's edges proved no hidden nests of mysterious critters or worrisome mold. The remains of a campfire suggested others had used this spot to camp as well. She would need shelter, food, and clean water. With her shelter secured, that left two vitals.

She would need drinking water first. Back in Silver Glen, they had old stills that stole the pure water from the dirt and grime that lurked in the lakewater. Of course, the mechanics and smiths had tools to craft such a device. Raven had only her fire. She knew the basics—let the sun do the work. She needed something to hold the seawater, something else to catch the vapor, and something to catch the clean water. She didn't have time to scour the island for parts.

She climbed through the window and to the shore. The loose sand gave in under her feet. The idea struck—sand. She walked to a wide stretch of sand and knelt. She summoned her flame on the sand. At first, she didn't think it would work, but she felt the sand starting to give in. She urged her flame to burn hotter.

By the time she had crafted the sand into a rudimentary glass still, sweat dripped down her face, and her magic whined for rest. The still was small, uneven, and a bit lumpy where bits of sand hadn't melted, but the basic shape was there. Raven used an old tin cup from the tower chamber and filled the base of the still. She set it in the sunlight.

Her dry tongue couldn't wait for the sun. She heated the water with the dregs of her magic. She watched the vapor gather on the top, more and more of it, until drops fell into the collection cup. Drops at a time. She dislodged the glass collection cup from the still with a clink; it was barely more than two gulps.

It was better than drinking seawater. In all of her books, nothing good came from drinking seawater.

She gathered palm fronds, coconuts, and driftwood, anything she thought might be of use. The sun heated the air and the humidity stuck her clothes to her skin, though the sea breeze made it bearable. As much as she wanted to, she couldn't strip—she had nothing to manage a sunburn.

By the time the sun began to set, she had a bed made, coconuts stored, and a firepit for when she didn't feel like using her magic.

As the sun set, as the colors of the sky streaked with dark golds, mauve, and indigo, Raven felt good about this Trial. She stood on the rocky shore as the colors brightened and then faded into twilight. She had removed her boots, trousers, and corset and relished the feeling of the cool sand under her bare feet and the sea breeze on her legs. As the sun sank, the temperature sank with it, though not by much.

Conrad had been right. The sunset over the ocean was breathtaking.

As the glow of twilight finally faded, Raven returned to the tower using her flame. She settled into her makeshift bed. As she had expected, it was not very comfortable.

If every Wraith had taken this Trial, it meant one of two things: either this old fort had a plethora of hidden treasures to be found, or Deikun replaced a treasure when someone found it. The latter implied that Deikun knew exactly where the treasures were and what explanation she needed to come up with for each one.

It didn't matter. She could handle it.

She would become a Wraith.

She slept terribly. The fronds did little to soften the stone floor, and each nighttime sound had her pulling her eyes open and summoning a fire—but each time, only the empty room greeted her. No monsters, no giant rats, no creeping spiders. Only shadows. By the time the sun began to glow, Raven gave up on getting any more sleep. She searched the island for a suitable stick, then used her magic, dagger, and stones to focus the end of the stick to a point. She found a fallen pillar that stretched into the sea, and she made way to the end of it. The warm salt water lapped over her ankles.

She crouched and waited, spear poised.

Raven could remember going fishing with her father. She'd been young. He had taught her how to wait, how to aim not at the fish but above it. It had been in the days when she didn't know what job she would grow into, when she still thought she would grow into the leading role her father held so effortlessly. It took a few dozen failures, but Raven speared a fish. After a small hoot of victory, she carried the fish back into her shelter, sparked a fire on the driftwood, and roasted the fish. She drank from the still and refilled it.

After breakfast, she started the dreadful and exciting work of exploring the ruins for treasure. Like a pirate, she told herself. Using her magic as a torch, she delved deeper into the shadow-laden corridors. While the sun and weather hadn't touched the interior walls, the dank and damp had. Some corridors had collapsed, others had puddles of filmy green water, and others had splotches of mold inching along the stones. She avoided the mold and stagnant water when she could, and when she couldn't, she held her shirt over her nose. Growing up in an underground mine, she had learned to avoid mold. It could be harmless, but it could also be toxic.

At least she wouldn't have to worry about burning off her magic—she would need all of it to make it through this nightmarish fort.

Despite the dank, the air reminded her of the Wraiths' stronghold. The air felt different, alive somehow, but steady. Indifferent. Her mind drifted over the word, *haunted*. More than once, Raven had been looking one direction, only to see the barest glimpse of movement from the other. She would whirl around, flame in hand, but she never saw anything or anyone. She heard rats scurrying, bats skittering, and gulls calling, but she never saw them. The absence of life bothered her. It felt worse than the mines, utterly closed off and forgotten by the world.

Had the grand master meant it when he said no one would fetch her body? At the time, she had agreed without thinking about what those words implied—that others had not returned, that their bodies hadn't been fetched either, that those bodies remained in the very ruins she exploded.

She shivered. She stopped looking so closely at the shadows after that. She didn't want to stumble across a body.

She wandered for what felt like hours, up and down crumbling staircases, through fallen archways and corridors, crawling through tiny passages underneath fallen columns and pillars, through decrepit chambers and rooms and closets. She had gone deep enough that no windows allowed her light. Water dripped endlessly, mimicking footsteps. The sea breeze whistled through impossible drafts, sounding like whispers.

Her sleeplessness caught up with her too soon, her stomach started to growl, and she hadn't a clue about how to get back to her camp. But she kept going.

She kept walking.

Kept wandering.

Even though she questioned her sense of direction—that crumbling archway looked familiar. Had she passed it before?

Exhausted, hungry, thirsty, and frustrated, Raven jumped the last four steps of a crumbling staircase to a corridor she hadn't seen before. Stone pillars lined the walls, and between each was a faded mural. Once, the hall might have been beautiful. An iron chandelier had once hung from the ceiling but now crumpled in a heap of rusted metal on the floor. The murals themselves, however, looked mostly intact.

Raven brought her flame closer to the first mural. The shadows lifted, the dust burned away, and the picture became one that she knew. She had seen it on maps in her mother's office—the continent—Gracita, Rhynwier, and Tinatun. But, it was not the same as she had seen. The three kingdoms were not named, and in the southwest corner of the map, where on every other map was nothing but open ocean, was a great land mass. Raven inched closer; there were no lines dividing kingdoms, only land.

At the top of the mural, beyond the northern mountains, a face overlooked the world. A man's face. His robes braided with the stone frame of the mural, and two carved feet rested at the bottom, touching the floor. Words in a language she had never seen before traced around the frame, the characters elegant and curving.

Raven felt a chill race through her bones. She knew who it was. The old god, the one the Gray Elite had tried to erase.

Raven stared into the stone eyes of the lost god; her breath quickened, and her heart stammered. She brought her flame to the next mural. The old god hovered above the mural as he did in the first, but this time, the continent had been divided into four kingdoms. The lines were not the same as the current borders, but the shapes were relatively the same. From his hand, four seeds dropped into the heart of each kingdom. Inside each seed, a symbol was carved: in Rhynwier, sky; in Gracita, stone; in Tinatun, water, and in the fourth kingdom in the southwest, a flame. The first three symbols decorated the walls of the Temple of the Three Sisters in Silver Glen, but Raven had never seen the fourth.

The grand master had said these ruins came from another time. He knew about these murals. He had to know.

In the next Mural, the seeds had grown into women. Raven's breath caught in her throat—she knew them. The seed of earth had become Solen, Goddess of Stone and Metal. From her, gears and tools grew. The seed of sky had become Wilyn, Goddess of the Forest and Stars. From her, trees flourished and flowers bloomed. The seed of water had become Minerva, Goddess of the Sea and Wind. Around her, snake-like creatures wove in and around.

The three sisters that she knew. They had come from the old god.

And then, in the southwest of the mural's map, the seed of flame had become a woman Raven had never seen before. A fourth Sister. From the fourth Sister, books and scrolls grew. A monster had been carved around her, fangs and bat-like wings. A dragon. Smoke billowed from its nostrils.

But it was not the books or scrolls or dragon that worried Raven. It was the face of the fourth Sister. It had been scratched from the mural, leaving a jagged dent in the stone where her face should have been. She doubted it had been from time—no other part of the murals had been damaged. Only the slice over the fourth Sister. Someone had purposefully carved her away.

Her eyes lingered on the fourth Sister. Four Sisters, not three. What had happened to the fourth? Why had history forgotten her? Had the Gray Elite erased her from history like it had the old god? Zander had once told her they wanted the Sisters gone too, and that they would succeed if left unchecked. Had they already erased one?

Raven pulled her lip between her teeth. Adding a fourth Sister felt blasphemous, yet something about it felt...right. Something deeper than her bones didn't balk at the idea, like her magic knew the fourth Sister had been real. Her magic accepted it, knew it.

"Magic works in its own way," Conrad had once said. "It doesn't work like human laws do or the way humans think it should. It does what it wants, however it wants to do it."

In the next mural, the old god remained at the top of the map. The Four Sisters stood in their kingdoms. Trees and stars spread around Wilyn; machinery spread over Solen's land; ships dotted the water around Minerva; and books stacked around the fourth Sister. The dragon had risen from the water, its wings spread, a flame shooting out of its mouth, reaching Solen's land.

Raven gasped—her flame nearly went out. She brought her light closer to the mural. There, where Solen and the fourth Sister collided, was an etching of what at first looked like a canon. The more Raven looked at it, the more she knew what it was: Altair's Augur.

The augur had been created between Solen and the fourth Sister?

Raven half ran and stumbled to the next mural. Altair's Augur had been carved with flames, and a hole had been carved where the old god had once been. His face, his hands, his braided robes, his feet—gone. Because of Altair's Augur. It had been used against him.

Her breath caught in her throat. What kind of power could erase gods?

Solen had not been happy. On the mural, she held her head in her hands. Wilyn and Minerva lifted their hands, water and stars in a flurry.

A hole had been carved in Solen's land. Raven shuddered. Legends told of Altair's Augur power and how it had destroyed an entire city in a single blast of blinding white light.

In the next mural, the Three Sisters combined their powers of earth, sky, and water. Vines of their magic swirled between them, a great storm. Lightning bolts struck the fourth Sister's land, killing the dragon, burning the books, and in the final mural, the map looked as Raven knew it. The fourth Sister was gone. No land existed in the southwest, only vast seas.

The fourth sister had been erased, just like the old god, just like the Gray Elite wanted to do to magic. But the Gray Elite had not erased the fourth Sister; the Three Sisters had. Raven returned to the mural depicting Altair's Augur, the collaboration between Solen and the fourth Sister. The fourth Sister's fire powered the machine, encircled it on the mural.

Even after the fourth Sister vanished, her fire remained with the augur. The centrum—it came from that power of Fire.

The same Fire that Raven now possessed.

Raven felt the world shift under her feet. She collapsed on the stone ground, breath catching, heart thudding. The world grayed. Darkness edged her vision.

She held the flame of the missing fourth Sister?

Deikun's words echoed through her mind, *unnaturally obtained*. Rosaria had said her magic was wild and untamed and violent.

She reached deep into her magic. It didn't feel like it could power such a machine. It didn't feel like the power of a goddess. Perhaps the centrum hadn't taken all of the fourth Sister's magic. Maybe it had left a fraction of it.

A chill shook her bones. Again, she felt like an intruder. She had taken a Sister's power.

Raven sat until the world righted itself and the darkness retreated. Her stomach grumbled and clenched with hunger. Raven tore her eyes off the mural and continued down the hall. She needed to find her way back before she collapsed from exhaustion—she would think of these things from the relative safety of her camp.

The Mural Hall led into another old part of the fort, what looked to have once been barracks or a meeting hall. The fort's lower halls didn't seem to have an organized layout, and the fallen walls, crumbling pillars, and water-logged stairwells didn't help.

Raven wandered for the majority of the day, and somehow she made it back to her camp in the tower. The sun had already started to set. Rather than fish, she used her magic to split a coconut. She stared listlessly at the gilded waters as she ate her fill of coconut meat and milk. She collapsed into her bed, not minding the stiff stones.

Her mind churned, her muscles ached, she felt bruises forming, and she hadn't seen anything she would consider treasure. That meant she would have to go back into the maze and hunt again.

But, tomorrow. Right now, she needed sleep.

It didn't take long to relax.

Raven hadn't spent so long by herself in... She didn't know how long. She liked the silence, the peace, but she longed for the company of the others. She missed Conrad's humor, Thalame's cynicism, Rosaria's heartfelt logic, Ivy's cleverness, and Zander's...everything. Thinking of them all, the air around her felt miserably empty.

Two days gone, five left. Plenty of time to hunt down treasure. And then she would be back with her friends.

On the morning of the third day, rather than going right into the fort, Raven explored more of the island. She burned her excess magic as she explored. The sun on her skin felt marvelous after a day spent almost entirely in the dark. She found evidence of humans, ancient and not so ancient—weathered lean-tos, frayed bits of rope, carvings that signaled three days, four days, and five days. Magicians on the Trial, she realized. Had they simply gotten lost and not returned to mark the sixth day, or had something happened to them?

She found a flattened piece of land that might have once been a farm, the remains of old pig pens, and a small gulf. In the base of the gulf, the wooden planks of a dock had long since rotted away into nothing. In the shallows, skeletons of old boats were half-buried in the silt and sand. Further out to sea, she spotted the remains of large boats, masts broken, hulls cracked. All sunken and forgotten.

Scattered along the sunken boats, she spotted what looked fearfully like bones. Human bones...skulls and ribs and spines. Sailors who went down with the ship. Bones scattered this side of the beach too. Half-buried in the sand. Leaning against what remained of the interior battlements, broke ribs and fractured skulls.

Had the fort been left to rot, or had something happened? The evidence—the sunken ships, the collapsed walls and corridors, the bones—suggested the fort had been subject to an attack. No repairs had happened. Whoever had held the fort had either lost or fled, never to return.

Raven meandered past a pile of bones, one of which still had a spearhead stuck in the eye socket. So many bones, so many people. Death had struck this island hard and left its mark.

Raven continued scouring the island, and around midday, she came across a berry bush growing in the shadow of a palm. Without deer or other wildlife to eat them, the berries remained untouched. She plucked one. It looked like a grape, only larger. The skin was a pale and translucent cyan. She'd never seen a berry like it, nor had she heard of a berry like it. She squeezed it and let a few drops of the juice land on her arm. The drops felt cool, but she felt no tingle, no pain, nothing. The drop rolled down her arm and to the ground.

In her favorite book, Leon Stark had proven berries to be safe or poisonous by rubbing the juice on his skin. If the juice irritated the skin, they were poisonous.

Her skin remained unharmed, albeit sticky.

And with no one to disprove that theory, she accepted it. She gathered a large handful of the sea-colored berries. On the way back to her tower, she plopped one berry at a time onto her tongue. They were bittersweet like a cranberry, juicy like a grape, and a bit tart like an apple. By the time she reached the window of her tower, she had eaten them all.

She put her hand on the windowsill and started to hoist herself through when her stomach gave a frightening lurch. She doubled over, half-falling onto the sandy ground. Her insides clenched, knotted, tearing her apart from the inside out and—

She emptied her stomach onto the beach. Her vision swayed, but she spotted cyan berries in her vomit.

The edges of her vision blackened. Clouds swirled low over the fort, funneling toward her tower in vicious shades of bleak gray and toxic green. The fading sunlight danced off the thickening clouds, dimming with every blink until only shadows remained. The wind picked up, pulsing in time with a growling thunder. Raven stumbled to her feet but collapsed onto a dry strip of sand. The sun-warmed sand turned to dust under her fingers. The dust snaked up her wrists, and talon-tipped fingers poked through.

Screaming, she fell backward and shook the dust off her skin.

The water slowly encroached on the beach, swallowing the land like it had the fourth Sister's island, higher and higher—Raven scrambled for her tower. The water wouldn't get her there! She fell through the window, leaving the water and sandy monsters behind. She crawled onto her bed of palm fronds.

The berries had not been all right. Sleep. She needed sleep. She shut her eyes, the treasures forgotten, the hunt pushed aside, the Trial paused. She needed to wait out the reaction.

She'd be fine. She'd be fine. She'd—

A hand grabbed her ankle and tugged. Raven kicked at the hand. The motion shook her roiling stomach and squeezing organs. The hand tightened its grip, the bony fingers biting into her skin, cutting through the leather of her boots.

She kicked at the hand with one foot and pulled on her other, but the hand didn't budge. "Stop," she whined. She pushed herself onto her hands, forced herself to sit up, intent on throwing up on whoever had come to annoy her in her weakened state.

But the words dried up on her tongue. A skeleton lay at the foot of her makeshift bed, fibers of old clothes hung in dirty tatters, eyes empty and dark, bones old and paled with time. Its bony hand clutched her ankle.

She swore it smiled, and underneath the howling wind, it laughed.

Raven screamed.

She kicked at the skeleton. The toe of her boot hooked into the eye, yanking the skull from the spine. It clattered against the wall. The rest of the skeleton didn't seem to mind—still, it laughed, a deep, raspy sound that came from everywhere. She clamored to her feet and stomped on its wrist, shattering the bones. It released her, though the laughter didn't cease.

All around the tower, skeletons rose from the ground, squeezing through the minute cracks in the floor, bone by bone. They crawled toward her as their bones pulled together, as if held by invisible tendons. Some wore sword belts, the leather dry and cracked. The skeletons stumbled onto feet, some wore boots, others did not, and some only had one boot. Some had cracked skulls, fractured bones, missing fingers or ribs. They wore ratty uniforms, but none Raven had seen before—dark trousers and shirts, tarnished silver buttons. The soldiers who had died here.

Ghosts. The dead come to throw the intruder from their home.

"No!" Raven shouted. She darted to the window, but a skull blocked her.

A skeleton hoisted itself up into the window, and a dozen more pushed to be next. They climbed out of the sand, out of the water, covered in seaweed and algae. She stumbled back as the skeleton reached for her, and her back hit the bony rib cage of another. A skeletal hand landed on her shoulder.

Screaming, Raven summoned her magic. Fire erupted from her palm, blasting the skeletons through the window. The fire scorched the stone, licked at the vines and moss, and seared the air around her. A skeleton grabbed her shoulder—she turned and smothered the tower in orange streaked white flames. The skeletons fell apart before her, turned back into the dust in the heat. A hand landed on her shoulder—another skeleton crawled through the window.

She blasted it back, but more lurched forward to take its place.

Her shelter was no longer safe.

She darted into the corridor. Skeletons came from every doorway, corridor, and window, falling from ledges, squeezing through the cracks and between fallen pillars, turning from dust and slivers to skeletons once more. Raven ran and blasted them out of her way, blasting and running, knocking anything and everything from her path.

Still, they kept coming.

There had to be somewhere safe. She refused to die like this, poisoned and attacked by the dead.

She skittered around a dark corridor, her flickering flame dancing shadows over the stone walls, and there, at the far end, stood a woman. She glowed bright against

503

the dank walls, her brown skin luminescent and dark curls escaping from her hood. She smiled at Raven and motioned for her to follow, but Raven thought she had been down this corridor the day before. The way the woman wanted her to go ended in a dead end.

The skeletons came closer.

Raven bolted after the stranger, down the dead-end corridor. The stranger seemed to vanish into the wall, and as Raven skidded to a halt, she noticed the narrow gap where the stone had shifted and broken. Raven crouched; she could not see the other side. Skeletons scraped against the stone behind her. With no other way forward, Raven crawled through the dark passage.

It came out into a half-collapsed corridor. On the other side, the strange woman stood. Raven straightened, and summoned a weak flame in one hand. She could barely see through the thick darkness. The glow of the woman seemed to take all the light her pitiful flame gave off, absorbing it.

The skeletons were right behind, clamoring against the stones, crawling through the narrow corridor, bones scraping against stone. Their low growls echoed off the stone, more chilling than any beast of the forest.

The strange woman glided down the dark hall, and Raven ran to keep up with her. She ran, ran, and ran—and then the floor vanished.

For a moment that seemed longer than it was, Raven was suspended in complete darkness. The dank air whipped past, and then—*splash*. Cool water engulfed her and doused her flame. She sank. Her clothes absorbed the water in an instant, soaking her to the bone.

Heart pounding, flame extinguished, she knew only black water.

The water muffled all sounds. She did not know up from down. She couldn't breathe. Her lungs burned, her panic flared, and as she reached out, she felt only stone.

Deeper she sank.

She would drown down here. Die like all the other fools who thought they could become a Wraith.

Dankness, everywhere. Impenetrable.

She would die. She would...

No.

She would not die down here. Raven refused to believe it. There had to be a way out of this, a way up or down or something. Her magic responded, to her determination or desperation, and she felt a tug. And, lungs threatening to burst, she followed it. She swam through the darkness with only her magic to guide her. An invisible path led her down, down, down, and then to the left, and then over, and then up, up, up—

She broke through the surface of the black water and took a gasp of dank, soured air. Again, she saw only darkness, but without the water, she summoned her fire.

504

She had come up in a half-submerged, lopsided corridor. The walls tilted to the right. The inky water reflected her flame like liquid gold. She climbed out and onto the soggy, mossy floor. Moss hung from the ceiling and clung to the walls. Mildew and spongy plants grew in every crack it could find. Water dripped endlessly.

Raven glanced at the way back. The rippling water was black as ink. The ceiling had collapsed, blocking the way out, unless she wanted to dive back into the water.

No way she was going back that way. She turned back toward the corridor. She had not been in this part of the ruins during her hunt. She didn't even know what part of the fort she'd gone to. It didn't matter. If she couldn't go back, she had to go forward.

But... Sisters.

She took a deep breath and then another. No more skeletons crawled out of the stone. It seemed their pursuit did not extend beyond the water. Standing on wobbly legs, her clothes and boots soaked through, she started down the lopsided corridor.

She kept one eye out for treasure and the other for a way out. She saw no more skeletons or ghosts or whatever they had been.

Raven moved slower than before. Her stomach clenched every few moments, and though she thought she might, she did not vomit again. She came to the end of a corridor and found a lopsided painting, the color faded and the frame rotting. Through holes in the canvas, she could see a thicker shadow behind it. The decaying strips of canvas gently moved. She yanked it off the wall—an easy feat—and revealed tightly spiraled stone steps. The steps rose up and out of sight through the darkness.

She held her flame aloft and started to climb. She had to duck slightly to keep her head from hitting the top of the stairs above her. Her flame shoved away the closest shadows, but they remained at the edge of her light. She thought for a foolish, hopeful moment that maybe Zander could see through the shadows—she didn't even know if he had that power, let alone use it so far away. Just the thought that he might be closer gave her a small comfort, despite the stretch of sea between them.

The stairs ended at another passage hidden by a painting. She shoved against the back of the painting, and the rusted fastenings gave with a vicious *creak*—the painting fell into the corridor beyond.

She stepped through and into a room full of shadows. No windows allowed in natural light, and by the look of it, no light had touched this part of the fort in a very long time. Raven's flame flickered against the coiled shadows, startling them away. The stone was darker, the stones themselves bigger, and the air danker. This part of the fort looked older. She stepped into the room; her flames illuminated a collapsed desk and rotting bookshelves, books and scrolls molded and sinking inward with time. A mural took up the wall across from the desk, the art style identical to those she had found during her hunt.

Stepping closer, she lifted her flame toward the stone. The mural depicted the continent as she knew it, three kingdoms and three Sisters. The old god hadn't been etched onto this mural; neither had the southwestern kingdom or the fourth Sister. Altair's Augur was gone. Gears and machines flourished around Solen; ships and sea life bloomed around Minerva; and trees and flowers grew around Wilyn.

And... Sisters. Raven brought her flame closer to the mural, to the hooded figure of Wilyn. Curls escaped the hood, and a kind smile stretched her lips.

Just like the strange woman who had guided Raven away from the skeletons.

Raven stared at the hooded figure of Wilyn. Had the Sister helped her, or had she been hallucinating? Had any of it even been real? Those skeletal hands had certainly felt real, and she had plunged into water—her soaked clothes proved that much.

Raven shook the thoughts from her mind. Too much to think about, too soon. She left the office and kept wandering, through half-rotten halls, lopsided corridors, and leaky ceilings. The temperature sank, and the already cool water soaking her clothes turned frigid. Still, she wandered.

Finally—shivering from cold, chafing from wet clothes, stomach growling—Raven came to a knocked-down wall. Through the holes, she spotted a familiar glow of sunlight. Distant, but sunlight nonetheless. She climbed through and into something of a throne room. A crumbling arcade lined the room. The ironwork torch brackets had rusted and flaked, most of them gone. Old pots held molded soil and long dead flowers, the stems shriveled and black. At the far end sat an old, ornate stone chair. A throne.

A skeleton sat on the throne, bones pale as moonlight, shoulders slumped. Raven shivered from something other than the cold. Though the ruler of this fort might appear dead and gone, she had the distinct feeling of being watched.

The glow of sunlight came from behind the throne, through another wall punctured by a fallen pillar.

Raven started across the throne room, toward the sunlight—as she moved, the angle of sunlight shifted, and a beam of light glinted off an ornate saber that rested across the dead ruler's thighs. Raven approached with caution, watching for movements of the white bones. The saber, unlike the rest of the fort, shined like new. The steel was spotless. A bejeweled handguard held a dozen small pearls and emeralds. Her flames reflected in the ruby on the pommel.

Treasure.

Raven paused before the dead ruler and ran her finger along the flat side of the blade. Smooth and cool, not a spec of rust. Someone had indeed placed this saber here recently. Had the grand master come all this way to put this saber here? Or had Malik done the chore?

Before she took the saber, she wandered into the adjoining room. It looked to have once been a meeting room, attached to the throne room within easy reach of the king. Just inside, a bejeweled shield rested against the wall. Not far from it, a golden bow rested on the wall.

Three ornate weapons. Three treasures?

Further exploration of the room led her to another secret passage, one whose painting had rotten away and left the room beyond exposed. It looked to have been used for storage. Resting on three separate barrels were a goblet, a lute, and a lantern. Each too shiny and new and smothered in jewels to have belonged to the fort itself. Six treasures placed in the same room.

She doubted the hider of the items would have been so careless, meaning they intended for her to find them all at once. Yet the grand master had told her to pick *one.*

She understood. She had to not only find the treasure room but pick a treasure and then explain its value. It was a test of survival and of person.

But which treasure?

Raven thought back to the murals she'd found, to the Sisters, and to all of her stepmother's stories of the Sisters and Mel's teachings. These objects had meaning.

The sword and goblet belonged to Solen, Goddess of Stone and Steel. The sword stood for those who wished to protect, those unafraid of violence, those willing to make change. The goblet stood for those who protected and healed from the inside, with food and drink.

The shield and lantern belonged to Minerva, Goddess of the Sea and Wind. The shield for those of unwavering faith, unafraid of sacrifice, those able to withstand the tempest. Those of inner strength. The lantern lit the way for those lost at sea, for those lighting the darkness for others, those who uncover secrets, those of the guiding light.

The arrow and lute belonged to Wilyn, Goddess of the Forest and Stars. Her arrow stood for stealth, for the silent protectors, for those who worked not for glory but for results, from the air and shadows. The lute stood for those who brightened the darkness within, those who bring joy in times of darkness.

And by picking a treasure, Raven would be picking a Sister.

Was there a wrong answer? If she picked the wrong treasure, would the Wraiths turn her away? Picking the sword might imply that she hadn't searched thoroughly and found the others. It might imply her shortsighted and inpatient.

Raven gathered all the treasure into the sunlit room—after carefully removing the sword from the skeleton, which did not move. She arranged them on the floor. Each glittered in her flame, rubies and diamonds and pearls. Each would be worth a fortune.

She heaved a sigh. Each object had its own set of traits. Depending on which she chose, it would imply that she had those traits. The object would reflect her strengths and weaknesses. But, what were her strengths and weaknesses? She didn't know. Logically, the shield would be the most awkward to get out. The goblet might be the easiest. Picking the shield might suggest stubbornness. The goblet might suggest laziness. She didn't like either of those.

The longer she stared at the treasures, the more uncertain she was. Her empty stomach played games with her mind. Though the outside air warmed the room, her clothes were still wet and cold. As the sunlight began to tilt toward the west, she gave up. She had time to make this impossible decision.

She wandered back through the throne room and through the corridors. Finding her way back to her shelter wasn't as hard as she feared. By the time she returned, the sun sank to the west, turning the ocean liquid gold.

She encountered no skeletons or ghosts.

Scorch marks darkened the walls like claw marks, and the room smelled like smoke. Too tired to dwell on it, she arranged what palm fronds remained, stripped herself of her wet clothes, and collapsed.

She slept deeply and woke to the grayed light of an overcast dawn. Over a breakfast of clean water and coconut, she mulled over what had happened. The berries, the skeletons, the ghost—she didn't know what to make of it all.

And which treasure should she pick? She feared what her choice would tell the grand master about her.

She fingered her dried clothes. They were stiff from stagnant water and stunk of mildew. She couldn't wander around the fort naked. Well, she could, but she didn't want to. She took the time to gather enough clean water to sate her thirst and rinse her clothes. It took a while to gather enough water, but she considered it worth it. She carefully used her magic to heat the water from the threads. One wrong move, and she would turn her clothes to ashes and have a very awkward meeting when the grand master returned to fetch her.

Once her clothes were dry, she wandered back to the throne room. She got lost only three times. Strangely enough, the corridors and halls were beginning to make sense.

The treasures remained where she had put them. She sat down, determined not to leave the room without an answer.

She left several hours later without an answer.

She spent the rest of the day cleaning up the mess she'd made of her tower and gathering a fresh armload of palm fronds and coconuts. That night, spearing for fish in her underthings, Raven glanced up at the sky. Inky clouds floated between her and the stars.

The experience of the adventure is the real treasure.

Raven inhaled sharply as her mother's voice resounded in her head as clear as if she stood on the rocky beach. Her mother, who had flown all over the world. Her mother, who had chosen herself above others. Her mother, who had flown at top speed to save the people Raven cared about. Her mother, who had once done this very Trial and become a Wraith.

Raven no longer felt anger toward her mother. She felt something far warmer: fondness and admiration.

Despite everything, Luckett was still her mother. And like it or not, she and her daughter shared a remarkable number of qualities. Didn't Raven choose herself over others when she went to catch the thief with Zander? Hadn't she picked adventure over safety in the mines? Hadn't she picked herself when she ran away from the Dwellers? And when she agreed to become a Wraith, she had thought of herself, her future, and what she wanted.

Despite everything, Raven was still her mother's daughter.

She had always been this way. She had always been her mother's daughter.

And her mother's words repeated in her mind as she cooked fish over the newly arranged firepit, as she picked the meat from the bones, as she fell asleep with the starry sky within her view.

R aven returned to the treasure room every day but hesitated to take anything.

At the end of her seven days, Raven returned to the dock at dawn. The rowboat appeared first as a speck and grew closer with every blink. She kept her hands behind her back. Grand Master Deikun, Malik, Elizi, and—Raven's breath caught at the sight of the fourth person in the boat. It was Zander. That he had come to see her made her heart swell.

The past week had been refreshing but also lonely.

Raven held her chin high and her shoulders steady. The boat glided to the dock and paused. Zander quickly looked her over—thankfully she had taken the time to bathe that morning. She hadn't had soap, but it had been better than wearing a week's worth of grime. Zander brought his sapphire eyes up to hers. Thoughts churned behind them. He had a lot he wanted to say, but he knew now wasn't the time.

The grand master gracefully climbed out of the boat and stood on the sturdy part of the dock, barring her exit into the boat.

Suddenly, her choice didn't feel so good. What if she had chosen wrong? What happened when someone failed the Trial? Would he kill her and be done with it?

"It is good to see you alive, magician. What treasure have you recovered?" His eyes were steady and curious.

Raven steeled herself by envisioning her mother. Then she brought her empty hands in front of her, palms up. Deikun stared at her hands, mouth tilted down, then at her. She met his stare, unafraid. In the boat, Zander, Malik, and Elizi looked horrified.

"You did not find a treasure?" Deikun's voice came out firm, but a twinkle in his eyes told her he suspected otherwise.

"I found them all," Raven said, her voice steady as her posture. She had gone over this speech a dozen times that morning. "The sword to cut down. The shield to defend. The arrow to strike from afar. The lute to entertain. The goblet to drink. The lantern to expose. I found them all, but none are the treasure that I chose."

Deikun lifted his brows. Behind him, Zander shifted in the boat, causing it to gently rock. Malik put a steady hand on his shoulders. Zander blinked at Raven; his sapphire eyes were stars in the daylight. She had missed those stars.

"The experience of an adventure cannot be defined in an ornate object," Raven explained.

The grand master tilted his chin in curiosity.

"I learned that my magic can help me see where my eyes cannot and to hear what my ears cannot. I learned to trust my magic. That experience cannot be measured in gold or jewels."

A long moment passed. The grand master blinked at her, and for a terrifying moment, she thought she had made an error—then he smiled.

Deikun threw his arms out, and said, "Welcome, magician, to the Wraiths."

Raven wanted to fall to the ground in relief, but she held her shoulders straight. She allowed a smile to creep over her lips. Zander sighed in relief and ran a hand through his hair. Malik released a held breath, a subtle action.

"Let us return," Deikun announced, and he climbed back into the boat.

Zander held his hand out for hers, and she accepted his offer as she eagerly joined them. She sat beside Zander while Malik sat beside the grand master. At Elizi's command, the boat gently glided away from the island and toward the mainland.

"How did it go?" Zander could likely smell the week on her skin, her hair, but he didn't say anything. Of course, having gone through the Trial himself, he understood exactly what she felt.

Raven met his eyes. She felt utterly exhausted. Worry over her choice of treasure had kept her tossing and turning. Everything ached from the wandering and exploring, and the strange skeleton chase. Her back ached from sleeping on a hard stone floor. And now that the survival had been taken from her shoulders, she felt beyond exhausted and spent.

"Fine, I suppose," Raven told Zander. "I'm tired and hungry."

Deikun gave her a knowing smile. "There will be a celebration dinner tonight in honor of your successful Trial," he told her. "After that, you will enter the temple for your Choosing. Once Chosen, you will be formally inducted into the Wraiths."

At the thought of a celebration dinner, her mouth began to water, but that there was more to becoming a Wraith sent her nerves rattling.

"My Choosing?" She looked helplessly from Deikun to Malik to Zander.

"It will be explained when the time comes," said Deikun. "Before that, we celebrate."

Neither Malik or Zander further explained, so she asked no more. Whatever the Choosing was, it couldn't possibly be worse than the Trial. So Raven let herself relax. Before her Choosing, she would celebrate. She would bathe, eat, and rest. She would be prepared for whatever came next.

Zander nudged her shoulder with his. She had unknowingly closed her eyes. She found the stars of his eyes and smiled at him to let him know that she was ready. For anything.

The boat glided between the cliffs and into the gulf. A gentle murmur had settled over the village since the last time Raven had seen it—a chatter of voices and life. Their boat paused against the dock, and Elizi tied it off. Deikun led them along the sandy path and to the shadowed temple. To Raven's surprise, Wraiths gathered in front of the temple; they stood on either side of the steps, leaving a path for the grand master. Deikun paused just inside the shadow of the cliff.

"A new Wraith will soon join us," he announced, his voice strong.

A single cheer came from the crowd, a single word from every mouth—a word Raven had never heard. Just as the cheer filled the air, it vanished.

"*Jul,*" Zander whispered. "It's an old word. It means success, happiness, and congratulations."

Deikun led Raven to the stronghold. Wraiths surrounded her, shaking her hand, offering smiles and congratulations, whispering kind words and praise. It felt so different than before. Where the Wraiths had been cold and indifferent, they were now warm and welcoming.

"There was a real chance you wouldn't make it back," Zander said as they started up the steps.

Deikun opened the doors to the stronghold with a wave of his hand. Unlike before, the torches were already lit.

"No one wanted to get close to you and then have you die."

It was such a morbid thought, but she understood.

Deikun turned and said to Malik, "See that the celebrations are set into motion for tonight."

Malik nodded and started back outside.

"Zander, see our newest member to the guest chambers," Deikun said. "They should be ready for you."

Zander nodded and offered his arm to Raven. She slipped her arm into his, and he guided her through a stone archway and into a darkly lit corridor. The corridor had been carved from the stone, though the walls had been carved with decorative lines and patterns. Fires burned in plates held aloft by carved hooded figures, spread just far enough to leave a line of shadow between each one. It smelled of smoke and stone, not unlike the mines of Silver Glen, but also of something else; something sweet she couldn't quite identify.

Magic, the childish part of her mind whispered.

She wanted to believe it, so she did.

"How many don't come back?" she asked. Her voice seemed to echo, but at the same time, it seemed to sink into the very stone.

"It's hard to say," Zander said grimly. "One in five, maybe. Not everyone can survive being alone for a week with nothing but the ocean. They either starve or drown or fall."

"I didn't see anyone," she whispered. Bodies, she meant, but she didn't want to voice it.

Zander's expression darkened. "If they aren't there when the grand master goes to get them, he sends a retrieval team. I know he says no one will get your body, but he sends someone. I... I went on a few during my training. We scour the old fort for bodies. It's not fun. Worse than the Trial."

She bit her lip. "I'm sorry."

"I've always said that we should at least warn magicians before tossing them onto an island," Zander said. "I thought I would have time to warn you, but..."

"I jumped in head first," she said, sighing.

Zander laughed. "Yeah, but apparently, I was wrong to worry. Of course, I knew you'd do it. And without breaking anything or getting some strange infection too."

"How would you know that?"

"You shook hands with three healers that I saw," Zander said, grinning. "They would have sensed anything wrong immediately."

Thalame had patted her shoulder, now that she thought about it.

"I learned how to scavenge in Silver Glen," Raven said proudly. "My father taught me how to fish, and luckily I prefer my food slightly burned." She started to mention the berries but paused.

Zander caught the hesitation and frowned. "What is it? Did something happen?"

"Well...yes and no."

He pulled her to a stop.

Half laughing, she said, "I found a berry bush."

Zander's brows came together and, in the next heartbeat, shot to his hairline. His mouth formed an O. "Rae...tell me you didn't eat them."

"Oh, I ate a handful," she said, her tone light.

Zander paled.

"I threw up immediately and saw skeletons coming out of the stone."

Zander gawked at her like she had gone mad.

"I found the passage that took me into the treasure room on my mad dash to get away from the skeletons," she said, poking his dropped chin.

He closed his mouth. She did not tell him about the ghostly vision of Wilyn. It felt too personal.

Zander let out a low laugh and continued down the corridor. "Sisters, Raven. You could have poisoned yourself beyond healing with those. They're called shade fruit. They only grow in the shade in the topics. They're powerful hallucinogens. I've heard shade is used a lot in the southern islands of Tinatun, but it's a diluted formula, not the straight berries."

"I felt horrible for several days." Raven had lived through that fight too. She had beaten the poison, beaten the Trial, and she could beat whatever this Choosing was too. "Can I ask you about what happens next?"

"I'm forbidden to tell you," Zander said plainly. "What? Don't give me that look. It's the truth. I swore an oath, Raven. A *magic* oath."

She pouted but didn't complain.

Zander guided her up a staircase and into a short corridor with a handful of dark wooden doors. He guided her to the last door. "This is the guest wing. No one else is staying up here, so you've got the place to yourself. Everything you need should be inside."

"Where will you be staying?"

"I've got a room a corridor away," Zander said. "You'll get your own room after your Choosing and the induction ceremony."

"You have a room here? Even if you're never here?"

"It's not really *my* room," Zander explained. "It's in the hall where the other Wraiths sleep." He stepped closer, mouth a straight line. "But I have a place here, among the Wraiths. As does every magician who has become a Wraith; as will you."

"That sounds nice," she said.

They stood alone in the corridor. The stone soaked up the sound, and it felt as though they were the only people for leagues. Raven glanced at the door to her guest room, then back to Zander's sapphire eyes.

He cupped her cheek. "I'm glad you made it back."

"I'm glad you were there to meet me," she said.

He leaned in, but she leaned away. Zander blinked, hurt flashing across his face.

"And I will kiss you twice after I wash the grime off myself." She smiled at his pout. She didn't give him a chance to argue. She patted his chest and let herself into her guest room.

It was a simple room. A candle burned on the bedside table. A narrow bed stood against the wall, made up with plain linens. A wooden folding screen divided the bed from the rest of the room. A washing basin stood on a stone pedestal underneath a carved clamshell; a rope hung underneath it. She tugged on the rope, and chilled water fell from the clam and into the basin. She released the rope; the water stopped flowing.

She didn't have the mind or patience to marvel at the inner workings. She pulled the rope and filled the tub. She found soap in the cabinet and used her magic to heat the water. She left her dirty clothes in a pile on the floor—Oh! A bath had never felt so good! She washed herself twice for good measure, relishing the feeling of the water, the soap, the softness of the skin left behind.

A drain at the bottom of the tub let the water flow out of sight. Towels had been stocked in the cabinet as well as a few essentials. After toweling off, Raven found a set of plain robes, not unlike the Wraiths wore, only unadorned and unarmored. She ran her hands over the simple material, soft and supple.

A Wraith. Her, a Wraith!

So much had happened in such a short period of time, her mind grappled to keep up with it all. For so long, every day had been the same. Now, every day was a surprise. And it had left her exhausted. She reclined back on the bed, wearing just the towel, intent on only a few moments' rest.

24

She woke sometime later to a knocking at the door.

"Raven?" came Zander's voice. "Are you in there? Raven?"

"I'm here," she said groggily, straining to sit up. Oh, she could sleep for days more. Her limbs begged to remain unused, but she sat up anyway.

The towel had gotten shoved to the floor sometime during her nap, leaving her naked and tangled in a mess of sheets. The handle on the door turned, and she grabbed the edge of the blanket and covered herself just as Zander stepped into the room.

"I came to see..." His words faded as his eyes fell on her. He blinked several times.

"You came to see?" Raven asked, chuckling at the wording. A mad blush heated her skin.

"...if you were awake," Zander said, each word carefully spoken. He dragged his eyes over her and finally met hers. "Dinner is ready, and it would be inappropriate to start the celebration of your success without you."

She maneuvered her body with the sheet, setting her bare feet on the floor. The sheet rose up her thighs. Dinner sounded marvelous, even more so than another nap. She lingered on the bedside, clutching the sheet to her chest. Zander stood dumbfounded in the doorway, and she relished it—she had gotten so few chances to stump him.

"I will be in the corridor," Zander said quickly. He stepped out and shut the door.

She dressed in the robes she'd found earlier and braided her wild hair over her shoulder. She dusted off her leather boots and tucked her ebony-handled dagger into the left one. The familiar weight settled against her leg.

She found Zander leaning against the wall with his arms crossed and one leg propped up. He wore fresh Wraith robes of dark indigo and gray.

"Your arm." Raven nodded to his mechanical arm. In the robes, only his brass hand was visible. "You've made progress."

Zander made a show of stretching his arms—both of them—in unison above his head. He brought his hands back down and flipped his mechanical wrist just so—with a delicate whirl of gears, the compass in his palm opened and quickly settled on north. "It's working like a dream," Zander said. "What about you? Considering you had an entire week to work on your magic?"

"I told the grand master the truth." She shrugged. "My magic helped me, but not just to cook dinner and clean water. It...guided me, if that makes sense."

"Can't say," Zander said. "Magic's odd like that. Everyone's magic is a little different, and considering yours is extremely different, it's impossible to say anything for certain."

Raven huffed and set her hands on her hips. "Enough talk. You mentioned food."

Zander extended his human arm for hers. She threaded her arm in his, and he guided her through the corridors and to the main chamber of the stronghold. Tables had been arranged from wall to wall, each laden with fruit, roasted meat and fish, breads, and sweets. Her mouth watered. Wraiths lingered around, chatting and laughing. The doors of the stronghold were open, and from somewhere in the village, music played.

A celebration.

Zander guided her toward the main doors, and on the way, she snagged a small loaf of dark bread with cinnamon and sugar baked in, a wooden skewer of pineapple, and a skewer of roasted pork. The sun hadn't yet set over the ocean, and the entire world seemed alight in bright golds and yellows and ambers. The shadow of the cliff extended over most of the village and gulf, but it did not dampen the spirits. Music sang from everywhere, strings and flutes and drums.

As Zander led Raven toward the gathering, a great shout of "*Jul!*" rose around them, and with her present, the celebration started.

Raven danced, ate her fill, and met as many other Wraiths as she could. They had heard stories of her from Thalame and Zander while she had been at her Trial, and all that she had done to agitate the Gray Elite. Everyone had heard about the melted Colossus by now, and everyone wanted to meet the girl who had done it. She found it both flattering and exhausting, but having slept and replenished her spirit with food and drink, she didn't mind. Luckily, the Wraiths had no qualms about her eating and greeting at the same time.

The sun sank, the stars glittered, and she danced on the beach. Though she would have liked to dance all night, her exhaustion caught up with her. When she could dance and eat no more, Zander guided her back into the stronghold.

Once in the relative calm of the corridors, she slipped her arm out of his and instead slipped it around his middle. She hugged him close, pressing her face into his shoulder. He smelled like the beach, like wet sand, woodsmoke, and briny sea breeze, but like him, dark and powerful.

"Have fun?" Zander asked.

She nodded against his shoulder.

He set his mechanical arm around her waist and stroked her hair with his other hand. She could stay like this for a long time.

"The Choosing isn't that bad," Zander whispered. "I was terrified before mine. I thought it would be worse than the island, but it wasn't. It's not bad at all."

"I don't want to talk about that right now," Raven said, though his words did provide a sense of comfort for the following morning. She pulled her head off his shoulder but didn't lean away.

"What do you want to talk about, then?"

She closed the gap between them in a heartbeat, pressing her mouth against his. She broke apart just long enough to say, "Nothing." She kissed him again.

Sisters, how she had missed Zander. How she had thought about him. How she had thought about this.

He pulled her closer and deepened the kiss. She ran her hand along the stubble of his jaw, down the contours of his throat, and to the folds of his robes. Having done up her own, she knew about how they worked, the hidden ties and clasps. She tugged the soft material away from his throat, and as her fingers graced his collarbone, he shifted—he pushed her against the wall. Her gasp was lost in the heat of his mouth. He laced his fingers with hers and pinned her hands above her head. He kissed her deeply, a kiss long overdue.

He pressed his body into hers. Her gasp evaporated on his lips. She nipped at his bottom lip, and a low moan escaped the back of his throat. He kissed her neck, his breath hot. Heat seared across her skin and through her bones, something other than her magic. Something hotter, something brighter. She needed more. She wanted more. Of this, of him.

She slid her calf along his. Up, down, then back up a little higher, a little higher, and then she hooked her leg around his waist. A low growl came from the back of his throat, rumbling against her skin. His teeth scraped along her jaw, nipped at her ear.

"Now would be the time to stop," Zander whispered, his voice husky. "Unless you want me to haul you to the nearest closet."

His voice sent a shiver down her back. She thought of a closet, dark and private, the cold floor against her back, of his... She hooked her other leg around his waist. He released a heavy sigh against her throat. He gave a single thrust of his hips into hers, to accentuate his meaning. To accentuate hers, she squeezed her legs tighter.

"Raven." His breath left his throat in a gasp, a sigh—she didn't know.

"If I wanted you to stop, I would have punched you by now," she said, shocked at the huskiness of her own voice.

Zander tightened his arms around her. In a swift motion, he pushed off from the wall, cradling her in his arms. He carried her into the guest corridor, into her room, and kicked the door closed. He laid her down on the bed. He removed his cowl and tunic, one tie and clasp at a time, leaving his chest exposed. She trailed her fingertips along the scars that crisscrossed his bronze skin, painting a story for each one. Fire burst through her veins as she touched him; the heat pulsed at the faintest brushes of his fingers and against her skin as she tugged at her robes.

His lips, his hands—he moved in such ways that had her seeing fantasies she'd never dreamed of! Her senses overheated. Everything blurred together and sharpened at once: the soft rustle of their robes hitting the floor, the thud of boots, the clicking of his belt unbuckling, and his skin against hers.

And the world exploded into stars and blinding colors.

Zander collapsed beside her. As the euphoria eased into something warmer, something steadier, Raven rolled onto her side. She waited for the feeling of being bare to make her blush, but it never came. Zander lay beside her, just as bare. She nestled her head onto his shoulder, and his heart beat under her cheek. She found his hand and laced her fingers with his.

25

Raven woke up to a gentle motion. She rolled over to see Zander sitting on the side of the bed, stretching his arms across his chest. His human arm flexed. His metal arm held, steel joints moved flawlessly, clicking and whirling. The scars along his shoulder had healed to pale bronze. The skin and metal met as if the metal had always been there.

His back held as many scars as his chest, and Raven absently traced her finger over one that slashed over his side. She dropped her hand back to the bed as he stood. He leaned over and pressed a kiss to her forehead, then started to dress. He picked up her robes from the floor and tossed them onto the bed.

She made no move. She hugged the pillow closer. She hadn't slept so well in what felt like months.

"I'd love to spend the morning cuddling," Zander said, buckling his belt, sapphire eyes rolling over her. "But, you've got an important meeting. It's bad form to be late to your Choosing."

She groaned, rolled onto her back, and stretched. Granted, she felt remarkably better than she had yesterday morning. Zander started to fill the basin, and Raven pulled on her robes. As she secured the clasp across her middle, she caught Zander watching. He wore that calm, arrogant smirk of his, the one that had left knots in her stomach from the first moment she'd seen it. Not that she would tell him that.

He splashed cool water on his face and tied back his hair; Raven combed hers and braided it back.

"You ready?" Zander asked into her neck. He punctuated his words with a kiss on her pulse.

"As ready as I can be," Raven said. "Though, are you sure they won't mind us being a little late?" She'd rather stay in here with him a while longer.

"As tempting as that is, it's not the Wraiths you've got to worry about today." Zander stepped away. "There's always tonight, and the night after that."

She hummed. Tonight seemed awfully far away. Changing the subject, she asked, "How's your arm?"

"It's still not quite one hundred percent." He thrust his metal arm to the side, fingers splayed. She heard the subtle grind of gears. He curled in his metal fingers and his human fingers; the metal took a heartbeat longer to respond. "Every day is a little better."

"Give it another week," Raven said.

He'd made so much progress in what time he'd had. Another week, two, three? He would be back to normal. Or, as normal as a metal arm could be.

Zander flexed his fingers again and then wiggled them at her. The tiny gears clicked, the joint of his wrist whirled. He stroked his metal thumb against her cheek.

"I could get used to this," he said.

Warmth spread through her limbs. "Your arm?" she asked, smirking. "You'd better. I don't think you can get the other one back."

He chuckled, but she saw it—a glimpse of something darker. "I meant I could get used to you. Waking up next to you. Seeing you first thing in the morning." He stepped closer, and that dark something vanished.

"Zander, are you turning sentimental on me?" She smiled; she couldn't help it. Zander had always been the tough guy, the snarky one. "Don't tell me you're going soft."

He snaked his arms around her and pulled her into an embrace. He kissed her temple. "I've not had a lot to be sentimental or soft about." His kiss found its way to her lips.

Say it, a little voice in her head said. *Say it. Say it. Say it.*

Her lips parted, she inhaled—a knock sounded on the door.

"Raven?" Malik called.

Zander let out a soft, disgruntled sigh.

"I'm awake," she called back.

The door started to open, and she and Zander stepped out of each other's arms. Malik looked as though he had slept well. Color brightened his cheeks and his eyes. He wore the robes of the Wraiths, as well as his rings and several fine silver chains around his neck. Each glinted in the candlelight.

"She's on her way to the Choosing," Zander said.

"It's not that." In a blink, Malik's gaze turned dire. "I'm actually looking for you, Zander. Deikun called an emergency meeting."

"What happened?" Zander asked.

"He didn't say," Malik said. "Only to spread the word."

"All right," Zander said.

Malik left, and Zander and Raven quickly readied. She straightened her robes and tightened the laces of her boots. She didn't know how to get ready for her Choosing. She double-checked to make sure her dagger was in place. Zander then led the way to the main chamber. Several other Wraiths had gathered for the emergency meeting, all in their armored gear. Tense whispers floated through the room. The tables remained from the celebration the night before, and platters of biscuits, bagels, and fruit had been served.

Raven and Zander sat at a table beside Thalame, and she took a large bite from a biscuit. Tiny seeds flecked the inside.

Grand Master Deikun stood at the end of the chamber, at a table with a few older Wraiths. Slowly, Wraiths filed in from the adjoining corridors. The hall gradually filled. At last, the grand master stood. Silence issued.

"As most of you know," started Deikun. He did not shout, yet his voice filled the room. "Raven completed the Trial and must attend her Choosing." An agreeable murmur followed. "But we have other news this morning. There is a Gray Elite caravan crossing into Tinatun to the west, transporting magicians. I am sending a small team to disrupt the caravan and retrieve the captive magicians. The scouts have reason to think they are sending the magicians to the coast to be shipped south. The Wraiths will not allow it."

A few of the Wraiths stood. Volunteers for the mission, Raven realized.

Zander stood, and her heart skidded.

"Your arm good enough, mate?" Thalame remained seated—he had once told Raven he didn't like fighting.

"My arm is more than good enough." Zander flexed his metal fingers. "This is my chance to prove it."

"Are you certain?" came the steady voice of Deikun.

"Yes," Zander said, bowing his head. "Allow me to prove my recovery on this mission."

Deikun held Zander's gaze a long moment, then nodded.

"Zander?" Raven started to stand, but Thalame put a hand on her shoulder.

"You're not a full Wraith," Thalame whispered. "The grand master wouldn't allow it. You've got to be Chosen first."

She bit her lip. She hadn't planned on being separated so soon.

Deikun scanned the volunteers. "All right. Those willing, meet me after breakfast in the Crystal Chamber."

Zander sat back down. "It'll be fine, Rae. This sort of thing is typical Wraith business. Nothing special. I can't go with you to the Choosing anyway, and they tend to last a while. I'll be back before you are."

She blinked; she hadn't planned on going anywhere either. Would the Choosing take place on another island? In the heart of the forest? Underground?

"You'll be fine." Zander nudged her knee with his. "It's not bad."

"Would you have told me that about the Trial?"

"No," he said. "I would have told you how horrible it was, and that you could die."

"So, there's no chance I'll die in the Choosing?"

"No."

"None at all?"

He shrugged. "I'm sure there's the smallest chance. If you somehow find a way to die during the Choosing, I'll be impressed."

Breakfast ended, and Malik motioned for Raven to follow. Zander stood, but rather than follow the other volunteers, he followed Malik.

"Don't you need to go with them?" Raven asked.

"In a few minutes." Zander laced his fingers with hers.

They followed Malik through a set of doors in the very back of the hall and down a spiraling stone staircase carved from the cliffside. The walls were smooth, too smooth to have been carved by tools or human hands. Sconces along the ceiling held flames, but she smelled no smoke, saw no candles. A chill ran up her spine as she realized why this place looked so familiar. It looked like the smooth stone of the Temple of the Three Sisters in Silver Glen.

Malik was leading her into a temple.

Her skin prickled.

The stairs ended before a grand set of stone doors, carved in the same fashion as the murals she'd found on the island. The carvings depicted the Three Sisters, their talents, their objects, and their elements. The mysterious fourth Sister was absent, and in her place on the door was a tree whose roots spread over the edges of the door. Had the doors in Silver Glen held such a tree? She couldn't remember. It felt like a lifetime ago that Mel had led her into the temple.

Malik paused before the doors, the flames casting his face in shadows.

Zander kissed her cheek and said, "You'll do fine, babe."

She blushed; she'd never been called *babe* before. "And I'll see you when I'm done? Babe?" It didn't sound as romantic when she said it.

Zander smiled and kissed the back of her hand. "Of course."

Say it. Say it. Say it.

Raven watched Zander go up the stairs and out of sight, and those words jumbled on her tongue. She swallowed them. When they met again, then.

"Ready?" Malik placed his hand against the seam of the doors.

She took a deep breath. "I'm ready."

The doors began to open. And she steeled herself to face her Choosing.

26

Raven stepped through the stone doors and into a dark chamber. The darkness swirled thick, like it had when she had first stepped into the Wraiths' stronghold. A magical darkness, meant to blind and hide. The doors began to close, and she glanced back at Malik. He stood on the other side, but he did not wear the same worry he had when he left her on the island. The light shrank into a sliver that divided her body in halves, then vanished as the doors closed.

For a terrifying heartbeat, she stood in total darkness. Alone. She repressed a shiver as she remembered the black water she'd fallen into, the darkness, the pressure, the inability to breathe—she took a gasping breath of the cool, cavernous air.

She would not drown. There was no water here.

And she had her magic. She brought a flame to life in her palm, dousing the back of the stone doors in bright red-orange. The stone was smooth. She turned to face the chamber; her light did not reach very far in, but it uncovered enough. She stood in a hall of plain stone walls and a gently curved ceiling.

With no other way to go, she started walking. A few steps in, torches burst to life on either side of her—eliciting a yelp of surprise from her. The flames were dull silver, ghosts of flames that had once been. The torches hung on iron brackets, the ironwork heavy and out of style. The torches brightened the corridor better than her flame, so she let it go out.

As she reached the edge of the torches' light, the next set burst to life with the same ghostly glow. The torches remained lit behind her, and when eight sets of torches burned, a multitude of torches burst to life at once.

She had reached the temple.

It looked identical to the one in Silver Gen. Three massive statues, one of each sister, stood at the cardinal points of the room. Each had been carved from the Sister's chosen stone: sandstone for Minerva; limestone for Solen; and marble for Wilyn. In the center of the chamber stood a circular platform, the edges carved with elegant lines that never intersected.

The Wraiths used a temple for the Choosing? Her heart thudded hard against her ribs—had the temple in Silver Glen once been used for the same purpose?

"Come forward," three voices spoke in unison, each female, each strong, and each proud. There was no mistaking the sound; the voices filled the room.

The Three Sisters.

A chill like Raven had never felt raced through her entire body. She forced her shaky legs forward, stepping onto the platform. Her legs shook too much to stand, so she sat. Her bones felt like they would rattle into nonexistence.

"A new face comes to us," said a voice from her left, from Solen's statue. Her voice was deep and somber, strong as steel.

"Another seeks to become a Wraith," said a voice from her right, from Minerva. Her voice was smooth and fluid, deep as the ocean.

"Another comes to be Chosen," said a voice in front of her, from Wilyn. Her voice was buttery and soft, a wind through the trees. Raven had the eeriest feeling that she had heard it before.

She could feel eyes on her, though she could not see anyone. She glanced into the eyes of Wilyn, but she saw only shadowed stone. But the Sisters were here, a part of them, somehow. That reality shook her deeper than she knew possible. The Sisters were real. And they were talking to her.

And in their silence, she realized they were waiting for her.

"Yes," she said, unsure of what else to say. "To be Chosen."

Her voice did not echo as theirs did, nor did it fill the chamber. She had never felt more insignificant.

"You have survived the Trial," said Solen.

"You have proven your worth of skill and persistence," said Minerva.

"You have shown your determination to live," said Wilyn.

"And now you have come to be Chosen," they said as one, the eerie cadence resounding.

"To be judged of character and mind," said Minerva.

"To be weighed of spirit," said Solen.

"To be Chosen by one of us," said Wilyn.

"To become a patron," they said together.

Raven swallowed. To be Chosen meant to be chosen by a Sister, a patron.

"But she has questions," added Solen.

"About that which has been erased," said Wilyn.

"About that which you now possess," Minerva said, her voice neither accusing nor mean.

"Speak," they said together.

Raven's hands shook. She balled them, but it didn't help. They knew about the murals, about what she had uncovered, and they knew the truth about her magic—that it wasn't hers. She swallowed.

"The murals I saw during the Trial," Raven said softly, her voice neither echoing nor brave. "There were four of you."

"Yes," Minerva said, regret in her voice. "Our forgotten Sister. Our father made four of us. From the depths of the ocean, he birthed me. From the deepest cavern, he birthed Solen. From the heart of the forest, he birthed Wilyn. And from the core of a volcano, he birthed Aeon."

"To each of us, he gifted a kingdom," said Solen. "And, for many years, we lived in peace. Our peoples thrived."

"But Aeon grew greedy and restless," said Wilyn. "She and her people were gifted with knowledge, and they wanted more."

"They wanted war," added Solen, her voice dark with remorse. "They sought to take."

"Aeon's people created a machine that would destroy any in their way and fortify them as the strongest kingdom of them all."

A deathly silence fell in the chamber.

"Altair's Augur," Raven whispered.

"Her people turned on her," said Solen. "But she allowed it. Her power became the machine, and war ensued. Many lives were lost. The era was darkened with fear."

"Our father sought to stop her, but she turned on him. Her people turned on him," said Wilyn.

"Our father could not stop her, so we did," said Minerva.

"Between the three of us, we stopped our sister and her people," said Wilyn.

"Her kingdom sank to the bottom of the ocean," said Minerva.

"Her name, erased," said Solen.

"The machine, hidden," said Minerva.

"Her power, contained," said Wilyn.

Again, silence thickened. Raven flattened her palms on her thighs. With every word, every piece of the story, her insides churned and shook. "Her power," she whispered. "It was contained in the machine."

"Her power became yours," Wilyn said, her voice soft, not unkind or accusing.

Raven felt that power tugging under her skin. She hadn't burned it off that morning. "I didn't mean to take it," Raven said.

"We know," Wilyn said. "You sought to keep the power away from those who would use it. You did not intend to use it yourself. You have become a vessel for Aeon's gift of fire. It is now yours."

"You chose to keep the world safe over your own safety," Minerva said proudly. "Without knowing what might happen to yourself."

"Your acts are commendable," Solen said.

"It shows a will to protect others, even strangers, and the world," said Wilyn.

"It is a will we wish more had," said Minerva.

Silence again fell, and Raven felt a question bubble up her throat. "In the ruins," she started, almost afraid of the answer. She cast her eyes toward Wilyn's statue. "I saw a woman. She helped me."

"She looked like me," Wilyn supplied. "Aeon. It would not be unthinkable that a part of her exists within the power that resides within you. A shadow of Aeon. She helped you survive?"

"She did," Raven said, nodding.

She thought of the hooded woman. It had been Aeon, the Sister whose face had been taken from the murals. The Sister who had been wiped from history for her greed and ambition. And a piece of that Sister resided within her magic? Raven looked at her hands. She hadn't felt anything, but then, she realized, that voice she hadn't heard in so long. It had been that sliver of Aeon. Something within her magic seemed to confirm it.

"She is not you, and you are not her," said Minerva. "Do not let that worry invade your senses. She cannot control you, though her power is now yours."

"Yours," echoed Wilyn. "Not hers."

"What you choose to do with it," said Solen, "time will tell."

"But now it is time for us to make a choice," Minerva said.

"To Choose," the three of them said together. "Let us begin."

The temperature in the chamber dropped. The blue light dimmed. The very stone seemed to hum with power. Raven felt the presence around her—all around, comforting and invasive. It felt heavy as water, soft as starlight, and strong as steel. Into her thoughts, her heart, her being.

A judgment.

She felt their voices, their words, their thoughts.

Solen admired her determination and her will in the face of danger and adversity. Minerva admired her bravery and her will to protect those around her. Wilyn admired her creativity and inner strength. Raven felt the Sisters confer amongst themselves, around her, about her. She felt the air changing and moving as light through water. She had proven herself in the eyes of each Sister. Any would gladly have her, but only one could Choose her.

The undulating air changed, then stopped. She felt the change, the difference—a decision had been made. And all at once, the presence vanished from around her. She gasped for a deep, much-needed breath. Had she even been breathing?

"Raven," came the soft, starry voice of Wilyn. "I Choose you as mine. I will be your patron. For your creativity, your passion, your desire, your ambition, your thirst for adventure, your strong heart."

"Do you accept?" said the Sisters as one.

"Yes," Raven said without thinking. "I accept."

"Welcome, Wraith," said Wilyn. Her Sisters echoed.

To be addressed as a Wraith felt unreal and fitting. Raven thought of Zander and Thalame, how powerful and dangerous they looked in their dark robes, leathers, and steel. The thought of herself in such a position felt tantalizing and empowering.

"Welcome, child," said Wilyn. "*Gorar gachy u kiwo.* May the stars forever guide you."

Raven felt a chill—her stepmother had often chimed those same words.

"Proceed the way you came," said Minerva. "Your new family is waiting for you."

"But be on guard," said Solen. "For choices lay on the horizon, both easy and most difficult."

"And remember," Wilyn said. "We are always there."

The air lightened and thinned. The silver light returned to its original brightness, which now felt too bright. Raven blinked; her eyes felt gummy, as though she hadn't opened them in some time. She climbed down from the platform; her limbs felt stiff and tired. Once on the temple floor, she stretched before heading down the corridor. The silver torches were still lit. As she proceeded toward the door, the torches went out behind her.

As she approached the doors, the last set of torches went out. For a terrifying moment, she stood in absolute darkness. Then the stone doors began to open.

Elizi sat on the bottom stair, cleaning a set of throwing knives. At the sight of Raven, she jumped to her feet. She dropped the cleaning rag and handed Raven a canteen. Raven gratefully accepted it. While she took a long drink, Elizi gathered the knives, which soon vanished into her robes. Raven corked the canteen and handed it back to Elizi. A quick glance around the chamber told her Malik hadn't stayed.

"How do you feel?" A faint accent sweetened Elizi's words. "You've been in there for a little more than a day."

Raven blinked. "What? A day? No, that's not possible."

"Time moves differently inside," said Elizi. "Time moves differently when the Sisters are speaking. You must be starving."

Raven put a hand over her stomach. "I don't feel hungry."

"It'll catch up to you." Elizi winked. "Come on. I'll walk you back to your room and send word for something to be brought up."

Raven rubbed her face as Elizi led her back up the stairs. An entire day had passed? When they entered the stronghold, the chaos of the celebration had been replaced with a calm murmur. No sooner had she sat on her bed than a tray of bread, hard cheese, and fruit appeared on her bedside table.

"Need anything else?" asked an older woman with freckles along her nose and charcoal in her dark hair.

Raven blinked. Elizi had disappeared.

"Don't worry." The older woman offered Raven a motherly smile. "I felt odd for days after my Choosing. It's like you're still walking through a dream."

"Yes, it does feel like that." Raven reached for the bread. Still warm. "Have the Wraiths who went to meet the Gray Elite caravan returned yet?"

The woman frowned. "No, but I wouldn't worry about it. It would have taken them several hours to get there, maybe longer. They'll return soon. With new faces, I hope."

Raven nodded. "Thank you."

"You are welcome," said the woman before she left.

Raven tore pieces of her bread and set them onto her tongue. She would tell Zander about her power's origin when he returned. She felt too weak to do much else. She ate her fill and then collapsed onto her bed. The pillow still smelled like Zander.

Raven woke feeling remarkably well rested. She took her time washing and dressed in a fresh set of deep plum and black robes that someone had brought up while she slept. The robes were silken and light as feathers, but strong and durable. They lacked the steel plating and weapon hiding spots of their typical gear, but she had only her dagger to wear. Someone had taken the tray too. She must have slept soundly for them to not have bothered her.

She stretched. Oh, she felt stiff. How long had she slept? Coupled with the time spent in the Choosing, her limbs felt leaden. Still, she was a Wraith. A Wraith! That knowledge sent a feverish excitement along her stiff limbs.

Raven made her way through the corridor and into the main room. She silently prided herself on not getting lost. The main doors were open, letting in glorious late afternoon sunlight. She made her way through the doors and down the sandy beach. The sunlight gleamed off the gulf in dazzling yellows and crystalline blues. To one side, a group of Wraiths jumped from a cliff halfway up the cove's wall and into the gulf below. On the other side, a group of older Wraiths sat in the shade, weaving baskets.

"Raven?" Malik appeared beside her. He wore fewer necklaces but just as many rings. His eyes searched hers, anxiety in his own. "You're awake."

"You're upset," she said.

Malik blinked, then half laughed. "You've got our mother's way of knowing things other people don't want to talk about."

"Not *other* people," Raven said. "You. You only have three faces: serious, mildly happy, and upset."

The corners of his lips twitched upward. "I can't argue with that."

"Is there something you want to talk about?" Raven asked. It seemed like a sisterly thing to do, and something a friend would do. And she felt incredibly light, like she could do anything, even help her half-brother with his problems.

"No," Malik said flatly.

"Let me rephrase," Raven said. "Is there something you *need* to talk about?"

He sighed. "No."

Raven held her gaze on him. She hadn't anticipated him telling her his deepest darkest secrets, but she hadn't anticipated a blunt refusal either.

"Walk with me." Malik held out his arm. She strung hers with his, and they started a slow meander along the gulf's shore. "I know we're family. I've never had a sister before. It's just been me for a long time, and I've not used to having people around. Especially those who care about my wellbeing."

529

"Our mother said she left you when you were little," Raven said, her voice low, not wanting to say something insensitive out loud.

"She did," Malik said. "Because she was a Wraith and because I had magic, she left me here. I grew up with one of the older Wraiths, a basket weaver." He glanced to the group of Wraiths weaving baskets. "I didn't understand why my mother didn't want me. I assumed I wasn't good enough for her. I grew up by myself. Because I had magic, I couldn't wander freely. And Wraiths come and go. I had few children my age, and I spent most of my time alone or with the Wraiths too old to go on missions. I learned a lot about magic from Deikun, and when I proved to have the gifts of a seeker, he took me under his wing."

"That sounds more exciting than growing up in a mine," Raven said. "My father didn't let us go outside without a reason, because he had this wild notion that we would get snatched by wandering automatons or Gray Elite soldiers."

"Yet you still ran back there to save them," Malik said.

Raven nodded. "I did. I might be resentful toward the people of Silver Glen for their backwater ways and old fashioned ideals, but they are still family. Of a sort." She hugged his arm. "I used to dream of flying through the clouds on an airship. Strange how it worked out."

"I knew my mother was a pirate, because the Wraiths told me," Malik said. "I always thought she would come back for me one day, and then she did, and I didn't know what to think about it."

"You don't sound happy about it," she said.

Malik sighed, considering. "Luckett is a great woman, but her mothering skills are...lacking." He offered her a small smile. "I remember your father. I remember the day I met him. I thought he was the greatest man in the world, because he could lift me above his head."

Raven felt her chest tighten. It felt strange to consider a time when her father, her mother, and Malik were together—before she was born. Her father...who was still up in the sky. Her thoughts snapped toward the sky.

She asked Malik, "Have you heard anything from the *Orion*?"

"I've kept Luckett updated on your Trial and Choosing." Malik glanced up, then quickly back down. "I only assume she relayed that information with your father, but Sisters only know what she told him, if she told him."

Malik paused underneath the shadow of a palm. "I remember the day we headed to Silver Glen, because your father wanted to. Because Mother was carrying you. I remember thinking that we would be a family. That everything would be as it should. But I was a child and foolish. You know how it turned out."

Raven pulled his arm closer, and by extension, him. "Wanting a family isn't foolish," she said. "Not even a little."

"It is when your mother is Bailey Luckett." Malik added in a hasty mutter, "And you share her taste in men."

"We're family," Raven said. "You said so."

Malik tore his eyes from the gulf and met hers. He looked bothered, but less than he had before. "Thank you, Raven. You have our mother in you, but you've got your father in you too."

"I accept that," Raven said. "I admire them both for their strengths." And she understood their faults, to a degree. "I wonder how they're getting along up there."

Malik let out a small, delicate laugh. "The *Orion* is a big ship, but Mother has a way of taking up a lot of space at once."

"As does my father," she added.

Malik cast his eyes back toward the gulf, toward the ocean visible between the cliffs, the expanse endless and blue.

"The team that went to find the Gray Elite caravan is late," Malik admitted, eyes on the ocean. "There are a hundred things that could have delayed them, but I don't like it. It might be my anxiety catching up to me and making me paranoid."

"Could something bad have happened?" Raven asked quietly.

"Something bad can always happen," Malik said with certainty. "But Wraiths are trained for bad situations. And, in all the time I've known Zander, he has repeatedly proven to be one of the toughest Wraiths out there. He fights with ferocity. I trained with him a few times, and he is a terrifying opponent."

She nodded, thinking of how his shadows had surged toward her, how they had taken down those automatons so effortlessly.

A boat rowed through the gulf's mouth, a fresh catch of fish on board. A few Wraiths waited by the dock, ready to help.

"Conrad is getting impatient," Malik said. Had Raven imagined the hitch in her brother's voice on the other boy's name?

"Is he here?" she asked, glancing around.

"No," Malik said quickly. "He cannot step into the village. He's been exiled." Malik sighed through his nose. "But he has been pacing by the gate every day, annoying the guards to no end, asking about you."

Raven glanced toward the path that led through the brush and palms to Wayward Point.

"He said he wanted you to see him when you returned from your Choosing," Malik said.

"He said?" she repeated. "He told you?"

Malik's face flushed deep scarlet. He looked away, and the panic of embarrassment flooded into his eyes.

"You went to see him?" she asked, curious. Before Malik could answer, she saw the answer in his eyes. Her smile turned wicked. "He came to see you? I thought he couldn't step foot into the village?"

"He shouldn't," Malik corrected, voice low. "The punishment for defying his exile is death, but only if he gets caught. Any Wraith can deliver the punishment."

Raven looked Malik up and down. Conrad had violated his exile, and he had gone to Malik. Yet Malik hadn't delivered punishment. He had broken the rules for Conrad.

"I thought you were the straight-laced type," Raven whispered.

He cleared his throat. "Have you eaten yet? I came out of my Choosing ravenous. I ate enough for two in my first meal."

Chuckling, she allowed the diversion in conversation.

Malik took Raven back to the kitchen, where he snagged her bread and cheese. While she ate, he led her through the village. Wraiths worked to repair huts, tend to gardens, and clean fish—only they used magic. Malik explained that jobs were given based on a magician's talents. Elizi had ferried almost every magician to the Trial since her induction. One Wraith could whisper to plants and make them grow faster. One man turned green fibers into dried rope in a few moments. It seemed every Wraith had a place in the village.

"We don't all stay here all the time," Malik said. "Wraiths travel all over, seeking magicians. Some follow the guidance of their patron Sister."

He introduced her to Wraiths as they approached, and now that she had gone through her Trial and Choosing, they could tell her about their own. She hadn't been the only one unprepared for a week's stay on an island, and she hadn't been the only one to eat the shade fruit. Other unfortunate Wraiths had seen ghouls rising from the waters, thought the island sinking, or felt spiders crawling under their skin.

No one else admitted to seeing a ghost guide, and Raven didn't volunteer that information.

The sun gradually sank, pulling its golden light across the gulf's calm waters. The waters turned molten, the shadows under the cliff thickened, and torches were lit in the village. Dinner was served, and Raven ate enough for two. She sat beside Malik and Thalame, but she kept one eye on the doors. The team sent to intercept the Gray Elite caravan hadn't returned.

Dinner ended, and Malik walked her back to her room in the guest wing. By the time they came to her door, exhaustion had settled into her bones.

"That strange feeling goes away," Malik said. "I remember feeling odd for days after my Choosing. It felt like a lucid dream."

"Is it because of what happened during the Choosing?" Raven whispered. "When the Sisters did...whatever they did?"

Malik shook his head. "I don't know. It's old magic, and no one alive understands what exactly happens."

Raven reached for her door, and Malik turned to leave.

"Do you think the team will come back tomorrow?" she asked.

Malik didn't answer immediately. "Odds are, yes. Goodnight, Raven."

"Goodnight."

When he left, Raven sat on the edge of her bed and clutched Zander's pillow to her chest. It didn't smell as much like him as it had the night before. His absence felt stronger this time, and she didn't like it.

The next morning, Raven meandered through the Wraiths' village. The day's work had begun. She didn't see Malik or Thalame, and her feet took her along the path that wound through the forest, up the cliffside, and toward Wayward Point. Few clouds marred the periwinkle sky, and the humid air clung Raven's thin robes to her skin, but the briny breeze blowing off the ocean was cool.

She came to the border of the Wraiths' village, signified by two stone pillars worn by time and weather and half-smothered in moss and vines. Walking through, she didn't spy any guards in the greenery, but she knew they were there somewhere.

Not far on the other side, a shadow fell into step beside her. A glance told her it was Conrad. Beads clinked in his braids. He wore the breezy clothes of Wayward Point, a thin sleeveless tunic and trousers the color of sand.

"About time," Conrad said. "I was starting to think they'd locked you down there."

"Malik was right," she said. "You're impatient."

"It's boring over here when all the Wraiths and excitement are over there," he said, pouting. He bent forward, searching her face. "What's wrong, little bird?"

"What makes you think something is wrong?"

"You and your brother share several expressions," Conrad said plainly.

She sighed. "Zander went on a mission to disrupt a Gray Elite caravan, and they're not back yet," she said in a single breath.

"Ah," he said, as though it explained it all. They walked for a while in silence, navigating the brambles and tree roots and bushes. As the path evened out enough they could walk side by side, he added, "I'm sure they're fine."

"How can you be sure?" Raven asked.

"How can you be sure they aren't?" Conrad asked with the same indifference as Malik. "Many things don't go as planned, and sometimes we have to improvise. You saw that with your own eyes in Moorin. There might have been more prisoners than they thought, and traveling with a crowd without attracting attention is hard."

"I hadn't thought about that," she said.

They came to the fork in the path.

"Do you have business to attend to?" Conrad asked.

She shrugged. "No. I just needed a walk."

"Good, then come and walk with me, little bird. I need the company, and I want to hear all about your Trial and Choosing." They started toward Wayward Point, and his grin widened, and his eyes grew curious. "Tell me, did you find the shade fruit?"

She laughed. They meandered through the outskirts of Wayward Point's oldest residences, and she talked. Conrad listened. She withheld the part of Aeon's ghost and the truth of her power. She didn't know what to think about it yet, and she wanted to talk to Zander about it first. As her story came to an end, they passed a small garden where a group of older women sat in a circle, each at a washboard, chattering in Tinatunian.

534

"You're lucky your magic helped you during the Trial," Conrad said, his words low as to not carry. "My magic doesn't heat water or cook fish. I knew how to start a fire and basic survival, but those berries got me. I started seeing mermaids calling me out to the sea. I swam out to sea, nearly drowned, but somehow managed to find dry land."

She grinned. "If it weren't for those berries, I might not have found the treasure."

"I can't believe you had the stones to come back empty-handed." Conrad shook his head at her. "And that old man let you in anyway." He harrumphed. "I brought back the lute."

"Can you play?"

"Not a single note," Conrad said. "But I like music, which was my answer, and people always forget about their troubles and dance. Music is a language everyone understands."

"Did your Choosing take a whole day?"

"Most of them take at least a day," Conrad said. "Time doesn't flow the same for the Sisters as it does for us, at least not when they commune. I think the longest Choosing lasted three days. The poor boy was nearly dry as death. Mine took about a day. It was exhausting in a different way, listening to the Sisters pick apart my qualities."

"Wilyn Chose me," Raven said. A prickling of panic seized her next thought. "Am I allowed to tell you that?"

Conrad shrugged. "I've never been told otherwise." He looked her up and down. "It fits. You did gravitate toward the sky. You have a strange love of airships. You like the stars."

"Some of that might be true," Raven said.

"It's legend that Wilyn has a soft spot for dreamers and hopeless romantics," Conrad said, winking.

"Then I would be among friends."

"Indeed, little bird." Conrad laughed. He glanced out to the sea. "Minerva Chose me, although she also threw me back out to the sea."

"Can you blame her?" Raven asked.

Conrad sighed deeply. "Legends say that Minerva is the stern one," he mumbled. "They also say she has a soft spot for pirates and treasure hunters, but I'm not so sure of that."

Because Conrad had stolen a treasure map from the Wraiths' archive.

"Do you regret it?" Raven asked. "Stealing the map, I mean."

"Yes and no," Conrad said, considering. "Yes, because I got kicked out of the best club on the continent, and Malik only glares at me now. No, because I found places so fantastic, I couldn't have dreamed them up. I know I am among the few humans to have stepped in certain places in the past one thousand years."

The huts parted, and they had a breathtaking view of the white sand beach and Linila Bay.

He sighed and looked to the endless sea with longing. "I've had incredible experiences on the sea during my exile, found myself, discovered far more than I intended. So...I suppose my final answer is no. I do not regret what I've done, because it's made me who I am."

Raven lifted her chin to the breeze. The salty air brushed her hair out of her face and away from her neck. Everything she had done, gone through, survived, had helped make her who she was. If she had stayed in Silver Glen, if she and Zander had returned there, if she had just stayed in the Dwellers' treehouse, so many things would have happened differently.

"Minerva told me to help you when we first met," Conrad admitted. "Well, she didn't say those words exactly. She told me to put that wooden coin in my pocket before I left to steal that stupid box, because someone would need it. She told me to go to the arena that day, because there was someone she wanted me to see. And I saw you." He chuckled. "If it weren't for that little bit of divine intervention, who knows where you would have ended up."

"I suppose I should thank her," Raven said.

"I should too," Conrad said. "I'm glad she sent me here. I almost ignored her, you know. Though, I feel like a better man for it all, and think of the adventure we've had! I know where I'd be had we not met. I'd be slumming it up on some ship headed southwest."

Raven's heart thumped hard. "What's to the southwest?"

Aeon's kingdom had been to the southwest, the kingdom her Sisters had sunk.

"Scattered islands and ruins, mostly," Conrad said casually, eyes drifting over the ocean's horizon. "It's a trove of adventures and treasure."

They wandered into Wayward Point's thriving market. Conrad bought two iced juices, one for each of them, and Raven brought hers to her lips just as a familiar voice drifted over the crowd in Tinatunian.

Raven didn't taste the passion fruit or citrus; she only felt sharp panic and fiery rage.

"You're looking pale, little bird." Conrad's eyes bored into hers with concern.

"That voice." Raven glanced over the crowd. Her eyes settled on the speaker, a Tinatunian woman in her twenties, smile broad and careless.

"Do you know her?" Conrad asked.

Raven felt rage bubble and boil under her skin. "That's the woman who sold me."

Raven balled her fists and felt flames licking her skin. She envisioned a dozen deaths for the woman who had saved her, then sold her—Nia. At the woman's name, her rage sprang—Conrad's fingers folded around her forearm. A sharp pain flickered down her arm and into that place deep inside where her magic slept.

A short gasp escaped her lips, and her magic shorted out. She turned a wide-eyed gaze to Conrad.

"Not here," he warned. "Magic upsets people when displayed openly. It also attracts the wrong kind of attention. Don't forget, not everyone looks kindly on the Wraiths."

"How did you—"

"We all have our talents," Conrad said, his voice rushed and low.

His seeker abilities to detect magic had shorted out her own.

She huffed, because she knew he was right. She turned her attention back to Nia, but she had already vanished into the crowd. Raven scanned the faces, but she didn't see Nia or the two other scavengers who had sold her into slavery.

"Come on, little bird." Conrad ushered her away. They returned to their walk of the market. "Take some deep, calming breaths."

She humored him by taking an exaggerated breath. Conrad offered her a small smile. They turned a corner into an alley and then onto a small side street.

"I didn't think I would ever see them again," Raven admitted. "I've thought about what I would do and say to them over and over, but...I hoped I'd not have to."

"Wayward Point does have its dark alleys," Conrad said with a heavy sigh. "Slavery just happens to be one of them."

"Is all of Tinatun like this place?"

"No." He shook his head. "Unlike Gracita and Rhynwier, Tinatun is divided into smaller provinces that act as their own kingdoms. This province is the least ruled, because the southern kings and queens don't like the Gray Elite. The southern peoples refer to their northern corner as the wild country. The wayward son, if you will." Conrad chuckled. "King Olino has openly hung pirates and gutted slavers, but since they are confined up here, and he's on the southern tip of the kingdom, he does not care."

Raven saw the distraction he offered, the chance to ask more about the vicious southern king and how Conrad knew such things. He offered a story while steering her away from the market. A part of her wanted to take the bait and forget about those scavengers, but another part knew she couldn't be the only unfortunate girl sold like meat. She had to do something, but what? What could she possibly do against an industry?

"You're looking glum," Conrad said in a sing-song tone. "Are you thinking those bad thoughts again?"

"I want to do something."

"I suppose we could hog-tie them and send them out to sea."

"Not just about the scavengers, but about the whole industry. Burn down every slaver hut or something."

"I don't have any advice on that, but I know what you need. Something cool to drink."

Conrad pulled her back toward the market and to a little tavern that sold cold drinks in coconuts. He bought her one but did not buy himself one. She sat at one of the little tables.

"Why don't you stay here and enjoy the drink," Conrad said, eyes across the market. "I've got someone I need to see about...something."

"Someone and something?"

Conrad winked. "It might not be strictly...Wraith approved or legal."

She frowned.

He sighed and said lowly, "It's a lead on old pirate treasure. I had a friend looking into it, and he's back. I need to catch him before he sells the information to someone else or gets himself killed in a bar fight. Both are likely."

She half laughed. She sipped loudly from the coconut, and Conrad vanished into the market. The coconut helped; she tasted sweet rum and something salty and sweet mixed with the coconut milk. As she sat there, she let her mind wander over foolish plans of revenge against the scavengers, against the slavers, against anyone who thought slavery fine. She had never felt such a strong sense of vengeance before, but she had never been tricked and damned. She had never experienced that side of humanity before, and she wanted to make sure no other lost girl or boy was tricked like she had been.

She hit the bottom of her coconut too soon, but she didn't want another. She could feel the loose feeling under her skin, the sense of detachment. It had not made her worry go away, but she cared less about it.

Conrad had not returned. She didn't see him in the market crowd either. The coconut vender spotted her—he had that look about him of one hoping for another sale. Raven stood, discarded her coconut, and started to meander through the busy market. She walked past the carts and stalls and stores with the same sense of amazement she'd felt when she first came to Wayward Point. She spotted scarves in every color and fabric, tropic clothes designed for heat, jewelry of every metal and stone and shade, food on sticks and food in melons. Voices chatted away in Tinatunian and her own tongue, the languages mixed together in a blur of sound.

She meandered past a tavern. The outside wall was covered in posters, including wanted posters. Raven had no intention to stop, but a familiar face among the others pulled her to a halt. It was a girl. The harshly drawn lines made her look vicious and beautiful, and the heavy lines of her eyes made her look clever and smart.

But it was the name under the poster that gave her pause—Raven Thane, wanted for the attempted assassination of General Oliver Deacon and other crimes.

She gawked. She knew about her bounty, but she hadn't seen a wanted poster.

She felt eyes on her. The guard by the tavern door looked her up and down. His eyes shifted to the poster. Before he could make a connection, Raven turned her back to him and started away. A few stalls down, she spotted another wanted poster. She pretended not to notice. She made a lap of the market, and she spotted no less than twenty wanted posters wearing her face.

Conrad's chime of laughter came from her left, and she turned down the alley. Footsteps followed—bare feet on the sandy ground. Her heart humped. Conrad wore boots. She walked a little faster. So did her stalker.

Before she reached the other end of the alley, a hand grabbed her wrist and whirled her around. Her panic flared, and it took a heartbeat for her to recognize the Tinatunian man who had grabbed her—one of the scavengers who had sold her. His black eyes pierced hers, and a wicked smile spread over his face. Her panic turned into rage.

"You," Raven spat.

"*Wawuw gai lu!*" he spat.

"I still don't understand." Raven started to summon flames.

"Look who found her way back," came a drawling female voice on the other side of the alley. At the sound of the voice, Raven's flames sputtered. Nia strolled into the alley. The other scavenger walked a step behind, wooden club over his shoulders. "You cost me money, girl."

Raven put her hand over her heart and asked innocently, "I cost you money? Hmm. I distinctly remember you walking away with a bag of tokens, marks, and piks when you sold me." Raven heated her wrist under the scavenger's hand—he yelped and yanked his hand away.

"*Aggi,*" the man spat, cradling his hand.

"You are one of them." Nia looked down her nose at Raven.

"And you are no longer a threat," Raven spat back. "But you have piqued my interest. How did I cost you money?"

"I bet against you in the *Chjelhu Tal,*" Nia said. "Half what we were paid for you. I thought he would rip you apart."

"And you bet wrong," Raven growled.

"Maybe." Nia chuckled. "But the Gray Elite will pay ten times what I got for you the first time."

Raven harrumphed, taunt on her tongue, when the scavenger behind her grabbed her arm. He pressed something smooth and cold against her neck. A stone. A needling sensation started where the stone met her skin and traveled inward, through her bloodstream, through her bones. Her panic reared, and she reached for her magic—flames sputtered. Pain flared in the place of her magic.

A cry ripped through her throat. Darkness surged on the edges of her vision, dark and cold and gripping.

She collapsed to the sand-packed ground.

The scavengers blurred above her. The sun turned them into shadows. Hands grabbed her, lifted her, but the darkness consumed her.

Raven came to against something hard. She blinked. Darkness swayed within her vision, and her body wobbled. The wooden ceiling came into view. She was lying on a stone floor in a windowless room. The only light came from a lantern in the hall, on the other side of an iron barred door.

"...when we've done half of the work?" came Nia's voice. One of the scavengers spat something in Tinatunian. "We want half the bounty."

A male voice sighed. "Fine. Half. But you'll wait here until the Gray Elite come to pick her up. I'm not shoving out any coin to you scumbags until I've got my half."

"She's not going anywhere," Nia spat. "We got her with a rune. She won't be using her *aggi* magic anytime soon."

The darkness retreated bit by bit. Raven could see the shadows of her captors in the hall outside the door. She reached for her magic, but it did not respond. The inferno had been reduced to a flicker.

A rune... She remembered seeing stones with runes painted and etched on them in the market. Is that what they'd done to her? The rune had shoved her magic out of her reach. It wasn't impossible; the Wraiths had been painting and tattooing runes to burn off excess magic, but this rune hadn't burned off her excess magic. It had stomped on it, suppressed it.

She tried to get up. They had tied her hands and ankles with rope.

The darkness faded from her vision and her mind. She could hear other people in other cells. Other prisoners.

"Fine," Nia spat. "We wait, and we get half."

"Fine."

A door slammed, and several sets of footsteps trailed into another room.

Raven let out a groan. What would Conrad think? Would he think she'd gone back to the stronghold without him? She couldn't count on him to save her, which left her on her own.

And they had sent word to the Gray Elite.

It will not hold you, said the voice in her mind, the ghost of Aeon.

Raven sighed. "And what do you want me to do about it?" she hissed at the voice. "I'm tied up and can't use my magic."

I can help you. Allow me control. I will bring you the revenge you desire.

Raven didn't like the sound of those words, yet she wanted revenge on those slavers, on the whole slaving industry for not only what they had done to her, but what they had done to so many others.

"Fine," Raven whispered.

A beat of silence, and then her magic flared through her bloodstream, burning off the icy remains of the rune's strange magic. Flames erupted from every pore, breathing through her skin and hair and clothes. The ropes on her wrists and ankles disintegrated. Flames spread through the fibers of her robes and spread across the dust and dirt and sand. They snaked up the wooden walls and reached across the iron door. They moved on their own once they touched the wooden walls, spreading up and down along the old dry wood. The flames raced to the ceiling, converging and spreading without mercy, without prejudice.

Screams sounded over the crackling wood and creaking stone. Panic filled the air. The other prisoners. Raven pushed herself over the burning stones and to her feet. No one deserved to be trapped like this.

She moved through the flames, her flames, and they licked at arms and legs but did not burn her. Her flames shoved the iron cell door out of its frame and raced along the hall, ripping doors from the other cells. At her command, the flames arched, leaving a path between them for the prisoners. They crept through the flames, fearful and worried.

They run like cowards!

Her flames consumed the building. They raced over the walls, the ceiling, the floor. They devoured everything.

See what we can do?

Raven stood among the flames, feeling the heat against her skin. The building crackled and groaned. Her flames consumed it all.

"Raven!"

She knew that voice, and she gravitated toward it. She walked through the wall of flame and into the cooler air of Wayward Point. The cool air seemed to steal her very breath.

"Raven?" Hands grabbed her shoulders. She blinked, and Conrad's worried face appeared in front of hers. "What happened?"

He pulled her away from the burning building. Something snapped—she gasped for breath. The flames had gone wild, and it was no longer her flames that consumed it, but the fire her's had sparked to life. It licked up the walls and reached into the air. Dark smoke trailing into the sky.

And people had stopped to watch.

"You might want this," Conrad said. He held his tunic in his hand.

Raven blinked—the flames had singed her robes, leaving them hanging on by tatters. She stood nearly naked. Something warm and slippery crawled under her skin, and a fierce blush turned her a deep shade of red. She hastily pulled his tunic over her head.

"We need to get out of here," Conrad said.

Already, people were hauling buckets of water to put out the fire. It didn't matter. Conrad pulled her away. He weaved through alleys, leading them farther away, until they left the chaos behind. When he paused in a quiet alley, Raven sank to the ground.

Conrad paced in front of her.

"What happened?" she asked after a time.

Conrad jerked to a halt and looked at her with wide eyes. "What happened?" A mad grin stretched across his face. "Little bird, you burned down one of the most profitable slave huts in Wayward Point. Extra points for doing it naked. You're insane, you know that?"

"I'm starting to question it," she said.

His grin waned. "Why is that?"

She looked down at her hands. How could she explain Aeon's strange influence? "It didn't feel like I was...me. It felt like someone else was controlling me."

Conrad tilted his head. "Hmm. Odd, though I've heard stress does strange things to people."

Raven inhaled deep. She didn't remember it clearly. She remembered waking up tied and helpless and then...fire. Power.

Conrad heaved a sigh. "Your turn. What happened?"

She told him about the wanted posters and the scavengers.

"I can't leave you alone for a minute." Conrad crossed his arms. "Come on, let's get you something else to wear."

He held out his arm, and she took it. He guided her away from the burning building as if it didn't exist. Raven soaked in the calm, desperately wishing her panic away.

"I suppose I shouldn't be surprised," Conrad said after a while. "You have spent a considerable amount of time with me. From here on out, little bird, you must promise to spend more time with your brother. Either to have his dire sense of the law rub off on you, or to have your chaotic whims rub off on him."

"Will the Wraiths be mad at me?" she asked.

"It's hard to tell," Conrad said. "You saved people, but you also made a scene."

They stopped at a small shop on the outskirts of the market, and Raven picked out a thin skirt that tied at her waist and brightly colored cropped shirt like she had seen many of the women wearing; much of her skin remained exposed, but the important things were covered. Conrad paid the merchant, who hadn't said a word about Raven's state of dress. Conrad then pulled his tunic back over his head.

"Did you find your friend?" Raven asked as they started away from the market.

"I did." Conrad's smile widened, and his eyes glittered—he had good news. He opened his mouth to tell her about it when Elizi slid out from an alley.

"There you are." Elizi stomped over. "I've been looking for you. I have news. Aside from whatever stunt you pulled." She motioned to the pillar of gray and black smoke.

Raven's heart plummeted. The Wraiths had already heard of her blunder? Had Elizi come to deliver the news of her exile?

"What other news?" Conrad asked, leaning forward.

"I take it you haven't heard, then," Elizi said. "Malik told me to find you when the news reached us. It's our missing team. It was a setup."

Elizi pulled a piece of folded paper from her robes and handed it to Conrad. He snatched it before Raven could and quickly unfolded it where she could see it. It was a wanted poster. Like her own, it bore the seal of the Gray Elite.

"By order of Emperor Renald the Fourth," read Conrad, "the public execution of the magician and assassin known as the Revenant will take place in the town square of the city of Kusmerk, tomorrow at sunset."

The Gray Elite had added a drawing of a masked figure with empty eyes and dark clothes.

The Revenant—Zander.

Raven couldn't breathe. She read the wanted poster again and again. The words blurred together, drowned out by her pounding heart and screaming mind. The Gray Elite had set the caravan up as a trap, and now they had Zander. They knew who and what he was, and they were going to kill him.

Conrad spat a curse. "The Gray Elite knew the Wraiths couldn't resist a crate of magicians so close to Wayward Point." He crumpled the wanted poster and threw it at the ground.

"You need to head back," Elizi said to Raven. "People are looking for you in new vigor."

"Come on, little bird." Conrad led her by the hand toward the stronghold, keeping to the side streets and alleys.

Once on the outskirts, they broke into a run. She forced her legs to move faster, over the sun-dried sand, through the trees and rocks, despite the stitch in her side and burning lungs. They neared the boundary pillars to the Wraith's village, but Conrad didn't slow down. They passed through. The guards didn't stop him.

By the time they reached the stronghold, her lungs felt like fire, and her side threatened to rip itself open. A group had gathered by the steps on the stronghold; Grand Master Deikun stood on the steps, worry creasing the skin between his brows.

"You shouldn't be here," came Malik's hiss. He appeared through the crowd and grabbed Conrad's arm. His eyes were wide with fear, not rage.

As if summoned by Conrad's presence, the grand master appeared beside Malik. Her brother's eyes grew wider still.

"This isn't about me," Conrad said to Malik. To Deikun, he said, "You're sending Wraiths after the others. I'm going."

The grand master considered him a long moment, then nodded. "If that is what you wish."

"It is," Conrad said with more determination than Raven had ever heard.

"I'm going too." Raven had hoped to say it with as much resolve as Conrad, but her voice fell flat and breathless.

At her, the grand master looked less enthused, almost pitied.

"It was a trap," Raven started, before the grand master could argue with her. "The Gray Elite set it up to catch Wraiths. They're going to execute Zander, and it's likely another trap they've set up for me. They know I'll go after him, and that's what they want."

"If that is what they want, then you shouldn't go," Malik said.

"It's why I should go," she countered.

Malik frowned. "Why risk yourself by going?"

"Because I want to make sure they know exactly who they're dealing with." Venom dripped from each word. The fury from before returned, hot and bright and powerful. This time, she controlled the fury. Flames danced around her hands. "I will make sure the Gray Elite never think about bothering me or Zander or the Wraiths again."

"Those are bold claims," said Deikun. Her flames reflected in his dark eyes. He didn't look enthused or impressed, though many Wraiths standing behind him did.

"Yes, they are." Raven nodded. She let her flames go out, but she could still feel the power. "I refuse to stand by and hide while Zander is killed because of me. I would rather let them kill me. I would rather die trying to save him than do nothing while he is hurt."

Again.

Conrad squeezed her hand. "And we have just a few hours to prepare. It will take us half a day to get there, and I would prefer not to be fashionably late."

"You will have to leave before dawn," Deikun announced for them all to hear. He glanced over the gathered. "Conrad and Raven cannot do this alone."

Hands shot into the air. Malik's curled fists shook at his sides.

"He's not a fighter," Conrad whispered to Raven, nodding toward Malik. "But he hates to stand by while others go fight."

Raven understood that feeling completely.

"The team is selected," the grand master announced over the crowd. "Those of you will get your rest. Your things will be packed and ready for you come the hour of departure."

Raven headed for the stronghold, as did several others, to sleep in the stone-walled rooms that held no sunlight so they would be ready to leave before dawn. Conrad followed her, and no one stopped him.

They would get there in time. They had to. Or Zander's head would roll, and she refused to allow that. If he died, if the Gray Elite killed him just to get at her, she would burn everything in Gracita to the ground. And she knew Aeon would help.

Raven just wished she knew if she wanted the forgotten Sister's help or not.

Raven couldn't sleep. A young Wraith brought her fresh robes, but she pretended to be asleep. Her new robes had plates of dark steel, hardened leather, and hidden pockets—the combat robes she had seen in Moorin. Along with her new robes, a tray of bread and butter, nuts, and dried berries rested on her bedside table. Raven tossed and turned. Her feverish magic churned under her skin, itching to incinerate any Gray Elite who dared to hurt Zander.

Was the thirst for vengeance her own or Aeon's?

In truth, she didn't know.

A knock sounded on her door, shattering what shallow sleep she had managed to find. Raven sat up as Elizi entered, her face solemn.

"It's time," said Elizi, her voice light as birdsong and as steady as the moon.

Raven did not trust her own voice to be as strong, so she said nothing. She sat up and tore a chunk of bread off with her teeth. It had gone stale.

"They're meeting in the hall when you're ready." Elizi departed without a sound.

Raven washed in cold water. She needed the shock. She ate what she could stomach, forcing her meal down. She would need her strength. She dressed in her new robes. Steel plates and hardened leather protected her vitals and made her feel heavy, but invulnerable and sturdy. She braided her hair back and tucked it under the hood.

Standing in her own Wraith gear, fire dancing under her skin, she felt a sense of power she had never felt before. She could save Zander. She would save him. She and the team of Wraiths going with her. The Gray Elite wouldn't see them coming.

She headed to the main hall. Conrad appeared beside her, dressed in the same dark robes. The next several moments blurred together. Malik appeared, worried but stoic. Thalame had volunteered to go, and he wore the same dark robes. He had gathered healing supplies along with daggers.

Along with Raven, Conrad, and Thalame, five other Wraiths had volunteered to go. The eight of them sat together in the hall, and Raven tried her best to listen as Deikun fed them the details. Kusmerk had been built over a series of bridges that stretched over the southern Gladia River. It meant there were few ways into the city and a lot of things could go wrong.

"The Gray Elite chose their location wisely," Deikun said grimly. "They will be patrolling the city."

Raven studied the hand-drawn map of Kusmerk spread over the table. Zander had once told her about a city built over a river, a feat by the Gray Elite to prove themselves above the laws of nature. The Gray Elite had wanted to prove their engineering and machines could do the impossible.

We will show them the power of nature.

In that moment, Raven agreed.

"Kusmerk also sits just within the border of Gracita," Malik added. "So you will have to sneak across."

"Sneaking across the border is one thing," said Thalame, crease between his brows. "But then we've got to find a way into the city once we're inside. You can bet all the piks in Wayward Point, they'll have the border guarded, as well as any way in or out of the city."

"You leave that to me," Conrad said, winking. "Kusmerk may look tough, but it's only tough on the outside."

"Now's not the time for vague nonsense," one of the other Wraiths said.

"I agree," Deikun said to Conrad. "What is your plan?"

Conrad sighed in defeat. He pointed to the map, his finger just below the city's edge. "Boats still have to pass underneath, and for the accomplished smuggler, the tangle of pipes and steel beams and maintenance halls are perfect for coming and going without going through all the trouble of the main gates."

"That'd work," Thalame said. "Assuming no one is afraid of cramped spaces?"

No one objected.

The door to the chamber opened, and a Wraith escorted two familiar faces. Raven jumped to her feet. Brent and Niall looked at the stronghold with a mixture of awe and uncertainty. Brent's gaze fell onto Raven, and relief replaced his worry.

"These are the two I told you about," Malik said to Deikun.

Thalame stood next, confusion on his brow. "What did I miss?"

"I reached out to our new friends regarding the situation," Malik said.

Niall paused at the table, eyes taking in the map. His gaze met Thalame's, then Raven's. "And we have the very thing that might save your necks—and Zander's."

Raven blinked at Brent.

"We've been busy." As Brent moved, the light shifted off the goggles around his neck. "Niall and I have been working on several projects, and Malik came by yesterday and told us what happened to Zander and what you were planning on doing."

"And this seems like the perfect time to test out something that we've been developing," Niall grinned.

"Unless you've got something that can get us to Kusmerk without being seen..." Thalame's brows rose. His confusion fell into a knowing smirk, along with a devilish twinkle in his eyes—one that Niall returned.

"That's right," Niall said.

"Did I miss the part where you announced it?" Conrad looked between Thalame and Raven.

"It's better if we show you," Brent said, excitement coursing through his every action.

They followed the tinkers out of the stronghold and to the gulf, to the shore, to a little boat.

"It's a boat?" one of the Wraiths deadpanned.

"No, this is the boat that will take you to the real surprise," Niall said plainly. "It wouldn't fit here in the shallows."

The Wraith sighed, as did Conrad.

Niall, Brent, Raven, Thalame, Malik, and Conrad went first—because only so many could fit in the boat at once. They rowed out of the gulf and to the open ocean, just a short way from the mouth. Raven spotted the dark shadow under the water first, then she spotted the thing above the shadow. She first thought it sea-foam covered driftwood, but as they rowed closer, it became a metal hatch. It had been painted the same pale green of the sea around it.

"What is it?" Raven asked, leaned over the side of the boat to see it better. The boat tilted, and Conrad pulled her back.

Niall hooked the oar on the hatch and pulled the boat right beside it. He smiled proudly and said, "Brent and I call it the *Barnacle*."

R aven gawked. Her friends—all that time spent scheming and thinking and building—they had built the perfect way into Kusmerk. A submersible machine.

"Would you like to look inside?" Niall's eyes were bright and his smile wide.

"Yes!" Raven said at once.

Niall knocked on the hatch. A few moments, then it opened from within. A familiar face appeared, her flaxen hair tied back, brassy goggles perched on her head, and her simple dress exchanged for fitted trousers, plain white shirt, and buttoned vest.

"Sweets?" Raven asked, delighted to see her friend.

"Hello again." Sweets leaned against the hatch's side. "What brings you all out to sea?"

Raven gathered herself and straightened her shoulders. "Permission to come aboard."

Sweets grinned. She ducked back down into the hatch, leaving it open, and Raven heard the *thunk-thunk* of boots on a metal ladder. Niall motioned for Raven to go first, and she eagerly climbed out of the boat and into the hatch. Her boots *thunk-thunk*ed as she climbed down into the *Barnacle*'s interior.

The submersible gently swayed, an unsteady but steady sensation. The *Barnacle* was larger on the inside than she thought it would be. The body was the size of a large bed, with benches that folded into the wall. Stubby brass lanterns were mounted on the walls, glowing bluish green. The brass and steel walls had been bolted and welded from oddly shaped scraps and gently curved to form the oval shape of the *Barnacle*. A narrow door in the back led to the engine room, a series of pipes and gauges and buzzing. With the eerie green light, the maze looked maddening.

Raven pressed her hand against the metal wall. She could hear the water moving on the other side, a deep, constant movement, like low-rolling thunder that never ended.

Conrad started down the ladder. His quick eyes took in the submersible, and he grimaced. "Cozy," he mumbled.

"I thought you loved the sea?" Raven asked.

"I'd rather be above the water," he mumbled.

"Think of it as a ship meant for deep sea," Niall said from that hatch. His voice echoed slightly.

Thalame climbed down next, looking more enthused as Conrad. "This is what you've been working on? How fast she go?"

"This baby isn't about speed," said Brent from above. "Not yet anyway."

Raven stepped into the bridge. Two seats had been welded to the floor and padded with brown leather. Sweets sat at one of them, arm thrown over the back of the seat.

The dashboard was filled with gauges, levers, switches, and dials—a colorful blend of brass and steel and iron. She spotted pieces of salvaged automatons. The steering wheel had been crafted from small automaton arms, bent at the elbow. The front of the *Barnacle* had two thick windows, through which Raven spotted a school of fish fluttering in the water beyond.

The green light of the lanterns filled the space, but the sunlight through the water made it glow; an undulating net of sunlight bathed the bridge and Sweets.

"Sisters," Raven breathed as she watched the fish weave back and forth, the sunlight glittering off each scale and tailfin.

"I know," Sweets said. "When Brent told me what they were working on, I didn't think it possible. But look at where we are now."

"The Gray Elite may have problems," came Conrad's voice behind Raven. He stood in the doorway to the bridge, taking in the view. "But they do know how to build a machine. If only they weren't so arrogant and hell-bent on proving themselves superior to everything else. Let that be a lesson, little bird." He winked.

Niall slid down the ladder. "Malik went back for the others. I offered, but he refused to come down. He looked a bit green too."

"He isn't a fan of the ocean," Conrad explained. "He has a fear of drowning, and he likely looks at this contraption as a coffin."

"A tour while we wait?" Niall motioned toward the small space.

Niall started with the lanterns. They did not hold candles; they held glowing crystals. Niall called them sunstones, a strange mineral-rich crystal from Tinatun's southern islands that soaked up the sun and radiated the light. The sunstones in the *Barnacle* held sunlight for two days, he said.

"We'll have plenty of light, but we have a limited air supply. We'll have to resurface every so often to replenish or suffocate," said Niall. "And the more people on board, the faster we'll go through that supply."

Conrad frowned. "This is starting to sound like a coffin."

The second boat arrived, and everyone except Malik climbed down. Conrad volunteered to go with Malik for the supplies. Malik did not turn down his company. Raven watched him vanish through the hatch, wondering what the two boys might have to say to one another when no one else could hear.

Thalame leaned into the bridge, grinning. "This is just what we needed. You came through again, mate."

Niall shrugged. "If it hadn't been for Brent, this idea would have never made it out of the workshop, let alone into the water."

"So, the new plan is," Thalame started, leaning against the bridge door, "we swim right underneath Kusmerk. We get in, grab Zander, and get out. The Gray Elite will never know we were there."

Raven frowned. "That will put a dent in my dramatics."

Thalame chuckled. "Can't say I'm sad about that. Your dramatics tend to endanger us all and piss off the Gray Elite."

"Speaking of dramatics." Sweets swiveled to see Raven better. "I heard you melted an automaton? A big one?"

Raven shrugged. "It might be true, but I don't like to brag."

Sweets's grin widened.

Water splashed from above—the rowboat and their supplies had returned. Whatever conversation Malik and Conrad had been having ended as the hatch opened.

"I'll tell you about it when we get back," Raven told Sweets. "Or Conrad can, he's a better storyteller than I am."

Raven stood aside while the Wraiths handed down the supplies. They had brought a fraction of the supplies they originally packed; they had planned on going over land, but the *Barnacle* had shortened their trip considerably. Supplies secured in the small hold, they bid farewell to Malik—he would be returning to the stronghold along with their rowboat. The sunlight squeezed out with a heavy clank as Brent closed and sealed the hatch.

Brent took to the engine room, and Niall sat behind the wheel. Sweets remained in the bridge's second chair.

"Ready when you are," Niall said into a brassy speaking tube beside the captain's chair.

"All systems go," came Brent's tinny confirmation from the speaking tube.

"Here we go." Niall pulled a lever. A *thunk* resounded through the *Barnacle*. A gurgle started below Raven's feet, and that gurgle burst into a roar. Raven tensed, but the roar settled into a purring buzz, one she had grown familiar with on the *Orion*. It was the sound of an engine working like it should.

With a few more levers and fluctuating gurgles, the *Barnacle* began to move. They dove deeper into the ocean until the sunlight dulled and the ocean opened up to a darkness below them. It reminded Raven of the night sky, endless and dark, only it had no stars or clouds. Only monsters and sunken kingdoms lurking at its depths.

Niall guided the *Barnacle* out to sea so they could move faster. He explained that once they entered the river, they wouldn't be able to move as fast. The engine would make too much noise, and even this deep, they didn't want to risk cavitating too much.

Raven resisted the urge to pace the length of the submersible. She settled on tapping her nails against the steel. They had a huge head start when they previously thought they would be short on time, and she reminded herself of that. They would have plenty of time to get to Zander. They would save him. She repeated those words over and over, but still her gut clenched, and her stomach twisted itself into unseemly knots. She watched the sea life go by, the schools of fish and bigger fish.

"Ever see a mermaid?" Conrad whispered, but he had spoken loud enough that others could hear him.

"Are they real?" she asked.

He winked. "According to pirate lore, they live in clans. Some live in the deepest depths, some in the shallows, and some in waterlogged ruins. They collect treasure from sunken ships and hoard it in their dens, like dragons, but cunning and shrewd. Legends tell that pirates and merchants of old made deals with a select few mermaid clans, dealing for lost treasures, and when I first set sail, I thought I would be the first of my generation to strike such a deal with a mermaid clan."

"Did you?" Raven whispered.

Conrad shrugged. "Mermaids are shrewd as they come, distrusting of humans, and firm believers in revenge. If I had, I would not tell you."

She pouted. "But, if mermaids exist, then that means I could find them for myself."

"You could, and you might live to tell the tale." Conrad smirked. "Legends suggest that mermaids are less hostile toward females."

"As they should be," Raven said.

Conrad laughed. "I suppose you're right."

"We're coming up on the river," said Niall.

Raven leaned forward to see what Niall saw. Ahead, the river plunged into the ocean. Niall guided the *Barnacle* toward the river's end. They rose toward the surface. The sound of the engines grew as they fought the current. Niall gently pulled a lever, and the engines worked harder. It took several long, loud moments, but they managed to enter the river. When they had gone far enough upstream that the current wouldn't sweep them into the sea, Niall calmed the engines.

"It'll be slower, but smoother," Niall explained. He relaxed in his chair, as did Sweets.

"And in a few hours," added Thalame, "we'll be underneath Kusmerk."

"Might as well make yourselves at home," Sweets added. "Apologies for the sparse interior. I wanted to add a few couches, but Brent said we didn't have time."

"We didn't!" came Brent's echoing voice from the speaking tube.

A few hours, Raven repeated to herself. Just a few hours. This time tomorrow, they would be celebrating another victory against the Gray Elite.

Compared to before, the *Barnacle* moved terribly slow—too slow. Didn't they realize Zander's life hung on the line?

"And we've plenty of time to prepare," said Conrad. "I've been to Kusmerk before, and I can give you something of a layout of the underside."

Conrad drew a map of Kusmerk's underside in the air. Raven couldn't picture it—smuggler ports, hidden berths, and maintenance tunnels. Her mind painted a dark, dangerous picture, and her resolve shuddered. Sisters... Was this how Zander felt when she had vanished from the treehouse? Lost and confused and overwhelmed? At least she knew where he was and how to get to him. She had just vanished. No word, no posted execution, no secret messages—he hadn't found a lead on her until they arrived in Moorin.

She couldn't imagine what it would feel like if Zander would have just vanished without a trace, if she had no idea of where to start looking, or how he'd vanished or why—just thinking about it made her anxious. If he had done to her what she had done to him...her nervous system would have likely imploded.

The sun filtered through the river and shimmered in beams as the *Barnacle* glided through the water. The light angled toward the west, gilding the surface of the river in shades of bronze.

Would the Gray Elite really execute Zander? Would his father not step in to save him? Or had General Winchester thrown his son aside? Raven took a deep breath to calm her nerves, an action that did not go unnoticed by Conrad or Thalame. Conrad continued to explain Kusmerk, and Thalame started to reach for her—to calm her emotions.

"No," Raven whispered.

Thalame hesitated. "You sure?"

"You can't hold my hand once we get there. If I don't take control of it now, I won't be of any use when it matters."

Thalame's hand returned to his side. He looked impressed by that answer. "Good on you, then. Let me know if you change your mind."

She nodded, though she knew she wouldn't change her mind. She needed to be in control. She needed to help them. They would need everyone to get Zander and themselves out safely. She took another deep, calming breath.

"There it is," Niall said from the bridge.

"Incredible," whispered Sweets.

Raven's cloud of thought shattered, and she jumped to her feet. She leaned into the bridge. There—a dark smudge on the other side of the water's surface. Kusmerk. It arched over the wide river, shadowing the water underneath it. Niall brought them closer to the surface. The smudge sharpened into a city. In Gray Elite fashion, many of the buildings ended in spirals and steeples. The buildings blended together in brightly colored steel, blues and purples and greens and golds. Kusmerk looked like a compact version of Moorin.

The ride had been smooth, as Niall had predicted. They had crossed the border into Gracita without detection. She knew stealth was the better approach, but a part of her still wanted to go in blazing and leave a trail of destruction behind her. She wanted there to be no mistaking who had come for Zander and who had bested the Gray Elite.

She wanted to burn the whole city to the ground.

Raven banished that line of thinking. She didn't know if it was her own or Aeon's.

"All right, here comes the slick maneuvering." Conrad moved into the bridge behind Niall's chair. There wasn't much room for him and Raven, but she didn't mind his proximity.

"You ready back there?" Niall said to the speaking tube.

"Ready," came Brent's reply. "Engaging silent running."

All but the smallest propeller shut off, and the *Barnacle* slowed to a crawl. They seemed to drift upstream, low enough to avoid detection and slow enough to avoid startling the fish. Like the engines, no one inside spoke. Soon the shadow of the city overtook them, leaving them with only the sunstones' glow.

Conrad navigated Niall through the dark undercarriage of Kusmerk. Above them, over the gushing of the river, came the muffled sound of a bustling dock—crews preparing ships, goods being loaded and unloaded, sailors lounging and laughing, orders being shouted, and somewhere a hurdy-gurdy played.

Kusmerk's grand bridge had three arches. The center arch allowed for ships and barges to pass through. The eastern and western arches were reserved for docking ships and business. Smuggler's Way was tucked into a corner of the eastern arch, a few berths hidden from obvious view and guarded by thugs. One of those berths would be a perfect place for the *Barnacle* to surface and wait.

Raven held her breath as Niall and Conrad navigated the near-total darkness of Smuggler's Way. In the glow of the sunstones, she could just make out the algae-covered stone walls. The *Barnacle* eased into one of the narrow berths and came to a halt.

"This is good," Conrad whispered.

"Shut her down," Niall said to Brent.

The *Barnacle* slowly rose through the water until the hatch broke the surface. Conrad volunteered to get out first, and no one objected. Conrad climbed up the ladder, and halfway there pulled a pistol from his waist. One of the Wraiths—Jack—stood on the ladder behind him. His magic commanded metals, and should the smugglers shoot first, Jack would halt the bullets midair. Conrad opened the hatch and climbed out. Yellow lantern light spilled into the *Barnacle*.

"It's ten tokens to park," came a gruff male voice from above. "Even if you ain't got no ship."

"The sea brought me in, not the wind," said Conrad. Coins jingled. "Here's for the berth."

"Aye," came the voice, a pitch friendlier. Footsteps carried it away.

Jack climbed out next, and Raven followed. Her boots landed on a wooden dock. They were inside the arch, between the stone and metal pillars. Lanterns and torches illuminated the space, albeit poorly. A wooden dock ran above the water, mismatched and stained and patched. A few other ships had docked; none looked friendly. The air smelled strongly of stagnant water and sweat. Smuggler's Way had a quiet air about it, though Raven could hear the distant clatter of the docks, shouting voices, stomping boots, and wind-rattled riggings.

Conrad nudged her. "Hood up." He pointed to the stone wall of wanted posters. Her own looked back at her.

Raven tucked her braid into her robes and pulled the hood over her head. She adjusted the silken cowl to be able to pull it up quickly over her nose and mouth if she needed to.

Conrad led the way down the narrow docks of Smuggler's Way. Few people lingered, but those who did wore pistols and short swords. Most wore hoods. Others still wore no shirt at all, openly displaying an upper body covered in tattoos. Luckily, no one seemed eager to give or get attention, and Raven fit in just fine among the underbelly. That thought both excited and despaired her.

Smuggler's Way opened to a broad and brightly lit corridor of berths. The ships were cleaner, and the crews were louder. At the end of the corridor, sunlight flared in the main archway, sparkling off the surface of the river. Conrad led them through a nook in the stone, through an alley between warehouses, and then down another. They paused at a metal door which read MAINTENANCE SHAFT 5. Conrad opened the door, revealing a ladder that led up into darkness.

"Unguarded?" Thalame whispered.

"I'm sure it's guarded by smugglers," Conrad whispered back. He then winked. "Or ghosts."

Conrad climbed up first, then Jack. Raven glanced up. The ladder led up through nearly complete darkness, and already she couldn't see Conrad. Jack was quickly fading into the dark too. Raven thought of Zander and started up. Thalame started up after her. The darkness closed in around her with every rung until she could barely see them. She made sure to leave space between herself and Jack; she'd rather not get kicked in the face.

They climbed and climbed, and then a squeal of metal on metal sounded—light spilled down the ladder. Raven winced in the sudden light.

"Here we are," Conrad said.

The ladder led into a maintenance room full of pipes, big and small, running horizontally along the ceiling, the walls, and the floor. Water gushed through the pipes, along with steam and Sisters knew what else. A constant sound of rushing and gushing filled the space, a monotonous whisper.

Conrad started down a narrow passage between walls of pipes, and they followed behind, single-file. He led them up a series of steep iron-grate stairs that might as well have been ladders, through corridors made of pipes so narrow, they had to walk sideways, and they steadily climbed up through the city's internals. As they trekked, the *thunk*ing of gears echoed without harmony. Steam engines pulled water from the river and pumped steam through pipes; for a city as big as Kusmerk, she couldn't imagine how many engines were needed or how much steam ran underneath the city. She had seen the maze that ran through the *Orion*, and three *Orion*s could easily fit within Kusmerk.

Up and up they climbed through the pipes. Raven felt like a rat, climbing between work spaces and rooms, underneath and beside human workers and automations. She heard the workers behind walls of pipes, working, whistling, and talking. Conrad never slowed and never lost his path, and it left her wondering how many times he had infiltrated Kusmerk this way.

Finally, their path led to a steel hatch. Conrad stood underneath it, leaning on the steep stairs, and knocked once, waited a beat, knocked twice, waited a beat, and knocked again.

A deadbolt slid back on the other side. The hatch opened; a woman stood on the other side with a pistol aimed at Conrad's head.

Raven's heart skipped a beat. In front of her, Jack's hand tightened into a fist. Despite knowing he could stop a bullet before it struck any of them, it didn't stop her panic.

"The weather is wonderful this afternoon," Conrad said calmly, as if no one threatened his life. "Not a cloud in the sky."

"Though Minerva knows we could use rain," said the woman.

"May the Sisters be kind," Conrad replied.

The woman removed her finger from the trigger and pointed the pistol skyward. "Hurry up, then."

Conrad climbed out.

Passwords, Raven realized. Conrad had given one to the man at the dock and another to this woman. They guarded Smuggler's Way.

Raven followed Jack though the hatch into a wooden-walled room full of barrels and crates. Conrad led them into a hallway and then into a low-key tavern. No one paid attention as they slipped into the barroom. The smell of grog and ale and fried food filled the air. The barroom itself had stone walls and hanging globes for light. Few windows let in the waning daylight, and each had a tight iron lattice. The bar itself was made of planks resting over thick barrels.

The clientele looked like smugglers, or other such criminals and lawbreakers. As the Wraiths made their way in and took to one of the booths, Raven realized that she didn't mind the crowd. Something like relief had gone over her that she did not have to act a certain way, that these people didn't care.

"All right," Conrad said with a sigh. He leaned back in the booth. "We've got several hours before sunset, plenty of time to relax and plan and then get into place. Tea anyone?"

"I could use something a lot stronger than tea," Thalame grumbled from beside Raven.

"Then you'd be useless," Jack deadpanned.

"Tea is fine," Thalame said, sighing.

"Barmaid?" Conrad called.

557

With an order of tea that came with a differently patterned china cup for each person, the team went over their plan once again. They had gone over it several times in the Barnacle, and each time made Raven feel slightly more prepared. Their plan wasn't perfect or without holes; there were too many unknowns to make a solid plan. As Conrad had explained, "Every plan needs room for adjustments and improvisations."

Zander would be executed in the Greens—a large public square. He would be in the open and exposed, more fitting for the dramatic show the Gray Elite advertised it as. However, as Thalame explained, "The more public an execution, the easier it'll be to get to Zander, but the more complicated our escape will be."

"Can't have it both ways," Conrad had mumbled to Raven.

Raven sipped her bitter tea and watched the sunlight fade too fast.

At last, when the afternoon light had turned golden, Thalame suggested they head out. "Better to be early than too late," he said grimly.

Raven couldn't bring herself to respond, so she nodded.

A horrible thought seared through her mind—what if they arrived too late?

The team followed Conrad out of the tavern and onto the narrow streets of Kusmerk. They had come up on the eastern side of the city. Lamps of stone and wrought iron lined the main streets. Lamplighters worked to get them lit before full dark, leaving the city with streaks of light and puddles of darkness. Conrad led the way, Raven walking a step behind him. Thalame maintained a steady presence at her side. She knew he did it on purpose. He was giving her the opportunity to lose her panic and dread, and a part of her wanted to grab his hand just to be able to think straight. She didn't.

Gulls and crows cawed overhead, blurs of gray and black in the darkness above the city. Conrad led them through narrow alleys strung with sagging silk streamers and clotheslines. Raven spotted a drain at the end of nearly every street, catching rainwater and whatever else, and each had an echoing trickle that gave the eerie impression that the city's innards were hollow. She knew otherwise; they were a mass of pipes and tanks.

They passed a group of sailors hurrying "to get a good seat," and Raven's heart plummeted.

Raven looked to the fading blue of the sky. Wilyn's Star had not yet appeared. She didn't know how the patron Sister thing worked, but in that moment, she asked for Zander's safety.

Conrad led them to the Greens, a large patch of too-green grass and thin birch trees located in the center of Kusmerk, directly on top of the largest archway. Shops lined the Greens, and most had already closed. At least a hundred people had already gathered, and countless more filed onto the Greens. Chatter filled the late summer evening as if they had gathered to watch a show, not a young man's execution.

Conrad led them around the Greens and into an alley parallel to the Greens. Raven caught glimpses of the Green and its crowd in the narrow gap between buildings.

"Why are there so many people?" Raven spat.

"Everyone's heard of the Revenant," Conrad whispered. "The Gray Elite have made sure everyone sees him as a horrid villain. It's made him quite popular."

"Now's not the time," Thalame said. "Joke when we're safe and on the way out of here."

As per their plan, they split up. They would surround the square. Raven went with Conrad, Jack, and a Wraith named Karl. They went along the northern side of the square. The closer they came to the center of the Greens, the thicker the crowd. People lounged on balconies and rooftops, ladies fanned themselves, and men sipped drinks like they had gone to a bar rather than an execution. Their breezy chatter drifted through the alleys, punctuated with bursts of laughter.

Rage burned under her skin. Monsters. All of them. Seeking out death like a game, a show, something to gawk at.

Conrad paused behind a three-story building of lavender-colored steel. He picked the lock on the backdoor, and they slipped inside. The shop was dark, closed for the event. Judging by the sterile setting, neatly stacked papers, shelves of ink bottles and quills, and shined floors, they had entered some sort of office space. Conrad led them up the back stairwell. They didn't encounter anyone one the stairs, but two men occupied the roof. Both wore fine suits and drank from crystal tumblers. They stood near the edge of the roof, looking down at the unfolding event.

"...told her I'd be watching from the office and invited her, but she scoffed and rolled her eyes," said the taller of the two men. "Said she'd rather watch from the street level."

"On the street where she belongs," said the shorter man, chuckling as he sipped his drink.

Conrad and Jack worked in perfect sync—in a blink, the two men were unconscious. They hadn't even spilled the drinks. Jack and Karl dragged the two men into the building. Raven didn't ask what they planned on doing with them. At the moment, she didn't care.

Conrad stepped up to the edge of the roof, lips parted to speak, but as he gazed down, the humor evaporated.

Her heart slammed against her ribs, and she dashed to the edge to see what he saw—her heart sputtered and stopped cold.

A wooden platform had been erected in the middle of the green. A dozen Gray Elite stood on the platform, and twice as many stood guard on the ground. An executioner in all black stood on the platform with a ceremonial ax resting over his shoulder. The fading sunlight glinted off the decorative metal.

But it was the boy kneeling in the center of the platform that made her heart stop. Zander—his mechanical arm had been torn from his body; metal scraps and wires dangled from his shoulder. Shackles chained his remaining wrist to his ankles.

The sight tore through her chest like it had been her own body ripped apart. His magic had allowed him to feel the arm too. He would have felt the arm being ripped apart. She couldn't breathe—her breath balled in her throat and stayed there.

Burn them. Burn them all. They deserve it for what they have done.

Rage bubbled and burned under her skin like a violent storm just waiting for the clouds to part. In that moment of blind rage, she agreed with Aeon. Those Gray Elite, those who had hurt him, deserved no less than her fire. They had hurt him just to get to her, to hurt her, to spite her.

"Oh, that's not good," Conrad said.

His voice brought Raven out of her rageful stupor. Blinking, she turned to him. He pointed downward with his eyes.

"See those automatons?"

She followed his line of sight. The guards on the ground she had initially believed to be Gray Elite were not. They were not human. Red eyes gleamed underneath Gray Elite caps. Each figure had the body shape and rigid posture; each had the same waxy beige skin tone.

"They're the same as the ones in the factory," Raven whispered.

"Oh, good," Conrad said sarcastically. "I was worried these were some new and improved auto-man with better marksmanship."

The automatons scanned the crowd with eyes of pale red. The crowd had put a distance between themselves and the humanoid automatons; no one wanted to be too close. The automatons also formed a protective circle around Zander.

Raven quickly counted. "There's so many of them," she whispered.

"Indeed," Conrad said.

When they had faced the humanoid automatons in the factory, the Wraiths had had the element of surprise and had outnumbered them. Now, the automatons outnumbered the Wraiths—and were armed with pistols.

Raven opened her mouth to voice her concerns when another thought struck and spilled out first, "I thought they could detect magic?"

"They can," said Conrad, his voice grim. "They would have sensed us the moment we entered the Greens. Most of the Wraiths have let their tattoos fade, and there won't be any mistaking what we are."

And Zander had let his tattoo fade. Had that been how they found him?

"It's more than we anticipated," whispered Karl.

"They don't seem interested in us," said Jack. "I'm a little offended."

"Because they don't want just any magician," Raven said bitterly. She swallowed and steeled herself. "They're after me."

"And they wouldn't risk losing you by chasing after any magician that distracts the automatons," Conrad finished.

More and more people arrived on the Greens to watch the execution. The moments ticked by faster than Raven wanted. The sun slowly slid to the west, turning the sunlight molten. Karl had left to see if he could talk with the other teams—thankfully, they had arrived early enough to do so. Raven tapped her fingers against the rooftop while Conrad paced. Jack glared at the automatons.

Hundreds of people had come to see Zander executed.

Burn them all.

A horn sounded—the crowd silenced. A broad-shouldered Gray Elite stepped onto the platform. He moved with a predator's grace and arrogance. He had sandy hair and a broad jaw, and even from this distance, she felt the coldness of his stare.

"General Deacon graces us with his presence," Conrad muttered.

General Oliver Deacon sauntered to the center of the platform. He said something to Zander, who tilted his head upward. Whatever Deacon had said, Zander spat at the general's feet. Deacon didn't react. Instead, the general sauntered away from Zander and spoke to the Gray Elite soldier. The soldier nodded.

"They're getting ready to start." Conrad's dark eyes scanned the crowd and the rooftops on the other side of the square, looking for the other Wraiths. Worry reflected in his eyes and his words.

Her thoughts churned fast—hers and Aeon's, but she didn't feel like arguing with a ghost.

Deacon stepped back onto the platform, ready to address the crowd.

"I have a new plan," Raven said quickly. A reckless, foolish, desperate plan.

"I'm all ears," said Conrad.

"You might not like it," she admitted. The sun touched the top of the western buildings, shading half the square and gilding the other.

"People of Kusmerk," boomed Deacon's voice.

"I don't have time to not like it, little bird," said Conrad. "Talk fast, or your boy's head is going to roll."

"For too long, the Revenant has terrorized our cities and murdered our people," boomed Deacon's voice. The square had gone utterly silent, and at the mention of the Revenant, agreeing boos echoed. "And today, the Revenant will face justice!"

A cheer sounded around the square.

Raven raced down the stairs of the office building and burst out the backdoor. Even as she moved, her plan sounded horrible. So many things could go wrong. Deadly wrong.

She bolted as silently as she could. Deacon was still talking, riling up the crowd against Zander, recounting his crimes and notable people he had assassinated. She didn't know how much longer Deacon would talk, and she wasted no time. She ran to the western side of the square, behind the platform. Because Deacon and Zander both faced away from her, fewer people had chosen the western side to watch. It left the alleys mostly clear, and those who lingered were looking at Deacon, not her.

She started through a crowded street and shouldered her way to the front. With the gilded evening sunlight, those she shoved didn't have a clear view of her face. A few muttered unkind things, but she ignored them.

She didn't care about these people, not when they hungered for Zander's blood.

Did it ever occur to you that the boy deserves such a death?

Raven slowed to a meander to garner less attention. This way, she appeared as just a girl wanting to get a better look.

He has killed people.

Raven mentally shushed Aeon's voice. She didn't want to think about these things. Not right now. She knew Zander had done things that, legally and morally, warranted execution. But that didn't matter when the Gray Elite used him as bait for her. She doubted they would care about his crimes if they had no means to use him to get to her.

And, she didn't care about legality—she cared about Zander.

She stepped onto the cushy grass of the Greens. People stood in clusters, nearly elbow to elbow, and it made shoving her way closer harder. The unkind words came with more venom.

"Should have gotten here earlier," spat one woman in an old frilly dress. She shoved Raven back.

We don't have time for this.

Raven grabbed the woman's wrist. Heat surged from her own. The woman shrieked, yanked her hand away, and before she could say or do anything more, Raven vanished into the crowd. The woman moped and whined, stealing attention

562

away from Raven. She should have felt bad for it, but in that moment, she felt little else besides anger.

She came to the edge of the crowd, or as close to the edge of the crowd as she could squeeze. People had packed themselves so tightly together, she couldn't elbow her way through. She'd already gotten called every demeaning name she knew and a few she didn't. The two young women she had pushed between both glared at her with enough venom to kill lesser wills. Raven ignored them. She could see the circle of humanoid automatons. Their pale red eyes kept watch, but none had signaled her approach.

Someone's elbow nudged Raven in the back, and she took a step forward. Her heel hit the edge of the drain between her feet.

"And today we close an era of panic and issue in an era of peace," came Deacon's voice.

"He certainly likes to hear himself talk," mumbled a tall man in front of Raven. "Why not get on with it already? I'm losing business."

"What's he waiting for? We skipped dinner to be here," said someone else.

The realization hit Raven hard—Deacon was stalling.

And she had fallen for it.

The absurdity of it all shattered her building panic and played into her rage. She laughed, stealing the attention of those around her.

Improvisation, like Conrad had said.

"The general is waiting for me," Raven said casually to the two men standing in front of her. "And for your own safety, I highly recommend you get out of the way."

The tall man half laughed, and the other muttered a curse under his breath.

"Suit yourselves." Raven grabbed the edge of the tall man's jacket and set it aflame.

He began to scream and writhe. He knocked people over in his desperate attempt to remove his jacket. He fell into the space between the crowd and the automatons, stomping his jacket into the grass.

Raven brought a flame to each hand. At once, the crowd around her scrambled to get away, stumbling over each other.

Like rats.

The automatons noticed, but none moved. She felt their pale red eyes on her. Waiting. One of the soldiers on the platform turned.

The executioner raised his ax. The steel caught the gilded light.

Together.

"Deacon!" Her voice rang out across the Greens, powerful and raw. As it coursed through the air, she heard another underneath her own, deeper and threatening—Aeon's.

At her call, everything stopped. The square went silent. Deacon slowly turned, not at all surprised. With a wave of his hand, the executioner swung down the ax. A scream ripped from her throat, and fire sizzled under her skin. The flames in her hand shot skyward, the red-orange burning white. The grass under her feet wilted and melted, the strong stench of burning hair filled the Greens.

The ax thunked into the platform in front of Zander.

Deacon's smug grin widened.

"On alert," Deacon ordered.

The eyes of the humanoid automatons flared blood red, and in one swift motion, each drew a pistol. A hundred pistols cocked, each aimed at her.

The crowd had begun to scream and panic. They flooded the alleys and streets in their desperate flight from the Greens.

"I didn't think you'd come." Deacon nodded to one of the Gray Elite, who yanked Zander to his feet. Zander awkwardly turned—he could barely move in the shackles.

Zander's sapphire eyes met hers and widened. Bruises spotted his face and vanished into his torn shirt. His bottom lip had split. He gently shook his head at Raven. He knew his odds; he knew hers.

She hadn't thought about her odds. She hadn't let herself consider failure.

Water sloshed under her feet, gurgling through the tangled mess of pipes snaking throughout Kusmerk's innards, to the thousands of grates, taps, and faucets scattered throughout the city. Steel creaked and groaned.

"You know what we want," Deacon said.

"I'm well aware," Raven said. "Unfortunately, I don't have it anymore. No one does. It's gone."

Deacon considered her.

The grate under her feet clattered as steam pushed against the underside. The automatons' red eyes were focused on her. They saw her. They sensed her magic. Yet they waited for their master's order. Raven didn't know how many pistols were aimed at her; she didn't want to know. If she played her game right, none of those bullets would hit her.

A crowd had lingered, watching from what they believed to be a safe distance. Raven saw them on the edge of her vision—she didn't take her eyes off Deacon.

"Can you blame me for not believing you?" Deacon said, still looking like he had won.

Columns of steam began to issue into the air around the Greens. Shouts of panic sounded from across the Greens, and the lingering crowd began to flee. She pushed her magic further; the steam thickened and gained momentum. Steam shot through every grate in the Greens. Deacon remained impassive, even as several of his soldiers glanced around nervously.

The stone under their feet creaked dangerously. A low rumble shook shop windows and streetlamps, making the flames within flicker.

Deacon's smug grin flattened.

The ground under their feet trembled, and the mild panic of the crowd grew into something wild. Raven pushed her magic to the edges of the arch, pipe to pipe.

The first pipe burst with a thunderous bang, echoing through every alley. A series of bursts followed, metal clanking and gears sticking.

The automatons started toward her. A wave of bullets popped; she summoned a wall of fire in front of her, burning white hot. Bullets melted as they hit the flame. Bystanders were not so lucky; grunts of pain and shock rattled through the crowd behind her.

"We want her alive!" Deacon roared over the panic. "Cease fire!"

The automatons came toward her. She sent her wall of fire toward them. This time, she knew what she was doing. This time, she was in control. She encapsulated the automatons, and they melted as the larger one had, only faster. Her magic burned at her command, hotter and faster and brighter. Her white flames met the gilded air, turning the dusky square a devastating gold.

She felt it under her skin, in her being. Aeon's fire. The power of a goddess. It flowed through her bones, her blood, her skin. It was her.

I once thought I was unstoppable.

The automatons didn't understand; they continued to march toward her, stumbling into the molten remains of the others. The crowd ran, gasping, crying, shouting, desperately fleeing. Their panic and fear fueled her power, and her fire burned higher. The fire under the square continued through the pipes, melting the metal, and the entire bridge trembled. The ground cried and whined, stone crunching, metal giving. The Gray Elite thought they would defy nature? She would show them.

I too sought to show them all my power.

The ground shifted. The stone gave a thunderous crash as a building on her right came tumbling down. Its neighbor followed, sending plumes of gray dust into the sky.

The bullets started again. She brought her fire wall up, but not in time. A bullet seared into her upper arm. Pain exploded inward. A scream ripped from her throat. She glanced at her arm, sure that her entire shoulder had been blown off. It hadn't. The bullet had caught a soft spot between the hardened leather and steel plate. Half an inch higher, and the bullet would have deflected off the steel.

Another bullet bounced off the steel on her other arm, and then another buried itself in her thigh. The pain seared down her leg. Screaming, she collapsed onto her knees. Her flames faltered. The white flickered and shifted back to red-orange. Hot but incapable of melting automatons. Pain overtook her senses. She tried to summon that power again but couldn't.

The haze over her awareness ebbed. Her distraction had worked: Zander was gone from the platform. Conrad had gotten to him in time. The executioner lay dead or unconscious. His clean ax lay on the ground by the stairs. By the warped bullets peppering the ground and the lack of blood, Jack had done his part.

And Raven had done hers. However stupid it had been.

Pipes burst, and steam hissed from the Greens. The ground shook. Metal creaked and bent. Stone crumbled. Her flames had caused catastrophic damage to the city's undercarriage. She fought to keep those flames alive, but with every pounding heartbeat, her flames shrank.

Automatons stepped through her flames, pistols raised.

Panic raced alongside the pain. They wouldn't kill her. Not her. They needed her. Deacon had said so.

She collapsed from the pain, and her magic collapsed with her. Her flames snuffed out all at once, and the steam began to cool. The automatons surrounded her, washing her in their blood-red light.

"Subject detained," said the flat, emotionless voice.

Raven couldn't think straight, not between the pain and the blood quickly soaking through her robes. Still, she knew her odds were not good.

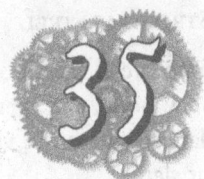

R aven gasped for her next breath. Between the automatons and through the thinning steam, she saw the extent of her display. Several buildings had collapsed. The ground continued to tremble and shake, and the stone and metal underneath creaked and rumbled.

"We need to get out of here," commanded a Gray Elite, a voice she didn't know. "This place is coming down."

"Start the engine!" boomed Deacon.

Raven couldn't move. Her bullet wounds oozed hot, sticky blood. The pain burned in a different way than her fire, a horrible way. It made the rest of her feel cold. With every heartbeat, the world dimmed, and her vision tunneled.

"Keep her alive!" barked Deacon, much closer now. His voice proximity sent a tremor down her spine, and the coldness rattled her nerves.

The general appeared beside the automatons, his glare vicious and his sneer vile. As he looked down at her, his grin turned victorious.

"And you thought you could win?" Deacon asked.

The world tilted, and she shut her eyes. Deacon barked orders at the Gray Elite, but the words blurred in her ears. Hard metal hands hauled her off the ground, away from the Greens. Raven felt blood seeping, felt it fleeing her body and leaving it a husk. She knew then, even if the automatons put her down, she wouldn't be able to go anywhere. She wouldn't be able to move.

Deacon was ordering his men into place, whatever that meant.

Raven waited for the Wraiths to jump from nowhere, to swoop down like the ancient beings they took their name from, to save her. Thalame would heal her, and then Zander would yell at her for endangering herself. Conrad would congratulate her on her dramatics. She would tell Zander she loved him.

But no one came.

The automatons carried her to a waiting airship, the engine purring. Balloons held it aloft, safe from the shaking ground.

"Hurry up! This place is coming down!" came a shout. Behind them, stone crumbled, and metal snapped.

They hauled her into the ship like cargo. As the automatons carried her over the gangplank, she saw the Greens. The bridge had started to crumble inward, exposing its mangled innards. Even as she watched, pieces of grass and entire trees and forgotten umbrellas vanished into the hole. Debris clattered into the maze of pipes. She imagined the hole going straight through, and things splashing into the river far below.

They entered the airship, blocking her view.

The automatons tossed her into a cell. Her body hit the steel floor, and pain radiated anew from every inch, every bone, and every fiber—a scream scratched the insides of her throat. Black stars danced across her vision. As her vision cleared, she blinked in time to see a barred door slam.

"The prisoner is secured," came a female voice.

"Get us out of here!"

The engines rumbled as the ship ascended, then evened into a purr.

Deacon appeared on the other side of the bars. He folded his arms behind his back and straightened his shoulders. "You think you've outsmarted me? You think I wouldn't be prepared for your little magic friends to come save that boy?" He chuckled.

It took all her effort to say, "They got away."

Though she had planned on getting away too.

"This wasn't about him or the Wraiths." He leaned closer to the bars. "This is about me getting what I want. What I want is the stone you stole from me."

He reached into the pocket of his jacket and pulled out the little iron box that had once held the centrum of Altair's Augur, the box she had emptied before giving to him. He clenched the box, then threw it at her. The iron smacked the wall beside her head and clattered to the floor.

A part of her magic recoiled. It remembered the box, being trapped.

"I was worried about where you would hide the stone, never mind how you managed to retrieve it without hurting yourself," Deacon said. "I didn't know how I'd track you or your friends down, and then your friend just happened to make a scene right outside my own front door." He chuckled, and his smile turned devilish. "You've had it all this time. I want it back."

"I'm not sure I can give it back." Raven gasped. Each word was hard to form. She had the feeling that if she died, the power would also go with her.

Deacon frowned. "That is yet to be decided."

Her blood seeped too fast. Darkness crept at the edges of her visions and on her thoughts, a gnawing sensation to rest.

"And if I die along the way?" she managed to gasp.

Deacon scoffed. "You'll live."

The general stepped aside, and a medic in white, gray, and yellow appeared. The medic stood by as Deacon opened the door. Raven closed her eyes and took a breath.

"Don't let her die, or I'll throw you from this aircraft," came Deacon's distant voice.

"Sir."

The door opened, footsteps approached, and Raven could barely open her eyes as the medic knelt over her.

And her world went black.

She dreamed of a temple made of volcanic stone. She knew the place; she knew the temple. She knew she need not fear an eruption, for the volcano would not disobey her. She sat in her tower, surrounded by books and scrolls. A light rain fell, pitter-pattering on the hibiscus flowers that grew on the mountainside. She reclined on her cushions and drew her legs closer. Her silken robes floated about her.

She reached her slender hand through the window. The cool raindrops splashed against her brown skin, cooling the incessant heat underneath. Below, the sun-drenched city stretched to the coast. Her people moved about the city, dots from this distance.

Footsteps sounded on the stone stairs. Who would dare intrude without a proper introduction? Her answer came as the dark-headed scholar fumbled up the last of the stairs. He bowed his head and mumbled his apologies in his soft voice.

"Altair? You've returned."

"I arrived this morning, my lady, and the news I bear could not wait. You were wise to send me to seek your sister's input. She has moved us along considerably."

She smiled. She had doubted her sister's helpfulness. It didn't matter. As Altair spread his latest diagrams on the table before her, chattering in his eager way, she felt a surge of pride. Their creation would change the world. She could feel it in her bones.

Thunder shook apart the world, ripping it at the seams. The temple crumbled, the books turned to dust, and the ocean washed away the village.

Raven sucked in her next breath—she woke. She blinked her eyes open. Everything ached. As the deadened sleep wore off, she became aware of the epicenters of the aching—two bullet wounds, one in her shoulder and one in her thigh.

She tried to summon her magic, but it didn't come. Flames flickered underneath her skin and died.

"Easy." A man in a Gray Elite uniform appeared beside her. He set a strong hand on her good shoulder and gently pushed her back onto the cot. He didn't look menacing. He had a boyish face and kind eyes.

"What happened?" Raven whispered.

The medic's brows rose. "What happened?" he whispered back. "You sank the Greens into the river."

Reality slammed into her senses. The execution, the Wraiths, Kusmerk. The Gray Elite had been waiting for her. She had been captured. Zander had been rescued. Deacon had taken her into an airship.

"Steady, now," said the medic.

She was no longer lying on the hard floor of the cell. She had been moved onto a canvas cot. Her arms and legs were secured. Heavy bandages wrapped her shoulder and thigh. Granted, she felt remarkably better, however she did not feel good; she felt groggy and wobbly, and she had to focus on breathing.

"Did I sink the whole city?" she asked.

"No, just the Greens. From what I've heard from the officers, most people made it out on time. But Kusmerk now has a hole in it. We barely made it out."

Raven took a deep breath.

"I gave you a serum to help with the pain and another to offset infection," said the medic, his tone professional. "You'll be a little wobbly for a while. I also gave you an experimental serum that disrupts magic, which will add to that wobbly sense. I've never used it. I'm not a magician, but I've been told it's like being under water."

That explained it, then.

The medic started to say something else, but Deacon's commanding voice boomed from somewhere in the ship. The medic's lips pursed, his shoulders straightened, and any emotion vanished from his face. As he stood, Raven noticed the porthole on the other side of the ship. The sky outside was dark, inky blue.

Deacon didn't appear. The medic changed her bandages, assured her that she would heal fine, threw a blanket over her, and then left her in the cell. Raven didn't mind. She didn't feel like forming sentences or thoughts. She didn't feel like anything at all. Over the rumble of the engine, she heard people talking. She recognized the cadence from the *Orion*—orders and information passing between pilot, captain, and crew.

The dark blue steadily brightened into the pale glow of dawn. The crew stayed clear of her cell, though a humanoid automaton stood on the other side of the doors. It watched her with pale red eyes. Guarding, not detecting.

Raven shifted her stare to the steel ceiling of her cell. As the serums wore off, the pain slithered back, but her thoughts un-muddied. That dream—it hadn't been a dream, had it? The temple had felt familiar, so had the man named Altair. She knew what she wanted to think, but it seemed ridiculous. Had she truly dreamed of Aeon and Altair? They had been talking about the augur. The diagrams Altair had laid before her had been of the cursed machine, hadn't they?

And it had, for better or worse, changed the world.

A dark bitterness agreed with her.

The glow of dawn brightened imperceptibly. She did not see Deacon. Each time she opened her eyes, the daylight appeared more yellow. They had sailed all night, or maybe even several days. She didn't know.

Gradually, the hum of other airships joined them in the sky. The rumbling doubled, tripled. The engines shifted, the daylight dimmed, and the sound echoed—they had entered an air dock. The airship rattled as it docked, then the engines quieted.

Deacon's commanding voice ordered the crew to, "Hurry up."

The medic appeared at her door again. Deacon stood behind him, glaring down at her like something nasty he'd stepped in. The medic prepared a syringe.

"What's that?" she asked, her voice breathy and dry.

"For the pain," the medic answered, though he did not look her in the eye as he said it. He injected the syringe into her uninjured arm. She felt the serum enter her system, cool and slippery. Whether for pain, infection, or anti-magic, she didn't know. It entered her bloodstream, and she felt its effects at once. Tendrils of unbearable exhaustion slithered through her bones and muscles and mind. She couldn't keep her eyes open, and in a few heartbeats, didn't want to.

A deep sleep settled over her body, and she welcomed it.

36

Raven slowly became aware. Her body felt sluggish and cold. She was moving. She blinked—a pair of Gray Elite soldiers carried her on a stretcher between them. Both wore impassive expressions. They were carrying her through a corridor of dark wooden paneling and arched ceilings and curling ironwork light fixtures. At first, she thought of Winchester house, but this house looked different. A different house. Still, the style resembled Lenhala. Deacon had taken her all the way to Lenhala.

She couldn't see where they were going. Her grogginess clung to her senses like a wet blanket. They went through a wide doorway and down a staircase. She didn't see any windows or even the glow of daylight. Old-fashioned sconces gave them the only light. Had they gone underground?

Humanoid automatons stood guard in the hall. The sconces exaggerated the shadows on their waxy faces and made their pale red eyes glow brighter.

They carried her down the corridor and through a narrow door. Bookshelves towered on either side of her, filled with tomes and glassy baubles and diagrams. Someone spoke. Their words melted together in her mind, though she knew she understood them. Deacon appeared beside her. He glanced down, his face impassive and bored—but his eyes gleamed. He thought he had won.

In that moment, Raven didn't know if he had or not.

Deacon motioned the soldiers forward. They carried her into a birdcage elevator with brass bars twisted together into an elegant arch. A globe hung from the center, bathing them all in dull yellow light. Deacon joined them, and the doors shut with a small clink; the gears had been oiled to silence. The birdcage began to descend with a *click-click-click* of a dozen head-sized gears, visible through the scrolling brass. The elevator came to a stop, the doors slid aside, and the Gray Elite carried her into a stone-walled corridor. With the flip of a heavy switch, mounted globes came to life along the corridor, their wiring exposed and hanging between each. Each globe flickered every few seconds, leaving a constant wiggle in the illumination.

The stone corridor went on—Raven used the time to fight the serum weighing her senses. With every heartbeat, her awareness solidified.

They went underneath a stone archway, the stones engraved with strange symbols she had never seen before. The echo of Deacon's footsteps shifted; he entered a larger chamber. They passed through the archway, and the ceiling on the other side rose into darkness. Because of the stretcher, she could only see above her. She spotted carvings on the gray stone wall, the lines slightly darker than the stone around it. Whorls and interlaced symbols like those on the archway decorated the stone as far as she could see in every direction.

She spotted a particular symbol on the wall, and in a flash of memory, she remembered it—she had seen similar symbols at the ruined fort, and on the books and scrolls from her dream of a kingdom that no longer existed. This chamber belonged to the same age.

That knowledge seared along her spine like lightning.

They set the stretcher down on what felt like stone. They unbound the straps on her shoulders, her arms, and then her legs. It didn't matter. In her sluggish state, she wouldn't be able to get away. Her numb legs barely twitched under her command. She would only fall on her face if she tried to run.

"Put her in the cage," commanded Deacon. His voice still sounded water-logged.

Gray Elite lifted her off the stretcher and carried her up a short set of stairs, onto a platform, and then into a cage no larger than a carriage. Rather than metal, the cage consisted of pillars roughly carved from clear crystal and obsidian. Some of the pillars twisted; others did not. The obsidian and crystal twisted together at the top of the cage.

They laid her on the floor. Her hands flopped to the cool floor, and as her skin came into contact with the obsidian, she *felt* it—a monstrosity of twisted obsidian and crystal loomed above her, taking the majority of the massive chamber. The sudden sensation overwhelmed everything else. She could feel the whorls carved into the obsidian, feel the lines, feel the symbols they created, feel the ancient magic it evoked. In the darkness, she could not see it, but she didn't need to see in order to know what it was. Altair's Augur. She felt its presence like a building storm, a great devouring beast of magic and metal. It yearned for her energy, her magic—its missing piece.

Raven gasped for breath she hadn't realized she needed. Her lungs expanded with gratitude. She blinked several times. The crystal pillars of the cage glowed a faint yellow. With every heartbeat, the yellow glow brightened elsewhere within the chamber—in the crystal of the augur. The pale energy flowed like water.

She could feel the augur's strange magic. It was...groggy. Her presence had stirred it from a deep, ageless slumber.

"Interesting," came a drawling male voice.

"Indeed," came Deacon's voice.

"The centrum has truly sunk into her flesh?"

"It would appear our sources were telling the truth." Deacon chuckled. "Sometimes the truth is stranger than fiction."

Raven recognized the first voice. She knew it. She tilted her head to the side, toward the voices. Deacon and a second man stood on the other side of the cage. Deacon wore his Gray Elite uniform. The second man wore a finely made suit of dark gray. He looked down at her with cruel sapphire eyes, cold and indifferent. She knew him at once. Brigadier General Winchester, Zander's father. She blinked.

Winchester stood beside Deacon like he belonged there, as if they weren't on opposite sides of a war.

"Oh, don't look so surprised," drawled Winchester. He smirked, looking so much like Zander yet vastly different at the same time. Zander may have his father's eyes and bronze skin, but he had never looked at her with such coldness.

"But you're a Hawk." Raven's voice came out scratchy and pitiful. Whether due to the machine or the serum, she didn't know, but it felt like her entire being was slowly leaking into the obsidian.

Winchester let out a controlled sigh. "Yes, yes, I suppose I am. But when it comes to an opportunity like this, a smart man seizes it."

Deacon nodded.

A hand squeezed around her lungs as realization set in. Winchester had betrayed the Hawks for power.

"What about your rebellion?" she asked.

Winchester chuckled. "The rebellion would never have won," he said with such assurance that it chilled her. "They were playing a game without an end. In the end, it's about power."

"And you would throw your son aside for it?"

Winchester glared at her, the coldness barely punctuated. "Zander made his choices, despite my warnings and guidance. If he chose to throw himself aside, then it is hardly my fault. I offered him a role in the new era, and he chose to rebel. I had the princess, and I would have put her on the throne. It would have appeased the Hawks, even if she had no political power. Besides, I still have one son who listens to me."

"We will put an end to this fruitless squabble." Deacon looked up at the augur. "It took some time, but we were able to configure this machine to hold a human instead of a box. Our little genius did a marvelous job."

"Oliver," Winchester warned. He pulled a golden pocket watch from his jacket. "We cannot be missed."

Deacon sighed. "You're right. Wouldn't want the uppers to suspect anything." He leaned in closer to the cage. "Sit tight. We will return soon."

The two men started away. Raven tilted her head as far as she could to see. Deacon left by the corridor they had carried her through. Winchester left through the opposite side, through a corridor that looked strikingly similar to the other.

And she was alone.

Alone with Altair's Augur and a body numbed with mystery serum. She supposed it could be worse. She just couldn't quite imagine how.

Raven didn't know how long she lay there. She and the machine had reached an equilibrium. It no longer tugged on her magic, but she tugged back. She felt the machine looming, felt it whispering in a language she somehow knew—wordless, silent, and persistent. It spoke sweetly, tenderly, and it needed her. She needed it.

This is what I have done. My creation.

"Is it what you thought would happen?" Raven asked the silence.

No. But I shouldn't be surprised. I should have seen it coming. I lost myself in my dream for power, my desire to change the world.

A soft footstep caught her attention, softer than either Deacon or Winchester. She sluggishly pulled her arm from over her eyes and turned her head. A short, narrow figure approached from the shadows. It took a long heartbeat for Raven to recognize the straw-colored hair.

"Ivy," Raven gasped. A surge of relief like she had never felt pulled her onto her feet. She clutched the pillars separating her from her friend. The obsidian felt cool to the touch.

Ivy, not Ivaline Pemberton, approached the cage. She wore slim-fitting trousers and a pale green vest over her dark blouse. She loosely crossed her arms, scanning the obsidian and crystal cage with indifference.

"Ivy?" Raven asked.

Ivy brought her eyes from the cage and finally looked at Raven.

"You have to get me out of here before they come back," Raven said.

"It took a while to figure out the right proportion of crystal and obsidian," Ivy said, her voice distant and clinical. She ran her fingers along the faintly growing crystal. "This is the fourth attempt. I never asked how much the materials cost. I didn't want to know."

"Ivy?" Raven's voice hitched on her friend's name. That joy of seeing Ivy turned to cold caution in a flash. "What are you talking about?"

"Because there's so little knowledge available about the magical properties of the materials," Ivy said, "I had so little to go on, so there was a lot of trial and error."

Raven blinked. She shook her head. Maybe the lingering effects of the serum were disrupting her mind. "Ivy," she said, rubbing her eyes. "I don't understand... Just... I need to get out of here. They gave me something to mess with my magic, I don't know what it was, but I need to get out here. There's got to be something around here to get this door open."

Ivy didn't move. She took a careful step forward. The kohl had been wiped hastily from her eyes, leaving streaks behind. It made it look as though she had been crying, but her eyes held no sadness. She did not approach the door.

"Ivy?" Raven asked.

"I can't do that."

"Why not?" Raven's heart sputtered in her chest, fear of what Ivy might say. She thought of what Deacon had said about the cage, about their *little genius*. "Ivy? What have you done?"

Ivy's blank face fell slightly. She inhaled and released it slowly. "I made a choice."

"And you chose *them*?" Raven whispered. She gave Ivy a moment to correct her, and when she didn't, Raven's hands tightened around the obsidian bars. "How could you choose them over your friends?"

"I chose myself," Ivy spat.

"You can't possibly believe a thing Deacon says," Raven said. "He's lying to you. Whatever he's promised you, he won't give to you. As soon as he gets what he wants, he'll get rid of you."

Ivy's eyes ran along the bars of the cage, all emotion erased. "Building it wasn't easy, you know. But I've watched Niall work so many times that I figured my way around the tools. He never wanted my help. He didn't think I could be anything other than Ivaline the Spy, gossiping and spreading rumors and pretending to be useful while everyone else went out to save magicians and sneak around." Her tone was light, almost bored. "That's what everyone else thought too. Thalame refused to train me like he trained you. He said I didn't need to know how to fight. He said I shouldn't get in situations where I had to fight."

Raven swallowed. She hadn't known that. She had assumed Ivy already knew how to fight like most of the other Dwellers. It had never occurred that she didn't.

"Thalame cares about you," Raven said. She had seen it on his face.

Ivy rolled her eyes.

"When we stopped at the treehouse and you weren't there, it was all over his face," Raven said.

Zander often wore that same face, worry underlined with the desire to keep her safe. And, like Zander, Thalame's plan had backfired.

Ivy let out a grievous sigh and took a step closer to the cage. She put her hand against one of the obsidian bars. "Obsidian is always cool to the touch. It doesn't soak in body heat like other materials. I could stand here and hold my hand against the same place for an hour, and it would still be cool to the touch."

"Ivy," Raven pleaded. How long before Deacon or Winchester came back? "It's not too late to change your mind. We can escape and contact the others before anyone notices."

"I was never useful." Ivy wasn't looking at Raven. Her eyes remained on the obsidian. "I'm not a magician. I'm no assassin. While my closest friends joined the Hawks or the Gray Elite or went south to become Wraiths, I was bedridden. When I was sick, I prayed every day for the Sisters to grant me magic too. Then I could be someone important, do something grand, just like my friends."

"You are important," Raven tried to tell her.

"When Zander told me about the Dwellers, I jumped on the chance to be a part of something bigger than myself. When my health returned, I did all I could to be useful. I recruited Niall from a Gray Elite sweatshop. I convinced Thalame to join after we saved him from a Gray Elite stronghold. I opened lines of communication between the Hawks, Gray Elite, and the Dwellers. But then other spies showed up, and other scouts, and then I wasn't as important."

"Ivy—"

"And then *you* showed up." Ivy brought her cold gaze to Raven. "I thought you would be different. Another girl for me to talk to. Another non-magician who might understand."

And Raven did understand, but her words failed her. She understood what Ivy felt, about uselessness, about being replaceable. She did not understand how Ivy could betray her friends so easily.

"And you had to go and find magic for yourself," Ivy spat, her tone spiteful. "And then I was alone again. The useless one who couldn't do anything but talk."

"You're not alone, Ivy," Raven said. She thought she had been too. "You have everyone in the treehouse. You have friends who would understand."

Ivy frowned. "They all think I'm just a frilly spy, good for nothing but gossiping. I could fight if they let me. I could be useful if they just gave me a chance."

The very chance that Deacon had provided. Raven felt spikes through her chest.

"How long?" Raven asked.

Ivy drew her hand away from the obsidian. She took a leisurely step toward the abandoned stretcher. "I was tired of being treated like a helpless little girl who couldn't do anything but bat her eyelashes. It felt like everyone stopped treating me like Ivy and started thinking I was really Ivaline, and that too much stress would send me to my deathbed." She heaved a sigh. "The Dwellers, the Hawks, the Wraiths...they all treated me like some precious doll that couldn't be taken down from the shelf. But the Gray Elite didn't see me that way. Deacon said I could be helpful. He gave me a chance, and I took it." Her straight-line lips twisted into a scowl. "Then I had my own secrets. I could choose what to tell the Dwellers, what to tell the Hawks, and what to tell the Gray Elite. I controlled what everyone heard. I controlled what others figured out and when and how."

And that control had given her the sense of power she craved.

Raven couldn't believe it. Ivy, sweet and smart Ivy, her friend and confidante, had betrayed them. She had been leaking information to the Gray Elite—to Deacon—and keeping information from the Dwellers—her friends. All because she had tasted power and wanted more.

"I messed up the blast on purpose," Ivy said after a beat of silence. "Back when Zander got thrown into the Hawks' dungeon and you and Thalame disguised yourselves and went in after him. I got left behind, again, to be the distraction. I purposefully messed it up so the Gray Elite would find the lair." A flicker of guilt came over her face. "No one told me to do it. I wanted to see what would happen. It made the night more interesting, wouldn't you say?" She offered Raven a half-smile.

Raven swallowed. Ivy had always had the capability for betrayal. Deacon just got her to switch sides.

"And when Thalame's word came that you had absorbed the centrum's power, and that's where your magic came from, I wanted to see what happened," Ivy said. "Deacon added another strand to the web."

"You told Deacon," Raven said.

"He tried not to act surprised," Ivy said, shrugging. "He thought you used the centrum to melt that Colossus. You did, just not in the way he assumed."

"And you just happened to tell him where and how to get me to expose myself," Raven added bitterly.

Ivy tilted one shoulder in a slight shrug. "I may have given him a few suggestions. I'm sorry to hear about Zander's arm, and his new arm. It was supposed to be a sneak attack, but the Gray Elite aren't as stealthy as the Wraiths. There was a struggle."

Raven seethed. The image of Zander kneeling on the execution platform—mechanical arm ripped from his body, the defeat in his eyes—evaporated any feeling of sympathy she had toward Ivy. Had she ever been a friend?

"But why help them and not us?" Raven asked.

"Because the Gray Elite have the upper hand," Ivy said like it was obvious. "What are a handful of rebels and magicians going to do against an empire of machines and soldiers?" A flicker of emotion came over her eyes. Ivy huffed, blinked, and the emotion vanished. "I've lived in the shadow of magicians all my life. Growing up, my father always talked about changing things, about Princess Rosaria, about Zander, about Ezra, all these great people who would be the face of the new era. I was never part of that. I was the sickly useless girl who couldn't do anything. I was never good enough. I never had anything interesting enough to say to please my parents. I couldn't save kingdoms or protect magic or usher in a new era." Ivy's breath had gone ragged. She took a deep breath, then another. "I *will* help usher in a new era. They were wrong."

"Yeah, they were. We were too," Raven said.

"It doesn't matter," Ivy said bitterly. She crossed her arms. "What's done is done. After the meeting with the Gray Elite, Deacon plans to show everyone just what his secret project can do. As we speak, an airship battalion is on their way from Moorin, just as your pirate friends are rushing to Lenhala to save you. They won't make it in time."

"You might be surprised," Raven said, though as the words left her mouth, her heart sputtered.

"They claim that rebels took out Kusmerk," Ivy said. "You did, kind of. You put a serious hole in the top of the bridge. Of course, the Gray Elite claim the rebels orchestrated it, and that the rebels are heading toward Lenhala on an airship. That's the same airship Deacon plans to test out Altair's Augur on."

Her heart sank. The *Orion*?

"Your friends are on that ship," Raven warned.

"No, *your* friends are on that ship," Ivy spat. "They were only my friends when they needed me. I was a means to an end, a line of communication."

"That's a lie, and you know it!" Raven's voice cracked. She banged her fists against the obsidian. "Deacon has poisoned your mind with all his talk, Ivy! Of course Thalame cares about you! Zander and Niall and I care too. You can't let that lying scum tell you what you should be thinking. Don't listen to him."

"Shut up!" Ivy covered her ears and turned her back to Raven. "Just shut up! You don't know what you're talking about! You don't understand!"

"Ivy—"

Ivy let out a disgruntled cry and stormed out of the chamber, through the dark corridor Winchester had gone down. Her footsteps echoed, then vanished.

And just like that, Raven was alone again. Alone with the augur. Moments passed, and Raven sank to the floor of the cage. With the silence, she felt the pull of the machine. It beckoned, yearned, and whispered in its strange, ancient language.

Zander gripped the railing of the Belt. The Orion raced through the sky. The wind shoved his hair away from his face. This side of the clouds made it impossible to know what was happening on the ground. A mechanic had patched his left arm, removing the dangling wires and twisted metal. The shoulder joint remained; his magic had accepted the socket, making it a part of him. They were throwing a new one together. It wouldn't be anything special, Niall had warned. Zander didn't care. He would give up his other arm to have Raven safe and sound on the Belt beside him.

"There you are," came Niall's voice. The tinker jogged down the Belt with a simple hobbled-together arm of steel scraps and brass. Niall stopped before Zander, panting. He'd likely run all the way from the workshop. Breath gathered, Niall held up the arm.

"Let's go." Zander motioned toward his left shoulder.

Niall braced Zander's shoulder with one hand and readied the arm's attaching joint against the socket. Zander gripped the Belt.

"On three," Niall warned. "One, two...three."

He thrust the arm into the socket. Bolts snapped into place, and Zander's magic raced up and down the arm, searching for the nerves he no longer had. A grunt of pain erupted from his throat, and his grip on the Belt turned white-knuckled. It felt like his arm was slowly waking up after being numb, the nerves and skin tingling and itching. With every passing second, the tingling subsided, and the strange numbness returned to the metal.

"How is it?" Niall asked.

Zander lifted his new metal arm and tested his range of motion. The wrist clicked too loudly, but he didn't complain. His metal arm moved a beat slower than his flesh and bones arm, but his other had started out slower too. It had become more responsive with every day. But they didn't have days.

"It'll do," Zander said. It didn't have all the extras the other had had, the compass, the compartments, the utility fingers.

"I met Thalame on the way up here." Niall leaned onto the railing. The wind caught his short braids and tossed them in the wind. "He sent word to Ivy in Lenhala, but he hasn't heard back."

"What?" Zander yanked his eyes from his arm to Niall.

"Our scouts came back and said they couldn't find her." Niall looked grim. "I don't know what it means, whether she ran into trouble on her own or something prevented her from getting to the scouts."

"It could be anything," Zander said. "Ivy's resourceful. She might not have been able to get to the scouts on short notice."

Niall nodded. "Thalame's not convinced. He's worried something happened."

Zander sighed through his nose. He had little right to condemn Thalame's thinking. He'd done the same when Raven hadn't come back to the treehouse that day. He had unwillingly envisioned her death a hundred different ways. Horrible scenarios had tortured his mind for days, until a whisper came of a girl fitting her description came from Wayward Point, then again from Moorin.

And then she was alive, the Wraiths thought her a traitor, and he thought he would have to end her life after all of that.

No, he couldn't tell Thalame not to think those things. He knew Thalame couldn't help it.

"There's more news," Niall said.

"Good news, right?" Zander deadpanned.

"Hardly. There's a Gray Elite Battalion heading for Lenhala."

Zander's breath left him, but he forced his exterior calm. He looked to the northwest, toward Moorin. If the Gray Elite thought a battalion necessary, what did they think was going to happen?

"They know we're coming," Zander said. "They either think we're coming in guns blazing, or they want us to think they're coming in guns blazing."

"We're not equipped for that kind of battle," Niall said. "Malik suggested to the captain that she send a small team of smaller, faster ships instead, but... As you can see, we are still heading to Lenhala."

"The Gray Elite threatened her daughter," Zander said. Luckett, he had gathered from his time with the Crusaders, held a grudge.

Niall looked skyward. "They are preparing for an attack anyway."

"We did say we could start a war." Zander counted on his fingers. "We stole the centrum, we made a fool out of Deacon, we rescued Rosaria, we destroyed that Colossus, we broke a pirate captain out of prison... Did I miss anything?"

"We rescued the Revenant from execution," Niall added darkly.

Zander ignored the tone. None of his friends had been pleased when they discovered that dirty little secret of his. "I'm not going to stand by and let them have Raven. I'd rather start a war. Besides, this is what the Hawks wanted all along. To push the Gray Elite into open war, to either win at last or lose and not worry about it anymore."

To win or die trying.

Niall frowned. "I don't like how you're thinking."

"Neither do I." Zander sighed and flexed his ten fingers. His new mechanical hand worked a little better than it had only moments ago. "Hopefully, if the Sisters are feeling kind, this will all be over quicker than we think, and we can all be laughing about it on the beach."

"All of us," Niall repeated.

Zander didn't comment. Niall knew just as he did that the odds of them all surviving whatever came were not very high.

But the odds had never stopped Zander before.

As soon as the official word came that the Gray Elite had sent a battalion to deal with the incoming rebel ship, Ivy had gone straight to the Hawks' lair. The new lair was an old inn downtown, a few notches up from their dungeon lair. It had an old sewer entrance, and with a few adjustments and simple construction, they had it connected to the old passageways.

The Hawk standing guard at the sewer entrance knew her; he offered her his hand. She took it because she wanted them all to think her a delicate lady. She didn't know why, but why break the charade without good reason?

Hawks and their associates lounged in the main floor's bar, pretending to drink. She didn't see Winchester among them, so she made her way upstairs to the meeting suite. She found him looking over maps of Lenhala and the surrounding countryside, including the escape tunnels the upper crust knew about—or rather, the tunnels the rich and important could afford to know about.

Ivy gently knocked on the door.

Winchester glanced up from his maps. He looked eerily like Zander. Sometimes, Zander's eyes went just as cold and detached.

"Yes?" Winchester asked, his tone that of a gentleman.

Ivy shut the office door, signaling the start of the meeting. She had seen Deacon do it. It was another power play. She refused to wait for him to invite her inside. Winchester said nothing. He straightened and folded his arms behind his back. She had his attention.

"I've just received word from the Dwellers," she said.

Winchester's brows rose. He had never been able to detect the Dwellers' spies, and it irritated and fascinated him.

"They know about the battalion," she said. "They're heading this way anyway, just not as fast, along with the pirate band known as the Crusaders."

"I didn't think pirates cared about our wars," Winchester said.

She shrugged. "I don't know why or how it happened or if it had anything to do with the battalion. Maybe they are rethinking their approach."

"What is your opinion on the matter?"

"I think bringing a sky city to an air fight is a horrible idea," Ivy answered. "I think they know that too. Smaller ships would work better. Especially considering they don't know where their target is."

Winchester hummed and looked back down at his maps. "The battalion is on course. Any pirate ship will be severely outgunned, and any smart pirate would know that. Of course, they'll have magicians on their side."

"Word is the Wraiths want nothing to do with this war," Ivy said.

Winchester glanced up.

"Kusmerk threw a wrench into those plans, but if what the scouts say is correct, few Wraiths are with them. Most returned to Tinatun to avoid the fighting."

Winchester offered a small smile of victory. "Those pacifists will hand the war to us. Anything else?"

"I went to see her." Ivy tried to look sad and guilty. It wasn't hard. Raven hadn't been happy when she'd realized what Ivy had done.

"And? Are her accommodations to her liking?"

"She didn't mention them," Ivy said, "although I'm sure she wouldn't mind a lantern or maybe a blanket. The tunnels are a bit chilly and dark."

Winchester gave a single huff of a laugh. "I will look into it."

His tone meant he wouldn't.

"That's all," Ivy said.

"Thank you," Winchester said.

Ivy let herself out in the hall, leaving the door open as she had found it. Only after she'd left the Hawks' den behind and stood within the cellar of Pemberton House did she release an aggravated breath. The role of Ivaline fell away like a damp towel. Ivaline would be ill today, she decided. Ivy didn't want to be in the city or deal with the gossip of the approaching battalion. Something told her it would be best to be inside.

A hot bath gave Ivy time to think. To go over all she'd said to Winchester, and all she hadn't said. She didn't know what had possessed her to take her message to Winchester. She didn't have the brain for strategy or the patience to consider all possible outcomes. She'd always been one to throw the dice and see what happened.

Ivy returned to the tunnels and made her way to the augur. She hated the machine. It was too big and too quiet, but not normal quiet. It was the quiet of a held breath.

The single lantern barely glowed, leaving the augur's chamber mostly dark. The machine itself emitted a strange glow but gave off little to no light. Raven had fallen asleep, curled on her side. Ivy replaced the lantern with another. She lit the candle within, brightening the platform. It would have a good day and a half of light in it.

Ivy tiptoed to the cage. Raven didn't move. As she'd suspected, her recommendation of a blanket had gone ignored. Ivy pulled the folded blanket from her satchel and tucked through the pillars. She started back to the surface. She didn't want to be in this cursed place any longer than she had to.

A few steps off the platform, she heard a shuffle. Ivy paused. A beat of silence passed, and then she glanced over her shoulder. Raven had tugged the blanket around herself. Ivy hesitated in case Raven said something. She hadn't prepared anything to say, and the panic her lack of preparation had caused bothered her. Raven didn't speak. She didn't move.

Ivy turned back and continued away, not minding if her steps echoed.

Raven dreamed of forgotten places. She dreamed of scattered islands and coral reefs, connected by bridges both high above the water and underneath; towering bookshelves of battered scrolls full of ancient knowledge since lost; temples of volcanic stone and cities built on sandy coasts.

She walked through a library with shelves three times her height. Windows let in clear sunlight and the briny sea breeze.

She walked along sand-packed streets. A language drifted on the breeze, one no longer spoken. The syllables were crisp and sing-song.

She walked through the market. Goods exchanged hands, fish and fruit and woven thread and silks in every color.

She stood in the dark chamber with Altair's Augur. She set her hand against the obsidian. The clear crystal began to glow pale yellow, then brighter, until it hummed with power. Her power. Her flames became white-hot starlight when it passed through the channeling crystal—a small slip of her sister's knowledge had led her to that discovery. Her power—and her, by extension—rushed through the crystal. She saw her target—the offending city that had slaughtered her people.

Her power burst from the machine, and the city vanished in a dazzling display of light. No rubble, no debris, no bodies. Gone.

It had been the final mistake.

Footsteps stirred Raven from her dream. It took a moment to realize the footsteps came from the present, not her dream. She blinked her eyes open, but sleep tugged on her awareness.

Voices were speaking lowly, too far away to understand. She knew the voices—Deacon and Winchester. She was too tired to care about what they said. How long had she slept? The shift between her dream and the present felt like a rift, and she was lost somewhere in the middle.

Ivy hadn't returned to talk since that first meeting, but Raven knew she'd visited. She had brought fresh candles so Raven wouldn't have to be in total darkness. Raven pulled the blanket closer to her chin. She wanted to go back to sleep. Her dreams were so much more pleasant than the augur's dark chamber.

But she felt the change in the air. It thrummed with tension and apprehension.

Deacon and Winchester continued to talk. Then, footsteps marched closer.

"We will find out," said Deacon.

"Are you sure it will even work with the centrum in this...state?" asked Winchester.

"We are about to find out," said Deacon, his voice cold and hungry.

Boots marched onto the platform. Raven turned her head to see Deacon standing before the platform. Winchester stood behind him, observing everything with his cold indifference. Deacon placed his hand on a panel she couldn't see, and then an eerie hum filled the chamber.

The augur came to life. The steady equilibrium she and the machine had reached shattered, and the machine ripped her magic away from her. Her energy pulsed through the crystal. She felt her body, lying in the cage. She could feel her throat stretching, hear herself screaming. She felt the machine—the crystals and magic. The machine whirled and sang, the ancient magic thrumming through the obsidian pillars. Her magic evoked the countless runes etched into the stone. The magic intensified; the thrumming grew stronger. The entire chamber hummed with a vicious, dangerous power.

Raven no longer felt herself. She felt magic and power. She was the device; the device was her.

Her being erupted into stars and white starlight. She rushed upward, guided along by the crystal paths, contained by the obsidian. Up and up, and then out. The sky above was blue. She was in a tower, contained. But she could see. A battle was happening. Airships littered the sky, guns firing in all directions.

Her power rushed up the crystal channelings, filling the containment. The containment began to swivel, guiding her.

And then, in a blast of light, she shot from the tower and into the battle.

She saw it all at once: the Gray Elite ships of white and yellow, the hobbled together pirate ships, the ships bearing the seal of the Hawks. Smoke and gunfire littered the air. The battalion had arrived. Hundreds of smaller airships, pristine and armed, zoomed and hummed. The battleship, a terror of steel and cannons, hung on the edge of the fight. Guns flashed. Ships were spiraling, engines smoking, balloons popped, wings torn.

Deacon had aimed the augur east, and she saw her planned destination. In the far distance, almost hidden by the clouds, was the *Orion*.

They would have her destroy her own family?

Her father was still onboard, as well as her stepmother and Lena. Luckett would be commanding her fleet from her office. All the people from Silver Glen. All her friends. The Crusaders.

She came close enough to the *Orion* to see the red of the Belt, the snapping of the rigging in the wind, the portholes. The young man with bronze skin and dark hair standing on the Belt, sapphire eyes wide.

No. She wouldn't let them control her. She would not allow Deacon to hurt anyone else. She would not allow him to use her to do it.

This power was *hers*.

And it obeyed only her.

She twisted herself, curving away from the *Orion*. She soared to the west, straight for the Gray Elite battleship.

She didn't catch the name on the steel hull. She didn't see the panicked faces of the crew as the blinding white light tore through the steel and leather like a blade through water. She felt it happen—the grand explosion, the utter obliteration, the seamless death and destruction. She felt the horror of it all, she felt the beauty in it.

She felt overwhelming exoneration and relief, and then everything blurred. Her magic had been expended. The augur calmed. The thrumming lessened.

Raven slammed into her own consciousness, her body still in the augur's cage, and her grogginess shattered into understanding. Lives had just been lost. She had killed people. She gasped for breath and curled into herself. It felt as though her bones had shattered and her blood had turned to sand.

Still...she had saved those she loved. She had turned her power onto the enemy instead.

The words did not make her feel better.

With every thudding heartbeat, the feeling went away. After her bones stopped hurting, she rolled onto her back. Deacon stood on the other side of the cage, looking smug. Winchester stood behind him, face blank.

"That is interesting." Deacon looked at her with the eyes of a madman. "Tell me, what did that feel like? Did it tear the magic from you? Do you remember it?"

"I was there," Raven said, her voice raw. "I was in the sky."

Deacon's grin turned devilish. He barked out a laugh. "You saw the whole thing, didn't you? We heard it, even from down here. I've never heard such a sound. A songbird of war. Tell me, did you see the looks on their faces as you killed them?"

"I didn't look," she said. A fragment of the wild flight slithered through her senses, the weightlessness, the utter power.

Deacon looked utterly delighted. Winchester, however, frowned. Raven met Winchester's skeptical eye. Did he suspect? The corners of her mouth tilted upward.

"What did you do?" Winchester asked.

She laughed; it came out a dry croak. "You don't know?"

"We are underground," said Winchester.

Deacon's mad grin fell. He looked between her and Winchester. "What? What did you do?" He grimaced. "The taste of power too much for you?"

She couldn't keep her lips from twitching into a smirk. "Too much for your fleet."

She watched her words sink into Deacon. His face fell, eyes widening. Winchester remained stony. From down here, they couldn't hear the peppering gunfire or the constant whirling of engines. They had only heard the blast—they hadn't seen it.

Deacon slammed a fist against the cage. "What did you do?"

She grinned. "Go upstairs and find out."

Deacon growled and again slammed his fist against the cage. Winchester started toward the far tunnel at a clipped pace. Deacon spat a curse, then he started toward the other tunnel.

Then both men were gone.

Raven reached for the blanket from where it lay across the cage. She felt horrible, like the augur had ripped her magic away and then stuffed what remained back into her body. When she reached inside, she found only embers.

Zander had always heard that in the moments before death, when the body realized what would happen and as the mind accepted the inevitable, one's life flashed before their eyes. But as he stood on the Belt and watched the beam of deadly light rush toward the Orion, his mind blanked. No memories came forward, no fears made themselves known—his mind hit the realization that he would die and cease to exist.

Altair's Augur would erase him and the *Orion* and everyone on board out of existence.

The beam, white as moonlight, gleamed off the Belt. The beam cut through the clouds, evaporating them into nothing. Zander felt the heat of it on his skin.

And then, by the grace of the Sisters, the beam *turned*. The light curved like a dove in mid-flight and surged toward the Gray Elite battleship. Zander took a shaky breath. Through the hole in the clouds, Zander watched the beam strike the battleship. In a dash of light and fire, the battleship was gone. The few remaining pieces fell to the ground.

Realization settled as his mind began to think again—the Gray Elite had fired the augur, but if Raven had the centrum— His breath caught. *Raven.*

Zander raced along the Belt and through the ship, toward the air docks. Sisters, let him be wrong! He ran himself breathless, but he didn't stop. He threw himself into the doors of the air docks and raced along the catwalks. He scanned the air docks for—

"Someone's in a hurry," Conrad said without turning around to look at Zander. He was fastening the special vest that pilots wore during combat, something the pirates had borrowed from a Gray Elite cache. He tightened a strap across his chest and glanced over his shoulder at Zander. His long braids had been tied back. His usual humor was gone.

"I'm going with you," Zander said at once.

Conrad's stoic expression betrayed no emotion. He knew Zander had been barred from combat due to his injuries. He knew the captain would be furious if he allowed Zander to go.

"You saw that light." Zander nodded toward the open dome where gunfire echoed like birds.

"I did." Conrad tightened the strap across his left shoulder. "I'm assuming we suspect the same?"

Zander stepped closer to Conrad. "It came from somewhere high. That's where she'll be. That's where we need to go."

"Are you sure?"

"She's down there," Zander whispered, urgency in every word. "Sisters only know what they did to her to get her to agree to something like that, if they didn't force her into it."

Conrad nodded, tightening a strap across his stomach.

The crew that had been prepping Conrad's small fighter ship backed away, giving the thumbs-up signal. Conrad climbed into the cockpit. As he started the first engine, he glanced at Zander with raised brows.

The crew released the ship from the rigging. Conrad's ship began to plummet. Zander rushed forward—amid the shouting and cursing of several Crusaders—and jumped. He fell through the air and landed with a thunk on top of Conrad's ship. He hooked his hands on the steel rods used to hook the ship into the air docks. Through the cockpit's window, Conrad was laughing.

The ship fell through the open air for a terrifying and exhilarating moment before the engines came to life. Zander let out a whoop. He had never felt a rush like this!

The engines *click-click*ed through a series of pitched purrs before settling into a constant roar. Conrad flew them toward Lenhala, toward the gunfight in the sky, and Zander held on with everything he had. The whipping air stung his eyes and tore at his hair. Conrad seemed to take his passenger into consideration; he did not twirl or pivot like the other Crusaders. They nimbly dodged while shooting; Conrad skirted the worst of the fight.

Zander had never seen an air fight. He'd heard about them from his father, from school, from other Gray Elite—but he had always heard it from the Gray Elite's side of victory. Hundreds of sleek metal ships zoomed around each other, peppering the air with gunfire, trying to knock the enemy from the air. The air rang with a constant barrage of bullets against the metal, the scream of engines pushed to their limits, the crunch of metal. Pieces of metal tumbled from the sky as ships were hit. The streets of Lenhala far below were empty; the people had either evacuated or gone underground.

A Gray Elite Buzzer went down—it filled the air with the worst screech Zander had ever heard.

Conrad steered them to the north. It didn't take long for Zander to see why; he aimed for an old watchtower, a remnant from when the City Watch guarded the city under the king's command. The tower had the right trajectory, and as Conrad circled the tower's open top, Zander's heart skipped a beat and then burned.

A mass of black stone and crystal had been partially uncovered. The black stone and crystal extended into a cannon—the barrel of the augur. It could be nothing else. That would lead him to Raven.

Zander knocked on the cockpit and pointed. Conrad angled them closer. Zander readied himself to jump. This time, his legs shook. Conrad wouldn't have the air space to catch him if he judged the distance wrong.

A bullet seared the air by Zander's cheek. He wrenched his head back, almost throwing himself off the ship's other side.

A Gray Elite Buzzer headed straight for them, and it opened fire. Conrad yanked the ship to the side, turning it to hide the engine under the thicker steel. Conrad maneuvered them around the other ship's gunfire. Zander flattened himself against the hull. The Buzzer came at them again.

It was guarding the tower. Zander spat a curse. That confirmed it—the Gray Elite were hiding something in that tower.

Too bad Zander already knew what it was.

Conrad and the Buzzer circled one another, trading bullets back and forth, and Zander felt his meager breakfast threatening to come back up. Conrad jerked the ship to the right, forcing Zander to hold on tighter or be thrown—something in his mechanical wrist popped. Zander felt the arm lose grip, felt the mechanism slacken, felt his magic shift within the bolts and gears.

One arm or five—he didn't care how many limbs he had to lose to get Raven out. Even if it killed him. She had risked everything to save him, and he would do the same for her.

Conrad shifted the other way, diving back toward the tower. Zander readied himself. He would have a small window. Conrad rolled the ship to avoid gunfire—Zander held his eyes on the tower, even as the world swiveled around him.

For all his shortcomings, Conrad could pilot the hell out of a ship. Zander vowed to buy him a tankard of the best ale if they both survived this.

The tower came closer. Conrad brought them in as close as it could, and Zander jumped. Bullets peppered the air. A few ricocheted off the fighter and sank into the stone of the tower. Conrad raced off, luring the Buzzer after him.

Zander's boots hit the stone ledge—for a terrifying moment, his weight pulled him backward, toward a deadly fall. Two Gray Elite stationed in the tower aimed their pistols at his chest. He thrust his weight forward and rolled onto the landing. As he rolled, he stole the soldiers' shadows. The Gray Elite fired. The bullets deflected off Zander's shadow shield. He commanded the shadows up, and in less than a heartbeat, he had the soldiers out cold.

He took a shaky, ragged breath.

He lifted his metal arm. Something had snapped in the mechanism. His fingers took twice as long to make a fist, and twice as long to uncurl. The little finger stuck out.

"Shit," he spat.

He dropped his arm. He couldn't do anything about it now.

He turned his attention to the partially uncovered cannon and yanked the tarp off. The mass of obsidian and crystal had been carved with ancient runes, most so complex and intricate, they made him dizzy. Obsidian entombed the crystal of the barrel, but beyond it, the two twisted together in thick ribbons. The crystal glowed a faint yellow. The cannon was aimed at the *Orion*, and it had fired—he had witnessed the blast—but the beam had altered course mid-flight.

Raven had done it. He knew she had. Somehow.

Somewhere in this mess, was Raven.

Zander put his hand against the barrel of the augur. After seeing what it had done to the battleship, every fiber of his being told him not to stand in front of it. He flattened his palm against the crystal. From his training as a Wraith, he knew obsidian did not react to magic while crystal absorbed it. The crystal would have channeled the magic while the obsidian kept it from leaving the desired pathway. His own magic reached into the faintly glowing crystal. Magic residue remained. He had felt the magic before—in Raven.

Her magic slowly crawled down the crystal. It headed below the tower.

He circled the tower's landing. On the far side, he found a trap door that led into a dark, narrow stairwell lit by scattered lanterns. Zander started down quietly. He sent his shadows ahead of him, testing for squeaky steps, feeling for signs of life. The lamps provided plenty of shadows too. With so many shadows, he didn't need light—he could move in near total darkness. That skill was what had made him the Revenant.

Another lifetime, he told himself.

Halfway down the tower, three Gray Elite started up from the street level. Zander halted. In the narrow stairwell, he had few options and little time to decide.

"This is stupid," one of them whined.

"Nah, I saw that ship drop something."

"Bloody waste of time," growled another.

Zander exhaled a breath of relief—he recognized none of the voices. He peered over the railing. He didn't recognize their faces either. That would make his job easier.

He readied himself, cleared his mind, and jumped over the railing. The Gray Elite noticed—as they drew weapons, Zander summoned a cocoon of shadows around himself. He landed on the stairs in front of the Gray Elite. Several bullets zinged off the shadows and landed in the stone. His shadows grabbed the closest soldier, knocked the saber from his hand, and sent him tumbling down the stairs. The saber clattered on the tower's bottom.

The shadows engulfed the second soldier. Zander grabbed his wrist and twisted, breaking his grip on his pistol. His shadows snapped his neck.

Zander maneuvered for the third Gray Elite. His shadows danced around him. The soldier had backed up several stairs. He fired—the bullet zinged off the shadows. Zander lunged. The Gray Elite came at him. In a regular fight, the guy might have had a chance. Zander didn't have time for a regular fight, not with Raven's life on the line.

The soldier slumped on the stairs, dead or out cold, he didn't know.

A bullet passed through a gap in the shadows. It banged off the metal of his arm. The impact sent a shockwave of pain through his shoulder and into his fingers; he grimaced, and his shadows quivered. The soldier he had knocked down the stairs now stood, aiming a pistol, a landing below. Zander threw his arm up—the second shot fired. The bullet careened through his weakened shadows and crashed into his metal palm.

The bullet tore through his metal hand, his wrist—shattering the metal on impact. Zander screamed—he felt the shattering through his entire being. His shadows dissolved. His metal arm fell limp against his side. Pieces clattered on the stairs, clinking and rolling, falling through the dark center of the tower.

The Gray Elite sneered. He aimed the third bullet at Zander's head. "Not so tough now," said the Gray Elite. He squeezed the trigger.

Zander summoned a shadow shield. The bullet zinged against it and fell to the floor. He formed a shadow spear and sent it at the Gray Elite. He didn't look—he looked at the stone above the soldier as the spear tore through flesh and bone. He didn't need to look. He heard it. He felt it through his magic. In his opinion, feeling it was worse than seeing.

The tower went quiet again. Zander let his magic fade and continued down the stairs without looking at the bodies he'd left behind. More bodies to leave behind him. Zander made his way to the bottom of the tower—an office. After a careless search, during which he didn't care if he shattered or broke anything, Zander discovered a secret passage behind—of all things—a painting.

It led into an old stone passage. Zander climbed through. It gradually declined, the sound softened and grew stale. Underground. It reminded him too much of the Hawk's lair, always gloomy and dank.

The passage ended in a sparse chamber lit with a single lamp. A brassy birdcage elevator had been built within the stone. A tangle of wires and gears were exposed—an obvious addition of the Gray Elite. Zander wrenched the elevator's door open. A panel held two buttons: up and down. Neither worked. Someone had turned the power off. Someone did not want anyone going down without permission.

Fine. He'd go the old fashioned way.

He used his magic to unscrew the hatch in the corner of the elevator's floor. Underneath, steel tracks, gears, and chains lined the darkness as far as he could see, for hauling the elevator up and down. Easy. Zander eased through the door and jumped onto the chain. It swung dangerously for several moments, during which his metal stub of an arm proved utterly useless.

As a Wraith, he had learned to climb impossible things. He'd climbed the steep cliffs of Wayward Point wearing nothing but trousers. If he could scale a slippery cliff during a thunderstorm without shoes, he could rappel down a chain in the dark with one arm.

His mechanical arm hung from his shoulder, dead weight. Every once in a while, a piece would fall and clink against the chain.

Still, he kept going.

He could do this. He had to do this.

His arm and thighs and back began to ache and burn. His hand slipped on the chain, and his entire body tensed.

And then, his grip faltered. His fingers spasmed.

And he fell through the dark elevator shaft.

Panic, hot and fluid, surged through his limbs. He reached for the walls, the chain, anything to stop his fall. His shadows reacted—his magic burned through the last of his rune, singeing the skin around it. A gasp of pain escaped his throat, echoing off the shaft.

Without the rune to dampen his magic, his shadows surged.

Zander latched onto a stone shelf. His hands found purchase, and his fall ended. His feet and knees slammed into stone.

After a terrifying moment, he allowed himself a breath.

And he realized he could feel his hands on the stone shelf—both of them.

A creak came from above, and in fear of being crushed by the elevator, he maneuvered his way down the stone wall and to the bottom of the shaft.

He landed on the stone floor of the shaft, and in the pale light that came from the elevator room beyond, he could see his hands—one of flesh and bone, one of shadow and scrap metal. His magic had created an arm for him, using the bits of broken metal for bones. He felt it too. Not like flesh and bone, but like his magic.

"Sisters," Zander breathed.

The elevator room was empty. A single lamp burned on a simple wooden table. The yellow light reflected off his new arm, making it look like a thousand flames danced within the shadows, and glinted off the protruding bits of steel and bronze.

He allowed himself a smirk and turned his new hand over in the light. He didn't even know his magic could do that. If he had, he would have had an arm days ago.

He tightened his shadow fingers into a fist. Oh, he could work with this.

Rosaria climbed into the airship behind Ezra. A Wraith who'd introduced himself as Jack only moments ago followed her. According to Ezra, Jack had been one of his contacts when smuggling magicians out of Gracita and into Tinatun. She had never met Jack, but if Ezra trusted him, then she would too.

Ezra situated himself in the pilot's chair. This particular ship had two leather-padded seats facing the dashboard of ramshackle gauges and mismatched dials, and then a third seat positioned sideways behind the co-pilot's seat. Rosaria, knowing next to nothing about flying, sat in the third seat. With a steel wall to her left and the back of the co-pilot's seat on her right, she felt moderately safe. Jack plopped into the co-pilot's seat.

The boys went through their list of jargon. Rosaria only half listened. She didn't care for flying. She knew what was about to happen, and her heart sped up and her skin broke into a sweat.

"We're ready to fly," Ezra called to the Crusaders waiting on the berth.

The Crusaders released the rigging. Rosaria dug her nails into the leather. She sucked in her next breath. The ship tipped forward and then fell out of the air docks. Her stomach rose into her throat, but she managed to withhold her gasp.

Ezra showed no fear. He wore his Gray Elite mask, calm and in control and ready for anything. He switched on the engines, the freefall ended with a swooping that echoed through her ribcage, and then they were flying toward Lenhala.

"Never gets old," said Jack.

Rosaria wanted to argue. She could go the rest of her life without falling out of another airship.

Ezra guided them the long way around the war-struck city. Even with her minimal view of the fight, she could hear it. The banging of guns and cannons, the smashing of metal, the scream of failing engines, the impact of fallen aircraft into the city below. Into her city. By the grace of the Sisters, if their plan worked, she would have a monstrous mess to clean up afterward.

They skirted the southern side of the cliffs, where age and weather and nature had left the rockface pocked with roots and sheer drops. Three large waterfalls cascaded down the cliffside and into the river far, far below.

"I hope you've got your info right," Jack said.

Ezra flashed him one of his winning smiles, but Rosaria saw what he hid underneath: fear and weariness. Then he steered them straight toward the leftmost waterfall.

Rosaria's heart plummeted. They raced toward the waterfall. The hum of the engine echoed off the cliffs. Water speckled the window, and the roar of the falls overtook all other sounds. The bow entered the falls—she gasped, anticipating the horrible crushing of metal against rock—the airship flew through the waterfall and into a long cavernous chamber lit by cloudy gaslights. The floor of the cavern had been painted in yellow and white: a Gray Elite airstrip.

Ezra brought the airship down, cut the engines, then turned around and grinned at Rosaria. "I told you I knew where it was."

Rosaria exhaled—it came out somewhere between a laugh and a groan. She couldn't fathom a response over her hammering heart. She wasn't cut out for these harrowing acts. Nevertheless, she banished the worry and panic from her face and met Ezra's smile with one of her own.

"I never doubted you," she said breathlessly.

"I did," Jack said. "Several times, and I might have wished a plague onto your house."

Ezra laughed and unhooked the leather belts holding him into his seat. Jack followed suit. Rosaria fumbled with her belt as Jack began unlatching the main door. Ezra took a small step in front of her in the moment before Jack pulled the door open, hand on the pistol at his side.

The door squealed open.

"Halt!" came a deep male voice.

Crossbows clicked. Pistols cocked.

"We are not enemies." Ezra stepped in front of Jack and revealed his empty hands. "It's me, Ezra Deacon."

"Hold your fire," came a voice that pricked against Rosaria's mind. "I can vouch for him."

"Exit your craft," said the deep male voice. "No sudden moves. Hands where we can see them."

Ezra exited first, followed by Jack, and then Rosaria. She mimicked their stance of hands up, fingers apart. A group of ten or so men and women stood around their airship, all aiming to kill. Some wore Gray Elite uniforms, others wore plain clothes, and others still wore hobbled together leather armor that looked like something the Hawks would have worn. Rosaria took it all in, just as the soldiers took her in. An arcade went along both walls of the long cavern, and she spotted several airships at the far end, poised for an easy takeoff.

"Make sure there's no one else," spat the man with the deep voice. He stood a head taller than Ezra and three times as wide. A scar traced a vicious line down his brown face.

Three soldiers entered the airship and began searching. Ezra held himself perfectly still, and Rosaria did the same. She had been through worse, she told herself.

"It's clear," came a female soldier from behind them.

The three soldiers did not return to the others. They remained behind.

"You vouch for them?" the first man asked.

"Yes." A younger man stepped forward beside the first. He held a pistol, but he did not hold his finger over the trigger like the others. The young man met her eye, and a small smile came over his lips. "This is Captain Ezra Deacon, Wraith Jack, and Princess Rosaria Whisehunt."

At her title, a murmur grew and dissipated within the span of a heartbeat.

"Bertrand," Rosaria whispered, more so to herself than to anyone.

Bertrand nodded. "I am glad to see you made it out of Moorin, Your Highness." He turned his attention to Ezra, and his expression turned dire. "We'd heard you'd been killed."

"I almost was," Ezra said. "My father discovered my treachery. I defected."

"And now you've sided with pirates?"

"Yes." Ezra wore no humor.

"This is Colonel Havelock." Bertrand motioned to the large man. "He has been leading this pocket of resistance."

Havelock returned his pistol to its holder and bowed his head at Rosaria. "It is an honor to meet you at last, Your Highness. It is our goal to return you to the throne."

Rosaria returned the bow, though she didn't have to. It felt disrespectful not to. Despite her questionable upbringing, Mrs. Winchester had taught her to always be respectful, even if the other person didn't deserve it.

"Let us speak elsewhere," Havelock said. "We have much to discuss and little time."

Havelock led them into the caves and to a meeting room. Askew wooden chairs circled an old and stained table as if a meeting had ended not that long ago. Introductions were quick. Havelock had served the Gray Elite faithfully until his daughter showed signs of magic. The Gray Elite warranted her death, but Havelock refused.

"As far as the Gray Elite know, my wife left me and stole my daughter," Havelock said without remorse. "They have been living in a small town in Tinatun. My daughter joined the Wraiths."

"Elizi," Jack said, nodding. "We've met."

Havelock nodded. "Is she here fighting?"

Jack hesitated, then nodded. "She is."

"If my plan goes the way I want, we will no longer have to hide our magicians." Ezra leaned onto the table, and the kind boy Rosaria had grown fond of vanished. A stern commander took his place, an unsettling replica of General Deacon. "My friends are fighting as we speak. Pirates, Hawks, rebels, and a handful of Wraiths. While they have the attention of the fleet, we are taking back the palace."

Havelock frowned, but he didn't interrupt.

"When the Gray Elite falter, Rosaria will be poised to reclaim her rightful place as queen," Ezra continued.

Just hearing those words spoken aloud sent a shiver along Rosaria's spine. She had often daydreamed of what it would be like to become queen, but those thoughts had never gained traction. She'd always known how slim her chances of becoming queen were.

"And you think that's going to work?" Havelock asked.

Ezra glanced at Rosaria. Havelock's stern stare followed. She held herself proud and firm. They all thought her a queen, and she needed to be one.

"Have you heard of the white fire?" Rosaria asked.

"Just old rumors," Havelock said. Skepticism furrowed his brow.

"It's not just rumors." Rosaria held every eye in the room, and the attention unnerved her. "There is an ancient Temple of the Three Sisters within the palace. It contains the white fire. It went out the day my parents were murdered. Only someone of royal blood can relight it, and by doing so, I will connect with the kingdom as my predecessors have done. It will magically tie me to the land, and it is the final push we need to cast the Gray Elite out of our kingdom."

"And having magic fire on our side will win this war?" asked Jack.

"It isn't just magic fire," Rosaria said. "It is a symbol. Anyone within sight will know that the Gray Elite have lost the palace and that I have claimed the throne and my kingdom."

"Anyone who served under your father will know it by sight," Havelock added lowly, remorse curving his words.

"Relighting the fire will also strengthen the magic of any magician in the city," Ezra added.

"It will give us more fire power," Jack added.

Havelock studied them for a long moment. "And I'm guessing you want our help in getting into the palace?"

"Correct," said Ezra.

Havelock retrieved a rolled map from a wooden cabinet and spread it over the table. It was a map of the palace and the surrounding streets, marked by countless pens and pins, leaving it nicked and endlessly illegible. Rosaria recognized the map from those she had seen growing up, the outer palace wall, the gardens, the rectangular palace itself. She had never thought of the palace as home. She had been too young when her parents died and her life had been ripped apart. Winchester house had been home. Over the past year, her life had been turned upside down over and over. Winchester house didn't feel like home anymore.

"We should be able to get in through the old Wraith quarters on the southeast corner of the palace grounds." Ezra pointed to the faded little building on the map. He glanced at Rosaria. "According to Zander, that's how you escaped that night."

The night General Winchester had taken her from the palace before the assassins could get to her.

Havelock hummed. "Right... We have a place not far from there. Two streets from the south wall."

"Which is why I came to you," Ezra said. "We don't have a lot of time. A storm is raging above, and we need to be ready when it calms."

"All right," started Havelock. "Give me half an hour. I'll grab a team, and we will meet you at the lift."

Bertrand led them to the lift room, a barren cave, save for the dusty gaslights and the birdcage elevator. Another rebel brought them canteens of fresh water and a small ration each. Without proper seating, Rosaria sat on the floor and leaned against the cavern wall. Ezra sat beside her.

"Ro," Ezra whispered, eyes on the lift. "On the chance that this mission goes wrong, I need to say something."

"This mission will not go wrong," she said firmly, though her own doubt quivered. There were a thousand things that could go wrong.

He offered her his charming boyish smile. "I wish I had a sliver of your confidence."

"I wish I had as much confidence as you think I do." She returned his smile. "But I also have something to ask of you."

Ezra's smile flattened. "Ro—"

"It's nothing morbid," she assured him. She held her open hand between them. He didn't hesitate to set his palm over hers and lace their fingers. "When this is over and I am queen, I will need a court of people I trust. I will also need an ambassador to the Gray Elite. I doubt our little coup will go over well with the emperor. I'll need someone clever and even tempered and brilliant with words."

Ezra blinked once. "Is this really the time to be thinking of things like this? We can find someone once the dust settles, and I'm sure—"

"I'm talking about *you*," she said, smiling.

His eyes widened, then guilt darkened his face. "I'm a defector. The Gray Elite wouldn't listen to me."

"They would if you are my ambassador," she said. "You defected because you did not believe in the Gray Elite's mission any longer. You saw the greater good and reached for it without worrying about the consequences for yourself. They will understand."

He half laughed. "Our views of the Gray Elite aren't quite the same."

"If not, there's always room in the court for a king consort," she said, squeezing his hands.

He blushed. He put his hand over his heart. "My lady, are you asking me to marry you?"

"Oh, I am merely suggesting," she said. "Should either of us ask such a thing, it would have to be under much more romantic conditions."

"I will keep that in mind," Ezra said.

They shared a quick, chaste kiss.

"What did you have to tell me?" Rosaria asked.

He grinned. "I was going to say I love you."

It was her turn to blush. "I would have said I love you too."

He started to speak, but the door to the little room opened and their rebel friends marched inside. Each had come armed and ready, daggers, pistols, sabers, and crossbows.

"You two ready?" asked Havelock.

"Yes, sir," Ezra said, standing.

"I'm ready." Rosaria stood.

Half the team went up first, and the second half, which included Ezra and Rosaria, went after. As the lift rose, Rosaria prayed to the Sisters for victory. She asked for confidence and guidance. The Sisters had long ago looked upon the people of Rhynwier with grace, and she prayed they would once again.

43

The elevator room had a single locked door. Zander's shadows slipped through the keyhole, and after prodding the tumblers, formed into the key. Unlike Raven, Zander couldn't easily blast through solid objects. He'd always preferred the stealth route.

The door swung open to a long, empty, sparsely lit corridor. He started down, feeling like an intruder. The tunnel reminded him of the one he'd found under his father's house, the tunnel that had gone to the augur's chamber. It likely connected to the other tunnels, including the one that led to Altair's Augur. That is where they would have taken Raven. They couldn't have activated the augur any other way.

The tunnel led steadily down. As he had imagined, other tunnels connected to it. It opened at the end, and his footsteps—as quiet as they were—echoed into the massive chamber beyond. The ceiling rose, carved with thousands of ancient runes, just like the augur's cannon.

His eyes fell on the monstrous machine that took over most of the room. Altair's Augur, a tangle of obsidian and crystal. It still hummed, still faintly glowed. It lifted the hair on his arm and on the back of his neck. Unlike the last time he had been there, a cage of obsidian and crystal had been crudely attached to the machine. Within the cage, a brown-haired girl lay unmoving.

Zander rushed up the platform's steps and collapsed by the cage. He grabbed an obsidian pillar with his human hand and grabbed a crystal bar with his shadow hand. At once he felt the leeching of his magic into the crystal—he wrenched his hand away. Where his shadow hand had touched the crystal, it glowed a faint blue. He set his shadow hand on obsidian instead. It felt cool.

"Raven?" he asked.

She didn't move. Her peachy skin had paled to a ghostly white, yet her chest gently rose and fell.

"Raven, wake up ," Zander pleaded.

She twitched. Her inhale came a little sharper.

"I'll get you out," he said.

Zander circled the cage. A heavy lock hung from the small door, and his magic cautiously entered the keyhole. As he found the right tumblers, Raven rolled onto her back. Her lips parted. His shadow-key found the right combination, he wrenched the lock from the door, and he crawled inside. He pressed his human hand against her cheek. Warm. A gentle exhale escaped her mouth and hit his thumb. He found her pulse. Alive. Zander released a breath of relief.

The strange leeching sensation he'd felt when he had touched the crystal radiated from all sides of the cage.

"I won't let them take you from me," Zander whispered.

He scooped Raven into his arms. The energy shifted as they exited, like the machine was trying to pull them back in. Not him, he realized, her.

They must have somehow used Raven in place of the centrum, harnessing her power as if she were the centrum. Which, he supposed, she was.

Outside the cage, the augur shuddered with her absence. The deep rumble shook the cavern. Zander felt a sharp panic tingle up and down his spine—he had heard that shudder before. He had thought it an earthquake. Someone had been tampering with the augur.

After the shudder, the augur whined, each tone lower than the one before. The augur gave a final, desperate whine.

"Tough shit," Zander spat at the device. "I need her more than you."

"I don't know about that."

Zander froze.

His father stood in the archway of the same corridor he had come through. He wore an immaculate suit of dark gray. General Winchester looked his son over, sneering. He looked like he always had, dark hair short and combed to the side in Gray Elite fashion, his shoes shined and spotless.

"I was starting to wonder if we would ever see each other again." His father sauntered into the chamber, his sapphire eyes roaming along Zander's arm of shadows and metal scraps. "You've been busy. I heard you were wounded in Moorin, but no one could tell me how badly."

"I lost my arm." Zander shrugged his shadow shoulder as much as he could while holding Raven. "Not that you'd care about that."

General Winchester's brows rose. "Would you believe me if I said I'm glad you're alive?"

"No," Zander said flatly, although a part of him desperately wanted to.

General Winchester shrugged. "Then, why would I tell you that if I knew you wouldn't believe me? Although, your mother will be ecstatic about your health. I'll make sure she knows."

Raven stirred in his arms. She took a deep breath, expanding her chest. Zander didn't dare take his eyes off his father. He reached out to her with his magic—hers responded. Her warm flame met his cool shadow halfway. The two energies laced together. With every passing heartbeat, her magic grew stronger. Replenishing.

"She's quite the catch." General Winchester nodded toward Raven. He didn't take his eyes off his son either. "Attractive and powerful."

Raven's magic curled around his, tightening in warning. A heartbeat later, he heard footsteps. Something was coming toward them from the opposite corridor. By the *thunk*ing footsteps, an automaton. Raven's magic released his own.

"Divide and conquer," Raven whispered, her voice hoarse.

"I'll take the old man," Zander whispered back.

General Winchester cocked his head, narrowing his eyes.

He'd wanted to punch his father for ten years. Since he'd shipped him south to become a Wraith, since he'd forced him into the role of assassin, since he'd stopped treating him like a son and, instead, a pawn.

Zander and Raven moved as one. He set her feet on the floor; she jumped from his arms. Zander gathered his shadows and went after his father. She and her flames surged down the opposite corridor. A squeal of metal sounded as the automaton halted.

General Winchester dodged his son's first punch. From within his suit jacket, he pulled out a small metal cylinder. With a click, the cylinder shot forward and extended into a steel cane. Zander dodged the first blow, but not the second. The steel cane thwacked him hard on his human shoulder, padded by the leather of his robes. It still stung.

Zander met his father's cane with a long dagger. Back and forth, they traded blows. Zander was fast, but so was his father. Before and after the Wraiths, General Winchester had trained with his sons, making sure both exceeded Gray Elite expectations. He trained with them as Hawks too. Despite his age, his father had kept up with his fitness.

But Zander had the advantage. He had his magic, his Wraith training, and the fierce determination to beat his revenge into his old man. The cane thwacked against the dagger. Zander started to feint to the left, preparing to go right with the dagger, and his father read those steps—as his father blocked his right side with his cane, a shadow-fist collided with his father's jaw on the left.

General Winchester stumbled back, and Zander let out a bark of a laugh. His father scowled and came back at him. Zander threw another shadow-fist, this time into his father's gut. His father stumbled backward into the wall of the corridor. His split lip bled onto his suit.

Zander had something witty on his tongue, but the stone around them gave a terrible shudder. General Winchester's eyes widened, as did Zander's. The shudder trembled through the stone, loosening rocks and dust. It did not come from the augur. It was no earthquake. The sound came from within the stone—the cavern was collapsing.

44

Zander ran one way, and Raven ran the other. As much as she wanted to look back at him, to make sure she hadn't imagined him, she didn't. She held her gaze straight ahead, at her target. They would have time for a better reunion when this was all over.

She met the automaton in the cavernous corridor. It stood seven feet and slim, its waxy skin a reddish brown. She didn't give it a chance—she engulfed it in flames. Her magic had dwindled from the augur's use, but she had enough. She pushed herself to burn hotter, and the red-orange flames flashed brilliant blue.

She felt her flames dancing around the automaton, licking its waxy flesh-like skin, but the automaton remained. She pulled her flames back. The flames danced red-orange around her fingers. The automaton still stood, not even singed.

"It's flame resistant," Ivy chimed from farther down the corridor. She stood in simple clothes, a hooded jacket pulled over her blonde hair. "Took ages to figure out."

Her magic guttered out, and she dismissed the flames around her hands. Sensing the window, the automaton came at Raven. Without her magic to rely on, she had few other options. She pulled two hidden daggers from her back—Deacon had disarmed her of the obvious weapons, but he hadn't searched her very thoroughly. She managed to dodge the automaton's grasping hands and used the right arm for leverage—she launched herself at the automaton's humanoid face. She didn't allow herself to think; she acted.

She had planned to pop the head off like she had seen other Wraiths do, however she lacked the grace. Her feet found no purchase on the waxy skin, and she slid right off the shoulder. She thrust one dagger into the automaton's shoulder, and as she tumbled off, her weight slammed into the hilt. The dagger sank into the waxy skin and caught in the mechanisms within, ripping it from Raven's grip. She smacked into the floor with the grace of a dead bird, but just as Thalame had taught her, she rolled and bounced back to her feet.

She had left a gash on the automaton's chest, exposing steely bones and mechanical insides.

"They ordered you to be captured alive," Ivy said like it was obvious. "They didn't mention uninjured. For your own safety—"

"Shut up," Raven spat. "I'm not going to just give up like you did."

Ivy frowned but held her tongue.

The automaton moved as if it hadn't been wounded, yet she spotted the twitch in its left side. It moved slower than the right. It came at her again. She dodged, but the automaton's fist smacked into her shoulder. She yelped and tumbled backward.

604

Any other Wraith would have popped the stupid head off. Raven didn't have years of training or the acrobatic skills the other Wraiths did.

Raven gathered her remaining magic, and as the automaton started toward her, she blasted everything she had into the gash on its chest. Blue flames erupted inside the automaton, melting whatever they touched. The automaton stumbled toward her, its arms and legs twitching, its internal workings crunching and squishing. Raven felt her magic squeezing, but she pushed her flames deeper, hotter. Gears melted. Joints twisted. Wires snapped. Her flames sliced through the engine and to the metal heart.

The automaton collapsed. Its fire-proof waxy skin slumped; the molten innards oozed from the seams.

Raven doubled over, panting.

"I hadn't thought of that." Ivy looked at the melted automaton with a clinical expression.

Raven glared at Ivy, her friend who'd betrayed her, who had built an automaton with fire-proof skin. She had something snarky to say—a crash sounded from above, echoing with a mighty thud through the stone.

"The air fight is more intense than the Gray Elite anticipated." Ivy brought her eyes to Raven. "They underestimated the *Orion*'s speed and the number of enemy ships, and then you dealt them a serious blow when you destroyed the battleship."

"I chose my side," Raven said firmly. "And I intend to fight for them until we win or I'm dead."

"I admire your tenacity," Ivy said, sounding just like the girl Raven had met in the woods all those weeks ago: optimistic, admirable, and kind.

"I wish I could say the same for you," Raven said. "It's not too late. You can still come with us. Turn on the Gray Elite."

The corridor shook. The very stone groaned and whined. Loosened rocks tumbled from the ceiling. Ivy's eyes widened. She took a step back, then another, and then bolted down the corridor.

"Ivy!" Raven shouted. She started after her.

The roar shook the tunnel; stone cracked. Ivy skidded to a halt, but only just in time. The ceiling collapsed, sending rocks and debris tumbling into her path. Ivy stumbled backward, smacking her head on the stone floor. She groaned and curled inward, but did not get up.

"Ivy?" Raven skidded to a halt beside Ivy's unconscious self. She pushed flaxen hair away from Ivy's temple. She didn't see a wound, but she had learned from Thalame that head injuries were never to be taken lightly.

The cavern shook dangerously. More rocks came loose. The walls shed layers of stone, knocking out the power to the lights and plunging parts of the corridor into darkness.

Raven shook Ivy's shoulder. Ivy came to, but her unfocused vision swam over Raven.

Raven pulled on Ivy's arm. "Come on!"

Ivy stumbled to her feet and leaned heavily on Raven. They ran as fast as they could back toward the augur. Ivy mumbled something, but Raven couldn't understand it over the rumbling of the cavern.

Zander met them by the augur. He'd taken a few blows but nothing bad.

"Ivy?" Zander looked the girl over. "Never mind, we've got to get out of here. Now. Give her to me."

Without waiting for permission, Zander hoisted Ivy into his arms.

"This way's blocked!" Raven said, pointing behind them.

Zander motioned her toward the other corridor, and they ran. Ivy told them to turn right at the fork, not left, and Zander listened to her without hesitation. Raven's heart squeezed. Even after all that Ivy had done, Raven still wanted to believe her.

The corridor gradually rose. The shaking lessened, but Raven could hear stone falling in the chamber behind them, crashing and shattering on the ground, clanking against the augur. She knew in her bones, it would take a lot more than a collapsing cavern to break the augur.

Zander guided them through the maze of stone corridors, steadily rising. When the walls no longer rumbled, they slowed to a walk.

"Where's your father?" Raven asked.

"He ran when the cave started to shake." Zander glanced behind them. "Sounds like it's really coming down."

"Something crashed on the ground above, something big," Raven said.

The tunnels led into a musty cellar, and a wooden staircase led them into a house. Zander kicked the door to the cellar closed. The dark paneling, red walls, and elaborate metalwork looked familiar, and as Zander led them into a lounge, it dawned on her. He'd led them to the Winchester house. Zander locked the lounge door behind them.

Raven meandered through the dainty furniture and to the tall windows. She pulled aside the heavy maroon drapes. Lenhala smoldered. Plumes of white and gray smoke billowed into the sky from the south, enough to shade the northern part of the city. The smell penetrated the lounge, smoke and burned metal and gunpowder. She could hear the constant *pop, pop, pop* of the air fight still raging.

"It sounds much worse from here," Raven whispered.

"It sounds much worse in the air," Zander said.

He set Ivy on the couch. She'd fallen unconscious along the way. Then he joined Raven at the window. The reflection of his shadow arm undulated like sea water, shimmering and dancing in the sunlight.

He whispered, "What the hell was Ivy doing down there?"

"Ivy sold us out," Raven said. The words felt like poison.

Zander's reflection gawked at her.

"I didn't want to believe it either. She came to see me while I was locked up down there. She told me that she'd led the Gray Elite to the Hawk's lair on purpose. She told Deacon that I had the centrum. She made the cage for the augur. She suggested Deacon use you against me."

"And Deacon knew exactly how to find us," Zander added. Gloom darkened his expression.

Raven turned from the window and meandered to the sofa. Zander sat in the chair beside her, glaring at Ivy.

"I couldn't just leave her down there," Raven said. The thought had never crossed her mind. "I know what she did was wrong, but she's still Ivy."

"You made the right choice." Zander held his hand out to her, and she took it. They sat there for a moment with the air fight raging in the skies.

"It's a mess out there," she said.

"War isn't supposed to be fun." Zander took a deep breath. "I can't believe you took down Kusmerk like that."

"It wasn't the original plan."

Zander half laughed. "That's what Conrad said."

"I improvised," Raven said. "My goal was to get you out. And it worked."

His small smile vanished. "And got yourself captured."

"That wasn't part of the plan either, but..." She sighed. How could she explain what happened in Kusmerk? "I wasn't entirely myself. My magic wasn't—isn't—entirely mine."

Zander frowned.

She explained it to him as best she could, how the centrum had once belonged to the fourth Sister, Aeon. She told him about Aeon, how her thirst for power had created the augur, how the augur had started an ancient war, and how her Sisters had struck her and her kingdom down.

"Aeon's power was fire, and it was somehow contained in the centrum," Raven explained. "And that power became mine, but it's not *just* mine. A sliver of Aeon remains, and she...took over in Kusmerk."

"You're...possessed?" Zander raised a brow.

"I don't know. It's strange, but since they used me in the augur, I haven't felt her presence. It's like the machine took that sliver of her away."

Zander held her under a piercing gaze, thinking. She shifted her own to the window. How many Crusaders had gone down? How many had been her friends?

"Rae?" Zander asked softly.

"I'm sorry," she said. "I know what I did was reckless. I just... I was thinking about you, not myself."

He tugged on her hand, pulling her attention back to him. "It'll be okay."

"And your arm?" Raven said, looking at the shadow-metal.

He flexed his shadow hand. The shadows moved like smoke but held the shape. "That's another story. I'll tell you about it later. Right now, we need to dust ourselves off and figure out our next move." He reached into his robes and withdrew a small black metal cylinder. "This is a flare. It lets friendly ships know that we need a pickup."

"Let's go." Raven stood. The floor wobbled, and at first, she thought it part of the battle. Zander grabbed her arm to steady her, and she realized the dizzy spell had been solely her.

"Easy." Zander stood, keeping his grip on her arm. "You sit with Ivy. I'll be right back."

Zander left, and Raven slumped in the chair. She missed the *Orion*. She missed the white sand beaches of Wayward Point. She missed calm and not having trouble following a step behind her.

Soon, she told herself, she would be lying on the sand with a coconut drink. Soon, this would all be over. Soon—because she knew they weren't done yet.

Zander returned a few moments later with a black bag. He set it on the table and pulled out a few small cloudy bottles and bags of dried meat and fruit. He uncorked one of the bottles and handed it to Raven, then opened the other for himself.

She sniffed it. It smelled cool and vaguely familiar. She took a drink. As it washed down her throat, a tingling sensation oozed into her limbs. The sensation settled, and she felt better, like she'd rested for several hours.

"What is this?" she asked. The bottle wore no label.

"Rejuvenation potion." Zander took a swig of his own. "It replenishes your magic and takes the sting off the depletion."

She'd taken a similar potion after their rescue from Moorin. She took another drink, finishing the small bottle.

They ate what they could. Despite how little she had eaten, she didn't have an appetite. By how Zander picked at his food, he didn't have much of one either. Ivy remained asleep. If she pretended, Raven didn't know. She didn't care. She felt like lying down for a long time too.

When Zander deemed their time up, he lifted Ivy into his arms, and they headed into the grand Winchester gardens. The sky gleamed in the late afternoon, the sunlight turning the smoke grayish gold. It smelled like gunpowder and molten steel, and though the air fight had calmed, sporadic gunshots still rang out. Raven glanced to the sky, but no airships battled over them. The fight kept to the southern parts of the city.

Despite the stench of the fight, the gardens smelled of ripening fruit trees and fresh soil. The bioluminescent flowers had dulled, their pedals folded as if in sleep.

Zander led them into the open patio and handed Raven the flare. She pried the tab off and yanked it back; blueish green smoke started to drift upward.

"Toss it up," Zander instructed. "It'll agitate the smoke and make it brighter."

She heaved and tossed. The smoke turned a vibrant sea green.

The flare reached the apex of the toss, and as it began to fall, a bullet zinged through the air—it hit the flare, knocking it out of the air and knocking it across the garden. It landed in the fountain. The smoke stopped.

General Deacon stepped out of the atrium. "Not so fast."

Gray Elite emerged from the garden—from behind trees, bushes, and under leafy camouflage—a hundred soldiers, at least. Each had a pistol or crossbow aimed at them. Raven sucked in a breath of surprise. They had been hiding in the garden? Of course, from the augur's chamber, the tunnels likely only led a handful of places.

"You're predictable," Deacon spat. He sauntered toward them. His usual smugness had been replaced with rage and disgust. "I knew you'd end up here. It's the only location you could have summoned a ship from."

"Wasn't hard to deduce," Zander added lowly.

Deacon scowled. "You've lost." He waved in the air. His Gray Elite moved closer in, but no one fired. "If you haven't noticed, the Gray Elite have proven superior yet again. Your pirate friends haven't the ships or the soldiers."

Raven glanced to the sky, to the guns and crossbows aimed at them, to the fallen and silent flare in the bottom of the fountain.

"I'm not so sure about that," Zander said. "From what I heard, your fleet was surprised. Not to mention that battleship that went down. To a bunch of pirates, of all things."

"Because of her." Deacon glared at Raven. His rage turned sinister and mad. "And with that kind of power at my disposal, the Gray Elite will overcome. This battle will be but a bump in our triumph over magic and rebels."

He said *magic* with more malice and bitterness than Raven thought possible.

"No, it won't." Raven steeled herself and straightened her shoulders. She took a step forward. Guns and crossbows followed her, more focused on her than Zander. "I control my magic, not you." Not Aeon. "You saw what I did. You will never have control of the augur. No one will, because it listens to me."

Deacon raised his pistol and aimed it at her head. He cocked it.

The sound reverberated down her spine, but she held her chin high and said, "And if I'm dead, the power is gone forever."

Deacon hesitated. She didn't know if the power would vanish with her death, but she spoke it as if she did. She knew Deacon couldn't afford to take that gamble. She couldn't either.

The Gray Elite didn't shift. They waited for their general's command. Then, the air filled with the roar of an incoming airship. Another followed. A small battle boomed—bullets zinging off metal, engines whirling and straining with the stress. Raven dared not take her eyes off Deacon.

The air exploded—one of the ships went down. It landed beyond the garden; the impact shuddered through the ground, shaking the trees in the garden and making the water in the fountain sputter and ripple. Metal ripped apart on impact, stone fractured, and glass shattered. A new plume of blackened smoke rose into the air, tinged with red.

Raven's heart hammered. Had that ship been Gray Elite or Crusader?

A ship flew over the garden, the victorious ship—and to Raven's utter glee, it bore the ramshackle metal shades of the Crusaders.

Raven laughed. "You've lost," she shouted to Deacon.

"And, if our timing is right," Zander added, "Rosaria will be relighting the white fire any moment."

Deacon's fingers flexed over the grip.

"I'm assuming your silence means you didn't foresee that coming?" Zander asked, his tone every bit the arrogant boy Raven had first met all those months ago.

"It doesn't matter," Deacon said. "It'll go out when she's dead. Just like her parents."

The Crusader ship doubled back. It fired a few warning shots into the tops of the trees, sending branches and fruit in every direction. The Gray Elite closest jumped out of the way, several yelping. The Crusader ship came back, circling the garden.

"That would be our exit," Zander mumbled.

"Shoot it down!" barked Deacon.

Half the Gray Elite aimed upward and fired. The shots shook the garden air, and Raven held her breath as those bullets smacked against the hull of the ship. Some sank in, some bounced off. The ship continued to circle.

Raven's eyes were on the sky. In her moment of distraction, the Gray Elite surged forward. The airship dove closer. A door opened, ropes descended, and pirates slid down the rope and to the ground. Each pirate let out a mighty war cry. Bullets and bolts banged and thwacks, hitting flesh, tree trunks, and the ground. Zander dropped to the ground, holding Ivy against him, and brought shadows on either side of them.

Deacon grabbed Raven and yanked her from the fight. She grabbed his hand, intending to burn him alive or until he released her, but Deacon had both strength and skill. He twisted her around, and her back slammed against his chest.

"Don't try it," he growled. He pressed the barrel of his pistol against her temple. "Unless you're willing to test your theory. I've got no problem with throwing your dead body into the machine."

He cocked the gun. She released her hands.

He started to walk backward, toward the house, and she had no choice but to walk with him. The fight unfolded in the garden. Bodies and blood and bullet shells. The airship circled overhead.

"You think you can make me do what you want?" she asked. "I'll just destroy something of yours again."

"And I'll destroy something of yours if you do," Deacon countered. "You think we don't have a dozen battleships waiting to head this way? The *Orion* will crash to the earth, and everyone on board will be killed. You think we don't have armies of automatons waiting for the order to march through Rhynwier and slaughter every last one of them?"

She heard the sounds—bullets and bolts tearing through flesh, yelps of pain. Bodies hit the ground, one after another. But as Deacon pulled her onto the back porch of the Winchester house, she saw something else—most of the bodies wore gray and yellow. Crusaders outgunned the Gray Elite.

Two Crusaders took watch over Ivy, and Zander joined the fight. He blasted two Gray Elite out of his way, searched the garden for Raven, and with a fearsome cry, charged for Deacon. Zander halted before the patio with death in his eyes.

"Let her go!" Zander's shadows curled around his hands like talons.

"Careful." Deacon wiggled the pistol he held to her head. "You wouldn't want me to do anything drastic."

Zander let his shadows fade. He straightened, took a breath, and drew Birdie. He aimed at Deacon, but she saw trepidation on his face. Zander could shoot a deer between the eyes at a hundred yards, but he wouldn't risk shooting her. Deacon pulled Raven closer. Zander's grim expression didn't wave, but his finger over the trigger did.

"Don't want to shoot her, do you?" Deacon taunted.

Raven tried to reach out to Zander with her magic, with that indescribable invisible force, like he had done in the augur's chamber. It took a moment to find that strange sense within herself, and another to send it out to Zander. Then, a cool wave of magic responded to her own—Zander's cool shadows. He didn't take his eyes off Deacon.

Trust me, she told him.

Zander swallowed. He took a slow inhale and blew his breath out. His magic responded, *Okay*.

Raven shifted her hand to her stomach. Deacon couldn't see her hand under his own arm, but Zander could see it clearly. She splayed her fingers wide—the countdown. Just like they used to do.

"You're not going to accomplish anything by taking her," Zander said, though his concentration flickered.

Raven put one finger down, *four*. Then another, *three*.

"Altair's Augur is mine!" Spittle flew from Deacon's mouth.

Raven put another finger down, *two*. Zander's finger settled over the trigger. Her heart hammered. She thought of how her mother would handle this, how Conrad would handle this. She steeled herself and put another finger down, *one*.

The fight in the garden had slowed, and those remaining were surrendering.

She inhaled, and as she curled her final finger toward her palm, as the countdown hit zero, she let her weight drop. Deacon's grip faltered and slipped; Birdie fired. The blast ripped through the air, and she felt the impact as the bullet hit Deacon. His arm slackened, he fell backward, and she tumbled to the ground with him. They hit the patio.

Raven rolled to the side, away from the body. Deacon looked skyward. He'd taken the bullet right between the eyes.

Zander appeared at her side, looking her over with wide eyes. He touched the sides of her head, searching for an accidental bullet wound. The assassin had vanished, and her Zander had returned.

612

"I'm fine," she said, though her quivering voice said otherwise. Her ears were ringing from the blast, but it faded with every heartbeat. "A refreshing cup of tea would be nice, but I'm okay."

"Sisters," Zander breathed, pushing his hair out of his face. "I aimed a gun at you."

"You fired a gun at me," she added.

He holstered Birdie and helped Raven to her feet. He then wrapped his arms around her and pressed a desperate kiss to her temple.

A redheaded Crusader jumped onto the patio and looked Deacon over. He nudged the body with the toe of his boot. "Safe to say he's dead, yeah?" he said in a rough accent.

In the garden, the Gray Elite were either dead or captured. The redheaded pirate let out a cry of victory—a cry echoed across the garden.

"We won," Zander breathed into Raven's hair. "Let's get the hell out of here."

Zander pulled Raven toward the hovering airship. She held onto him. If he let go, she would surely collapse. The bodies, despite them being mostly enemies, churned her stomach. Blood and gunpowder stained the air. The already wilted-looking flowers had been trampled.

A second Crusader ship appeared in the sky, and rope ladders fell from the doorway. Zander helped Raven onto one of those ladders, and he climbed behind her. Raven spotted Ivy—a Crusader carried her on his back. Ivy hung on, which meant she had woken up again. Once inside the ship, Raven slumped against the far wall. Zander sat beside her. They sat close to make room for all the others.

"What now?" she breathed.

"Well, with the general dead and Rosaria in position, our chances of winning just rose considerably," Zander said.

"I thought we already won?"

"We won this fight," Zander said. "We took down Deacon, but he's just one of countless power-hungry wolves in the Gray Elite."

The airship started away, and one of the Crusaders threw a flare out of the door. It spewed golden smoke. As they circled back around, Raven spotted at least a dozen golden flares following suit—a signal.

"We let the others know the general is dead," Zander said. "And our princess knows it's time."

The airship flew over the palace. Raven felt the white fire before she saw it. Her magic swelled, and she felt as light as air. From Zander's subtle intake of breath, he felt it too. Before she could question the strange sensation, she saw it. In the palace's center tower, a white fire burned.

"I've only ever read about the white fire," Zander breathed. "It boosts magic and protects it."

"It also ties the ruler to the land," said a man in Wraith gear from the cockpit. "Every magician in the kingdom will know that a queen has risen, and that this century of war is over."

They circled the palace several times, as did several others, before heading back to the *Orion*. From the air, Raven saw the devastation. The southern part of Lenhala smoldered. Airship crashes spotted the district, buildings had collapsed with the impact, and several fires had spread.

"What about all the people?" Raven asked. Smoke billowed from a high rise, and most of the windows had been shattered.

"Evacuated," said Zander. "Anyone with Gray Elite connections knew about the incoming attack and fled or hid early. Sirens warned everyone else."

Raven nodded at the news. She felt a strange numbness. She had heard the battle, the engines, the gunfight, the crashes, but seeing the ruins left behind gave her a different kind of pitting.

They flew back to the *Orion*. It remained hidden on the other side of the clouds and a layer of smoke. Their airship nimbly rose into the air docks, and the crew rushed to fasten it into the rigging. The air docks buzzed with activity, ships in repair, pilots limping along the catwalks, and medics tending to those who couldn't wait. One of the Crusaders from another ship carried Ivy along the catwalks.

Only she and Zander knew of her treachery. The Crusaders would tend to her injuries.

A medic rushed along the catwalk, sweaty and out of breath. He motioned to Raven and asked, "You hurt?"

"No." Raven looked to Zander, to his shadow-metal arm. He shook his head at the medic.

The medic rushed to help others, and Raven and Zander retreated through the *Orion* and to the Belt. Raven leaned onto the railing and took the deep breath she'd needed days ago. Zander joined her, and her eyes wandered over his shadow arm.

"How did you know you could do that?"

"I didn't until I did it." Zander flexed his shadow fingers. "It takes energy, but without the rune, I can handle it."

"And if you grow tired?"

Zander released his control. The shadows dissolved, exposing the damaged metal arm. The hand and wrist and part of the forearm had been shattered. A few pieces of metal fell onto the Belt.

Raven pretended to consider it. "It's not as attractive."

"I'm sure the mechanics can build me another." Zander brought his shadow arm back. "But since they're probably busy with damaged ships, I can wait."

Zander offered her his human hand. She took it. She felt the gentle caress of his magic against hers.

"Can you feel that?" he whispered.

"Yes." She responded to his touch with her own.

Zander's eyes softened. "According to the Wraiths, to touch someone else's magic with your own is more intimate than skin."

"It feels that way," she said.

When their magic touched, it felt like their souls connected. She felt his being, his essence—she couldn't describe it. And by the softness in his eyes, he could feel hers.

She stepped closer. "What would happen if... I mean, what if our magic were to be touching, and then we were also touching...in other places?"

A mischievous grin spread over Zander's face, and a warm tingle surged down her spine and into her toes. He kissed her, a kiss full of desire and longing. He pulled away, but not far. His warm breath hit her lips.

"This is nice," she said, cheeks heating, "but I was thinking more of bedroom touching."

Zander laughed, his breath husky and deep. "I was too, but I don't think that's appropriate for this part of the ship."

She laughed in return. She leaned into his chest and wrapped her arms around his middle. She felt bruises lining her arms and legs, but she ignored them. She had more pressing matters.

"Zander," she started. Her magic caressed his.

"Hmm?"

"I love you," she whispered.

His magic threaded with hers, and his lips found her temple.

"I should have said so weeks ago," she added.

"I love you more than I thought myself capable of loving anyone," he said, lips against her temple. "I knew there was something about you when I met you in Silver Glen. You kept staring at me like I was some wild mongrel that wandered into your house."

"You were," she said, laughing. He'd looked it too.

He hugged her closer.

A bell sounded—the official victory. The last of the Gray Elite ships had retreated, and the surrender had been made. Even from this part of the ship, a resonant cheer could be heard.

Raven and Zander made their way to the air docks to be among the crowd welcoming their pilots back. Most stood along the mezzanine—out of the way—and whistled as each ship came in, as each pilot exited, while the mechanics and medics scrambled from ship to ship. Mechanics tended to the worst of the ships; medics tended to the worst of the injured. The lesser injured were carted along the catwalks and to the hospital. She found Malik on the mezzanine, looking pale and nervous. He couldn't stand still; his fingers twitched on his arm, his feet tapped, and he swayed back and forth in agitation. He stared at each ship as it came in, waiting for the pilot. She didn't need to ask who he was waiting for.

"I'm sure he's all right." Raven gave his arm a sisterly squeeze of affection, like Lena had done to her so many times. "He's a good pilot."

"One of the finest," Malik said dryly. He cleared his throat. "A ship will be ready shortly to take you down to the palace, if you wish. Several Wraiths are already there."

"That's good," Zander said.

One by one, the berths filled.

Among the last to enter the docks was a ship with a smoking hole dangerously close to the engine. It wobbled as it docked. Malik's breath hitched, and he started along the catwalks toward the ship. No one told him to stand back.

Raven remembered Ezra limping out of his damaged airship, bleeding and barely conscious. She found herself holding her breath as Malik approached the ship. The crew checked the hole by the engine first, and medics stood ready for the pilot. The cockpit slid open, and Conrad ungracefully climbed to the dock. He wobbled but remained standing. He bore no obvious wounds or blood stains; he looked unenthused and weary.

Malik pushed his way to the berth. Conrad gave him a tired smile, but Malik didn't give him the chance to say anything—he threw his arms around Conrad's neck.

Raven released a breath of relief.

"What?" Zander asked. "You think Conrad wouldn't come back?"

"I had considered it."

Zander chuckled. "He's too stubborn and clever to die, or the Wraiths would have done him in years ago."

She laughed, and it felt joyous on her lungs.

Conrad and Malik parted. Conrad's lips moved. Malik frowned, looking like he might slap him—instead, he kissed him.

Zander nudged Raven and gave her a knowing smile.

"Mother did say Malik and I had similar tastes in men," Raven said.

He raised a brow. "And what tastes are those?"

She took a long moment to look him up and down, considering. "The bad ones."

He smirked, and butterflies let loose in her ribcage. "Bad as in good, or bad as in bad?"

Raven only smiled and laced her fingers with his.

Raven had fallen asleep to thoughts of a new era. She woke to Zander's gentle breathing and her darkened cabin aboard the Orion. Zander slept in Rosaria's bunk; Rosaria had opted to stay in the palace with a few trusted companions, including Ezra. She had a few Wraiths with her, so Raven wasn't worried for her safety.

She climbed out of her bunk. Zander slept on his stomach, and his human arm dangled off the side of the bed. She couldn't see his other arm. A mechanic had removed the broken bits of metal. They hadn't replaced it—Zander had told them not to. When he had explained what had happened with his magic, Niall and Brent had shared an expression. They had a plan, but neither told Zander what it was.

She washed her hands and face, pulled on her Wraith robes from the day before, and tiptoed into the corridor. Despite the early hour, the airship buzzed with activity. Raven made her way to the holding cells belowdecks, past the purring engines, past the mechanic workshops and smiths. The holding cells were on the lowest part of the ship. The Crusader guarding the iron door was leaning against the wall, puffing on a sweet-smelling cigar. Two pistols hung off his hips, and two daggers crisscrossed his back. Gray streaked his black hair and his beard. An old scar stretched from his cheekbone to his jaw, and the hair didn't grow there.

"I want to see a prisoner," Raven said.

"Awful early," he said.

"The sun is up," Raven said.

He chuckled. "You're starting to sound like the captain."

Raven shrugged. The news of her being Luckett's daughter had made the rounds. The Crusader unlocked the heavy door and pulled it open—it gave a vicious squeal of metal on metal.

Raven walked into the holding cells. It was a corridor of plain steel and iron, lined with iron-barred doors. Dirty globes hung from the ceiling. No windows allowed in sunlight. The holding cells were not friendly or welcoming, and Raven hated them. She reasoned that those thrown into the holding cells had done something wrong and didn't deserve to sit in a friendly, welcoming place. Thankfully, most of the cells were empty.

Ivy's cell was at the end of the corridor. Thalame leaned against the iron bars of the cell, looking like he hadn't slept. He had been busy tending to the wounded all night, and he had still been at it when Raven had gone to bed. Ivy sat cross-legged on the cot. She wore the same trousers and blouse as the day before.

"How are you?" Raven asked Ivy.

"I'm awake," Ivy said. She didn't have the same cool demeanor as she'd had in the cavern. She sounded defeated and tired. Her voice was hoarse. "Thalame said he fixed my head."

"Concussion," Thalame said to Raven. Dark circles hung under his eyes. The way he said it made Raven think it had been much worse than a concussion, but she didn't push him for the truth.

"Raven, tell Thalame to go get some sleep," Ivy said. "He's being grumpy."

Thalame grimaced and left. Several cells down, he muttered something too low for Raven to hear. The iron door creaked open and closed once more.

"He's persistent." Ivy gazed at the ceiling. "He said he'd forgive me if I apologized."

"Did you?"

Ivy shook her head. "Not yet."

Raven scowled. "Why not?"

Ivy's gaze slid to Raven. "I don't feel sorry."

Raven wanted to shake her friend until she felt sorry for what she had done, all the trouble she had caused. All the lives she had cost.

"You look mad," Ivy deadpanned.

Raven's rage bubbled. "Of course I'm mad! Your stupid decisions got us in this mess. If you hadn't sold us out to Deacon, none of this would have happened. They wouldn't have known where to find Zander, they wouldn't have caught me, and they wouldn't have used me to..." Raven sucked back a hot rush of tears. "I killed people. They forced me to. I don't even know how many people."

Ivy stilled.

"And you're pretending like it was nothing," Raven spat.

"I suppose this means you won't be asking me to apologize like Thalame."

Raven wanted Ivy to feel sorry for what she had done, but by the empty expression on the girl's face, she did not. Yelling would not help things, despite how much she wanted to scream at Ivy.

"Thalame will wait until you are sorry," Raven said, her words threaded with the tears she had pushed down. She wiped at her eyes with the back of her hand.

"Will you?" Ivy asked softly.

"I don't know." Raven sniffled and swallowed the rest of her tears. "You know, if anyone else had done what you did, they would have been tried as a war criminal and executed."

That punctuated Ivy's stony expression. Her brows rose, and her lips twitched.

"I don't know what Luckett is planning on doing with you." Raven let those words sink in. Luckett had not been happy with having Ivy on board; however, Ivy's fate in Lenhala would have been much worse. "I only asked her not to throw you overboard."

A moment passed, then Ivy said quietly, "Thank you." Another long moment passed, and Raven turned to go, when Ivy spoke again, "Do you think Thalame hates me?"

"No," Raven said at once. "I think he might love you." Raven didn't know for certain what Thalame's feelings were, but in some way, whether platonically or romantically, he did care for Ivy.

"Is that so?" Ivy sighed. "He's not very good at showing it."

Raven didn't feel like talking about boys with Ivy. She didn't feel like talking with Ivy at all. She had come to see her because she knew, deep down, she needed to. "We're friends. We care about you, despite the horrible decisions you've made, and despite how much it doesn't feel like it right now."

Ivy sighed and returned her gaze to the ceiling. "Like you're friends with Conrad? He's a pirate and a thief and a liar. He's been kicked out of the Wraiths for stealing. I hear there's people in Tinatun who want him dead."

"Yes, like I'm friends with Conrad, only he never stabbed me in the back."

Ivy didn't say anything.

A horn sounded within the ship—the signal to switch shifts in the engine room. She'd only heard it a few times; it didn't sound in the upper parts of the ship.

Raven stepped away from the bars.

"I'm thinking about moving to Wayward Point when this is all over," Ivy said casually, eyes on the ceiling. "I could use a beach after all this."

After a long pause, Raven started back to the upper deck. They had a lot of things to do in the next few days, and she didn't have time to nag Ivy. She could wait for the other girl to feel remorse.

Raven headed up to the captain's office near the bridge. Her mother had requested—a bit aggressively—for Raven to join her and Malik for tea.

A week passed in a blur of news and gossip. Raven made several trips from the *Orion* to Lenhala's new royal palace, where Rosaria and her inner circle of trusted companions oversaw the rebuilding of Rhynwier. The people had started to return to their homes and business. Teams swept the city for debris and bodies.

With the Gray Elite's retreat and subsequent surrender, Rosaria reclaimed her throne. Her ragtag team of Wraiths, rebels, and Hawks became her Royal Guard, led by the newly appointed Captain Havelock. The Hawks had sworn allegiance to her immediately, though Raven had noted the absence of Zander's father. Zander noted a few other Hawks who had failed to show. Rosaria also extended a welcome to those of the Gray Elite who wished to remain in Lenhala; it was their home too, she had reasoned.

The Gray Elite had not been happy about the entire ordeal. The emperor had sent a delegation to speak with Rosaria three days after the official surrender. Raven had attended as a Wraith, alongside a few others, as security for Rosaria. The emperor offered a treaty, which Rosaria picked apart during the meeting. Rosaria had borrowed a few of the Crusaders scouts and spread rumors that she had taken control of Altair's Augur. They said it curved upon her command and destroyed the Gray Elite Battleship at her will. It made the delegation nervous. Rosaria demanded the Gray Elite and its automatons leave Rhynwier, and she asked for peace between their two peoples.

It had been a dreadful meeting full of politics and court-trained smiles and duplicitous words, but Rosaria had navigated her way with ease and grace. Luckily, all Raven had to do was look intimidating. Her dark robes with plated steel and hardened leather made her part easy to manage.

By the end of the first week, Raven was exhausted.

It would be a long road uphill, as Rosaria had claimed. She had ten years of Gray Elite tyranny to undo, hundreds of villages to help rebuild, and an economy to piece back together.

The day of Rosaria's coronation dawned bright and clear. The growing court had been hard at work cleaning and preparing the palace. Many Wraiths came in their full gear, Raven and Zander among them. Rosaria entered the throne room in a simple gown of ivory and a cape of gold.

She made her way through the throne room to the newly crafted throne; behind it, a portion of white fire burned in a silver cask. Captain Havelock stood on one side, and Ezra Deacon stood on the other. Ezra had traded his Gray Elite uniform for a suit of brown and ivory. An aged woman—one of the few scholars to have escaped the palace massacre and newly appointed Chief of Council—held the crown while Rosaria recited an ancient oath of justice and loyalty.

Then the old woman placed the crown upon Rosaria's head.

"May the Sisters look upon your rule with grace." Her frail voice wobbled and tears lined her eyes. "Rise, Queen Rosaria Whisehunt."

Rosaria stood. The crown gleamed in the midmorning sunlight streaming in through the tall windows. As she stood, every knee in the room bent.

The new era had dawned. Raven felt it in her bones. It tingled on her skin. Everything would be changing.

Following the coronation, Queen Rosaria gave her first speech from the palace steps. Hundreds had come to see her. She spoke of a bright future, renewed independence, and a thriving economy. Magicians would no longer be hunted. Automatons would no longer replace human workers. The Gray Elite would have no power over the people. Along with the Wraiths and the Hawks, Rosaria would usher in an era of peace and prosperity. They would rebuild Lenhala and all the villages and cities that had once dotted the kingdom. They would become the mighty and brave kingdom they once had been. They would rebuild the kingdom the Gray Elite had tried to slay.

Rosaria's first act as queen was to lift the ban on magic and magicians. For her second, she appointed Ezra Deacon as her ambassador. She ordered the automaton statues removed and commissioned new statues of the Sisters. It stirred mild unrest, but Rosaria announced that those upset by the change in leadership were free to leave, for Rhynwier would return to the Sisters.

The Order of the Hawk returned to the surface and stood behind Queen Rosaria. Some had even found old uniforms bearing the royal coat of arms—a hawk in flight. The old Wraith quarters would again house Wraiths, and the ancient order agreed to set up a headquarters in Lenhala. Elizi had volunteered to oversee the new faction.

The evening after the coronation, Raven stood in the vast palace grounds and bid farewell to her friend from Silver Glen. Most had come down from the *Orion* to see their new queen crowned, but now it was time for them to go home. Luckett had offered to ferry them. Most had already returned to the *Orion*. Raven had wished luck and happiness to Brent and Sweets, who hadn't decided if they were going to stay in Silver Glen or travel.

Only Raven's father, stepmother, and sister remained on the ground. A Crusader ship waited to take them back up to the *Orion*.

Lena hugged Raven tight, as did her stepmother.

"You take care of yourself," said her stepmother.

"And write every week," Lena added. "I want to hear about all of your adventures."

"As long as you write back," Raven said.

Her stepmother and Lena climbed aboard the waiting airship. Her father stood with his arms crossed, looking as commanding as ever.

"You'll always have a home in Silver Glen," he said. "No matter how much time passes or where you go."

She nodded. "Thanks, Dad."

Samuel's gaze shifted over her shoulder. Footsteps sounded against the grass, and then Zander appeared at her side. For a long moment, the two men stared at one another.

"You mind yourself." Samuel extended his hand to Zander.

"I will, sir." Zander shook his hand.

"Take care of her," Samuel said to Zander. He turned to Raven and added, "Take care of him."

"You make it sound easy." Raven smiled at Zander.

"You know," her father started, eyes on the horizon, "without the Gray Elite and their automatons, there's no need to hide so far north or in the dank mines. There are plenty of places to make a new home."

Samuel brought his eyes back to Raven, and she saw something within them she had never seen before—a twinkle of excitement, a glimmer of the sky sailor he had once been.

"Wherever you end up, send us a letter," Raven said. "We can't visit if we don't know where to go."

"That I'll do," her father said.

"Bye, Dad," Raven said.

"See you, Samuel," said Zander.

Her father huff-laughed, then took them both in an embrace. He kissed his daughter's head, then joined the others in the airship. Raven watched it rise through the clouds to the waiting *Orion*.

Raven inhaled and released a calming breath.

"What do you think?" Zander asked.

"I think it's strange watching my family fly away, but at the same time it feels..." She didn't know the words to use. "It feels like my father is allowing me to grow up."

A crash came from the far side of the grounds, where a team of royal guards were busy taking down an automaton statue. One of the statues had fallen into the grassy earth, barely missing one of the guards. A beat of silence passed, and then laughter rang through the yard.

"We've got a lot of work to do," Raven said.

Zander sighed. "Can't say I'm looking forward to it."

While the Orion took the people of Silver Glen home—wherever home ended up being—Raven and Zander remained in Lenhala to help the Hawks and Wraiths rebuild. Magicians no longer had to hide, and over the next several weeks, magic shops dotted the city. The Wraiths offered to start a school for magicians, just like there had been one hundred years before, to teach young magicians how to control their gifts.

Zander and Raven—being Wraiths—had beds in the Wraiths' new headquarters. Being friends with the queen, they were offered quarters in the palace. Raven hadn't hesitated to pick the palace. The room she and Zander shared had come with a large amount of dust, dirty floors, and a musty smell of disuse. It also had a beautiful view of the grounds.

Three weeks into their stay at the palace, three weeks of cleaning, rebuilding, organizing, discussing, and taking down Gray Elite emblems, Raven collapsed into the cushy bed and groaned into the pillow. Her wet hair flopped around her face. She hadn't the energy to braid it back. She'd barely had the energy to pull on one of the summer nightdresses she'd accumulated. The one she chose was pale blue with a calf-length pleated skirt and short sleeves.

Zander stepped out of the grand bathroom they'd spent an entire day deep cleaning. He wore only a towel around his waist, and his real hand and his shadow hand worked to tie his wet hair into a knot behind his head.

"I don't think I'll be able to sleep on anything other than silk again," she whined.

Zander chuckled. "There goes that camping trip into the mountains I was planning."

"Just pack silk sheets." She turned her head to see him. They had been so busy, she'd barely seen Zander more than a few minutes at a time and in the evenings when they were both exhausted.

Zander was sorting through his side of their walk-in closet. He pulled a gray sleeping shirt over his head. It fell to his knees. He looked exhausted and bothered. While she had spent the day with Rosaria, Zander had gone to the Winchester house to sort things out.

"Any word of your father?"

"No." Zander deflated. "They haven't found his body among the dead, so he's still out there. I bet he slipped out with the other refugees going to Gracita. With him presumed dead, the estate falls to my mother, but she doesn't want it."

"Do you want it?"

"No," Zander said without hesitation. "She's already passed it to Baxter, who has claimed innocence of our father's double dealings. Baxter claims to be a Hawk and loyal to the queen."

"Is he?"

"I don't know," Zander whispered. "Baxter grew up with Rosaria too. She sees him as a brother. Regardless of what he is, Ro won't throw him in the dungeon." Zander rubbed his face. "It's fine. I don't want an estate. I'd end up selling it. At least my brother will get use out of it. My mother says she's going to stay with relatives in Moorin, but it's a lie and everyone knows it. She's going to go wherever my father is." He let out a grievous groan. "It doesn't matter. If my old man wants to stay over there, I don't care. Sisters... How could I have been blind to his true nature? How could I not know he doubled-crossed the Hawks?"

"He saw a chance for power." Brigadier General Winchester had said as much to her. "He didn't think the Hawks had a real chance."

Zander leaned against the thick bedpost. "If I did half the things he did, would you still follow me around?"

"First," Raven started with a pointed tone, "I do not follow you around. We happen to share a path most of the time. Second, if you did half the stupid stuff your father has done, I would have punched you ages ago."

"I expect no less." Zander's expression became dire. "I expect you to keep me from becoming my father. I don't want to end up like him."

"Only if you keep me from becoming mine," she said.

His brow furrowed. "What's wrong with your father?"

"Oh, don't get me wrong, he's a great father, but he's a stick in the mud."

Zander chuckled. "He's protective."

"*Over*protective," she corrected.

"He doesn't want anything to happen to you, and neither do I," Zander said. "I know you can take care of yourself, and now he does too. At least you can most of the time."

She let out a soft laugh and shut her eyes.

"Don't fall asleep yet." Zander strode to the bed and trailed his shadow fingers along her shoulder blades.

She hummed her disapproval. "We can do that tomorrow."

He laughed, low and husky. "Not that. I've got something else planned. Come on. Get up."

She reluctantly pushed herself into a sitting position. Zander stood by the balcony doors. Heavy brocade curtains hung over the windows and the doors. It had taken days for the musty smell to dissipate, and some magic.

"Do I need shoes?" Raven asked.

"Nah."

Zander opened the balcony doors and stepped out. Raven followed. The stone was cool under Raven's bare feet, and a gentle breeze blew from the north, pushing the stale smoke to the south. The royal grounds stretched on, dark and green and teeming with cicadas. Stars littered the sky. With the lights of Lenhala dimmed, the stars glowed brighter.

Raven looked around the balcony. It looked exactly the same as it had before. She glanced over the balcony to the grounds. They also looked the same.

"And we're out here because...?" Raven frowned at Zander, and her next words dissolved. Zander stood with his shadow arm behind his back and his human hand extended.

"We're out here because we have a dance we never finished," Zander said. "I promised we would dance under the stars, and this seems like the right place. I don't think I can find anything nicer than a private suite in a palace."

Raven didn't have words. She'd almost forgotten all about that. She gave him a tired, happy smile and slid her hand into his. Zander swept her into his arms, and they danced around the balcony. Her pleated skirt fluttered as he twirled her. Without music, they invented their own rhythm.

Zander spun her away and then back in, meeting her lips with his own. Raven traced her fingers along his clean-shaven jaw and tilted her head, deepening the kiss. His arms tightened around her middle. All the things she had been worried about seemed farther away.

He mumbled against his lips, "Still too tired?"

She grinned. Yes, she was exhausted, but too tired? "Not anymore."

Zander pulled her back into the bedroom, kicking the balcony doors closed. They collapsed into the silk sheets in a tangle of limbs and laughter. Raven had gotten used to Zander in the past few weeks, and he hadn't been able to make her blush as easily.

After, Raven snuggled into his neck. Zander hugged her close. A beat of silence passed, and within it, Raven fell asleep. In the next moment, sunlight glowed behind the closed curtains. Zander slept soundly beside her. Raven lay there a while, taking in the sight of the grand room, the golds and creams. She woke to the same view every morning, but a part of it still didn't feel real.

On the way to breakfast, a courier intercepted Raven. He handed her a letter.

"Who's it from?" Zander asked.

Raven ripped the letter open and read it over quickly. "My mother." She read it again, slower. "They've returned to Lenhala. My father and the others have relocated, and Mom wants to know if we need a lift."

"What do you think?" Zander asked, brows raised. "We *have* been in Lenhala a while."

"Hmm... I think I need to eat before I make big decisions." Raven tucked the letter into her pocket.

They had eaten breakfast every morning in a small parlor that overlooked the eastern grounds. Rosaria and Ezra were already seated, and royal guards stood by the doors. After tea, Raven relayed her mother's message to Rosaria.

"The city's restoration is going well," Rosaria said. "I don't want you to feel like you have to stay here. You've already done beyond what I could have asked. If you wish to travel with your mother, you have my blessing. Only, mind the piracy. I can't allow it when it's blatant."

"I will take your warning to my mother." Raven turned to Zander. "While staying here has been amazing, I want to see the rest of the world."

With their queen's permission, Zander and Raven boarded a crusader airship that afternoon. She watched the city of Lenhala shrink from the porthole, the towering buildings and homes in the middle of repair, steadied with scaffolding. Then, they punched through the clouds. The *Orion* waited for them, looking like a dream. The afternoon sunlight glinted off the steel rigging, the crimson Belt, and the sky-blue balloons.

Once aboard, they made their way to the Belt.

Far below, on the other side of the wispy clouds, Lenhala gradually drifted west as the *Orion* drifted east.

"Well, what do you want to do now?" Zander asked, leaning onto the railing. "We probably have ten minutes before your mother sends for you."

Raven took a long moment to think it over. What did she want to do? She looked out over the horizon, endless in every direction.

"I want to see what else is out there," Raven said. "I want to see the coast of Rhynwier. I want to see how far the beaches stretch in Tinatun. I want to see if there are sea monsters and mermaids in the southern seas. I want to see how high the mountains go. I want to see everything."

"Everything?" Zander raised a brow. The sun glided his dark hair in shades of gold. "That is a tall order. Luckily, we happen to have use of a sky city. And, from what I hear, the captain likes you. She might take requests."

Raven grinned and leaned away from the railing. "Then let's go request our next adventure."

She grabbed his hand and tugged him back into the ship. As they made their way to the bridge, she couldn't stop smiling. All those years of daydreaming, and she couldn't wait to see what adventures she and Zander might find together.

Acknowledgments

I put off writing this part until I couldn't. I started writing *Hard as Stone* sometime in early 2018. The third and final book was released late 2022. Almost four years. While that doesn't seem like a long time, it was. A lot happened in those four years. I left my amazing part-time job at a library for a full-time job at a law office—quite the law office because it was turning me into a toxic alcoholic—and spent a month and a half pretending to be a full-time writer. (I was job-hunting the whole time.) I ended up working in an office supply store, and I was there when the pandemic began, and I was still there when all the other business shut down. Except the one I worked at. I left retail to work full-time in the medical field. Despite all the life changes and end-of-the-world anxiety, I managed to be a writer.

I'm fairly certain that if I stopped being a writer, I would implode. I don't plan on trying any time soon.

Hard as Stone is my first finished and published series. It is beyond strange and fulfilling to be on the other side. First and foremost, an ocean's worth of gratitude is due for the wonderful team at Authors 4 Authors—Rebecca, Renee, and Brandi—for believing in Raven and Zander from the first page and using their brilliant editing powers to take this trilogy from first draft to published omnibus.

I also need to extend a thank you to every coworker between 2018 and 2022 who, after learning I was an author, asked me about my books, proceeded to buy a copy of my books, and then tell other people about my books. Thank you for nerding out about me when I didn't feel good enough to nerd out about myself. An extra thank you to KK for squealing at my Amazon Author page, as if that made all the difference, and to Cathy for liking all my weird TikTok's.

And of course, Mom, because when I called in tears during my lunch at the law office, you said it was okay and I didn't have to work there if I hated it that much. And for always buying a copy of my books, even if they just end up stacked on your nightstand.

And I am eternally grateful for every single reader who picked up a copy of Hard as Stone, for giving me and Raven a chance, for seeing this adventure through to the end. I tip my hat at thee.

About the Author

Beatrice B. Morgan lives in southern Illinois. When she isn't reading or writing, she is most likely playing a video game. She is a night owl, caffeine addict, yoga enthusiast, dog person, hopeless romantic, optimist, and shameless Ravenclaw.

Follow her online:

bbmorgan.com
Twitter: @BBMorgan_W
Facebook: @BBMorganBooks

ALSO BY BEATRICE B. MORGAN

STARS AND BONES:
Thief in the Castle

The notorious Juniper Thimble is destined for execution. Caught stealing the king's crown—in addition to her long list of crimes—she has only one way out. Juniper must survive the biggest, most deadly con of her life, commissioned by the king himself. Disguised as the crown prince's lover, she is forced to protect him with her life...literally. Guarded by a surly squire, relentlessly attacked by demons, and surrounded by mysteriously disappearing servants, Juniper must dispatch the threat to the prince's life before they find out who she really is.

books2read.com/thiefinthecastle

Authors 4 Authors
Publishing

A publishing company for authors, run by authors, blending the best of traditional and independent publishing

We specialize in speculative fiction: science fiction, fantasy, paranormal, and romance. Get lost in another world!

Check out our collection at https://books2read.com/rl/a4a
or visit Authors4AuthorsPublishing.com/books

For updates, scan the QR code or visit our website to join our semi-monthly newsletter!

Want more heart-pounding YA? We recommend:

FYR
by Lisa Borne Graves

At seventeen, Toury arrives in Fyr, where magic is power, a prince's love is deadly, and female autonomy is a dream. Formerly a loner and burden to her adoptive parents, she ruins her chances of a fresh start by offending an ogler who just happens to be the prince.

Alex, the Prince of Fyr, is no novice when it comes to pressure. He has to face his father's ailing health, the expectation to marry soon, and the hidden necromancers trying to take over the realm by exploiting his dark curse. At least there's hope in a cheeky savior, but Earth girls aren't so easy.

books2read.com/fyr

www.ingramcontent.com/pod-product-compliance
Lightning Source LLC
Chambersburg PA
CBHW010731130726
47899CB00015B/3107